KU-464-559

We were able to purchase this book thanks to the support of the Wendover Community Library Trust and friends' group.

B14 840 460 5

BABEL

ALSO BY R.F. KUANG

The Poppy War
The Dragon Republic
The Burning God

BABEL

OR

THE NECESSITY OF VIOLENCE

An Arcane History of the Oxford
Translators' Revolution

ROYAL INSTITUTE OF TRANSLATION
UNIVERSITY OF OXFORD

R.F. KUANG

HARPER
Voyager

Harper*Voyager*
An imprint of HarperCollins*Publishers* Ltd
1 London Bridge Street
London SE1 9GF

www.harpercollins.co.uk

HarperCollins*Publishers*
Macken House, 39/40 Mayor Street Upper
Dublin1, D01 C9W8, Ireland

First published by HarperCollins*Publishers* 2022

15

Copyright © Rebecca Kuang 2022

Maps of Oxford and Babel copyright © Nicolette Caven 2022

Crest illustration copyright © HarperCollins*Publishers* 2022

R.F. Kuang asserts the moral right to
be identified as the author of this work

A catalogue record for this book is available
from the British Library

ISBN: 978-0-00-850181-5 (HB)
ISBN: 978-0-00-850182-2 (TPB)

This novel is entirely a work of fiction.
The names, characters and incidents portrayed in it are the work
of the author's imagination. Any resemblance to actual persons, living
or dead, events or localities is entirely coincidental.

Set in Adobe Caslon Pro

Printed and bound in the UK using 100% renewable
electricity by CPI Group (UK) Ltd

All rights reserved. No part of this publication may be reproduced,
stored in a retrieval system, or transmitted, in any form or by any means,
electronic, mechanical, photocopying, recording or otherwise,
without the prior permission of the publishers.

MIX
Paper | Supporting
responsible forestry
FSC
www.fsc.org   FSC™ C007454

This book is produced from independently certified FSC™ paper
to ensure responsible forest management.

For more information visit: www.harpercollins.co.uk/green

To Bennett,
who is all the light and laughter in the world.

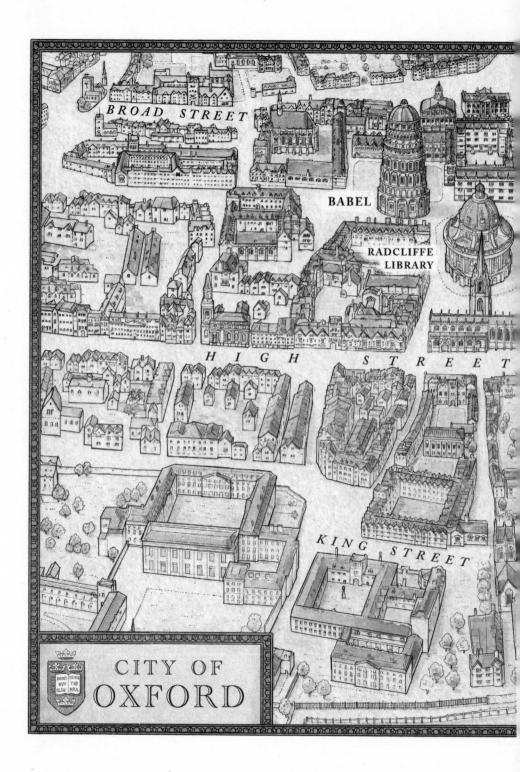

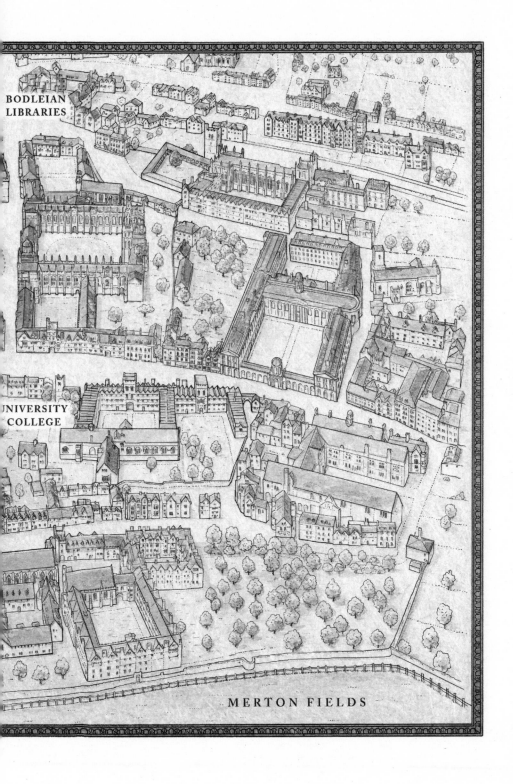

BODLEIAN
LIBRARIES

UNIVERSITY
COLLEGE

MERTON FIELDS

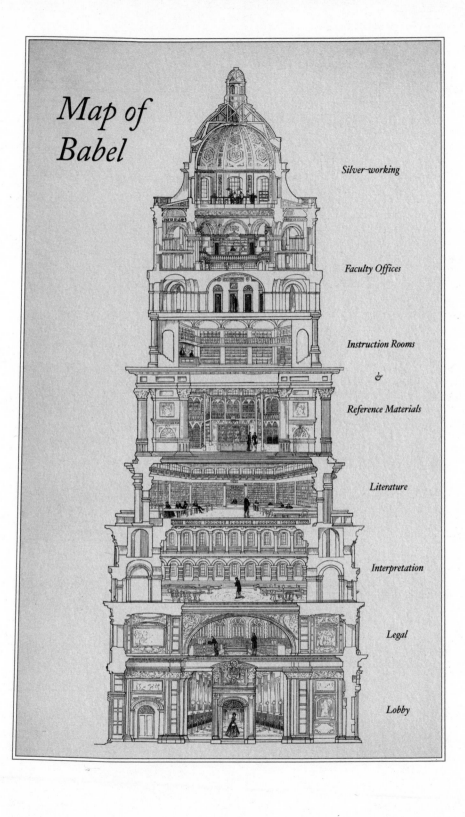

Map of
Babel

Silver-working

Faculty Offices

Instruction Rooms

&

Reference Materials

Literature

Interpretation

Legal

Lobby

Author's Note on
Her Representations of Historical England,
and of the University of Oxford in Particular

The trouble with writing an Oxford novel is that anyone who has spent time at Oxford will scrutinize your text to determine if your representation of Oxford aligns with their own memories of the place. Worse if you are an American writing about Oxford, for what do Americans know about anything? I offer my defence here:

Babel is a work of speculative fiction and so takes place in a fantastical version of Oxford in the 1830s, whose history was thoroughly altered by silver-work (more on that shortly). Still, I've tried to remain as faithful to the historical record on life in early Victorian Oxford as possible, and to introduce falsehoods only when they serve the narrative. For references on early nineteenth-century Oxford, I've relied on James J. Moore's highly entertaining *The Historical Handbook and Guide to Oxford* (1878), as well as *The History of the University of Oxford* volumes VI and VII, edited by M.G. Brock and M.C. Curthoys (1997 and 2000, respectively) among others.

For rhetoric and the general texture of life (such as early nineteenth-century Oxford slang, which differs quite a lot from contemporary Oxford slang),* I have made use of primary sources such as Alex Chalmers's *A History of the Colleges, Halls, and Public Buildings Attached to the University of Oxford, Including the Lives of the Founders* (1810), G.V. Cox's *Recollections of Oxford* (1868), Thomas Mozley's *Reminiscences: Chiefly of Oriel College and the Oxford Movement* (1882), and W. Tuckwell's *Reminiscences of Oxford* (1908). Since fiction can also tell us much about life the way it was lived, or

---

* For example, I never heard anyone refer to High Street as 'The High' when I was at Oxford, but G.V. Cox tells us otherwise.

at least the way it was perceived, I have also dropped in details from novels such as Cuthbert M. Bede's *The Adventures of Mr. Verdant Green* (1857), Thomas Hughes's *Tom Brown at Oxford* (1861), and William Makepeace Thackeray's *The History of Pendennis* (1850). For everything else, I've relied on my memories and my imagination.

For those familiar with Oxford and thus eager to cry, 'No, that's not how things are!', I'll now explain some peculiarities. The Oxford Union was not established until 1856, so in this novel it is referred to by the name of its predecessor, the United Debating Society (founded in 1823). My beloved Vaults & Garden café did not exist until 2003, but I spent so much time there (and ate so many scones there) that I couldn't deny Robin and company those same pleasures. The Twisted Root as described does not exist, and as far as I'm aware no pub exists in Oxford of that name. There is also no Taylor's on Winchester Road though I am pretty fond of the Taylors on High Street. The Oxford Martyrs Monument does exist, but was not completed until 1843, three years after the conclusion of this novel. I've moved the date of its construction up just a little bit, all for the sake of a cute reference. The coronation of Queen Victoria happened in June 1838, not 1839. The Oxford-to-Paddington railway line was not laid until 1844, but here it was constructed several years earlier for two reasons: first, because it makes sense given the altered history; and second, because I needed to get my characters to London a bit faster.

I took a lot of artistic liberties with the commemoration ball, which looks a lot more like a contemporary Oxbridge May/Commemoration Ball than any kind of early-Victorian social event. For instance, I'm aware that oysters were a staple of the early-Victorian poor, but I choose to make them a delicacy because that was my first impression of the 2019 May Ball at Magdalene College, Cambridge – heaps and heaps of oysters on ice (I hadn't brought a purse, and was juggling my phone, champagne glass, and oyster in one hand, and spilled champagne all over an old man's nice dress shoes as a result).

Some may be puzzled by the precise placement of the Royal Institute of Translation, also known as Babel. That is because I've warped geography to make space for it. Imagine a green between the Bodleian Libraries, the Sheldonian, and the Radcliffe Camera. Now make it much bigger, and put Babel right in the centre.

If you find any other inconsistencies, feel free to remind yourself this is a work of fiction.

BOOK I

ROYAL INSTITUTE OF TRANSLATION
UNIVERSITY OF OXFORD

CHAPTER ONE

⊶⊷

Que siempre la lengua fue compañera del imperio; y de tal manera lo siguió, que junta mente començaron, crecieron y florecieron, y después junta fue la caida de entrambos.

Language was always the companion of empire, and as such, together they begin, grow, and flourish. And later, together, they fall.

ANTONIO DE NEBRIJA,
Gramática de la lengua castellana

By the time Professor Richard Lovell found his way through Canton's narrow alleys to the faded address in his diary, the boy was the only one in the house left alive.

The air was rank, the floors slippery. A jug of water sat full, untouched by the bed. At first the boy had been too scared of retching to drink; now he was too weak to lift the jug. He was still conscious, though he'd sunk into a drowsy, half-dreaming haze. Soon, he knew, he'd fall into a deep sleep and fail to wake up. That was what had happened to his grandparents a week ago, then his aunts a day after, and then Miss Betty, the Englishwoman, a day after that.

His mother had perished that morning. He lay beside her body, watching as the blues and purples deepened across her skin. The last thing she'd said to him was his name, two syllables mouthed without breath. Her face had then gone slack and uneven. Her tongue lolled out of her mouth. The boy tried to close her filmy eyes, but her lids kept sliding back open.

No one answered when Professor Lovell knocked. No one exclaimed in surprise when he kicked through the front door – locked, because plague thieves were stripping the houses in the neighbourhood bare, and though there was little of value in their home, the boy and his mother had wanted a few hours of peace before the sickness took them too. The boy heard all the commotion from upstairs, but he couldn't bring himself to care.

By then he only wanted to die.

Professor Lovell made his way up the stairs, crossed the room, and stood over the boy for a long moment. He did not notice, or chose not to notice, the dead woman on the bed. The boy lay still in his shadow, wondering if this tall, pale figure in black had come to reap his soul.

'How do you feel?' Professor Lovell asked.

The boy's breathing was too laboured to answer.

Professor Lovell knelt beside the bed. He drew a slim silver bar out of his front pocket and placed it over the boy's bare chest. The boy flinched; the metal stung like ice.

'*Triacle*,' Professor Lovell said first in French. Then, in English, 'Treacle.'

The bar glowed a pale white. There came an eerie sound from nowhere; a ringing, a singing. The boy whined and curled onto his side, his tongue prodding confusedly around his mouth.

'Bear with it,' murmured Professor Lovell. 'Swallow what you taste.'

Seconds trickled by. The boy's breathing steadied. He opened his eyes. He saw Professor Lovell more clearly now, could make out the slate-grey eyes and curved nose – *yīnggōubí*, they called it, a hawk's-beak nose – that could only belong on a foreigner's face.

'How do you feel now?' asked Professor Lovell.

The boy took another deep breath. Then he said, in surprisingly good English, 'It's sweet. It tastes so sweet . . .'

'Good. That means it worked.' Professor Lovell slipped the bar back into his pocket. 'Is there anyone else alive here?'

'No,' whispered the boy. 'Just me.'

'Is there anything you can't leave behind?'

The boy was silent for a moment. A fly landed on his mother's cheek and crawled across her nose. He wanted to brush it off, but he didn't have the strength to lift his hand.

'I can't take a body,' said Professor Lovell. 'Not where we're going.'

The boy stared at his mother for a long moment.

'My books,' he said at last. 'Under the bed.'

Professor Lovell bent beneath the bed and pulled out four thick volumes. Books written in English, spines battered from use, some pages worn so thin that the print was barely still legible. The professor flipped through them, smiling despite himself, and placed them in his bag. Then he slid his arms under the boy's thin frame and lifted him out of the house.

In 1829, the plague that later became known as Asiatic Cholera made its way from Calcutta across the Bay of Bengal to the Far East – first to Siam, then Manila, then finally the shores of China on merchant ships whose dehydrated, sunken-eyed sailors dumped their waste into the Pearl River, contaminating the waters where thousands drank, laundered, swam, and bathed. It hit Canton like a tidal wave, rapidly working its way from the docks to the inland residential areas. The boy's neighbourhood had succumbed within weeks, whole families perishing helplessly in their homes. When Professor Lovell carried the boy out of Canton's alleys, everyone else on his street was already dead.

The boy learned all this when he awoke in a clean, well-lit room in the English Factory, wrapped in blankets softer and whiter than anything he'd ever touched. These only slightly reduced his discomfort. He was terribly hot, and his tongue sat in his mouth like a dense, sandy stone. He felt as though he were floating far above his body. Every time the professor spoke, sharp pangs shot through his temples, accompanied by flashes of red.

'You're very lucky,' said Professor Lovell. 'This illness kills almost everything it touches.'

The boy stared, fascinated by this foreigner's long face and pale grey eyes. If he let his gaze drift out of focus, the foreigner morphed into a giant bird. A crow. No, a raptor. Something vicious and strong.

'Can you understand what I'm saying?'

The boy wet his parched lips and uttered a response.

Professor Lovell shook his head. 'English. Use your English.'

The boy's throat burned. He coughed.

'I know you have English.' Professor Lovell's voice sounded like a warning. 'Use it.'

'My mother,' breathed the boy. 'You forgot my mother.'

Professor Lovell did not respond. Promptly he stood and brushed at his knees before he left, though the boy could scarcely see how any dust could have accumulated in the few minutes in which he'd been sitting down.

* * *

The next morning the boy was able to finish a bowl of broth without retching. The morning after that he managed to stand without much vertigo, though his knees trembled so badly from disuse he had to clutch the bedframe to keep from falling over. His fever receded; his appetite improved. When he woke again that afternoon, he found the bowl replaced with a plate with two thick slices of bread and a hunk of roast beef. He devoured these with his bare hands, famished.

He spent most of the day in dreamless sleep, which was regularly interrupted by the arrival of one Mrs Piper – a cheery, round woman who plumped his pillows, wiped his forehead with deliciously cool wet cloths, and spoke English with such a peculiar accent that the boy always had to ask her several times to repeat herself.

'My word,' she chuckled the first time he did this. 'Must be you've never met a Scot.'

'A . . . Scot? What is a Scot?'

'Don't you worry about that.' She patted his cheek. 'You'll learn the lay of Great Britain soon enough.'

That evening, Mrs Piper brought him his dinner – bread and beef again – along with news that the professor wanted to see him in his office. 'It's just upstairs. The second door to the right. Finish your food first; he's not going anywhere.'

The boy ate quickly and, with Mrs Piper's help, got dressed. He didn't know where the clothes had come from – they were Western in style, and fitted his short, skinny frame surprisingly well – but he was too tired then to inquire further.

As he made his way up the stairs he trembled, whether from fatigue or trepidation, he didn't know. The door to the professor's study was shut. He paused a moment to catch his breath, and then he knocked.

'Come in,' called the professor.

The door was very heavy. The boy had to lean hard against the wood to budge it open. Inside, he was overwhelmed by the musky, inky scent of books. There were stacks and stacks of them; some were arrayed neatly on shelves, while others were messily piled up in precarious pyramids throughout the room; some were strewn across the floor, while others teetered on the desks that seemed arranged at random within the dimly lit labyrinth.

'Over here.' The professor was nearly hidden behind the bookcases. The boy wound his way tentatively across the room, afraid the slightest wrong move might send the pyramids tumbling.

'Don't be shy.' The professor sat behind a grand desk covered with books, loose papers, and envelopes. He gestured for the boy to take a seat across from him. 'Did they let you read much here? English wasn't a problem?'

'I read some.' The boy sat gingerly, taking care not to tread on the volumes – Richard Hakluyt's travel notes, he noticed – amassed by his feet. 'We didn't have many books. I ended up re-reading what we had.'

For someone who had never left Canton in his life, the boy's English was remarkably good. He spoke with only a trace of an accent. This was thanks to an Englishwoman – one Miss Elizabeth Slate, whom the boy had called Miss Betty, and who had lived with his household for as long as he could remember. He never quite understood what she was doing there – his family was certainly not wealthy enough to employ any servants, especially not a foreigner – but someone must have been paying her wages because she had never left, not even when the plague hit. Her Cantonese was passably good, decent enough for her to make her way around town without trouble, but with the boy, she spoke exclusively in English. Her sole duty seemed to be taking care of him, and it was through conversation with her, and later with British sailors at the docks, that the boy had become fluent.

He could read the language better than he spoke it. Ever since the boy turned four, he had received a large parcel twice a year filled entirely with books written in English. The return address was a residence in Hampstead just outside London – a place Miss Betty seemed unfamiliar with, and which the boy of course knew nothing about. Regardless, he and Miss Betty used to sit together under candlelight, laboriously tracing their fingers over each word as they sounded them out loud. When he grew older, he spent entire afternoons poring over the worn pages on his own. But a dozen books were hardly enough to last six months; he always read each one so many times over he'd nearly memorized them by the time the next shipment came.

He realized now, without quite grasping the larger picture, that those parcels must have come from the professor.

'I do quite enjoy it,' he supplied feebly. Then, thinking he ought to say a bit more, 'And no – English was not a problem.'

'Very good.' Professor Lovell picked a volume off the shelf behind him and slid it across the table. 'I suppose you haven't seen this one before?'

The boy glanced at the title. *The Wealth of Nations*, by Adam Smith. He shook his head. 'I'm sorry, no.'

'That's fine.' The professor opened the book to a page in the middle and pointed. 'Read out loud for me. Start here.'

The boy swallowed, coughed to clear his throat, and began to read. The book was intimidatingly thick, the font very small, and the prose proved considerably more difficult than the breezy adventure novels he'd read with Miss Betty. His tongue tripped over words he didn't know, words he could only guess at and sound out.

'The par . . . particular ad-advantage which each col-o-colonizing country derives from the col . . . colonies which par . . . particularly belong to it, are of two different kinds; first, those common advantages which every empire de . . . rives?' He cleared his throat. 'Derives . . . from the provinces subject to its dom . . . dom . . ."'

'That's enough.'

He had no idea what he'd just read. 'Sir, what does—'

'No, that's all right,' said the professor. 'I hardly expect you to understand international economics. You did very well.' He set the book aside, reached into his desk drawer, and pulled out a silver bar. 'Remember this?'

The boy stared, wide-eyed, too apprehensive even to touch it.

He'd seen bars like that before. They were rare in Canton, but everyone knew about them. *Yínfúlù*, silver talismans. He'd seen them embedded in the prows of ships, carved into the sides of palanquins, and installed over the doors of warehouses in the foreign quarter. He'd never figured out precisely what they were, and no one in his household could explain. His grandmother called them rich men's magic spells, metal amulets carrying blessings from the gods. His mother thought they contained trapped demons who could be summoned to accomplish their masters' orders. Even Miss Betty, who made loud her disdain for indigenous Chinese superstition and constantly criticized his mother's heeding of hungry ghosts, found them unnerving.

---

* In Book IV, Chapter VII of *The Wealth of Nations*, Adam Smith argues against colonialism on the grounds that the defence of colonies is a drain on resources, and that the economic gains of the monopolistic colonial trade are an illusion. He writes: 'Great Britain derives nothing but loss from the dominion which she assumes over her colonies.' This view was not widely shared at the time.

'They're witchcraft,' she'd said when he asked. 'They're devil's work is what they are.'

So the boy didn't know what to make of this *yínfúlù*, except that it was a bar just like this one that had several days ago saved his life.

'Go on.' Professor Lovell held it out towards him. 'Have a look. It won't bite.'

The boy hesitated, then received it in both hands. The bar was very smooth and cold to the touch, but otherwise it seemed quite ordinary. If there was a demon trapped inside, it hid itself well.

'Can you read what it says?'

The boy looked closer and noticed there was indeed writing, tiny words engraved neatly on either side of the bar: English letters on one side, Chinese characters on the other. 'Yes.'

'Say them out loud. Chinese first, then English. Speak very clearly.'

The boy recognized the Chinese characters, though the calligraphy looked a bit strange, as if drawn by someone who had seen them and copied them out radical by radical without knowing what they meant. They read: 囫圇吞棗.

'*Húlún tūn zǎo*,' he read slowly, taking care to enunciate every syllable. He switched to English. 'To accept without thinking.'

The bar began to hum.

Immediately his tongue swelled up, obstructing his airway. The boy grasped, choking, at his throat. The bar dropped to his lap, where it vibrated wildly, dancing as if possessed. A cloyingly sweet taste filled his mouth. *Like dates*, the boy thought faintly, black pushing in at the edges of his vision. Strong, jammy dates, so ripe they were sickening. He was drowning in them. His throat was wholly blocked, he couldn't breathe—

'Here.' Professor Lovell leaned over and pulled the bar from his lap. The choking sensation vanished. The boy slumped over the desk, gulping for air.

'Interesting,' said Professor Lovell. 'I've never known it to have such a strong effect. What does your mouth taste of?'

'*Hóngzǎo*.' Tears streamed down the boy's face. Hastily he switched to English. 'Dates.'

'That's good. That's very good.' Professor Lovell observed him for a long moment, then dropped the bar back into the drawer. 'Excellent, in fact.'

The boy wiped tears from his eyes, sniffling. Professor Lovell sat back, waiting for the boy to recover somewhat before he continued. 'In two days, Mrs Piper and I will depart this country for a city called London in a country called England. I'm sure you've heard of both.'

The boy gave an uncertain nod. London existed to him like Lilliput did: a faraway, imaginary, fantasy place where no one looked, dressed, or spoke remotely like him.

'I propose to bring you with us. You will live at my estate, and I will provide you with room and board until you've grown old enough to make your own living. In return, you will take courses in a curriculum of my design. It will be language work – Latin, Greek, and of course, Mandarin. You will enjoy an easy, comfortable life, and the best education that one can afford. All I expect in return is that you apply yourself diligently to your studies.'

Professor Lovell clasped his hands together as if in prayer. The boy found his tone confusing. It was utterly flat and dispassionate. He could not tell if Professor Lovell *wanted* him in London or not; indeed, this seemed less like an adoption and more like a business proposal.

'I urge you to strongly consider it,' Professor Lovell continued. 'Your mother and grandparents are dead, your father unknown, and you have no extended family. Stay here, and you won't have a penny to your name. All you will ever know is poverty, disease, and starvation. You'll find work on the docks if you're lucky, but you're still small yet, so you'll spend a few years begging or stealing. Assuming you reach adulthood, the best you can hope for is backbreaking labour on the ships.'

The boy found himself staring, fascinated, at Professor Lovell's face as he spoke. It was not as though he had never encountered an Englishman before. He had met plenty of sailors at the docks, had seen the entire range of white men's faces, from the broad and ruddy to the diseased and liver-spotted to the long, pale, and severe. But the professor's face presented an entirely different puzzle. His had all the components of a standard human face – eyes, lips, nose, teeth, all healthy and normal. His voice was a low, somewhat flat, but nevertheless human voice. But when he spoke, his tone and expression were entirely devoid of emotion. He was a blank slate. The boy could not guess his feelings at all. As the professor described the boy's early, inevitable death, he could have been reciting ingredients for a stew.

'Why?' asked the boy.

'Why what?'

'Why do you want me?'

The professor nodded to the drawer which contained the silver bar. 'Because you can do *that*.'

Only then did the boy realize that this had been a test.

'These are the terms of my guardianship.' Professor Lovell slid a two-page document across the desk. The boy glanced down, then gave up trying to skim it; the tight, looping penmanship looked nigh illegible. 'They're quite simple, but take care to read the entire thing before you sign it. Will you do this tonight before you go to bed?'

The boy was too shaken to do anything but nod.

'Very good,' said Professor Lovell. 'One more thing. It occurs to me you need a name.'

'I have a name,' said the boy. 'It's—'

'No, that won't do. No Englishman can pronounce that. Did Miss Slate give you a name?'

She had, in fact. When the boy turned four, she had insisted he adopt a name by which Englishmen could take him seriously, though she'd never elaborated which Englishmen those might be. They'd chosen something at random from a children's rhyming book, and the boy liked how firm and round the syllables felt on his tongue, so he harboured no complaint. But no one else in the household had ever used it, and soon Miss Betty had dropped it as well. The boy had to think hard for a moment before he remembered.

'Robin.'*

Professor Lovell was quiet for a moment. His expression confused the boy – his brows were furrowed, as if in anger, but one side of his mouth curled up, as if delighted. 'How about a surname?'

'I have a surname.'

'One that will do in London. Pick anything you like.'

The boy blinked at him. 'Pick . . . a surname?'

Family names were not things to be dropped and replaced at whim, he thought. They marked lineage; they marked belonging.

'The English reinvent their names all the time,' said Professor Lovell. 'The only families who keep theirs do it because they have titles to hold

---

* *I killed Cock Robin.*
  Who saw him die?

on to, and you certainly haven't got any. You only need a handle to introduce yourself by. Any name will do.'

'Then can I take yours? Lovell?'

'Oh, no,' said Professor Lovell. 'They'll think I'm your father.'

'Oh – of course.' The boy's eyes cast desperately around the room,
searching for some word or sound to latch on to. They landed on a familiar volume on the shelf above Professor Lovell's head – *Gulliver's Travels*.
A stranger in a strange land, who had to learn the local languages if he
wished not to die. He thought he understood now how Gulliver felt.

'Swift?' he ventured. 'Unless—'

To his surprise, Professor Lovell laughed. Laughter was strange
coming out of that severe mouth; it sounded too abrupt, almost cruel,
and the boy couldn't help but flinch. 'Very good. Robin Swift you'll be.
Mr Swift, good to meet you.'

He rose and extended his hand across the desk. The boy had seen
foreign sailors greeting each other at the docks, so he knew what to
do. He met that large, dry, uncomfortably cool hand with his own.
They shook.

Two days later, Professor Lovell, Mrs Piper, and the newly christened
Robin Swift set sail for London. By then, thanks to many hours of bed
rest and a steady diet of hot milk and Mrs Piper's abundant cooking,
Robin was well enough to walk on his own. He lugged a trunk heavy
with books up the gangplank, struggling to keep pace with the professor.

Canton's harbour, the mouth from which China encountered the
world, was a universe of languages. Loud and rapid Portuguese, French,
Dutch, Swedish, Danish, English, and Chinese floated through the
salty air, intermingling in an implausibly mutually intelligible pidgin
which almost everyone understood, but which only a few could
speak with ease. Robin knew it well. He'd gained his first instruction
in foreign languages running about the quays; he'd often translated
for sailors in exchange for a tossed penny and a smile. Never had he
imagined he might follow the linguistic fragments of this pidgin back
to their source.

They walked down the waterfront to join the boarding line for the
Countess of Harcourt, one of the East India Company ships that took
on a small number of commercial passengers on each voyage. The sea
was loud and choppy that day. Robin shivered as frigid seaside gusts cut

viciously through his coat. He badly wanted to be on the ship, inside a cabin or anywhere with walls, but something held up the boarding line. Professor Lovell stepped to the side to have a look. Robin followed him. At the top of the gangplank, a crewman was berating a passenger, acerbic English vowels piercing through the morning chill.

'Can't you understand what I'm saying? *Knee how? Lay ho?* Anything?'

The target of his ire was a Chinese labourer, stooped from the weight of the rucksack he wore slung over one shoulder. If the labourer uttered a response, Robin couldn't hear it.

'Can't understand a word I'm saying,' complained the crewman. He turned to the crowd. 'Can anyone tell this fellow he can't come aboard?'

'Oh, that poor man.' Mrs Piper nudged Professor Lovell's arm. 'Can you translate?'

'I don't speak the Cantonese dialect,' said Professor Lovell. 'Robin, go on up there.'

Robin hesitated, suddenly frightened.

'*Go.*' Professor Lovell pushed him up the plank.

Robin stumbled forward into the fray. Both the crewman and the labourer turned to look at him. The crewman merely looked annoyed, but the labourer seemed relieved – he seemed to recognize immediately in Robin's face an ally, the only other Chinese person in sight.

'What's the matter?' Robin asked him in Cantonese.

'He won't let me aboard,' the labourer said urgently. 'But I have a contract with this ship until London, look, it says so right here.'

He shoved a folded sheet of paper at Robin.

Robin opened it. The paper was written in English, and it did indeed look like a lascar contract – a certificate of pay to last for the length of one voyage from Canton to London, to be specific. Robin had seen such contracts before; they had grown increasingly common over the past several years as the demand for indentured Chinese servants grew concurrently with overseas difficulties with the slave trade. This was not the first contract he'd translated; he'd seen work orders for Chinese labourers to board for destinations as far away as Portugal, India, and the West Indies.

It all looked in order to Robin. 'So what's the problem?'

'What's he telling you?' asked the crewman. 'Tell him that contract's no good. I can't have Chinamen on this ship. Last ship I sailed that carried a Chinaman got filthy with lice. I'm not taking risks on people who can't wash. Couldn't even understand the word *bath* if I yelled it at him, this one. Hello? Boy? Do you understand what I'm saying?'

'Yes, yes.' Robin switched hastily back to English. 'Yes, I'm just – give me a moment, I'm just trying to . . .'

But what should he say?

The labourer, uncomprehending, cast Robin an imploring look. His face was creased and sun-browned, leathered in a way that made him look sixty, though he was likely only in his thirties. All lascars aged quickly; the work wrecked their bodies. Robin had seen that face a thousand times before at the docks. Some tossed him sweets; some knew him well enough to greet him by name. He associated that face with his own kind. But he'd never seen one of his elders turn to him with such total helplessness.

Guilt twisted his gut. Words collected on his tongue, cruel and terrible words, but he could not turn them into a sentence.

'Robin.' Professor Lovell was at his side, gripping his shoulder so tightly it hurt. 'Translate, please.'

This all hinged on him, Robin realized. The choice was his. Only he could determine the truth, because only he could communicate it to all parties.

But what could he possibly say? He saw the crewman's blistering irritation. He saw the rustling impatience of the other passengers in the queue. They were tired, they were cold, they couldn't understand why they hadn't boarded yet. He felt Professor Lovell's thumb digging a groove into his collarbone, and a thought struck him – a thought so frightening that it made his knees tremble – which was that should he pose too much of a problem, should he stir up trouble, then the *Countess of Harcourt* might simply leave him behind onshore as well.

'Your contract's no good here,' he murmured to the labourer. 'Try the next ship.'

The labourer gaped in disbelief. 'Did you read it? It says London, it says the East India Company, it says *this* ship, the *Countess*—'

Robin shook his head. 'It's no good,' he said, then repeated this line, as if doing so might make it true. 'It's no good, you'll have to try the next ship.'

'What's wrong with it?' demanded the labourer.

Robin could hardly force his words out. 'It's just no good.'

The labourer gaped at him. A thousand emotions worked through that weathered face – indignation, frustration, and finally, resignation. Robin had been afraid the labourer might argue, might fight, but quickly it became clear that for this man, such treatment was nothing new. This had happened before. The labourer turned and made his way down the gangplank, shoving passengers aside as he did. In a few moments he was gone from sight.

Robin felt very dizzy. He escaped back down the gangplank to Mrs Piper's side. 'I'm cold.'

'Oh, you're shaking, poor thing.' She was immediately on him like a mother hen, enveloping him within her shawl. She spoke a sharp word to Professor Lovell. He sighed, nodded; then they bustled through to the front of the line, from which they were whisked straight to their cabins while a porter collected their luggage and carried it behind them.

An hour later, the *Countess of Harcourt* left the port.

Robin was settled on his bunk with a thick blanket wrapped around his shoulders, and he would have happily stayed there all day, but Mrs Piper urged him back above deck to watch the receding shoreline. He felt a sharp ache in his chest as Canton disappeared over the horizon, and then a raw emptiness, as if a grappling hook had yanked his heart out of his body. It had not registered until now that he would not step foot on his native shore again for many years, if ever. He wasn't sure what to make of this fact. The word *loss* was inadequate. Loss just meant a lack, meant something was missing, but it did not encompass the totality of this severance, this terrifying un-anchoring from all that he'd ever known.

He watched the ocean for a long time, indifferent to the wind, staring until even his imagined vision of the shore faded away.

He spent the first few days of the voyage sleeping. He was still recuperating; Mrs Piper insisted he take daily walks above deck for his health, but initially he could manage only a few minutes at a time before he had to lie down. He was fortunate to be spared the nausea of seasickness; a childhood along docks and rivers had habituated his senses to the roiling instability. When he felt strong enough to spend whole afternoons above deck, he loved sitting by the railings, watching the ceaseless waves changing colour with the sky, feeling the ocean spray on his face.

Occasionally Professor Lovell would chat with him as they paced the deck together. Robin learned quickly that the professor was a precise and reticent man. He offered up information when he thought Robin needed it, but otherwise, he was happy to let questions lie.

He told Robin they would reside in his estate in Hampstead when they reached England. He did not say whether he had family at that estate. He confirmed that he had paid Miss Betty all those years, but did not explain why. He intimated that he'd known Robin's mother, which was how he'd known Robin's address, but he did not elaborate on the nature of their relationship or how they'd met. The only time he acknowledged their prior acquaintance was when he asked Robin how his family came to live in that riverside shack.

'They were a well-off merchant family when I knew them,' he said. 'Had an estate in Peking before they moved south. What was it, gambling? I suppose it was the brother, wasn't it?'

Months ago Robin would have spat at anyone for speaking so cruelly about his family. But here, alone in the middle of the ocean with no relatives and nothing to his name, he could not summon the ire. He had no fire left in him. He was only scared, and so very tired.

In any case, all this accorded with what Robin had been told of his family's previous wealth, which had been squandered completely in the years after his birth. His mother had complained about it bitterly and often. Robin was fuzzy on the details, but the story involved what so many tales of decline in Qing dynasty China did: an aging patriarch, a profligate son, malicious and manipulative friends, and a helpless daughter whom, for some mysterious reason, no one would marry. Once, he'd been told, he'd slept in a lacquered crib. Once, they'd enjoyed a dozen servants and a chef who cooked rare delicacies imported from northern markets. Once, they'd lived in an estate that could have housed five families, with peacocks roaming about the yard. But all Robin had ever known was the little house on the river.

'My mother said that my uncle lost all their money at the opium houses,' Robin told him. 'Debtors seized their estate, and we had to move. Then my uncle went missing when I was three, and it was just us and my aunts and grandparents. And Miss Betty.'

Professor Lovell made a noncommittal hum of sympathy. 'That's too bad.'

Apart from these talks, the professor spent most of the day holed up in his cabin. They saw him only semi-regularly in the mess for dinners;

more often Mrs Piper had to fill a plate with hardtack and dried pork and take it to his room.

'He's working on his translations,' Mrs Piper told Robin. 'He's always picking up scrolls and old books on these trips, you see, and he likes to get a head start on rendering them into English before he gets back to London. They keep him so busy there – he's a very important man, a fellow of the Royal Asiatic Society, you know – and he says sea voyages are the only time he gets any peace and quiet. Isn't that funny. He bought some nice rhyming dictionaries in Macau – lovely things, though he won't let me touch them, the pages are so fragile.'

Robin was startled to hear that they'd been to Macau. He had not been aware of any Macau trip; naively, he'd imagined he was the only reason why Professor Lovell had come to China at all. 'How long were you there? In Macau, I mean.'

'Oh, two weeks and some change. It would have been just two, but we were held up at customs. They don't like letting foreign women onto the mainland – I had to dress up and pretend to be the professor's uncle, can you imagine!'

Two weeks.

Two weeks ago, Robin's mother was still alive.

'Are you all right, dear?' Mrs Piper ruffled his hair. 'You look pale.'

Robin nodded, and swallowed down the words he knew he could not say.

He had no right to be resentful. Professor Lovell had promised him everything, and owed him nothing. Robin did not yet fully understand the rules of this world he was about to enter, but he understood the necessity of gratitude. Of deference. One did not spite one's saviours.

'Do you want me to take this plate down to the professor?' he asked.

'Thank you, dear. That's very sweet of you. Come and meet me above deck afterwards and we'll watch the sun go down.'

Time blurred. The sun rose and set, but without the regularity of routine – he had no chores, no water to fetch or errands to run – the days all seemed the same no matter the hour. Robin slept, reread his old books, and paced the decks. Occasionally he struck up a conversation with the other passengers, who always seemed delighted to hear a near pitch-perfect Londoner's accent out of the mouth of this little Oriental boy. Recalling Professor Lovell's words, he tried very hard to live exclusively in English. When thoughts popped up in Chinese, he quashed them.

He quashed his memories too. His life in Canton – his mother, his grandparents, a decade of running about the docks – it all proved surprisingly easy to shed, perhaps because this passage was so jarring, the break so complete. He'd left behind everything he'd known. There was nothing to cling to, nothing to escape back to. His world now was Professor Lovell, Mrs Piper, and the promise of a country on the other side of the ocean. He buried his past life, not because it was so terrible but because abandoning it was the only way to survive. He pulled on his English accent like a new coat, adjusted everything he could about himself to make it fit, and, within weeks, wore it with comfort. In weeks, no one was asking him to speak a few words in Chinese for their entertainment. In weeks, no one seemed to remember he was Chinese at all.

One morning, Mrs Piper woke him very early. He made some noises of protest, but she insisted. 'Come, dear, you won't want to miss this.' Yawning, he pulled on a jacket. He was still rubbing his eyes when they emerged above deck into a cold morning shrouded in mist so thick Robin could hardly see the prow of the ship. But then the fog cleared, and a grey-black silhouette emerged over the horizon, and that was the first glimpse Robin ever had of London: the Silver City, the heart of the British Empire, and in that era, the largest and richest city in the world.

CHAPTER TWO

———— ∞∞∞ ————

That vast metropolis, The fountain of my country's destiny
And of the destiny of earth itself

WILLIAM WORDSWORTH,
The Prelude

London was drab and grey; was exploding in colour; was a raucous din, bursting with life; was eerily quiet, haunted by ghosts and graveyards. As the *Countess of Harcourt* sailed inland down the River Thames into the dockyards at the beating heart of the capital, Robin saw immediately that London was, like Canton, a city of contradictions and multitudes, as was any city that acted as a mouth to the world.

But unlike Canton, London had a mechanical heartbeat. Silver hummed through the city. It glimmered from the wheels of cabs and carriages and from horses' hooves; shone from buildings under windows and over doorways; lay buried under the streets and up in the ticking arms of clock towers; was displayed in shopfronts whose signs proudly boasted the magical amplifications of their breads, boots, and baubles. The lifeblood of London carried a sharp, tinny timbre wholly unlike the rickety, clacking bamboo that underwrote Canton. It was artificial, metallic – the sound of a knife screeching across a sharpening steel; it was the monstrous industrial labyrinth of William Blake's 'cruel Works / Of many Wheels I view, wheel without wheel, with cogs tyrannic, moving by compulsion each other'.*

London had accumulated the lion's share of both the world's silver ore and the world's languages, and the result was a city that was bigger, heavier, faster, and brighter than nature allowed. London was voracious,

---

* William Blake, 'Jerusalem', 1804.

was growing fat on its spoils and still, somehow, starved. London was both unimaginably rich and wretchedly poor. London – lovely, ugly, sprawling, cramped, belching, sniffing, virtuous, hypocritical, silver-gilded London – was near to a reckoning, for the day would come when it either devoured itself from inside or cast outwards for new delicacies, labour, capital, and culture on which to feed.

But the scales had not yet tipped, and the revels, for now, could be sustained. When Robin, Professor Lovell, and Mrs Piper stepped ashore at the Port of London, the docks were a flurry of the colonial trade at its apex. Ships heavy with chests of tea, cotton, and tobacco, their masts and crossbeams studded with silver that made them sail more quickly and safely, sat waiting to be emptied in preparation for the next voyage to India, to the West Indies, to Africa, to the Far East. They sent British wares across the world. They brought back chests of silver.

Silver bars had been used in London – and indeed, throughout the world – for a millennium, but not since the height of the Spanish Empire had any place in the world been so rich in or so reliant on silver's power. Silver lining the canals made the water fresher and cleaner than any river like the Thames had a right to be. Silver in the gutters disguised the stink of rain, sludge, and sewage with the scent of invisible roses. Silver in the clock towers made the bells chime for miles and miles further than they should have, until the notes clashed discordantly against each other throughout the city and over the countryside.

Silver was in the seats of the two-wheeled Hansom cabs Professor Lovell hailed when they had cleared customs – one for the three of them, and a second for their trunks. As they settled in, tightly nestled against each other in the tiny carriage, Professor Lovell reached over his knees and pointed out a silver bar embedded in the floor of the carriage.

'Can you read what that says?' he asked.

Robin bent over, squinting. 'Speed. And . . . spes?'

'Spēs,' said Professor Lovell. 'It's Latin. It's the root word of the English *speed*, and it means a nexus of things involving hope, fortune, success, and reaching one's goal. Makes the carriages run a bit more safely and quickly.'

Robin frowned, running his finger along the bar. It seemed so small, too innocuous to produce such a profound effect. 'But how?' And a second, more urgent question. 'Will *I*—'

'In time.' Professor Lovell patted him on the shoulder. 'But yes, Robin

Swift. You'll be one of the few scholars in the world that knows the secrets of silver-working. That's what I've brought you here to do.'

Two hours in the cab brought them to a village called Hampstead several miles north of London proper, where Professor Lovell owned a four-storey house made of pale red brick and white stucco, surrounded by a generous swath of neat green shrubbery.

'Your room is at the top,' Professor Lovell told Robin as he unlocked the door. 'Up the stairs and to the right.'

The house was very dark and chilly inside. Mrs Piper went about pulling open the curtains, while Robin dragged his trunk up the spiralling staircase and down the hall as instructed. His room consisted of only a little furniture – a writing desk, a bed, and a sitting chair – and was bare of any decorations or possessions except for the corner bookshelf, which was packed with so many titles that his treasured collection felt paltry in comparison.

Curious, Robin approached. Had those books been prepared especially for him? That felt unlikely, though many of the titles looked like things he would enjoy – the top shelf alone had a number of Swifts and Defoes, novels by his favourite authors he hadn't known existed. Ah, there was *Gulliver's Travels*. He pulled the book off the shelf. It seemed well-worn, some pages creased and dog-eared and others stained by tea or coffee.

He replaced the book, confused. Someone else must have lived in this room before him. Some other boy, perhaps – someone his age, who loved Jonathan Swift just as much, who had read this copy of *Gulliver's Travels* so many times that the ink at the top right where one's finger turned the page was starting to fade.

But who could that have been? He'd assumed Professor Lovell had no children.

'Robin!' Mrs Piper bellowed from downstairs. 'You're wanted outside.'

Robin hurried back down the stairs. Professor Lovell waited by the door, looking impatiently at his pocket-watch.

'Will your room do?' he asked. 'Has everything you need?'

Robin nodded effusively. 'Oh, yes.'

'Good.' Professor Lovell nodded to the waiting cab. 'Get in, we've got to make you an Englishman.'

He meant this literally. For the rest of the afternoon, Professor Lovell took Robin on a series of errands in the service of assimilating him into British civil society. They saw a physician who weighed him, examined him, and reluctantly declared him fit for life on the island: 'No tropical diseases nor fleas, thank heavens. He's a bit small for his age, but raise him on mutton and mash and he'll be fine. Now let's have a smallpox jab – roll that sleeve up, please, thank you. It won't hurt. Count to three.' They saw a barber, who clipped Robin's unruly, chin-length curls into a short, neat crop above his ears. They saw a hatter, a bootmaker, and finally a tailor, who measured every inch of Robin's body and showed him several bolts of cloth among which Robin, overwhelmed, chose at random.

As the afternoon wound down, they went to the courthouse for an appointment with a solicitor who drafted a set of papers which, Robin was told, would make him a legal citizen of the United Kingdom and a ward under the guardianship of Professor Richard Linton Lovell.

Professor Lovell signed his name with a flourish. Then Robin went up to the solicitor's desk. The surface was too high for him, so a clerk dragged over a bench on which he could stand.

'I thought I had signed this already.' Robin glanced down. The language seemed quite similar to the guardianship contract that Professor Lovell had given him in Canton.

'Those were the terms between you and me,' said Professor Lovell. '*This* makes you an Englishman.'

Robin scanned the looping script – *guardian, orphan, minor, custody*. 'You're claiming me as a son?'

'I'm claiming you as a ward. That's different.'

Why?, he almost asked. Something important hinged on that question, though he was still too young to know what precisely it was. A moment stretched between them, pregnant with possibility. The solicitor scratched his nose. Professor Lovell cleared his throat. But the moment passed without comment. Professor Lovell was not forthcoming, and Robin already knew better than to press. He signed.

The sun had long set by the time they returned to Hampstead. Robin asked if he might head up to bed, but Professor Lovell urged him to the dining room.

'You can't disappoint Mrs Piper; she's been in the kitchen all afternoon. At least push your food around on your plate for a bit.'

Mrs Piper and her kitchen had enjoyed a glorious reunion. The dining room table, which seemed ridiculously large for just the two of them, was piled with pitchers of milk, white rolls of bread, roast carrots and potatoes, gravy, something still simmering in a silver-gilded tureen, and what looked like an entire glazed chicken. Robin hadn't eaten since that morning; he should have been famished, but he was so exhausted that the sight of all that food made his stomach twist.

Instead, he turned his eyes to a painting that hung behind the table. It was impossible to ignore; it dominated the entire room. It depicted a beautiful city at dusk, but it was not London, he didn't think. It seemed more dignified. More ancient.

'Ah. Now that,' Professor Lovell followed his gaze, 'is Oxford.'

Oxford. He'd heard that word before, but he wasn't sure where. He tried to parse the name, the way he did with all unfamiliar English words. 'A . . . a cow-trading centre? Is it a market?'

'A university,' said Professor Lovell. 'A place where all the great minds of the nation can congregate in research, study, and instruction. It's a wonderful place, Robin.'

He pointed to a grand domed building in the middle of the painting. 'This is the Radcliffe Library. And this,' he gestured to a tower beside it, the tallest building in the landscape, 'is the Royal Institute of Translation. This is where I teach, and where I spend the majority of the year when I'm not in London.'

'It's lovely,' said Robin.

'Oh, yes.' Professor Lovell spoke with uncharacteristic warmth. 'It's the loveliest place on earth.'

He spread his hands through the air, as if envisioning Oxford before him. 'Imagine a town of scholars, all researching the most marvellous, fascinating things. Science. Mathematics. Languages. Literature. Imagine building after building filled with more books than you've seen in your entire life. Imagine quiet, solitude, and a serene place to think.' He sighed. 'London is a blathering mess. It's impossible to get anything done here; the city's too loud, and it demands too much of you. You can escape out to places like Hampstead, but the screaming core draws you back in whether you like it or not. But Oxford gives you all the tools you need for your work – food, clothes, books, tea – and then it leaves you alone. It is the centre of all knowledge and innovation in the civilized world. And, should you progress sufficiently well in your studies here, you might one day be lucky enough to call it home.'

The only appropriate response here seemed to be an awed silence. Professor Lovell gazed wistfully at the painting. Robin tried to match his enthusiasm, but could not help glancing sideways at the professor. The softness in his eyes, the *longing*, startled him. In the little time he'd known him, Robin had never seen Professor Lovell express such fondness for anything.

Robin's lessons began the next day.

As soon as breakfast concluded, Professor Lovell instructed Robin to wash and return to the drawing room in ten minutes. There waited a portly, smiling gentleman named Mr Felton – a first class at Oxford, an Oriel man, mind you – and yes, he'd make sure Robin was up to Oxford's Latinate speed. The boy was starting a bit late compared to his peers, but if he studied hard, that could be easily remedied.

Thus began a morning of memorizing basic vocabulary – *agricola, terra, aqua* – which was daunting, but then seemed easy compared to the head-spinning explanations of declensions and conjugations which followed. Robin had never been taught the fundamentals of grammar – he knew what worked in English because it *sounded* right – and so in learning Latin, he learned the basic parts of language itself. Noun, verb, subject, predicate, copula; then the nominative, genitive, accusative cases . . . He absorbed a bewildering amount of material over the next three hours, and had forgotten half of it by the time the lesson ended, but he came away with a deep appreciation of language and all the words for what you could do with it.

'That's all right, lad.' Mr Felton, thankfully, was a patient fellow, and seemed sympathetic to the mental brutalization he'd subjected Robin to. 'You'll have much more fun after we've finished laying the groundwork. Just wait until we get to Cicero.' He peered down at Robin's notes. 'But you've got to be more careful with your spelling.'

Robin couldn't see where he'd gone wrong. 'How do you mean?'

'You've forgotten nearly all the macron marks.'

'Oh.' Robin suppressed a noise of impatience; he was very hungry, and just wanted to be done so he could go to lunch. 'Those.'

Mr Felton rapped the table with his knuckles. 'Even the length of a single vowel matters, Robin Swift. Consider the Bible. The original

Hebrew text never specifies what sort of forbidden fruit the serpent persuades Eve to eat. But in Latin, *malum* means "bad" and *mālum*,' he wrote the words out for Robin, emphasizing the macron with force, 'means "apple". It was a short leap from there to blaming the apple for the original sin. But for all we know, the real culprit could be a persimmon.'

Mr Felton departed at lunchtime, after assigning a list of nearly a hundred vocabulary words to memorize before the following morning. Robin ate alone in the drawing room, mechanically shoving ham and potatoes into his mouth as he blinked uncomprehendingly at his grammar.

'More potatoes, dear?' Mrs Piper asked.

'No, thank you.' The heavy food, combined with the tiny font of his readings, was making him sleepy. His head throbbed; what he really would have liked then was a long nap.

But there was no reprieve. At two on the dot, a thin, grey-whiskered gentleman who introduced himself as Mr Chester arrived at the house, and for the next three hours, they commenced Robin's education in Ancient Greek.

Greek was an exercise in making the familiar strange. Its alphabet mapped onto the Roman alphabet, but only partly so, and often letters did not sound how they looked – a rho (P) was not a *P*, and an eta (H) was not an *H*. Like Latin, it made use of conjugations and declensions, but there were a good deal more moods, tenses, and voices to keep track of. Its inventory of sounds seemed further from English than Latin's did, and Robin kept struggling not to make Greek tones sound like Chinese tones. Mr Chester was harsher than Mr Felton, and became snippy and irritable when Robin kept flubbing his verb endings. By the end of the afternoon, Robin felt so lost that it was all he could do to simply repeat the sounds Mr Chester spat at him.

Mr Chester left at five, after also assigning a mountain of readings that hurt Robin to look at. He carried the texts to his room, then stumbled, head spinning, to the dining room for supper.

'How did your classes go?' Professor Lovell inquired.

Robin hesitated. 'Just fine.'

Professor Lovell's mouth quirked up in a smile. 'It's a bit much, isn't it?'

Robin sighed. 'Just a tad, sir.'

'But that's the beauty of learning a new language. It *should* feel like an enormous undertaking. It ought to intimidate you. It makes you appreciate the complexity of the ones you know already.'

'But I don't see why they have to be *quite* so complicated,' Robin said with sudden vehemence. He couldn't help it; his frustration had been mounting since noon. 'I mean, why so many rules? Why so many *endings*? Chinese doesn't have any of those; we haven't got tenses or declensions or conjugations. Chinese is much simpler—'

'You're wrong there,' said Professor Lovell. 'Every language is complex in its own way. Latin just happens to work its complexity into the shape of the word. Its morphological richness is an asset, not an obstacle. Consider the sentence *He will learn. Tā huì xué.* Three words in both English and Chinese. In Latin, it takes only one. *Disce.* Much more elegant, you see?'

Robin wasn't sure he did.

This routine – Latin in the morning, Greek in the afternoon – became Robin's life for the foreseeable future. He was grateful for this, despite the toil. At last, he had some structure to his days. He felt less unrooted and bewildered now – he had a purpose, he had a place, and even though he still couldn't quite fathom why this life had fallen to *him*, of all the dock boys in Canton, he took to his duties with determined, uncomplaining diligence.

Twice a week he had conversational practice with Professor Lovell in Mandarin.* At first, he could not understand the point. These dialogues felt artificial, stilted, and most of all, unnecessary. He was fluent already; he didn't stumble over vocabulary recall or pronunciations the way he

---

* As Robin's family had only recently migrated south, he had grown up speaking both Mandarin and Cantonese. But his Cantonese, Professor Lovell informed him, could now be forgotten. Mandarin was the language of the Qing imperial court in Peking, the language of officials and scholars, and therefore the only dialect that mattered.

This view is a side effect of the British Academy's path dependency on scant previous Western research. Matteo Ricci's Portuguese-Chinese dictionary was of the Mandarin dialect he learned at the Ming court; Francisco Varo, Joseph Prémare, and Robert Morrison's Chinese dictionaries were also of Mandarin. Britain's Sinologists of that era, then, were far more focused on Mandarin than on other dialects. And so Robin was asked to forget his preferred native tongue.

did when he and Mr Felton conversed in Latin. Why should he answer such basic questions as how he found his dinner, or what he thought about the weather?

But Professor Lovell was adamant. 'Languages are easier to forget than you imagine,' he said. 'Once you stop living in the world of Chinese, you stop thinking in Chinese.'

'But I thought you wanted me to start thinking in English,' Robin said, confused.

'I want you to *live* in English,' said Professor Lovell. 'This is true. But I still need you to practise your Chinese. Words and phrases you think are carved into your bones can disappear in no time.'

He spoke as if this had happened before.

'You've grown up with solid foundations in Mandarin, Cantonese, and English. That's very fortunate – there are adults who spend their lifetimes trying to achieve what you have. And even if they do, they achieve only a passable fluency – enough to get by, if they think hard and recall vocabulary before speaking – but nothing close to a native fluency where words come unbidden, without lag or labour. You, on the other hand, have already mastered the hardest parts of two language systems – the accents and rhythm, those unconscious quirks that adults take forever to learn, and even then, not quite. But you must *maintain* them. You can't squander your natural gifts.'

'But I don't understand,' said Robin. 'If my talents lie in Chinese, then what do I need Latin and Greek for?'

Professor Lovell chuckled. 'To understand English.'

'But I know English.'

'Not as well as you think you do. Plenty of people speak it, but few of them really *know* it, its roots and skeletons. But you need to know the history, shape, and depths of a language, particularly if you plan to manipulate it as you will one day learn to do. And you'll need to attain that mastery of Chinese as well. That begins with practising what you have.'

Professor Lovell was right. It was, Robin discovered, startlingly easy to lose a language that had once felt as familiar as his own skin. In London, without another Chinese person in sight, at least not in the circles of London where he lived, his mother tongue sounded like babble. Uttered in that drawing room, the most quintessentially English of spaces, it didn't feel like it belonged. It felt made-up. And it scared him, sometimes, how often his memory would lapse, how the syllables he'd grown up around could suddenly sound so unfamiliar.

He put twice the effort into Chinese that he did into Greek and Latin. For hours a day he practised writing out his characters, labouring over every stroke until he achieved a perfect replica of the characters in print. He reached into his memory to recall how Chinese conversations felt, how Mandarin sounded when it rolled naturally off his tongue, when he didn't have to pause to remember the tones of the next word he uttered.

But he *was* forgetting. That terrified him. Sometimes, during practice conversations, he found himself blanking on a word he used to toss around constantly. And sometimes he sounded, to his own ears, like a European sailor imitating Chinese without knowing what he said.

He could fix it, though. He would. Through practice, through memorization, through daily compositions – it wasn't the same as living and breathing Mandarin, but it was close enough. He was of an age when the language had made a permanent impression on his mind. But he had to try, really try, to make sure that he did not stop dreaming in his native tongue.

At least thrice a week Professor Lovell received a variety of guests in his sitting room. Robin supposed they must have also been scholars, for often they came bearing stacks of books or bound manuscripts, which they would pore over and debate about until the late hours of the night. Several of these men, it turned out, could speak Chinese, and Robin sometimes hid out over the banister, eavesdropping on the very strange sound of Englishmen discussing the finer points of Classical Chinese grammar over afternoon tea. 'It's just a final particle,' one of them would insist, while the others cried, 'Well, they can't *all* be final particles.'

Professor Lovell seemed to prefer that Robin keep out of sight when company came. He never explicitly forbade Robin's presence, but he would make a note to say that Mr Woodbridge and Mr Ratcliffe were visiting at eight, which Robin interpreted to mean that he ought to make himself scarce.

Robin had no issue with this arrangement. Admittedly, he found their conversations fascinating – they spoke often of far-flung things like expeditions to the West Indies, negotiations over cotton prints in India, and violent unrest throughout the Near East. But as a group, they were frightening; a procession of solemn, erudite men, all dressed in black like a murder of crows, each more intimidating than the last.

The only time he barged in on one of these gatherings was by accident. He'd been out in the garden, taking his daily physician-recommended turn, when he overheard the professor and his guests loudly discussing Canton.

'Napier's an idiot,' Professor Lovell was saying. 'He's playing his hand too early – there's no subtlety. Parliament's not ready, and he's irritating the compradors besides.'

'You think the Tories will want to move in at any point?' asked a man with a very deep voice.

'Perhaps. But they'll have to get a better stronghold in Canton if they're going to bring ships in.'

At this point Robin could not help but venture into the sitting room. 'What about Canton?'

The gentlemen all turned to regard him at once. There were four of them, all very tall, and all either spectacled or monocled.

'What about Canton?' Robin asked again, suddenly nervous.

'Shush,' said Professor Lovell. 'Robin, your shoes are filthy, you're tracking mud everywhere. Take them off and go and have a bath.'

Robin persisted. 'Is King George going to declare war on Canton?'

'He can't declare war on Canton, Robin. No one declares war on cities.'

'Then is King George going to invade China?' he persisted.

For some reason this made the gentlemen laugh.

'Would that we could,' said the man with the deep voice. 'It'd make this whole enterprise a lot easier, wouldn't it?'

A man with a great grey beard peered down at Robin. 'And where would your loyalties lie? Here, or back home?'

'My goodness.' The fourth man, whose pale blue eyes Robin found unnerving, bent down to inspect him, as if through a massive, invisible magnifying glass. 'Is this the new one? He's even more of your spitting image than the last—'

Professor Lovell's voice cut through the room like glass. 'Hayward.'

'Really, it's *uncanny*, I mean, look at his eyes. Not the colour, but the *shape*—'

'*Hayward.*'

Robin glanced back and forth between them, baffled.

'That's quite enough,' said Professor Lovell. 'Robin, *go.*'

Robin muttered an apology and hurried up the stairs, muddy boots forgotten. Over his shoulder, he heard fragments of Professor Lovell's response: 'He doesn't know, I don't like giving him ideas . . . No, Hayward, I won't—' But by the time he reached the safety of the landing, where he could lean over the banister and listen in without being caught, they had already changed the topic to Afghanistan.

That night, Robin stood before his mirror, staring intently at his face for so long that eventually it began to seem alien.

His aunts liked to say he had the kind of face that could blend in anywhere – his hair and eyes, both a softer shade of brown than the indigo-black that coloured the rest of his family, could have plausibly marked him as either the son of a Portuguese sailor or the heir to the Qing Emperor. But Robin had always attributed this to some accidental arrangement of nature that ascribed him features that could have belonged anywhere on the spectrum of either race, white or yellow.

He had never wondered whether he might not be full-blooded Chinese.

But what was the alternative? That his father was white? That his father was—

Look at his eyes.

That was incontrovertible proof, wasn't it?

Then why would his father not claim Robin as his own? Why was he only a ward, and not a son?

But even then, Robin was not too young to understand there were some truths that could not be uttered, that life as normal was only possible if they were never acknowledged. He had a roof over his head, three guaranteed meals a day, and access to more books than he could read in a lifetime. He did not, he knew, have the right to demand anything more.

He made a decision then. He would never question Professor Lovell, never probe at the empty space where the truth belonged. As long as Professor Lovell did not accept him as a son, Robin would not attempt to claim him as a father. A lie was not a lie if it was never uttered; questions that were never asked did not need answers. They would both remain perfectly content to linger in the liminal, endless space between truth and denial.

He dried himself, dressed, and sat down at his desk to finish his translation exercise for the evening. He and Mr Felton had moved on to Tacitus's *Agricola* now.

Auferre trucidare rapere falsis nominibus imperium atque ubi solitudinem faciunt pacem appellant.

Robin parsed the sentence, consulted his dictionary to check that *auferre* meant what he thought it did, then wrote out his translation.*

When Michaelmas term began in early October, Professor Lovell departed for Oxford, where he would stay for the next eight weeks. He would do this for each of Oxford's three academic terms, returning only during the breaks. Robin relished these periods; even though his classes did not pause, it felt possible to breathe and relax then without risk of disappointing his guardian at every turn.

It also meant that, without Professor Lovell breathing over his shoulder, he had the freedom to explore the city.

Professor Lovell gave him no allowance, but Mrs Piper occasionally let him have some small change for fares, which he saved up until he could get to Covent Garden by carriage. When he learned from a paperboy about the horse-drawn omnibus service, he rode it almost every weekend, crisscrossing the heart of London from Paddington Green to the Bank. His first few trips alone terrified him; several times he grew convinced he would never find his way back to Hampstead again and would be doomed to live out his life as a waif on the streets. But he persisted. He refused to be cowed by London's complexity, for wasn't Canton, too, a labyrinth? He determined to make the place home by walking every inch of it. Bit by bit London grew to feel less overwhelming, less like a belching, contorted pit of monsters that might swallow him up at any corner and more like a navigable maze whose tricks and turns he could anticipate.

He read the city. London in the 1830s was exploding with print. Newspapers, magazines, journals, quarterlies, weeklies, monthlies, and books of every genre were flying off the shelves, tossed on doorsteps, and hawked from the corners of nearly every street. He pored over newsstand copies of *The Times*, the *Standard*, and the *Morning Post*; he read, though did not fully comprehend, articles in academic journals like *Edinburgh*

---

* 'Robbery, butchery, and theft – they call these things empire, and where they create a desert, they call it peace.'

Review and *Quarterly Review*, he read penny satirical papers like *Figaro in London*, melodramatic pseudo-news like colourful crime reports and a series on the dying confessions of condemned prisoners. For cheaper stuff, he entertained himself with the *Bawbee Bagpipe*. He stumbled on a series called *The Pickwick Papers* by someone named Charles Dickens, who was very funny but seemed to hate very much anyone who was not white. He discovered Fleet Street, the heart of London publishing, where newspapers came off the printing presses still hot. He went back there time and time again, bringing home stacks of yesterday's papers for free from piles that were dumped on the corner.

He didn't understand half of what he read, even if he could decipher all the individual words. The texts were packed with political allusions, inside jokes, slang, and conventions that he'd never learned. In lieu of a childhood spent absorbing it all in London, he tried devouring the corpus instead, tried to plough through references to things like Tories, Whigs, Chartists, and Reformers and memorize what they were. He learned what the Corn Laws were and what they had to do with a Frenchman named Napoleon. He learned who the Catholics and Protestants were, and how the (he thought, at least) small doctrinal differences between the two were apparently a matter of great and bloody importance. He learned that being English was not the same as being British, though he was still hard-pressed to articulate the difference between the two.

He read the city, and he learned its language. New words in English were a game to him, for in understanding the word he always came to understand something about English history or culture itself. He delighted when common words were, unexpectedly, formed from other words he knew. *Hussy* was a compound of *house* and *wife*. *Holiday* was a compound of *holy* and *day*. *Bedlam* came, implausibly, from *Bethlehem*. *Goodbye* was, incredibly, a shortened version of *God be with you*. In London's East End he encountered Cockney rhyming slang, which initially presented a great mystery, for he had no clue how *Hampstead* could come to mean 'teeth.'* But once he learned about the omitted rhyming component, he had great fun coming up with his own. (Mrs Piper was not very amused when he began referring to dinner as the 'meal of saints'.)†

---

* *Hampstead Heath* rhymes with *teeth*. Example: 'She's still got all her baby hampsteads.'

† Dinner, sinner.

Long after he learned the proper meanings of words and phrases that had once confused him, his mind still formed funny associations around them. He imagined the Cabinet as a series of massive shelves where men in fancy dress were arranged like dolls. He thought the Whigs were named for their wigs, and the Tories for the young Princess Victoria. He imagined Marylebone was composed of marble and bone, that Belgravia was a land of bells and graves, and that Chelsea was named for shells and the sea. Professor Lovell kept a shelf of Alexander Pope titles in his library, and for a full year Robin thought *The Rape of the Lock* was about fornication with an iron bolt instead of the theft of hair.*

He learned that a pound was worth twenty shillings, and a shilling was worth twelve pence – clarity on florins, groats, and farthings would have to come in time. He learned there were many types of British people, just as there were many types of Chinese people, and that being Irish or Welsh was distinct in important ways from being English. He learned Mrs Piper was from a place called Scotland, which made her a Scot, and also explained why her accent, lilting and rhotic, sounded so different from Professor Lovell's crisp, straight intonations.

He learned that London in 1830 was a city that could not decide what it wanted to be. The Silver City was the largest financial centre of the world, the leading edge of industry and technology. But its profits were not shared equally. London was as much a city of plays at Covent Garden and balls in Mayfair as it was a city of teeming slums around St Giles. London was a city of reformers, a place where the likes of William Wilberforce and Robert Wedderburn had urged the abolition of slavery; where the Spa Fields riots had ended with the leaders charged for high treason; where Owenites had tried to get everyone to join their utopian socialist communities (he was still not sure what socialism was yet); and where Mary Wollstonecraft's *Vindication of the Rights of Woman*, published only forty years ago, had inspired waves of loud, proud feminists and suffragists in its wake. He discovered that in Parliament, in town halls, and on the streets, reformers of every stripe were fighting for the soul of London, while a conservative, landed ruling class fought back against attempts at change at every turn.

He did not understand these political struggles, not then. He only

---

* A reasonable error. By *rape*, Pope meant 'to snatch, to take by force', which is an older meaning derived from the Latin *rapere*.

sensed that London, and England at large, was very divided about what it was and what it wanted to be. And he understood that silver lay behind it all. For when the Radicals wrote about the perils of industrialization, and when the Conservatives refuted this with proof of the booming economy; when any of the political parties spoke about slums, housing, roads, transportation, agriculture, and manufacturing; when anyone spoke about Britain and the Empire's future at all, the word was always there in papers, pamphlets, magazines, and even prayer books: *silver, silver, silver.*

From Mrs Piper, he learned more than he'd imagined possible about English food and England. Adjusting to this new palate took some time. He had never thought much about food when he lived in Canton – the porridge, steamed buns, dumplings, and vegetable dishes that comprised his daily meals had seemed unremarkable to him. They were the staples of a poor family's diet, a far cry from high Chinese cuisine. Now he was astonished by how much he missed them. The English made regular use of only two flavours – salty and not salty – and did not seem to recognize any of the others. For a country that profited so well from trading in spices, its citizens were violently averse to actually using them; in all his time in Hampstead, he never tasted a dish that could be properly described as 'seasoned', let alone 'spicy'.

He took more pleasure in learning about the food than in eating it. This education came unprompted – dear Mrs Piper was the chatty sort, and would happily lecture as she served up lunch if Robin displayed even the slightest interest in what was on his plate. He was told that potatoes, which he found quite tasty in any form, were not to be served around important company, for they were considered lower-class. He found that newly invented silver-gilded dishes were used to keep food warm throughout a meal, but that it was rude to reveal this trickery to guests, and so the bars were always embedded on the very bottoms of the platters. He learned that the practice of serving food in successive courses was adopted from the French, and that the reason it was not yet a universal norm was a lingering resentment over that little man Napoleon. He learned, but did not quite understand, the subtle distinctions between lunch, luncheon, and a noon dinner. He learned he had the Roman Catholics to thank for his favourite almond cheesecakes, for the prohibition of dairy during fast days had forced English cooks to innovate with almond milk.

One night Mrs Piper brought out a round, flat circle: some kind of baked dough that had been cut into triangular wedges. Robin took one and tentatively bit at the corner. It was very thick and floury, much denser than the fluffy white rolls his mother used to steam every week. It was not unpleasant, just surprisingly heavy. He took a large gulp of water to guide the bolus down, then asked, 'What's this?'

'That's a bannock, dear,' said Mrs Piper.

'Scone,' corrected Professor Lovell.

'It's properly a *bannock*—'

'The scones are the pieces,' said Professor Lovell. 'The bannock is the entire cake.'

'Now look here, this is a bannock, and all the itty pieces are bannocks as well. Scones are those dry, crumbly things you English love to shove in your mouths—'

'I assume you're excepting your own scones, Mrs Piper. No one in their right mind would accuse those of being dry.'

Mrs Piper did not succumb to flattery. 'It's a bannock. *They're* bannocks. My grandmother called them bannocks, my mother called them bannocks, so bannocks they are.'

'Why's it – why are they – called bannocks?' Robin asked. The sound of the word made him imagine a monster of the hills, some clawed and gristly thing that wouldn't be satisfied unless given a sacrifice of bread.

'Because of Latin,' said Professor Lovell. 'Bannock comes from *panicium*, meaning "baked bread".'

This seemed plausible, if disappointingly mundane. Robin took another bite of the bannock, or scone, and this time relished the thick, satisfying way it settled on his stomach.

He and Mrs Piper quickly bonded over a deep love of scones. She made them every which way – plain, served with a bit of clotted cream and raspberry jam; savoury and studded with cheese and garlic chives; or dotted through with bits of dried fruit. Robin liked them best plain – why ruin what was, in his opinion, perfect from conception? He had just learned about Platonic forms, and was convinced scones were the Platonic ideal of bread. And Mrs Piper's clotted cream was wonderful, light and nutty and refreshing all at once. Some households simmered milk for nearly a full day on the stove to get that layer of cream on top, she told him, but last Christmas Professor Lovell had brought her a clever silver-work contraption that could separate the cream in seconds.

Professor Lovell liked plain scones the least, though, so sultana scones were the staple of their afternoon teas.

'Why are they called sultanas?' Robin asked. 'They're just raisins, aren't they?'

'I'm not sure, dear,' said Mrs Piper. 'Perhaps it's where they're from. *Sultana* does sound rather Oriental, doesn't it? Richard, where are these grown? India?'

'Asia Minor,' said Professor Lovell. 'And they're sultanas, not sultans, because they haven't got seeds.'

Mrs Piper winked at Robin. 'Well, there you have it. It's all about the seeds.'

Robin didn't understand this joke, but he knew he didn't like sultanas in his scones; when Professor Lovell wasn't looking, he picked out his sultanas, slathered the denuded scone in clotted cream, and popped it in his mouth.

Apart from scones, Robin's other great indulgence was novels. The two dozen tomes he'd received every year in Canton had been a meagre trickle. Now he had access to a veritable flood. He was never without a book, but he had to get creative in squeezing leisure reading into his schedule – he read at the table, scarfing down Mrs Piper's meals without a second thought to what he was putting in his mouth; he read while walking in the garden, though this made him dizzy; he even tried reading in the bath, but the wet, crumpled fingerprints he left on a new edition of Defoe's *Colonel Jack* shamed him enough to make him give up the practice.

He enjoyed novels more than anything else. Dickens's serials were well and fun, but what a pleasure it was to hold the weight of an entire, finished story in his hands. He read any genre he could get his hands on. He enjoyed all of Jane Austen's oeuvre, though it took much consulting with Mrs Piper to understand the social conventions Austen described. (Where was Antigua? And why was Sir Thomas Bertram always going there?)* He devoured the travel literature of Thomas Hope and James Morier, through whom he met the Greeks and the Persians,

---

* Because he owned slaves.

or at least some fanciful version of them. He greatly enjoyed Mary Shelley's *Frankenstein*, though he could not say the same of the poems by her less talented husband, whom he found overly dramatic.

Upon his return from Oxford that first term, Professor Lovell took Robin to a bookshop – Hatchards on Piccadilly, just opposite Fortnum & Mason. Robin paused outside the green-painted entrance, gaping. He'd passed by bookshops many times during his jaunts about the city, but never had he imagined he might be allowed to go inside. He had somehow developed the idea that bookshops were only for wealthy grown-ups, that he'd be dragged out by the ear if he dared to enter.

Professor Lovell smiled when he saw Robin hesitating at the doors.

'And this is just a shop for the public,' he said. 'Wait until you see a college library.'

Inside, the heady wood-dust smell of freshly printed books was over-whelming. If tobacco smelled like this, Robin thought, he'd huff it every day. He stepped towards the closest shelf, hand lifted tentatively towards the books on display, too afraid to touch them – they seemed so new and crisp; their spines were uncracked, their pages smooth and bright. Robin was used to well-worn, waterlogged tomes; even his Classics grammars were decades old. These shiny, freshly bound things seemed like a dif-ferent class of object, things to be admired from a distance rather than handled and read.

'Pick one,' said Professor Lovell. 'You ought to know the feeling of acquiring your first book.'

Pick *one*? Just one, of all these treasures? Robin didn't know the first title from the second, and he was too dazzled by the sheer amount of text to flip through and decide. His eyes alighted on a title: *The King's Own* by Frederick Marryat, an author he was, so far, unfamiliar with. But new, he thought, was good.

'Hm. Marryat. I haven't read him, but I'm told he's popular with boys your age.' Professor Lovell turned the book over in his hands. 'This one, then? You're sure?'

Robin nodded. If he didn't decide now, he knew, he'd never leave. He was like a starved man in a pastry shop, dazzled by his options, but he did not want to try the professor's patience.

Outside, the professor handed him the brown-paper-wrapped parcel. Robin hugged it to his chest, willing himself not to rip it open until they'd returned home. He thanked Professor Lovell profusely, and stopped only when he noticed this made the professor look somewhat uncomfortable. But then the professor asked him whether it felt good to hold the new book in his hands. Robin enthusiastically agreed and, for the first time he could remember, they traded smiles.

Robin had planned to save *The King's Own* until that weekend, when he had a whole afternoon without classes to slowly savour its pages. But Thursday afternoon came, and he found he couldn't wait. After Mr Felton left, he wolfed down the plate of bread and cheese Mrs Piper had set out and hurried upstairs to the library, where he curled up in his favourite armchair and started to read.

He was immediately enchanted. *The King's Own* was a tale of naval exploits; of revenge, daring, and struggle; of ship battles and far-flung travels. His mind drifted to his own voyage from Canton, and he reframed those memories in the context of the novel, imagined himself battling pirates, building rafts, winning medals for courage and valour—

The door creaked open.

'What are you doing?' asked Professor Lovell.

Robin glanced up. His mental image of the Royal Navy navigating choppy waters had been so vivid, it took him a moment to remember where he was.

'Robin,' Professor Lovell said again, '*what are you doing?*'

Suddenly the library felt very cold; the golden afternoon darkened. Robin followed Professor Lovell's gaze to the ticking clock above the door. He'd completely forgotten the time. But those hands couldn't possibly be right, it couldn't have been *three hours* since he'd sat down to read.

'I'm sorry,' he said, still somewhat dazed. He felt like a traveller from far away, plucked from the Indian Ocean and dropped into this dim, chilly study. 'I didn't – I lost track of time.'

He couldn't read Professor Lovell's expression at all. That scared him. That inscrutable wall, that inhuman blankness, was infinitely more frightening than fury would have been.

'Mr Chester has been downstairs for over an hour,' said Professor Lovell. 'I wouldn't have kept him waiting for even ten minutes, but I've only just returned to the house.'

Robin's gut twisted with guilt. 'I'm very sorry, sir—'

'What are you reading?' Professor Lovell interrupted.

Robin hesitated for a moment, then held out *The King's Own*.[*] 'The book you bought me, sir – there's a big battle going on, I just wanted to see what—'

'Do you think it matters what that infernal book is about?'

In years to come, whenever Robin looked back on that memory, he was appalled by how brazenly he had acted next. He must have been panicked out of his mind, because it was absurdly foolish, in retrospect, how he had simply closed the Marryat book and headed for the door, as if he could merely hurry down to class, as if a fault of this magnitude could be so easily forgotten.

As he neared the door, Professor Lovell drew his hand back and brought his knuckles hard against Robin's left cheek.

The force of the blow thrust him to the floor. He didn't register pain so much as shock; the reverberation in his temples didn't *hurt*, not yet – that came later, after several seconds passed and the blood began rushing to his head.

Professor Lovell wasn't finished. As Robin rose to his knees, dazed, the professor pulled the poker from beside the fireplace and swung it diagonally against the right side of Robin's torso. Then he brought it down again. And again.

Robin would have been more frightened if he'd ever suspected Professor Lovell of violence, but this beating was so unexpected, so wholly out of character, that it felt surreal more than anything else. It didn't occur to him to beg, to cry, or even to scream. Even as the poker cracked against his ribs for the eighth, ninth, tenth, time – even as he tasted blood on his teeth – all he felt was a deep bewilderment that this was happening at all. It felt absurd. He seemed to be caught in a dream.

Professor Lovell, too, did not look like a man in the throes of a tempestuous rage. He was not shouting; his eyes were not wild; his cheeks had not even turned red. He seemed simply, with every hard and deliberate

---

[*] This was to be the last Marryat title Robin ever read. It was just as well. Frederick Marryat's novels, though full of the high seas adventuring and valour that endeared them to young English boys, also portrayed Black people as happy, satisfied slaves and American Indians as either noble savages or dissolute drunks. Chinese and Indians he described as 'races of inferior stature and effeminate in person'.

blow, to be attempting to inflict maximum pain with the minimum risk of permanent injury. For he did not strike Robin's head, nor did he apply so much force that Robin's ribs would crack. No; he only dealt bruises that could be easily hidden and that, in time, would heal completely.

He knew very well what he was doing. He seemed to have done this before.

After twelve strikes, it all stopped. With just as much poise and precision, Professor Lovell returned the poker to the mantel, stepped back, and sat down at the table, regarding Robin silently as the boy climbed to his knees and wiped the blood, as best he could, from his face.

After a very long silence, he spoke. 'When I brought you from Canton, I made clear my expectations.'

A sob had finally built up in Robin's throat, a choking, delayed emotional reaction, but he swallowed it down. He was terrified of what Professor Lovell would do if he made a noise.

'Get up,' Professor Lovell said coldly. 'Sit down.'

Automatically, Robin obeyed. One of his molars felt loose. He probed at it, wincing when a fresh, salty spurt of blood coated his tongue.

'Look at me,' Professor Lovell said.

Robin lifted his eyes.

'Well, that's one good thing about you,' said Professor Lovell. 'When you're beaten, you don't cry.'

Robin's nose prickled. Tears threatened to burst forth, and he strained to hold them back. He felt as if a spike were being driven through his temples. He was so overcome with pain then that he could not breathe, and still it seemed the most important thing was to display no hint of suffering at all. He had never felt so wretched in his life. He wanted to die.

'I won't tolerate laziness under this roof,' said Professor Lovell. 'Translation is no easy occupation, Robin. It demands focus. Discipline. You are already at a disadvantage for your lack of an early education in Latin and Greek, and you've only six years to make up the difference before you begin at Oxford. You cannot sloth. You cannot waste time on daydreams.'

He sighed. 'I hoped, based on Miss Slate's reports, that you had grown to be a diligent and hardworking boy. I see now that I was wrong. Laziness and deceit are common traits among your kind. This is why China remains an indolent and backwards country while her neighbours hurtle towards progress. You are, by nature, foolish, weak-minded, and disinclined to hard work. You must resist these traits, Robin. You must learn to overcome the pollution of your blood. I've gambled greatly on your capacity to do so. Prove to me that it was worth it, or purchase your own passage back to Canton.' He cocked his head. 'Do you wish to return to Canton?'

Robin swallowed. 'No.'

He meant it. Even after this, even after the miseries of his classes, he could not imagine an alternate future for himself. Canton meant poverty, insignificance, and ignorance. Canton meant the plague. Canton meant no more books. London meant all the material comforts he could ask for. London meant, someday, Oxford.

'Then decide now, Robin. Dedicate yourself to excelling at your studies, make the sacrifices that entails, and promise me you will never embarrass me so much again. Or take the first packet home. You'll be back on the streets with no family, no skills, and no money. You'll never get the kinds of opportunities I'm offering you again. You'll only ever dream of seeing London again, much less Oxford. You will never, *ever* touch a silver bar.' Professor Lovell leaned back, regarding Robin through cold, scrutinizing eyes. 'So. Choose.'

Robin whispered a response.

'Louder. In English.'

'I'm sorry,' Robin said hoarsely. 'I want to stay.'

'Good.' Professor Lovell stood up. 'Mr Chester is waiting downstairs. Collect yourself and go to class.'

Somehow Robin made it through the entirety of that class, sniffling, too dazed to focus, a great bruise blooming on his face while his torso throbbed from a dozen invisible hurts. Mercifully, Mr Chester said nothing about the incident. Robin went through a list of conjugations and got all of them wrong. Mr Chester patiently corrected him in a pleasant if forcedly even tone. Robin's tardiness had not shortened the class – they went far past suppertime, and those were the longest three hours of Robin's life.

The next morning, Professor Lovell acted as if nothing had happened. When Robin came down for breakfast, the professor asked if he'd finished his translations. Robin said he had. Mrs Piper brought out eggs and ham for breakfast, and they ate in a somewhat frenzied silence. It hurt to chew, and at times to swallow – Robin's face had swollen even more overnight – but Mrs Piper only suggested he cut his ham into smaller pieces when he coughed. They all finished their tea. Mrs Piper cleared the plates away, and Robin went to retrieve his Latin textbooks before Mr Felton arrived.

It never occurred to Robin to run, not then, and not once in the weeks that followed. Some other child might have been frightened, might have seized the first chance to escape into London's streets. Some other child suited to better, kinder treatment might have realized that such nonchalance on the part of adults like Mrs Piper, Mr Felton, and Mr Chester to a badly bruised eleven-year-old was frightfully wrong. But Robin was so grateful for this return to equilibrium that he couldn't find it in himself to even resent what had happened.

After all, it never happened again. Robin made sure it did not. He spent the next six years studying to the point of exhaustion. With the threat of expatriation looming constantly above him, he devoted his life to becoming the student Professor Lovell wanted to see.

Greek and Latin grew more entertaining after the first year, after he'd assembled enough building blocks of each language to piece together fragments of meaning for himself. From then on it felt less like groping in the dark whenever he encountered a new text and more like filling in the blanks. Figuring out the precise grammatical formulation of a phrase that had been frustrating him gave him the same sort of satisfaction he derived from reshelving a book where it belonged or finding a missing sock – all the pieces fitted together, and everything was whole and complete.

In Latin, he read through Cicero, Livy, Virgil, Horace, Caesar, and Juvenal; in Greek, he tackled Xenophon, Homer, Lysias, and Plato. In time, he realized he was quite good at languages. His memory was strong, and he had a knack for tones and rhythm. He soon reached a level of fluency in both Greek and Latin that any Oxford undergraduate would have been jealous of. In time, Professor Lovell stopped commenting on his inherited inclination to sloth, and instead nodded in approval at every update on Robin's rapid progress through the canon.

History, meanwhile, marched on around them. In 1830, King George IV had died and was succeeded by his younger brother, William IV, the eternal compromiser who pleased no one. In 1831, another cholera epidemic swept through London, leaving thirty thousand dead in its wake. The brunt of its impact fell on the poor and the destitute; those living in close, cramped quarters who could not escape each other's tainted miasmas.* But the neighbourhood in Hampstead was untouched – to Professor Lovell and his friends in their remote walled estates, the epidemic was something to mention in passing, wince about in sympathy, and quickly forget.

In 1833, a momentous thing happened – slavery was abolished in England and its colonies, to be replaced by a six-year apprenticeship term as a transition to freedom. Among Professor Lovell's interlocutors, this news was taken with the mild disappointment of a lost cricket match.

'Well, that's ruined the West Indies for us,' Mr Hallows complained. 'The abolitionists with their damned moralizing. I still believe this obsession with abolition is a product of the British needing to at least feel culturally superior now that they've lost America. And on what grounds? It isn't as if those poor fellows aren't equally enslaved back in Africa under those tyrants they call kings.'†

'I wouldn't give up on the West Indies just yet,' Professor Lovell said. 'They're still allowing a legal kind of forced labour—'

'But without ownership, it takes the teeth out of it all.'

'Perhaps that's for the best, though – freedmen do work better than slaves after all, and slavery is in fact more expensive than a free labour market—'

'You've been reading too much of Smith. Hobart and MacQueen had the right idea – just smuggle in a ship full of Chinamen,‡ that'll do the trick. They're so very industrious and orderly, Richard should know—'

---

* As the weekly papers recorded the climbing death counts, Robin asked Mrs Piper why the doctors could not simply go around healing the sick with silver, as Professor Lovell had done to him. 'Silver is expensive,' responded Mrs Piper, and that was the last they ever spoke of it.

† Here Mr Hallows forgets that chattel slavery, wherein slaves were treated as property and not persons, is a wholly European invention.

‡ Indeed, in the wake of Haiti's liberation, the British began toying with the idea of importing labourers of other races, such as the Chinese ('a sober, patient, industrious people'), as a possible alternative to African slave labour. The *Fortitude* experiment of 1806 attempted to establish a colony of two hundred Chinese labourers in Trinidad to create a 'barrier between us and the Negroes'. The colony failed, and most labourers soon returned to their native China. Still, the idea of replacing African labour with Chinese labour remained attractive to British entrepreneurs, and would be continually revived throughout the nineteenth century.

'No, Richard thinks they're lazy, don't you, Richard?'

'Now, what *I* wish,' interrupted Mr Ratcliffe, 'is that all these women would stop taking part in those anti-slavery debates. They see too much of themselves in their situation; it puts ideas in their head.'

'What,' asked Professor Lovell, 'is Mrs Ratcliffe unsatisfied with her domestic situation?'

'She'd like to think that it's a hop and a skip from abolition to women's suffrage.' Mr Ratcliffe let out a nasty laugh. 'That would be the day.'

And with that, the conversation turned to the absurdity of women's rights.

Never, Robin thought, would he understand these men, who talked of the world and its movements like a grand chess game, where countries and peoples were pieces to be moved and manipulated at will.

But if the world was an abstract object for them, it was even more abstract to him, for he had no stake in any of these matters. Robin processed that era through the myopic world of Lovell Manor. Reforms, colonial uprisings, slave revolts, women's suffrage, and the latest Parliamentary debates all meant nothing to him. All that mattered were the dead languages before him, and the fact that one day, a day that drew ever closer as the years trickled by, he would matriculate at the university he knew only from the painting on the wall – the city of knowledge, the city of dreaming spires.

It all ended without circumstance, without celebration. One day Mr Chester told Robin as he packed up his books that he'd enjoyed their lessons, and that he wished him well at university. This was how Robin discovered he was to be sent up to Oxford the next week.

'Oh, yes,' said Professor Lovell when asked. 'Did I forget to tell you? I've written to the college. They'll be expecting you.'

Supposedly there was an application process, some exchange of letters of introduction and guarantees of funding that secured his position. Robin was involved with none of this. Professor Lovell simply informed him he was due to move into his new lodgings on 29th September, so he'd best have his bags packed by the evening of the 28th. 'You'll arrive a few days before the start of term. We'll ride up together.'

The night before they left, Mrs Piper baked Robin a plate of small, hard, round biscuits so rich and crumbly they seemed to melt away in his mouth.

'It's shortbread,' she explained. 'Now, they're very rich, so don't eat them all at once. I don't make them much, as Richard thinks sugar ruins a boy, but you've deserved it.'

'Shortbread,' Robin repeated. 'Because they don't last long?'

They had been playing this game since the night of the bannock debate.

'No, dear.' She laughed. 'Because of the crumble. Fat "shortens" the pastry. That's what *short* means, you know – it's how we get the word *shortening*.'

He swallowed the sweet, fatty lump and chased it down with a gulp of milk. 'I'll miss your etymology lessons, Mrs Piper.'

To his surprise, her eyes turned red at the corners. Her voice grew thick. 'Write home whenever you need a sack of victuals,' she said. 'I don't know much of what goes on inside those colleges, but I know their food is something awful.'

CHAPTER THREE

But this shall never be: to us remains
One city that has nothing of the beast,
That was not built for gross, material gains,
Sharp, wolfish power or empire's glutted feast.

C.S. Lewis, 'Oxford'

The next morning Robin and Professor Lovell took a cab to a station in central London, where they transferred to a stagecoach bound all the way for Oxford. As they waited to board, Robin entertained himself by trying to guess at the etymology of *stagecoach*. *Coach* was obvious, but why *stage*? Was it because the flat, wide carriage looked something like a stage? Because entire troupes of actors might have travelled thus, or performed atop one? But that was a stretch. A carriage looked like a lot of things, but he couldn't imagine how a stage – a raised public platform – was the obvious association. Why not a basketcoach? An omnicoach?

'Because the journey happens in stages,' Professor Lovell explained when Robin gave up. 'Horses don't want to run all the way from London to Oxford, and usually neither do we. But I detest travellers' inns, so we're doing the single-day run; it's about ten hours with no stops, so use that lavatory before we go.'

They shared their stagecoach with nine other passengers – a well-dressed little family of four and a group of slouching gentlemen in drab suits and elbow patches who Robin assumed were all professors. Robin sat squeezed between Professor Lovell and one of the suited men. It was too early for conversation. As the carriage bounced along the cobblestones, the passengers either dozed or stared blankly in various directions.

It took Robin a while to realize the woman across from him was staring over her knitting. When he met her eyes, she promptly turned to Professor Lovell and asked, 'Is that an Oriental?'

Professor Lovell jerked his head up, roused from slumber. 'I beg your pardon?'

'I was asking about your boy,' said the woman. 'Is he from Peking?'

Robin glanced at Professor Lovell, suddenly very curious what he might say.

But Professor Lovell only shook his head. 'Canton,' he said curtly. 'Further south.'

'Ah,' said the woman, clearly disappointed when he wouldn't elaborate.

Professor Lovell went back to sleep. The woman looked Robin up and down again with an unsettlingly eager curiosity, then turned her attention to her children. Robin remained silent. Suddenly his chest felt very tight, though he couldn't understand why this was.

The children wouldn't stop staring at him; their eyes were wide and their mouths gaped in a way that would have been precious if they didn't make Robin feel as if he'd sprouted another head. After a moment the boy tugged on his mother's sleeve and made her bend down so he could whisper in her ear.

'Oh.' She chuckled, then glanced at Robin. 'He'd like to know if you can see.'

'I – what?'

'If you can see?' The woman raised her voice and overenunciated her every syllable, as if Robin had difficulty hearing. (This had happened often to Robin on the *Countess of Harcourt*; he could never understand why people treated those who couldn't understand English as if they were deaf.) 'With your eyes like that – can you see everything? Or is it only in little slits?'

'I can see perfectly well,' Robin said quietly.

The boy, disappointed, turned his attention to pinching his sister. The woman resumed her knitting as if nothing had happened.

The little family got off at Reading. Robin found he breathed more easily when they were gone. He could also stretch his legs over the aisle to give his stiff knees a respite without the mother shooting him a startled, suspicious look, as if she'd caught him in the act of trying to pick her pockets.

* * *

The last ten or so miles to Oxford were an idyllic stretch of green pasture-land, punctuated by the occasional herd of cows. Robin tried reading a guidebook entitled *The University of Oxford and Her Colleges*, but found himself with a throbbing headache, and so began nodding off. Some stagecoaches were outfitted with silver-work to make the ride feel as smooth as skates on ice, but theirs was an older model, and the constant jostling was exhausting. He awoke to wheels rumbling against cobble-stones and glanced around to discover they had arrived in the middle of High Street, right before the walled gates of his new home.

Oxford was composed of twenty-two colleges, all with their own residential complexes, coats of arms, dining halls, customs, and tradi-tions. Christ Church, Trinity, St John's, and All Souls boasted the largest endowments and therefore the nicest grounds. 'You'll want to make friends there, if only to have a look at the gardens,' said Professor Lovell. 'You can safely ignore anyone from Worcester or Hertford. They're poor and ugly,' whether he was referring to the people or the gardens, Robin couldn't be sure, 'and their food is bad.' One of the other gentlemen gave him a sour look as they stepped off the coach.

Robin would live in University College. His guidebook informed him that it was commonly referred to as 'Univ', that it housed all students enrolled in the Royal Institute of Translation, and that in aesthetic it was 'sombre and venerable, a look befitting of the university's oldest daugh-ter'. It certainly looked like a Gothic sanctuary; its front wall was all turrets and uniform windows against smooth white stone.

'Well, here you are.' Professor Lovell stood with his hands shoved in his pockets, looking slightly uncomfortable. Now that they'd been to the porter's lodge, acquired Robin's keys, and dragged Robin's trunks off High Street onto the paved sidewalk, it seemed obvious that a parting was imminent. Professor Lovell simply didn't know how to go about it. 'Well,' he said again. 'You have a few days before classes start, so you ought to spend them getting to know the city. You've got a map – yes, there – though the place is small enough you'll learn it by heart after a few strolls. Perhaps seek out the members of your cohort; they'll likely have moved in by now. My residence here is up north in Jericho; I've written you direc-tions in that envelope. Mrs Piper will join me there next week, and we'll expect you at dinner the Saturday after next. She'll be very happy to see you.' All this he rattled off like a memorized checklist. He seemed to have a hard time looking Robin in the eyes. 'Are you all set?'

'Oh, yes,' said Robin. 'I'll be very happy to see Mrs Piper as well.'

They blinked at each other. Robin felt that surely there were other words that should be said, words to mark this occasion – his growing up, leaving home, his entering university – as momentous. But he couldn't imagine what they might be, and apparently neither could Professor Lovell.

'Well, then.' Professor Lovell gave him a curt nod and turned halfway towards High Street, as if confirming he was no longer needed. 'You can manage your trunks?'

'Yes, sir.'

'Well, then,' Professor Lovell said again, then headed back out to High Street.

It was an awkward phrase to end on, two words that suggested more to come. Robin watched him for a moment, half expecting him to turn around, but Professor Lovell seemed focused solely on hailing a cab. Strange, yes. But this did not bother Robin. This was how things had always been between them: conversations unfinished, words best left unsaid.

Robin's lodgings were in Number 4, Magpie Lane[*] – a green-painted building halfway down the crooked, narrow alley that connected High Street and Merton Street. Someone else was already standing at the front door, fiddling with the lock. He had to be a new student – satchels and trunks were scattered on the cobblestones around him.

He was, Robin saw as he drew closer, very clearly not native to England. South Asia was more likely. Robin had seen sailors with the same colouring in Canton, all from ships arriving from India. The stranger had smooth dusky skin, a tall and graceful build, and the longest, darkest eyelashes that Robin had ever seen. His eyes flickered up and down Robin's frame before settling on his face, questioning – determining, Robin suspected, just how foreign Robin was in return.

'I'm Robin,' Robin burst out. 'Robin Swift.'

'Ramiz Rafi Mirza,' the other boy pronounced proudly, extending his hand. He spoke with such proper English diction he sounded nearly like Professor Lovell. 'Or just Ramy, if you like. And you – you're here for the Translation Institute, aren't you?'

---

[*] Formerly known as Gropecunt Lane, Magpie Lane was originally, as the name suggests, a street of brothels. This was not mentioned in Robin's guidebook.

'I am,' said Robin, then added, on a hunch, 'I'm from Canton.'

Ramy's face relaxed. 'Calcutta.'

'Did you just get in?'

'To Oxford, yes. To England, no – I came in through Liverpool on a ship four years ago and I've been holed up in a big, boring estate in Yorkshire until now. My guardian wanted me to acclimatize to English society before I matriculated.'

'Mine too,' Robin said eagerly. 'What did you think?'

'Awful weather.' One side of Ramy's mouth quirked up. 'And the only thing I can eat here is fish.'

They beamed at each other.

Robin felt a strange, bursting feeling in his chest then. He'd never met someone else in his situation, or anything like it, and he strongly suspected that should he keep probing, he would uncover a dozen more similarities. He had a thousand questions, but he didn't know where to start. Was Ramy also orphaned? Who was his sponsor? What was Calcutta like? Had he been back since? What brought him to Oxford? He was suddenly anxious – he felt his tongue stiffen, unable to choose a word – and there was also the matter of the keys, and their scattered trunks, which made the alley look as if a hurricane had emptied a ship's hold onto the street—

'Should we—' Robin managed, just as Ramy asked, 'Shall we open that door?'

They both laughed. Ramy smiled. 'Let's drag these inside.' He nudged a trunk with his toe. 'Then I've got a box of very nice sweets which I think we should open, yes?'

Their quarters were across the hall from one another – rooms six and seven. Each unit consisted of a large bedroom and a sitting room equipped with a low table, empty bookshelves, and a couch. The couch and table both seemed too formal, so they sat cross-legged on the floor of Ramy's room, blinking like shy children as they regarded each other, unsure what to do with their hands.

Ramy pulled a colourfully wrapped parcel from one of his trunks and set it on the floor between them. 'Sending-off gift from Sir Horace Wilson, my guardian. He gave me a bottle of port, too, but I threw that away. What would you like?' Ramy ripped the parcel open. 'There's toffee, caramel, peanut brittle, chocolates, and all kinds of candied fruits . . .'

'Oh, goodness – I'll have some toffee, thank you.' Robin hadn't spoken to another person near his age in as long as he could remember.* He was only now realizing how badly he wanted a friend, but he didn't know how to make one, and the prospect of trying but failing suddenly terrified him. What if Ramy found him dull? Annoying? Oversolicitous?

He took a bite of toffee, swallowed, and placed his hands in his lap.

'So,' he said. 'Tell me about Calcutta?'

Ramy grinned.

In the years to come, Robin would return so many times to this night. He was forever astonished by its mysterious alchemy, by how easily two badly socialized, restrictively raised strangers had transformed into kindred spirits in the span of minutes. Ramy seemed just as flushed and excited as Robin felt. They talked and talked. No topics seemed taboo; everything they brought up was either a point of instant agreement – scones are better without sultanas, thank you – or a cause for fascinating debate – no, London's lovely, actually; you country mice are just prejudiced because you're jealous. Only don't swim in the Thames.

At some point they began reciting poems to each other – lovely chains of Urdu couplets Ramy told him were called ghazals, and Tang poetry which Robin frankly didn't love but which sounded impressive. And he so badly wanted to impress Ramy. He was so witty, so well-read and funny. He had sharp, scathing opinions on everything – British cuisine, British manners, and the Oxbridge rivalry ('Oxford is larger than Cambridge, but Cambridge is prettier, and anyhow I think they only established Cambridge as overflow for the mediocre talent.') He'd travelled half the world; he'd been to Lucknow, Madras, Lisbon, Paris, and Madrid. He described his native India as a paradise: 'The mangoes, Birdie' (he'd already started calling Robin 'Birdie'), 'they're ridiculously juicy, you can't buy anything similar on this sorry little island. It's been years since I've had one. I'd give anything to see a proper Bengal mango.'

---

* There had once been a boy named Henry Little who'd visited Hampstead with his father, one of Professor Lovell's colleagues in the Royal Asiatic Society. Robin tried to engage him in conversation about scones, which he thought as good an opening salvo as any, but Henry Little merely reached out and stretched Robin's eyelids out so hard that Robin, startled, kicked him in the shin. Robin was banished to his room, and Henry Little to the garden; Professor Lovell had not invited his colleagues to bring their children over since then.

'I've read *Arabian Nights*,' Robin offered, drunk on excitement and trying to seem worldly as well.

'Calcutta's not in the Arab world, Birdie.'

'I know.' Robin blushed. 'I just meant—'

But Ramy had already moved on. 'You didn't tell me you read Arabic!'

'I don't, I read it in translation.'

Ramy sighed. 'Whose?'

Robin tried hard to remember. 'Jonathan Scott's?'

'That's a terrible translation.' Ramy waved his arm. 'Throw it away. For one thing, it's not even a direct translation – it went into French first, and then English – and for another, it's not remotely like the original. What's more, Galland – Antoine Galland, the French translator – did his very best to Frenchify the dialogue and to erase all cultural details he thought would confuse the reader. He translates Haroun Alraschid's concubines as *dames ses favourites*. Favourite ladies. How do you get "favourite ladies" from "concubines"? And he entirely cuts out some of the more erotic passages, and injects cultural explanations whenever he feels like it – tell me, how would you like to read an epic with a doddering Frenchman breathing down your neck at all the raunchy bits?'

Ramy gesticulated wildly as he spoke. It was clear he wasn't truly angry, just passionate and clearly brilliant, so invested in the truth he needed the whole world to know. Robin leaned back and watched Ramy's lovely, agitated face, both amazed and delighted.

He could have cried then. He'd been so desperately lonely, and had only now realized it, and now he *wasn't*, and this felt so good he didn't know what to do with himself.

When at last they grew too sleepy to finish their sentences, the sweets were half-gone and Ramy's floor was littered with wrappers. Yawning, they waved each other good night. Robin tripped back to his own quarters, swung the door shut, then turned around to face his empty rooms. This was his home for the next four years – the bed under the low, sloping ceiling where he would wake every morning, the leaking tap over the sink where he would wash his face, and the desk in the corner that he would hunch over every evening, scribbling by candlelight until wax dripped onto the floorboards.

For the first time since he'd arrived at Oxford, it struck him that he was to make a life here. He imagined it stretched out before him: the gradual accumulation of books and trinkets in those spare bookshelves;

the wear and tear of those crisp new linen shirts still packed in his trunks, the change of seasons seen and heard through the wind-rattled window above his bed that wouldn't quite shut. And Ramy, right across the hall.

This wouldn't be so bad.

The bed was unmade, but he was too tired now to fiddle with the sheets or search for covers, so he curled up on his side and pulled his coat over him. In a very short while he was fast asleep and smiling.

Classes would not begin until the third of October, which left three full days in which Robin and Ramy were free to explore the city.

These were three of the happiest days of Robin's life. He had no readings or classes; no recitations or compositions to prepare. For the first time in his life he was in full control of his own purse and schedule, and he went mad with freedom.

They spent their first day shopping. They went to Ede & Ravenscroft to be fitted for gowns; to Thornton's Bookshop for the entirety of their course list; to the home-goods stands at Cornmarket for teapots, spoons, bed linens, and Argand lamps. After acquiring everything they assumed necessary for student life, they both found they had a generous fraction of their stipends left over, with no danger of running out – their scholarship allowed them to withdraw the same amount from the bursary every month.

So they were profligate. They bought bags of candied nuts and caramels. They rented the college punts and spent the afternoon driving each other into the Cherwell's banks. They went to the Queen's Lane coffeehouse, at which they spent a ridiculous amount of money on a variety of pastries neither of them had ever tried. Ramy was very fond of flapjacks – 'They make oats taste *so good*,' he said, 'I understand the joys of being a horse,' – while Robin preferred sticky sweet buns so drenched in sugar they made his teeth ache for hours.

In Oxford, they stuck out like sore thumbs. This rattled Robin at first. In London, which was slightly more cosmopolitan, foreigners never drew such prolonged stares. But Oxford's townsfolk seemed constantly startled by their presence. Ramy attracted more attention than Robin did. Robin was foreign only when viewed up close and in certain lights, but Ramy was immediately, visibly other.

'Oh, yes,' he said, when the baker asked if he was from Hindustan, speaking in an exaggerated accent Robin had never heard before. 'I've got quite a big family there. Don't tell anyone, but I'm actually royalty, fourth in line to the throne – what throne? Oh, just a regional one; our political system is very complicated. But I wanted to experience a normal life – get a proper British education, you know – so I've left my palace for here.'

'Why did you talk like that?' Robin asked him once they were out of earshot. 'And what do you mean, you're actually royalty?'

'Whenever the English see me, they try to determine what kind of story they know me from,' Ramy said. 'Either I'm a dirty thieving lascar, or I'm a servant in some nabob's house. And I realized in Yorkshire that it's easier if they think I'm a Mughal prince.'

'I've always just tried to blend in,' said Robin.

'But that's impossible for me,' said Ramy. 'I have to play a part. Back in Calcutta, we all tell the story of Sake Dean Mahomed, the first Muslim from Bengal to become a rich man in England. He has a white Irish wife. He owns property in London. And you know how he did it? He opened a restaurant, which failed; and then he tried to be hired as a butler or valet, which also failed. And then he had the brilliant idea of opening a shampoo house in Brighton.' Ramy chuckled. 'Come and get your healing vapours! Be massaged with Indian oils! It cures asthma and rheumatism; it heals paralysis. Of course, we don't believe that at home. But all Dean Mahomed had to do was give himself some medical credentials, convince the world of this magical Oriental cure, and then he had them eating out of the palm of his hand. So what does that tell you, Birdie? If they're going to tell stories about you, use it to your advantage. The English are never going to think I'm posh, but if I fit into their fantasy, then they'll at least think I'm royalty.'

That marked the difference between them. Ever since his arrival in London, Robin had tried to keep his head down and assimilate, to play down his otherness. He thought the more unremarkable he seemed, the less attention he would draw. But Ramy, who had no choice but to stand out, had decided he might as well dazzle. He was bold to the extreme. Robin found him incredible and a little bit terrifying.

'Does *Mirza* really mean "prince"?' Robin asked, after he'd overheard Ramy declare this to a shopkeeper for the third time.

'Sure. Well, really, it's a title – it's derived from the Persian *Amīrzādeh*, but "prince" comes close enough.'

'Then are you—?'

'No.' Ramy snorted. 'Well. Perhaps once. That's the family story, anyhow; my father says we were aristocrats in the Mughal court, or something like that. But not anymore.'

'What happened?'

Ramy gave him a long look. 'The British, Birdie. Keep up.'

That evening they paid far too much money for a hamper of rolls, cheese, and sweet grapes, which they brought to a hill in South Park on the eastern part of campus for a picnic. They found a quiet spot near a thicket of trees, secluded enough that Ramy could conduct his sunset prayer, and sat cross-legged on the grass, pulling bread apart with their bare hands, interrogating each other about their lives with the eager fascination of boys who, for many years, thought they were the only ones in their particular situation.

Ramy deduced very quickly that Professor Lovell was Robin's father. 'Has to be, right? Otherwise, why's he so cagey about it? And otherwise to that otherwise, how'd he come to know your mother? Does he know that you know, or is he really still trying to hide it?'

Robin found his frankness alarming. He'd got so used to ignoring the issue that it was odd to hear it described in such blunt terms. 'I don't know. About any of it, I mean.'

'Hm. Does he look like you?'

'A bit, I think. He teaches here, he does East Asian languages – you'll meet him, you'll see.'

'You've never asked him about it?'

'I've never tried,' said Robin. 'I ... I don't know what he would say.' No, that wasn't true. 'I mean, I just don't think he would answer.'

They'd known each other for less than a day at that point, yet Ramy could read Robin's face well enough not to push the subject.

Ramy was far more open about his own background. He had spent the first thirteen years of his life in Calcutta, the older brother to three younger sisters in a family employed by a wealthy nabob named Sir Horace Wilson, and the next four in a Yorkshire countryside estate as a consequence of impressing Wilson, reading Greek and Latin, and trying not to claw out his eyes from boredom.

'Lucky you got your education in London,' Ramy said. 'At least you had somewhere to go at the weekends. My whole adolescence was hills and moors, and not a single person under forty in sight. Did you ever see the King?'

This was another talent of Ramy's: switching subjects so nimbly that Robin found himself struggling to keep up.

'William? No, not really, he doesn't come out in public much. Especially recently, what with the Factory Act and the Poor Law – the reformers were always rioting in the streets, it wouldn't have been safe.'

'Reformers,' Ramy repeated jealously. '*Lucky* you. All that ever happened in Yorkshire was a marriage or two. Sometimes the hens got out, on a good day.'

'I didn't get to participate, though,' Robin said. 'My days were rather monotonous, to be honest. Endless studying – all in preparation for here.'

'But we're here now.'

'Cheers to that.' Robin settled back with a sigh. Ramy passed him a cup – he'd been mixing elderflower syrup with honey and water – and they clinked and drank.

From their vantage point at South Park they could look over the whole of the university, draped in a golden blanket at sunset. The light made Ramy's eyes glow, made his skin shine like burnished bronze. Robin had the absurd impulse to place his hand against Ramy's cheek; indeed, he'd half lifted up his arm before his mind caught up with his body.

Ramy glanced down at him. A curl of black hair fell in his eyes. Robin found it absurdly charming. 'You all right?'

Robin leaned back on his elbows, turning his gaze to the city. Professor Lovell was right, he thought. This was the loveliest place on earth.

'I'm all right,' he said. 'I'm just perfect.'

The other residents of Number 4, Magpie Lane filled in over the weekend. None of them were translation students. They introduced themselves as they moved in: Colin Thornhill, a wide-eyed and effusive solicitor-in-training who talked only in full paragraphs and about himself; Bill Jameson, an affable redhead studying to be a surgeon who seemed perpetually worried about how much things cost; and at the end of the hall, a pair of twin brothers, Edgar and Edward Sharp, who were second years nominally pursuing an education in the Classics but who, as they loudly proclaimed, were more 'just interested in the social aspect until we come into our inheritances.'

On Saturday night, they congregated for drinks in the common room adjoining the shared kitchen. Bill, Colin, and the Sharps were all seated around the low table when Ramy and Robin walked in. They'd been told to come at nine, but the wine had clearly been flowing for a while – empty bottles littered the floor around them, and the Sharp brothers were slouched against each other, both visibly drunk.

Colin was holding forth on the differences between the student gowns. 'You can tell everything about a man from his gown,' he said importantly. He had a peculiar, overpronounced, suspiciously exaggerated accent that Robin couldn't place but quite disliked. 'The bachelor's gown loops at the elbow and terminates at a point. The gentleman-commoner's gown is silk and plaited at the sleeves. The commoner's gown has no sleeves, and has plaits at the shoulder, and you can tell the servitors and the commoners apart because their gowns don't have plaits, and their caps don't have tassels—'

'Good Lord,' said Ramy as he sat down. 'Has he been going on about this all this time?'

'For ten minutes at least,' Bill said.

'Oh, but proper academic dress is of the utmost importance,' Colin insisted. 'It's how we display our status as Oxford men. It's considered one of the seven deadly sins to wear an ordinary tweed cap with a gown, or to use a walking stick with a gown. And I once heard of a fellow who, not knowing the kinds of gowns, told the tailor he was a scholar, so of course he needed a scholar's gown, only to be laughed out of hall the next day when it transpired that he was not a scholar, for he'd won no scholarship, but merely a paying *commoner*—'

'So what gowns do we wear?' Ramy cut in. 'Just so I know if we told our tailor the right thing.'

'Depends,' Colin said. 'Are you a gentleman-commoner or a servitor? I pay tuition, but not everyone does – what's your arrangement with the bursar?'

'Don't know,' said Ramy. 'Do you think the black robes will do? All I know is we got the black ones.'

Robin snorted. Colin's eyes bulged slightly. 'Yes, but the sleeves—'

'Leave off him,' Bill said, smiling. 'Colin's very concerned with status.'

'They take gowns very seriously here,' Colin said solemnly. 'I read it in my guidebook. They won't even let you into lectures if you're not in the proper attire. So are you a gentleman-commoner or a servitor?'

'They're neither.' Edward turned to Robin. 'You're Babblers, aren't you? I heard all Babblers are on scholarships.'

'Babblers?' Robin repeated. It was the first time he'd heard the term.

'The Translation Institute,' Edward said impatiently. 'You've got to be, right? They don't let your kind in otherwise.'

'Our kind?' Ramy arched an eyebrow.

'So what are you, anyway?' Edgar Sharp asked abruptly. He'd seemed on the verge of falling asleep, but now he made a mighty effort to sit up, squinting as if trying to see Ramy through a fog. 'A Negro? A Turk?'

'I'm from Calcutta,' Ramy snapped. 'Which makes me Indian, if you like.'

'Hm,' said Edward.

'"London streets, where the turbaned Moslem, bearded Jew, and woolly Afric, meet the brown Hindu,"' said Edgar in a sing-song tone. Beside him, his twin snorted and took another swig of port.

Ramy, for once, had no riposte; he only blinked at Edgar, amazed.

'Right,' Bill said, picking at his ear. 'Well.'

'Is that Anna Barbauld?' Colin asked. 'Lovely poet. Not as deft with wordplay as the male poets, of course, but my father loves her stuff. Very romantic.'

'And you're a Chinaman, aren't you?' Edgar fixed his lidded gaze on Robin. 'Is it true that the Chinese break their women's feet with bindings so that they can't walk?'

'What?' Colin snorted. 'That's ridiculous.'

'I read about it,' Edgar insisted. 'Tell me, is it meant to be erotic? Or is it just so that they can't run away?'

'I mean . . .' Robin had no idea where to begin with this. 'It's not done everywhere – my mother didn't have her feet bound, and there's quite a lot of opposition where I'm from—'

'So it's true,' Edgar crowed. 'My God. You people are perverse.'

'Do you really drink little boys' urine for medicine?' Edward inquired. 'How's it collected?'

'Suppose you shut up and stick to dribbling wine down your front,' Ramy said sharply.

Any hopes of fraternity fizzled out quite quickly after that. A round of whist was proposed, but the Sharp brothers did not know the rules and were too drunk to learn. Bill begged a headache and left for bed early. Colin went on another long tirade about the intricacies of hall etiquette, including the very long Latin grace he suggested they all learn by heart that night, but no one listened. The Sharp brothers, in a strange show of contrition, then asked Robin and Ramy some polite if inane questions about translation, but it was clear they were not too interested in the answers. Whatever esteemed company the Sharps were seeking at Oxford, they had clearly not found it here. In half an hour the gathering was over, and all parties slunk back to their respective rooms.

Some noise had been made that night about a house breakfast. But when Ramy and Robin appeared in the kitchen the next morning, they found a note for them on the table.

We've gone to a café the Sharps know in Iffley. Didn't think you'd like it – see you later. – CT

'I suppose,' Ramy said drily, 'it's going to be them and us.'
Robin didn't mind this one bit. 'I like just us.'
Ramy cast him a smile.
They spent their third day together touring the jewels of the university. Oxford in 1836 was in an era of becoming, an insatiable creature feeding on the wealth which it bred. The colleges were constantly renovating; buying up more land from the city; replacing medieval buildings with newer, lovelier halls; constructing new libraries to house recently acquired collections. Almost every building in Oxford had a name – derived not from function or location, but from the wealthy and powerful individual who inspired its creation. There was the massive, imposing Ashmolean Museum, which housed the cabinet of curiosities donated by Elias Ashmole, including a dodo's head, hippopotamus skulls, and a three-inch-long sheep's horn that was supposed to have grown out of the head of an old woman in Cheshire named Mary Davis; the Radcliffe Library, a domed library that somehow appeared even larger and grander from the inside than from the outside; and the Sheldonian Theatre, ringed by massive stone busts known as the Emperor Heads, all of whom looked like ordinary men who had stumbled upon Medusa.
And there was the Bodleian – oh, the Bodleian, a national treasure in its own right: home of the largest collection of manuscripts in England ('Cambridge has only got a hundred thousand titles,' sniffed the clerk who admitted them, 'and Edinburgh's only got a paltry sixty-three'),

whose collection only continued to expand under the proud leadership of the Reverend Doctor Bulkeley Bandinel, who had a book-buying budget of nearly £2,000 a year.

It was the Reverend Doctor Bandinel himself who came to greet them on their first tour of their library and guided them to the Translators' Reading Room. 'Couldn't let a clerk do it,' he sighed. 'Normally we let the fools wander about on their own and ask around for directions if they get lost. But you translators – you truly appreciate what's going on here.'

He was a heavy-set man with droopy eyes and a similarly droopy demeanour whose mouth seemed permanently slumped in a frown. Yet as he moved through the building, his eyes lit up with genuine pleasure. 'We'll start in the main wings, then traipse over to the Duke Humphreys. Follow along, feel free to have a look – books are meant to be touched, otherwise they're useless, so don't be nervous. We're quite proud of our last few major acquisitions. There's the Richard Gough map collection donated in 1809 – the British Museum didn't want them, can you believe it? And then the Malone donation ten or so years ago – it greatly expanded our Shakespearean materials. Oh, and just two years ago, we received the Francis Douce collection – that's thirteen thousand volumes in French and English, though I suppose neither of you is specializing in French ... Arabic? Oh, yes – right this way; the Institute has the bulk of Arabic materials at Oxford, but I've got some poetry volumes from Egypt and Syria that may interest you ...'

They left the Bodleian dazed, impressed, and a bit intimidated by the sheer amount of material at their disposal. Ramy made an imitation of Reverend Doctor Bandinel's hanging jowls, but could summon no real malice; it was difficult to disdain a man who so clearly adored the accumulation of knowledge for knowledge's sake.

They ended the day with a tour of University College by Billings, a senior porter. It turned out that thus far they had seen only a small corner of their new home. The college, which lay just to the east of the houses on Magpie Lane, boasted two green quadrangle courtyards and an arrangement of stone buildings that resembled castle keeps. As they walked, Billings rattled off a list of namesakes and biographies of those namesakes, including donors, architects, and otherwise significant figures. ' ... now, the statues over the entrances are of Queen Anne and Queen Mary, and in the interior, James II and Dr Radcliffe ... And those brilliant painted windows in the chapel were done by Abraham van Linge in 1640, yes, they've held up very well, and the glass painter Henry Giles of York did the east window . . . There's no service on, so we can take a poke around inside; follow me.'

Inside the chapel, Billings paused before a bas-relief monument. 'I suppose you'll know who that is, being translation students and all.'

They knew. Robin and Ramy both had been hearing the name constantly since their arrival at Oxford. The bas-relief was a memorial to the University College alum and widely recognized genius who in 1786 published a foundational text identifying Proto-Indo-European as a predecessor language linking Latin, Sanskrit, and Greek. He was now perhaps the single best-known translator on the continent, save for his nephew, the recently graduated Sterling Jones.

'It's Sir William Jones.' Robin found the scene depicted in the frieze somewhat discomfiting. Jones was positioned at a writing desk, one leg crossed pertly over the other, while three figures, clearly meant to be Indians, sat submissively on the floor before him like children receiving a lesson.

Billings looked proud. 'That's right. Here he is translating a digest on the Hindu laws, and there are some Brahmins on the floor to assist him. We are, I believe, the only college whose walls are graced with Indians. But then Univ has always had a special link to the colonies.* And those tigers' heads, as you know, are emblematic of Bengal.'

'Why's he the only one with a table?' Ramy asked. 'Why are the Brahmins on the floor?'

'Well, I suppose Hindus preferred it that way,' said Billings. 'They like sitting cross-legged, you see, for they find it more comfortable.'

'Very illuminating,' said Ramy. 'I never knew.'

They spent Sunday night in the depths of the Bodleian bookcases. They'd been assigned a reading list upon registration, but both, faced with a sudden deluge of freedom, had left it off until the last possible moment. The Bodleian was supposed to close by 8.00 p.m. on weekends. They reached its doors at 7.45 p.m., but mention of the Translation Institute

---

* This was true. University College had produced, among others, a Chief Justice of Bengal (Sir Robert Chambers), a Chief Justice of Bombay (Sir Edward West), and a Chief Justice of Calcutta (Sir William Jones). All were white men.

seemed to hold immense power, for when Ramy explained what they needed, the clerks told them they could stay as late as they liked. The doors would be unlocked for the night staff; they could leave at their own convenience.

By the time they emerged from the stacks, satchels heavy with books and eyes dizzy from squinting at tiny fonts, the sun had long gone down. At night, the moon conspired with streetlamps to bathe the city in a faint, otherworldly glow. The cobblestones beneath their feet seemed like roads leading into and out of different centuries. This could be the Oxford of the Reformation, or the Oxford of the Middle Ages. They moved within a timeless space, shared by the ghosts of scholars past.

The journey back to college took less than five minutes, but they detoured up and around Broad Street to lengthen their walk. This was the first time they'd been out so late; they wanted to savour the city at night. They moved in silence, neither daring to break the spell.

A burst of laughter drifted from across the stone walls when they passed New College. As they turned down Holywell Lane, they saw a group of six or seven students, all garbed in black gowns, though from the sway of their walk they must have just departed not from a lecture but from a pub.

'Balliol, you think?' Ramy murmured.

Robin snorted.

They'd been three days at University College, but they'd already learned the intercollegiate pecking order and associated stereotypes. Exeter was genteel but unintellectual; Brasenose was rowdy and lush with wine. Their neighbouring Queen's and Merton were safely ignored. Balliol boys, who paid near the highest tuitions at the University, next to Oriel, were better known for running up the tab than for showing up for their tutorials.

The students glanced their way as they approached. Robin and Ramy nodded towards them, and a few of them nodded back, a mutual acknowledgment between gentlemen of the university.

The street was wide, and the two groups were walking on opposite sides. They would have passed each other without commotion, except that one of the boys pointed suddenly at Ramy and shouted, 'What's that? Did you see that?'

His friends pulled him along, laughing.

'Come on, Mark,' one said. 'Let them go—'

'Hold it,' said the boy called Mark. He shrugged his friends off. He stood still on the street, squinting at Ramy with drunken concentration. His hand hung in midair, still pointing. 'Look at his face – you see it?'

'Mark, please,' said the boy furthest down the road. 'Don't be an idiot.'

None of them were laughing any more.

'That's a Hindu,' said Mark. 'What's a Hindu doing here?'

'Sometimes they visit,' said one of the other boys. 'Remember the two foreigners last week, those Persian sultans or whatever they were—'

'I think I do, those fellows in turbans—'

'But he's got a gown.' Mark raised his voice at Ramy. 'Hey! What have you got a gown for?'

His tone turned vicious. The atmosphere was no longer so cordial; the scholarly fraternity, if it had ever existed, evaporated.

'You can't wear a gown,' Mark insisted. 'Take that off.'

Ramy took a step forward.

Robin gripped his arm. 'Don't.'

'Hello, I'm talking to you.' Mark was now crossing the street towards them. 'What's the matter? Can't you speak English? Take off that gown, do you hear me? Take it off.'

Clearly Ramy wanted to fight – his fists were clenched, his knees bent in preparation to spring. If Mark drew any closer, this night would end in blood.

So Robin began to run.

He hated it as he did so, he felt like such a coward, but it was the only act he could imagine that didn't end in catastrophe. For he knew that Ramy, shocked, would follow. Indeed – seconds later he heard Ramy's footsteps behind him, his hard breathing, the curses he muttered under his breath as they sprinted down Holywell.

The laughter – for there was laughter again, though it was no longer born of mirth – seemed to amplify behind them. The Balliol boys hooted like monkeys; their cackles stretched alongside their shadows against the brick walls. For a moment Robin was terrified they were being chased, that the boys were hot on their heels, footsteps hammering all around them. But it was only the blood thundering in his ears. The boys had not followed them; they were too drunk, too easily amused, and certainly, by now, distracted in pursuit of their next entertainment.

Even so, Robin didn't stop until they reached High Street. The way was clear. They were alone, panting in the dark.

'Damn it,' Ramy muttered. 'Damn it—'

'I'm sorry,' Robin said.

'Don't be,' Ramy said, though he wouldn't meet Robin's eye. 'You did the right thing.'

Robin wasn't sure either of them believed that.

They were much further from home now, but they were at least back under the streetlamps, where they could see trouble coming from further off.

They walked awhile in silence. Robin could think of nothing appropriate to say; any words that came to mind died immediately on his tongue.

'Damn it,' Ramy said again. He stopped abruptly, one hand on his satchel. 'I think – hold on.' He dug through his books, then cursed again. 'I left my notebook behind.'

Robin's gut twisted. 'On Holywell?'

'In the Bod.' Ramy pressed his fingertips against the bridge of his nose and groaned. 'I know where – right on the corner of the desk; I was going to place it on top because I didn't want the pages crumpled, only I got so tired I must have forgotten.'

'Can't you leave it until tomorrow? I don't think the clerks will move it, and if they do we could just ask—'

'No, it's got my revision notes, and I'm nervous they'll make us do a recitation tomorrow. I'll just head back—'

'I'll get it,' Robin said quickly. This felt like the right thing to do; it felt like making amends.

Ramy frowned. 'Are you sure?'

There was no fight in his voice. They both knew what Robin would not say out loud – that Robin, at least, could pass for white in the dark, and that if Robin came across the Balliol boys alone, they wouldn't give him a second glance.

'I won't be twenty minutes,' Robin vowed. 'I'll drop it outside your door when I'm back.'

Oxford took on a sinister air now that he was alone; the lights were no longer warm but eerie, stretching and warping his shadow against the cobblestones. The Bodleian was locked, but a night clerk noticed him waving at the window and let him in. He was, thankfully, one of the staff from before, and he let Robin into the west wing without question. The

Reading Room was pitch-black and freezing. All the lamps were off; Robin could only just see by the moonlight streaming in at the far end of the room. Shivering, he snatched Ramy's notebook, shoved it into his satchel, and hurried out the door.

He'd just made it past the quadrangle when he heard whispers.

He should have quickened his pace, but something – the tones, the shape of the words – compelled him to stop. Only after he'd paused to strain his ears did he realize he was listening to Chinese. One Chinese phrase, uttered over and over again with increasing urgency.

'*Wúxíng.*'

Robin crept cautiously around the walled corner.

There were three people in the middle of Holywell Street, all slim youths dressed entirely in black, two men and a woman. They were struggling with a trunk. The bottom must have dropped out, because what were unmistakably silver bars were strewn across the cobblestones.

All three glanced up as Robin approached. The man whispering furiously in Chinese had his back to Robin; he turned around last, only after his associates had gone stock-still. He met Robin's eyes. Robin's heart caught in his throat.

He could have been looking in a mirror.

Those were his brown eyes. His own straight nose, his own chestnut hair that even fell over his eyes the same way, swooping messily from left to right.

The man held a silver bar in his hand.

Robin realized instantly what he was trying to do. *Wúxíng* – in Chinese, 'formless, shapeless, incorporeal'.* The closest English translation was 'invisible'. These people, whoever they were, were trying to hide. But something had gone wrong, for the silver bar was only barely working; the three youths' images flickered under the streetlamp, and occasionally they seemed translucent, but they were decidedly not hidden.

Robin's doppelgänger cast him a plaintive look.

'Help me,' he begged. Then in Chinese, '*Bāngmáng.*'†

---

* 無 (*wú*) means 'negative, not, without'; 形 (*xíng*) means 'appearance, form, shape'. 無行 means not just invisible, but intangible. To illustrate: the poet Zhang Shunmin of the Northern Song dynasty wrote once that '詩是無形的畫，畫是有形詩'; that poems were incorporeal (*wúxíng*) paintings, and paintings were corporeal poems.

† 幫忙 (*bāngmáng*), 'to help, to lend a hand'.

Robin didn't know what it was that compelled him to act – the recent terror of the Balliol boys, the utter absurdity of this scene, or the disorienting sight of his doppelgänger's face – but he stepped forward and put his hand on the bar. His doppelgänger relinquished it without a word.

'*Wúxíng*,' Robin said, thinking of the myths his mother had told him, of spirits and ghosts hiding in the dark. Of shapelessness, of nonbeing. 'Invisible.'

The bar vibrated in his hand. He heard a sound from nowhere, a breathy sigh.

All four of them disappeared.

No, *disappeared* was not quite the word for it. Robin didn't have the words for it; it was lost in translation, a concept that neither the Chinese nor the English could fully describe. They existed, but in no human form. They were not merely beings that couldn't be seen. They weren't beings at all. They were shapeless. They drifted, expanded; they were the air, the brick walls, the cobblestones. Robin had no awareness of his body, where he ended and the bar began – he was the silver, the stones, the night.

Cold fear shot through his mind. *What if I can't go back?*

Seconds later a constable rushed up to the end of the street. Robin caught his breath, squeezing the bar so hard that pangs of pain shot up his arm.

The constable stared right at him, squinting, seeing nothing but darkness.

'They're not down here,' he called over his shoulder. 'Try chasing them up Parks . . .'

His voice faded as he sprinted away.

Robin dropped the bar. He couldn't maintain his hold on it; he was barely aware of its presence anymore. He didn't so much as use his hand and open his fingers as he did violently thrust the bar away to try to separate his essence from the silver.

It worked. The thieves rematerialized in the night.

'Hurry,' urged the other man, a youth with pale blond hair. 'Shove it in your shirts and let's leave the trunk behind.'

'We can't just leave it,' said the woman. 'They'll trace it.'

'Pick up the pieces then, come on.'

All three began scooping the silver bars off the ground. Robin hesitated for a moment, arms hanging awkwardly at his sides. Then he bent down to help them.

The absurdity of this had not yet sunk in. Dimly he realized that whatever was happening had to be very illegal. These youths could not be associated with Oxford, the Bodleian, or the Translation Institute, or else they wouldn't be skulking about at midnight, clad in black and hiding from the police.

The right and obvious thing to do was to raise the alarm.

But somehow, helping seemed the only option. He didn't question this logic, he simply acted. It felt like falling into a dream, like stepping into a play where he already knew his lines, though everything else was a mystery. This was an illusion with its own internal logic, and for some reason he couldn't quite name, he didn't want to break it.

At last all the silver bars had been shoved down shirt fronts and into pockets. Robin gave the ones he'd picked up to his doppelgänger. Their fingers touched, and Robin felt a chill.

'Let's go,' said the blond man.

But none of them moved. They all looked at Robin, visibly uncertain what to do with him.

'What if he—' began the woman.

'He won't,' Robin's doppelgänger said firmly. 'Will you?'

'Of course not,' Robin whispered.

The blond man looked unconvinced. 'Would be easier to just—'

'No. Not this time.' Robin's doppelgänger looked Robin up and down for a moment, then seemed to come to a decision. 'You're a translator, aren't you?'

'Yes,' Robin breathed. 'Yes, I've only just got here.'

'The Twisted Root,' said his doppelgänger. 'Find me there.'

The woman and the blond man exchanged a glance. The woman opened her mouth as if to object, paused, and then closed it.

'Fine,' said the blond man. 'Now let's go.'

'Wait,' Robin said desperately. 'Who are – when should—'

But the thieves had broken into a run.

They were startlingly fast. Just seconds later, the street was empty. They'd left no trace they'd ever been there – they'd picked up every last bar, had even run away with the broken ruins of the trunk. They could have been ghosts. Robin could have imagined this entire encounter, and the world would have looked no different at all.

*   *   *

Ramy was still awake when Robin returned. He opened his door at the first knock.

'Thanks,' he said, taking the notebook.

'Of course.'

They stood looking at each other in silence.

There was no question about what had happened. They were both shaken by the sudden realization that they did not belong in this place, that despite their affiliation with the Translation Institute and despite their gowns and pretensions, their bodies were not safe on the streets. They were men at Oxford; they were not Oxford men. But the enormity of this knowledge was so devastating, such a vicious antithesis to the three golden days they'd blindly enjoyed, that neither of them could say it out loud.

And they never would say it out loud. It hurt too much to consider the truth. It was so much easier to pretend; to keep spinning the fantasy for as long as they could.

'Well,' Robin said lamely, 'good night.'

Ramy nodded and, without speaking, closed his door.

CHAPTER FOUR

———⊕———

So the Lord scattered them abroad from there over the face of all the earth, and they left off building the city. Therefore its name was called Babel, because there the Lord confused the language of all the earth; and from there the Lord scattered them abroad over the face of all the earth.

Genesis 11:8–9, Revised Standard Version

Sleep felt impossible. Robin kept seeing the face of his doppelgänger floating in the dark. Had he, fatigued and rattled, imagined the whole thing? But the streetlamps had shone so brightly, and his twin's features – his fear, his panic – were so sharply etched into his memory. He knew it was not a projection. It had not quite felt like looking into a mirror, where all his features were reflected backwards, a false representation of what the world saw, but a gut recognition of sameness. Whatever was in that man's face was in his as well.

Was that why he had helped him? Some instinctive sympathy?

He was only beginning to fathom the weight of his actions. He'd stolen from the university. Was it a test? Stranger rituals were practised at Oxford. Had he passed or failed? Or would constables come banging on his door the next morning and ask him to leave?

But I can't be sent down, he thought. *I've only just got here.* Suddenly the delights of Oxford – the warmth of his bed, the smell of new books and new clothes – made him squirm in discomfort, for now all he could think about was how soon he might lose it all. He tossed and turned in sweaty sheets, conjuring up more and more detailed visions of how the morning might go – how the constables would pull him from his bed, how they'd shackle his wrists and drag him to the gaol, how Professor Lovell would sternly ask Robin never to contact him or Mrs Piper again.

At last he fell asleep from exhaustion. He woke to a persistent tapping at his door.

'What are you doing?' Ramy demanded. 'You haven't even *washed*?'

Robin blinked at him. 'What's going on?'

'It's Monday morning, you dolt.' Ramy was already dressed in his black gown, cap in hand. 'We're due at the tower in twenty minutes.'

They made it in time, but barely; they were half running down the greens of the quadrangle to the Institute, gowns flapping in the wind, when the bells rang for nine.

Two slim youths awaited them on the green – the other half of their cohort, Robin assumed. One was white; the other was Black.

'Hello,' said the white one as they approached. 'You're late.'

Robin gaped at her, trying to catch his breath. 'You're a girl.'

This was a shock. Robin and Ramy had both grown up in sterile, isolated environments, kept far away from girls their own age. The feminine was an idea that existed in theory, the stuff of novels or a rare phenomenon to be glimpsed from across the street. The best description Robin knew of women came from a treatise he'd once flipped through by a Mrs Sarah Ellis,* which labelled girls 'gentle, inoffensive, delicate, and passively amiable'. As far as Robin was concerned, girls were mysterious subjects imbued not with a rich inner life but with qualities that made them otherworldly, inscrutable, and possibly not human at all.

'Sorry – I mean, hello,' he managed. 'I didn't mean to – anyhow.'

Ramy was less subtle. 'Why are you girls?'

The white girl gave him a look of such withering scorn that Robin wilted on Ramy's behalf.

'Well,' she drawled, 'I suppose we decided to be girls because being boys seems to require giving up half your brain cells.'

'The university has asked us to dress like this so as to not upset or distract the young gentlemen,' the Black girl explained. Her English carried a faint accent, which Robin thought resembled French, though

---

* Sarah Stickney Ellis, a well-known author, published several books (including *The Wives of England, The Mothers of England,* and *The Daughters of England*) arguing that women had a moral imperative to improve society through domestic propriety and virtuous conduct. Robin had no strong opinion on the matter; he'd picked up her work by accident.

he wasn't sure. She shook her left leg at him, displaying trousers so crisp and stiff they looked like they'd been purchased yesterday. 'Not every faculty is as liberal as the Translation Institute, you see.'

'Is it uncomfortable?' Robin asked, trying valiantly to prove his own lack of prejudice. 'Wearing trousers, I mean?'

'It's not, in fact, since we have two legs and not fish tails.' She extended her hand to him. 'Victoire Desgraves.'

He shook it. 'Robin Swift.'

She arched an eyebrow. 'Swift? But surely—'

'Letitia Price,' the white girl interjected. 'Letty, if you like. And you?'

'Ramiz.' Ramy halfway extended his hand, as if unsure whether he wanted to touch the girls or not. Letty decided for him and shook it; Ramy winced in discomfort. 'Ramiz Mirza. Ramy to friends.'

'Hello, Ramiz.' Letty glanced around. 'So we're the whole cohort, then.'

Victoire gave a little sigh. '*Ce sont des idiots,*' she said to Letty.

'*Je suis tout à fait d'accord,*' Letty murmured back.

They both burst into giggles. Robin could not understand French, but felt distinctly that he had been judged and found wanting.

'There you are.'

They were saved from further conversation by a tall, slender Black man who shook all their hands and introduced himself as Anthony Ribben, a postgraduate specializing in French, Spanish, and German. 'My guardian fancied himself a Romanticist,' he explained. 'He hoped I'd follow his passion for poetry, but when it became apparent I had more than just a passing talent for languages, he had me sent here.'

He paused expectantly, which prompted them to respond with their own languages.

'Urdu, Arabic, and Persian,' said Ramy.

'French and Kreyòl,' said Victoire. 'I mean – Haitian Creole, if you think that counts.'

'That counts,' Anthony said cheerfully.

'French and German,' said Letty.

'Chinese,' Robin said, feeling somewhat inadequate. 'And Latin and Greek.'

'Well, we've all got Latin and Greek,' said Letty. 'It's an entry requirement, isn't it?'

Robin's cheeks flushed; he hadn't known.

Anthony looked amused. 'A nicely cosmopolitan group, aren't you? Welcome to Oxford! How are you finding it?'

'Lovely,' said Victoire. 'Though . . . I don't know, it's strange. It doesn't quite feel real. It feels like I'm at the theatre, and I keep waiting for the curtains to come down.'

'That doesn't go away.' Anthony headed towards the tower, gesturing for them to follow. 'Especially once you've gone through these doors. They've asked me to show you about the Institute until eleven, and then I'll leave you with Professor Playfair. Will this be your first time inside?'

They gazed up at the tower. It was a magnificent building – a gleaming white edifice built in the neoclassical style, eight storeys tall and ringed with ornamental pillars and high stained-glass windows. It dominated the skyline of High Street, and made the nearby Radcliffe Library and University Church of St Mary the Virgin look quite pathetic in comparison. Ramy and Robin had walked past it countless times over the weekend, marvelling at it together, but always from a distance. They hadn't dared approach. Not then.

'Magnificent, isn't it?' Anthony sighed with satisfaction. 'You never get used to the sight. Welcome to your home for the next four years, believe it or not. We call it Babel.'

'Babel,' Robin repeated. 'Is that why—?'

'Why they call us Babblers?' Anthony nodded. 'A joke as old as the Institute itself. But some first year at Balliol thinks he conceived it for the first time every September, and so we've been doomed to that unwieldy moniker for decades.'

He strode briskly up the front steps. At the top a blue and gold seal was carved into the stone before the door, the Oxford University coat of arms. *Dominus illuminatio mea*, it read. *The Lord is my light.* The moment Anthony's foot touched the seal, the heavy wooden door swung out on its own accord, revealing a golden, lamplit interior of staircases, bustling dark-robed scholars, and books upon books upon books.

Robin paused, too dazzled to follow. Of all the marvels of Oxford, Babel seemed the most impossible – a tower out of time, a vision from a dream. Those stained-glass windows, that high, imposing dome; it all seemed to have been pulled straight from the painting in Professor Lovell's dining room and dropped whole onto this drab grey street. An illumination in a medieval manuscript; a door to a fairy land. It seemed impossible that they should come here every day to study, that they had the right to enter at all.

Yet here it stood, right in front of them, waiting.

Anthony beckoned, beaming. 'Well, come on in.'

'Translation agencies have always been indispensable tools of – nay, the centres of – great civilizations. In 1527, Charles V of Spain created the Secretaría de Interpretación de Lenguas, whose employees juggled over a dozen languages in service of governing his empire's territories. The Royal Institute of Translation was founded in London in the early seventeenth century, though it didn't move to its current home in Oxford until 1715 and the end of the War of the Spanish Succession, after which the British decided it might be prudent to train young lads to speak the languages of the colonies the Spanish had just lost. Yes, I've memorized all this, and no, I didn't write it, but I've been giving this tour since my first year on account of my immense personal charisma, so I've got quite good at it. Through the foyer this way.'

Anthony had the rare skill of talking smoothly while walking backwards. 'There's eight floors to Babel,' he said. 'The Book of Jubilees claims the historical Tower of Babel reached a height of over five thousand cubits – that's nearly two miles – which is of course impossible, though our Babel *is* the tallest building in Oxford, and likely all of England, excepting St Paul's. We're nearly three hundred feet tall, not counting the basement, which means our total height is twice that of the Radcliffe Library—'

Victoire lifted her hand. 'Is the tower—'

'Larger on the inside than it seems on the outside?' Anthony asked. 'Indeed.' Robin had not noticed this at first, but now felt disoriented by the contradiction. Babel's exterior was massive, but it still did not appear tall enough to admit the high ceilings and towering shelves of each interior floor. 'It's a pretty trick of silver-working, though I'm not sure of the match-pair involved. It's been like this since I got here; we take it for granted.'

Anthony guided them through a throng of townsfolk standing in busy queues before cashier windows. 'We're in the lobby now – all business gets conducted here. Local tradesmen ordering bars for their equipment, city officials requesting public works maintenance, that sort of thing. It's the only area of the tower accessible to civilians, though they don't interact with scholars much – we've got clerks to process their requests.' Anthony waved for them to follow him up the central staircase. 'This way.'

The second floor was the Legal Department, which was full of dour-faced scholars scratching at paper and flipping through thick, musty reference volumes.

'It's always busy here,' said Anthony. 'International treaties, overseas trade, that sort of thing. The gears of empire, the stuff that makes the world go round. Most Babel students end up here after graduation, as the pay is good and they're always hiring. They do quite a lot of pro bono work here, too – the whole southwest quadrant is a team working on translating the Code Napoléon into other European languages.* But we charge a pretty penny for the rest. This is the floor that draws the largest income – except silver-working, of course.'

'Where's silver-working?' Victoire asked.

'Eighth floor. Up at the very top.'

'For the view?' Letty asked.

'For the fires,' said Anthony. 'When fires start you'd rather they be at the top of the building so everyone has time to get out.'

No one could tell if he was joking.†

Anthony led them up another flight of stairs. 'The third floor is the landing base for the live interpreters.' He gestured around the largely empty room, which showed few signs of use except for several stained teacups lying askew and the occasional stack of paper on a desk corner. 'They're almost never here, but they need a place to prepare briefing files in confidence when they are, so they get this entire space. They accompany dignitaries and foreign service officials on their trips abroad, attending balls in Russia and taking tea with sheikhs in Arabia and whatnot. I'm told all the travel gets quite exhausting, so there aren't too

---

* This is, frankly, quite a generous description of the Legal Department. One could also argue that the business of translators in Legal was manipulating language to create favourable terms for European parties. One example is the alleged sale of land by King Paspehay to the English in Virginia 'for copper', despite the obvious difficulty of translating precisely the notions of European kingship or land as property into Algonquin languages. The Legal solution to these issues was simply to declare that the Algonquins were too savage to have developed those concepts, and it was a good thing the English were there to teach them.

† He was not. The eighth floor of the Institute had been reconstructed seven times since the building's initial construction.

many career interpreters who come out of Babel. They're usually natural polyglots who picked up their languages elsewhere – they had mission-ary parents, or they spent summers with foreign relatives, for example. Babel graduates tend to avoid it.'

'Why?' Ramy asked. 'It sounds fun.'

'It's a cushy posting if what you want is to travel abroad on someone else's money,' said Anthony. 'But academics by nature are a solitary, sed-entary lot. Travel sounds fun until you realize what you really want is to stay at home with a cup of tea and a stack of books by a warm fire.'

'You have a dim view of academics,' said Victoire.

'I have a view informed by experience. You'll understand in time. Alums who apply for interpreting jobs always quit within the first two years. Even Sterling Jones – Sir William Jones's nephew, mind you – couldn't hack it for more than eight months, and they had *him* travelling first class wherever he went. Anyway, live interpretation isn't considered all that glamorous, because all that really matters is that you get your basic points across without offending anyone. You don't get to play around with the intricacies of language, which is of course where the *real* fun is.'

The fourth floor was a good deal busier than the third. The schol-ars also appeared to be younger: messy-haired and patch-sleeved types compared with the polished, well-dressed folks in Legal.

'Literature,' Anthony explained. 'That is, the businesses of translating foreign novels, stories, and poems into English and – less frequently – vice versa. It's a bit low on the prestige rung, to be honest, but it's a more coveted placement than interpretation. One considers a postgraduation appointment to Literature the natural first step towards becoming a Babel professor.'

'Some of us actually like it here, mind you.' A young man wearing postgraduate gowns strode up next to Anthony. 'These are the first years?'

'That's all of them.'

'Not a big class, are you?' The man waved cheerfully at them. 'Hello. Vimal Srinivasan. I've just graduated last term; I do Sanskrit, Tamil, Telugu, and German.'*

---

* A good amount of foundational Western scholarship on Sanskrit was done by German Romantics such as Herder, Schlegel, and Bopp. Not all of their mono-graphs had been translated into English – at least, not well – and so most students studying Sanskrit at Babel were also required to learn German.

'Does everyone here introduce themselves with their languages?' Ramy asked.

'Of course,' Vimal said. 'Your languages determine how interesting you are. Orientalists are fascinating. Classicists are dull. Anyhow, welcome to the best floor in the tower.'

Victoire was peering around the shelves with great interest. 'So do you get your hands on every book that's published abroad?'

'Most of them, yes,' said Vimal.

'All the French releases? As soon as they come out?'

'Yes, greedy,' he said, with absolutely no malice. 'You'll find our book-buying budget is effectively limitless, and our librarians like to maintain a thorough collection. Though we can't translate everything that comes through here; we just haven't the manpower. Translating ancient texts still occupies a good part of our time.'

'Which is why they're the only department that runs a deficit every year,' said Anthony.

'Bettering one's understanding of the human condition is not a matter of profit.' Vimal sniffed. 'We're always updating the classics – between the past century and now, we've become a lot better at certain languages, and there's no reason why classics should remain so inaccessible. I'm currently working on a better Latin version of the *Bhagavad Gita*—'

'Never mind that Schlegel just put one out,' Anthony quipped.

'Over ten years ago,' Vimal dismissed. 'And the Schlegel *Gita* is dreadful; he said himself that he hadn't grasped the basic philosophy that underlies the whole thing. Which shows, because he's used about seven different words for yoga—'

'Anyway,' Anthony said, ushering them away, 'that's Literature. One of the worst applications of a Babel education, if you ask me.'

'You don't approve?' Robin asked. He shared Victoire's delight; a life spent on the fourth floor, he thought, would be wonderful.

'Me, no.' Anthony chuckled. 'I'm here for silver-working. I think the Literature Department are an indulgent lot, as Vimal knows. See, the sad thing is, they could be the most dangerous scholars of them all, because they're the ones who really *understand* languages – know how they live and breathe and how they can make our blood pump, or our skin prickle, with just a turn of phrase. But they're too obsessed fiddling with their lovely images to bother with how all that living energy might be channelled into something far more powerful. I mean, of course, silver.'

The fifth and sixth floors housed both instruction rooms and reference materials – the primers, grammars, readers, thesauruses, and at least four different editions of every dictionary published in what Anthony claimed was every language spoken in the world.

'Well, the dictionaries are really scattered all over the tower, but here's where you come if you need to do some archival heavy lifting,' Anthony explained. 'Right in the middle, you see, so no one ever has to walk more than four flights to get what they need.'

In the centre of the sixth floor, a series of red-bound books sat on crimson velvet cloth beneath a glass display case. The way the soft lamplight gleamed against their leather covers made them look quite magical – more like magicians' grimoires than common reference materials.

'These are the Grammaticas,' said Anthony. 'They look impressive, but it's all right, you can touch. They're meant to be consulted. Just wipe your fingers on the velvet first.'

The Grammaticas were bound volumes of varying thicknesses but identical binding, arranged alphabetically by the Romanized name of the language and by publication date within those languages. Some Grammatica sets – notably the European languages – took up entire display cases on their own; others, largely the Oriental languages, contained very few volumes. The Chinese Grammaticas spanned only three volumes; the Japanese and Korean Grammaticas contained only one volume each. Tagalog, surprisingly, spanned five volumes.

'But we can't take credit for that,' said Anthony. 'All of that translation work was done by the Spanish; that's why you'll also see Spanish-to-English translator credits behind the cover pages. And a good deal of the Caribbean and South Asian Grammaticas – here they are – are still in progress. Those languages weren't of interest at Babel until after the Peace of Paris, which of course dumped a great deal of territory into Britain's imperial holdings. Similarly, you'll find most of the African Grammaticas are translated into English from German – it's the German missionaries and philologists who are doing the most work there; we haven't had anyone doing African languages for years.'

Robin couldn't help himself. He reached eagerly for the Oriental language Grammaticas and began thumbing through the front material. Written on the cover page of each volume in very neat, tiny handwriting were the names of those scholars who had produced the first edition of each Grammatica. Nathaniel Halhed had written the Bengali

Grammatica, Sir William Jones the Sanskrit Grammatica. This was a pattern, Robin noticed – the initial authors all tended to be white British men rather than native speakers of those languages.

'It's only recently that we've done much in Oriental languages at all,' said Anthony. 'We were lagging behind the French there for quite a while. Sir William Jones made some headway introducing Sanskrit, Arabic, and Persian to the courses lists when he was a fellow here – he started the Persian Grammatica in 1771 – but he was the only one doing any serious work in those languages until 1803.'

'What happened then?' asked Robin.

'Then Richard Lovell joined the faculty,' said Anthony. 'I hear he's something like a genius with Far Eastern languages. He's contributed two volumes to the Chinese Grammatica alone.'

Reverently, Robin reached out and pulled the first volume of the Chinese Grammatica towards him. The tome felt inordinately heavy, each page weighted down by ink. He recognized Professor Lovell's cramped, neat handwriting on each page. It covered an astonishing breadth of research. He put the volume down, struck with the unsettling realization that Professor Lovell – a foreigner – knew more about his mother tongue than he did.

'Why are these under display cases?' asked Victoire. 'Seems rather difficult to take them out.'

'Because these are the only editions in Oxford,' said Anthony. 'There are backups at Cambridge, Edinburgh, and the Foreign Offices in London. Those are updated annually to account for new findings. But these are the only comprehensive, authoritative collections of knowledge of every language that exist. New work is added by hand, you'll notice – it costs too much to reprint every time new additions are made, and besides, our printing presses can't handle that many foreign scripts.'

'So if a fire tore through Babel, we could lose a full year of research?' asked Ramy.

'A year? Try decades. But that'll never happen.' Anthony tapped the table, which Robin noticed was inlaid with dozens of slim silver bars. 'The Grammaticas are better protected than the Princess Victoria. These books are impervious to fire, flood, and attempted removal by anyone who isn't in the Institute register. If anyone tried to steal or damage one of these, they'd be struck by an unseen force so powerful they'd lose all sense of self and purpose until the police arrived.'

'The bars can do that?' Robin asked, alarmed.

'Well, something close,' Anthony said. 'I'm just guessing. Professor Playfair does the protective wards, and he likes to be mysterious about them. But yes, the security of this tower would astound you. It looks like your standard Oxford building, but if anyone ever tried to break in, they'd find themselves bleeding out on the street. I've seen it happen.'

'That's a lot of protection for a research building,' said Robin. His palms felt suddenly clammy; he wiped them on his gown.

'Well, of course,' said Anthony. 'There's more silver in these walls than in the vaults of the Bank of England.'

'Truly?' Letty asked.

'Of course,' said Anthony. 'Babel is one of the richest places in the entire country. Would you like to see why?'

They nodded. Anthony snapped his fingers and beckoned for them to follow him up the stairs.

The eighth floor was the only part of Babel that lay hidden behind doors and walls. The other seven were designed following an open floor plan, with no barriers surrounding the staircase, but the stairs to the eighth floor led to a brick hallway which in turn led to a heavy wooden door.

'Fire barrier,' Anthony explained. 'In case of accidents. Seals off the rest of the building so that the Grammaticas don't get burnt if something up here explodes.' He leaned his weight against the door and pushed.

The eighth floor looked more like a workshop than a research library. Scholars stood bent around worktables like mechanics, holding assortments of engraving tools to silver bars of all shapes and sizes. Whirring, humming, drilling sounds filled the air. Something exploded near the window, causing a shower of sparks followed by a round of cursing, but no one so much as glanced up.

A portly, grey-haired white man stood waiting for them in front of the workstations. He had a broad, smile-wrinkled face and the sort of twinkling eyes that could have placed him anywhere between forty and sixty. His black master's gowns were coated with so much silver dust that he shimmered whenever he moved. His eyebrows were thick, dark, and extraordinarily expressive; they seemed ready to leap off his face with enthusiasm whenever he spoke.

'Good morning,' he said. 'I'm Professor Jerome Playfair, chair of the faculty. I dabble in French and Italian, but my first love is German.

Thank you, Anthony, you're free to go. Are you and Woodhouse all set for your Jamaica trip?'

'Not yet,' said Anthony. 'Still need to track down the Patois primer. I suspect Gideon took it without signing it out again.'

'Get on, then.'

Anthony nodded, tipped an imaginary hat at Robin's cohort, and retreated back through the heavy door.

Professor Playfair beamed at them. 'So now you've seen Babel. How are we all doing?'

For a moment, no one spoke. Letty, Ramy, and Victoire all seemed as stunned as Robin felt. They'd been exposed to a great deal of information at once, and the effect was that Robin wasn't sure the ground he stood on was real.

Professor Playfair chuckled. 'I know. I had the same impression on my first day here as well. It's rather like an induction into a hidden world, isn't it? Like taking food in the seelie court. Once you know what happens in the tower, the mundane world doesn't seem half as interesting.'

'It's dazzling, sir,' said Letty. 'Incredible.'

Professor Playfair winked at her. 'It's the most wonderful place on earth.'

He cleared his throat. 'Now I'd like to tell a story. Forgive me for being dramatic, but I like to mark this occasion – your first day, after all, in what I believe is the most important research centre in the world. Would that be all right?'

He didn't need their approval, but they nodded regardless.

'Thank you. Now, we know this following story from Herodotus.' He paced several steps before them, like a player marking out his position on the stage. 'He tells us of the Egyptian king Psammetichus, who once formed a pact with Ionian sea raiders to defeat the eleven kings who had betrayed him. After he had overthrown his enemies, he gave large tracts of land to his Ionian allies. But Psammetichus wanted an even better guarantee that the Ionians would not turn on him as his former allies once had. He wanted to prevent wars based on misunderstandings. So he sent young Egyptian boys to live with the Ionians and learn Greek so that when they grew up, they could serve as interpreters between the two peoples.

'Here at Babel, we take inspiration from Psammetichus.' He peered around, and his sparkling gaze landed on each of them in turn as he spoke. 'Translation, from time immemorial, has been the facilitator of peace. Translation makes possible communication, which in turn makes possible the kind of diplomacy, trade, and cooperation between foreign peoples that brings wealth and prosperity to all.

'You've noticed by now, surely, that Babel alone among the Oxford faculties accepts students not of European origin. Nowhere else in this country will you find Hindus, Muslims, Africans, and Chinamen studying under the same roof. We accept you not despite, but *because* of your foreign backgrounds.' Professor Playfair emphasized this last part as if it was a matter of great pride. 'Because of your origins, you have the gift of languages those born in England cannot imitate. And you, like Psammetichus's boys, are the tongues that will speak this vision of global harmony into being.'

He clasped his hands before him as if in prayer. 'Anyhow. The postgrads make fun of me for that spiel every year. They think it's trite. But I think the situation calls for such gravity, don't you? After all, we're here to make the unknown known, to make the other familiar. We're here to make magic with words.'

This was, Robin thought, the kindest thing anyone had ever had to say about his being foreign-born. And though the story made his gut squirm – for he had read the relevant passage of Herodotus, and recalled that the Egyptian boys were nevertheless slaves – he felt also a thrum of excitement at the thought that perhaps his unbelonging did not doom him to existing forever on the margins, that perhaps, instead, it made him special.

Next, Professor Playfair gathered them around an empty worktable for a demonstration. 'Now, the common man thinks that silver-working is equivalent to sorcery.' He rolled his sleeves up to his elbows as he spoke, shouting so they could hear him over the din. 'They think that the power of the bars lies in the silver itself, that silver is some inherently magical substance which contains the power to alter the world.'

He unlocked the left drawer and pulled out a blank silver bar. 'They're not wholly wrong. There is indeed something special about silver that makes it an ideal vehicle for what we do. I like to think that it was blessed by the gods – it's refined with mercury, after all, and Mercury is the messenger god, no? Mercury, Hermes. Does silver not then have an inextricable link to hermeneutics? But let's not get too romantic. No, the power of the bar lies in words. More specifically, the stuff of language that words are incapable of expressing – the stuff that gets lost when we move between one language and another. The silver catches what's lost and manifests it into being.'

He glanced up, took in their baffled faces. 'You have questions. Don't worry. You won't start working with silver until near the end of your third year. You'll have plenty of time to catch up on the relevant theory before then. What matters now is that you understand the magnitude of what we do here.' He reached for an engraving pen. 'Which is, of course, the casting of spells.'

He began carving a word into one end of the bar. 'I'm just showing you a simple one. The effect will be quite subtle, but see if you feel it.'

He finished writing on that end, then held it up to show them. 'Heimlich. German for the secret and clandestine, which is how I'll translate it to English. But heimlich means more than just secrets. We derive heimlich from a Proto-Germanic word that means "home". Put together this constellation of meaning, and what do you get? Something like the secret, private feeling you get from being somewhere you belong, secluded from the outside world.'

As he spoke, he wrote the word clandestine on the flip side of the bar. The moment he finished, the silver began to vibrate.

'Heimlich,' he said. 'Clandestine.'

Once again Robin heard a singing without a source, an inhuman voice from nowhere.

The world shifted. Something bound them – some intangible barrier blurred the air around them, drowned out the surrounding noise, made it feel as though they were the only ones on a floor they knew was crowded with scholars. They were safe here. They were alone. This was their tower, their refuge.*

They were no strangers to this magic. They had all seen silver-work in effect before; in England it was impossible to avoid. But it was one thing to know the bars could work, that silver-work was simply the foundation of a functioning, advanced society. It was another thing to witness with their own eyes the warping of reality, the way words seized what no words could describe and invoked a physical effect that should not be.

---

* Cf. the related German unheimlich.

Victoire had her hand to her mouth. Letty was breathing hard. Ramy blinked very rapidly, as if trying to hold back tears.

And Robin, watching the still quivering bar, saw clearly now that it was all worth it. The loneliness, the beatings, the long and aching hours of study, the ingesting of languages like bitter tonic so that he could one day do *this* – it was *all* worth it.

'One last thing,' Professor Playfair said as he accompanied them down the stairs. 'We'll need to take your blood.'

'I beg your pardon?' asked Letty.

'Your blood. It won't take long.' Professor Playfair led them through the lobby to a small, windowless room hidden behind the shelves, which was empty save for a plain table and four chairs. He gestured for them to sit, then strode to the back wall, where a series of drawers were concealed inside the stone. He pulled out the top drawer, revealing stacks and stacks of tiny glass vials within. Each one was labelled with the name of the scholar whose blood it contained.

'It's for the wards,' Professor Playfair explained. 'Babel sees more robbery attempts than all of the banks in London combined. The doors keep most of the riffraff out, but the wards need some way to distinguish scholars from intruders. We've tried hair and fingernails, but they're too easy to steal.'

'Thieves can steal blood,' said Ramy.

'They can,' said Professor Playfair. 'But they'd have to be much more determined about the whole endeavour, wouldn't they?'

He pulled a handful of syringes from the bottom drawer. 'Sleeves up, please.'

Reluctantly, they pushed up their gowns.

'Shouldn't we have a nurse in here?' asked Victoire.

'Don't you worry.' Professor Playfair tapped the needle. 'I'm quite good at this. Won't take me too long to find a vein. Who's first?'

Robin volunteered; he didn't want to suffer the anticipation of watching the others. Ramy went next, and then Victoire, and then Letty. The whole procedure took less than fifteen minutes, with none the worse for the wear, though Letty had turned disturbingly green by the time the needle left her arm.

'Have a hearty lunch,' Professor Playfair told her. 'Blood pudding's good, if they have any.'

Four new glass vials were added to the drawer, all labelled with neat, tiny handwriting.

'Now you're part of the tower,' Professor Playfair told them as he locked the drawers. 'Now the tower knows you.'

Ramy made a face. 'Bit creepy, isn't it?'

'Not at all,' said Professor Playfair. 'You're in the place where magic is made. It's got all the trappings of a modern university, but at its heart, Babel isn't so different from the alchemists' lairs of old. But unlike the alchemists, we've actually figured out the key to the transformation of a thing. It's not in the material substance. It's in the name.'

Babel shared a buttery in the Radcliffe quadrangle with several other humanities faculties. The food there was supposedly very good, but it was closed until start of classes tomorrow, so instead they headed back to the college just in time for the tail end of lunch service. All the hot food was gone, but afternoon tea and its trappings were on offer until supper. They loaded trays with teacups, teapots, sugar bowls, milk jugs, and scones, then navigated the long wooden tables in hall until they found an unoccupied one in the corner.

'So you're from Canton, then?' asked Letty. She had a very forceful personality, Robin had noticed; she asked all her questions, even the benign ones, in the tone of an interrogator.

He'd just bitten into a scone; it was dry and stale, and he had to take a sip of tea before he could answer. She turned her gaze on Ramy before he could. 'And you – Madras? Bombay?'

'Calcutta,' Ramy said pleasantly.

'My father was stationed in Calcutta,' she said. 'Three years, from 1825 to 1828. Could be you saw him around.'

'Lovely,' said Ramy as he slathered jam over his scone. 'Could be he pointed a gun at my sisters once.'

Robin snorted, but Letty blanched. 'I'm only saying I've met Hindus before—'

'I'm Muslim.'

'Well, I'm just saying—'

'And you know,' now Ramy was buttering his scone with great vim, 'it's very irritating, actually, the way everyone wants to equate India with Hinduism. "Oh, Muslim rule is an aberration, an intrusion; the Mughals just interlopers, but *tradition* – that's Sanskrit, that's the Upanishads."'

He lifted his scone to his mouth. 'But you don't even know what any of those words mean, do you?'

They'd got off to a bad start. Ramy's humour did not always work on new acquaintances. One needed to take his glib tirades in one's stride, and Letitia Price seemed capable of anything but that.

'So, Babel,' Robin interjected before Ramy could say anything else. 'Nice building.'

Letty cast him an amazed look. 'Quite.'

Ramy, rolling his eyes, coughed and set down his scone.

They sipped their tea in silence. Victoire clinked her spoon nervously around her cup. Robin stared out of the window. Ramy tapped his fingers against the table but stopped when Letty shot him a glare.

'How have you found the place?' Victoire tried valiantly to rescue their conversation. 'Oxfordshire, I mean. I feel like we've only seen a fraction of it so far, it's so big. I mean, not like London or Paris, but there are so many hidden corners, don't you think?'

'It's incredible,' Robin said with a bit too much enthusiasm. 'It's unreal, every single building – we spent the first three days just walking around, staring. We saw all the tourist attractions – the Oxford Museum, the Christ Church gardens—'

Victoire arched an eyebrow. 'And they're letting you in wherever you go?'

'Actually, no.' Ramy set down his teacup. 'Remember, Birdie, the Ashmolean—'

'Right,' said Robin. 'They seemed so certain we were going to steal something, they made us turn out our pockets on the way in and out, as if they were convinced we'd stolen the Alfred Jewel.'

'They wouldn't let us in at all,' Victoire said. 'They said unchaperoned ladies weren't allowed.'

Ramy snorted. 'Why?'

'Probably because of our nervous dispositions,' said Letty. 'They couldn't have us fainting against the paintings.'

'But the colours are *so* exciting,' said Victoire.

'Battlefields and breasts.' Letty put the back of her hand to her forehead. 'Too much for my nerves.'

'So what'd you do?' Ramy asked.

'We came back when a different docent was on shift and pretended this time to be men.' Victoire deepened her voice. 'Excuse me, we're just countryside lads visiting our cousins here and we've nothing to do when they're in class—'

Robin laughed. 'You didn't.'

'It worked,' Victoire insisted.

'I don't believe you.'

'No, really.' Victoire smiled. She had, Robin noticed, enormous and very pretty doe-like eyes. He liked listening to her speak; every sentence felt like she was pulling laughter out from inside him. 'They must have thought we were about twelve, but it worked like a dream—'

'Until you got excited,' Letty cut in.

'All right, it worked until we were *just* past the docent—'

'But then she saw a Rembrandt she liked and let out this squeak—' Letty made a chirping noise. Victoire shoved at her shoulder, but she was laughing too.

'"Excuse me, miss."' Victoire pulled down her chin in imitation of the disapproving docent. '"You're not supposed to be here, I think you've got turned around—"'

'So it was nerves, after all—'

That was all it took. The ice melted. In an instant they were all laughing – a bit harder, perhaps, than the joke justified, but what mattered was that they were laughing at all.

'Has anyone else found you out?' Ramy asked.

'No, they all just think we're particularly slim freshers,' Letty said. 'Though once someone yelled at Victoire to take off her gown.'

'He tried to pull it off me.' Victoire's gaze dropped to her lap. 'Letty had to beat him off with her umbrella.'

'Similar thing happened to us,' Ramy said. 'Some drunkards from Balliol started shouting at us one night.'

'They don't like dark skin in their uniforms,' said Victoire.

'No,' said Ramy, 'they don't.'

'I'm so sorry,' said Victoire. 'Did they – I mean, did you get away all right?'

Robin cast Ramy a concerned glance, but Ramy's eyes were still crinkled with good humour.

'Oh, yes.' He threw his arm around Robin's shoulders. 'I was ready to break some noses, but this one did the prudent thing – started running like the hounds of hell were behind him – so then I couldn't do anything but run as well.'

'I don't like conflict,' Robin said, blushing.

'Oh, no,' said Ramy. 'You'd disappear into the stones if you could.'

'You could have stayed,' Robin quipped. 'Fought them off single-handed.'

'What, and leave you to the scary dark?' Ramy grinned. 'Anyway, you looked absurd. Sprinting like your bladder was bursting and you couldn't find a privy.'

And then they were laughing again.

Soon it became apparent that no topics were off limits. They could talk about anything, share all the indescribable humiliations they felt being in a place they were not supposed to be, all the lurking unease that until now they'd kept to themselves. They offered up everything about themselves because they had, at last, found the only group of people for whom their experiences were not so unique or baffling.

Next they traded stories about their educations before Oxford. Babel, apparently, always anointed its chosen ones at a young age. Letty, who was from down south in Brighton, had dazzled family friends with her prodigious memory ever since she could speak; one such friend, who knew some Oxford dons, secured her a set of tutors and had her drilled in French, German, Latin, and Greek until she was old enough to matriculate.

'Though I almost didn't make it.' Letty blinked, eyelashes fluttering madly. 'Father said he'd never pay for a woman's education, so I'm grateful for the scholarship. I had to sell a set of bracelets to pay for the coach fare up.'

Victoire, like Robin and Ramy, had come to Europe with a guardian. 'Paris,' she clarified. 'He was a Frenchman, but he had acquaintances at the Institute, and he was going to write to them when I was old enough. Only then he died, and for a while I wasn't sure I'd get to come.' Her voice faltered a bit. She took a sip of tea. 'But I managed to get in touch with them, and they arranged to bring me over,' she concluded vaguely.

Robin suspected this was not the full extent of this story, but he, too, was practised in the art of papering over pain, and he did not pry.

One thing united them all – without Babel, they had nowhere in this country to go. They'd been chosen for privileges they couldn't have ever imagined, funded by powerful and wealthy men whose motives they did not fully understand, and they were acutely aware these could be lost at any moment. That precariousness made them simultaneously bold and terrified. They had the keys to the kingdom; they did not want to give them back.

By the time they'd finished their tea, they were almost in love with each other – not quite yet, because true love took time and memories, but as close to love as first impressions could take them. The days had not yet come when Ramy wore Victoire's sloppily knitted scarves with pride, when Robin learned exactly how long Ramy liked his tea steeped so he could have it ready when he inevitably came to the Buttery late from his Arabic tutorial, or when they all knew Letty was about to come to class with a paper bag full of lemon biscuits because it was a Wednesday morning and Taylor's bakery put out lemon biscuits on Wednesdays. But that afternoon they could see with certainty the kind of friends they would be, and loving that vision was close enough.

Later, when everything went sideways and the world broke in half, Robin would think back to this day, to this hour at this table, and wonder why they had been so quick, so carelessly eager to trust one another. Why had they refused to see the myriad ways they could hurt each other? Why had they not paused to interrogate their differences in birth, in raising, that meant they were not and could never be on the same side?

But the answer was obvious – that they were all four of them drowning in the unfamiliar, and they saw in each other a raft, and clinging to one another was the only way to stay afloat.

The girls were not allowed to live in college, which was why they hadn't crossed paths with Robin and Ramy until the first day of instruction. Instead, Victoire and Letty lodged about two miles away in the servant annex of one of the Oxford day schools, which was apparently a common arrangement for Babel's female students. Robin and Ramy accompanied them home because it seemed the gentlemanly thing to do, but Robin hoped this would not become a nightly routine, as the road really was quite far away and there was no omnibus at this hour.

'They couldn't put you anywhere closer?' Ramy asked.

Victoire shook her head. 'All of the colleges said our proximity risked corrupting the gentlemen.'

'Well, that's not fair,' said Ramy.

Letty shot him a droll look. 'Say more.'

'But it's not so bad,' said Victoire. 'There are some fun pubs on this street – we like the Four Horsemen, the Twisted Root, and there's this place called Rooks and Pawns where you can play chess—'

'Sorry,' said Robin. 'Did you say the Twisted Root?'

'It's up ahead on Harrow Lane near the bridge,' said Victoire. 'You won't like it, though. We took a peek and walked right back out – it's awfully dirty inside. Run your finger around the glass and you'll find a wadge of grease and dirt a quarter of an inch thick.'

'Not a haunt for students, then?'

'No, Oxford boys wouldn't be seen dead there. It's for town, not gown.'

Letty pointed out a herd of meandering cows up ahead, and Robin let the conversation drift. Later, after they'd seen the girls safely home, he told Ramy to head back to Magpie Lane on his own.

'I forgot I've got to go and see Professor Lovell,' he said. Jericho was conveniently closer to this part of town than it was to Univ. 'It's a long walk; I don't want to drag you over there.'

'I thought your dinner wasn't until next weekend,' said Ramy.

'It is, but I've just remembered I was supposed to visit sooner.' Robin cleared his throat; he felt terrible lying to Ramy's face. 'Mrs Piper said she had some cakes for me.'

'Thank heavens.' Amazingly, Ramy suspected nothing. 'Lunch was inedible. Are you sure you don't want company?'

'I'm all right. It's been quite a day, and I'm tired, and I think it'll be nice just to walk for a bit in silence.'

'Fair enough,' Ramy said pleasantly.

They parted on Woodstock Road. Ramy went down south straight back to the college. Robin cut right in search of the bridge Victoire had pointed out, unsure of what he was looking for except for the memory of a whispered phrase.

The answer found him. Halfway through Harrow Lane he heard a second pair of footsteps behind him. He glanced over his shoulder and saw a dark figure following him up the narrow road.

'Took you long enough,' said his doppelgänger. 'I've been skulking here all day.'

'Who are you?' Robin demanded. 'What are you – why do you have my face?'

'Not here,' said his doppelgänger. 'The pub's round this corner, let's go inside—'

'Answer me,' Robin demanded. A belated sense of danger had only now kicked in; his mouth had gone dry; his heart was hammering furiously. 'Who are you?'

'You're Robin Swift,' said the man. 'You grew up without a father but with an inexplicable English nursemaid and a never-ending supply of books in English, and when Professor Lovell turned up to carry you off to England, you said farewell to your motherland for good. You think the professor might be your father, but he hasn't admitted that you are his own. You're quite sure he never will. Does that make sense?'

Robin couldn't speak. His mouth opened, and his jaw worked pointlessly, but he simply had nothing to say.

'Come with me,' said his doppelgänger. 'Let's have a drink.'

BOOK II

ROYAL INSTITUTE OF TRANSLATION
UNIVERSITY OF OXFORD

CHAPTER FIVE

⎯⎯⟨∞⟩⎯⎯

*'I don't care for hard names,' interrupted Monks with a jeering laugh.
'You know the fact, and that's enough for me.'*

CHARLES DICKENS, *Oliver Twist*

They found a table in the back corner of the Twisted Root. Robin's doppelgänger ordered them two glasses of a light golden ale. Robin drained half his glass in three desperate gulps and felt somewhat steadier, though no less confused.

'My name,' said his doppelgänger, 'is Griffin Lovell.'

Upon closer inspection, he and Robin were not so alike after all. He was several years older, and his face bore a hard maturity that Robin's hadn't yet acquired. His voice was deeper, less forgiving, more assertive. He was several inches taller than Robin, though he was also much thinner; indeed, he appeared composed entirely of sharp edges and angles. His hair was darker, his skin paler. He looked like a print illustration of Robin, the lighting contrasts amplified and the colour blanched out.

He's even more of your spitting image than the last.

'Lovell,' Robin repeated, trying to find his bearings. 'Then you're—?'

'He'll never admit it,' said Griffin. 'But he won't with you either, will he? Do you know he's got a wife and children?'

Robin choked. 'What?'

'It's true. A girl and a boy, seven and three. Darling Philippa and little Dick. The wife's name is Johanna. He's got them squirrelled away in a lovely estate in Yorkshire. It's partly how he gets funding for voyages abroad – he came from nothing, but she's terribly rich. Five hundred pounds a year, I'm told.'

'But then does—?'

'Does she know about us? Absolutely not. Though I don't think she'd care if she did, apart from the obvious reputational problems. There's no love lost in that marriage. He wanted an estate and she wanted bragging rights. They see each other about twice a year, and the rest of his time he lives here, or in Hampstead. We're the children he spends the most time with, funnily enough.' Griffin cocked his head. 'At least, you are.'

'Am I dreaming?' Robin mumbled.

'You wish. You look ghastly. Drink.'

Robin reached mechanically for his glass. He was no longer trembling, but his head felt very fuzzy. Drinking didn't help, but it at least gave him something to do with his hands.

'I'm sure you've got loads of questions,' said Griffin. 'I'll try to answer them, but you'll have to be patient. I've got questions too. What do you call yourself?'

'Robin Swift,' said Robin, puzzled. 'You know that.'

'But that's the name you prefer?'

Robin was not sure what he meant by this. 'I mean, there's my first – I mean, my Chinese name, but no one – I don't—'

'Fine,' said Griffin. 'Swift. Nice name. How'd you come up with that?'

'*Gulliver's Travels*,' Robin admitted. It sounded very silly when he said it out loud. Everything about Griffin made him feel like a child in contrast. 'It – it's one of my favourite books. Professor Lovell said to pick whatever I liked, and that was the first name that came to mind.'

Griffin's lip curled. 'He's softened a bit, then. Me, he took to a street corner before we signed the papers and told me foundlings were often named after the places they'd been abandoned. Said I could walk the city until I found a word that didn't sound too ridiculous.'

'Did you?'

'Sure. Harley. Nowhere special in particular, I just saw it above a shop and I liked the way it sounded. The shapes your mouth has to make, the release of the second syllable. But I'm no Harley, I'm a Lovell, just as you're no Swift.'

'So we're—'

'Half-brothers,' said Griffin. 'Hello, brother. It's lovely to meet you.'

Robin set down his glass. 'I'd like to have the full story now.'

'Fair enough.' Griffin leaned forward. At dinnertime the Twisted Root was just crowded enough that the hubbub cast a shroud of noise over any individual conversation, but still Griffin lowered his voice to such a quiet murmur that Robin had to strain to hear. 'Here's the long and short of it. I'm a criminal. My colleagues and I regularly steal silver, manuscripts, and engraving materials from Babel and funnel them across England to our associates throughout the world. What you did last night was treason, and if anyone found out, you'd be locked up in Newgate for twenty years at least, but only after they'd tortured you in an attempt to get to us.' All this he uttered very quickly, with hardly any change in tone or volume. When finished, he leaned back, looking satisfied.

Robin did the only thing he could think to do, which was take another heady gulp of ale. When he set the glass down, temples throbbing, the only word he managed was 'Why?'

'Easy,' said Griffin. 'There's people who need silver more than wealthy Londoners.'

'But – I mean, who?'

Griffin didn't respond at once. He looked Robin up and down for several seconds, examining his face as if searching for something – some further resemblance, some crucial, innate quality. Then he asked, 'Why did your mother die?'

'Cholera,' Robin said after a pause. 'There was an outbreak—'

'I didn't ask how,' said Griffin. 'I asked why.'

I don't know why, Robin wanted to say, but he did. He'd always known, he'd just forced himself not to dwell on it. In all this time, he had never let himself ask this particular formulation of the question.

Oh, two weeks and some change, said Mrs Piper. They'd been in China for over two weeks.

His eyes stung. He blinked. 'How do you know about my mother?'

Griffin leaned back, arms folded behind his head. 'Why don't you finish that drink?'

Outside, Griffin set off briskly down Harrow Lane, tossing rapid-fire questions from out of the side of his mouth. 'So where are you from?'

'Canton.'

'I was born in Macau. I don't remember if I ever went to Canton. So when did he bring you over?'

'To London?'

'No, you dolt, to Manila. Yes, London.'

His brother, Robin thought, could be quite an ass. 'Six – no, seven years ago now.'

'Incredible.' Griffin turned left onto Banbury Road without warning;

Robin hastened to follow. 'No wonder he never went looking for me. Had something better to focus on, didn't he?'

Robin lurched forward, tripping on the cobblestones. He righted himself and hurried after Griffin. He'd never had ale before, only weak wines at Mrs Piper's table, and the hops left his tongue feeling numb. He had a strong urge to vomit. Why had he drunk so much? He felt dazed, twice as slow at putting together his thoughts – but of course that was the point. It was clear Griffin had wanted him off-kilter, unguarded. Robin suspected Griffin liked to keep people unbalanced.

'Where are we going?' he asked.

'South. Then west. Doesn't matter; it's just that the best way to avoid being overheard is to always be on the move.' Griffin pivoted down Canterbury Road. 'If you're standing still, then your tail can hide and catch the whole conversation, but it makes things harder for them when you're weaving about.'

'Your tail?'

'One should always assume.'

'Can we go to a bakery, then?'

'A bakery?'

'I told my friend I'd gone to see Mrs Piper.' Robin's head was still spinning, but the memory of his lie stuck out with clarity. 'I can't go home empty-handed.'

'Fine.' Griffin led them down Winchester Road. 'Will Taylor's do? There's nothing else still open.'

Robin ducked inside the shop and hastily purchased a selection of the plainest pastries he could find – he didn't want Ramy to grow suspicious the next time they passed Taylor's glass display. He had a burlap sack in his room; he could discard the shop boxes when he got home and dump the cakes in there.

Griffin's paranoia had infected him. He felt marked, coated in scarlet paint, certain that someone would call him a thief even as he paid. He couldn't meet the baker's eye as he received his change.

'Anyhow,' Griffin said when Robin emerged. 'How would you like to steal for us?'

'Steal?' They were strolling at an absurd pace again. 'You mean from Babel?'

'Obviously, yes. Keep up.'

'But why do you need me?'

'Because you're a part of the institution and we're not. Your blood's in the tower, which means there are doors you can open that we can't.'

'But why . . .' Robin's tongue kept tripping over a flood of questions. 'What for? What do you do with what you steal?'

'Just what I told you. We redistribute it. We're Robin Hood. Ha, ha. Robin. No? All right. We send bars and silver-working materials all over the world to people who need them – people who don't have the luxury of being rich and British. People like your mother. See, Babel's a dazzling place, but it's only dazzling because it sells its match-pairs to a very limited customer base.' Griffin glanced over his shoulder. There was no one around them save a washerwoman lugging a basket down the other end of the street, but he quickened his pace regardless. 'So are you in?'

'I – I don't know.' Robin blinked. 'I can't just – I mean, I still have so many questions.'

Griffin shrugged. 'So ask anything you want. Go on.'

'I – all right.' Robin tried to arrange his confusion into sequential order. 'Who are you?'

'Griffin Lovell.'

'No, the collective *you*—'

'The Hermes Society,' Griffin said promptly. 'Just Hermes, if you like.'

'The Hermes Society.' Robin turned that name over in his mouth. 'Why—'

'It's a joke. Silver and mercury, Mercury and Hermes, Hermes and hermeneutics. I don't know who came up with it.'

'And you're a clandestine society? No one knows about you?'

'Certainly Babel does. We've had a – well, it's been quite back and forth, shall we say? But they don't know much, and certainly not as much as they'd like to. We're very good at staying in the shadows.'

Not that good, Robin thought, thinking of curses in the dark, silver scattered across cobblestones. He said instead, 'How many of you are there?'

'Can't tell you.'

'Do you have a headquarters?'

'Yes.'

'Will you show me where it is?'

Griffin laughed. 'Absolutely not.'

'But – there's more of you, surely?' Robin persisted. 'You could at least introduce me—'

'Can't, and won't,' said Griffin. 'We've just barely met, brother. For all I know, you could go running to Playfair the moment we part.'

'But then how—' Robin threw up his arms in frustration. 'I mean, you're giving me nothing, and asking me for everything.'

'Yes, brother, that's really how secret societies with any degree of competence work. I don't know what sort of person you are, and I'd be a fool to tell you more.'

'You see why this makes things very difficult for me, though?' Robin thought Griffin was brushing off some rather reasonable concerns. 'I don't know a thing about you either. You could be lying, you could be trying to frame me—'

'If that were true you'd have been sent down by now. So that's out. What do you think we're lying about?'

'Could be you're not using the silver to help other people at all,' said Robin. 'Could be the Hermes Society is a great fraud, could be you're reselling what you steal to get rich—'

'Do I look like I'm getting rich?'

Robin took in Griffin's lean, underfed frame, his frayed black coat, and his unkempt hair. No – he had to admit, the Hermes Society did not seem like a scheme for personal profit. Perhaps Griffin was using the stolen silver for some other secret means, but personal gain did not seem like one of them.

'I know it's a lot at once,' Griffin said. 'But you've simply got to trust me. There's no other way.'

'I want to. I mean – I'm just – this is so much.' Robin shook his head. 'I've only just arrived here, I've only just seen Babel for the first time, and I don't know you or this place well enough to have the slightest idea what's going on—'

'Then why'd you do it?' Griffin asked.

'I – what?'

'Last night.' Griffin cast him a sideways look. 'You helped us, without question. You didn't even hesitate. Why?'

'I don't know,' Robin said truthfully.

He'd asked himself this a thousand times. Why had he activated that bar? It wasn't merely because the whole situation – the midnight hour, the moonlight glow – had been so dreamlike that rules and consequences seemed to disappear, or because the sight of his doppelgänger had made him doubt reality itself. He'd felt some deeper compulsion he couldn't explain. 'It just seemed right.'

'What, you didn't realize you were helping a ring of thieves?'

'I knew you were thieves,' Robin said. 'I just . . . I didn't think you were doing anything wrong.'

'I'd trust your instinct on that,' said Griffin. 'Trust *me*. Trust that we're doing the right thing.'

'And what is the right thing?' Robin asked. 'In your view? What's all this for?'

Griffin smiled. It was a peculiar, condescending smile, a mask of amusement that didn't reach his eyes. 'Now you're asking the right questions.'

They'd looped back round to Banbury Road. The University Parks loomed lush before them, and Robin half hoped they would cut south to Parks Road – it was getting late, and the night was quite cold – but Griffin took them north, further from the city centre.

'Do you know what the majority of bars are used for in this country?'

Robin took a wild guess. 'Doctors' practices?'

'Ha. Adorable. No, they're used for sitting room decorations. That's right – alarm clocks that sound like real roosters, lights that dim and brighten on vocal demand, curtains that change colour throughout the day, that sort of thing. Because they're fun, and because the British upper class can afford them, and whatever rich Britons want, they get.'

'Fine,' said Robin. 'But just because Babel sells bars to meet popular demand—'

Griffin cut him off. 'Would you like to know the second and third largest sources of income at Babel?'

'Legal?'

'No. Militaries, both state and private,' said Griffin. 'And then slave traders. Legal makes pennies in comparison.'

'That's . . . that's impossible.'

'No, that's just how the world works. Let me paint you a picture, brother. You've noticed by now that London sits at the centre of a vast empire that won't stop growing. The single most important enabler of this growth is Babel. Babel collects foreign languages and foreign talent the same way it hoards silver and uses them to produce translation magic that benefits England and England only. The vast majority of all silver bars in use in the world are in London. The newest, most powerful bars in use rely on Chinese, Sanskrit, and Arabic to work, but you'll count less than a thousand bars in the countries where those languages are widely spoken, and then only in the homes of the wealthy and powerful. And that's wrong. That's predatory. That's fundamentally unjust.'

Griffin had a habit of crisply punctuating each sentence with an open hand, like a conductor bearing down again and again over the same note. 'But how does this happen?' he continued. 'How does all the power from foreign languages just somehow accrue to England? This is no accident; this is a deliberate exploitation of foreign culture and foreign resources. The professors like to pretend that the tower is a refuge for pure knowledge, that it sits above the mundane concerns of business and commerce, but it does not. It's intricately tied to the business of colonialism. It *is* the business of colonialism. Ask yourself why the Literature Department only translates works into English and not the other way around, or what the interpreters are being sent abroad to *do*. Everything Babel does is in the service of expanding the Empire. Consider – Sir Horace Wilson, who's the first endowed chair in Sanskrit in Oxford history, spends half his time conducting tutorials for Christian missionaries.

'The point of it all is to keep amassing silver. We possess all this silver because we cajole, manipulate, and threaten other countries into trade deals that keep the cash flowing homeward. And we enforce those trade deals with the very same silver bars, now inscribed with Babel's work, that make our ships faster, our soldiers hardier, and our guns more deadly. It's a vicious circle of profit, and unless some outside force breaks the cycle, sooner or later Britain will possess all the wealth in the world.

'We are that outside force. Hermes. We funnel silver away to people, communities, and movements that deserve it. We aid slave revolts. Resistance movements. We melt down silver bars made for cleaning doilies and use them to cure disease instead.' Griffin slowed down; turned to look Robin in the eyes. '*That's* what this is all for.'

This was, Robin had to admit, a very compelling theory of the world. Only it seemed to implicate nearly everything he held dear. 'I – I see.'

'So why the hesitation?'

Why indeed? Robin tried to sort through his confusion, to find a reason for prudence that did not simply boil down to fear. But that was precisely it – fear of consequences, fear of breaking the gorgeous illusion of the Oxford he'd won admission to, the one Griffin had just sullied before he'd been able to properly enjoy it.

'It's just so sudden,' he said. 'And I've only just met you, there's so much I don't know.'

'That's the thing about secret societies,' said Griffin. 'They're easy to romanticize. You think it's this long courting process – that you'll be inducted, shown a whole new world, shown all the levers and people at play. If you've formed your only impression of secret societies from novels and penny dreadfuls, then you might expect rituals and passwords and secret meetings in abandoned warehouses.

'But that's not how things work, brother. This is not a penny dreadful. Real life is messy, scary, and uncertain.' Griffin's tone softened. 'You should understand, what I'm asking you to do is very dangerous. People die over these bars – I've watched friends die over these bars. Babel would like to crush the life out of us, and you don't want to know what happens to the Hermes members they catch. We exist because we're decentralized. We don't put all of our information in one place. So I can't ask you to take your time reviewing all the information. I'm asking you to take a chance on a conviction.'

For the first time, Robin registered that Griffin was not as confident, not as intimidating as his rapid-fire speech made him sound. He stood, hands wedged in his pockets, shoulders hunched and shivering against the biting autumn wind. And he was so visibly nervous. He was twitching, fidgeting; his eyes darted over his shoulder every time he finished a sentence. Robin was confused, distressed, but Griffin was *scared*.

'It's got to be like this,' Griffin insisted. 'Minimal information. Quick judgment calls. I'd love to show you my whole world – I promise, it's not fun being alone – but the fact remains you're a Babel student who I've known for less than a day. The time may come when I trust you with everything, but that'll only be when you've proven yourself, and when I've got no other options. For now, I've told you what we do, and what we need from you. Will you join us?'

This audience, Robin realized, was drawing to an end. He was being asked to make a final decision – and if he said no, he suspected, then Griffin would simply vanish from the Oxford he knew, would fade so effectively into the shadows that Robin would be left wondering if he'd imagined the entire encounter. 'I want to – I do, really, but I still don't – I just need time to think. Please.'

He knew this would frustrate Griffin. But Robin was terrified. He felt he'd been led to the edge of a precipice and told, with no assurances, to jump. He felt as he had seven years ago, when Professor Lovell had slid a contract before him and calmly asked that he sign away his future. Only then he'd had nothing, so there had been nothing to lose. This time he had everything – food, clothing, shelter – and no guarantee of survival at the other end.

'Five days, then,' said Griffin. He looked cross, but he made no recriminations. 'You get five days. There's a lone birch in the Merton College gardens – you'll know it when you see it. Scratch a cross in the trunk by Saturday if it's a yes. Don't bother if it's a no.'

'Just five?'

'If you don't know the layout of this place by then, kid, there's no getting through to you at all.' Griffin clapped him on the shoulder. 'Do you know the way home?'

'I – no, actually.' Robin hadn't been paying attention; he had no idea where they were. The buildings had receded into the background; now they were surrounded only by rolling green.

'We're in Summertown,' said Griffin. 'Pretty, though a bit boring. Woodstock's at the end of this green – just take a left and walk all the way down south until things start looking familiar. We'll part here. Five days.' Griffin turned to go.

'Wait – how do I reach you?' Robin asked. Now that Griffin's departure seemed imminent, he was somehow reluctant to part ways. He had a sudden fear that if he let Griffin out of his sight then he might disappear for good, that this would all turn out to be a dream.

'I told you – you don't,' said Griffin. 'If there's a cross on the tree, I reach you. Gives me insurance in case you turn out to be an informant, you see?'

'Then what am I supposed to do in the meantime?'

'What do you mean? You're still a Babel student. Act like one. Go to class. Go out drinking and get into brawls. No – you're soft. Don't get into brawls.'

'I . . . fine. All right.'

'Anything else?'

Anything else? Robin wanted to laugh. He had a thousand other questions, none of which he thought Griffin would answer. He took the chance on just one. 'Does he know about you?'

'Who?'

'Our – Professor Lovell.'

'Ah.' This time, Griffin did not glibly rattle off an answer. This time, he paused before he spoke. 'I'm not sure.'

This surprised Robin. 'You don't know?'

'I left Babel after my third year,' Griffin said quietly. 'I'd been with Hermes since I started, but I was on the inside like you. Then something happened, and it wasn't safe anymore, so I ran. And since then I've ...' He trailed off, then cleared his throat. 'But that's beside the point. All you need to know is you probably shouldn't mention my name at dinner.'

'Well, that goes without saying.'

Griffin turned to go, paused, then turned back around. 'One more thing. Where do you live?'

'Hm? Univ – we're all at University College.'

'I know that. What room?'

'Oh.' Robin blushed. 'Number four, Magpie Lane, room seven. The house with the green roof. I'm in the corner. With the sloping windows facing Oriel chapel.'

'I know it.' The sun had long set. Robin could no longer see Griffin's face, half-hidden in shadow. 'That used to be my room.'

Chapter Six

'The question is,' said Alice, 'whether you can make words mean so many different things.'

'The question is,' said Humpty Dumpty, 'which is to be master, that's all.'

Lewis Carroll, *Through the Looking-Glass*

Professor Playfair's introductory class to Translation Theory met at Tuesday mornings on the fifth floor of the tower. They'd barely been seated when he began to lecture, filling the narrow classroom with his booming showman's voice.

'By now you are each passably fluent in at least three languages, which is a feat in its own right. Today, however, I will try to impress upon you the unique difficulty of translation. Consider how tricky it is merely to say the word *hello*. Hello seems so easy! *Bonjour. Ciao. Hallo.* And on and on. But then say we are translating from Italian into English. In Italian, *ciao* can be used upon greeting or upon parting – it does not specify either, it simply marks etiquette at the point of contact. It is derived from the Venetian *s-ciào vostro*, meaning something akin to "your obedient servant". But I digress. The point is, when we bring *ciao* into English – if we are translating a scene where the characters disperse, for example – we must impose that *ciao* has been said as goodbye. Sometimes this is obvious from context, but sometimes not – sometimes we must add new words in our translation. So already things are complicated, and we haven't moved past hello.

'The first lesson any good translator internalizes is that there exists no one-to-one correlation between words or even concepts from one language to another. The Swiss philologist Johann Breitinger, who claimed that languages were merely "collections of totally equivalent words and locutions which are interchangeable, and which fully correspond to each other in meaning", was dreadfully wrong. Language is not like maths. And even maths differs depending on the language* – but we will revisit that later.'

Robin found himself searching Professor Playfair's face as he spoke. He was not sure what he was looking for. Some evidence of evil, perhaps. The cruel, selfish, lurking monster Griffin had sketched. But Professor Playfair seemed only a cheerful, beaming scholar, enamoured by the beauty of words. Indeed, in daylight, in the classroom, his brother's grand conspiracies felt quite ridiculous.

'Language does not exist as a nomenclature for a set of universal concepts,' Professor Playfair went on. 'If it did, then translation would not be a highly skilled profession – we would simply sit a class full of dewy-eyed freshers down with dictionaries and have the completed works of the Buddha on our shelves in no time. Instead, we have to learn to dance between that age-old dichotomy, helpfully elucidated by Cicero and Hieronymus: *verbum e verbo* and *sensum e sensu*. Can anyone—'

'Word for word,' Letty said promptly. 'And sense for sense.'

'Good,' said Professor Playfair. 'That is the dilemma. Do we take words as our unit of translation, or do we subordinate accuracy of individual words to the overall spirit of the text?'

'I don't understand,' said Letty. 'Shouldn't a faithful translation of individual words produce an equally faithful text?'

'It would,' said Professor Playfair, 'if, again, words existed in relation to each other in the same way in every language. But they do not. The words *schlecht* and *schlimm* both mean "bad" in German, but how do you know when to use one or the other? When do we use *fleuve* or *rivière* in French? How do we render the French *esprit* into English? We ought not merely translate each word on its own, but must rather evoke the sense of how they fit the whole of the passage. But how can that be

---

* This is true. Mathematics is not divorced from culture. Take counting systems – not all languages use base ten. Or geometry – Euclidean geometry assumes a conception of space not shared by all. One of the greatest intellectual shifts in history involves the transition from Roman numerals to the more elegant Arabic numerals, whose place-value notation and concept of zero, signifying nothing, made possible new forms of mental arithmetic. Old habits died hard; in 1299, merchants in Florence were banned by the Florentine Arte del Cambio from using both zero and Arabic numerals: 'He shall write openly and fully by letter.'

done, if languages are indeed so different? These differences aren't trivial, mind you – Erasmus wrote an entire treatise on why he rendered the Greek *logos* into the Latin *sermo* in his translation of the New Testament. Translating word-for-word is simply inadequate.'

'*That servile path thou nobly dost decline,*' Ramy recited, '*of tracing word by word, and line by line.*'

'*Those are the laboured births of slavish brains, not the effect of poetry, but pains,*' Professor Playfair finished. 'John Denham. Very nice, Mr Mirza. So you see, translators do not so much deliver a message as they rewrite the original. And herein lies the difficulty – rewriting is still writing, and writing always reflects the author's ideology and biases. After all, the Latin *translatio* means "to carry across". Translation involves a spatial dimension – a literal transportation of texts across conquered territory, words delivered like spices from an alien land. Words mean something quite different when they journey from the palaces of Rome to the tea-rooms of today's Britain.

'And we have not yet moved past the lexical. If translation were only a matter of finding the right themes, the right general ideas, then theoretically we could eventually make our meaning clear, couldn't we? But something gets in the way – syntax, grammar, morphology and orthography, all the things that form the bones of a language. Consider the Heinrich Heine poem "Ein Fichtenbaum". It's short, and its message is quite easy to grasp. A pine tree, longing for a palm tree, represents a man's desire for a woman. Yet translating it into English has been devilishly tricky, because English doesn't have genders like German does. So there's no way to convey the binary opposition between the masculine *ein Fichtenbaum* and the feminine *einer Palme*. You see? So we must proceed from the starting assumption that distortion is inevitable. The question is how to distort with deliberation.'

He tapped the book lying on his desk. 'You've all finished Tytler, yes?'

They nodded. They'd been assigned the introductory chapter of *Essay on Principles of Translation* by Lord Alexander Fraser Tytler Woodhouselee the night before.

'Then you'll have read that Tytler recommends three basic principles. Which are – yes, Miss Desgraves?'

'First, that the translation conveys a complete and accurate idea of the original,' said Victoire. 'Second, that the translation mirrors the style and manner of writing of the original. And third, that the translation should read with all the ease of the original composition.'

She spoke with such confident precision, Robin thought she must have been reading from the text. He was very impressed when he glanced over and saw her consulting nothing but blank space. Ramy, too, had this talent for perfect recall – Robin was beginning to feel a bit intimidated by his cohort.

'Very good,' said Professor Playfair. 'This sounds basic enough. But what do we mean by the "style and manner" of the original? What does it mean for a composition to read "easily"? What audience do we have in mind when we make these claims? These are the questions we will tackle this term, and such fascinating questions they are.' He clasped his hands together. 'Allow me again to descend into theatrics by discussing our namesake, Babel – yes, dear students, I can't quite escape the romanticism of this institution. Indulge me, please.'

His tone conveyed no regret at all. Professor Playfair loved this dramatic mysticism, these monologues that must have been rehearsed and perfected over years of teaching. But no one complained. They loved it too.

'It is often argued that the greatest tragedy of the Old Testament was not man's exile from the Garden of Eden, but the fall of the Tower of Babel. For Adam and Eve, though cast from grace, could still speak and comprehend the language of angels. But when men in their hubris decided to build a path to heaven, God confounded their understanding. He divided and confused them and scattered them about the face of the earth.

'What was lost at Babel was not merely human unity, but the original language – something primordial and innate, perfectly understandable and lacking nothing in form or content. Biblical scholars call it the Adamic language. Some think it is Hebrew. Some think it is a real but ancient language that has been lost to time. Some think it is a new, artificial language that we ought to invent. Some think French fulfils this role; some think English, once it's finished robbing and morphing, might.'

'Oh, no, this one is easy,' said Ramy. 'It's Syriac.'

'Very funny, Mr Mirza.' Robin did not know if Ramy was indeed joking, but no one else made a comment. Professor Playfair ploughed ahead. 'For me, however, it matters not what the Adamic language was, for it's clear we have lost any access to it. We will never speak the divine language. But by amassing all the world's languages under this roof, by collecting the full range of human expressions, or as near to it as we can get, we can try. We will never touch heaven from this mortal plane, but our confusion is not infinite. We can, through perfecting the arts of translation, achieve what humanity lost at Babel.' Professor Playfair sighed, moved by his own performance. Robin thought he saw actual tears form in the corners of his eyes.

'Magic.' Professor Playfair pressed a hand against his chest. 'What we are doing is magic. It won't always feel that way – indeed, when you do tonight's exercise, it'll feel more like folding laundry than chasing the ephemeral. But never forget the audacity of what you are attempting. Never forget that you are defying a curse laid by God.'

Robin raised his hand. 'Do you mean, then, that our purpose here is to bring mankind closer together as well?'

Professor Playfair cocked his head. 'What do you mean by that?'

'I only . . .' Robin faltered. It sounded silly as he said it, a child's fancy, not a serious scholarly query. Letty and Victoire were frowning at him; even Ramy was wrinkling his nose. Robin tried again – he knew what he meant to ask, only he couldn't think of an elegant or subtle way to phrase it. 'Well – since in the Bible, God split mankind apart. And I wonder if – if the purpose of translation, then, is to bring mankind back together. If we translate to – I don't know, bring about that paradise again, on earth, between nations.'

Professor Playfair looked baffled by this. But quickly his features reassembled into a sprightly beam. 'Well, of course. Such is the project of empire – and why, therefore, we translate at the pleasure of the Crown.'

Mondays, Thursdays, and Fridays they had language tutorials, which, after Professor Playfair's lecture, felt like reassuring solid ground.

They were required to take Latin together three times a week, regardless of regional speciality. (Greek, at this stage, could be dropped for anyone not specializing in Classics.) Latin was taught by a woman named Professor Margaret Craft, who could not have been more different from Professor Playfair. She rarely smiled. She delivered her lectures without feeling and by rote memory, never glancing once at her notes, although she flipped through these as she spoke, as if she'd long ago memorized her place on the page. She did not ask their names – she only ever referred to them with a pointed finger and a cold, abrupt 'You.' She came off at first as utterly humourless, but when Ramy read aloud one of Ovid's dryer injections – *fugiebat enim,* 'for she was fleeing', after Jove begs Io not to flee – she burst out in a fit of girlish laughter that made her seem twenty years younger; indeed, like a schoolgirl who might have sat among them. Then the moment passed, and her mask resumed its place.

Robin did not like her. Her lecturing voice had an awkward, unnatural rhythm with unexpected pauses that made it hard to follow her line of argument, and the two hours they spent in her classroom seemed to drag for an eternity. Letty, however, seemed rapt. She gazed at Professor Craft with shining admiration. When they filed out at the end of class, Robin hung by the door to wait as she collected her things so they could all walk to the Buttery together. But she instead went up to Professor Craft's desk.

'Professor, I was wondering if I could speak with you for—'

Professor Craft rose. 'Class is over, Miss Price.'

'I know, but I wanted to ask you for a moment – if you have spare time – I mean, just as a woman at Oxford, I mean, there aren't so many of us, and I hoped to hear your advice—'

Robin felt then he should stop listening, out of some vague sense of chivalry, but Professor Craft's chilly voice cut through the air before he could reach the stairs.

'Babel hardly discriminates against women. It's simply that so few of our sex are interested in languages.'

'But you're the only woman professor at Babel, and we all – that is, all the girls here and I – we think that's quite admirable, so I wanted—'

'To know how it's done? Hard work and innate brilliance. You know that already.'

'It's different for women, though, and surely you've experienced—'

'When I have relevant topics for discussion, I will bring them up in class, Miss Price. But class is over. And you're now infringing on my time.'

Robin hastened around the corner and down the winding steps before Letty could see him. When she sat down with her plate in the Buttery, he saw her eyes were a bit pink around the edges. But he pretended not to notice, and if Ramy or Victoire did, they said nothing.

*   *   *

On Wednesday afternoon, Robin had his solo tutorial in Chinese. He'd half expected to find Professor Lovell in the classroom, but his instructor turned out to be Professor Anand Chakravarti, a genial and understated man who spoke English with such a pitch-perfect Londoner's accent that he might have been raised in Kensington.

Chinese class was a wholly different exercise from Latin. Professor Chakravarti didn't lecture at Robin or make him do recitations. He conducted this tutorial as a conversation. He asked questions, Robin tried his best to answer, and they both tried to make sense out of what he'd said.

Professor Chakravarti began with questions so basic that Robin at first couldn't see how they were worth answering, until he picked apart their implications and realized they were far beyond his scope of understanding. What was a word? What was the smallest possible unit of meaning, and why was that different from a word? Was a word different from a character? In what ways was Chinese speech different from Chinese writing?

It was an odd exercise to analyse and dismantle a language he thought he knew like the back of his hand, to learn to classify words by ideogram or pictogram, and to memorize an entire vocabulary of new terms, most having to do with morphology or orthography. It was like tunnelling into the crevasses of his own mind, peeling things apart to see how they worked, and it both intrigued and unsettled him.

Then came the harder questions. Which Chinese words could be traced back to recognizable pictures? Which couldn't? Why was the character for 'woman' – 女 – also the radical used in the character for 'slavery'? In the character for 'good'?

'I don't know,' Robin admitted. 'Why is it? Are slavery and goodness both innately feminine?'

Professor Chakravarti shrugged. 'I don't know either. These are questions Richard and I are still trying to answer. We're far from a satisfactory edition of the Chinese Grammatica, you see. When I was studying Chinese, I had no good Chinese-English resources – I had to make do with Abel-Rémusat's *Elémens de la grammaire chinoise* and Fourmont's *Grammatica Sinica*. Can you imagine? I still associate both Chinese and French with a headache. But I think we've made progress today, actually.'

Then Robin realized what his place here was. He was not simply a student but a colleague, a rare native speaker capable of expanding the bounds of Babel's scant existing knowledge. *Or a silver mine to be plundered*, said Griffin's voice, though he pushed the thought away.

The truth was, it felt exciting to contribute to the Grammaticas. But he still had much to learn. The second half of their tutorial was spent on readings in Classical Chinese, which Robin had dabbled in at Professor Lovell's home but had never tackled in a systematic manner. Classical Chinese was to vernacular Mandarin what Latin was to English; one could guess at the gist of a phrase, but the rules of grammar were unintuitive and impossible to grasp without rigorous reading practice. Punctuation was a guessing game. Nouns could be verbs when they felt like it. Often, characters had different and contradictory meanings, either of which produced valid possible interpretations – the character 篤, for instance, could mean both 'to restrict' and 'large, substantial'.

That afternoon they tackled the *Shijing* – the Book of Songs – which was written in a discursive context so far removed from contemporary China that even readers of the Han period would have considered it written in a foreign language.

'I propose we break here,' Professor Chakravarti said after twenty minutes of debating the character 不, which in most contexts meant a negative 'no, not', but in the given context seemed instead like a word of praise, which didn't track with anything they knew about the word. 'I suspect we'll have to leave this as an open question.'

'But I don't understand,' Robin said, frustrated. 'How can we just not know? Could we ask someone about all this? Couldn't we go on a research trip to Peking?'

'We could,' said Professor Chakravarti. 'But it makes things a bit hard when the Qing Emperor has decreed it punishable by death to teach a foreigner Chinese, you see.' He patted Robin's shoulder. 'We make do with what we have. You're the next best thing.'

'Isn't there anyone else here who speaks Chinese?' Robin asked. 'Am I the only student?'

A strange look came over Professor Chakravarti's face then. Robin was not supposed to know about Griffin, he realized. Probably Professor Lovell had sworn the rest of the faculty to secrecy; probably, according to the official record, Griffin did not exist.

Still, he couldn't help but press. 'I heard there was another student, a few years before me. Also from the coast.'

'Oh – yes, I suppose there was.' Professor Chakravarti's fingers drummed anxiously against the desk. 'A nice boy, though not quite as diligent as you are. Griffin Harley.'

'*Was?* What happened to him?'

'Well – it's a sad story, really. He passed away. Just before his fourth year.' Professor Chakravarti scratched his temple. 'He fell ill on an over-seas research trip and didn't make it home. It happens all the time.'

'It does?'

'Yes, there's always a certain . . . risk, entailed in the profession. There's so much travel, you know. You expect attrition.'

'But I still don't understand,' said Robin. 'Surely there's any number of Chinese students who would love to study in England.'

Professor Chakravarti's fingers quickened against the wood. 'Well, yes. But first there's the matter of national loyalties. It's no good recruiting scholars who might run home to the Qing government at any moment, you know. Second, Richard is of the opinion that . . . well. One requires a certain upbringing.'

'Like mine?'

'Like yours. Otherwise, Richard thinks . . .' Professor Chakravarti was using this construction quite a lot, Robin noticed, 'that the Chinese tend towards certain natural inclinations. Which is to say, he doesn't think Chinese students would acclimatize well here.'

Lowly, uncivilized stock. 'I see.'

'But that doesn't mean you,' Professor Chakravarti said quickly. 'You're raised properly, and all that. Wonderfully diligent, I don't expect that will be a problem.'

'Yes.' Robin swallowed. His throat felt very tight. 'I've been very lucky.'

On the second Saturday after his arrival to Oxford, Robin made his way north for dinner with his guardian.

Professor Lovell's Oxford residence was only a shade more humble than his Hampstead estate. It was a bit smaller, and enjoyed a mere front and back garden instead of an expansive green, but it was still more than someone on a professor's salary should have been able to afford. Trees bearing plump red cherries lined the hedges by the front door, though cherries could hardly still be in season at the turn of autumn. Robin sus-pected that if he bent down to check the grass by their roots, he would find silver bars in the soil.

'Dear boy!' He'd scarce rung the bell when Mrs Piper was upon him, brushing leaves from his jacket and turning him in circles to examine his reedy frame. 'My heavens, you're so thin already—'

'The food's horrible,' he said. A great big smile spread over his face; he hadn't realized how much he'd missed her. 'Just like you said. Dinner yesterday was salt herrings—'

She gasped. 'No.'

'—cold beef—'

'*No!*'

'—and stale bread.'

'Inhumane. Don't you worry, I've cooked enough to make up for it.' She patted his cheeks. 'How's college life besides? How do you like wearing those floppy black gowns? Have you made any friends?'

Robin was about to answer when Professor Lovell came down the stairs.

'Hello, Robin,' he said. 'Come in. Mrs Piper, his coat—' Robin shrugged it off and handed it to Mrs Piper, who examined the ink-stained cuffs with disapproval. 'How goes the term?'

'Challenging, just as you warned.' Robin felt older as he spoke, his voice somehow deeper. He'd left home only a week ago, but he felt like he'd aged years, and could present himself now as a young man and not a boy. 'But challenging in a way that's enjoyable. I'm learning quite a lot.'

'Professor Chakravarti says you've made some good contributions to the Grammatica.'

'Not as much as I'd like,' said Robin. 'There are particles in Classical Chinese that I've just no idea what to do with. Half the time our translations feel like guesswork.'

'I've felt that way for decades.' Professor Lovell gestured towards the dining room. 'Shall we?'

They might as well have been back in Hampstead. The long table was arranged precisely the same way Robin was used to, with him and Professor Lovell sitting at opposite ends and a painting to Robin's right, which this time depicted the Thames rather than Oxford's Broad Street. Mrs Piper poured their wine and, with a wink at Robin, disappeared back into the kitchen.

Professor Lovell raised his glass to him, then drank. 'You're taking theory with Jerome and Latin with Margaret, correct?'

'Right. It's fairly good going.' Robin took a sip of wine. 'Though Professor Craft lectures like she wouldn't notice if she were speaking to an empty room, and Professor Playfair seems to have missed a calling for the stage.'

Professor Lovell chuckled. Robin smiled, despite himself; he had never been able to make his guardian laugh before.

'Did he give you his Psammetichus speech?'

'He did,' said Robin. 'Did all that really happen?'

'Who knows, except that Herodotus tells us so,' said Professor Lovell. 'There's another good Herodotus story, again about Psammetichus. Psammetichus wanted to determine which language was the foundation of all earthly languages, so he gave two newborn infants to a shepherd with the instructions that they should not be allowed to hear human speech. For a while all they did was babble, as infants do. Then one day one of the infants stretched out his little hands to the shepherd and exclaimed *bekos*, which is the Phrygian word for bread. And so Psammetichus decided the Phrygians must have been the first race on earth, and Phrygian the first language. Pretty story, isn't it?'

'I'm assuming no one accepts that argument,' said Robin.

'Heavens, no.'

'But could that really work?' asked Robin. 'Could we actually learn anything from what infants utter?'

'Not that I'm aware of,' said Professor Lovell. 'The issue is it's impossible to isolate infants from an environment with language if you want them to develop as infants should. Might be interesting to buy a child and see – but, well, no.' Professor Lovell tilted his head. 'It's fun to entertain the possibility of an original language, though.'

'Professor Playfair mentioned something similar,' said Robin. 'About a perfect, innate, and unadulterated language. The Adamic language.'

He felt more confident talking to the professor now that he'd spent some time at Babel. They were on more of an equal footing; they could communicate as colleagues. Dinner felt less like an interrogation and more like a casual conversation between two scholars in the same fascinating field.

'The Adamic language.' Professor Lovell made a face. 'I don't know why he fills your minds with that stuff. It's a pretty metaphor, certainly, but every few years we get an undergraduate who's determined to discover the Adamic language in Proto-Indo-European, or otherwise wholly invent it on his own, and it always takes either a stern talking-to or a few weeks of failure for him to come back to his senses.'

'You don't think that an original language exists?' Robin asked.

'Of course I don't. The most devout Christians think it does, but you'd think if the Holy Word were so innate and unambiguous, there'd be less debate about its contents.' He shook his head. 'There are those who think that the Adamic language might be English – might *become* English – purely because the English language has enough military might and power behind it to credibly crowd out competitors, but then we must also remember that it was barely a century ago that Voltaire declared that French was the universal language. That was, of course, before Waterloo. Webb and Leibniz once speculated that Chinese might, in fact, have once been universally intelligible due to its ideogrammatic nature, but Percy debunks this by arguing Chinese is a derivative of Egyptian hieroglyphs. My point being, these things are contingent. Dominant languages might keep a little staying power even after their armies decline – Portuguese, for instance, has far outstayed its welcome – but they always fade from relevance eventually. But I do think there is a pure realm of meaning – a language in between, where all concepts are perfectly expressed, which we have not been able to approximate. There is a sense, a feeling of when we have got it right.'

'Like Voltaire,' Robin said, emboldened by his wine and rather excited that he could remember the relevant quote. 'Like what he writes in his preface to his translation of Shakespeare. *I have tried to soar with the author where he soars.*'

'Quite right,' said Professor Lovell. 'But how does Frere put it? *The language of translation ought, we think, as far as possible, to be a pure, impalpable, and invisible element, the medium of thought and feeling, and nothing more.* But what do we know of thought and feeling except as expressed through language?'

'Is that what powers the silver bars?' Robin asked. This conversation was starting to get away from him; he sensed a depth to Professor Lovell's theorizing into which he wasn't prepared to follow, and he needed to bring things back to the material before he got lost. 'Do they work by capturing that pure meaning – whatever gets lost when we invoke it through crude approximations?'

Professor Lovell nodded. 'It is as close to a theoretical explanation as we can get. But I also think that as languages evolve, as their speakers become more worldly and sophisticated, as they gorge on other concepts and swell and morph to encompass more over time – we approach something close to that language. There's less room for mis-understanding. And we've only begun to work out what that means for silver-working.'

'I suppose that means the Romanticists might eventually run out of things to say,' said Robin.

He was only joking, but Professor Lovell nodded vigorously at this. 'You're quite right. French, Italian, and Spanish dominate the faculty, but their new contributions to the silver-working ledgers dwindle by the year. There's simply too much communication across the continent. Too many loanwords. Connotations change and converge as French and Spanish grow closer to English, and vice versa. Decades from now, the silver bars we use from Romance languages might no longer have any effect. No, if we want to innovate, then we must look to the East. We need languages that aren't spoken in Europe.'

'That's why you specialize in Chinese,' said Robin.

'Precisely.' Professor Lovell nodded. 'China, I'm quite sure, is the future.'

'And that's why you and Professor Chakravarti have been trying to diversify the cohorts?'

'Who's been gossiping to you about departmental politics?' Professor Lovell chuckled. 'Yes, there are hurt feelings this year because we only took one Classicist, and a woman at that. But that's how it has to be. The cohort above you are going to have a tough time finding jobs.'

'If we're talking about the spread of language, I wanted to ask . . .' Robin cleared his throat. 'Where do all those bars go? I mean, who buys them?'

Professor Lovell gave him a curious look. 'To those who can afford them, of course.'

'But Britain is the only place where I've ever seen silver bars in wide use,' said Robin. 'They're not nearly so popular in Canton, or, I've heard, in Calcutta. And it strikes me – I don't know, it seems a bit strange that the British are the only ones who get to use them when the Chinese and Indians are contributing the crucial components of their functioning.'

'But that's simple economics,' said Professor Lovell. 'It takes a great deal of cash to purchase what we create. The British happen to be able to afford it. We have deals with Chinese and Indian merchants too, but they're often less able to pay the export fees.'

'But we have silver bars in charities and hospitals and orphanages here,' said Robin. 'We have bars that can help people who need them most. None of that exists anywhere else in the world.'

He was playing a dangerous game, he knew. But he had to seek clarity. He could not construct Professor Lovell and all his colleagues as the enemy in his mind, could not wholly buy into Griffin's damning assessment of Babel, without some confirmation.

'Well, we can't expend energy researching any frivolous application,' Professor Lovell scoffed.

Robin tried a different line of argument. 'It's just that – well, it only seems fair there ought to be some kind of exchange.' He was regretting now that he'd drunk so much. He felt loose, vulnerable. Too passionate for what should have been an intellectual discussion. 'We take their languages, their ways of seeing and describing the world. We ought to give them something in return.'

'But language,' said Professor Lovell, 'is not like a commercial good, like tea or silks, to be bought and paid for. Language is an infinite resource. And if we learn it, if we use it – who are we stealing from?'

There was some logic in this, but the conclusion still made Robin uncomfortable. Surely things were not so simple; surely this still masked some unfair coercion or exploitation. But he could not formulate an objection, could not figure out where the fault in the argument lay.

'The Qing Emperor has one of the largest silver reserves in the world,' said Professor Lovell. 'He has plenty of scholars. He even has linguists who understand English. So why doesn't he fill his court with silver bars? Why is it that the Chinese, rich as their language is, have no grammars of their own?'

'It could be they don't have the resources to get started,' said Robin.

'Then why should we just hand them to them?'

'But that's not the point – the point is that they need it, so why doesn't Babel send scholars abroad on exchange programmes? Why don't we teach them how it's done?'

'Could be that all nations hoard their most precious resources.'

'Or that you're hoarding knowledge that should be freely shared,' said Robin. 'Because if language is free, if knowledge is free, then why are all the Grammaticas under lock and key in the tower? Why don't we ever host foreign scholars, or send scholars to help open translation centres elsewhere in the world?'

'Because as the Royal Institute of Translation, we serve the interests of the Crown.'

'That seems fundamentally unjust.'

'Is that what you believe?' A cold edge crept into Professor Lovell's voice. 'Robin Swift, do you think what we do here is fundamentally unjust?'

'I only want to know,' said Robin, 'why silver could not save my mother.'

There was a brief silence.

'Well, I'm sorry about your mother.' Professor Lovell picked up his knife and began cutting into his steak. He seemed flustered, discomfited. 'But the Asiatic Cholera was a product of Canton's poor public hygiene, not the unequal distribution of bars. And anyhow, there's no silver match-pair that can bring back the dead—'

'What excuse is that?' Robin set down his glass. He was properly drunk now, and that made him combative. 'You *had* the bars – they're easy to make, you told me so yourself – so *why*—'

'For God's sake,' snapped Professor Lovell. 'She was only just a woman.'

The doorbell rang. Robin flinched; his fork clattered against his plate and fell to the floor. He scooped it up, deeply embarrassed. Mrs Piper's voice carried down the hall. 'Oh, what a surprise! They're having dinner now, I'll bring you in—' and then a blond, handsome, and elegantly dressed gentleman strode into the dining room, bearing a stack of books in his hand.

'Sterling!' Professor Lovell set down his knife and stood to greet the stranger. 'I thought you were coming in late.'

'Finished up in London earlier than expected—' Sterling's eyes caught Robin's, and the whole of him went rigid. 'Oh, hello.'

'Hello,' Robin said, flustered and shy. This was the famous Sterling Jones, he realized. William Jones's nephew, the star of the faculty. 'It's – nice to meet you.'

Sterling said nothing, only perused him for a long moment. His mouth twisted oddly, though Robin could not read the attendant expression. 'My goodness.'

Professor Lovell cleared his throat. 'Sterling.'

Sterling's eyes lingered on Robin's face for another moment, and then he looked away.

'Welcome, anyhow.' He said this like an afterthought; he had already turned his back on Robin, and the words sounded forced and awkward. He set the books on the table. 'You were right, Dick, it's precisely the Ricci dictionaries that are the key. We've been missing what happens when we go through Portuguese. *That*, I can help with. Now I think if we daisy-chain the characters I've marked here, and here—'

Professor Lovell was flipping through the pages. 'This is waterlogged. I hope you didn't pay him in full—'

'I paid *nothing*, Dick, do you think me a fool?'

'Well, after Macau—'

They fell into a heated discussion. Robin was entirely forgotten.

He looked on, feeling tipsy and out of place. His cheeks burned. He had not finished his food, but it seemed very awkward to keep eating now. He had no appetite besides. His earlier confidence vanished. He felt again like a stupid little boy, laughed away and dismissed by those crow-like visitors in Professor Lovell's sitting room.

And he wondered at the contradiction: that he despised them, that he knew they could be up to no good, and that still he wanted to be respected by them enough to be included in their ranks. It was a very strange mix of emotions. He hadn't the faintest idea how to sort through them.

But we haven't finished, he wanted to tell his father. *We were discussing my mother.*

He felt his chest constrict, as if his heart were a caged beast straining to burst out. That was curious. This dismissal was nothing he hadn't experienced before. Professor Lovell had never acknowledged Robin's feelings, or offered care or comfort, only abruptly changed the subject, only thrown up a cold, indifferent wall, only minimized Robin's hurts so that it seemed frivolous to bring them up at all. Robin had grown used to it by now.

Only now – perhaps because of the wine, or perhaps it had all been building up for so long that things were past the tipping point – he felt he wanted to scream. Cry. Kick the wall. Anything, if only to make his father look him in the face.

'Oh, Robin.' Professor Lovell glanced up. 'Tell Mrs Piper we'd like some coffees before you go, will you?'

Robin grabbed his coat and left the room.

*   *   *

He did not turn from High Street onto Magpie Lane.

Instead he went further and passed into the grounds of Merton College. At night, the gardens were twisted and eerie; black branches reached like fingers from behind a bolted iron gate. Robin fiddled uselessly with the lock, then hauled himself panting over a narrow gap between the spikes. He wandered a few feet into the garden before realizing he did not know what a birch looked like.

He stepped back and glanced around, feeling rather foolish. Then a patch of white caught his eye – a pale tree, surrounded by a cluster of mulberry bushes, trimmed to curl slightly upwards as if in adulation. A knob protruded from the white tree's trunk; in the moonlight, it looked like a bald head. A crystal ball.

As good a guess as any, Robin thought.

He thought of his brother in his flapping raven's cloak, brushing his fingers over this pale wood by moonlight. Griffin did love his theatrics.

He wondered at the hot coil in his chest. The long, sobering walk had not dimmed his anger. He still felt ready to scream. Had dinner with his father infuriated him so? Was this the righteous indignation that Griffin spoke of? But what he felt was not as simple as revolutionary flame. What he felt in his heart was not conviction so much as doubt, resentment, and a deep confusion.

He hated this place. He loved it. He resented how it treated him. He still wanted to be a part of it – because it felt so good to be a part of it, to speak to its professors as an intellectual equal, to be in on the great game.

One nasty thought crept into his mind – *It's because you're a wounded little boy, and you wish they had paid you more attention* – but he pushed this away. Surely he could not be so petty; surely he was not merely lashing out at his father because he felt dismissed.

He had seen and heard enough. He knew what Babel was at its roots, and he knew enough to trust his gut.

He ran his finger over the wood. His nails would not do. A knife would have been ideal, but he'd never carried one. At last, he pulled a fountain pen from his pocket and pressed the tip into the knob. The wood gave purchase. He scratched hard several times to make the cross visible – his fingers ached, and the nib was irreversibly ruined – but at last he left his mark.

CHAPTER SEVEN

Quot linguas quis callet, tot homines valet.
The more languages you speak, the more men you are worth.

CHARLES V

The following Monday, Robin returned to his room after class to find a slip of paper wedged under his windowsill. He snatched it up. Heart hammering, he shut his door and sat down on the floor, squinting at Griffin's cramped handwriting.

The note was in Chinese. Robin read it twice, then backwards, then forwards again, perplexed. Griffin seemed to have strung together characters utterly at random and the sentences did not make sense – no, they could not even be described as sentences, for although there was punctuation, the characters were arranged without care for grammar or syntax. This was a cipher, surely, but Griffin had not given Robin a key, and Robin could think of no literary allusions or subtle hints Griffin might have dropped to help him decode this nonsense.

At last he realized he was going about it all wrong. This was not Chinese. Griffin had merely used Chinese characters to convey words in a language Robin suspected was English. He ripped a sheet of paper from his diary, placed it next to Griffin's note, and wrote out the romanization of each character. Some of the words took guesswork, since romanized Chinese words had very different spelling patterns to English words, but in the end, through working out several common change patterns – *tè* always meant 'the', *ü* was *oo* – Robin broke the code.

The next rainy night. Open the door at precisely midnight, wait inside the foyer, then walk back out at five past. Speak to no one. Go straight home after.

Do not deviate from my instructions. Memorize, then burn.

Curt, direct, and minimally informative – just like Griffin. It rained constantly at Oxford. The next rainy night could be tomorrow.

Robin read the note again and again until he'd committed the details to memory, then tossed both the original and his decryption into the fireplace, watching intently until every scrap had shrivelled to ash.

On Wednesday, it poured. It had been misty all afternoon, and Robin had watched the darkening sky with accumulating dread. When he left Professor Chakravarti's office at six, a soft drizzle was slowly turning the pavement grey. By the time he reached Magpie Lane, the rain had thickened to a steady patter.

He locked himself in his room, put his assigned Latin readings on his desk, and tried to at least stare at them until the hour came.

By half past eleven, the rain had announced its permanence. It was the kind of rain that sounded cold; even in the absence of vicious winds, snow, or hail, the very pattering against cobblestones felt like cubes of ice hammering against one's skin. Robin saw now the reasoning behind Griffin's instructions – on a night like this, you couldn't see more than a few feet past your own nose, and even if you could, you wouldn't care to look. Rain like this made you walk with your head down, shoulders hunched, indifferent to the world until you got to somewhere warm.

At a quarter to midnight, Robin threw on a coat and stepped into the hallway.

'Where are you going?'

He froze. He'd thought Ramy was asleep.

'Forgot something in the stacks,' he whispered.

Ramy cocked his head. 'Again?'

'I suppose it's our curse,' Robin whispered, trying to keep his expression blank.

'It's pouring. Go and get it tomorrow.' Ramy frowned. 'What is it?'

My readings, Robin almost said, but that couldn't be right, because he'd purportedly been working on them all night. 'Ah – just my diary. It'll keep me up if I leave it, I'm nervous about anyone seeing my notes—'

'What's in there, a love letter?'

'No, it's just – it makes me nervous.'

Either he was a spectacular liar, or Ramy was too sleepy to care. 'Make sure I get up tomorrow,' he said, yawning. 'I'm spending all night with Dryden, and I don't like it.'

'Will do,' Robin promised, and hastened out the door.

The punishing rainfall made the ten-minute walk up High Street feel like an eternity. Babel shone in the distance like a warm candle, each floor still fully lit as if it were the middle of the afternoon, though hardly any silhouettes were visible through the windows. Babel's scholars worked round the clock, but most took their books home with them by nine or ten, and anyone still there at midnight was not likely to leave the tower until morning.

When he reached the green, he paused and peered around. He saw no one. Griffin's letter had been so vague; he didn't know if he should wait until he glimpsed one of the Hermes operatives, or if he should go ahead and follow his orders precisely.

Do not deviate from my instructions.

The bells rang for midnight. He hurried up to the entrance, mouth dry, breathless. When he reached the stone steps, two figures materialized from the darkness – both black-clad youths whose faces he could not make out in the rain.

'Go on,' one of them whispered. 'Hurry.'

Robin stepped up to the door. 'Robin Swift,' he said, softly but clearly.

The wards recognized his blood. The lock clicked.

Robin pulled the door open and paused for the briefest moment on the doorstep, just long enough for the figures behind him to slink into the tower. He never saw their faces. They dashed up the staircase like wraiths, quick and silent. Robin stood in the foyer, shivering as rain dripped down his forehead, watching the clock as the seconds ticked towards the five-minute mark.

It was all so easy. When the time came, Robin turned and strode out the door. He felt a slight bump at his waist, but otherwise perceived nothing: no whispers, no clinks of silver bars. The Hermes operatives were swallowed by the dark. In seconds, it was as if they had never been there at all.

Robin turned and walked back toward Magpie Lane, shivering violently, dizzy with the sheer audacity of what he'd just done.

He slept badly. He kept tossing in his bed in a nightmarish fugue, soaking his sheets with sweat, tortured by half dreams, anxious extrapolations in which the police kicked down his door and dragged him off to gaol, declaring they'd seen everything and knew everything. He did not fall properly asleep until the early morning, and by then he was so exhausted he missed the morning bells. He did not awake until the scout knocked at his door, asking if he'd like his floors swept that day.

'Oh – yes, sorry, just give me a moment and I'll be out.' He splashed water on his face, dressed, and dashed out the door. His cohort had arranged to meet in a study room on the fifth floor to compare their translations before class, and now he was terribly late.

'There you are,' said Ramy when he arrived. He, Letty, and Victoire were all seated around a square table. 'I'm sorry I left without you, but I thought you'd gone already – I knocked twice but you never answered.'

'It's all right.' Robin took a seat. 'I didn't sleep well – must have been the thunder, I think.'

'Are you feeling all right?' Victoire looked concerned. 'You're sort of . . .' She waved a hand vaguely before her face. 'Pale?'

'Just nightmares,' he said. 'Happens, um, sometimes.'

This excuse sounded stupid the moment it left his mouth, but Victoire gave his hand a sympathetic pat. 'Of course.'

'Could we start?' Letty asked sharply. 'We've just been dithering around with vocabulary because Ramy wouldn't let us go on without you.'

Robin hastily shuffled through his pages until he found last night's assigned Ovid. 'Sorry – yes, of course.'

He'd feared he would never sit through the entire meeting. But somehow, the warm sunlight against the cool wood, the scratch of ink against parchment, and Letty's crisp, clear dictation pulled his exhausted mind into focus, made Latin, not his impending expulsion, seem like the most pressing order of the day.

The study meeting turned out much livelier than expected. Robin, who was used to reading his translations out loud to Mr Chester, who drolly corrected him as he went, was not anticipating such hearty debate over turns of phrase, punctuation, or how much repetition was too much. It quickly became apparent they had drastically different translation styles. Letty, who was a stickler for grammatical structures that adhered to the Latin as much as possible, seemed ready to forgive the most astoundingly awkward manipulations of prose, while Ramy, her polar opposite, was always ready to abandon technical accuracy for rhetorical flourishes he insisted would better deliver the point, even when this meant insertion of completely novel clauses. Victoire seemed constantly frustrated with the limits of English – 'It's so awkward, French would suit this better' – and Letty always vehemently agreed, which made Ramy snort, at which point the topic of Ovid was abandoned for a repeat of the Napoleonic Wars.

'Feeling better?' Ramy asked Robin when they adjourned.

He was, actually. It felt good to sink into the refuge of a dead language, to fight a rhetorical war whose stakes could not really touch him. He was astonished by how ordinary the rest of the day felt, how calmly he could sit among his cohort as Professor Playfair lectured and pretend that Tytler was the foremost subject on his mind. In the light of day, the exploits of last night seemed a faraway dream. The tangible and solid consisted of Oxford, of coursework and professors and freshly baked scones and clotted cream.

Still, he could not erase the lurking dread that this was all a cruel joke, that the curtains would come down any minute on this charade. For how could there not be some consequence? Such an act of betrayal – of stealing from Babel itself, the institution to which he'd literally given his blood – should surely have made this life impossible.

Anxiety hit him properly midafternoon. What had last night seemed like such a thrilling, righteous mission now seemed incredibly stupid. He couldn't focus on Latin; Professor Craft had to snap her fingers in front of his eyes before he realized she'd asked him three times over to scan a line. He kept imagining horrible scenarios with vivid detail – how the constables would burst in, point, and yell, *There he is, the thief;* how his cohort would stare, stunned; how Professor Lovell, who was for some reason both prosecutor and judge, would coldly sentence Robin to the noose. He imagined the fireplace poker, coming down again and again, cold and methodical, snapping every single one of his bones.

But the visions remained only that. No one came to arrest him. Their class proceeded slowly, blandly, uninterrupted. His terror faded. By the time Robin and his cohort reassembled in hall for supper, he found it astonishingly easy to pretend to himself that last night had never happened. And once they were seated with their food – cold potatoes and steak so tough it took all their might to hack off chewable bits – laughing at Professor Craft's irritated corrections of Ramy's embellished translations, it indeed felt like only a distant memory.

A new note awaited him under the windowsill when he returned home that night. He unfolded it with shaking hands. The message scrawled within was very brief, and this time Robin managed to decode it in his head.

Await further contact.

His disappointment confused him. Hadn't he spent the day wishing he'd never been ensnared in this nightmare? He could just imagine Griffin's mocking voice – *What, did you want a pat on the back? A biscuit for a job well done?*

He now found himself hoping for more. But he had no way of knowing when he might hear from Griffin again. Griffin had warned Robin their contact would be sporadic, that entire terms might pass before he was in touch again. Robin would be summoned when he was needed, and no sooner. He found no note at his windowsill the next evening, or the evening after that.

Days passed, and then weeks.

You're still a Babel student, Griffin had told him. *Act like one.*

It turned out this was very easy to do. As the memories of Griffin and Hermes receded into the back of his mind, into nightmares and the dark, his life at Oxford and at Babel rose to the forefront in glaring, dazzling colour.

It stunned him, how quickly he fell in love with the place and the people. He hadn't even noticed it happening. His first term had him spinning in place, dazed and exhausted; his classes and coursework formed a rote pattern of frenzied readings and late, bleary-eyed nights against which his cohort was his only source of joy and solace. The girls, bless them, quickly forgave Robin and Ramy for their first impressions. Robin discovered he and Victoire shared the same unabashed love of literature of all kinds from Gothic horrors to romances, and they took great pleasure in swapping and discussing the latest batch of penny dreadfuls brought in from London. And Letty, once she'd been persuaded the boys were indeed not too stupid to be at Oxford, became a great deal more tolerable. She turned out to possess both an acerbic wit and a keen understanding of the British class structure by virtue of her upbringing, which made for infinitely amusing commentary when it wasn't aimed at either of them.

'Colin's the sort of bottom-feeding middle-class leech who likes to pretend he's got connections because his family knows a mathematics tutor in Cambridge,' she would say after a visit to Magpie Lane. 'If he wants to be a solicitor, he could just get an apprenticeship at the Inns of

Court, but he's here because he wants the prestige and connections, only he's not half charming enough to acquire them. He's got the personality of a wet towel: damp, and he clings.'

At this point she would do an impression of Colin's wide-eyed, over-solicitous greetings while the rest of them roared with laughter.

Ramy, Victoire, and Letty – they became the colours of Robin's life, the only regular contact he had with the world outside his coursework. They needed each other because they had no one else. The older students at Babel were aggressively insular; they were too busy, too intimidatingly brilliant and impressive. Two weeks into the term Letty boldly asked a graduate fellow named Gabriel if she might join the French reading group, but was swiftly rejected with the particular disdain only the French could muster. Robin tried to befriend a Japanese third-year student named Ilse Dejima,* who spoke with a faint Dutch accent. They crossed paths often on their ways in and out of Professor Chakravarti's office, but the few times he tried to say hello to her she made a face as if he were mud on her boots.

They tried to befriend the second-year cohort, too, a group of five white boys who lived just across the way on Merton Street. But this went south immediately when one of them, Philip Wright, told Robin at a faculty dinner that the first-year cohort was largely international only because of departmental politics. 'The board of undergraduate studies is always fighting over whether to prioritize European languages, or other . . . more exotic languages. Chakravarti and Lovell have been making a stink about diversifying the student body for years. They didn't like that my cohort are all Classicists. I assume they were overcorrecting with you.'

Robin tried to be polite. 'I'm not sure why that's such a bad thing.'

'Well, it's not a *bad* thing per se, but it does mean spots taken away from equally qualified candidates who passed the entrance exams.'

'I didn't take any entrance exams,' said Robin.

'Precisely.' Philip sniffed, and did not say another word to Robin for the entire evening.

So it was Ramy, Letty, and Victoire who became such constant

---

* Like Robin, Ilse was known to the English not by her birth name but by an adopted name; a combination of a chosen Anglicized name (Ilse) and the island from which she'd come (Dejima).

interlocutors that Robin started seeing Oxford through their eyes. Ramy would adore that purple scarf hanging in the window of Ede & Ravenscroft; Letty would laugh herself silly at the puppy-eyed young man sitting outside Queen's Lane Coffeehouse with a book of sonnets; Victoire would be so excited that a new batch of scones had just been put out at Vaults & Garden but because she would be stuck in her French tutorial until noon, Robin absolutely had to buy one, wrap it up in his pocket, and save it for her for when class was let out. Even his course readings became more exciting when he began seeing them as source material for cutting observations, complaining or humorous, to be shared later with the group.

They were not without their rifts. They argued endlessly, the way bright young people with well-fed egos and too many opinions do. Robin and Victoire had a long-running debate over the superiority of English versus French literature, wherein both were oddly, fiercely loyal to their adopted countries. Victoire insisted that England's best theorists could not hold a candle to Voltaire or Diderot, and Robin would have given her the benefit of the doubt if only she didn't keep scoffing at the translations he took out from the Bodleian on the grounds that 'They're nothing compared to the original, you might as well not read it at all.' Victoire and Letty, though normally quite close, seemed to always get snippy on issues of money and whether Letty truly counted as poor as she claimed to be just because her father had cut her off.* And Letty and Ramy bickered most of all, largely over Ramy's claim that Letty had never stepped foot in the colonies and therefore shouldn't opine on the supposed benefits of the British presence in India.

'I do know a thing or two about India,' Letty would insist. 'I've read all sorts of essays, I've read Hamilton's *Translation of the Letters of a Hindoo Rajah*—'

'Oh, yes?' Ramy would ask. 'The one where India is a lovely Hindu nation, overrun by tyrannical Muslim invaders? That one?'

At which point Letty would always get defensive, sullen, and irritable

---

* The boys stayed out of this one. Privately, Ramy thought Letty had a fair point that as a woman, she was entitled to inherit none of the Price estate to begin with. Robin thought it was a bit rich for her to call herself 'impoverished' when they were all receiving stipends sizable enough that they could dine out whenever they felt like it.

until the next day. But this was not entirely her fault. Ramy seemed particularly determined to provoke her, to dismantle her every assertion. Proud, proper Letty with her stiff upper lip represented everything Ramy disdained about the English, and Robin suspected Ramy would not be satisfied until he'd got Letty to declare treason against her own country.

Still, their fights could not really pull them apart. Rather, these arguments only drew them closer together, sharpened their edges, and defined the ways they fitted differently into the puzzle of their cohort. They spent all their time together. On weekends, they sat at a corner table outside the Vaults & Garden café, interrogating Letty on the oddities of English, of which only she was a native speaker. ('What does *corned* mean?' Robin would demand. 'What is corned beef? What are you all doing to your beef?" 'And what is a welcher?'† Victoire would ask, looking up from her latest penny serial. 'Letitia, please, what in God's name is a jigger-dubber?'‡)

When Ramy complained that the food in hall was so bad that he was visibly dropping weight (this was true; the Univ kitchens, when they weren't serving the same rotation of tough boiled meat, unsalted roast vegetables, and indistinguishable pottages, put out inexplicable and inedible dishes with names like 'India Pickle', 'Turtle Dressed the West India Way', and something called 'China Chilo', very little of which was halal), they stole into the kitchen and cobbled a dish out of chickpeas, potatoes, and an assortment of spices Ramy had scrounged together from Oxford's markets. The result was a lumpy scarlet stew so spicy that they all felt like they'd been punched in the nose. Ramy refused to accept defeat; instead, he argued, this was further proof of his grand thesis that there was something fundamentally wrong with the British, since if they'd been able to get their hands on real turmeric and mustard seeds then the dish would have tasted much better.

'There are Indian restaurants in London,' Letty objected. 'You can get curries with rice in Piccadilly—'

---

* Robin, Victoire, and Ramy were all very disappointed to learn that corned beef had nothing to do with corn, but with the size of rock salt crystals used to cure said beef.

† A swindler, a grifter.

‡ Thief's slang for a gaoler (*jigger* meaning 'door', and *dubber* meaning 'closer').

'Only if you want bland mash,' Ramy scoffed. 'Finish your chickpeas.'

Letty, sniffling miserably, refused to take another bite. Robin and Victoire stoically kept shovelling spoonfuls into their mouths. Ramy told them they were all cowards – in Calcutta, he claimed, infants could eat ghost peppers without batting an eye. But even he had trouble finishing the fiery-red mass on his plate.

Robin didn't realize what he had, what he'd been searching for and had finally obtained, until one night halfway through the term when they were all in Victoire's rooms. Hers were improbably the largest of any of their quarters because none of the other boarders wanted to share with her, which meant not only did she have a bedroom all to herself but also the bathroom and the spacious sitting room where they'd taken to congregating to finish their coursework after the Bodleian closed at nine. That night they were playing cards, not studying, because Professor Craft was in London for a conference, which meant they had the evening off. But the cards were soon forgotten because an intense stench of ripe pears suddenly pervaded the room and none of them could figure out what it was, because they hadn't been eating pears, and because Victoire swore she didn't have any stashed away in her room.

Then Victoire was rolling on the ground, both laughing and shrieking because Letty kept screaming, 'Where is the pear? Where is it, Victoire? Where is the pear?' Ramy made a joke about the Spanish Inquisition, so Letty, playing along, ordered Victoire to turn out all her coat pockets to prove none of them concealed the core. Victoire obeyed but turned up nothing, which sent them into further shrieks of hysterics. And Robin sat at the table, watching them, smiling as he waited for the card game to resume until he realized that it wouldn't because they were all laughing too much and, besides, Ramy's cards were splayed across the floor face-up, so continuing was pointless. Then he blinked, because he'd just registered what this most mundane and extraordinary moment meant – that in the space of several weeks, they had become what he'd never found in Hampstead, what he thought he'd never have again after Canton: a circle of people he loved so fiercely his chest hurt when he thought about them.

A family.

He felt a crush of guilt then for loving them, and Oxford, as much as he did.

He adored it here; he really did. For all the daily slights he suffered, walking through campus delighted him. He simply could not maintain, as Griffin did, an attitude of constant suspicion or rebellion; he could not acquire Griffin's hatred of this place.

Yet didn't he have a right to be happy? He had never felt such warmth in his chest until now, had never looked forward to getting up in the morning as he did now. Babel, his friends, and Oxford – they had unlocked a part of him, a place of sunshine and belonging, that he never thought he'd feel again. The world felt less dark.

He was a child starved of affection, which he now had in abundance – and was it so wrong for him to cling to what he had?

He was not ready to commit fully to Hermes. But by God, he would have killed for any of his cohort.

Later, it would amaze Robin that it never seriously crossed his mind to tell any of them about the Hermes Society. After all, by the end of Michaelmas term, he had come to trust them with his life; he had no doubt that if he fell into the frozen Isis, any one of them would have dived in to save him. Yet Griffin and the Hermes Society belonged to bad dreams and shadows; his cohort was sun and warmth and laughter, and he could not imagine bringing those worlds together.

Only once was he ever tempted to say something. At lunch one day, Ramy and Letty were arguing – once again – over the British presence in India. Ramy regarded the occupation of Bengal as an ongoing travesty; Letty thought the British victory at Plassey was more than fair retaliation for what she considered the horrific treatment of hostages by Siraj-ud-daulah, and that the British need never have intervened if the Mughals had not been such terrible rulers.

'And it's not as if you have had it all so bad,' said Letty. 'There are plenty of Indians in the civil administration, as long as they're qualified—'

'Yes, where "qualified" means an elite class that speaks English and acts like toadies to the British,' said Ramy. 'We're not being ruled, we're being misruled. What's happening to my country is nothing short of robbery. It's not open trade; it's financial bleeding, it's looting, and sacking. We've never needed their help, and they've only constructed that narrative out of a misplaced sense of superiority.'

'If you think that, then what are you doing in England?' Letty challenged.

Ramy looked at her as if she were crazy. 'Learning, woman.'

'Ah, to acquire the weapons to bring down the Empire?' She scoffed. 'You're going to take some silver bars home and start a revolution, are you? Shall we march into Babel and declare your intentions?'

For once, Ramy did not have a quick riposte. 'It's not as simple as that,' he said after a pause.

'Oh, really?' Letty had found the spot where it hurt; now she was like a dog with a bone and she wouldn't let go. 'Because it seems to me that the fact that you're here, enjoying an English education, is precisely what makes the English superior. Unless there's a better language institute in Calcutta?'

'There's plenty of brilliant madrasas in India,' Ramy snapped. 'What makes the English superior is guns. Guns, and the willingness to use them on innocent people.'

'So you're here to ship silver back to those mutinying sepoys, are you?'

Perhaps he should, Robin almost said. *Perhaps that's precisely what the world needs.*

But he stopped himself before he opened his mouth. Not because he was afraid of breaking Griffin's confidence, but because he could not bear how this confession would shatter the life they'd built for themselves. And because he himself could not resolve the contradiction of his willingness to thrive at Babel even as it became clearer, day by day, how obviously unjust were the foundations of its fortunes. The only way he could justify his happiness here, to keep dancing on the edges of two worlds, was to continue awaiting Griffin's correspondence at night – a hidden, silent rebellion whose main purpose was to assuage his guilt over the fact that all this gold and glitter had to come at a cost.

CHAPTER EIGHT

*We then used to consider it not the least vulgar for a parcel of lads who
had been whipped three months previous, and were not allowed more
than three glasses of port at home, to sit down to pineapples and ices at
each other's rooms, and fuddle themselves with champagne and claret.*

WILLIAM MAKEPEACE THACKERAY,
The Book of Snobs

In the last weeks of November, Robin assisted in three more thefts for
the Hermes Society. They all followed the efficient, clockwork routine
of the first – a note by his windowsill, a rainy night, a midnight rendezvous, and minimal contact with his accomplices save for a quick glance
and nod. He never got a closer look at the other operatives. He didn't
know if they were the same people every time. He never found out what
they stole or what they used it for. All he knew was that Griffin had said
his contribution aided a vaguely defined fight against empire, and all he
could do was trust Griffin's word.

He kept hoping that Griffin would summon him for another chat
outside the Twisted Root, but it seemed his half-brother was too busy
leading a global organization of which Robin was only a very small part.

Robin was nearly caught during his fourth theft, when a third year
named Cathy O'Nell strode through the front door as he was waiting
in the foyer. Cathy was, unfortunately, one of the chattier upperclassmen; she specialized in Gaelic, and perhaps due to the sheer loneliness
of being one of two people in her subfield, she went out of her way to
befriend everyone in the faculty.

'Robin!' She beamed at him. 'What are you doing here so late?'

'Forgot my Dryden reading,' he lied, patting his pocket as if he'd just
stashed the book there. 'Turns out I left it in the lobby.'

'Oh, Dryden, that's miserable. I remember Playfair had us discussing him for weeks. Thorough, but dry.'

'Awfully dry.' He hoped badly she'd get on with it; it was already five past twelve.

'Is he making you compare translations in class?' Cathy asked. 'Once he interrogated me for nearly half an hour over my word choice of *red* instead of *apple-like*. I'd nearly sweated through my shirt by the end.'

Six minutes past. Robin's eyes darted to the staircase, then back at Cathy, then back at the staircase until he realized Cathy was watching him expectantly.

'Oh.' He blinked. 'Erm. Speaking of Dryden, I should really get on—'

'Oh, I'm sorry, the first year is really so difficult and here I am keeping you—'

'Anyway, nice to see you—'

'Let me know if I can be of any assistance,' she said cheerfully. 'It's a lot at first, but the terms do get easier, I promise.'

'Sure. I will do – bye.' He felt awful being so curt. She was so nice, and such offers were particularly generous coming from the upperclassmen. But all he could think of then was his accomplices upstairs, and what might happen if they came down at the same time that Cathy went up.

'Good luck, then.' Cathy gave him a little wave and headed into the lobby. Robin backed into the foyer and prayed she did not turn around.

An eternity later, two black-clad figures hurried down the opposite staircase.

'What'd she say?' one of them whispered. His voice seemed strangely familiar, though Robin was too distracted to try to place it then.

'Just being friendly.' Robin pushed the door open, and the three of them hurried out into the cool night. 'Are you all right?'

But there was no answer. They'd already taken off, leaving him alone in the dark and the rain.

A more cautious personality would have quit Hermes then, would not have risked his entire future on such razor-thin possibilities. But Robin did go back to do it again. He assisted in a fifth theft, and then a sixth. Michaelmas term ended, the winter holidays sped by, and Hilary term began. His heartbeat no longer pounded in his ears when he approached the tower at midnight. The minutes between entrance and exit no longer felt like purgatory. It all started to feel easy, this simple act of opening a door twice; so easy that by the seventh theft, he had convinced himself he was not doing anything dangerous at all.

'You're very efficient,' said Griffin. 'They like working with you, you know. You stick to the instructions and don't embellish.'

A week into Hilary term, Griffin had finally deigned to meet Robin again in person. Once more they strode briskly around Oxford, this time following the Thames down south towards Kennington. The meeting felt like a midterm progress report with a harsh and rarely available supervisor, and Robin found himself basking in the praise, trying and failing not to come off as a giddy kid brother.

'So I'm doing a good job?'

'You're doing very well. I'm quite pleased.'

'So you'll tell me more about Hermes now?' Robin asked. 'Or at least tell me where the bars are going? What you're doing with them?'

Griffin chuckled. 'Patience.'

They walked in silence for a stretch. There had been a storm just that morning. The Isis flowed fast and loud under a misty, darkening sky. It was the kind of evening when the world seemed drained of colour, a painting in progress, a sketch really, existing in greys and shadows only.

'I have another question, then,' said Robin. 'And I know you won't tell me much about Hermes now. But at least tell me how this all ends up.'

'How what ends up?'

'I mean – my situation. This current arrangement feels fine – as long as I'm not caught, I mean – but it seems, I don't know, rather unsustainable.'

'Of course it's unsustainable,' said Griffin. 'You'll study hard and graduate, and then they'll ask you to do all kinds of unsavoury things for the Empire. Or they'll catch you, as you said. It all comes to a head eventually, like it did for us.'

'Does everyone at Hermes leave Babel?'

'I know very few who have stayed.'

Robin was not sure how to feel about this. He often lulled himself into the fantasy of the post-Babel life – a cushy fellowship, if he wanted it; a guarantee of more fully funded years of study in those gorgeous libraries, living in comfortable college housing and tutoring rich undergraduates in Latin if he wanted extra pocket money; or an exciting career travelling overseas with the book buyers and simultaneous interpreters. In the *Zhuangzi*, which he'd just translated with Professor Chakravarti, the phrase *tǎntú*[*] literally meant 'a flat road', metaphorically, 'a tranquil life'. This was what he wanted: a smooth, even path to a future with no surprises.

The only obstacle, of course, was his conscience.

'You'll remain at Babel as long as you're able,' said Griffin. 'I mean, you ought to – heaven knows, we need more people on the inside. But it gets harder and harder, you see. You'll find you can't reconcile your sense of ethics with what they ask you to do. What happens when they direct you to military research? When they send you to the frontier in New Zealand, or the Cape Colony?'

'You can't just avoid those assignments?'

Griffin laughed. 'Military contracts compose over half of the work orders. They're a necessary part of the tenure application. And they pay well too – most of the senior faculty got rich fighting Napoleon. How do you think dear old Dad's able to maintain three houses? It's violent work that sustains the fantasy.'

'So then what?' Robin asked. 'How do I leave?'

'Simple. You fake your death, and then you go underground.'

'Is that what you did?'

'About five years ago, yes. You will too, eventually. And then you'll become a shadow on the campus you once had the run of, and pray that some other first year will find it in their conscience to grant you access to your old libraries.' Griffin shot him a sideways look. 'You're not happy with this answer, are you?'

Robin hesitated. He wasn't quite sure how to verbalize his discomfort. Yes, there was a certain appeal to abandoning the Oxford life for Hermes. He wanted to do what Griffin did; he wanted access to Hermes's inner workings, wanted to see where the stolen bars went and what was done with them. He wanted to see the hidden world.

But if he went, he knew, he could never come back.

'It just seems so hard to be cut off,' he said. 'From everything.'

'Do you know how the Romans fattened up their dormice?' Griffin asked.

Robin sighed. 'Griffin.'

'Your tutors had you read Varro, didn't they? He describes a *glirarium* in the *Res Rustica*.[†] It's quite an elegant contraption. You make a

---

[*] 坦途.

[†] 'On Agriculture'.

jar, only it's perforated with holes so the dormice can breathe, and the surfaces are polished so smooth that escape is impossible. You put food in the hollows, and you make sure there are some ledges and walkways so the dormice don't get too bored. Most importantly, you keep it dark, so the dormice always think it's time to hibernate. All they do is sleep and fatten themselves up.'

'All right,' Robin said impatiently. 'All right. I get the picture.'

'I know it's difficult,' said Griffin. 'It's hard to give up the trappings of your station. You still love your stipend and scholar's gowns and wine parties, I'm sure—'

'It's not the wine parties,' Robin insisted. 'I don't – I mean, I don't go to wine parties. And it's not about the stipend, or the stupid gowns. It's just that – I don't know, it's such a leap.'

How could he explain it? Babel represented more than material comforts. Babel was the reason he belonged in England, why he was not begging on the streets of Canton. Babel was the only place where his talents mattered. Babel was security. And perhaps all that was morally compromised, yes – but was it so wrong to want to survive?

'Don't trouble yourself,' said Griffin. 'No one's asking you to leave Oxford. It's not prudent, strategically speaking. See, I'm free, and I'm happy on the outside, but I also can't get into the tower. We're trapped in a symbiotic relationship with the levers of power. We need their silver. We need their tools. And, loath as we are to admit it, we benefit from their research.'

He gave Robin a shove. It was meant as a fraternal gesture, but neither of them was very practised at those, and it came off as more threatening than perhaps Griffin intended. 'You do your reading and you stay on the inside. Don't you worry about the contradiction. Your guilt is assuaged, for now. Enjoy your *glirarium*, little dormouse.'

Griffin left him at the corner of Woodstock. Robin watched his narrow frame disappear into the streets, his coat flapping around him like the wings of a giant bird, and wondered at how he could both admire and resent someone so much at the same time.

In Classical Chinese, the characters 二心 referred to disloyal or traitorous intentions; literally, they translated as 'two hearts'. And Robin found himself in the impossible position of loving that which he betrayed, twice.

He did adore Oxford, and his life at Oxford. It was very nice to be among the Babblers, who were in many ways the most privileged group of students there. If they flaunted their Babel affiliation, they were allowed in any of the college libraries, including the absurdly gorgeous Codrington, which didn't actually hold any reference materials they needed, but which they haunted regardless because its high walls and marble floors made them feel so very grand. All their living expenses were taken care of. Unlike the other servitors, they never had to serve food in hall or clean tutors' rooms. Their room, board, and tuition were paid directly by Babel, so they never even saw the bill – on top of that, they received their stipend of twenty shillings a month, and were also given access to a discretionary fund they could use to purchase whatever course materials they liked. If they could make even the flimsiest case that a gold-capped fountain pen would aid their studies, then Babel paid for it.

The significance of this never crossed Robin's mind until one night he stumbled upon Bill Jameson in the common room, scratching numbers onto a sheet of scrap paper with a wretched look on his face.

'This month's battels,' he explained to Robin. 'I've overspent what they sent me from home – I keep coming up short.'

The numbers on the paper astonished Robin; he had never imagined Oxford tuition could be so expensive.

'What are you going to do?' he asked.

'I've got a few things I can pawn to make up the difference until next month. Or I'll pass on a few meals until then.' Jameson glanced up. He looked desperately uncomfortable. 'I say, and I do hate to ask, but do you think—'

'Of course,' Robin said hastily. 'How much do you need?'

'I wouldn't, but the costs this term – they're charging us to dissect corpses for Anatomy, I really—'

'Don't mention it.' Robin reached into his pocket, pulled out his purse, and began counting out coins. He felt awfully pretentious as he did this – he'd just retrieved his stipend from the bursar that morning, and he hoped Jameson did not think he always walked around with such a stuffed purse. 'Would that cover meals, at least?'

'You're an angel, Swift. I'll pay you back first thing next month.' Jameson sighed and shook his head. 'Babel. They take care of you, don't they?'

They did. Not only was Babel very rich, it was also respected. Theirs was by far the most prestigious faculty at Oxford. It was Babel that new undergraduates bragged about when showing their visiting relatives around campus. It was a Babel student who invariably won Oxford's yearly Chancellor's Prize, given to the best composition of Latin verse, as well as the Kennicott Hebrew Scholarship. It was Babel undergraduates who were invited to special receptions* with the politicians, aristocrats, and the unimaginably wealthy who made up the lobby clientele. Once it was rumoured that Princess Victoria herself would be in attendance at the faculty's annual garden party; this turned out to be false, but she did give them a new marble fountain which was installed on the green a week later, and which Professor Playfair enchanted to shoot high, glistening arcs of water at all hours of the day.

By the middle of Hilary term, like every Babel cohort before them, Robin, Ramy, Victoire, and Letty had absorbed the insufferable superiority of scholars who knew they had the run of campus. They took much amusement in how visiting scholars, who either condescended to or ignored them in hall, started fawning and shaking their hands when they revealed they studied translation. They dropped mention of how they had access to the Senior Common Room, which was both very nice and inaccessible to other undergraduates, though in truth they rarely spent much time there, as it was difficult to have a plain conversation when an ancient, wrinkled don sat snoring in the corner.

Victoire and Letty, who now understood that the presence of women at Oxford was more of an open secret than an outright taboo, began slowly growing out their hair. One day Letty even appeared in hall for dinner wearing a skirt instead of trousers. The Univ boys whispered and pointed, but the staff said nothing, and she was served her three courses and wine without incident.

But there were also significant ways in which they did not belong. No one would serve Ramy at any of their favourite pubs if he was the

---

* These receptions were entertaining at first, but quickly grew tiresome when it became apparent that Babel scholars were there less as distinguished guests and more as zoo animals on display, expected to dance and perform for wealthy donors. Robin, Victoire, and Ramy were always treated as national representatives of the countries they appeared to hail from. Robin had to put up with excruciating small talk about Chinese botanical gardens and lacquerware; Ramy was expected to elaborate on the inner workings of the 'Hindu race', whatever that meant; and Victoire, bizarrely, was always being asked for speculation advice in the Cape.

first to arrive. Letty and Victoire could not take books out of the library without a male student present to vouch for them. Victoire was assumed by shopkeepers to be Letty or Robin's maid. Porters regularly asked all four of them if they could please not step on the green for it was off limits, while the other boys trampled over the so-called delicate grass all around them.

What's more, it took them all several months to learn to speak like Oxfordians. Oxford English was different from London English, and was developed largely by the undergraduate tendency to corrupt and abbreviate just about everything. *Magdalene* was pronounced *maudlin*; by the same token, *St Aldate's* had become *St Old's*. The Magna Vacatio became the Long Vacation became the Long. New College became New; St Edmund's became Teddy. It took months before Robin was used to uttering 'Univ' when he meant 'University College'. A *spread* was a party with a sizable number of guests; a *pidge* was short for *pigeonhole*, which in turn meant one of the wooden cubbies where their post was sorted.

Fluency also entailed a whole host of social rules and unspoken conventions that Robin feared he might never fully grasp. None of them could quite understand the particular etiquette of calling cards, for instance, or how it was that one wormed oneself into the social ecosystem of the college in the first place, or how the many distinct but overlapping tiers of said ecosystem worked.* They were always hearing rumours of wild parties, nights at the pub spinning out of control, secret society meetings, and teas where so-and-so had been devastatingly rude to his tutor or where so-and-so had insulted someone else's sister, but they never witnessed these events in person.

'How is it we don't get invited to wine parties?' Ramy asked. 'We're delightful.'

'You don't drink wine,' Victoire pointed out.

'Well, I'd like to appreciate the *ambience*—'

'It's because you don't throw any wine parties yourself,' said Letty. 'It's a give-and-take economy. Have either of you ever delivered a calling card?'

---

* Through Colin Thornhill and the Sharp brothers, Robin became aware of various 'sets' of people one might run with, which included 'fast men', 'slow men', 'reading men', 'gentlemen', 'cads', 'sinners', 'smilers', and 'saints'. He thought perhaps he qualified as a 'reading man'. He hoped he was not a 'cad'.

'I don't think I've ever *seen* a calling card,' said Robin. 'Is there an art to it?'

'Oh, they're easy enough,' said Ramy. '*To Pendennis, Esq., Infernal beast, I will give you lashings of booze tonight. Confound you, your enemy, Mirza.* No?'

'Very civil.' Letty snorted. 'Small wonder you aren't college royalty.'

They were decidedly not college royalty. Not even the white Babblers in the years above them were college royalty, for Babel kept them all too busy with coursework to enjoy a social life. That label could only describe a second year at Univ named Elton Pendennis and his friends. They were all gentlemen-commoners, which meant they'd paid higher fees to the university to avoid entrance examinations and to enjoy the privileges of fellows of the college. They sat at high table in hall, they lodged in apartments far nicer than the Magpie Lane dormitories, and they played snooker in the Senior Common Room whenever they liked. They enjoyed hunting, tennis, and billiards at the weekends and headed to London by coach every month for dinner parties and balls. They never did their shopping on High Street; all the newest fashions and cigars and accessories were brought straight from London to their quarters by salesmen who did not even bother quoting prices.

Letty, who'd grown up around boys like Pendennis, made him and his friends the target of a running stream of vituperation. 'Rich boys studying on their father's money. I bet they've never cracked open a textbook in their lives. I don't know why Elton thinks he's so handsome. Those lips are girlish; he shouldn't pout so. Those double-breasted purple jackets look ridiculous. And I don't know why he keeps telling everyone that he has an understanding with Clara Lilly. I know Clara and she's as good as engaged to the Woolcotts' oldest boy . . .'

Still, Robin could not help but envy those boys – those born into this world, who uttered its codes as native speakers. When he saw Elton Pendennis and his crowd strolling and laughing across the green, he couldn't help but imagine, just for a moment, what it might be like to be a part of that circle. He wanted Pendennis's life, not so much for its material pleasures – the wine, the cigars, the clothes, the dinners – but for what it represented: the assurance that one would always be welcome in England. If he could only attain Pendennis's fluency, or at least an imitation of it, then he, too, would blend into the tapestry of this idyllic campus life. And he would no longer be the foreigner, second-guessing his pronunciation at every turn, but a native whose belonging could not possibly be questioned or revoked.

It was a great shock when one night Robin found a card made of embossed stationery waiting in his pidge. It read:

Robin Swift—
Would appreciate the pleasure of your company for drinks next Friday – seven o'clock if you like to be there at the start or any reasonable time thereafter we are not fussy.

It was signed, in a very impressive calligraphy that took Robin a moment to decipher, *Elton Pendennis.*

'I think you're making a rather big deal of this,' said Ramy when Robin showed them the card. 'Don't tell me you'll actually go.'

'I don't want to be rude,' Robin said weakly.

'Who cares if Pendennis thinks you're rude? He didn't invite you for your impeccable manners, he just wants to be friends with someone at Babel.'

'Thank you, Ramy.'

Ramy brushed this off. 'The question is, why *you*? I'm infinitely more charming.'

'You're not genteel enough,' Victoire said. 'Robin is.'

'I don't understand what anyone means by *genteel*,' said Ramy. 'People always throw it around in reference to the high- and well-born. But what's it actually *mean*? Does it just mean that you're very wealthy?'

'I mean it in the context of manners,' said Victoire.

'Very funny,' said Ramy. 'But it's not manners that's the issue, I think. It's that Robin passes as white and we don't.'

Robin could not believe they were being so rude about this. 'Is it impossible they might just want my company?'

'Not impossible, just unlikely. You're horrible with people you don't know.'

'I am not.'

'You are too. You always clam up and retreat into the corner like they're about to shoot you.' Ramy folded his arms and cocked his head. 'What do you want to dine with them for?'

'I don't know. It's just a wine party.'

'A wine party, and then what?' Ramy persisted. 'You think they'll make you one of the lads? Are you hoping they'll take you to the Bullingdon Club?'

The club on Bullingdon Green was an exclusive eating and sporting establishment where young men could while away the afternoon hunting or playing cricket. Membership was assigned on mysterious grounds that seemed to strongly correlate with wealth and influence. For all of Babel's prestige, none of the Babel students Robin knew had any expectations they might ever be invited.

'Perhaps,' said Robin, just to be contrary. 'It'd be nice to have a look inside.'

'You're excited,' Ramy accused. 'You hope they love you.'

'It's all right to admit you're jealous.'

'Don't come crying when they pour wine all down your shirt and call you names.'

Robin grinned. 'You won't defend my honour?'

Ramy swatted his shoulder. 'Steal an ashtray for me; I'll pawn it to pay off Jameson's battels.'

For some reason it was Letty who most ardently opposed Robin's accepting Pendennis's invitation. When they left the coffee shop for the library, long after the conversation had drifted elsewhere, she tugged at his elbow until they fell back several paces behind Ramy and Victoire.

'Those boys are no good,' she said. 'They're lushes, they're indolent, they're bad influences.'

Robin laughed. 'It's only a wine party, Letty.'

'So why do you want to go?' she pressed. 'You hardly even drink.'

He could not understand why she was making such a big deal of this. 'I'm just curious, that's all. It's probably going to be awful.'

'So don't show up,' she insisted. 'Just throw the card away.'

'Well no, that's rude. And I really haven't anything on that night—'

'You could spend it with us,' she said. 'Ramy wants to cook something.'

'Ramy's always cooking something, and it always tastes awful.'

'Oh, then are you hoping they'll bring you into the ranks?' She arched an eyebrow. 'Swift and Pendennis, bosom friends, is that what you want?'

He felt a flare of irritation. 'Are you really that terrified I'll make some other friends? Trust me, Letitia, nothing could beat your company.'

'I see.' To his shock, her voice broke. Her eyes, he noticed, had turned very red. Was she about to cry? What was wrong with her? 'So that's how it is.'

'It's only a wine party,' he said, frustrated. 'What's the matter, Letty?'

'Never mind,' she said, and quickened her pace. 'Have drinks with whoever you like.'

'I will,' he snapped, but she'd already left him far behind.

At ten to seven the following Friday, Robin put on his one nice jacket, pulled a bottle of port he'd bought at Taylor's from under his bed, and walked to the flats on Merton Street. He had no trouble finding Elton Pendennis's rooms. Even before he'd made his way down the street, he heard loud voices and somewhat arrhythmic piano music floating out of the windows.

He had to knock several times before someone heard him. The door swung open, revealing a tow-haired boy whose name Robin vaguely remembered as St Cloud.

'Oh,' he said, looking Robin up and down through lidded eyes. He seemed quite drunk. 'You came.'

'It seemed polite,' Robin said. 'As I was invited?' He hated how his voice crawled up into a question.

St Cloud blinked at him, then turned and gestured vaguely inside. 'Well, come on.'

Indoors, three other boys were seated on lounge chairs in the sitting room, which was so thick with cigar smoke that Robin coughed upon entering.

The boys were all crowded around Elton Pendennis like leaves around a bloom. Up close, the reports of his good looks seemed not to be exaggerated one bit. He was one of the handsomest men Robin had ever encountered, a Byronic hero incarnate. His hooded eyes were framed by thick, dark lashes; his plump lips would have looked girlish, as Letty had accused, if they weren't set off by such a strong, square jaw.

'It's not the company, it's the *ennui*,' he was saying. 'London's fun for a season, but then you start seeing all the same faces again year after year, and the girls don't ever get any prettier, just older. Once you've been to one ball you might have been to them all. You know, one of my father's friends once promised his closest acquaintances that he could liven up their gatherings. He prepared an elaborate dinner party, then told his servants to go out and extend an invitation to all the beggars and home-less sops they came across. When his friends arrived, they saw those motley stragglers, punch-drunk and dancing on tables – it was hilarious, I wish I'd been invited myself.'

The joke ended here; the audience laughed on cue. Pendennis, his monologue complete, looked up. 'Oh, hello. Robin Swift, isn't it?'

By now Robin's tentative optimism that this would be a good time had evaporated. He felt drained. 'That's me.'

'Elton Pendennis,' said Pendennis, extending a hand for Robin to shake. 'We're very happy you could make it.'

He pointed around the room with his cigar, wafting smoke about as he made introductions. 'That's Vincy Woolcombe.' A red-headed boy sitting next to Pendennis gave Robin a friendly wave. 'Milton St Cloud, who's been providing our musical entertainment.' The tow-haired, freck-led St Cloud, who'd taken his seat in front of the piano, nodded lazily, then resumed plunking out a tuneless sequence. 'And Colin Thornhill – you know him.'

'We're neighbours on Magpie Lane,' Colin said eagerly. 'Robin's in room seven, and I'm number three—'

'So you've said,' Pendennis said. 'Many times, in fact.'

Colin faltered. Robin wished Ramy were there to see; he'd never met someone capable of eviscerating Colin with a single glance.

'Thirsty?' Pendennis asked. Assembled on the table was such a rich collection of liquor it made Robin dizzy to look at it. 'Help yourself to anything you want. We can never agree on the same drink. Port and sherry's being decanted over there – oh, I see you've brought something, just put it on the table.' Pendennis did not even look at the bottle. 'Here's absinthe, there's the rum – oh, there's only a bit of gin left, but feel free to finish the bottle, it isn't very good. And we've ordered a dessert from Sadler's, so please help yourself, otherwise it'll go bad sitting out like that.'

'Just some wine,' Robin said. 'If you have it.'

His cohort rarely drank together, out of deference to Ramy, and he had yet to acquire the detailed knowledge of types and makes of alcohol and what one's choice of drink said about one's character. But Professor Lovell always drank wine at dinner, so wine seemed safe.

'Of course. There's a claret, or port and Madeira if you want some-thing stronger. Cigar?'

'Oh – no, that's all right, but Madeira's good, thanks.' Robin retreated to the one open seat, bearing a very full glass.

'So you're a Babbler,' said Pendennis, leaning back against the chair.

Robin sipped his wine, trying to match Pendennis's listless affect. How did one make such a relaxed position look so elegant? 'That's what they call us.'

'What's it you do? Chinese?'

'Mandarin's my speciality,' said Robin. 'Though I'm also studying comparisons to Japanese and, eventually, Sanskrit—'

'So you are a Chinaman, then?' Pendennis pressed. 'We weren't sure – I think you look English, but Colin swore you were an Oriental.'

'I was born in Canton,' Robin said patiently. 'Though I'd say I'm English as well—'

'I know China,' Woolcombe interjected. 'Kubla Khan.'

There was a short pause.

'Yes,' Robin said, wondering if that utterance was supposed to mean anything.

'The Coleridge poem,' Woolcombe clarified. 'A very Oriental work of literature. Yet somehow, very Romantic as well.'

'How interesting,' Robin said, trying his best to be polite. 'I'll have to read it.'

Silence descended again. Robin felt some pressure to sustain the conversation, so he tried turning the question around. 'So what – I mean, what are you all going to do? With your degrees, I mean.'

They laughed. Pendennis rested his chin on his hand. '*Do*,' he drawled, 'is such a proletarian word. I prefer the life of the mind.'

'Don't listen to him,' said Woolcombe. 'He's going to live off his estate and subject all his guests to grand philosophical observations until he dies. I'll be a clergyman, Colin a solicitor. Milton's going to be a doctor, if he can find it in him to go to lectures.'

'So you're not training for any profession here?' Robin asked Pendennis.

'I write,' Pendennis said with very deliberate indifference, the way people who are very conceited throw out morsels of information they hope become objects of fascination. 'I write poetry. I haven't produced much so far—'

'Show him,' Colin cried, right on cue. 'Do show him. Robin, it's ever so profound, wait until you hear it—'

'All right.' Pendennis leaned forward, still feigning reluctance, and reached for a stack of papers that Robin realized had been set out for display on the coffee table this entire time. 'Now, this one is a reply to Shelley's "Ozymandias",* which is as you know an ode to the unforgiving ravaging of time against all great empires and their legacies. Only I've argued that, in the modern era, legacies can be built to last and indeed there are great men of the sort at Oxford capable of such a monumental task.' He cleared his throat. 'I've opened with the same line as Shelley – *I met a traveller from an antique land . . .*'

Robin leaned back and drained the rest of his Madeira. Several seconds passed before he realized that the poem had ended, and his appraisal was required.

'We have translators working on poetry at Babel,' he said blandly, for lack of anything better to say.

'Of course that's not the same,' Pendennis said. 'Translating poetry is for those who haven't the creative fire themselves. They can only seek residual fame cribbing off the work of others.'

Robin scoffed. 'I don't think that's true.'

'You wouldn't know,' said Pendennis. 'You're not a poet.'

'Actually—' Robin fidgeted with the stem of his glass for a moment, then decided to keep talking. 'I think translation can be much harder than original composition in many ways. The poet is free to say whatever he likes, you see – he can choose from any number of linguistic tricks in the language he's composing in. Word choice, word order, sound – they all matter, and without any one of them the whole thing falls apart. That's why Shelley writes that translating poetry is about as wise as casting a violet into a crucible.† So the translator needs to be translator, liter- ary critic, and poet all at once – he must read the original well enough to understand all the machinery at play, to convey its meaning with as

---

* Many romantic Univ undergraduates fancied themselves successors to Percy Bysshe Shelley, who rarely attended lectures, was expelled for refusing to admit authorship of a pamphlet titled 'The Necessity of Atheism', married a nice girl named Mary, and later drowned in a violent storm off the Gulf of Larici.

† Robin, despite his general dislike of Shelley, had still read his thoughts on trans- lation, which he grudgingly respected: 'Hence the vanity of translation; it were as wise to cast a violet into a crucible that you might discover the formal principle of its colour and odour, as seek to transfuse from one language into another the cre- ations of a poet. The plant must spring again from its seed, or it will bear no flower – and this is the burthen of the curse of Babel.'

much accuracy as possible, then rearrange the translated meaning into an aesthetically pleasing structure in the target language that, by his judgment, matches the original. The poet runs untrammelled across the meadow. The translator dances in shackles.'

By the end of this spiel Pendennis and his friends were staring at him, slack-jawed and bemused, as if they weren't sure what to make of him.

'Dancing in shackles,' Woolcombe said after a pause. 'That's lovely.'

'But I'm not a poet,' Robin said, a bit more viciously than he'd intended. 'So really what do I know?'

His anxiety had dissipated entirely. He no longer felt concerned about how he presented, about whether his jacket was properly buttoned or he'd left crumbs on the side of his mouth. He didn't want Pendennis's approval. He didn't care for any of these boys' approval at all.

The truth of this encounter hit him with such clarity that he nearly laughed out loud. They were not appraising him for membership. They were trying to impress him – and by impressing him, to display their own superiority, to prove that to be a Babbler was not as good as being one of Elton Pendennis's friends.

But Robin was not impressed. Was this the pinnacle of Oxford society? *This?* He felt a profuse pity for them – these boys who considered themselves aesthetes, who thought their lives were as rarefied as the examined life could be. But they would never engrave a word in a silver bar and feel the weight of its meaning reverberate in their fingers. They would never change the fabric of the world by simply wishing it.

'Is that what they teach you at Babel, then?' Woolcombe looked slightly awed. No one, it seemed, ever talked back to Elton Pendennis.

'That and then some,' Robin said. He felt a heady rush every time he spoke. These boys were nothing; he could decimate them with a word if he so desired. He could jump up on the couch and hurl his wine against the curtains without consequence, because he simply did not care. This rush of heady confidence was wholly foreign to him, but it felt very good. 'Of course, the real point of Babel is silver-working. All that stuff about poetry is just the underlying theory.'

He was talking off the top of his head here. He had only a very vague idea of the underlying theory behind silver-working, but whatever he'd just said sounded good and played off even better.

'Have you done silver-working?' St Cloud pressed. Pendennis shot him an irritated look, but St Cloud persisted. 'Is it difficult?'

'I'm only still learning the fundamentals,' Robin said. 'We have two years of coursework, then one year of apprenticeship on one of the floors, and then I'll be engraving bars on my own.'

'Can you show us?' Pendennis asked. 'Could I do it?'

'It wouldn't work for you.'

'Why not?' Pendennis asked. 'I know Latin and Greek.'

'You don't know them well enough,' said Robin. 'You've got to live and breathe a language, not just muddle through a text now and then. Do you dream in languages other than English?'

'Do you?' Pendennis shot back.

'Well, of course,' said Robin. 'After all, I'm a Chinaman.'

The room lapsed once again into uncertain silence. Robin decided to put them out of their misery. 'Thank you for the invitation,' he said, standing up. 'But I ought to head to the library.'

'Of course,' said Pendennis. 'I'm sure they keep you very busy.'

No one said anything as Robin retrieved his coat. Pendennis watched him lazily through lidded eyes, slowly sipping his Madeira. Colin was blinking very rapidly; his mouth opened once or twice, but nothing came out. Milton made a desultory gesture at getting up to walk him to the door, but Robin waved him back down.

'You can find your way out?' Pendennis asked.

'I'm sure I'm fine,' Robin called over his shoulder as he left. 'This place isn't that large.'

The next morning, he recounted everything to his cohort to uproarious laughter.

'Recite his poem again to me,' Victoire begged. 'Please.'

'I don't remember it all,' said Robin. 'But let me think – wait, yes, there was another line, *the blood of a nation ran in his noble cheeks—*'

'No – oh, God—'

'*And the spirit of Waterloo in his widow's peak—*'

'I don't know what you're all talking about,' said Ramy. 'The man's a poetic genius.'

Only Letty did not laugh. 'I'm sorry you didn't have a good time,' she said frostily.

'You were right,' Robin said, trying to be generous. 'They're fools, all right? I should never have abandoned your side, dear, sweet, sober Letty. You are always right about everything.'

Letty did not respond. She picked up her books, dusted off her trousers, and stormed out of the Buttery. Victoire stood halfway up as if about to chase after her, then sighed, shook her head, and sat down.

'Let her go,' Ramy said. 'Let's not spoil a good afternoon.'

'Is she like this always?' Robin asked. 'I can't see how you can stand living with her.'

'You rile her up,' Victoire said.

'Don't defend her—'

'You do,' said Victoire. 'You both do, don't pretend otherwise; you like making her snap.'

'Only because she's so up her own backside all the time,' Ramy scoffed. 'Is she an entirely different person with you, then, or have you merely adapted?'

Victoire glanced back and forth between them. She seemed to be trying to decide something. Then she asked, 'Did you know she had a brother?'

'What, some nabob in Calcutta?' Ramy asked.

'He's dead,' said Victoire. 'He died a year ago.'

'Oh.' Ramy blinked. 'Pity.'

'His name was Lincoln. Lincoln and Letty Price. They were so close when they were children that all their family's friends called them the twins. He came to Oxford some years before her, but he hadn't half the mind for books as she does, and every holiday he and their father would fight viciously over how he was squandering his education. He was much more like Pendennis than like any of us, if you know what I mean. One night he went out drinking. The police came to Letty's house the next morning, told them they'd found Lincoln's body under a cart. He'd fallen asleep by the road, and the driver hadn't noticed him under the wheels until hours later. He must have died sometime before dawn.'

Ramy and Robin were quiet; neither could think of anything to say. They felt rather like chastised schoolboys, as if Victoire were their stern governess.

'She came up to Oxford a few months later,' said Victoire. 'Did you know Babel has a general entrance exam for applicants who don't come specially recommended? She took it and passed. It was the only faculty at Oxford that would take women. She'd always wanted to come to Babel – she'd studied for it her whole life – but her father kept refusing to let her go to school. It wasn't until Lincoln died that her father let her come and take his place. Bad to have a daughter at Oxford, but worse to have no children at Oxford at all. Isn't that terrible?'

'I didn't know,' Robin said, ashamed.

'I don't think you two quite understand how hard it is to be a woman here,' said Victoire. 'They're liberal on paper, certainly. But they think so very little of us. Our landlady roots through our things when we're out as if she's searching for evidence that we've taken lovers. Every weakness we display is a testament to the worst theories about us, which is that we're fragile, we're hysterical, and we're too naturally weak-minded to handle the kind of work we're set to do.'

'I suppose that means we're to excuse her constantly walking around like she's got a rod up her bum,' Ramy muttered.

Victoire shot him a droll look. 'She's unbearable sometimes, yes. But she's not trying to be cruel. She's scared she isn't supposed to be here. She's scared everyone wishes she were her brother, and she's scared she'll be sent home if she steps even slightly out of line. Above all, she's scared that either of you might go down Lincoln's path. Go easy on her, you two. You don't know how much of her behaviour is dictated by fear.'

'Her behaviour,' said Ramy, 'is dictated by self-absorption.'

'Be that as it may, I have to live with her.' Victoire's face tightened; she looked very annoyed with the both of them. 'So do pardon me if I try to keep the peace.'

Letty's sulks never lasted long, and she soon expressed her tacit forgiveness. When they filed into Professor Playfair's office the next day, she returned Robin's tentative smile with her own. Victoire nodded when he glanced her way. They were all on the same page, it seemed; Letty knew that Robin and Ramy knew, she knew they were sorry, and she herself was sorry and more than a bit embarrassed for being so dramatic. There was nothing else to be said.

Meanwhile, there were more exciting debates to be had. In Professor Playfair's class that term, they were hung up on the idea of fidelity.

'Translators are always being accused of faithlessness,' boomed Professor Playfair. 'So what does that entail, this faithfulness? Fidelity to whom? The text? The audience? The author? Is fidelity separate from style? From beauty? Let us begin with what Dryden wrote about the *Aeneid. I have endeavoured to make Virgil speak such English as he would himself have spoken, if he had been born in England, and in this present age.'* He looked around the classroom. 'Does anyone here think that is fidelity?'

'I'll bite,' said Ramy. 'No, I don't think that can possibly be right. Virgil belonged to a particular time and place. Isn't it more unfaithful to strip all that away, to make him speak like any Englishman you might run into on the street?'

Professor Playfair shrugged. 'Is it not also unfaithful to make Virgil sound like a stuffy foreigner, rather than a man you would happily carry on a conversation with? Or, as Guthrie did, to cast Cicero as a member of the English Parliament? But I confess, these methods are question-able. You take things too far, and you get something like Pope's transla-tion of the *Iliad.'*

'I thought Pope was one of the greatest poets of his time,' Letty said.

'Perhaps in his original work,' said Professor Playfair. 'But he injects the text with so many Britishisms that he makes Homer sound like an eighteenth-century English aristocrat. Surely this does not accompany our image of the Greeks and Trojans at war.'

'Sounds like typical English arrogance,' said Ramy.

'It isn't only the English that do this,' said Professor Playfair. 'Recall how Herder attacks the French neoclassicists for making Homer a captive, clad in French clothes, and following French customs, lest he offend. And all the well-known translators in Persia favoured the "spirit" of translation rather than word-for-word accuracy – indeed, they often found it appropriate to change European names into Persian and replace aphorisms in the target languages with Persian verse and proverbs. Was that wrong, do you think? Unfaithful?'

Ramy had no rejoinder.

Professor Playfair ploughed on. 'There is no right answer, of course. None of the theorists before you have solved it either. This is the ongoing debate of our field. Schleiermacher argued that translations should be sufficiently unnatural that they clearly present themselves as foreign texts. He argued there were two options: either the translator leaves the author in peace and moves the reader towards him; or he leaves the reader in peace and moves the author towards him. Schleiermacher chose the former. Yet the dominant strain in England now is the latter – to make translations sound so natural to the English reader that they do not read as translations at all.

'Which seems right to you? Do we try our hardest, as translators, to render ourselves invisible? Or do we remind our reader that what they are reading was not written in their native language?'

'That's an impossible question,' said Victoire. 'Either you situate the text in its time and place, or you bring it to where you are, here and now. You're always giving something up.'

'Is faithful translation impossible, then?' Professor Playfair challenged. 'Can we never communicate with integrity across time, across space?'

'I suppose not,' Victoire said reluctantly.

'But what is the opposite of fidelity?' asked Professor Playfair. He was approaching the end of this dialectic; now he needed only to draw it to a close with a punch. 'Betrayal. Translation means doing violence upon the original, means warping and distorting it for foreign, unintended eyes. So then where does that leave us? How can we conclude, except by acknowledging that an act of translation is then necessarily always an act of betrayal?'

He closed this profound statement as he always did, by looking at each of them in turn. And as Robin's eyes met Professor Playfair's, he felt a deep, vinegary squirm of guilt in his gut.

CHAPTER NINE

Translators are of the same faithless and stolid race that they have ever been: the particle of gold they bring us over is hidden from all but the most patient eye, among shiploads of yellow sand and sulphur.

THOMAS CARLYLE, 'State of German Literature'

Babel students did not take qualifying exams until the end of their third year, so Trinity flew by with no more and no less stress than the previous two terms. Somewhere in this flurry of papers, readings, and doomed late-night attempts to perfect Ramy's potato curry, their first year came to an end.

It was customary for rising second years to go abroad during the summer for language immersion. Ramy spent June and July in Madrid learning Spanish and studying the Umayyad archives. Letty went to Frankfurt, where she apparently read nothing but incomprehensible German philosophy, and Victoire to Strasbourg, from which she returned with insufferable opinions on food and fine dining.* Robin had hoped he might have the chance to visit Japan that summer, but he was sent instead to the Anglo-Chinese College in Malacca to maintain his Mandarin. The college, which was run by Protestant missionaries, enforced an exhausting routine of prayers, readings in the classics, and courses in medicine, moral philosophy, and logic. Never did he get the chance to wander out of the compound onto Heeren Street, where the Chinese residents lived; instead, those weeks were an unbroken stream of sun, sand, and endless Bible study meetings among white Protestants.

---

* For example: 'You know how the French refer to an unfortunate situation? *Triste comme un repas sans fromage.* Sad as a meal without cheese. Which is, really, the state of all English cheese.'

He was very glad when summer ended. They all returned to Oxford sun-darkened and at least a stone heavier each from eating better than they had all term. Still, none of them would have extended their breaks if they could have done. They'd missed each other, they'd missed Oxford with its rain and dreadful food, and they'd missed the academic rigour of Babel. Their minds, enriched with new sounds and words, were like sleek muscles waiting to be stretched.

They were ready to make magic.

This year, they were finally allowed access to the silver-working department. They would not be allowed to make their own engravings until year four, but this term they would begin a preparatory theory course called Etymology – taught, Robin learned with some trepidation, by Professor Lovell.

On the first day of term, they went up to the eighth floor for a special introductory seminar with Professor Playfair.

'Welcome back.' Normally he lectured in a plain suit, but today he'd donned a black master's gown with tassels that swished dramatically around his ankles. 'The last time you were allowed on this floor, you saw the extent of the magic we create here. Today, we'll dismantle its mysteries. Have a seat.'

They settled into chairs at the nearest workstations. Letty moved aside a stack of books on hers so she could see better, but Professor Playfair barked suddenly, 'Don't touch that.'

Letty flinched. 'Pardon?'

'That's Evie's desk,' said Professor Playfair. 'Can't you see the plaque?'

There was, indeed, a small bronze plaque affixed to the front of the desk. They craned their necks to read it. *Desk Belonging to Eveline Brooke*, it read. *Do not touch.*

Letty gathered her things, stood up, and took the seat next to Ramy. 'I'm sorry,' she mumbled, cheeks scarlet.

They sat in silence for a moment, not sure what to do. They'd never seen Professor Playfair so upset. But just as abruptly, his features rearranged themselves back into his regular warmth and, with a slight hop, he began to lecture as if nothing had happened.

'The core principle underlying silver-working is untranslatability. When we say a word or phrase is untranslatable, we mean that it lacks a precise equivalent in another language. Even if its meaning can be partially captured in several words or sentences, something is still lost – something that falls into semantic gaps which are, of course, created by cultural differences in lived experience. Take the Chinese concept *dao*, which we translate sometimes as "the way", "the path", or "the way things ought to be". Yet none of those truly encapsulates the meaning of *dao*, a little word that requires an entire philosophical tome to explain. Are you with me so far?'

They nodded. This was nothing more than the thesis Professor Playfair had hammered into their heads all of last term – that all translation involved some degree of warp and distortion. Finally, it appeared, they were going to do something with this distortion.

'No translation can perfectly carry over the meaning of the original. But what is meaning? Does *meaning* refer to something that supersedes the words we use to describe our world? I think, intuitively, yes. Otherwise we would have no basis for critiquing a translation as accurate or inaccurate, not without some unspeakable sense of what it lacked. Humboldt,* for instance, argues that words are connected to the concepts they describe by something invisible, intangible – a mystical realm of meaning and ideas, emanating from a pure mental energy which only takes form when we ascribe it an imperfect signifier.'

Professor Playfair tapped the desk in front of him, where a number of silver bars, both blank and engraved, had been arranged in a neat row. 'That pure realm of meaning – whatever it is, wherever it exists – is the core of our craft. The basic principles of silver-working are very simple. You inscribe a word or phrase in one language on one side, and a corresponding word or phrase in a different language on the other. Because translation can never be perfect, the necessary distortions – the meanings lost or warped in the journey – are caught, and then manifested by the silver. And that, dear students, is as close to magic as anything within the realm of natural science.' He appraised them. 'Are you still with me?'

They looked more unsure now.

'I think, Professor,' said Victoire. 'If you gave us an example ...'

---

* Karl Wilhelm von Humboldt is perhaps most famous for writing in 1836 'On the Structural Difference of Human Languages and Its Influence on the Intellectual Development of the Human Race', in which he argues, among other things, that a culture's language is deeply tied to the mental capacities and characteristics of those who speak it, which explains why Latin and Greek are better suited for sophisticated intellectual reasoning than, say, Arabic.

'Of course.' Professor Playfair picked up the bar on the far right. 'We've sold quite a few copies of this bar to fishermen. The Greek *kárabos* has a number of different meanings including "boat", "crab", or "beetle". Where do you think the associations come from?'

'Function?' Ramy ventured. 'Were the boats used for catching crabs?'

'Good try, but no.'

'The shape,' Robin guessed. As he spoke it made more sense. 'Think of a galley with rows of oars. They'd look like little scuttling legs, wouldn't they? Wait – scuttle, sculler . . . '

'You're getting carried away, Mr Swift. But you're on the right path. Focus on *kárabos* for now. From *kárabos* we get *caravel*, which is a quick and lightweight ship. Both words mean "ship", but only *kárabos* retains the sea-creature associations in the original Greek. Are you following?'

They nodded.

He tapped the ends of the bar, where the words *kárabos* and *caravel* were written on opposite sides. 'Affix this to a fishing ship, and you'll find it yields a better load than any of its sister crafts. These bars were quite popular in the last century, until overuse meant fishing yields dropped down to what they were before. The bars can warp reality to some extent, but they can't materialize new fish. You'd need a better word for that. Is this all starting to make sense?'

They nodded again.

'Now, this is one of our most widely replicated bars. You'll find these in doctors' bags throughout England.' He lifted the second bar to the right. '*Triacle* and *treacle*.'

Robin reeled back, startled. It was the bar, or a copy of the bar, that Professor Lovell had used to save him in Canton. The first enchanted silver he'd ever touched.

'It is most often used to create a sugary home remedy that acts as an antidote to most types of poison. An ingenious discovery by a student named Evie Brooke – yes, that Evie – who realized the word *treacle* was first recorded in the seventeenth century in relation to the heavy use of sugar to disguise the bad taste of medicine. She then traced that back to the Old French *triacle*, meaning "antidote" or "cure from snakebite", then the Latin *theriaca*, and finally to the Greek *theriake*, both meaning "antidote".'

'But the match-pair is only between English and French,' said Victoire. 'How—'

'Daisy-chaining,' said Professor Playfair. He turned the bar around to show them the Latin and Greek engraved along the sides. 'It's a technique that invokes older etymologies as guides, shepherding meaning across miles and centuries. You might also think of it as extra stakes for a tent. It keeps the whole thing stable and helps us identify with accuracy the distortion we're trying to capture. But that's quite an advanced technique – don't worry about that for now.'

He lifted the third bar to the right. 'Here's something I came up with quite recently on commission for the Duke of Wellington.' He uttered this with evident pride. 'The Greek word *idiótes* can mean a fool, as our *idiot* implies. But it also carries the definition of one who is private, unengaged with worldly affairs – his idiocy is derived not from lack of natural faculties, but from ignorance and lack of education. When we translate *idiótes* to *idiot*, it has the effect of removing knowledge. This bar, then, can make you forget, quite abruptly, things you thought you'd learned. Very nice when you're trying to get enemy spies to forget what they've seen."

Professor Playfair put the bar down. 'So there it is. It's all quite easy once you've grasped the basic principle. We capture what is lost in translation – for there is always something lost in translation – and the bar manifests it into being. Simple enough?'

'But that's absurdly powerful,' said Letty. 'You could do anything with those bars. You could be God—'

'Not quite, Miss Price. We are restrained by the natural evolution of languages. Even words that diverge in meaning still have quite a close relationship with each other. This limits the magnitude of change the bars can effect. For example, you can't use them to bring back the dead, because we haven't found a good match-pair in a language where life and death are not in opposition to each other. Besides that, there's one other rather severe limitation to the bars – one that keeps every peasant in England from running around wielding them like talismans. Can anyone guess what it is?'

---

* The military applications of this match-pair were really not as useful as Professor Playfair made them sound. It was impossible to specify *which* pieces of knowledge one wanted to remove, and often the match-pair only caused enemy soldiers to forget how to lace their boots, or how to speak the fragmented English they knew. The Duke of Wellington was not impressed.

Victoire raised her hand. 'You need a fluent speaker.'

'Quite right,' said Professor Playfair. 'Words have no meaning unless there is someone present who can understand them. And it can't be a shallow level of understanding – you can't simply tell a farmer what *triacle* means in French and expect that the bar will work. You need to be able to think in a language – to live and breathe it, not just recognize it as a smattering of letters on a page. This is also why invented languages* will never work, and why ancient languages like Old English have lost their effect. Old English would be a silver-worker's dream – we've got such extensive dictionaries and we can trace the etymology quite clearly, so the bars would be wonderfully exact. But nobody thinks in Old English. Nobody lives and breathes in Old English. It's partly for this reason that the Classics education at Oxford is so rigorous. Fluency in Latin and Greek are still mandatory for many degrees, though the reformers have been agitating for years for us to drop those requirements. But if we ever did so, half the silver bars in Oxford would stop working.'

'That's why we're here,' said Ramy. 'We're already fluent.'

'That's why you're here,' Professor Playfair agreed. 'Psammetichus's boys. Wonderful, no, to hold such power by virtue of your foreign birth? I'm quite good with new languages, yet it would take me years to invoke Urdu the way you can without hesitation.'

'How do the bars work if a fluent speaker must be present?' Victoire asked. 'Shouldn't they lose their effect as soon as the translator leaves the room?'

'Very good question.' Professor Playfair held up the first and second bars. Placed side by side, the second bar was clearly slightly longer than the first. 'Now you've raised the issue of endurance. Several things affect the endurance of a bar's effect. First is the concentration and amount of silver. Both these bars are over ninety per cent silver – the rest is a copper

---

* In the late eighteenth century, there had been a brief craze of the silver-working potential of created languages such as the abbess Hildegard of Bingen's mystical Lingua Ignota, which had a glossary of over a thousand words; John Wilkins's language of truth, which involved an elaborate classification scheme for every known thing in the universe; and Sir Thomas Urquhart of Cromarty's 'Universal Language', which attempted to reduce the world to a perfectly rational expression of arithmetic. All these faltered upon a common obstacle that later became accepted as basic truth at Babel: that languages are more than mere ciphers, and must be used to express oneself to others.

alloy, which is used often in coins – but the *triacle* bar is about twenty per cent larger, which means it'll last a few months longer, depending on frequency and intensity of use.'

He lowered the bars. 'Many of the cheaper bars you see around London don't last quite as long. Very few of them are actually silver all the way through. More often, they're just a thin sheen of silver coating over wood or some other cheap metal. They run out of charge in a matter of weeks, after which they need to be touched up, as we put it.'

'For a fee?' Robin asked.

Professor Playfair nodded, smiling. 'Something has to pay for your stipends.'

'So that's all it takes to maintain a bar?' asked Letty. 'Just having a translator speak the words in the match-pair?'

'It's a bit more complicated than that,' said Professor Playfair. 'Sometimes the engravings have to be reinscribed, or the bars have to be refitted—'

'How much do you charge for those services, though?' Letty pressed. 'A dozen shillings, I've heard? Is it really worth so much to perform a little touch-up?'

Professor Playfair's grin widened. He looked rather like a boy who'd been caught sticking his thumb in a pie. 'It pays well to perform what the general public thinks of as magic, doesn't it?'

'Then the expense is entirely invented?' Robin asked.

This came out more sharply than he'd intended. But he was thinking, then, of the choleric plague that had swept through London; of how Mrs Piper explained the poor simply could not be helped, for silverwork was so terribly costly.

'Oh, yes.' Professor Playfair seemed to find this all very funny. 'We hold the secrets, and we can set whatever terms we like. That's the beauty of being cleverer than everyone else. Now, one last thing before we conclude.' He plucked up one gleaming blank bar from the far end of the table. 'I must issue a warning. There is one match-pair that you must never, ever attempt. Can anyone guess what that is?'

'Good and evil,' said Letty.

'Good guess, but no.'

'The names of God,' said Ramy.

'We trust you not to be that stupid. No, this one's trickier.'

No one else had the answer.

'It's translation,' said Professor Playfair. 'Simply, the words for translation itself.'

As he spoke, he engraved a word quickly on one side of the bar, and then showed them what he'd written: *Translate*.

'The verb *translate* has slightly different connotations in each language. The English, Spanish, and French words – *translate*, *traducir*, and *traduire* – come from the Latin *translat*, which means "to carry across". But we get something different once we move past Romance languages.' He began inscribing a new set of letters on the other side. 'The Chinese *fānyì*, for example, connotes turning or flipping something over, while the second character *yì* comes with a connotation of change and exchange. In Arabic, *tarjama* can refer both to biography and translation. In Sanskrit, the word for translation is *anuvad*, which also means "to say or repeat after and again". The difference here is temporal, rather than the spatial metaphor of Latin. In Igbo, the two words for translation – *tapia* and *kowa* – both involve narration, deconstruction, and reconstruction, a breaking into pieces that makes possible a change in form. And so on. The differences and their implications are infinite. As such, there are no languages in which translation means exactly the same thing.'

He showed them what he'd written on the other side. Italian – *tradurre*. He put it on the table.

'Translate,' he said. '*Tradurre.*'

The moment he lifted his hand from the bar, it began to shake.

Amazed, they watched as the bar trembled with greater and greater violence. It was awful to witness. The bar seemed to have come alive, as if possessed by some spirit desperately trying to break free, or at least to split itself apart. It made no sound other than a fierce rattling against the table, but Robin heard in his mind a tortured, accompanying scream.

'The translation match-pair creates a paradox,' Professor Playfair said calmly as the bar started shaking so hard that it leapt inches off the table in its throes. 'It attempts to create a purer translation, something that will align to the metaphors associated with each word, but this is of course impossible, because no perfect translations are possible.'

Cracks formed in the bar, thin veins that branched, split, and widened.

'The manifestation has nowhere to go except the bar itself. So it creates an ongoing cycle until, at last, the bar breaks down. And ... this happens.'

The bar leapt high into the air and shattered into hundreds of tiny pieces that scattered across the tables, the chairs, the floor. Robin's cohort backed away, flinching. Professor Playfair did not bat an eye. 'Do not try it. Not even out of curiosity. This silver,' he kicked at one of the fallen shards, 'cannot be reused. Even if it's melted down and reforged, any bars made with even an ounce of it will be impotent. Even worse, the effect is contagious. You activate the bar when it's on a pile of silver, and it spreads to everything it's in contact with. Easy way to waste a couple dozen pounds if you're not careful.' He placed the engraving pen back on the worktable. 'Is this understood?'

They nodded.

'Good. Never forget this. The ultimate viability of translation is a fascinating philosophical question – it is, after all, what lies at the heart of the story of Babel. But such theoretical questions are best left for the classroom. Not for experiments that might bring down the building.'

'Anthony was right,' said Victoire. 'Why would anyone bother with the Literature Department when there's silver-working?'

They sat around their regular table at the Buttery, feeling rather dizzy with power. They'd been repeating the same sentiments about silver-working since class had been let out, but it didn't matter; it all felt so novel, so incredible. The whole world had seemed different when they stepped out of the tower. They'd entered the wizard's house, had watched him mix his potions and cast his spells, and now nothing would satisfy them until they'd tried it themselves.

'Did I hear my name?' Anthony slid into the seat across Robin. He peered around at their faces, then smiled knowingly. 'Oh, I remember this look. Did Playfair give you his demonstration today?'

'Is that what you do all day?' Victoire asked him excitedly. 'Tinker with match-pairs?'

'Close enough,' said Anthony. 'It involves a lot more thumbing through etymological dictionaries than tinkering per se, but once you've seized upon something that might work, things get really fun. Right now I'm playing with a pair I think might be useful in bakeries. *Flour* and *flower*.'

'Aren't those just entirely different words?' asked Letty.

'You would think,' said Anthony. 'But if you go back to the Anglo-French original of the thirteenth century, you'll find they were originally the same word – *flower* simply referred to the finest part of grain meal. Over time, *flower* and *flour* diverged to represent different objects. But if this bar works right, then I should be able to install it in milling machines to refine flour with more efficiency.' He sighed. 'I'm not sure it will work. But I expect a lifetime of free scones from Vaults if it does.'

'Do you get royalties?' asked Victoire. 'Every time they make a copy of your bars, I mean?'

'Oh, no. I get a modest sum, but all proceeding profits go to the tower. They do add my name to the ledger of match-pairs, though. I've got six in there so far. And there are only about twelve hundred active match-pairs currently in use throughout the Empire, so that's about the highest academic laurel you can claim. Better than publishing a paper anywhere else.'

'Hold on,' said Ramy. 'Isn't twelve hundred quite low? I mean, match-pairs have been in use since the Roman Empire, so how—'

'How is it that we haven't covered the country in silver expressing every match-pair possible?'

'Right,' said Ramy. 'Or at least, come up with more than twelve hundred.'

'Well, think about it,' said Anthony. 'The problem should be obvious. Languages affect each other; they inject new meaning into each other, and like water rushing out of a dam, the more porous the barriers are, the weaker the force. Most of the silver bars that power London are translations from Latin, French, and German. But those bars are losing their efficacy. As linguistic flow spreads across continents – as words like *saute* and *gratin* become a standard part of the English lexicon – the semantic warp loses its potency.'

'Professor Lovell told me something similar,' said Robin, remembering. 'He's convinced that Romance languages will yield fewer returns as time goes on.'

'He's right,' said Anthony. 'So much has been translated from other European languages to English and vice versa in this century. We seem unable to kick our addiction to the Germans and their philosophers, or to the Italians and their poets. So, Romance Languages is really the most threatened branch of the faculty, as much as they'd like to pretend they own the building. The Classics are getting less promising as well. Latin and Greek will hang on for a bit, since fluency in either is still the purview of the elites, but Latin, at least, is getting more colloquial than you'd think. Somewhere on the eighth floor there's a postdoc working on a revival of Manx and Cornish, but no one thinks that's going to succeed. Same with Gaelic, but don't tell Cathy. That's why you three are so valuable.' Anthony pointed at them all in turn except for Letty. 'You know languages they haven't milked to exhaustion yet.'

'What about me?' Letty said indignantly.

'Well, you're all right for a bit, but only because Britain's developed its sense of national identity in opposition to the French. The French are superstitious heathens; we are Protestants. The French wear wooden shoes, so we wear leather. We'll resist French incursion on our language yet. But it's really the colonies and the semi-colonies – Robin and China, Ramy and India; boys, you're uncharted territory. You're the stuff that everyone's fighting over.'

'You say it like it's a resource,' said Ramy.

'Well, certainly. Language is a resource just like gold and silver. People have fought and died over those Grammaticas.'

'But that's absurd,' said Letty. 'Language is just words, just thoughts – you can't constrain the use of a language.'

'Can't you?' asked Anthony. 'Do you know the official punishment in China for teaching Mandarin to a foreigner is death?'

Letty turned to Robin. 'Is that true?'

'I think it is,' said Robin. 'Professor Chakravarti told me the same thing. The Qing government are – they're scared. They're scared of the outside.'

'You see?' asked Anthony. 'Languages aren't just made of words. They're modes of looking at the world. They're the keys to civilization. And that's knowledge worth killing for.'

'Words tell stories.' This was how Professor Lovell opened their first class that afternoon, held in a spare, windowless room on the tower's fifth floor. 'Specifically, the history of those words – how they came into use, and how their meanings morphed into what they mean today – tell us just as much about a people, if not more, than any other kind of historical artefact. Take the word *knave*. Where do you think it comes from?'

'Playing cards, right? You've got your king, queen . . .' Letty started, then broke off when she realized the argument was circular. 'Oh, never mind.'

Professor Lovell shook his head. 'The Old English *cnafa* refers to a boy servant, or young male servant. We confirm this with its German cognate *Knabe*, which is an old term for *boy*. So knaves were originally young boys who attended to knights. But when the institution of knight-hood crumbled at the end of the sixteenth century, and when lords real-ized they could hire cheaper and better professional armies, hundreds of knaves found themselves unemployed. So they did what any young men down on their luck would do – they fell in with highwaymen and robbers and became the lowlife scoundrels that we label as knaves now. So the history of the word does not describe just a change in language, but a change in an entire social order.'

Professor Lovell was not a passionate lecturer, nor a natural performer. He looked ill at ease before an audience; his movements were stilted and abrupt, and he spoke in a dry, sombre, straightforward manner. Still, every word out of his mouth was perfectly timed, well considered, and fascinating.

In the days before this lecture, Robin had dreaded taking a class with his guardian. But it turned out not to be awkward or embarrassing. Pro-fessor Lovell treated him just like he had in front of company back in Hampstead – distant, formal, his eyes flitting always over Robin's face without landing, like the space where he existed could not be seen.

'We get the word *etymology* from the Greek étymon,' continued Professor Lovell. 'The true sense of a word, from *étumos*, the "true or actual". So we can think of etymology as an exercise in tracing how far a word has strayed from its roots. For they travel marvellous distances, both literally and metaphorically.' He looked suddenly at Robin. 'What's the word for a great storm in Mandarin?'

Robin gave a start. 'Ah – *fēngbào*?'*

'No, give me something bigger.'

'*Táifēng*?'†

'Good.' Professor Lovell pointed to Victoire. 'And what weather patterns are always drifting across the Caribbean?'

'Typhoons,' she said, then blinked. '*Taifeng*? Typhoon? How—'

'We start with Greco-Latin,' said Professor Lovell. 'Typhon was a monster, one of the sons of Gaia and Tartarus, a devastating creature with a hundred serpentine heads. At some point he became associated

---

* 風暴.

† 颱風.

with violent winds, because later the Arabs started using *tūfān* to describe violent, windy storms. From Arabic it hopped over to Portuguese, which was brought to China on explorers' ships.'

'But *táifēng* isn't just a loanword,' said Robin. 'It means something in Chinese – *tái* is great, and *fēng* is wind–'

'And you don't think the Chinese could have come up with a transliteration that had its own meaning?' asked Professor Lovell. 'This happens all the time. Phonological calques are often semantic calques as well. Words spread. And you can trace contact points of human history from words that have uncannily similar pronunciations. Languages are only shifting sets of symbols – stable enough to make mutual discourse possible, but fluid enough to reflect changing social dynamics. When we invoke words in silver, we call to mind that changing history.'

Letty raised her hand. 'I have a question about method.'

'Go on.'

'Historical research is well and fine,' said Letty. 'All you have to do is look at artefacts, documents, and the like. But how do you research the history of *words*? How do you determine how far they've travelled?'

Professor Lovell looked very pleased by this question. 'Reading,' he said. 'There is no other way around it. You compile all the sources you can get your hands on, and then you sit down to solve puzzles. You look for patterns and irregularities. We know, for instance, that the final Latin *m* was not pronounced in classical times, because inscriptions at Pompeii are misspelled in a way that leaves the *m* out. This is how we pin down sound changes. Once we do that, we can predict how words should have evolved, and if they don't match our predictions, then perhaps our hypothesis about linked origins is wrong. Etymology is detective work across centuries, and it's devilishly hard work, like finding a needle in a haystack. But our particular needles, I'd say, are quite worth the search.'

That year, using English as an example, they began the task of studying how languages grew, changed, morphed, multiplied, diverged, and converged. They studied sound changes; why the English *knee* had a silent *k* that was pronounced in the German counterpart; why the stop consonants of Latin, Greek, and Sanskrit had such a regular correspondence with consonants in Germanic languages. They read Bopp, Grimm, and Rask in translation; they read the *Etymologiae* of Isidorus. They studied semantic shifts, syntactical change, dialectical divergence, and borrowing, as well as the reconstructive methods one might use to piece together the relationships between languages that at first glance seemed to have nothing to do with each other. They dug through languages like they were mines, searching for valuable veins of common heritage and distorted meaning.

It changed the way they spoke. Constantly they trailed off in the middle of sentences. They could not utter even common phrases and aphorisms without pausing to wonder where those words came from. Such interrogations infiltrated all their conversations, became the default way they made sense of each other and everything else.[*] They could no longer look at the world and not see stories, histories, layered everywhere like centuries' worth of sediment.

And the influences on English were so much deeper and more diverse than they thought. *Chit* came from the Marathi *chitti*, meaning 'letter' or 'note'. *Coffee* had made its way into English by way of Dutch (*koffie*), Turkish (*kahveh*), and originally Arabic (*qahwah*). Tabby cats were named after a striped silk that was in turn named for its place of origin: a quarter of Baghdad named al-'Attābiyya. Even basic words for clothes all came from somewhere. *Damask* came from cloth made in Damascus; *gingham* came from the Malay word *genggang*, meaning 'striped'; *calico* referred to Calicut in Kerala, and *taffeta*, Ramy told them, had its roots in the Persian word *tafte*, meaning 'a shiny cloth'. But not all English words had their roots in such far-flung or noble origins. The curious thing about etymology, they soon learned, was that anything could influence a language, from the consumption habits of the rich and worldly to the so-called vulgar utterances of the poor and wretched. The lowly cants, the supposed secret languages of thieves, vagabonds, and foreigners, had contributed such common words such as *bilk*, *booty*, and *bauble*.

English did not just borrow words from other languages; it was stuffed to the brim with foreign influences, a Frankenstein vernacular. And Robin found it incredible, how this country, whose citizens prided themselves so much on being better than the rest of the world, could not make it through an afternoon tea without borrowed goods.

---

[*] '*Awkward*,' Victoire would say, pointing to Robin, 'comes from the Old Norse *aufgr*, which means "turned the wrong way round, like a turtle on its back".'
'Then *Victoire* must derive from *vicious*, not *Victoria*, for you are nothing but vice,' Robin would retort.

In addition to Etymology, they each took on an extra language that year. The point was not to attain fluency in this language, but to, through the process of its acquisition, deepen their understanding of their focus languages. Letty and Ramy began studying Proto-Indo-European with Professor De Vreese. Victoire proposed a number of West African languages she hoped to learn to the advisory board, but was rejected on the grounds that Babel possessed insufficient resources for proper instruction in any of them. She ended up studying Spanish – Spanish contact was relevant to the Haitian-Dominican border, Professor Play-fair argued – but was none too happy about it.

Robin took Sanskrit with Professor Chakravarti, who began their first lesson by scolding Robin for having no knowledge of the language to begin with. 'They should teach Sanskrit to China scholars from the beginning. Sanskrit came to China by way of Buddhist texts, and this caused a veritable explosion of linguistic innovation, as Buddhism introduced dozens of concepts that Chinese had no easy word for. *Nun*, or *bhiksunī* in Sanskrit, became *ni*.[*] *Nirvana* became *nièpán*.[†] Core Chinese concepts like hell, consciousness, and calamity come from Sanskrit. You can't begin to understand Chinese today without also understanding Buddhism, which means understanding Sanskrit. It's like trying to understand multiplication before you know how to draw numbers.'

Robin thought it was a bit unfair to accuse him of learning out of order a language he'd spoken from birth, but he played along. 'Where do we start, then?'

'The alphabet,' Professor Chakravarti said cheerfully. 'Back to basic building blocks. Take out your pen and trace these letters until you've developed a muscle memory for them – I expect it'll take you about half an hour. Go on.'

Latin, translation theory, etymology, focus languages, and a new research language – it was an absurdly heavy class load, especially when each professor assigned coursework as if none of the other courses existed. The faculty was utterly unsympathetic. 'The Germans have this lovely word, *Sitzfleisch*,' Professor Playfair said pleasantly when Ramy protested that they had over forty hours of reading a week. 'Translated

---

[*] 尼.

[†] 涅槃.

literally, it means "sitting meat". Which all goes to say, sometimes you need simply to sit on your bottom and get things done.'

Still, they found their moments of joy. Oxford had now begun to feel like a home of sorts, and they carved their own pockets into it, spaces where they were not just tolerated but in which they thrived. They'd learned which coffee houses would serve them without fuss, and which ones would either pretend Ramy did not exist or complain he was too dirty to sit on their chairs. They learned which pubs they could frequent after dark without harassment. They sat in the audience of the United Debating Society and gave themselves stitches trying to contain their laughter as boys like Colin Thornhill and Elton Pendennis shouted about justice, liberty, and equality until they were red in their faces.

Robin took up rowing at Anthony's insistence. 'It's no good for you to stay cooped up in the library all the time,' he told him. 'One needs to stretch one's muscles for the brain to work properly. Get the blood flowing. Try it, it'll be good for you.'

As it happened, he adored it. He found great pleasure in the rhythmic straining motion of pulling a single oar against the water again and again. His arms grew stronger; his legs, somehow, felt longer. Gradually he lost his hunched-over reediness and acquired a filled-in look, which gave him deep satisfaction every morning when he glanced at the mirror. He started looking forward to chilly mornings on the Isis, when the rest of the town hadn't woken up yet, when the only sound he could hear for miles around was the birds chirping and the pleasant splash of blades sinking into the water.

The girls tried, but failed, to sneak their way into the boat club. They weren't nearly tall enough to row, and coxing involved too much shouting for them to pretend they were men. But weeks later, Robin began hearing rumours of two vicious additions to the Univ fencing team, though Victoire and Letty at first claimed innocence upon interrogation.

'It's the aggression that's the attraction,' Victoire finally confessed. 'It's so funny to watch. These boys always come out so strong at the front, and they lose all sight of strategy.'

Letty agreed. 'Then it's a simple matter of keeping your head and pricking them where they're not guarded. That's all it takes.'

In the winter, the Isis froze over and they went skating, which none of them save Letty had ever done before. They laced their boots on as tight as they could go – 'Tighter,' said Letty, 'they can't wobble, else you'll break your ankles' – and staggered onto the ice, clutching each other for balance as they teetered forth, though usually this only meant that they all fell when one did. Then Ramy realized if he leaned forward and bent his knees, he could drive himself faster and faster, and by the third day he was skating circles around the rest, even Letty, who pretended to be upset when he skidded in her path but who couldn't stop laughing regardless.

There was a solid, enduring quality to their friendship now. They were no longer dazzled and frightened first years, clinging to each other for stability. Instead they were weary veterans united by their trials, hardened soldiers who could lean against each other for anything. Meticulous Letty, despite her grumbling, would always mark up a translation, no matter how late at night or early in the morning. Victoire was like a vault; she would listen to any amount of complaining and petty griping without letting slip to the subjects thereof. And Robin could knock on Ramy's door at any time, day or night, if he needed a cup of tea, or something to laugh about, or someone to cry with.

When the new cohort – no girls, and four baby-faced boys – had appeared at Babel that autumn, they'd given them scarcely any attention. They had, without consciously intending to, become just like the upperclassmen they had so envied during their first term. What they'd perceived as snobbery and haughtiness, it turned out, was only exhaustion. Older students had no intention of bullying newer ones. They simply didn't have the time.

They became what they'd aspired to be since their first year – aloof, brilliant, and fatigued to the bone. They were miserable. They slept and ate too little, read too much, and fell completely out of touch with matters outside Oxford or Babel. They ignored the life of the world; they lived only the life of the mind. They adored it.

And Robin, despite everything, hoped the day Griffin prophesied would never come, that he could live hanging in this balance forever. For he had never been happier than he was now: stretched thin, too preoccupied with the next thing before him to pay any attention to how it all fitted together.

In late Michaelmas a French chemist named Louis-Jacques-Mandé Daguerre came to Babel with a curious object in tow. It was a heliographic camera obscura, he announced, and could be capable of replicating still images using exposed copper plates and light-sensitive compounds, although he couldn't quite get the mechanics right. Could the Babblers take a look and see if they could improve it somehow?

The problem of Daguerre's camera became the talk of the tower. The faculty made it a competition – any student cleared for silver-work who could solve Daguerre's problem was entitled to have their name on his patent, and a percentage of the riches that were sure to follow. For two weeks, the eighth floor frothed with silent frenzy as fourth years and graduate fellows flipped through etymological dictionaries, trying to find a set of words that would get at the right nexus of meaning involving light, colour, image, and imitation.

It was Anthony Ribben who finally cracked it. As per contractual terms with Daguerre, the actual patented match-pair was kept a secret, but rumour was that Anthony had done something with the Latin *imago*, which in addition to meaning 'a likeness' or 'imitation' also implied a ghost or phantom. Other rumours held that Anthony had found some way to dissolve the silver bar to create fumes from heated mercury. Whatever it was, Anthony could not say, but he was paid handsomely for his efforts.

The camera worked. Magically, the exact likeness of a captured subject could be replicated on a sheet of paper in marvellously little time. Daguerre's device – the daguerreotype, they called it – became a local sensation. Everyone wanted their picture taken. Daguerre and the Babel faculty put on a three-day exhibition in the tower lobby, and eager members of the public formed lines that wrapped around the street.

Robin was nervous about a Sanskrit translation due the next day, but Letty insisted they all go in for a portrait. 'Don't you want a memento of us?' she asked. 'Preserved at this moment in time?'

Robin shrugged. 'Not really.'

'Well, I do,' she said stubbornly. 'I want to remember exactly how we were now, in this year, in 1837. I never want to forget.'

They assembled themselves before the camera. Letty and Victoire sat down in chairs, hands folded stiffly in their laps. Robin and Ramy stood behind them, uncertain what to do with their hands. Should they place them on the girls' shoulders? On the chairs?

'Arms by your sides,' said the photographer. 'Hold still as best you can. No – first, cluster a bit closer – there you go.'

Robin smiled, realized he couldn't keep his mouth stretched wide for that long, and promptly dropped it.

The next day, they retrieved their finished portrait from a clerk in the lobby.

'Please,' said Victoire. 'That looks nothing like us at all.'

But Letty was delighted; she insisted they go shopping for a frame. 'I'll hang it over my mantel, what do you think?'

'I'd rather you throw that away,' said Ramy. 'It's unnerving.'

'It is not,' said Letty. She seemed bewitched as she observed the print, as if she'd seen actual magic. 'It's us. Frozen in time, captured in a moment we'll never get back as long as we live. It's wonderful.'

Robin, too, thought the photograph looked strange, though he did not say so aloud. All of their expressions were artificial, masks of faint discomfort. The camera had distorted and flattened the spirit that bound them, and the invisible warmth and camaraderie between them appeared now like a stilted, forced closeness. Photography, he thought, was also a kind of translation, and they had all come out the poorer for it.

Violets cast into crucibles, indeed.

CHAPTER TEN

To preserve the principles of their pupils they confine them to the safe and elegant imbecilities of classical learning. A genuine Oxford tutor would shudder to hear his young men disputing upon moral and political truth, forming and pulling down theories, and indulging in all the boldness of political discussion. He would augur nothing from it but impiety to God, and treason to Kings.

SYDNEY SMITH, 'Edgeworth's *Professional Education*'

Near the end of Michaelmas term that year, Griffin seemed to be around more than usual. Robin had been starting to wonder where he'd gone; since he'd got back from Malacca, his assignments had dropped from twice a month to once to none. But in December, Robin began to receive notes instructing him to meet Griffin outside the Twisted Root every few days, where they commenced their usual routine of walking frantically round the city. Usually these were preludes to planned thefts. But occasionally Griffin seemed to have no agenda in mind, and instead wanted only to chat. Robin eagerly awaited these talks; they were the only times when his brother seemed less mysterious, more human, more flesh and bone. But Griffin never answered the questions Robin really wanted to discuss, which were what Hermes did with the materials he helped steal, and how the revolution, if there was one, was proceeding. 'I still don't trust you,' he would say. 'You're still too new.'

I don't trust you either, Robin thought but didn't say. Instead, he probed at things in a roundabout way. 'How long has Hermes been around?'

Griffin shot him a droll look. 'I know what you're doing.'

'I just want to know if it's a modern invention, or, or—'

'I don't know. I've no idea. Decades at least, perhaps longer, but I've never found out. Why don't you ask what you really want to know?'

'Because you won't tell me.'

'Try me.'

'Fine. Then if it's been around for longer, I can't understand ...'

'You can't see why we haven't won already. Is that it?'

'No. I just don't see what difference it makes,' said Robin. 'Babel is – Babel. And you're just—'

'A small cluster of exiled scholars chipping away at the behemoth?' Griffin supplied. 'Say what you mean, brother, don't dither.'

'I was going to say "massively outnumbered idealists", but yes. I mean – please, Griffin, it's just hard to keep faith when it's unclear what effect there is to anything I do.'

Griffin slowed his pace. He was silent for a few seconds, considering, and then he said, 'I'm going to paint you a picture. Where does silver come from?'

'Griffin, honestly—'

'Indulge me.'

'I've got class in ten minutes.'

'And it's not a simple answer. Craft won't throw you out for being late just once. Where does silver come from?'

'I don't know. Mines?'

Griffin sighed heavily. 'Don't they teach you anything?'

'Griffin—'

'Just listen. Silver's been around forever. The Athenians were mining it in Attica, and the Romans, as you know, used silver to expand their empire once they realized what it could do. But silver didn't become international currency, didn't facilitate a trade network spanning continents, until much later. There simply wasn't enough of it. Then in the sixteenth century, the Hapsburgs – the first truly global empire – stumbled upon massive silver deposits in the Andes. The Spaniards brought it out of the mountains, courtesy of indigenous miners you can be certain weren't paid fairly for their labour,* and minted it into their little pieces of eight, which brought riches flowing into Seville and Madrid.

---

* An understatement. A few short decades after Potosí's 'discovery' in 1545, the silver city had become a death trap for enslaved Africans and drafted indigenous labourers working amidst mercury vapour, foul water, and toxic waste. Spain's 'King of Mountains and Envy of Kings' was a pyramid built on bodies lost to disease, forced marches, malnutrition, overwork, and a poisoned environment.

'Silver made them rich – rich enough to buy printed cotton cloth from India, which they used to pay for bound slaves from Africa, who they put to work on plantations in their colonies. So the Spanish become richer and richer, and everywhere they go they leave death, slavery, and impoverishment in their wake. You see the patterns so far, surely?'

Griffin, when lecturing, bore a peculiar resemblance to Professor Lovell. Both made very sharp gestures with their hands, as if punctuating their lengthy diatribes with hand movements instead of full stops, and both spoke in a very precise, syncopated manner. They also shared a fondness for Socratic questioning. 'Jump forward two hundred years, and what do you have?'

Robin sighed, but played along. 'All the silver, and all the power, flows from the New World to Europe.'

'Right,' said Griffin. 'Silver accrues where it's already in use. The Spanish held the lead for a long time, while the Dutch, British, and French were nipping at their heels. Jump ahead another century, and Spain's a shadow of what it once was; the Napoleonic wars have eroded France's power, and now glorious Britannia is on top. Largest silver reserves in Europe. Best translation institute in the world by far. The best navy on the seas, cemented after Trafalgar, meaning this island is well on its way to ruling the world, isn't it? But something funny's been happening over the last century. Something that's been giving Parliament and all the British trading companies quite a headache. Can you guess what it is?'

'Don't tell me we're running out of silver.'

Griffin grinned. 'They're running out of silver. Can you guess where it's all flowing now?'

This Robin knew the answer to, only because he'd heard Professor Lovell and his friends complaining about it for years during those sitting room nights in Hampstead. 'China.'

'China. This country is gorging itself on imports from the Orient. They can't get enough of China's porcelain, lacquered cabinets, and silks. And tea. Heavens. Do you know how much tea gets exported from China to England every year? At least thirty million pounds' worth. The British love tea so much that Parliament used to insist that the East India Company always keep a year's worth of supply in stock in case of shortages. We spend millions and millions on tea from China every year, and we pay for it in silver.

'But China has no reciprocal appetite for British goods. When the Qianlong Emperor received a display of British manufactured items from Lord Macartney, do you know what his response was? *Strange and costly objects do not interest me.* The Chinese don't need anything we're selling; they can produce everything they want on their own. So silver keeps flowing to China, and there's nothing the British can do about it because they can't alter supply and demand. One day it won't matter how much translation talent we have, because the silver reserves will simply not exist to put it to use. The British Empire will crumble as a consequence of its own greed. Meanwhile, silver will accrue in new centres of power – places that have heretofore had their resources stolen and exploited. They'll have the raw materials. All they'll need then are silver-workers, and the talent will go where the work is; it always does. So it's all as simple as running out the Empire. The cycles of history will do the rest, and you've only got to help us speed it along.'

'But that's . . .' Robin trailed off, struggling to find the words to phrase his objection. 'That's so abstract, so simple, it can't possibly – I mean, certainly you can't predict history like this with such broad strokes—'

'There's quite a lot you can predict.' Griffin shot Robin a sideways look. 'But that's the problem with a Babel education, isn't it? They teach you languages and translation, but never history, never science, never international politics. They don't tell you about the armies that back dialects.'

'But what does it all look like?' Robin persisted. 'What you're describing, I mean – how is this going to come about? A global war? A slow economic decline until the world looks entirely different?'

'I don't know,' said Griffin. 'No one knows precisely what the future looks like. Whether the levers of power move to China, or to the Americas, or whether Britain's going to fight tooth and nail to hold on to its place – that's impossible to foretell.'

'Then how do you know that what you're doing has any effect?'

'I can't predict how every encounter will shake out,' Griffin clarified. 'But I do know this. The wealth of Britain depends on coercive extraction. And as Britain grows, only two options remain: either her mechanisms of coercion become vastly more brutal, or she collapses. The former's more likely. But it might bring about the latter.'

'It's such an uneven fight, though,' Robin said helplessly. 'You on one side, the whole of the Empire on the other.'

'Only if you think the Empire is inevitable,' said Griffin. 'But it's not.

Take this current moment. We are just at the tail end of a great crisis in the Atlantic, after the monarchic empires have fallen one after the other. Britain and France lost in America, and then they went to war against each other to nobody's benefit. Now we're watching a new consolidation of power, that's true – Britain got Bengal, it got Dutch Java and the Cape Colony – and if it gets what it wants in China, if it can reverse this trade imbalance, it's going to be unstoppable.

'But nothing's written in stone – or even silver, as it were. So much rests on these contingencies, and it's at these tipping points where we can push and pull. Where individual choices, where even the smallest of resistance armies make a difference. Take Barbados, for example. Take Jamaica. We sent bars there to the revolts—'

'Those slave revolts were crushed,' said Robin.

'But slavery's been abolished, hasn't it?' said Griffin. 'At least in British territories. No – I'm not saying everything's good and fixed, and I'm not saying we can fully take the credit for British legislation; I'm sure the abolitionists would take umbrage at that. But I am saying that if you think the 1833 Act passed because of the moral sensibilities of the British, you're wrong. They passed that bill because they couldn't keep absorbing the losses.'

He waved a hand, gesturing at an invisible map. 'It's junctures like that where we have control. If we push in the right spots – if we create losses where the Empire can't stand to suffer them – then we've moved things to the breaking point. Then the future becomes fluid, and change is possible. History isn't a premade tapestry that we've got to suffer, a closed world with no exit. We can form it. Make it. We just have to *choose* to make it.'

'You really believe that,' said Robin, amazed. Griffin's faith astounded him. For Robin, such abstract reasoning was a reason to divest from the world, to retreat into the safety of dead languages and books. For Griffin, it was a rallying call.

'I have to,' said Griffin. 'Otherwise, you're right. Otherwise we've got nothing.'

After that conversation, Griffin seemed to have decided Robin wasn't about to betray the Hermes Society, for Robin's assignments vastly increased in number. Not all of his missions involved theft. More often Griffin made requests for materials – etymological handbooks,

Grammatica pages, orthography charts – which were easily acquired, copied out, and returned without drawing attention. Still, he had to be clever with when and how he took the books out, as he'd attract suspicion if he kept sneaking away materials unrelated to his focus areas. One time Ilse, the upperclassman from Japan, demanded to know what he was doing with the Old German Grammatica, and he had to stammer out a story about pulling the title by accident in the course of trying to trace a Chinese word back to Hittite origins. No matter that he was at the entirely wrong section of the library. Ilse seemed ready to believe he was simply that dim.

By and large, Griffin's requests were painless. It was all less romantic than Robin had imagined – and, perhaps, hoped for. There were no thrilling escapades or coded conversations spoken on bridges over running water. It was all so mundane. The great achievement of the Hermes Society, Robin learned, was how effectively it rendered itself invisible, how completely it concealed information even from its members. If one day Griffin disappeared, then Robin would be hard-pressed to prove to anyone the Hermes Society ever existed except as a figment of his imagination. He often felt that he wasn't a part of a secret society at all, but rather of a large, boring bureaucracy that functioned with exquisite coordination.

Even the thefts became routine. Babel's professors seemed wholly unaware that anything was being stolen at all. The Hermes Society took silver only in amounts small enough to mask with some accounting trickery, for the virtue of a humanities faculty, Griffin explained, was that everyone was hopeless with numbers.

'Playfair would let entire crates of silver disappear if no one checked him,' he told Robin. 'Do you think he keeps tidy books? The man can barely add figures in two digits.'

Some days Griffin did not mention Hermes at all, but instead spent the hour it took to reach Port Meadow and back inquiring about Robin's life at Oxford – his rowing exploits, his favourite bookshops, his thoughts on the food in hall and in the Buttery.

Robin answered cautiously. He kept waiting for the ball to drop, for Griffin to spin this conversation into an argument, for his own preference for plain scones to become the proof of his infatuation with the bourgeoisie. But Griffin only kept asking, and gradually it dawned on Robin that perhaps Griffin just missed being a student.

'I do love the campus at Christmastime,' said Griffin one night. 'It's the season when Oxford leans most into the magic of itself.'

The sun had set. The air had gone from pleasantly chilly to bone-cuttingly cold, but the city was bright with Christmas candles, and a light trickle of snow floated down around them. It was lovely. Robin slowed his pace, wanting to savour the scene, but Griffin, he noticed, was shivering madly.

'Griffin, don't . . .' Robin hesitated; he didn't know how to ask politely. 'Is that the only coat you have?'

Griffin recoiled like a dog rising on its hackles. 'Why?'

'It's just – I've got a stipend, if you wanted to buy something warmer—'

'Don't patronize me.' Robin regretted instantly that he'd ever brought it up. Griffin was too proud. He could take no charity; he could not even take sympathy. 'I don't need your money.'

'Suit yourself,' said Robin, wounded.

They walked for another block in silence. Then Griffin asked, in an obvious attempt at an olive branch, 'What's on for Christmas?'

'First there'll be dinner in hall.'

'So endless Latin prayers, rubber goose, and a Christmas pudding that's indistinguishable from pig slop. What's really on?'

Robin grinned. 'Mrs Piper has some pies waiting for me in Jericho.'

'Steak and kidney?'

'Chicken and leek. My favourite. And a lemon tart for Letty, and a chocolate pecan dessert pie for Ramy and Victoire—'

'Bless your Mrs Piper,' Griffin said. 'The professor had some frigid crone named Mrs Peterhouse in my time. Couldn't cook to save her life, no, but always remembered to say something about half-breeds whenever I was in earshot. He didn't like that either, though; I suppose that's why he let her go.'

They turned left onto Cornmarket. They were very near the tower now, and Griffin seemed fidgety; Robin suspected they would soon part ways.

'Before I forget.' Griffin reached into his coat, pulled out a wrapped parcel, and tossed it at Robin. 'I got you something.'

Surprised, Robin pulled at the string. 'A tool?'

'Just a present. Merry Christmas.'

Robin tore away the paper, which revealed a lovely, freshly printed volume.

'You said you liked Dickens,' said Griffin. 'They'd just bound the seri-alization of his latest – you might have already read it, but I thought you'd like it all in one piece.'

He'd bought Robin the three-volume set of *Oliver Twist*. For a moment Robin could only stammer – he hadn't known they were exchanging gifts, he hadn't bought anything for Griffin – but Griffin waved this off. 'That's all right, I'm older than you, don't embarrass me.'

Only later, after Griffin had disappeared down Broad Street, coat flapping around his ankles, would Robin realize this selection had been Griffin's idea of a joke.

Come back with me, he almost said when they parted. *Come to hall. Come back and have Christmas dinner.*

But that was impossible. Robin's life was split into two, and Griffin existed in the shadow world, hidden from sight. Robin could never bring him back to Magpie Lane. Could never introduce him to his friends. Could never, in daylight, call him brother.

'Well.' Griffin cleared his throat. 'Next time, then.'

'When will that be?'

'Don't know yet.' He was already walking away, snow filling in his footsteps. 'Watch your window.'

On the first day of Hilary term, the main entrance to Babel was blocked off by four armed policemen. They appeared to be engaged with someone or something inside, though whatever it was, Robin could not see over the crowd of shivering scholars.

'What's happened?' Ramy asked the girls.

'They're saying it was a break-in,' said Victoire. 'Someone wanted to pilfer some silver, I suppose.'

'So what, the police were here at precisely the right time?' asked Robin.

'He set off some alarm when he tried to get through the door,' said Letty. 'And the police, I think, came quickly.'

A fifth and sixth policeman emerged from the building, dragging the man Robin assumed was the thief between them. He was middle-aged, dark-haired, bearded, and dressed in very grimy clothes. Not Hermes, then, Robin thought with some relief. The thief's face was contorted in pain, and his moans floated over the crowd as the police pulled him down the steps towards a waiting cab. They left a streak of blood on the cobblestones behind them.

'He's got about five bullets in him.' Anthony Ribben appeared beside them. He looked like he might vomit. 'Nice to see the wards are working, I suppose.'

Robin balked. 'Wards did that?'

'The tower's protected by the most sophisticated security system in the country,' said Anthony. 'It's not just the Grammaticas that are guarded. There's about half a million pounds' worth of silver in this building, and only spindly academics around to defend it. Of course the doors are warded.'

Robin's heart was beating very quickly; he could hear it in his eardrums. 'By what?'

'They never tell us the match-pairs; they're very private about it. Playfair updates them every few months, which is about as often as someone attempts a theft. I must say, I like this set much better – the last set tore gaping wounds in the trespasser's limbs using ancient knives rumoured to be from Alexandria. It got blood all over the inside carpet; you can still see the brown spots if you look carefully. We spent weeks guessing which words Playfair used, but no one's been able to crack it.'

Victoire's eyes followed the departing cab. 'What do you think will happen to him?'

'Oh, he'll probably be on the first ship to Australia,' said Anthony. 'Provided he doesn't bleed out on the way to the police station.'

'Routine pickup,' said Griffin. 'In and out – you won't even see we're there. The timing's a bit tricky, though, so be on call all night.' He nudged Robin's shoulder. 'What's wrong?'

Robin blinked and glanced up. 'Hm?'

'You look spooked.'

'I just . . .' Robin deliberated for a moment, then blurted, 'You know about the wards, right?'

'What?'

'We saw a man break in this morning. And the wards, they triggered some sort of gun, and it shot him full of bullets—'

'Well, of course.' Griffin looked puzzled. 'Don't tell me that's news to you. Babel's got ridiculous wards – didn't they rub that into your faces during the first week?'

'They've updated them, though. That's what I'm trying to tell you, they can tell when a thief's walking through now—'

'The bars aren't that sophisticated,' Griffin said dismissively. 'They're designed to discriminate between students, their guests, and strangers to the Institute. What do you think would happen if the traps sprang on a translator who needed to take some bars home overnight? Or someone bringing his wife to the faculty without first clearing it with Playfair? You're completely safe.'

'But how do you *know?*' Robin sounded more petulant than he'd intended. He cleared his throat, tried to deepen his voice without being obvious about it. 'You didn't see what I saw, you don't know what the new match-pairs are—'

'You're in no danger. Here – take this, if you're worried.' Griffin rummaged in his pocket, then tossed Robin a bar. *Wúxíng*, it read. Invisible. It was the same bar he'd used the first night they met.

'For a quick getaway,' said Griffin. 'If things really do go wrong. And you might need to use it on your comrades regardless – it's hard to get a chest that size out of the city unseen.'

Robin slid the bar into his inner pocket. 'You could be less flippant about all this, you know.'

Griffin's lip curled. 'What, now is when you're scared?'

'It's just . . .' Robin considered for a moment, shook his head, then decided to say it. 'It just feels like – I mean, I'm the one who's always at risk, while you're just—'

'Just what?' Griffin asked sharply.

He'd strayed into dangerous territory. He knew, from the way Griffin's eyes flashed, he'd wandered too close to where it hurt. A month ago, when their relationship was more precarious, he might have changed the subject. But he couldn't hold his silence now. He felt irritated and belittled just then, and with that came a hot desire to hurt.

'Why aren't you coming on this one?' he asked. 'Why can't you use the bar yourself?'

Griffin blinked slowly. Then he said, in a tone so level it must have been forced, 'I can't. You know I can't.'

'Why not?'

'Because I don't dream in Chinese.' His expression did not change, nor did his tone, but the condescending fury seeped through his words nonetheless. Watching him speak then was uncanny. He looked so like their father. 'I'm your failed predecessor, you see. Dear old Papa took me out of the country too early. I've got a natural ear for tones, but that's it. My fluency is largely artificial. I don't have memories in Chinese. I don't dream in it. I've got the recall, I've got the language skills, but I can't reliably make the bars work. Half the time they do nothing at all.' His throat pulsed. 'Our father got it right with you. He left you to ferment until you were literate. But he brought me here before I'd formed enough connections, enough memories. What's more, he was the only person I ever spoke Mandarin with, when my Cantonese was far better to begin with. And that's lost now. I don't think in it, and I certainly don't dream in it.'

Robin thought of the thieves in the alley, of Griffin's desperate whispers as he tried to make them disappear. What would he do if he'd lost his own Chinese? The very idea filled him with horror.

'You get it,' Griffin said, watching him. 'You know how it feels for your native tongue to slip away. You caught it in time. I didn't.'

'I'm so sorry,' said Robin. 'I didn't know.'

'Don't be sorry,' Griffin said drily. '*You* didn't ruin my life.'

Robin could see Oxford now through Griffin's eyes – an institution that never valued him, that had only ever ostracized and belittled him. He imagined Griffin coming up through Babel, trying desperately to win Professor Lovell's approval, but never able to get the silver to work consistently. How awful it would have felt to reach for flimsy Chinese from a barely remembered life, knowing full well that it was the only thing that gave him value here.

Small wonder Griffin was furious. Small wonder he hated Babel with such vehemence. Griffin had been robbed of everything – a mother tongue, a motherland, a family.

'So I need you, darling brother.' Griffin reached out, ruffled his hair. His touch was so forceful it hurt. 'You're the real thing. You're indispensable.'

Robin knew better than to respond.

'Keep an eye on your window.' There was no warmth in Griffin's eyes. 'Things are moving fast. And this one's important.'

Robin swallowed his objections and nodded. 'Right.'

One week later, Robin came back from dinner with Professor Lovell to find the scrap of paper he'd been dreading wedged under his window.

Tonight, it read. *Eleven.*

It was already 10.45. Robin hastily threw on the coat he'd just hung up, grabbed the *wúxíng* bar out of his drawer, and dashed back out into the rain.

He checked the back of the note for other details as he walked, but Griffin had included no further instructions. This wasn't necessarily a problem – Robin assumed this meant he should simply let whatever accomplices showed up in and out of the tower – but the hour was surprisingly early, and he realized belatedly that he hadn't brought anything with him – no books, no satchel, not even an umbrella – that would justify a late-night trip to the tower.

But he couldn't fail to show at all. As the bells struck eleven, he dashed across the green and yanked the door open. This was nothing he hadn't done a dozen times before – open sesame, close sesame, and stay out of the way. As long as Robin's blood was stored in those stone walls, the wards shouldn't sound.

Two Hermes operatives followed him through and disappeared up the stairs. Robin hung around the foyer as usual, keeping an eye out for nocturnal scholars, counting down the seconds until it was time to leave. At five past eleven, the Hermes operatives hurried downstairs. One of them carried a set of engraving tools, the other a chest of silver bars.

'Well done,' whispered one. 'Let's go.'

Robin nodded and opened the door to let them out. The moment they stepped foot over the barrier, an awful cacophony split the air – a screaming, a howling, the grinding of metal gears in some invisible mechanism. It was a threat and a warning, the hybrid of ancient horror and the modern capacity for spilling blood. Behind them, the panels in the door shifted, revealing a dark cavity within.

Without another word, the Hermes operatives dashed towards the green.

Robin hesitated, trying to decide whether to follow. He might get away – the trap was loud, but seemed slow-acting. He glanced down and saw both his feet were planted squarely on the university's coat of arms. Suppose the ward was only triggered if he stepped off?

One way to find out. He took a deep breath, then dashed down the stairs. He heard a bang, then felt a searing pain in his left arm. He couldn't tell where he'd been hit. The pain seemed to come from everywhere, less a singular wound and more a burning agony that spread through his entire arm. It was on fire, it was exploding, the whole limb was going to fall off. He kept running. Bullets fired into the air behind him. He ducked and jumped at random; he'd read somewhere this was how to dodge gunshots, but had no idea if it was true. He heard more bangs, but felt no corresponding explosions of pain. He made it down the length of the green and turned left onto Broad Street, out of sight and out of range.

Then the pain and fear caught up with him. His knees shook. He took two more steps and collapsed against the wall, fighting the urge to vomit. His head swam. He couldn't outrun the police if they came. Not like this, not with blood dripping down his arm and black creeping at the edges of his vision. *Focus.* He fumbled for the bar in his pocket. His left hand was slippery, dark with blood; the very sight set off another wave of vertigo.

'*Wúxíng*,' he whispered frantically, trying to concentrate, to imagine the world in Chinese. He was nothing. He was formless. '*Invisible*.'

It didn't work. He couldn't make it work; he couldn't switch modes to Chinese when all he could think about was the awful pain.

'Hey there! You – stop!'

It was Professor Playfair. Robin flinched, prepared for the worst, but the professor's face creased into a warm, concerned smile. 'Oh, hello, Swift. Didn't realize that was you. Are you quite all right? There's a ruckus on at the building.'

'Professor, I . . . ' Robin hadn't the faintest clue what to say, so he decided it was best just to babble. 'I don't – I was near it, but I don't know if . . . '

'Did you see anyone?' asked Professor Playfair. 'The wards are meant to shoot the intruder, you know, but the gears seem to have stuck after last time. Might have still hit him, though – did you see anyone with a limp, anyone who looked like they were in pain?'

'No, I didn't – I was almost to the green when the alarms went off, but I hadn't turned the corner.' Was Professor Playfair nodding in sympathy? Robin hardly dared believe his luck. 'Is it – was there a thief?'

'Perhaps not. Don't you worry.' Professor Playfair reached out and patted him on the shoulder. The impact sent another horrible wave of pain through his whole upper body, and Robin clenched his teeth to keep from crying out. 'The wards get finicky sometimes – perhaps it's time to replace them. Pity, I liked this version. Are you all right?'

Robin nodded and blinked, trying his hardest to keep his voice level. 'Just scared, I suppose – I mean, after what we saw last week . . . '

'Ah, right. Awful, wasn't it? Nice to know that my little idea worked, though. They wouldn't even let me test it out on dogs beforehand. Good thing it wasn't you it malfunctioned on.' Professor Playfair barked out a laugh. 'Might have pumped you full of lead.'

'Right,' Robin said weakly. 'So . . . so glad.'

'You're fine. Have a whisky with hot water, that'll help with the shock.'

'Yes, I think . . . I think that sounds nice.' Robin turned to go.

'Didn't you say you were on your way in?' Professor Playfair asked.

Robin had this lie ready. 'I was feeling anxious, so I thought I'd get a head start on a paper for Professor Lovell. But I'm a bit shaken up, and I don't think I'll do any good work if I start now, so I think I'd rather just head to bed.'

'Of course.' Professor Playfair patted his shoulder again. It felt more forceful this time; Robin's eyes bulged. 'Richard would say you're being lazy, but I quite understand. You're still only in your second year, you can afford to be lazy. Go home and sleep.'

Professor Playfair gave him a last cheerful nod and strolled off towards the tower, where the alarms were still wailing. Robin took a deep breath and hobbled away, striving with all his might not to collapse on the street.

Somehow he made it back to Magpie Lane. The bleeding still had not stopped, but after wiping his arm with a wet towel, he saw to his relief that the bullet had not lodged in his arm. It had only grazed a notch into the flesh above his elbow, about a third of an inch deep. The wound looked reassuringly small when he wiped the blood away. He didn't know how to dress it properly – he imagined it might involve a needle and thread – but it would be foolish to go and seek the college nurse at this hour.

He gritted his teeth against the pain, trying to remember what useful advice he'd picked up from adventure novels. Alcohol – he needed to disinfect the wound. He rummaged around his shelves until he found a half-empty bottle of brandy, a Christmas gift from Victoire. He dribbled it over his arm, hissing from the sting, then swallowed down several mouthfuls for good measure. Next he found a clean shirt, which he ripped up to make bandages. These he wrapped tightly around his arm using his teeth – he'd read that pressure helped stanch the bleeding. He didn't know what else he ought to do. Should he simply wait, now, for the wound to close up on its own?

His head swam. Was he dizzy from blood loss, or was that only the brandy at work?

Find Ramy, he thought. *Find Ramy, he'll help.*

No. Calling on Ramy would implicate him. Robin would die before he jeopardized Ramy.

He sat against the wall, head tilted towards the roof, and took several deep breaths. He just had to get through this night. It took several shirts – he'd have to go to the tailor, make up some story about a laundry disaster – but eventually, the bleeding was stemmed. At last, exhausted, he slumped over and fell asleep.

The next day, after wincing through three hours of class, Robin went to the medical library and rooted through the stacks until he found a physician's handbook on field wounds. Then he went to Cornmarket, bought a needle and thread, and hurried home to suture his arm back together.

He lit a candle, sterilized the needle over the flame, and after many fumbled tries, managed to thread it. Then he sat down and held the sharp point above his raw, wounded flesh.

He couldn't do it. He kept bringing the needle close to the wound and then, anticipating the pain, pulling it away. He reached for the brandy and took three massive gulps. He waited several minutes until the alcohol had settled nicely in his stomach and his extremities had begun tingling pleasantly. This was where he needed to be – dull enough not to mind the pain, alert enough to sew himself together. He tried again. It was easier this time, though he still had to stop to jam a wadded cloth in his mouth to keep from yelling. At last he made the final stitch. His forehead dripped with sweat; tears flowed freely down his cheeks. Somehow, he found the strength to snip the thread, tie the sutures off with his teeth, and toss the bloody needle into the sink. Then he collapsed back on his bed and, curling onto his side, finished the rest of the bottle.

Griffin was not in touch that night.

Robin knew it was foolish to expect he would be. Griffin, upon learning what had happened, would likely have gone underground, and for good reason. Robin wouldn't be surprised if he didn't hear from Griffin for an entire term. Still, he felt an overwhelming, black wave of resentment.

He'd *told* Griffin this would happen. He'd warned him, he'd told him exactly what he'd seen. This had been utterly avoidable.

He wanted their next meeting to happen sooner just so he could yell at him, say he'd told him so, that Griffin should have listened. That if Griffin weren't so arrogant, perhaps his little brother wouldn't have a line of messy stitches up his arm. But the appointment didn't come. Griffin left no notes in his window the next night, or the night after. He seemed to have disappeared without a trace from Oxford, leaving Robin with no way of contacting him or Hermes at all.

He couldn't talk to Griffin. Couldn't confide in Victoire, Letty, or Ramy. He had only himself for company that night, crying miserably over the empty bottle while his arm throbbed. And for the first time since he'd arrived at Oxford, Robin felt truly alone.

CHAPTER ELEVEN

_But slaves we are, and labour in another man's plantation; we dress
the vineyard, but the wine is the owner's._

JOHN DRYDEN, extract from the 'Dedication'
to his translation of the _Aeneid_

Robin saw none of Griffin for the rest of Hilary Term, or Trinity.
In truth, he hardly noticed; his second-year coursework only got
more difficult as the weeks went on, and he barely had time to dwell on
his resentment.

Summer came, though it was not a summer at all but rather an accel-
erated term, and his days were occupied with frantically cramming Sanskrit vocabulary for an assessment the week before next Michaelmas
began. Then they were third-year students, a status that entailed all the
exhaustion of Babel with none of its novelties. Oxford lost its charm
that September; the golden sunsets and bright blue skies replaced by
an endless chill and fog. It rained an inordinate amount, and the storm
winds felt uniquely vicious compared to previous years. Their umbrel-
las kept breaking. Their socks were always wet. Rowing that term was
cancelled.*

That was just as well. None of them had time for sports anymore. The
third year at Babel was traditionally known as the Siberian winter, and
the reason became obvious when they were issued their courses lists.

---

* Two weeks into Michaelmas several freshers at Balliol had rented several punting
boats and, in their drunken revels, created a traffic jam in the middle of the Cherwell that piled up three barges and one houseboat, costing incalculable pounds in
damages. As punishment, the university had suspended all races until next year.

They were all continuing in their tertiary languages and in Latin, which was rumoured to become devilishly difficult when Tacitus entered the picture. They were also continuing in Translation Theory with Professor Playfair and Etymology with Professor Lovell, though the workload for each course had now doubled, as they were expected to produce a five-page paper for each class every week.

Most importantly, they were all assigned supervisors with whom they would pursue an independent research project. This counted as their proto-dissertation – their first piece of work that would, if completed successfully, be preserved on Babel's shelves as a true piece of scholarly contribution.

Ramy and Victoire were both immediately unhappy with their supervisors. Ramy had been invited by Professor Joseph Harding to contribute to an editorial round of the Persian Grammatica, which was nominally a great honour.[*] But Ramy couldn't see the romance in such a project.

'Initially I proposed a translation of Ibn Khaldun's manuscripts,' he told them. 'The ones Silvestre de Sacy's got hold of. But Harding objected that the French Orientalists were already working on that, and that it was unlikely I could get Paris to lend them to me for the term. So then I asked if I might just translate Omar ibn Said's Arabic essays into English, given that they've just been sitting around for a near decade in our collections, but Harding said that was unnecessary because abolition had already passed into law in England, can you believe it?[†] As if America doesn't exist? At last Harding said if I wanted to do something authoritative, then I could edit the citations in the Persian Grammatica, so he's got me reading Schlegel now. *Über die Sprache und Weisheit der Indier*. And you know what? Schlegel wasn't even in India when he

---

[*] It took a great deal of rigour and scrutiny to contribute anything to a Grammatica. Oxford was still smarting from the embarrassments dealt by a former visiting lecturer named George Psalmanazar, a Frenchman who, claiming to be from Formosa, passed off his pale skin by saying that Formosans lived underground. He had lectured and published on the Formosan languages for decades before he was exposed as a complete fraud.

[†] Omar ibn Said was a West African Islamic scholar captured into slavery in 1807. When he wrote his autobiographical essay in 1831, he was still enslaved by American politician James Owen in North Carolina. He would remain enslaved for the rest of his life.

wrote that. He wrote it all from Paris. How do you write a definitive text on the "language and wisdom" of India from Paris?'*

Yet Ramy's indignation seemed trivial compared to what Victoire was dealing with. She was working with Professor Hugo Leblanc, with whom she'd studied French for two years with no trouble, but who now became a source of ceaseless frustration.

'It's impossible,' she said. 'I want to work on Kreyòl, which he's not wholly opposed to despite thinking it's a degenerate language, but all he wants to know about is Vodou.'

'That pagan religion?' Letty asked.

Victoire shot her a scathing look. 'The *religion*, yes. He keeps asking about Vodou spells and poems, which he can't access, of course, because they're in Kreyòl.'

Letty looked confused. 'But isn't that just the same thing as French?'

'Not even remotely,' said Victoire. 'French is the lexifier, yes, but Kreyòl is its own language, with its own grammatical rules. French and Kreyòl are not mutually intelligible. You could have studied French for a decade, but a Kreyòl poem might still be impossible to decipher without a dictionary. Leblanc doesn't have a dictionary – there *is* no dictionary, not yet – so I'm the next best thing.'

'Then what's the problem?' asked Ramy. 'Seems like you've got a pretty good project, there.'

Victoire looked uncomfortable. 'Because the texts he wants translated are – I don't know, they're special texts. Texts that mean something.'

'Texts so special that they shouldn't even be translated?' Letty asked.

'They're heritage,' insisted Victoire. 'They're sacred beliefs—'

'Not *your* beliefs, surely—'

'Perhaps not,' said Victoire. 'I haven't – I mean, I don't know. But they're not meant to be shared. Would you be content to sit hour after hour with a white man as he asks you the story behind every metaphor, every god's name, so he can pilfer through your people's beliefs for a match-pair that might make a silver bar glow?'

Letty looked unconvinced. 'But it's not *real*, is it?'

---

* This was only the beginning of the multiple flaws of Schlegel's work. Islam he considered a 'dead empty Theism'. He also assumed that Egyptians were descended from Indians, and argued Chinese and Hebrew were inferior to German and Sanskrit because they lacked inflection.

'Of course it's real.'

'Oh, please, Victoire.'

'It's real in a sense you can never know.' Victoire was growing agitated. 'In a sense that only someone from Haiti could have access to. But not in the sense that Leblanc is imagining.'

Letty sighed. 'So why don't you tell him just that?'

'You don't think I've tried?' Victoire snapped. 'Have you ever tried to convince a Babel professor not to pursue something?'

'Well anyhow,' said Letty, annoyed and defensive now and therefore vicious, 'what would you know about Vodou? Didn't you grow up in France?'

This was the worst reply she could have made. Victoire clamped her mouth shut and looked away. The conversation died. An awkward silence descended, which neither Victoire nor Letty made any attempt to break. Robin and Ramy exchanged a glance, clueless, foolish. Something had gone terribly wrong, a taboo had been breached, but they were all too afraid to probe at precisely what.

Robin and Letty were passably happy with their projects, plodding and time-consuming as they were. Robin was working with Professor Chakravarti to complete a list of Sanskrit loanwords to Chinese, and Letty was working with Professor Leblanc to wade through French scientific papers for possibly useful and untranslatable metaphors in the realm of mathematics and engineering. They learned to avoid discussing the details around Ramy and Victoire. They all used platitudes with each other; Robin and Letty were always 'making good progress' while Ramy and Victoire were 'struggling on as usual'.

Privately, Letty was not so generous. The subject of Professor Leblanc had become a sticking point between her and Victoire, who was hurt and astounded by Letty's lack of sympathy, while Letty thought Victoire was being too sensitive about it all.

'She's brought this on herself,' she complained to Robin. 'She could make this so much easier if she'd just do the research – I mean, no one's done a third-year project in Haitian Creole, there's barely even a Grammatica. She could be the very first!'

There was no debating with Letty when she was in these moods – it was obvious she only wanted an audience to vent to – but Robin tried anyway. 'Suppose it means more to her than you realize.'

'But it doesn't. I know it doesn't! She's not the slightest bit religious; I mean, she's *civilized*—'

He whistled. 'That's a loaded word, Letty.'

'You know what I mean,' she huffed. 'She's not Haitian. She's *French*. And I just don't see why she has to be so difficult.'

Halfway into Michaelmas, Letty and Victoire were hardly talking to each other. They always came to class several minutes apart, and Robin wondered if it took skill to space out their departures so that they never crossed paths on the long walk down.

The girls were not the only ones suffering fractures. The atmosphere of those days was oppressive. Something had seemed to break between them all – no, *break* was perhaps too strong a word, for they still clung to each other with the force of people who had no one else. But their bond had twisted in a decidedly hurtful direction. They still spent nearly all their waking moments together, but they dreaded each other's company. Everything was an unintended slight or deliberate offence – if Robin complained about Sanskrit, it was insensitive to the fact that Professor Harding kept insisting Sanskrit was one of Ramy's languages when it wasn't; if Ramy was pleased he and Professor Harding had finally agreed on a research direction, it was a callous remark to Victoire, who had got nowhere with Professor Leblanc. They used to find solace in their solidarity, but now they saw each other only as reminders of their own misery.

The worst, from Robin's perspective, was that something had changed suddenly and mysteriously between Letty and Ramy. Their interactions were as heated as ever – Ramy never ceased to make fun, and Letty never ceased to flare up in response. But now Letty's rejoinders had acquired an oddly victimized tone. She snapped at the smallest, often intangible slights. Ramy in return had got more cruel and more snide in a way that was hard to describe. Robin didn't know what to do about this, nor did he have the faintest clue what it was all about, other than that it gave him strange pangs in his chest whenever he watched these exchanges happen.

'She's just being Letty,' said Ramy when pressed about it. 'She wants attention, and she thinks throwing a tantrum is the way to get it.'

'Did you do something to upset her?' Robin asked.

'Other than generally exist? I don't think so.' Ramy seemed bored by the subject. 'Suppose we get on with this translation? Everything's all right, Birdie, I promise.'

But things were decidedly not all right. Things were in fact very weird. Ramy and Letty seemed unable to stand each other, and at the same time, they gravitated around each other; they could not speak normally without fiercely opposing each other in a way that made them the protagonists of the conversation. If Ramy wanted coffee, Letty wanted tea; if Ramy thought that a painting on the wall was pretty, then Letty suddenly had twelve reasons why it exemplified the worst of the Royal Academy's adherence to artistic conventionalism.

Robin found it unbearable. One night, during a fitful burst of sleep, he had a sudden and violent fantasy of pushing Letty into the Cherwell. When he awoke he searched himself for any hint of guilt, but could find none; the thought of Letty drenched and sputtering brought just as much vicious satisfaction in the sober light of day.

There was at least the distraction of their third-year apprenticeships, for which they would each assist a faculty member in their silver-working duties throughout the term. 'Theory comes from the Greek theōria, meaning a sight or spectacle, whose root also gives us the word theatre.' So Professor Playfair expounded before he sent them off with their respective supervisors. 'But it is not enough to merely watch the operations. You must get your hands dirty. You must understand how the metal sings.'

In practice this meant a lot of unpaid donkey work. To Robin's disappointment, the apprentices spent very little time on the eighth floor, where all the exciting research happened. Instead, three times a week, he accompanied Professor Chakravarti on trips around Oxford, helping with silver-work installation and upkeep. He learned how to polish silver until it shone (oxidation and tarnishing greatly dampened the match-pair effect), how to choose between different sizes of engraving styluses to painstakingly restore an inscription to its original clarity, and how to deftly slide the bars in and out of their specially welded fixtures. It was too bad that Griffin had gone underground, he thought, for his apprenticeship gave him almost unrestricted access to the tower's tools and raw materials. He wouldn't have had to let thieves in at midnight. Amidst whole drawers of engraving equipment and absent-minded professors who wouldn't have noticed a thing, he could have plucked whatever he liked from the tower at will.

'How often do you have to do this?' he asked.

'Oh, it never ends,' said Professor Chakravarti. 'It's how we make all our money, you see. The bars fetch a high price, but it's the upkeep that's the real grift. The workload is a bit harder on myself and Richard, though, since there are so few Sinologists.'

That afternoon they were doing a house call on an estate in Wolvercote, where a silver-work installation in the back garden had ceased to function despite a twelve-month warranty. They'd had some trouble getting through the front gate – the housekeeper seemed unconvinced they were Babel scholars, and rather suspicious that they were here to rob the place – but after supplying various proofs of identification, including the recitations of many Latin graces, they were at last invited in.

'Happens about twice a month,' Professor Chakravarti told Robin, though he looked quite put off. 'You get used to it. They don't give Richard half the trouble.'*

The housekeeper led them through the estate to a very lush, pretty garden with a burbling, serpentine stream and several large rocks arranged at random. It was designed in the Chinese style, they were informed, which had become very popular in that era after William Chambers's Oriental landscaping designs were shown for the first time in Kew Gardens. Robin could not recall ever seeing anything like this in Canton, but he nodded along appreciatively until the housekeeper had gone.

'Well, the problem here's obvious.' Professor Chakravarti pushed some shrubbery aside to reveal the fence corner where the silver-work was installed. 'They've been pushing a cart back and forth over the bar. It's rubbed the engraving half off. That's their own fault – this won't qualify under the warranty.'

He let Robin extract it from its fixture, then turned the bar around to show him the inscription. On one side: *garden*; on the other, the character 齋, which could mean a landscape garden, but more generally evoked a place for private withdrawal, to retreat from the world, with connotations of ritual purification, cleansing, alms-giving, and Daoist acts of repentance.

---

* Many of Babel's customers were ready to believe that their silver-work made use of foreign languages, but not that their maintenance involved foreign-born scholars, and more than once Professor Chakravarti had had to enlist one of the white fourth years to accompany him and Robin on trips just to get them through the door.

'The idea is to make their gardens nicer and quieter than the hubbub of Oxford allows. Keeps out the riffraff. The effect is quite subtle, if we're being honest; we didn't do all that much testing, but there's really no limit to what the wealthy will throw money at.' Professor Chakravarti whittled at the bar as he spoke. 'Hm. We'll see if that'll do the trick.'

He let Robin reinstall the bar, then bent down to check his work. Satisfied, he stood and brushed his hands on his trousers. 'Would you like to activate it?'

'I just – what, say the words?' Robin had seen the professors do the same many times, though he couldn't imagine it was all that easy. Then again, he recalled, the *wùxíng* bar had worked for him on the first try.

'Well, it's a particular kind of mental state. You do speak the words, but more importantly, you hold two meanings in your head at once. You exist in both linguistic worlds simultaneously, and you imagine traversing them. Does that make sense?'

'I – I think so, sir.' Robin frowned at the bar. 'That's really all it takes?'

'Oh, no, I'm being careless. There are some good mental heuristics you'll learn during your fourth year, and some theory seminars you'll have to sit through, but when it comes down to it, it's about the feeling.' Professor Chakravarti seemed rather bored; Robin got the impression he was still very irritated by this household and wanted to be away as quickly as possible. 'Go on.'

'Well – all right.' Robin placed his hand on the bar. '*Zhāi*. Garden.'

He felt a slight thrum beneath his fingertips. The garden did seem quieter then, more serene, though he couldn't tell if this was his doing or his imagination. 'Have we done it?'

'Well, we'd better hope so.' Professor Chakravarti slung his tool bag over his shoulder. He was not concerned enough to check. 'Come on, let's go and get paid.'

'Do you always need to speak the match-pair to make it work?' Robin asked as they walked back to campus. 'It seems untenable – that is, there are so many bars, and so few translators.'

'Well, that depends on a number of things,' said Professor Chakravarti. 'To begin with, the nature of the impact. With some bars, you want a temporary manifestation. Suppose you need a short and extreme physical effect – a lot of military bars work this way. Then they need to be activated each time upon use, and they're designed so that the effects don't last long. But other bars have an enduring effect – like the wards in the tower, for example, or the bars installed in ships and carriages.'

'What makes them last longer?'

'The number of carats, to start with. Finer silver endures, and the higher the percentage of other alloys, the shorter the time of effect. But there are also subtle differences in the way they're smelted and engraved; you'll learn soon enough.' Professor Chakravarti shot him a smile. 'You're eager to get started, aren't you?'

'It's just very exciting, sir.'

'That'll wear off,' said Professor Chakravarti. 'Walk around town muttering the same words over and over again, and soon you start feeling like a parrot instead of a magician.'

One afternoon, they arrived at the Ashmolean Museum to fix a silver bar that no number of incantations would activate. The English side read *verify*, and the Chinese side used the character 参, meaning 'to validate'. It could also mean 'to juxtapose', 'to arrange side by side', and 'to compare things'. The Ashmolean staff had been using this to compare fraudulent artifacts against the real ones, but recently it had failed several test runs, which the staff wisely conducted before appraising new acquisitions.

They carefully inspected the bar under a hand-held microscope, but neither the Chinese nor the English calligraphy showed any sign of erosion. Even after Professor Chakravarti went over the whole thing with his smallest engraving stylus, it still failed to activate.

He sighed. 'Wrap that up and put it in my bag, won't you?'

Robin obeyed. 'What's wrong?'

'Its resonance link has stopped working. It happens sometimes, especially with some of the older match-pairs.'

'What's a resonance link?'

'Off to the tower,' said Professor Chakravarti, already walking away. 'You'll see what I mean.'

Back at Babel, Professor Chakravarti led Robin up to the southern wing of the eighth floor, past the worktables. Robin had never been in this area before. All of his visits to the eighth floor had been restricted to the workshop, which occupied most of what the eye saw past the thick fire door. But another set of doors blocked off the southern wing, bolted shut with three sets of locks, which Professor Chakravarti now opened with a jangling ring of keys.

'I'm really not supposed to show you just yet.' Professor Chakravarti winked at him. 'Privileged information and all that. But there's no other way to explain.'

He undid the final lock. They stepped through.

It was like entering a fun house exhibit, or the inside of a giant piano. Massive silver rods of varying heights and lengths stood upright all across the floor. Some were waist high; others towered above him, stretching from the floor to the ceiling, with just enough room between them for one to step nimbly through without touching any. They reminded Robin rather of church organs; he had a strange impulse to take a mallet and strike them all at once.

'Resonance is a way of cutting costs,' Professor Chakravarti explained. 'We need to save the higher-carat silver for bars with endurance needs – the bars that go into the Navy, that protect merchant ships, and the like. So we use silver with a higher percentage of alloys for the bars that operate on English land, since we can keep them fuelled with resonance.'

Robin peered around, amazed. 'But how does it all work?'

'It's easiest to think of Babel as the centre, and all the resonance-dependent bars in England as the periphery. The periphery draws on the centre for power.' Professor Chakravarti gestured around him. Each rod, Robin noticed, appeared to be vibrating at a very high frequency, but though it felt as if the tower should be ringing with discordant notes, the air was still and silent. 'These rods, engraved with commonly used match-pairs, sustain linked bars throughout the country. The manifesting power comes from the rod, you see, which means that the bars outside don't require such constant reactivation.'

'Like British outposts in the colonies,' said Robin. 'Calling upon home for soldiers and supplies.'

'A convenient metaphor, yes.'

'So do these resonate with every bar in England?' Robin saw in his mind an invisible network of meaning stretching over the country, keeping the silver-work alive. It was quite terrifying to consider. 'I'd have thought there would be more of them.'

'Not quite. There are much smaller resonance centres across the country – there's one in Edinburgh, for example, and one in Cambridge. The effect does weaken with distance. But the lion's share is in Oxford – it spreads the Translation Institute too far out to maintain multiple centres, as you need trained translators for the upkeep.'

Robin bent to examine one of the closest rods. In addition to the match-pair, written in large calligraphy at the top, he saw a series of letters and symbols that he could make no sense of. 'How's the link forged, then?'

'It's a complicated process.' Professor Chakravarti led Robin to a slender rod near the south-side window. He knelt down, retrieved the Ashmolean bar from his bag, and held it up against the rod. Robin noticed then a number of etchings in the side of the rod that corresponded with similar etchings in the bar. 'They've got to be smelted from the same material. And then there's a good deal of etymological symbol work – you'll learn all of that in your fourth year, if you specialize in silver-working. We actually use an invented alphabet, based on a manuscript first discovered by an alchemist from Prague in the seventeenth century.* It's so that no one outside Babel can replicate our process. For now, you can think of all this adjustment as deepening the bond of connection.'

'But I thought fake languages didn't work to activate the bars,' said Robin.

'They don't to *manifest* meaning,' said Professor Chakravarti. 'As a linking mechanism, however, they work quite well. We could do with basic numbers, but Playfair likes his mysteries. Keeps things proprietary.'

Robin stood awhile in silence, watching as Professor Chakravarti adjusted the etchings on the Ashmolean bar with a fine stylus, examined them with a lens, and then made corresponding adjustments to the resonance rod. The whole process took about fifteen minutes. At last, Professor Chakravarti wrapped the Ashmolean bar back up in velvet, returned it to his bag, and stood up. 'That should do the trick. We'll head back to the museum tomorrow.'

---

* The manuscript in question – named the Baresch Codex after the alchemist who brought it to public attention – is a vellum-bound codex of what appears to be magic, science, or botany. It is written in an alphabet combining some Latin symbols and wholly unfamiliar symbols; this alphabet employs no capitalization and no punctuation marks. The script appears closest to Latin, and indeed makes use of Latin abbreviations, but the manuscript's purpose and meaning have remained a mystery since its discovery. The manuscript was acquired by Babel in the mid-eighteenth century, and many Babel scholars since have failed to translate it; the alphabet used for resonance links takes inspiration from the manuscript's symbols but represents no progress in deciphering the original.

Robin had been reading the rods, noticing what a large percentage of them appeared to use Chinese match-pairs. 'You and Professor Lovell have to maintain all of these?'

'Oh, yes,' said Professor Chakravarti. 'There's no one else who can do it. Your graduation will make three.'

'They need us,' Robin marvelled. It was strange to think the functioning of an entire empire depended on just a handful of people.

'They need us so terribly,' agreed Professor Chakravarti. 'And it's good, in our situation, to be needed.'

They stood together at the window. Looking out over Oxford, Robin had the impression that the whole city was like a finely tuned music box, relying wholly on its silver gears to keep running; and that if the silver ever ran out, if these resonance rods ever collapsed, then the whole of Oxford would stop abruptly in its tracks. The bell towers would go mute, the cabs would halt on the roads, and the townsfolk would freeze in motion on the street, limbs lifted in midair, mouths open in midspeech.

But he couldn't imagine that it would ever run out. London, and Babel, were getting richer every day, for the same ships fuelled by long-enduring silver-work brought back chests and chests of silver in return. There wasn't a market on earth that could resist British incursion, not even the Far East. The only thing that would disrupt the inflow of silver was the collapse of the entire global economy, and since that was ridiculous, the Silver City, and the delights of Oxford, seemed eternal.

One day in mid-January, they showed up at the tower to find all the upperclassmen and graduate fellows wearing black under their gowns.

'It's for Anthony Ribben,' explained Professor Playfair when they filed into his seminar. He himself was wearing a shirt of lilac blue.

'What about Anthony?' Letty asked.

'I see.' Professor Playfair's face tightened. 'They haven't told you.'

'Told us what?'

'Anthony went missing during a research expedition to Barbados last summer,' said Professor Playfair. 'He disappeared the night before his ship was due to return to Bristol, and we haven't heard from him since. We're presuming he's dead. His colleagues on the eighth floor are quite upset; I believe they'll be wearing black for the rest of the week. A few of the other cohorts and fellows have joined in, if you care to participate.'

He said this with such casual unconcern that they might have been discussing whether they wanted to go punting that afternoon. Robin gaped at him. 'But isn't he – aren't you – I mean, doesn't he have family? Have they been told?'

Professor Playfair scribbled an outline for that day's lecture on the chalkboard as he answered. 'Anthony has no family except his guardian. Mr Falwell's been notified by post, and I hear he's quite upset.'

'My God,' said Letty. 'That's terrible.'

She said this with a solicitous glance at Victoire, who among them had known Anthony the best. But Victoire looked surprisingly unfazed; she didn't seem shocked or upset so much as vaguely uncomfortable. Indeed, she looked as if she hoped they might change topics as quickly as possible. Professor Playfair was more than happy to oblige.

'Well, on to business,' he said. 'We left off last Friday on the innovations of the German Romantics ...'

Babel did not mourn Anthony. The faculty did not so much as hold a memorial service. The next time Robin went up to the silver-working floor, a wheat-haired graduate fellow he didn't know had taken over Anthony's workstation.

'It's disgusting,' Letty said. 'Can you believe – I mean, a Babel graduate, and they just act like he was never here?'

Her distress belied a deeper terror, a terror which Robin felt as well, which was that Anthony had been expendable. That they were all expendable. That this tower – this place where they had for the first time found belonging – treasured and loved them when they were alive and useful but didn't, in fact, care about them at all. That they were, in the end, only vessels for the languages they spoke.

No one said that out loud. It came too close to breaking the spell.

Of them all, Robin had assumed Victoire would be most devastated. She and Anthony had grown quite close over the years; they were two of only a handful of Black scholars in the tower, and they were both born in the West Indies. Occasionally he'd seen them talking, heads bent together, as they walked from the tower to the Buttery.

But he never once saw her cry that winter. He wanted to comfort her, but he did not know how, especially as it seemed impossible to broach the topic with her. Whenever Anthony was brought up, she flinched, blinked rapidly, and then tried very hard to change the subject.

'Did you know Anthony was a slave?' Letty asked one night in hall. Unlike Victoire, she was determined to raise the issue at every opportunity; indeed, she was obsessed with Anthony's death in a way that felt uncomfortably, performatively righteous. 'Or would have been. His master didn't want him freed when abolition took effect, so he was going to take him to America, and he only got to stay at Oxford because Babel paid for his freedom. *Paid*. Can you believe it?'

Robin glanced to Victoire, but her face had not changed one bit.

'Letty,' she said very calmly, 'I am trying to eat.'

Chapter Twelve

'In a word, I was too cowardly to do what I knew to be right, as I had been too cowardly to avoid doing what I knew to be wrong.'

CHARLES DICKENS, *Great Expectations*

They were well into Hilary term before Griffin resurfaced. So many months had passed by then that Robin had stopped checking his window with his usual rigour, and he would have missed the note if he had not spotted a magpie trying in vain to retrieve it from under the pane.

The note instructed Robin to show up at the Twisted Root at half past two the next day, but Griffin was nearly an hour late. When he did arrive, Robin was astounded by his haggard appearance. The sheer act of walking through the pub seemed to exhaust him; by the time he sat down, he was breathing as hard as if he'd just run the length of Parks. He'd clearly not had a change of clothes in days; his smell wafted, attracting glares. He moved with a slight limp, and Robin glimpsed bandages under his shirt every time he raised his arm.

Robin was not sure what to do with this. He'd had a rant prepared for this meeting, but the words died at the sight of his brother's obvious misery. Instead, he sat silently as Griffin ordered shepherd's pie and two glasses of ale.

'Term going all right?' Griffin asked.

'It's fine,' said Robin. 'I'm, uh, working on an independent project now.'

'With whom?'

Robin scratched at his shirt collar. He felt stupid bringing it up at all. 'Chakravarti.'

'That's nice.' The ale arrived. Griffin drained his glass, set it down, and winced. 'That's lovely.'

'The rest of my cohort's not too happy with their assignments, though.'

'Of course they aren't.' Griffin snorted. 'Babel's never going to let you do the research you ought to be doing. Only the research that fills the coffers.'

A long silence passed. Robin felt vaguely guilty, though he had no good reason to be; still, a worm of discomfort ate further into his gut with every passing second. Food came. The plate was steaming hot, but Griffin wolfed his down like a man starved. And he just might have been, too; when he bent over his place, his collarbones protruded in a way that hurt to look at.

'Say . . . ' Robin cleared his throat, unsure how to ask. 'Griffin, is everything—'

'Sorry.' Griffin put his fork down. 'I'm just – I only got back to Oxford last night, and I'm exhausted.'

Robin sighed. 'Sure.'

'Anyhow, here's a list of texts I need from the library.' Griffin reached into his front pocket and pulled out a crumpled note. 'You might have some trouble finding the Arabic volumes – I've transliterated the titles for you, which will get you to the right shelf, but then you'll have to identify them on your own. But they're in the Bodleian, not the tower, so you won't have to worry about someone wondering what you're up to.'

Robin took the note. 'That's it?'

'That's it.'

'*Really?*' Robin couldn't suppress it anymore. He expected callousness from Griffin, but not this blank pretence of ignorance. His sympathy evaporated, along with his patience; now the resentment, which he'd kept simmering for a year, rushed to the fore. 'You're sure?'

Griffin cast him a wary look. 'What's the matter?'

'We're not going to talk about last time?' Robin demanded.

'Last time?'

'When the alarm went off. We sprang a trap, we sprang a *gun*—'

'You were fine.'

'I was *shot*,' Robin hissed. 'What happened? Someone messed up, and

I know it wasn't me, because I was right where I was supposed to be, meaning you were wrong about the alarms—'

'These things happen.' Griffin shrugged. 'The good thing is that no one got caught—'

'I was *shot* in the *arm*.'

'So I heard.' Griffin peered over the table, as if he could see Robin's wound through his shirt sleeve. 'You seem quite all right, though.'

'I had to stitch myself together—'

'Well done, you. Smarter than going to the college nurse. You didn't, did you?'

'What is *wrong* with you?'

'Keep your voice down,' said Griffin.

'Keep my—'

'I don't see why we're labouring the point. I made a mistake, you got away, it won't happen again. We're going to stop sending people in with you. Instead you'll drop off the contraband outside on your own—'

'That's not the point,' Robin hissed once more. 'You let me get hurt. Then you left me out in the cold.'

'Please don't be so dramatic.' Griffin sighed. 'Accidents happen. And you're fine.' He paused, considering, and then said more quietly, 'Look, if this will make you feel better, there's a safe house on St Aldate's we use when we need to hide out for a bit. There's a basement door by the church – it looks rusted shut, but you've only got to look for where the bar's installed and say the words. It leads to a tunnel end that got overlooked when they did the renovations—'

Robin shook his arm at Griffin. 'A safe house doesn't fix this.'

'We'll be better next time,' Griffin insisted. 'That was a slip-up, that was my fault, we're adjusting for it. So calm down before someone overhears.' He settled back in his chair. 'Now. I've been out of town for months, so I need to hear what's been going on at the tower, and I'd like you to be efficient about it, please.'

Robin could have hit him then. He would have, if it would not have attracted stares, if Griffin were not so clearly already in pain.

He was getting nothing out of his brother, he knew. Griffin, like Professor Lovell, could be astonishingly single-minded; if something did not suit them, they simply failed to acknowledge it, and indeed any

attempt to procure acknowledgment would only end in more frustration. He had the fleeting impulse simply to stand up and walk away, if
only to see Griffin's expression. But that would grant no lasting satisfaction. If he turned back around, Griffin would mock him; if he kept
walking out, he would only have severed his own ties to Hermes. So he
did what he did best, with father and brother both – he swallowed his
frustrations and resigned himself to letting Griffin set the terms of the
conversation.

'Not much,' he said after a calming breath. 'The professors haven't
been travelling abroad recently, and I don't think the wards have changed
since last time either. Oh – something terrible happened. A graduate
fellow – Anthony Ribben—'

'Sure, I know Anthony,' Griffin said, then cleared his throat. 'Knew,
I mean. Same cohort.'

'So you've heard?' Robin asked.

'Heard what?'

'That he's dead.'

'What? No.' Griffin's voice was oddly flat. 'No, I just meant – I knew
him before I left. He's dead?'

'Lost at sea sailing back from the West Indies, apparently,' said Robin.

'Terrible,' Griffin said blandly. 'Just awful.'

'That's all?' Robin asked.

'What do you want me to say?'

'He was your classmate!'

'I hate to tell you, but these incidents aren't uncommon. Voyages are
dangerous. Someone goes missing every few years.'

'But it's just . . . it feels wrong. That they won't even give him a memorial. They're just carrying on like it never happened. It's . . .' Robin trailed
off. Suddenly he wanted to cry. He felt foolish for bringing this up. He
didn't know what he had wanted – some kind of validation, perhaps, that
Anthony's life had mattered and that he could not be so easily forgotten.
But Griffin, he should have known, was the worst person from whom
to seek comfort.

Griffin was silent for a long time. He stared out of the window, brows
furrowed in concentration as if he were pondering something. He didn't
seem to be listening to Robin at all. Then he cocked his head, opened
his mouth, closed it, then opened it again. 'You know, that's not a surprise. The way Babel treats its students, particularly those they recruit

from abroad. You're an asset to them, but that's all you are. A translation machine. And once you fail them, you're out.'

'But he didn't fail, he *died*.'

'Same thing.' Griffin stood up and grabbed his coat. 'Anyhow. I want those texts within the week; I'll leave you instructions on where to drop them.'

'We're done?' Robin asked, startled. He felt a fresh wave of disappointment. He didn't know what he wanted from Griffin, or indeed if Griffin was capable of giving it, but still he'd hoped for more than this.

'I've places to be,' Griffin said without turning round. He was already on his way out. 'Watch your window.'

It was, by every measure, a very bad year.

Something had poisoned Oxford, had sucked out everything about the university that gave Robin joy. The nights felt colder, the rains heavier. The tower no longer felt like a paradise but a prison. Coursework was torture. He and his friends took no pleasure in their studies; they felt neither the thrilling discovery of their first year nor the satisfaction of actually working with silver that might one day come with their fourth.

The older cohorts assured them that this always happened, that the third-year slump was normal and inevitable. But that year seemed a markedly bad year in several other respects. For one, the number of assaults on the tower rose alarmingly. Before, Babel could expect two to three attempted break-ins per year, all of which were the subject of great spectacle as the students crowded around the doors to see what cruel effect Playfair's wards had wrought that time. But by February of that year, the attempted thefts started happening nearly every week, and the students began to grow sick of the sight of policemen dragging maimed perpetrators down the cobblestones.

They weren't only targeted by thieves. The base of the tower was constantly being defiled, usually with urine, broken bottles, and spilt booze. Twice they discovered graffiti painted overnight in large, crooked scarlet letters. TONGUES OF SATAN read the one on the back wall; DEVIL'S SILVER read the one beneath the first-floor window.

Another morning, Robin and his cohort arrived to find dozens of townsmen assembled on the green, shouting viciously at the scholars going in and out of the front door. They approached cautiously. The crowd was a bit frightening, but not so dense that they couldn't weave their way through. Perhaps it said something that they were willing to risk a mob rather than miss class, but it really looked like they might get by without harassment until a large man stepped in front of Victoire and began snarling something in a rough and incomprehensible northern accent.

'I don't know you,' Victoire gasped. 'I don't know what you're—'

'Christ!' Ramy lurched forward like he'd been shot. Victoire yelped. Robin's heart stopped. But it was only an egg, he saw; it was aimed at Victoire, and Ramy had lurched because he'd stepped forward to protect her. Victoire flinched back, arms shielding her face; Ramy put an arm around her shoulder and ushered her up the front steps.

'What is wrong with you?' Letty screamed.

The man who'd thrown the egg shouted something unintelligible in return. Hastily Robin clenched Letty's hand and dragged her through the door behind Ramy and Victoire.

'Are you all right?' he asked.

Victoire was trembling so hard she could barely speak. 'Fine, I'm fine – oh, Ramy, let me, I've got a handkerchief...'

'Don't worry.' Ramy shrugged off his jacket. 'It's a lost cause, I'll buy a new one.'

Inside the lobby, students and clients alike were clustered at the wall, watching the crowd through the windows. Robin's first instinct was to wonder if this was the work of Hermes. But it couldn't be – Griffin's thefts were so meticulously planned; they belied a far more sophisticated apparatus than this furious mob.

'Do you know what's going on?' Robin asked Cathy O'Nell.

'They're mill workers, I think,' said Cathy. 'I heard Babel's just signed a contract with mill owners north of here and that's put all these people out of work.'

'All these people?' Ramy asked. 'With just some silver bars?'

'Oh, they've laid off several hundred workers,' said Vimal, who'd over-heard. 'Supposedly it's a brilliant match-pair, something Professor Play-fair came up with, and it's netted us enough to fund renovations for the entire east wing of the lobby. Which doesn't surprise me, if it can do the work of all those men combined.'

'But it's quite sad, isn't it?' mused Cathy. 'I wonder what they'll do now.'

'What do you mean?' asked Robin.

Cathy gestured to the window. 'Well, how are they going to provide for their families?'

It shamed Robin that he hadn't even considered this.

Upstairs in their Etymology class, Professor Lovell expressed a decidedly more cruel opinion. 'Don't worry about them. Just the usual riffraff. Drunkards, malcontents from up north, lowlifes with no better way to express their opinions than shouting about them on the street. I'd prefer they wrote a letter, of course, but I doubt half of them can read.'

'Is it true they're out of work?' asked Victoire.

'Well, of course. The sort of labour they do is redundant now. It should have been made redundant long ago; there's simply no reason that weaving, spinning, carding, or roving hasn't all been mechanized already. This is simply human progress.'

'They seem rather cross about it,' Ramy observed.

'Oh, they're furious for sure,' said Professor Lovell. 'You can imagine why. What has silver-working done for this country over the past decade? Increased agricultural and industrial productivity to an unimaginable extent. It's made factories so efficient they can run with a quarter of their workers. Take the textile industry – Kay's flying shuttle, Arkwright's water frame, Crompton's spinning mule, and Cartwright's loom were all made possible with silver-working. Silver-working has catapulted Britain ahead of every other nation, and put thousands of labourers out of work in the process. So instead of using their wits to learn a skill that might actually be useful, they've decided to whine about it on our front steps. Those protests outside aren't anything new, you know. There's a sickness in this country.' Professor Lovell spoke now with a sudden, nasty vehemence. 'It started with the Luddites – some idiot workers in Nottingham who thought they'd rather smash machinery than adapt to progress – and it's spread across England since. There are people all over the country who'd rather see us dead. It's not just Babel that gets attacked like this; no, we don't even see the worst of it, since our security's better than most. Up north, those men are pulling off arson, they're stoning building owners, they're throwing acid on factory managers. They can't seem to stop smashing looms in Lancashire. No, this isn't the first time our faculty have received death threats, it's only the first time they've dared to come as far south as Oxford.'

'Do you get death threats?' Letty asked, alarmed.

'Of course. I get more and more every year.'

'But doesn't it bother you?'

Professor Lovell scoffed. 'Never. I look at those men, and I think of the vast differences between us. I am where I am because I believe in knowledge and scientific progress, and I have used them to my advantage. They are where they are because they have stubbornly refused to move forward with the future. Men like that don't scare me. Men like that make me laugh.'

'Is it going to be like this all year?' Victoire asked in a small voice. 'Out on the green, I mean.'

'Not for long,' Professor Lovell assured her. 'No, they'll have cleared off by this evening. Those men have no persistence. They'll be gone by sunset once they get hungry, or once they wander off in search of a drink. And if they don't, the wards and the police will move them on.'

But Professor Lovell was wrong. This wasn't the work of an isolated handful of discontents, nor did they simply dissipate overnight. The police did clear the crowd away that morning, but they returned in smaller numbers; several times a week, a dozen or so men showed up to harass scholars on their way into the tower. One morning, the entire building had to be evacuated when a package making a ticking noise was delivered to Professor Playfair's office. It turned out to be a clock connected to an explosive. Fortunately, rain had soaked through the package, eroding the fuse.

'But what happens when it doesn't rain?' Ramy asked.

No one had a good answer to that.

Security at the tower doubled overnight. The post was now received and sorted by newly hired clerks at a processing centre halfway across Oxford. A rotating team of policemen guarded the tower entrance at all hours. Professor Playfair installed a new set of silver bars over the front door, though as usual he refused to reveal what match-pairs he'd inscribed them with, or what they would do when triggered.

These protests were not the symptoms of a minor disturbance. Something was happening throughout England, a set of changes the consequences of which they were only beginning to fathom. Oxford, which consistently ran about a century behind the rest of England's major cities, could only pretend to be immune to change for so long. The vicissitudes of the world outside had now become impossible to ignore. This was about more than mill workers. Reform, unrest, and inequality were the keywords of the decade. The full impact of a so-called silver industrial revolution, a term coined by Peter Gaskell just six years before, was just beginning to be felt across the country. Silver-powered machines of the kind William Blake dubbed 'dark Satanic Mills' were rapidly replacing artisanal labour, but rather than bringing prosperity to all, they had instead created an economic recession, had caused a widening gap between the rich and poor that would soon become the stuff of novels by Disraeli and Dickens. Rural agriculture was in decline; men, women, and children moved en masse to urban centres to work in factories, where they laboured unimaginably long hours and lost limbs and lives in frightful accidents. The New Poor Law of 1834, which had been designed to reduce the costs of poverty relief more than anything else, was fundamentally cruel and punitive in design; it withheld financial aid unless applicants moved into a workhouse, and those workhouses were designed to be so miserable no one would want to live in them. Professor Lovell's promised future of progress and enlightenment seemed only to have wrought poverty and suffering; the new jobs he thought the displaced workers should take up never materialized. Truly, the only ones who seemed to profit from the silver industrial revolution were those who were already rich, and the select few others who were cunning or lucky enough to make themselves so.

These currents were unsustainable. The gears of history were turning fast in England. The world was getting smaller, more mechanized, and more unequal, and it was as yet unclear where things would end up, or what that would mean for Babel, or for the Empire itself.

Robin and his cohort, though, did what scholars always did, which was to bend their heads over their books and focus solely on their research. The protestors eventually dispersed after troops sent in from London dragged the ringleaders off to Newgate. The scholars stopped holding their breath every time they ascended the steps to the tower. They learned to put up with the swarming police presence, along with the fact that now it took twice as long for new books and correspondence to arrive. They stopped reading the editorials in the *Oxford Chronicle*, which was a newly minted proreform, pro-Radical publication that seemed intent on destroying their reputation.

Still, they couldn't quite ignore the headlines, hawked from every
street corner on their way to the tower:

BABEL A THREAT TO THE NATIONAL ECONOMY?
FOREIGN BARS SEND DOZENS TO THE WORKHOUSE
SAY NO TO SILVER!

It should have been distressing. In truth, though, Robin found it was
actually quite easy to put up with any degree of social unrest, as long as
one got used to looking away.

One stormy night, on his way to dinner at Professor Lovell's home,
Robin glimpsed a family sitting at the corner of Woodstock Road
holding out tin mugs for alms. Beggars were a common sight in Oxford's
outskirts, but entire families were rare. The two small children gave him
little waves as he approached, and the sight of their pale, rain-streaked
faces made him feel guilty enough to stop and fish several pennies out
of his pocket.

'Thank you,' murmured the father. 'God bless you.'

The man's beard had grown out, and his clothes had got a good deal
tattier, but Robin still recognized him – he was, without question, one of
the men who had screamed obscenities at him on his way into the tower
several weeks ago. He met Robin's eyes. It wasn't clear if he recognized
Robin as well; he opened his mouth to say something, but Robin quickened his pace, and whatever the man might have called after him was
soon drowned out by the wind and the rain.

He didn't mention the family to Mrs Piper or Professor Lovell. He
didn't want to dwell on all the things they represented – the fact that
for all of his professed allegiance to revolution, for his commitment to
equality and to helping those who were without, he had no experience
of true poverty at all. He'd seen hard times in Canton, but he had never
not known where his next meal might come from or where he would
sleep at night. He had never looked at his family and wondered what
it might take to keep them alive. For all his identification with the
poor orphan Oliver Twist, for all his bitter self-pity, the fact remained
that since the day he had set foot in England, he had not once gone to
sleep hungry.

That night he ate his dinner, smiled at Mrs Piper's compliments, and
shared a bottle of wine with Professor Lovell. He walked a different

route back to the college. The next month, he forgot to take the same detour on his way up, but it didn't matter – by then, the little family was already gone.

Looming exams made a bad year awful. Babel scholars underwent two rounds of exams – one at the end of their third year, and another during their fourth. These were staggered throughout the calendar; the fourth years sat their exams in the middle of Hilary term, while the third years had until Trinity term. The effect was that starting after the winter holidays, the mood in the tower was utterly changed. The libraries and study rooms were packed during all hours by nervous fourth years who flinched whenever someone breathed and looked ready to murder whenever someone dared to so much as whisper.

Traditionally, Babel publicly announced the fourth years' marks at the end of the examination period. At noon on Friday of that week, a bell rang three times throughout the tower. Everyone stood and hurried downstairs to the lobby, where that afternoon's clients were being ushered out the door. Professor Playfair stood on a table at the centre of the room. He was dressed in an ornate gown with purple edges, holding aloft the kind of curling scroll that Robin had only ever seen in medieval illuminations. Once the tower had been cleared of everyone not affiliated with the faculty, he cleared his throat and intoned, 'The following degree candidates have passed their qualifying exams with distinction. Matthew Houndslow—'

Someone in the back corner let out a loud shriek.

'Adam Moorhead.'

A student near the front sat plumb down on the floor in the middle of the lobby, both hands clasped over his mouth.

'This is inhumane,' Ramy whispered.

'Most cruel and unusual,' Robin agreed. But he couldn't take his eye off the proceedings. He wasn't up for examination yet, but it was so much closer now, and his heart was pounding hard with vicarious terror. As horrific as this was, it was also still exciting, this public declaration of who had proven themselves brilliant and who hadn't.

Only Matthew and Adam had won distinction. Professor Playfair announced a merit (James Fairfield) and a pass (Luke McCaffrey), then said in a very sombre voice, 'The following candidate failed their qualifying exams, and will not be asked to return to the Royal Institute of

Translation for a postgraduate fellowship, nor will they be awarded a degree. Philip Wright.'

Wright was the French and German specialist who had sat beside Robin at the faculty dinner during his first year. Over the years, he had grown thin and haggard-looking. He was one of the students who constantly lurked around at the library looking as if he hadn't bathed or shaved in days, staring at the stack of papers before him with a mixture of panic and bewilderment.

'You've been offered every lenience,' Professor Playfair said. 'You've been granted more accommodations than was good for you, I think. Now it's time to acknowledge this is the end of your time here, Mr Wright.'

Wright made as if to approach Professor Playfair, but two graduate fellows seized him by the arms and pulled him back. He began to beg, babbling about how his exam response had been misinterpreted, how he could clarify everything if only he got another chance. Professor Playfair stood placidly with his hands held behind his back, pretending not to listen.

'What happened?' Robin asked Vimal.

'Gave a folk etymology instead of a real one.' Vimal shook his head dramatically. 'Tried to link canards to canaries, you see, except canaries aren't related to canard ducks – they're from the Canary Islands, which are named after dogs—'

The rest of his explanation eluded Robin.

Professor Playfair pulled a glass vial out of his inner pocket – the vial, Robin assumed, that contained Wright's blood. He placed it on the table and stomped down. Glass shards and brown flecks scattered across the floor. Wright began howling. It wasn't clear what the breaking of the vial had actually done to him – all four limbs seemed intact, as far as Robin could tell, and there was no fresh blood – but Wright collapsed to the floor, clutching his midriff as if he'd been impaled.

'Horrific,' said Letty, awed.

'Positively medieval,' Victoire agreed.

They had never witnessed a failure before. They could not tear their eyes away.

It took a third graduate fellow to pull Wright to his feet, drag him to the front door, and fling him unceremoniously down the steps. Everyone else watched, mouths hanging open. Such a grotesque ceremony seemed unbefitting of a modern academic institution. Yet this was utterly appropriate. Oxford, and Babel by extension, were, at their roots, ancient religious institutions, and for all their contemporary sophistication, the rituals that comprised university life were still based in medieval mysticism. Oxford was Anglicanism was Christianity, which meant blood, flesh, and dirt.*

The door slammed shut. Professor Playfair dusted off his gown, hopped down from the table, and turned around to face the rest of them.

'Well, that's taken care of.' He beamed. 'Happy exams. Congratulations all.'

Two days later Griffin asked Robin to meet him at a tavern in Iffley, nearly an hour's walk from the college. It was a dim, noisy place. It took Robin a moment to find his brother, who was sitting slouched near the back. Whatever he'd been up to since their last meeting, he apparently hadn't been eating; he had two steaming shepherd's pies before him and was wolfing one down with no fear of scalding his tongue.

'What is this place?' Robin asked.

'I get supper here sometimes,' said Griffin. 'The food's awful but there's a lot of it, and importantly, nobody from the university ever comes out here. It's too close to the – what did Playfair call them? The locals.'

He looked worse than he'd been all term – visibly exhausted, hollow-cheeked, and whittled down to a sharp, lean core. He gave off the air of a shipwreck survivor, of someone who'd travelled long distances and barely made it out alive – though of course he wouldn't tell Robin where he'd been. His black coat, hanging off the chair behind him, reeked.

'Are you all right?' Robin pointed to Griffin's left arm. It was wrapped in bandages, but whatever wound lay beneath was clearly still open, because the dark stain over his forearm had spread visibly since Robin had sat down.

---

* And even this exam ritual was rather tame compared to the way things were done in the late eighteenth century. Back then fourth years were subject to what was called the 'door test', in which recent examinees lined up to walk through the entrance the morning after grading finished. Those who had passed would step through the door with no trouble; those who had failed would be treated by the tower as trespassers, and suffer whatever violent punishment the current wards were designed to inflict. This practice was finally abolished on the grounds that maiming was not proportionate punishment for academic underperformance, but Professor Playfair still lobbied annually to bring it back.

'Oh.' Griffin glanced at his arm. 'That's nothing, it's just taking forever to close up.'

'So it's something.'

'Bah.'

'It looks bad.' Robin chuckled, and what came next sounded more bitter than he'd intended. 'You should suture it. Brandy helps.'

'Ha. No, we've got someone. I'll have it looked at later.' Griffin pulled his sleeve over the bandages. 'Anyhow. I need you ready next week. It's very touch-and-go, so I don't yet have a good idea of the time or day, but it's a big one – they're expecting a massive shipment of silver in from Magniac & Smith, and we'd love to get a crate during the unloading. It'll take a large distraction, of course. I might need to store some explosives in your room for quick access—'

Robin recoiled. 'Explosives?'

'I forgot you scare easily.' Griffin waved a hand. 'It's all right, I'll show you how to set them off before the day, and if you plan it well enough then no one will get hurt—'

'No,' said Robin. 'No, that's it, I'm done – this is absurd, I'm not doing this.'

Griffin arched a brow. 'Where's all this coming from?'

'I've just seen someone expelled—'

'Oh.' Griffin laughed. 'Who was it this year?'

'Wright,' said Robin. 'They crushed a vial of his blood. They threw him out of the tower, locked him out, cut him off from everything and everyone—'

'But that won't happen to you; you're too brilliant. Or am I keeping you from your revision?'

'Opening doors is one thing,' said Robin. 'Setting explosives is quite another.'

'It'll be fine, just trust me—'

'But I don't,' Robin blurted. His heart beat very quickly, but it was too late now to hold his silence. He had to say it all at once; he couldn't keep biting down on his words forever. 'I *don't* trust you. You're getting messy.'

Griffin's brows shot up. 'Messy?'

'You don't show up for weeks, and when you do you're late half the time; your instructions are all scratched out and revised so many times that it takes skill, really, to decipher what they say. Babel's security has nearly tripled, but you don't seem interested in working out how to deal with it. And you still haven't explained what happened last time, or what your new workaround for the wards is. I was shot in the arm and you don't seem to care—'

'I said I'm sorry about that,' Griffin said wearily. 'Won't happen again.'

'But why should I believe you?'

'Because this one's important.' Griffin leaned forward. 'This could change everything, could shift the balance—'

'Tell me how, then. Tell me more. This doesn't work when you always keep me in the dark.'

'Look, I told you about St Aldate's, didn't I?' Griffin looked frustrated. 'You know I can't say more. You're still too new, you don't understand the risks—'

'The *risks*? I'm the one taking risks, I'm putting my entire future on the line—'

'Funny,' said Griffin. 'And here I thought the Hermes Society was your future.'

'You know what I mean.'

'Yes, it's quite clear.' Griffin's lip curled. He looked very much like their father just then. 'You have such a great fear of freedom, brother. It's shackling you. You've identified so hard with the colonizer, you think any threat to them is a threat to you. When are you going to realize you can't be one of them?'

'Stop deflecting,' said Robin. 'You always deflect. When I say my future, I don't mean a cushy post. I mean *survival*. So tell me why this matters. Why now? Why this one?'

'Robin—'

'You are asking me to put my life on the line for the invisible,' Robin snapped. 'And I'm just asking you to give me a reason.'

Griffin was silent for a moment. He glanced round the room, tapping his fingers against the table, and then said in a very low voice, 'Afghanistan.'

'What's going on in Afghanistan?'

'Don't you read the news? The British are going to pull Afghanistan into their sphere of influence. But there are plans in motion to make sure that doesn't happen – and that I really can't tell you about, brother—'

But Robin was laughing. 'Afghanistan? Really?'

'Is this funny?' asked Griffin.

'You're all talk,' Robin said, amazed. Something in his mind shattered then – the illusion that he ought to admire Griffin, that Hermes mattered at all. 'It makes you feel important, doesn't it? Acting like you've got some leverage over the world? I've seen the men who really pull the levers, and they're nothing like you. They don't have to scramble for power. They don't organize silly midnight heists and put their kid brothers in jeopardy in some wild attempt to obtain it. They've already got it.'

Griffin's eyes narrowed. 'What does that mean?'

'What do you *do*?' Robin demanded. 'Really, Griffin, what on earth have you ever done? The Empire's still standing. Babel's still there. The sun rises, and Britain's still got her claws everywhere in the world, and silver keeps flowing in without end. None of this matters.'

'Tell me you don't really think that.'

'No, I just—' Robin felt a sharp twinge of guilt. He'd spoken too harshly perhaps, but his point, he thought, was fair. 'I just can't see what any of this achieves. And you're asking me to give up so much in return. I want to help you, Griffin. But I also want to survive.'

Griffin did not respond for a long while. Robin sat watching him, growing increasingly uncomfortable as he calmly finished the last of his shepherd's pie. Then he set down his fork and meticulously wiped his mouth with a napkin.

'You know the funny thing about Afghanistan?' Griffin's voice was very soft. 'The British aren't going to invade with English troops. They're going to invade with troops from Bengal and Bombay. They're going to have sepoys fight the Afghans, just like they had sepoys fight and die for them at Irrawaddy, because those Indian troops have the same logic you do, which is that it's better to be a servant of the Empire, brutal coercion and all, than to resist. Because it's safe. Because it's stable, because it lets them survive. And that's how they win, brother. They pit us against each other. They tear us apart.'

'I'm not out for good,' Robin said hastily. 'I just – I mean, just until this year is over, or until things have blown over—'

'That's not how this works,' said Griffin. 'You're in or you're not. Afghanistan isn't waiting.'

Robin drew in a shaky breath. 'Then I'm out.'

'Very well.' Griffin dropped his napkin and stood up. 'Only keep your mouth shut, will you? Otherwise I'll have to come and tie up loose ends, and I don't like to be messy.'

'I won't tell a soul. You have my word—'

'I don't really care about your word,' said Griffin. 'But I do know where you sleep.'

There was nothing Robin could say to that. He knew Griffin was not bluffing, but also that if Griffin really did not trust him, he would not make it back to the college alive. They watched each other for a long time, unspeaking.

At last, Griffin shook his head and said, 'You're lost, brother. You're a ship adrift, searching for familiar shores. I understand what it is you want. I sought it too. But there is no homeland. It's gone.' He paused beside Robin on his way to the door. His fingers landed on Robin's shoulder, squeezed so hard they hurt. 'But realize this, brother. You fly no one's flag. You're free to seek your own harbour. And you can do so much more than tread water.'

BOOK III

ROYAL INSTITUTE OF TRANSLATION

UNIVERSITY OF OXFORD

BOOK III

CHAPTER THIRTEEN

Mountains will be in labour, the birth will be a single laughable little mouse.

HORACE, *Ars Poetica*, trans. E.C. Wickham

Griffin made good on his word. He never left another note for Robin. At first, Robin was sure Griffin would merely take some time to sulk before pestering him again for smaller, more routine errands. But a week became a month, which became a term. He'd expected Griffin to be a bit more vindictive – to leave a recriminating farewell letter, at least. For the first few days after their falling-out, he flinched every time a stranger glanced his way on the street, convinced that the Hermes Society had decided it best to tie up this loose end.

But Griffin had cut him out entirely.

He tried not to let his conscience bother him. Hermes was not going anywhere. There would always be battles to fight. They would all be there waiting when Robin was ready to rejoin them, he was sure. And he could do nothing for Hermes if he did not remain firmly ensconced within Babel's ecosystem. Griffin had said it himself – they needed people on the inside. Wasn't that reason enough to stay right where he was?

Meanwhile, there were third-year exams. End-of-year exams were quite a matter of ceremony at Oxford. Up until the last years of the previous century, viva voce exams – oral questioning ordeals made public for crowds of spectators to witness – had been the norm, although by the early 1830s the regular BA degree required only five written examinations and one viva voce exam, on the grounds that oral responses were too difficult to assess objectively and were unnecessarily cruel besides. By 1836, spectators were no longer allowed at the vivas either, and the townspeople lost a great source of annual entertainment.

Instead, Robin's cohort was told to expect a three-hour essay exam in each of their research languages; a three-hour essay exam in Etymology; a viva voce exam in Translation Theory, and a silver-working test. They could not stay on at Babel if they failed any of their language or theory exams, and if they failed the silver-working test, they could not, in the future, work on the eighth floor.*

The viva voce would be done in front of a panel of three professors led by Professor Playfair, who was a notoriously tough examiner, and who was rumoured to make at least two students dissolve into tears every year. '*Balderdash*,' he would drawl slowly, 'is a word which used to refer to the cursed concoction created by bartenders when they'd nearly run out of every drink at the end of the night. Ale, wine, cider, milk – they'd dump it all in and hope their patrons wouldn't mind, since after all the goal was simply to get drunk. But this is Oxford University, not the Turf Tavern after midnight, and we are in need of something slightly more illuminating than getting sloshed. Would you like to try again?'

Time, which had felt infinite during their first and second years, now ran quickly down the hourglass. No longer could they put off their readings to have a lark on the river under the assumption there was always the opportunity later to catch up. Exams were in five weeks, then four, then three. When Trinity term drew to an end, the last day of class should have culminated in a golden afternoon, in desserts and elderflower cordial and punting on the Cherwell. But the moment the bells rang at four, they packed up their books and walked straight from Professor Craft's classroom to one of the study rooms on the fifth floor, where they would wall themselves in, every day for the next thirteen days, to pore over dictionaries and translated passages and vocabulary lists until their temples throbbed.

---

* Though many Babel graduates were happy to work in Literature or Legal, the silver-working exam had higher stakes for scholars of foreign origin, who found it difficult to find prestigious postings in departments other than the eighth floor, where their fluency in non-European languages was most valuable. Griffin, upon failing his silver-working test, had been offered a continuation track in Legal. But Professor Lovell had always expressed the belief that nothing except silver-working mattered, and that every other department was for unimaginative, untalented fools. Poor Griffin, who had been raised under his contemptuous and exacting roof, agreed.

Acting from generosity, or perhaps sadism, the Babel faculty made available a set of silver bars for examinees to use as study aids. These bars were engraved with a match-pair using the English word *meticulous* and its Latin forerunner *metus*, meaning 'fear, dread'. The modern usage of *meticulous* had arisen just a few decades before in France, with the connotation of being fearful of making a mistake. The effect of the bars was to induce a chilling anxiety whenever the user erred in their work.

Ramy hated and refused to use them. 'It doesn't tell you where you went wrong,' he complained. 'It just makes you want to vomit for no reason you can discern.'

'Well, you could do with more caution,' Letty grumbled, returning his marked-up composition. 'You've made at least twelve errors on this page, and your sentences are far too long—'

'They're not too long; they're Ciceronian.'

'You can't just excuse all bad writing on the grounds that it's *Ciceronian*—'

Ramy waved a hand dismissively. 'That's fine, Letty, I cranked that one out in ten minutes.'

'But it's not about speed. It's about precision—'

'The more I get done, the larger range I've acquired for the possible paper questions,' said Ramy. 'And that's what we've really got to prepare for. I don't want to go blank when the paper's in front of me.'

This was a valid worry. Stress had the unique ability to wipe students' minds clear of things they had been studying for years. During the fourth-year exams last year, one examinee was rumoured to have become so paranoid that he declared not only that he could not finish the exam but that he was lying about being fluent in French at all. (He was in fact a native speaker.) They all thought they were immune to this particular folly until one day, a week before exams, Letty suddenly broke down crying and declared she knew not a word of German, not a single word, that she was a fraud and her entire career at Babel had been based on pretence. None of them understood this rant until much later, for she had indeed delivered it in German.

Failure of memory was only the first symptom to come. Never had Robin's anxiety over his marks made him so physically ill. First came a persistent, throbbing headache, and then the constant urge to throw up every time he stood or moved. Waves of tremors kept coming over him with no warning; often his hand shook so hard that he had difficulty gripping his pen. Once, during a practice paper, he found his vision blacking out; he couldn't think, couldn't remember a single word, couldn't even see. It took him nearly ten minutes to recover. He couldn't make himself eat. He was somehow both exhausted all the time and unable to sleep from a surplus of nervous energy.

Then, like all good Oxford upperclassmen, he found himself losing his mind. His grip on reality, already tenuous from sustained isolation in a city of scholars, became even more fragmented. Hours of revision had interfered with his processing of signs and symbols, his belief in what was real and what was not. The abstract was factual and important; daily exigencies like porridge and eggs were suspect. Everyday dialogue became a chore; small talk was a horror, and he lost his grip on what basic salutations meant. When the porter asked him if he'd had a good one, he stood still and mute for a good thirty seconds, unable to process what was meant by 'good', or indeed, 'one'.

'Oh, same,' Ramy said cheerfully when Robin brought this up. 'It's awful. I can't have basic conversations anymore – I keep on wondering what the words really mean.'

'I'm walking into walls,' said Victoire. 'The world keeps disappearing around me, and all I can perceive are vocabulary lists.'

'It's tea leaves for me,' said Letty. 'They keep looking like glyphs, and I really did find myself trying to gloss one the other day – I'd even started copying it out on paper and everything.'

It relieved Robin to hear he wasn't the only one seeing things, because the visions worried him the most. He'd begun to hallucinate entire persons. Once when hunting through the bookshelves at Thornton's for a poetry anthology on their Latin reading list, Robin glimpsed what he thought was a familiar profile by the door. He walked closer. His eyes had not betrayed him – Anthony Ribben was paying for a paper-wrapped parcel, hale and healthy as could be.

'Anthony—' Robin blurted.

Anthony glanced up. He saw Robin. His eyes widened. Robin started forward, confused yet elated, but Anthony hastily pushed several coins at the bookseller and darted out of the shop. By the time Robin made his way out onto Magdalene Street, Anthony had disappeared from sight. Robin stared around for several seconds, then returned to the bookshop, wondering if it was possible he'd mistaken

a stranger for Anthony. But there were not many young Black men in
Oxford. Which meant either he'd been lied to about Anthony's death
– that indeed, all of Babel's faculty had done it as some elaborate hoax
– or he'd imagined the whole thing. In his current state, he found the
latter far more likely.

The exam they all dreaded most was the silver-working test. During the
last week of Trinity term, they'd been informed they'd have to devise a
unique match-pair and engrave it in front of a proctor. In their fourth
year, once they had finished their apprenticeships, they would learn proper
techniques of match-pair design, engraving, and experimentation for magnitude and duration of effect, as well as the intricacies of resonance links
and spoken manifestation. But for now, armed with just the basic principles of how match-pairs worked, they had only to achieve any effect at all.
It did not need to be perfect; indeed, first tries never were. But they had
to do something. They had to prove they possessed the undefinable stuff,
the inimitable instinct for *meaning*, that made a translator a silver-worker.

Help from postgraduates here was technically forbidden, but sweet,
kind Cathy O'Nell surreptitiously slipped Robin a faded yellow pamphlet on the basics of match-pair research one afternoon when she
caught him looking dazed and scared in the library.

'It's just in the open stacks,' she said sympathetically. 'We've all used
it; have a read through and you'll be fine.'

The pamphlet was rather dated – it was written in 1798, and employed
many archaic spellings – but did contain a number of brief, easily digest-
ible tips. The first was to stay away from religion. This one they already
knew from dozens of horror stories. It was theology that had got Oxford
interested in Oriental languages in the first place – the only reason
Hebrew, Arabic, and Syriac had initially become subjects of academic
study was the translation of religious texts. But the Holy Word, it turned
out, was both unpredictable and unforgiving on silver. There was a desk
in the north wing of the eighth floor that no one dared approach because
it still occasionally emitted smoke from an unseen source. There, it was
rumoured, some foolish graduate fellow had attempted to translate on
silver the name of God.

More helpful was the second lesson in the pamphlet, which was to
focus their research by looking for cognates. Cognates – words in different
languages that shared a common ancestor and often similar meanings as

well* – were often the best clues for fruitful match-pairs, since they were on such close branches of the etymological tree. But the difficulty with cognates was that often their meanings were so close that there was little distortion in translation, and thus little effect that the bars could manifest. There was, after all, no significant difference between the word *chocolate* in English and in Spanish. Moreover, in looking for cognates, one had to be wary of false friends – words which seemed like cognates but had utterly different origins and meanings. The English *have* did not come from the Latin *habere* ('to hold, to possess'), for example, but from the Latin *capere* ('to seek'). And the Italian *cognato* did not mean 'cognate' like one might hope, but rather 'brother-in-law'.

False friends were especially tricky when their meanings appeared related as well. The Persian word *farang*, which was used to refer to Europeans, appeared to be a cognate of the English *foreign*. But *farang* actually arose from a reference to the Franks, and morphed to encompass Western Europeans. The English *foreign*, on the other hand, originated from the Latin *fores*, meaning 'doors'. Linking *farang* and *foreign*, then, produced nothing.†

The third lesson in the pamphlet introduced a technique called daisy-chaining. This they vaguely recalled from Professor Playfair's demonstration. If the words in their binary match-pair had evolved too far apart in meaning for a translation to be plausible, one could try adding a third or even fourth language as an intermediary. If all these words were engraved in chronological order of evolution, this could guide the distortion of meaning more precisely in the way they intended. Another related technique was the identification of a second etymon: another source that may have interfered in the evolution of meaning. The French *fermer* ('to close, to lock') was for instance quite obviously based on the Latin *firmāre* ('to make hard, to strengthen') but had also been influenced by the Latin *ferrum*, meaning 'iron'. *Fermer*, *firmāre*, and *ferrum* could then, hypothetically, create an unbreakable lock.

---

* The English *night* and Spanish *noche*, for example, are both derived from the Latin *nox*.

† A trap as tricky as false friends is folk etymologies: incorrect etymologies assigned by popular belief to words that in fact had different origins. The word *handiron*, for instance, means a metal tool to support logs in a fireplace. One is tempted to assume its etymology involved the words *hand* and *iron* separately. But *handiron* is truly derived from the French *andier*, which became *andire* in English.

All these techniques sounded good in theory. They were much harder to replicate. The difficult part, after all, was coming up with a suitable match-pair in the first place. For inspiration, they took out a copy of the Current Ledger – the comprehensive list of match-pairs in use across the Empire in that year – and skimmed through it for ideas.

'Look,' said Letty, pointing at a line on the first page. 'I've figured out how they make those driverless trams run.'

'Which trams?' asked Ramy.

'Haven't you seen them running around in London?' said Letty. 'They move of their own accord, but there's no one driving them.'

'I always thought there was some internal mechanism,' said Robin. 'Like an engine, surely—'

'That's true of the larger ones,' said Letty. 'But the smaller cargo trams aren't that big. Haven't you noticed they seem to pull themselves?' She jabbed excitedly at the page. 'There are bars in the track. *Track* is related to *trecken*, from Middle Dutch, which means to pull – especially when you go through the French intermediary. And now you have two words that mean what we think of as a track, but only one of them involves a moving force. The result is the tracks pull the carts forward themselves. That's brilliant.'

'Oh, good,' said Ramy. 'We've only got to revolutionize transportation infrastructure during our exams, and we'll be set.'

They could have spent hours alone reading the ledger, which was full of endlessly interesting and astonishingly brilliant innovations. Many, Robin discovered, had been devised by Professor Lovell. One particularly ingenious pair was the translation from the Chinese character *gǔ* (古) meaning 'old or aged', and the English 'old'. The Chinese *gǔ* carried a connotation of durability and strength; indeed, the same character 古 was present in the character *gù* (固), which meant 'hard, strong, or solid'. Linking the concepts of durability and antiquity helped prevent machinery from decaying over time; in fact, the longer it was in use, the more reliable it became.

'Who's Eveline Brooke?' Ramy asked, flipping through the most recent entries near the back.

'Eveline Brooke?' Robin repeated. 'Why does that sound familiar?'

'Whoever she is, she's a genius.' Ramy pointed at a page. 'Look, she's got over twelve match-pairs in 1833 alone. Most of the graduate fellows haven't got more than five.'

'Hold on,' said Letty. 'Do you mean Evie?'

Ramy frowned. 'Evie?'

'The desk,' Letty said. 'Remember? That time Playfair snapped at me for sitting in the wrong chair? He said it was Evie's chair.'

'Suppose she's very particular,' Victoire said. 'And she doesn't like when people mess with her things.'

'But no one's moved any of her things since that morning,' said Letty. 'I've noticed. It's been months. And those books and pens are right where she left them. So either she's particular about her things to a frightening degree, or she hasn't been back at that desk at all.'

As they flipped through the ledger, another theory became more evident. Evie had been wildly prolific between the years 1833 and 1834, but by 1835, her research had dropped completely off the record. Not a single innovation in the past five years. They'd never met an Evie Brooke at any of the departmental parties or dinners; she'd given no lectures, no seminars. Whoever Eveline Brooke was, as brilliant as she'd been, she was clearly no longer at Babel.

'Hold on,' said Victoire. 'Suppose she graduated in 1833. That would have put her in the same class as Sterling Jones. And Anthony.'

And Griffin, Robin realized, though he did not say this out loud.

'Perhaps she was also lost at sea,' said Letty.

'A cursed class, then, that,' observed Ramy.

The room suddenly felt very cold.

'Suppose we get back to revising,' Victoire suggested. No one disagreed.

In the late hours of the night, when they'd been staring at their books for so long that they could no longer think straight, they made a game of conceiving implausible match-pairs that might help them pass.

Robin won one night with *jīxīn*. 'In Canton, mothers would send their sons off to the imperial exams with a breakfast of chicken hearts,' he explained. 'Because chicken hearts – *jīxīn* – sounds similar to *jìxìng*, which means memory."

'What would that do?' Ramy snorted. 'Scatter bloody chicken bits all over your paper?'

'Or make your heart the size of a chicken's,' said Victoire. 'Imagine,

---

* *Jīxīn*: 雞心; *jìxìng*: 記性.

one moment you've got a normal-size heart and the next it's smaller than a thimble, and it can't pump all the blood you need to survive, so you collapse—'

'Christ, Victoire,' said Robin. 'That's morbid.'

'No, this is easy,' said Letty. 'It's a metaphor of sacrifice – the key is the trade. The chicken's blood – the chicken's heart – is what supports your memory. So you've only got to slaughter a chicken to the gods and you'll pass.'

They stared at each other. It was very late, and none of them had got enough sleep. They were all presently suffering the peculiar madness of the very scared and very determined, the madness that made academia feel as dangerous as the battlefield.

If Letty had suggested they plunder a henhouse right then, none of them would have hesitated to follow.

The fated week came. They were as prepared as they could be. They'd been promised a fair exam as long as they did their work, and they had done their work. They were frightened, of course, but warily confident. These exams, after all, were precisely what they had been trained to do for the last two and a half years; no more and no less.

Professor Chakravarti's paper was easiest of all. Robin had to translate, unseen, a five-hundred-character-long passage in Classical Chinese that Professor Chakravarti had composed. It was a charming parable about a virtuous man who loses one goat in a mulberry field but finds another. Robin realized after the exam that he'd mistranslated *yànshǐ*, which meant 'romantic history', as the tamer 'colourful history',* which missed the tone of the passage somewhat, but hoped the ambiguities between 'sexual' and 'colourful' in English would be enough to fudge things over.

Professor Craft had written a devilishly difficult paper prompt about the fluid roles of the *interpretes* in the writings of Cicero. They were not simply interpreters, but played a number of roles such as brokers, mediators, and occasionally bribers. Robin's cohort were instructed to elaborate, then, on the use of language in this context. Robin scribbled an eight-page essay on how the term *interpretes* was, for Cicero, ultimately

---

* A reasonable mistake. The characters in *yànshǐ* are 艷史. 史, *shǐ*, means 'history'. 艷, *yàn*, can mean both 'colourful' and 'sexual, romantic'.

value neutral in comparison to Herodotus's *hermeneus*, one of whom was killed by Themistocles for using Greek on behalf of the Persians. He concluded with some comments on linguistic propriety and loyalty. He was truly unsure how he'd performed when he walked out of the examination room – his mind had resorted to the funny trick of ceasing to understand what he'd argued as soon as he dotted the last sentence, but the inky lines had looked robust, and he knew he'd at least sounded good.

Professor Lovell's paper involved two prompts. The first was a challenge to translate three pages of a children's nonsense alphabet rhyme (*'A* is for the apricot, which was eaten by a Bear') into a language of their choosing. Robin spent fifteen minutes trying to match Chinese characters ordered by their romanizations before giving up and going the easy route, which was just to do it all in Latin. The second page contained an Ancient Egyptian fable told through hieroglyphs and its accompanying English translation with the instructions to identify as best they could, with no prior knowledge of the source language, the difficulties in conveying it into the target language. Here, Robin's facility with the pictorial nature of Chinese characters helped greatly; he came up with something about ideographic power and subtle visual implications and managed to get it all down before time ran out.

The viva voce was not as bad as it could have been. Professor Playfair was as harsh as promised, but still an incorrigible showman, and Robin's anxiety dissipated as he realized how much of Playfair's loud condescension and indignation was for theatrics. 'Schlegel wrote in 1803 that the time was not so far away that German would be the speaking voice of the civilized world,' said Professor Playfair. 'Discuss.' Robin had fortunately read this piece by Schlegel in translation, and he knew Schlegel was referring to the unique and complex flexibility of German, which Robin proceeded to argue was an underestimation of other Occidental languages such as English (which Schlegel accused in that same piece of 'monosyllabic brevity') and French. This sentiment was also – Robin recalled hastily as his time ran out – the grasping argument of a German aware that the Germanic empire could offer no resistance to the increasingly dominant French, and who sought refuge instead in cultural and intellectual hegemony. This answer was neither particularly brilliant nor original, but it was correct, and Professor Playfair followed up on only a handful of technicalities before dismissing Robin from the room.

*   *   *

Their silver-working test was scheduled for the last day. They were instructed to report to the eighth floor in thirty-minute increments – Letty first at noon, then Robin, then Ramy, then Victoire at half past one.

At half past noon, Robin walked up all seven flights of the tower and stood waiting outside the windowless room at the back of the southern wing. His mouth was very dry. It was a sunny afternoon in May, but he couldn't stop the shivering in his knees.

It was simple, he told himself. Just two words – he needed only to write down two simple words, and then it would be over. No cause for panic.

But fear, was, of course, not rational. His imagination ran wild with the thousand and one things that could go wrong. He could drop the bar on the floor, he could suffer a lapse of memory the moment he walked through the door, or he could forget a brush stroke or spell the English word wrong despite practising both a hundred times. Or it could fail to work. It could simply fail to work, and he would never get a position on the eighth floor. It could all be over that quickly.

The door swung open. Letty emerged, pale-faced and shaking. Robin wanted to ask her how it had gone, but she brushed past him and hurried down the stairs.

'Robin.' Professor Chakravarti poked his head out the door. 'Come on in.'

Robin took a deep breath and stepped forward.

The room had been cleared of chairs, books, and shelves – anything valuable or breakable. Only one desk remained, in the corner, and that was bare save for a single blank silver bar and an engraving stylus.

'Well, Robin.' Professor Chakravarti clasped his hands behind his back. 'What do you have for me?'

Robin's teeth were chattering too hard for him to speak. He hadn't known how debilitatingly scared he would be. The written exams had involved their fair share of shakes and retching, but when it came down to it, when his pen hit parchment, it felt routine. It had been nothing more and nothing less than the accumulation of everything he'd practised for the past three years. This was something else entirely. He had no idea what to expect.

'It's all right, Robin,' Professor Chakravarti said gently. 'It'll work. You've just got to focus. It's nothing you won't do a hundred times in your career.'

Robin took a deep breath and exhaled. 'It's something very basic. It's – theoretically, metaphorically, I mean, it's a bit messy, and I don't think it'll work—'

'Well, why don't you walk me through the theory first and then we'll see.'

'*Míngbái*,' Robin blurted. 'Mandarin. It means – so it means, "to understand", right? But the characters are loaded with imagery. *Míng* – bright, a light, clear. And *bái* – white, like the colour. So it doesn't just mean to understand, or to realize – it has the visual component of making clear, to shine a light on.' He paused to clear his throat. He was not quite so nervous anymore – the match-pair he'd prepared did sound better when he spoke it out loud. In fact, it seemed halfway plausible. 'So – now this is the part I'm not very sure about, because I don't know what the light will be associated with. But it should be a way of making things clear, of revealing things, I think.'

Professor Chakravarti gave him an encouraging smile. 'Well, why don't we see what it does?'

Robin took the bar in trembling hands and positioned the tip of the stylus against the smooth, blank surface. It took an unexpected amount of force to make the stylus etch out a clear line. This was, somehow, calming – it made him focus on keeping the pressure steady instead of the thousand other things he could do wrong.

He finished writing.

'*Míngbái*,' he said, holding up the bar so that Professor Chakravarti could see. 明白. Then he flipped it over. 'Understand.'

Something pulsed in the silver – something alive, something forceful and bold; a gale of wind, a crashing wave; and in that fraction of a second Robin felt the source of its power, that sublime, unnameable place where meaning was created, that place which words approximated but could not, could never pin down; the place which could only be invoked, imperfectly, but even so would make its presence felt. A bright, warm sphere of light shone out of the bar and grew until it enveloped them both. Robin had not specified what sort of understanding this light would signify; he had not planned that far; yet in that moment he knew perfectly and, from the look on Professor Chakravarti's face, his supervisor did too.

He dropped the bar. It stopped glowing. It lay inert on the desk between them, a perfectly ordinary hunk of metal.

'Very good,' was all Professor Chakravarti said. 'Will you retrieve Mr Mirza?'

Letty was waiting for him outside the tower. She'd calmed significantly; the colour had returned to her cheeks, and her eyes were no longer wide with panic. She must have just dashed to the bakery up the street, for she held a crumpled paper bag in her hands.

'Lemon biscuit?' she asked as he approached.

He realized he was starving. 'Yes please, thanks.'

She passed him the bag. 'How'd it go?'

'All right. It wasn't the precise effect I wanted, but it was something.' Robin hesitated, biscuit halfway to his mouth, not wanting to celebrate nor elaborate in case she'd failed.

But she beamed at him. 'Same. I just wanted something to happen, and then it did, and oh, Robin, it was so wonderful—'

'Like rewriting the world,' he said.

'Like drawing with the hand of God,' she said. 'Like nothing I'd ever felt before.'

They grinned at each other. Robin savoured the taste of the biscuit melting in his mouth – he saw why these were Letty's favourite; they were so buttery that they dissolved instantly, and the lemony sweetness spread across his tongue like honey. They'd done it. Everything was okay; the world could keep moving; nothing else mattered, because they'd done it.

The bells rang for one o'clock, and the doors opened again. Ramy strode out, grinning widely.

'It worked for you too, eh?' He helped himself to a biscuit.

'How do you know?' asked Robin.

'Because Letty's eating,' he said, chewing. 'If either of you'd failed, she'd be pummelling these biscuits to crumbs.'

Victoire took the longest. It was nearly an hour before she emerged from the building, scowling and flustered. Immediately Ramy was at her side, one arm slung around her shoulder. 'What happened? Are you all right?'

'I gave them a Kreyòl-French match-pair,' Victoire said. 'And it worked, worked like a charm, only Professor Leblanc said they couldn't put it in the Current Ledger because he didn't see how a Kreyòl match-pair would be useful to anyone who doesn't speak Kreyòl. And then I said it'd be of great use to people in Haiti, and then he laughed.'

'Oh, dear.' Letty rubbed her shoulder. 'Did they let you try a different one?'

She'd asked the wrong question. Robin saw a flash of irritation in Victoire's eyes, but it was gone in an instant. She sighed and nodded. 'Yes, the French-English one didn't work quite so well, and I was a bit too shaken so I think my handwriting was off, but it did have some effect.'

Letty made a sympathetic noise. 'I'm sure you'll pass.'

Victoire reached for a biscuit. 'Oh, I passed.'

'How do you know?'

Victoire shot her a puzzled look. 'I asked. Professor Leblanc said I'd passed. He said we'd all passed. What, none of you knew?'

They stared at her for a moment in surprise, and then they burst out into laughter.

If only one could engrave entire memories in silver, thought Robin, to be manifested again and again for years to come – not the cruel distortion of the daguerreotype, but a pure and impossible distillation of emotions and sensations. For simple ink on paper was not enough to describe this golden afternoon; the warmth of uncomplicated friendship, all fights forgotten, all sins forgiven; the sunlight melting away the memory of the classroom chill; the sticky taste of lemon on their tongues and their startled, delighted relief.

CHAPTER FOURTEEN

All we to-night are dreaming, —
To smile and sigh, to love and change:

Oh, in our heart's recesses,
We dress in fancies quite as strange

WINTHROP MACKWORTH PRAED,
'The Fancy Ball'

A nd then they were free. Not for long – they had the summer off, and then they would repeat all the miseries they'd just endured, with twice the agony, during their fourth-year exams. But September felt so far away. It was only May, and the whole summer lay before them. It felt now as if they had all the time in the world to do nothing but be happy, if they could just remember how.

Every three years University College held a commemoration ball. These balls were the pinnacle of Oxford social life; they were a chance for colleges to show off their lovely grounds and prodigious wine cellars, for the richer colleges to flaunt their endowments, and for the poorer colleges to try to claw their way up the ladder of prestige. Balls let colleges fling all their excess wealth that they didn't, for some reason, allocate to students in need at a grand occasion for their wealthy alumni, the financial justification being that wealth attracted wealth, and there was no better way to solicit donations for hall renovations than showing the old boys a good time. And what a very good time it was. Colleges competed each year to break records for sheer indulgence and spectacle. The wine flowed all night, the music never stopped, and those who danced into the early hours could expect breakfast brought round on silver trays when the sun came up.

Letty insisted they all purchase tickets. 'It's exactly what we need. We deserve some indulgence after that nightmare. You'll come with me to London, Victoire, we'll go to be fitted for gowns—'

'Absolutely not,' said Victoire.

'Why? We have the money. And you'd look dazzling in emerald, or perhaps a white silk—'

'Those tailors are not going to dress me,' said Victoire. 'And the only way they'll let me into the shop is if I pretend to be your maid.'

Letty was shaken, but only for a moment. Robin saw her hastily rearrange her features into a forced smile. Letty was relieved to be back in Victoire's good graces, he knew, and she'd do anything to stay there. 'That's all right, you can make do with one of mine. You're a bit taller, but I can let out the hem. And I've got so much jewellery to lend you – I can write back to Brighton and see if they'll send me some of Mama's old things. She had all these lovely pins – I'd love to see what I can do with your hair—'

'I don't think you understand,' Victoire said, quietly but firmly. 'I really don't want—'

'Please, darling, it'll be no fun without you. I'll buy your ticket.'

'Oh,' said Victoire, 'please, I don't want to owe you—'

'You can buy ours,' said Ramy.

Letty rolled her eyes at him. 'Buy your own.'

'Dunno, Letty. Three pounds? That's quite pricey.'

'Work one of the silver shifts,' Letty said. 'They're only for an hour.'

'Birdie doesn't like crowded spaces,' said Ramy.

'I don't,' Robin said gamely. 'Get too nervous. Can't breathe.'

'Don't be ridiculous,' Letty scoffed. 'Balls are wonderful. You've never seen anything like it. Lincoln brought me as his date to one at Balliol – oh, the whole place was transformed. I saw stage acts that you can't even see in London. And they're only once every three years; we won't be undergraduates next time. I'd give anything to feel that way again.'

They cast each other helpless looks. The dead brother settled the conversation. Letty knew it, and was not afraid to invoke him.

So Robin and Ramy signed up to work the ball. University College had devised a labour-for-entry scheme for students too poor to afford the ticket price, and Babel students were particularly lucky here, for instead of catering drinks or taking coats, they could work what were called 'silver shifts'. This did not take much work other than periodically checking that the bars commissioned to enhance the decorations, lights, and music hadn't been removed or slipped out of their temporary installations, but the colleges did not seem to know this, and Babel had no good reason to inform them.

On the day of the ball, Robin and Ramy shoved their frock coats and waistcoats into canvas bags and walked past the ticket lines curling around the corner to the kitchen entrance at the back of the college.

University College had outdone itself. It exhausted the eye; there was too much to take in at once – oysters on enormous pyramids of ice; long tables bearing all kinds of sweet cakes, biscuits, and tarts; champagne flutes going round on precariously balanced plates; and floating fairy lights that pulsed through an array of colours. Stages had been erected overnight in every quad of the college, upon which a variety of harpists, players, and pianists performed. An opera singer, it was rumoured, had been brought in from Italy to perform in hall; every now and then, Robin thought he could hear her higher notes piercing through the din. Acrobats cavorted on the green, twisting up and down long silken sheets and spinning silver rings around their wrists and ankles. They were dressed in vaguely foreign garb. Robin scrutinized their faces, wondering where they were from. It was the oddest thing: their eyes and lips were made up in an exaggeratedly Oriental fashion, yet beneath the paint they seemed as if they could have been plucked off the streets of London.

'So much for Anglican principles,' Ramy said. 'This is a proper bacchanalia.'

'You think they'll run out of oysters?' Robin asked. He'd never tried them before; they apparently upset Professor Lovell's stomach, so Mrs Piper never bought them. The gloopy meat and shiny shells looked both disgusting and very enticing. 'I just want to know how they taste.'

'I'll go and grab one for you,' said Ramy. 'Those lights are about to slip, by the way, you should – there you go.'

Ramy disappeared into the crowd. Robin sat atop his ladder and pretended to work. Privately, he was grateful for the job. It was humiliating to wear servant's blacks while his fellow students danced around him, yes, but it was at least a gentler way to ease into the frenzy of the night. He liked being hidden safely in the corner with something to do with his hands; this way the ball was not quite so overwhelming. And he truly liked discovering what ingenious silver match-pairs Babel had provided for the ball. One, certainly devised by Professor Lovell, paired the Chinese four-word idiom 百卉千葩 with the English translation 'a hundred plants and thousand flowers'. The connotation of the Chinese original, which invoked rich, dazzling, and myriad colours, made the roses redder, the blooming violets larger and more vibrant.

'No oysters,' said Ramy. 'But I brought you some of these truffle things, I don't know what they are exactly but people kept snagging them off plates.' He passed a chocolate truffle up the ladder and popped the other one in his mouth. 'Oh – ugh. Never mind. Don't eat that.'

'I wonder what it is?' Robin held the truffle up to his eyes. 'Is this pale mushy part supposed to be cheese?'

'I shudder to think what else it could be,' said Ramy.

'You know,' said Robin, 'there's a Chinese character, *xiǎn,*[*] which can mean "rare, fresh, and tasty". But it can also mean "meagre and scanty".'

Ramy spat the truffle into a napkin. 'Your point?'

'Sometimes rare and expensive things are worse.'

'Don't tell the English that, it'll shatter their entire sense of taste.' Ramy glanced out over the crowd. 'Oh, look who's arrived.'

Letty pushed her way through the throng towards them, tugging Victoire along behind her.

'You're – goodness.' Robin hurried down the ladder. 'You're incredible.'

He meant it. Victoire and Letty were unrecognizable. He'd grown so used to seeing them in shirts and trousers that he forgot sometimes they were women at all. Tonight, he recalled, they were creatures of a different dimension. Letty wore a dress of a pale, floaty blue material that matched her eyes. Her sleeves were quite enormous – she looked as if she could have concealed an entire leg of mutton up there – but that appeared to be the fashion of the year, for colourful, billowing sleeves filled the college grounds. Letty was in fact quite pretty, Robin realized; he'd only never noticed it before – under the soft fairy lights, her arched eyebrows and her sharply angled jaw did not look cold and austere, but regal and elegant.

'How'd you get your hair like that?' Ramy demanded.

---

* 鲜.

Pale, bouncy ringlets framed Letty's face, defying gravity. 'Why, curl papers.'

'You mean witchcraft,' said Ramy. 'That's not natural.'

Letty snorted. 'You need to meet more women.'

'Where at, Oxford lecture halls?'

She laughed.

It was Victoire, however, who'd truly been transformed. She glowed against the deep emerald fabric of her gown. Her sleeves, too, ballooned outwards, but on her they seemed rather adorable, like a protective ring of clouds. Her hair was twisted into an elegant knot at the top of her head, fastened with two coral pins, and a string of the same coral beads shone like constellations around her neck. She was lovely. She knew it, too; as she took in Robin's expression a smile bloomed over her face.

'I've done a good job, haven't I?' Letty surveyed Victoire with pride. 'And to think she didn't want to come.'

'She looks like starlight,' said Robin.

Victoire blushed.

'Hello, there.' Colin Thornhill strode up to them. He seemed quite drunk; there was a dazed, unfocused look in his eyes. 'I see even Babblers have deigned to come.'

'Hello, Colin,' Robin said warily.

'Good party, isn't it? The opera girl was a little pitchy, but perhaps it was only the acoustics in the chapel – it's really not a proper performance venue, you need a bigger space so the sound doesn't get lost.' Without looking at her, Colin held his wineglass out in front of Victoire's face. 'Get rid of this and get me a burgundy, will you?'

Victoire blinked at him, astonished. 'Get your own.'

'What, aren't you working this thing?'

'She's a student,' Ramy snapped. 'You've met her before.'

'Have I?' Colin really was very drunk; he kept swaying on his feet, and his pale cheeks had turned a deep ruddy colour. The glass hung so precariously from his fingertips that Robin was afraid it would shatter. 'Well. They all look the same to me.'

'The waiters are in black, and they've got trays,' Victoire said patiently. Robin was amazed at her restraint; he would have slapped the glass from Colin's hand. 'Though I think you might try some water.'

Colin narrowed his eyes at Victoire, as if trying to see her in better detail. Robin tensed, but Colin only laughed, murmured something

under his breath that sounded like the words 'She looks like a Tregear,'*
and walked off.

'Ass,' Ramy muttered.

'Do I look like I'm serving staff?' Victoire asked anxiously. 'And what's
a Tregear?'

'Never mind,' Robin said quickly. 'Just – ignore Colin, he's an idiot.'

'And you look *ethereal*,' Letty assured her. 'We've all just got to relax,
everyone – here.' She extended her arm to Ramy. 'Your shift's done now,
isn't it? Dance with me.'

He laughed. 'Absolutely not.'

'Come on.' She seized his hands and tugged him towards the dancing
crowd. 'This waltz isn't hard, I'll teach you the steps—'

'No, really, stop.' Ramy extricated his hands from hers.

Letty crossed her arms. 'Well, it's no fun just sitting here.'

'We're sitting here because we're already barely tolerated, and because
as long as we don't move too quickly or speak too loudly, we can blend
into the background or at least pretend to be serving staff. That's how
this works, Letty. A brown man at an Oxford ball is a fun curiosity as
long as he keeps to himself and manages not to offend anyone, but if
I dance with you, then someone's going to hit me, or worse.'

She huffed. 'Don't be dramatic.'

'I'm only being prudent, dear.'

One of the Sharp brothers drifted by just then and extended his hand
to Letty. It seemed a rather rude and perfunctory gesture, but Letty
took it without comment and left, tossing Ramy a nasty look over her
shoulder as she sauntered off.

'Good for her,' Ramy muttered. 'And good riddance.'

Robin turned to Victoire. 'You're feeling all right?'

'I don't know.' She looked very nervous. 'I feel – I don't know, exposed.
Put on display. I told Letty they'd think I was staff—'

'Don't mind Colin,' said Robin. 'He's a prat.'

She looked unconvinced. 'Aren't they all like Colin, though?'

'Hello, there.' A red-haired boy in a purple waistcoat swooped upon

---

* Gabriel Shire Tregear, a London-based print seller and flaming racist, issued a
series of caricature prints known as 'Tregear's Black Jokes' in the 1830s which aimed
to ridicule the presence of Black people in social situations where Tregear thought
they did not belong.

them. It was Vincy Woolcombe – the least awful of Pendennis's friends, Robin recalled. Robin opened his mouth to greet him, but Woolcombe's eyes slid over him completely; he was solely focused on Victoire. 'You're in our college, aren't you?'

Victoire glanced around for a moment before realizing Woolcombe was indeed addressing her. 'Yes, I—'

'You're Victoire?' he asked. 'Victoire Desgraves?'

'Yes,' she said, standing up a bit straighter. 'How did you know my name?'

'Well, there are only two of you in your year,' said Woolcombe. 'Woman translators. You must be brilliant to be at Babel. Of course we know your names.'

Victoire's mouth was slightly open, but she said nothing; she seemed unable to determine whether Woolcombe was about to make fun of her or not.

'*J'ai entendu dire que tu venais de Paris.*' Woolcombe dipped his head in a slight bow. '*Les parisiennes sont les plus belles.*'

Victoire smiled, surprised. '*Ton français est assez bon.*'

Robin watched this exchange, impressed. Perhaps Woolcombe was not so terrible after all – perhaps he was only a prat in association with Pendennis. He, too, wondered briefly if Woolcombe was having fun at Victoire's expense, but there were no leering friends in sight; no one was glancing surreptitiously over their shoulders and pretending not to laugh.

'Summers in Marseilles,' said Woolcombe. 'My mother is of French extraction; she insisted I learn. Would you say it's passable?'

'You exaggerate the vowels a bit,' Victoire said earnestly, 'but otherwise, not bad.'

Woolcombe, to his credit, did not seem offended at this correction. 'I'm glad to hear it. Would you like to dance?'

Victoire lifted her hand, hesitated, then glanced at Robin and Ramy as if asking their thoughts.

'Go,' Ramy said. 'Enjoy.'

She took Woolcombe's hand, and he spun her away.

That left Robin alone with Ramy. Their shifts were ended; the bells had rung for eleven several minutes ago. They both pulled on their dress coats – identical black garments they'd purchased at the last moment from Ede & Ravenscroft – but continued lingering in safety by the back wall. Robin had made a perfunctory attempt to enter the fray, but quickly retreated in horror – everyone he was vaguely familiar with stood in tight conversational clusters and either ignored him completely as he approached, which made him feel oafish and awkward, or asked him about working at Babel, since that was apparently all they knew about him. Except whenever this happened, he was assaulted with a dozen questions on every side, all having to do with China and the Orient and silver-working. Once he'd escaped back to the cool quiet by the wall, he was so frightened and exhausted that he couldn't bear doing it again.

Ramy, ever loyal, stayed at his side. They watched the proceedings in silence for a bit. Robin snatched a glass of claret from a passing waiter and downed it faster than he should have, just to dull his fear of the noise and the crowd.

At last, Ramy asked, 'Well, are you going to ask anyone to dance?'

'I don't know how,' said Robin. He peered out at the throng, but all the girls in their bright balloon sleeves looked one and the same to him.

'To dance? Or to ask?'

'Well – both. But certainly the latter. It seems you need to know them socially before it's appropriate.'

'Oh, you're handsome enough,' said Ramy. 'And you're a Babbler. I'm sure one of them would say yes.'

Robin's mind was spinning with claret, or else he wouldn't have managed what he said next. 'Why won't you dance with Letty?'

'I'm not looking to start a row.'

'No, really.'

'Please, Birdie.' Ramy sighed. 'You know how it is.'

'She wants you,' Robin said. He'd only just realized this, and now that he said it out loud, it seemed so obvious that he felt stupid for not seeing it earlier. 'Very badly. So why—'

'Don't you know why?'

Their eyes met. Robin felt a prickle at the back of his neck. The space between them felt very charged, like the moment between lightning and thunder, and Robin had no idea what was going on or what would happen next, only that it all felt very strange and terrifying, like teetering over the edge of a windy, roaring cliff.

Abruptly Ramy stood. 'There's trouble over there.'

Across the quad, Letty and Victoire stood backs against the wall,

surrounded on all sides by a pack of leering boys. Pendennis and Woolcombe were among them. Victoire was hugging her arms across her
chest, Letty saying something very quickly that they couldn't make out.

'Better have a look,' said Ramy.

'Right.' Robin followed him through the crowd.

'It's not funny,' Letty was snarling. Her cheeks were blotchy with
rage. She held both her fists up like a boxer might; they trembled as she
spoke. 'We're not showgirls, you can't just—'

'But we're so curious,' said Pendennis, drawling and drunk. 'Are they
really different colours? We'd like to see – you're wearing such low-cuts,
it tantalizes the imagination—'

He reached an arm towards her shoulder. Letty drew her hand back
and smacked him full across the face. Pendennis recoiled. His face was
transformed, beastly with fury. He took a step towards Letty, and for a
moment it seemed as if he really might hit her back. Letty flinched away.

Robin rushed up between them. 'Leave,' he told Victoire and Letty.
They darted towards Ramy, who took their hands and pulled them
towards the back gate.

Pendennis turned on Robin.

Robin had no idea what would happen next. Pendennis was taller, a
bit heavier, and likely stronger, but he was swaying on his feet, his gaze
unfocused. If this became a fight, it would be a clumsy, undignified one.
No one would be seriously hurt. He might even land Pendennis on the
ground and skirt away before Pendennis got his wits about him. But
the college had strict rules against brawling, there were quite a lot of
witnesses, and Robin did not want to know how he would fare against
Pendennis's word before a disciplinary board.

'We can fight,' Robin breathed. 'If that's what you want. But you're
holding a glass of Madeira, and do you really want to spend the night
with red all down your front?'

Pendennis's eyes dipped to his wineglass, then back up to Robin.

'Chink,' he said in a very ugly voice. 'You're just a dressed-up Chinkee,
you know that, Swift?'

Robin's fists tightened. 'And are you going to let a Chinkee ruin
your ball?'

Pendennis sneered, but it was clear the danger had passed. As long as
Robin swallowed his pride, as long as he told himself it was only words
Pendennis had hurled his way, words that meant nothing at all, he could

simply turn and follow Ramy, Victoire, and Letty out of the college unscathed.

Outside, the cool night breeze was welcome relief against their reddened, overheated faces.

'What happened?' Robin asked. 'What were they saying?'

'It's nothing,' Victoire said. She was shivering violently; Robin pulled off his jacket and wrapped it around her shoulders.

'It's not nothing,' snapped Letty. 'That bastard Thornhill started going on about the different colours of our – our – you know, for biological reasons, and then Pendennis decided we ought to show them—'

'It doesn't matter,' said Victoire. 'Let's just walk.'

'I'll kill him,' Robin swore. 'I'm going back in. I'm going to kill him—'

'Please don't.' Victoire seized his arm. 'Don't make this worse, please.'

'This is your fault,' Ramy told Letty.

'*Mine?* How—'

'None of us wanted to come. Victoire told you it'd end badly, and still you forced us out here—'

'Forced?' Letty gave a sharp laugh. 'You seemed to be having a nice enough time, with your chocolates and truffles—'

'Yes, until Pendennis and his lot tried to violate our Victoire—'

'They had a go at me too, you know.' This was a bizarre line of argument, and Robin was not sure why Letty made it at all, but she said it with vehemence. Her voice went up by several octaves. 'It wasn't just because she's—'

'Stop!' Victoire shouted. Tears streamed down her face. 'Stop it, it's no one's fault, we just – I should have known better. We shouldn't have come.'

'I'm sorry,' Letty said in a very small voice. 'Victoire, love, I didn't . . .'

'It's fine.' Victoire shook her head. 'There's no reason why you'd – never mind.' She took a shaky breath. 'Let's just be out of here, can we, please? I want to go home.'

'Home?' Ramy stopped walking. 'What do you mean, home? It's a night for celebration.'

'Are you mad? I'm going to bed.' Victoire picked at the skirt of her gown, muddied now, at the bottom. 'And I'm getting out of this, I'm getting rid of these *stupid* sleeves—'

'No, you're not.' Ramy gave her a gentle tug towards High Street. 'You got dressed up for a ball. You deserve a ball. So let's have one.'

Ramy's plan, he revealed, was for them to spend the night on Babel's roof – just the four of them, a basket of sweets (the kitchens were very easy to steal from if you looked like staff), and the telescope under a clear night sky.* But when they turned the corner on the green, they saw lights and moving silhouettes through the windows of the first floor. Someone was in there.

'Wait—' Letty began, but Ramy jumped lightly up the steps and pushed the door open.

Fairy lights bobbed all around the lobby, which was crowded with students and graduate fellows. Robin recognized Cathy O'Nell, Vimal Srinivasan, and Ilse Dejima among them. Some danced, some chatted with wineglasses in hands, and some stood with heads bent over work-tables dragged down from the eighth floor, watching intently as a graduate fellow etched an engraving into a silver bar. Something went poof, and the room filled with the scent of roses. Everyone cheered.

Finally someone noticed them. 'Third years!' Vimal cried, waving them in. 'What took you so long?'

'We were at the college,' said Ramy. 'We didn't know there was a private party.'

'You should have invited them,' said a dark-haired German girl whose name Robin thought might be Minna. She danced in place as she spoke, and her head kept bobbing heavily to the left. 'So cruel of you, to let them go to that horror show.'

'One does not appreciate heaven until one has known hell,' said Vimal. 'Revelations. Or Mark. Or something like that.'

'That's not in the Bible,' said Minna.

'Well,' Vimal said dismissively, 'I wouldn't know.'

'That was cruel of you,' said Letty.

'Make haste,' Vimal called over his shoulder. 'Give the girl some wine.'

---

* In the mid-eighteenth century, Babel scholars were briefly seized by an astrology fad, and several state-of-the-art telescopes were ordered for the roof on behalf of scholars who thought they could derive useful match-pairs from the names of star signs. These efforts never yielded anything interesting, as astrology is fake, but the stargazing was pleasant.

Glasses were handed round; port was poured. Soon Robin was very pleasantly drunk, head buzzing, limbs floating. He leaned against the shelves, slightly out of breath from waltzing with Victoire, and basked in the marvellousness of it all. Vimal was now on the table, dancing a vigorous jig with Minna. On the opposite table, Matthew Houndslow, winner of that year's most prestigious postgraduate fellowship, was inscribing a silver bar with a match-pair that caused bright spheres of pink and purple light to bob around the room.

'*Ibasho*,' said Ilse Dejima.

Robin turned to her. She'd never spoken to him before; he wasn't sure if she'd meant to address him. But there was no one else around. 'Pardon?'

'*Ibasho*,' she repeated, swaying. Her arms floated in front of her, either dancing or conducting the music, he couldn't tell which. For that matter, he couldn't tell where the music was coming from at all. 'It doesn't translate well into English. It means "whereabouts". A place where one feels like home, where they feel like themselves.'

She wrote out the kanji characters for him in the air – 居場所 – and he recognized their Chinese equivalents. The character for a residence. The characters for a place.

In the months to come, whenever he thought back on this night, he could only grasp a handful of clear memories – after three glasses of port, it all turned into a pleasant haze. Vaguely he remembered dancing to some frantic Celtic tune on tables pushed together, then playing some kind of language game that mostly involved a lot of shouting and rapid rhyming, and laughing so hard his sides hurt. He remembered Ramy sitting with Victoire in a corner, doing silly impersonations of the professors until her tears were dry, and then until they were both crying from laughter. 'I despise women,' intoned Ramy in Professor Craft's severe monotone. 'They're flighty, easily distracted, and in general unsuited for the sort of rigorous study that an academic life demands.'

He remembered English phrases rising unbidden to his mind as he watched the revels; phrases from songs and poems that he wasn't quite sure on the meaning of, but which looked and sounded right – and perhaps that was just what poetry was? Meaning through sound? Through spelling? He couldn't remember whether he merely thought it, or if he asked it out loud to everyone he came across, but he found himself consumed with the question 'What is the light fantastic?'*

And he remembered sitting on the stairs deep into the night with Letty, who wept furiously into his shoulder. 'I wish he would see me,' she kept repeating through her hiccups. 'Why won't he see me?' And though Robin could think of any number of reasons – because Ramy was a brown man in England and Letty the daughter of an admiral; because Ramy did not want to be shot in the street; or because Ramy simply did not love her like she loved him, and she'd badly mistaken his general kindness and ostentatious verve for special attention, because Letty was the kind of girl who was used to, and had come to always expect, special attention – he knew better than to tell her the truth. What Letty wanted then was not honest counsel, but someone to comfort and love her and give her, if not the attention she craved, then some facsimile of it. So he let her sob against him, soaking the front of his shirt in tears, and rubbed circles in her back as he murmured mindlessly that he didn't understand – was Ramy a fool? What wasn't to love about her? She was gorgeous, gorgeous, she made Aphrodite herself jealous – indeed, he intoned, she ought to feel lucky she hadn't been turned into a mayfly already. This made Letty giggle, which stopped her crying somewhat, and that was good; that meant he'd done his job.

He had the oddest feeling of disappearing as he spoke, of fading into the background of a painting depicting a story which must have been old as history. And perhaps it was the drink, but he was fascinated by the way he seemed to drift outside himself, to watch from the awning as her hiccuping sobs and his murmurs mingled, floated, and became puffs of condensation against the cold stained-glass windows.

They were all very drunk by the time the party broke up – except for Ramy, who was drunk anyway on exhaustion and laughter – which was the only reason it seemed a good idea to wander through the cemetery behind St Giles, taking the long way round north, to where the girls lived. Ramy murmured a quiet *du'a*, and they traipsed through the gate. At first it seemed a great adventure as they stumbled against each other, laughing, as they picked their way around the tombstones. But then

---

* Milton, 1645:
  'Come, and trip as ye go,
  On the light fantastick toe.'

the air seemed to change very quickly. The warmth of the streetlamps dimmed; the tombstone shadows stretched long, shifting, as if belying some presence that did not want them there. Robin felt a sudden, chilling dread. It was not illegal to walk through the cemetery, but suddenly it seemed a horrific violation to trespass these grounds in their state.

Ramy had felt it too. 'Let's hurry.'

Robin nodded. They began weaving faster among the tombstones. 'Shouldn't be out here after Maghrib,' Ramy muttered. 'Should have listened to my mother—'

'Hold on,' said Victoire. 'Letty's still – Letty?'

They turned around. Letty had fallen behind several rows back. She stood before a tombstone.

'Look.' She pointed, her eyes wide. 'It's her.'

'Her who?' asked Ramy.

But Letty only stood there, staring.

They doubled back to join her before the weathered stone. *Eveline Brooke*, it read. *Dearly beloved daughter, scholar. 1813–1834.*

'Eveline,' said Robin. 'Is that—'

'Evie,' said Letty. 'The girl with the desk. The girl with all the match-pairs on the ledger. She's dead. All this time. She's been dead for five years.'

Suddenly the night air felt icy. The lingering warmth of port had evaporated with their laughter; now they were sober, cold, and very scared. Victoire pulled her shawl tighter around her shoulders. 'What do you think happened to her?'

'Probably just something mundane.' Ramy made a valiant effort to dispel the gloom. 'Probably she fell sick, or had an accident, or overexhausted herself. Could be she went skating without a scarf. Could be she got so wrapped up in her research she forgot to eat.'

But Robin suspected Evie Brooke's death was about more than some mundane bout of illness. Anthony's disappearance had left hardly a trace on the faculty. Professor Playfair seemed by now to have forgotten he'd ever existed; he'd not uttered a word about Anthony since the day he'd announced his death. Yet he'd kept Evie's work desk undisturbed for five years and counting.

Eveline Brooke had been someone special. And something awful had happened here.

'Suppose we go home,' Victoire whispered after a while.

They must have been in the graveyard for quite some time. The dark sky was slowly giving way to pale light, the chill condensing into morning dew. The ball was over. The last night of term had ended, had given way to endless summer. Wordlessly, they took each other's hands and walked home.

Chapter Fifteen

As the days take on a mellower light, and the apple at last hangs really
    finish'd and indolent-ripe on the tree,
Then for the teeming quietest, happiest days of all!

WALT WHITMAN, 'Halcyon Days'

Robin received his exam marks in his pidge the next morning (Merit in Translation Theory and Latin, Distinction in Etymology, Chinese, and Sanskrit), along with the following note printed on thick, creamy paper: *The board of undergraduate studies at the Royal Institute of Translation is pleased to inform you that you have been invited to continue your tenure as undergraduate scholar for the following year.*

Only when he had the papers in hand did it all seem real. He'd passed; they'd all passed. For at least another year, they had a home. They had room and board paid for, a steady allowance, and access to all of Oxford's intellectual riches. They would not be forced to leave Babel. They could breathe easy again.

Oxford in June was hot, sticky, golden, and beautiful. They had no pressing summer assignments – they could do further research on their independent projects if they liked, though generally, the weeks between the end of Trinity and the start of next Michaelmas were tacitly acknowledged as a reward, and brief respite, that incoming fourth years deserved.

Those were the happiest days of their lives. They had picnics of ripe, bursting grapes; fresh rolls; and Camembert cheese on the hills of South Park. They went punting up and down the Cherwell – Robin and Ramy got passably good at it, but the girls could not seem to manage the art of pushing them straight ahead instead of sideways into the bank. They walked the seven miles north to Woodstock to tour Blenheim Palace, but did not go in, as the sightseeing fee was exorbitant. A visiting acting troupe from London put on some excerpts of Shakespeare at the Sheldonian; they were undeniably awful, and the heckling from badly behaved undergraduates probably made them worse, but quality was not the point.

Near the end of June, all anyone could talk about was the coronation of Queen Victoria. Many of the students and fellows still on campus took coaches to Didcot for the train to London the day before, but those who remained in Oxford were treated to a dazzling lighting-up show. There were rumours of a grand dinner to be put on for Oxford's poor and homeless, but the city authorities argued that the richness of roast beef and plum pudding would put the poor in such a state of excitement that they would lose their ability to properly enjoy the illumination.* So the poor went hungry that night, but at least the lights were lovely. Robin, Ramy, and Victoire strolled with Letty down High Street with mugs of cold cider in hand, trying to conjure up the same sense of patriotism visible in everyone else.

Near the end of summer they took a weekend trip to London, where they drank in the vitality and variety that Oxford, suspended centuries in the past, so lacked. They went to Drury Lane and saw a show – the acting wasn't very good, but the garish make-up and the ingenue's pitchy warbling kept them fascinated for the full three-hour run time. They browsed the stalls at New Cut for plump strawberries, copper trinkets, and sachets of supposedly exotic teas; tossed pennies to dancing monkeys and organ-grinders; dodged beckoning prostitutes; perused street stands of counterfeit silver bars with amusement;† had dinner at an 'Authentick Indian' curry house that disappointed Ramy but satisfied the rest of them; and slept overnight in a single crowded townhouse room on Doughty Street. Robin and Ramy lay on the floor swaddled

---

* In that time, the authorities in Oxford, like those in London, seemed to think the poor were akin to little children, or animals, rather than grown, intelligent adults.

† As with all valuable and expensive things, there was a massive underground market for counterfeit and amateur silver bars. At New Cut, one could buy charms to Banish Rodents, to Cure Common Ailments, and to Attract Wealthy Young Gentlemen. Most were composed without a basic understanding of the principles of silver-working, and involved elaborate spells in made-up languages often in imitation of Oriental languages. Yet some were, occasionally, rather incisive applications of folk etymology. For this reason, Professor Playfair conducted an annual survey of contraband silver match-pairs, though the use of this survey was a matter of utmost secrecy.

in coats while the girls huddled on the narrow bed, all of them giggling and whispering until long past midnight.

The next day they took a walking tour of the city that ended by the Port of London, where they strolled down to the docks and marvelled at the massive ships, their great white sails, and the complex interlacing of their masts and rigging. They tried identifying the flags and company logos of the departing vessels, speculating on where they might be coming from or going. Greece? Canada? Sweden? Portugal?

'A year from now we'll be getting on one of these,' said Letty. 'Where do you think it'll be sailing to?'

Every graduating cohort at Babel went on a grand, fully compensated international voyage at the conclusion of fourth-year exams. These voyages usually corresponded with some Babel business – graduates had served as live interpreters at the court of Nicholas I, hunted for cuneiform tablets in the ruins of Mesopotamia, and once, accidentally, caused a near diplomatic breakdown in Paris – but they were primarily a chance for the graduates to simply see the world, and to soak in the foreign linguistic environments they had been sequestered from during their years of study. Languages had to be lived to be understood, and Oxford was, after all, the opposite of real life.

Ramy was convinced their class would be sent to either China or India. 'There's simply so much happening. The East India Company's lost its monopoly in Canton, which means they'll need translators for all kinds of business reorientations. I'd give my left arm for it to be Calcutta. You'll love it – we'll go and stay with my family for a bit; I've written to them all about you, they even know Letty can't take her tea too hot. Or perhaps we'll go to Canton – wouldn't that be lovely, Birdie? When's the last time you were home?'

Robin wasn't sure he wanted to return to Canton. He'd considered it a few times, but couldn't summon any feelings of excitement, only a confused, vaguely guilty dread. Nothing awaited him there; no friends, no family, just a city he only half remembered. Rather, he was afraid of how he might react if he did go home; if he stepped back into the world of a forgotten childhood. What if, upon return, he couldn't bring himself to leave?

Worse, what if he felt nothing at all?

'More likely we'll be sent somewhere like Mauritius,' he said. 'Let the girls make use of their French.'

'You think Mauritian Creole is anything like Haitian Creole?' Letty asked Victoire.

'I'm not sure they'll be mutually intelligible,' said Victoire. 'They're both French-based, of course, but Kreyòl takes grammar cues from the Fon language, while Mauritian Creole . . . hm. I don't know. There's no Grammatica, so I've nothing to consult.'

'Perhaps you'll write one,' said Letty.

Victoire cast her a small smile. 'Perhaps.'

The happiest development of that summer was that Victoire and Letty had gone back to being friends. In fact, all the strange, ill-defined awfulness of their third year had evaporated with the news that they'd passed their exams. Letty no longer grated on Robin's nerves, and Ramy no longer made Letty scowl every time he opened his mouth.

To be fair, their fights were tabled rather than resolved. They had not really confronted the reasons why they'd fallen out, but they were all willing to blame it on stress. There would be a time when they had to face up to their very real differences, when they would hash things out instead of always changing the subject, but for now they were content to enjoy the summer and to remember again what it was like to love one another.

For these, truly, were the last of the golden days. That summer felt all the more precious because they all knew it couldn't last, that such delights were only so because of the endless, exhausting nights that had earned them. Soon year four would start, then graduating exams, and then work. None of them knew what life might look like after that, but surely they could not remain a cohort forever. Surely, eventually, they had to leave the city of dreaming spires; had to take up their respective posts and repay all that Babel had given them. But the future, vague as it was frightening, was easily ignored for now; it paled so against the brilliance of the present.

In January of 1838, the inventor Samuel Morse had given a demonstration in Morristown, New Jersey, showing off a device that could transmit messages over long distances using electrical impulses to convey a series of dots and dashes. Sceptical, the United States Congress declined to grant him funding to build a line connecting the capitol in Washington, DC, with other cities, and would drag their feet in doing so for another five years. But scholars at the Royal Institute of Translation, as soon as they heard that Morse's device worked, went overseas and cajoled Morse into making a months-long visit to Oxford, where the silver-working department was amazed that this device required no match-pairs to work, but instead ran on pure electricity. By July 1839, Babel hosted the first working telegraph line in England, which was connected to the British Foreign Office in London.*

Morse's original code transmitted only numerals, under the assumption that the receiver could look up the corresponding words in a guidebook. This was fine for conversations that involved a limited vocabulary – train signals, weather reports, and certain kinds of military communications. But soon after Morse's arrival, Professors De Vreese and Playfair developed an alphanumeric code that allowed exchange of messages of any kind.† This expanded the telegraph's possible uses to the commercial, personal, and beyond. Word spread quickly that Babel had means of communicating instantaneously with London from Oxford. Soon clients – largely businessmen, government officials, and the occasional clergyman – were crammed in the lobby and lined up around the block clutching messages they needed sent. Professor Lovell, exasperated by the clamour, wanted to set the defensive wards on crowd. But calmer, more financially attuned heads prevailed. Professor Playfair, seeing great potential for profit, ordered that the northwest wing of the lobby, which was formerly used for storage, be converted into a telegraph office.

The next obstacle was staffing the office with operators. Students were the obvious source of free labour, and so every Babel undergraduate and graduate fellow was required to learn Morse code. This took only a matter of days, since Morse code was the rare language that did in fact have a perfect one-to-one correlation between language symbols, provided one was communicating in English. When September bled into October and Michaelmas term began that autumn, all students on campus were assigned to work at least one three-hour shift a week. And so, at nine o'clock every Sunday night, Robin dragged himself to the

---

* In doing so, Babel and Morse greatly upset the inventors William Cooke and Charles Wheatstone, whose own telegraph machine had been installed on the Great Western Railway just two years prior. However, Cooke and Wheatstone's telegraph used moving needles to point to a preset board of symbols, which did not afford nearly the range of communication that Morse's simpler, click-based telegraph did.

† In an act of incredible academic generosity, they allowed this improved system to also be referred to as the Morse Code.

little lobby office and sat by the telegraph machine with a stack of course readings, waiting for the needle to buzz into life.

The advantage of the late shift was that the tower received very little correspondence during those hours, since everyone in the London office would have already gone home. All Robin had to do was stay awake from nine to midnight, in case any urgent missives arrived. Otherwise, he was free to do as he liked, and he usually spent these hours reading or revising his compositions for the next morning's class.

Occasionally he glanced out of the window, squinting across the quad to relieve the strain of the dim light on his eyes. The green was usually empty. High Street, so busy during the day, was eerie late at night; when the sun had gone down, when all the light came from pale streetlamps or from candles inside windows, it looked like another, parallel Oxford, an Oxford of the faerie realm. On cloudless nights especially, Oxford was transformed, its streets clear, its stones silent, its spires and turrets promising riddles and adventures and a world of abstraction in which one could get lost forever.

On one such night, Robin glanced up from his translation of Sima Qian's histories and saw two black-clad figures striding briskly towards the tower. His stomach dropped.

Only when they reached the front steps, when the lights from inside the tower shone against their faces, did he realize it was Ramy and Victoire.

Robin sat frozen at his desk, unsure what to do. They were here on Hermes business. They had to be. Nothing else explained the attire; the furtive glances; the late night trip to the tower when Robin knew they had no business being there, because he'd seen them finish their papers for Professor Craft's seminar on the floor of Ramy's room just several hours before.

Had Griffin recruited them? Certainly, that was it, Robin thought ruefully. He'd given up on Robin, so he'd gone for the others in his cohort instead.

Of course he wouldn't report them – that was not in question. But should he *help* them? No, perhaps not – the tower was not wholly empty; there were researchers still on the eighth floor, and if he startled Ramy and Victoire, he might attract unwanted attention. The only choice seemed to be to do nothing. If he pretended never to notice, and if they succeeded in whatever it was they wanted, then the fragile equilibrium of their lives at Babel would not be disturbed. Then they could maintain the thin veneer of deniability Robin had lived with for years. Reality was, after all, just so malleable – facts could be forgotten, truths suppressed, lives seen from only one angle like a trick prism, if only one resolved never to look too closely.

Ramy and Victoire slipped through the door and up the stairs. Robin trained his eyes on his translation, trying not to strain his ear for any hint of what they might be doing. Ten minutes later, he heard descending footsteps. They'd got what they'd come for. Soon they'd be back out the door. Then the moment would pass, and the calm would resume, and Robin could consign this to the back of his mind with all the other unpleasant truths he hadn't the will to untangle—

A shrieking, inhuman wail pierced the tower. He heard a great crash, then a bout of cursing. He jumped up and dashed out of the lobby.

Ramy and Victoire were trapped just outside the front door, ensnared in a web of glistening silvery string that doubled and multiplied before his eyes, new strands lashing around their wrists, waists, ankles, and throats with every passing second. A smattering of items lay scattered at their feet – six silver bars, two old books, one engraving stylus. Items Babel scholars regularly took home at the end of the day.

Except, it appeared, Professor Playfair had successfully changed the wards. He'd achieved even more than Robin had feared – he'd altered them to detect not only which people and things were passing through, but whether their purposes were legitimate.

'Birdie,' gasped Ramy. Silver webs tightened around his neck; his eyes bulged. 'Help—'

'Hold still.' Robin yanked at the strands. They were sticky but pliable, breakable; impossible to escape alone but not without help. He freed Ramy's neck and hands first, then together they pulled Victoire out of the web, though Robin's legs became entangled in the process. The web, it seemed, gave only if it could take. But its vicious lashing had ceased; whatever match-pair triggered the alarm seemed to have calmed. Ramy pulled his ankles free and stepped back. For a moment they all regarded each other under the moonlight, baffled.

'You too?' Victoire finally asked.

'Looks like it,' said Robin. 'Did Griffin send you?'

'Griffin?' Victoire looked bewildered. 'No, Anthony—'

'Anthony *Ribben*?'

'Of course,' said Ramy. 'Who else?'

'But he's *dead*—'

'This can wait,' Victoire interrupted. 'Listen, the sirens—'

'Damn it,' said Ramy. 'Robin, lean this way—'

'There's no time,' said Robin. He couldn't move his legs. The strings had ceased multiplying – perhaps because Robin was not the thief – but the web was now impossibly dense, stretching across the entire front entrance, and if Ramy came any closer, he feared, they'd both be trapped. 'Leave me.'

They both began to protest. He shook his head. 'It has to be me. I haven't conspired, I have no idea what's going on—'

'Isn't it obvious?' Ramy demanded. 'We're—'

'It's *not* obvious, so don't tell me,' Robin hissed. The siren's wailing was endless; soon the police would be at the green. 'Say nothing. I know nothing, and when they question me, that's what I'll say. Just hurry and go, please, I'll think of something.'

'You're sure—' Victoire began.

'*Go*,' Robin insisted.

Ramy opened his mouth, closed it, then bent down to scoop up the stolen materials. Victoire followed suit. They left just two bars behind – *clever*, Robin thought, for that was some evidence that Robin had been working alone, that he had no accomplices who'd disappeared with all the contraband. Then they dashed down the steps, across the green and into the alley.

'Who's there?' someone shouted. Robin saw lamps bobbing at the other end of the quadrangle. He twisted his head and squinted towards Broad Street, trying and failing to glimpse any trace of his friends. They'd got away, it had worked, the police were coming only for the tower. Only for him.

He took a shaky breath, then turned to face the light.

Angry shouts, bright lamps in his face, firm hands on his arms. Robin hardly processed what happened over the next several minutes; he was aware only of his vague, incoherent rambles, a cacophony of policemen yelling different orders and questions in his ear. He tried piecing together an excuse, some story about seeing thieves caught in the webbing, and how they'd snagged him when he went to stop them, but that was incoherent upon utterance, and the police only laughed. Eventually they prised him free of the web and led him back into the tower to a small, windowless room in the lobby, empty save for a single chair. The door had a small grate at eye level covered by a sliding flap; it resembled a jail cell more than a reading room. He wondered if he was not the first Hermes operative to be detained here. He wondered if the faint brown splotch in the corner might be dried blood.

'You'll stay here,' said the constable in charge as he cuffed Robin's hands behind his back. 'Till the professor arrives.'

They locked the door and left. They had not said which professor, or when they would return. Not knowing was torture. Robin sat and waited, knees jangling, arms shuddering miserably from waves and waves of nauseating adrenaline.

He was finished. There was, surely, no coming back from this. It was so difficult to be expelled from Babel, which invested so much in its hard-sought talent that previous Babel undergraduates had been pardoned for almost every kind of offence save for murder.[*] But surely thievery and treason were grounds for expulsion. And then what? A cell in the city gaol? In Newgate? Would they hang him? Or would he simply be put on a ship and sent back to where he had come from, where he had no friends, no family, and no prospects?

An image rose in his mind, one he had locked away for nearly a decade now – a hot, airless room, the smell of sick, his mother lying stiff beside him, her drawn cheeks turning blue before his eyes. The last ten years – Hampstead, Oxford, Babel – had all been a miraculous enchantment, but he had broken the rules – had broken the spell – and soon the glamour would fall away and he would be back among the poor, the sick, the dying, the dead.

The door creaked open.

'Robin.'

It was Professor Lovell. Robin searched his eyes for a shred of something – kindness, disappointment, or anger – anything that might prophesy what he should expect. But his father's expression, as ever before, was only a blank, inscrutable mask. 'Good morning.'

*   *   *

---

[*] A list of offences that Babel undergraduates had got away with in the past included public intoxication, brawling, cockfighting, and intentionally adding vulgarities to a recital of the Latin grace before dinner in hall.

'Have a seat.' The first thing Professor Lovell had done was unlock Robin's cuffs. Then he'd led him up the stairs to his office on the seventh floor, where now they sat facing each other as casually as if convening for a weekly tutorial.

'You're very lucky the police contacted me first. Imagine if they'd found Jerome instead. You'd be missing your legs right now.' Professor Lovell leaned forward, hands clasped over his desk. 'How long have you been pilfering resources for the Hermes Society?'

Robin blanched. He had not expected Professor Lovell to be so direct. This question was very dangerous. Professor Lovell evidently knew about Hermes. But how *much* did he know? How much could Robin lie about? Perhaps he was bluffing, and perhaps Robin could fumble his way out of this if he minced his words in just the right way.

'Tell the truth,' Professor Lovell said in a hard, flat voice. 'That's the only thing that will save you now.'

'Three months,' Robin breathed. Three months felt less damning than three years, but long enough to sound plausible. 'Only – only since the summer.'

'I see.' There was no ire in Professor Lovell's voice. The calm made him terrifyingly unreadable. Robin would have preferred that he screamed.

'Sir, I—'

'Quiet,' Professor Lovell said.

Robin clamped his mouth shut. It didn't matter. He didn't know what he would have said. There was no explaining himself out of this mess, no possible exoneration. He could only face up to the stark evidence of his betrayal and await the consequences. But if he could keep Ramy and Victoire's names out of this, if he could convince Professor Lovell that he'd acted alone, that would be enough.

'To think,' Professor Lovell said after a long while, 'that you would have turned out so abominably ungrateful.'

He leaned back, shook his head. 'I have done more for you than you could ever imagine. You were a dock boy in Canton. Your mother was an outcast. Even if your father had been Chinese,' Professor Lovell's throat pulsed then, and this was as much of an admission as he would ever make, Robin knew, 'your station would have been the same. You would have scraped along for pennies your entire life. You never would have seen the shores of England. You never would have read Horace, Homer, or Thucydides – you never would have opened a book, for that matter. You would have lived and died in squalor and ignorance, never imagining the world of opportunities that I have afforded you. I lifted you from destitution. I gifted you the world.'

'Sir, I didn't—'

'How *dare* you? How dare you spit in the face of all you were given?'

'Sir—'

'Do you know how privileged you've been by this university?' Professor Lovell's voice remained unchanged in volume, but each syllable grew longer, first drawled and then spat out as if he were biting the words off at the ends. 'Do you know how much most households pay to send their sons to Oxford? You enjoy rooms and lodging at no cost. You're blessed with a monthly allowance. You have access to the largest stores of knowledge in the world. Did you think your situation was common?'

A hundred arguments swam through Robin's head – that he had not requested these privileges of Oxford, had not chosen to be spirited out of Canton at all, that the generosities of the university should not demand his constant, unswerving loyalty to the Crown and its colonial projects, and if it did, then that was a peculiar form of bondage he had never agreed to. That he had not wished for this fate until it was thrust upon him, decided for him. That he didn't know what life he would have chosen – this one, or a life in which he'd grown up in Canton, among people who looked and spoke like him.

But what did it matter? Professor Lovell would hardly sympathize. All that mattered was that Robin was guilty.

'Was it fun for you?' Professor Lovell's lip curled. 'Did you get a thrill out of it? Oh, you must have. I imagine you considered yourself the hero of one of your little stories – a regular Dick Turpin, didn't you? You always did love your penny dreadfuls. A weary student by day, and a dashing thief by night? Was it romantic, Robin Swift?'

'No.' Robin squared his shoulders and tried, at least, not to sound so pathetically scared. If he was going to be punished, he might as well own his principles. 'No, I was doing the right thing.'

'Oh? And what is the right thing?'

'I know you don't care. But I did it, and I'm not sorry, and you can do whatever you like—'

'No, Robin. Tell me what you were fighting for.' Professor Lovell leaned back, steepled his fingers together, and nodded. As if this were an examination. As if he were really listening. 'Go, on, convince me. Try to recruit me. Do your very best.'

'The way Babel hoards materials isn't just,' said Robin.

'Oh! It's not just!'

'It's not right,' Robin continued angrily. 'It's selfish. All our silver goes to luxury, to the military, to making lace and weapons when there are people dying of simple things these bars could fix. It's not right that you recruit students from other countries to work your translation centre and that their motherlands receive nothing in return.'

He knew these arguments well. He was parroting what Griffin had told him, truths he had come to internalize. Yet in the face of Professor Lovell's stony silence, it all seemed so silly. His voice sounded frail and tinny, desperately unsure of itself.

'And if you are indeed so disgusted by the ways Babel enriches itself,' continued Professor Lovell, 'how is it that you seemed delighted, always, to take its money?'

Robin flinched. 'I didn't – I didn't *ask*—' But this was incoherent upon utterance. He trailed off, cheeks burning.

'You drink the champagne, Robin. You take your allowance. You live in your furnished room on Magpie Lane, you parade down the streets in your robes and tailored clothes, all paid for by the school, and yet you say all this money comes from blood. This does not bother you?'

And that was the heart of it all, wasn't it? Robin had always been willing, in theory, to give up only some things for a revolution he halfway believed in. He was fine with resistance as long as it didn't hurt him. And the contradiction was fine, as long as he didn't think too hard about it, or look too closely. But spelled out like this, in such bleak terms, it seemed inarguable that far from being a revolutionary, Robin, in fact, had no convictions whatsoever.

Professor Lovell's lip curled again. 'Not so bothered by empire, now, are you?'

'It's not just,' Robin repeated. 'It's not fair—'

'*Fair*,' mimicked Professor Lovell. 'Suppose you invented the spinning wheel. Are you suddenly obligated to share your profits with everyone who still spins by hand?'

'But that's not the same—'

'And are we obligated to distribute silver bars all around the world to backward countries who have had every opportunity to construct their own centres of translation? It takes no great investment to study foreign languages. Why must it be Britain's problem if other nations fail to take advantage of what they have?'

Robin opened his mouth to reply, but could think of nothing to say. Why was it so difficult to find the words? There was something wrong with this argument, but once again, he could not figure out what. Free trade, open borders, equal access to the same knowledge – it all sounded so fine in theory. But if the playing field really was so even, why had all the profits accumulated in Britain? Were the British really so much more clever and industrious? Had they simply played the game, fair and square, and won?

'Who recruited you?' Professor Lovell inquired. 'They must not have done a very good job.'

Robin did not respond.

'Was it Griffin Harley?'

Robin flinched, and that was confession enough.

'Of course. Griffin.' Professor Lovell spat the name like a curse. He watched Robin for a long moment, scrutinizing his face as if he could find the ghost of his elder son in the younger. Then he asked, in a strangely soft tone, 'Do you know what happened to Eveline Brooke?'

'No,' Robin said, even as he thought *yes*; he did know, not the particulars of the story but its general outline. He had nearly put it all together by now, though he'd held off sliding in the final piece, because he did not want to know, and did not want it to be true.

'She was brilliant,' said Professor Lovell. 'The best student we've ever had. The pride and joy of the university. Did you know it was Griffin who murdered her?'

Robin recoiled. 'No, that's not—'

'He never told you? I'm surprised, to be honest. I would have expected him to gloat.' Professor Lovell's eyes were very dark. 'Then let me enlighten you. Five years ago, Evie – poor, innocent Evie – was working on the eighth floor after midnight. She'd kept her lamp on, but she hadn't realized the rest of the lights were off. That's how Evie was. When she was caught up in her work, she lost track of what was going on around her. Nothing existed for her but the research.

'Griffin Harley entered the tower at about two in the morning. He didn't see Evie – she was working in the back corner behind the workstations. He thought he was alone. And Griffin proceeded to do what

Griffin does best – pilfer and steal, root through precious manuscripts to smuggle them to God knows where. He was nearly at the door when he realized Evie had seen him.'

Professor Lovell fell silent. Robin was confused by this pause, until he saw, to his astonishment, that his eyes were red and wet at the corners. Professor Lovell, who'd never shown the slightest ounce of feeling in all the years Robin had known him, was crying.

'She never did anything.' His voice was hoarse. 'She didn't raise the alarm. She didn't scream. She never had the chance. Eveline Brooke was simply in the wrong place at the wrong time. But Griffin was so afraid she might turn him in that he killed her anyway. I found her the next morning.'

He reached out and tapped the worn silver bar lying at the corner of his desk. Robin had seen it many times before, but Professor Lovell had always kept it turned away, half-hidden behind a picture frame, and he'd never been bold enough to ask. Professor Lovell flipped it over. 'Do you know what this match-pair does?'

Robin glanced down. The front side read 爆. His gut twisted. He was too afraid to look at the back.

'*Bào*,' said Professor Lovell. 'The radical for fire. And beside it, the radical for violence, cruelty, and turbulence; the same radical which on its own can mean untamed, savage brutality; the same radical used in the words for *thunder* and *cruelty*.* And he translated it against *burst*, the tamest English translation possible, so tame that it hardly translates as such at all – so that all of that force, that destruction, was trapped in the silver. It exploded against her chest. Sprang her ribs apart like an open birdcage. And then he left her there, lying among the shelves, books still in hand. When I saw her, her blood had pooled across half the floor. Stained every page red.' He slid the bar across the table. 'Hold it.'

Robin flinched. 'Sir?'

'Pick it up,' snapped Professor Lovell. 'Feel the weight of it.'

Robin reached out and closed his fingers around the bar. It was terribly cold to the touch, colder than any other silver he'd encountered, and inordinately heavy. Yes, he could believe that this bar had murdered someone. It seemed to hum with trapped, furious potential, a lit grenade, waiting to go off.

---

* The character 爆 is composed of two radicals: 火 and 暴.

He knew it was pointless to ask, but he had to regardless. 'How do you know it was Griffin?'

'We've had no other students in Chinese in the past ten years,' said Professor Lovell. 'Do you suppose I did it? Or Professor Chakravarti?'

Was he lying? It was possible – this story was so grotesque, Robin nearly didn't believe it, didn't want to believe that Griffin could be capable of something like murder.

But wasn't he? Griffin, who spoke of Babel faculty as if they were enemy combatants, who sent his own brother repeatedly into the fray without care for the consequences, who was so convinced of the Manichaean justice of the war he fought that he could see little else. Wouldn't Griffin have murdered a defenceless girl, if it meant keeping Hermes secure?

'I'm sorry,' Robin whispered. 'I didn't know.'

'This is who you've thrown your lot in with,' said Professor Lovell. 'A liar and a killer. Do you imagine you're aiding some movement of global liberation, Robin? Don't be naive. You're aiding Griffin's delusions of grandeur. And for what?' He nodded to Robin's shoulder. 'A bullet in your arm?'

'How did you—'

'Professor Playfair observed you might have hurt your arm rowing. I am not quite so easily deceived.' Professor Lovell clasped his hands over the desk and leaned back. 'So. The choice ought to be very obvious, I think. Babel, or Hermes.'

Robin frowned. 'Sir?'

'Babel, or Hermes? It's quite simple. You may decide.'

Robin felt like a broken instrument, capable of uttering only one sound. 'Sir, I don't . . .'

'Did you think you would be expelled?'

'Well – *yes*, wouldn't—'

'It's not quite so easy to leave Babel, I'm afraid. You've strayed down the wrong path, but I believe it was as a result of vicious influences – influences crueller and wilier than you could have been expected to handle. You're naive, yes. And a disappointment. But you're not finished. This does not need to end with gaol or prison.' Professor Lovell tapped his fingers against the desk. 'But it would be very helpful if you could give us something useful.'

'Useful?'

'Information, Robin. Help us find them. Help us root them out.'

'But I don't know anything about them,' said Robin. 'I don't even know any of their names, except Griffin's.'

'Really.'

'It's true, it's how they operate – they're so decentralized, they don't tell new associates anything. In case—' Robin swallowed. 'In case something like this happens.'

'How unfortunate. You're quite sure?'

'Yes, I really don't—'

'Say what you mean, Robin. Don't dither.'

Robin flinched. Those were precisely the same words Griffin had used; he remembered. And Griffin had said it exactly the same way Professor Lovell did now, cold and imperious, as if he'd already won the argument, as if any response Robin made was bound to be nonsense.

And Robin could imagine Griffin's smirk just now; knew exactly what he would say – *of course you'll choose your creature comforts, you coddled little scholar*. But what right did Griffin have to judge his choices? Staying at Babel, at Oxford, wasn't indulgence; it was survival. It was his only ticket into this country, the one thing between him and the streets.

He felt a sudden flare of hatred towards Griffin. Robin had asked for none of this, and now his future – and Ramy's and Victoire's futures – hung in the balance. And where was Griffin? Where was he when Robin had been shot? Vanished. He'd used them to do his bidding, then abandoned them when things went sour. At least if Griffin went to prison, he deserved it.

'If it's loyalty that's keeping you quiet, then there's nothing else to be done,' said Professor Lovell. 'But I think we can work together still. I think you're not quite ready to leave Babel. Don't you?'

Robin took a deep breath.

What was he giving up, really? The Hermes Society had abandoned him, had ignored his warnings and endangered his two dearest friends. He owed them nothing.

In the days and weeks that followed he would try to persuade himself that this was a moment of strategic concession, not of betrayal. That he was not giving up much of importance – Griffin himself had said they had multiple safe houses, hadn't he? – and that this way Ramy and Victoire were protected, he was not expelled, and all the lines of communication existed still for some future cooperation with Hermes. But he'd never quite talk himself out of the nasty truth – that this was not about Hermes, nor about Ramy or Victoire, but about self-preservation.

'St Aldate's,' he said. 'The back entrance to the church. There's a door near the basement that looks rusted shut, but Griffin has a key. They use it as a safe room.'

Professor Lovell scribbled this down. 'How often does he go there?'

'I don't know.'

'What's in there?'

'I don't know,' Robin said again. 'I never went myself. Truly, he told me very little. I'm sorry.'

Professor Lovell cast him a long, cool look, then appeared to relent.

'I know you're better than this.' He leaned forward over his desk. 'You are unlike Griffin in every way possible. You're humble, you're bright, and you work hard. You are less corrupted by your heritage than he was. If I'd only just met you, I'd be hard pressed to guess you were a Chinaman at all. You have prodigious talent, and talent deserves a second chance. But careful, boy.' He gestured to the door. 'There won't be a third.'

Robin stood up, then glanced down at his hand. He noticed he'd been clutching the bar that had killed Evie Brooke this whole time. It felt simultaneously very hot and very cold, and he had the strange fear that if he touched it for a moment longer, it might erode a hole through his palm. He held it out. 'Here, sir—'

'Keep it,' said Professor Lovell.

'Sir?'

'I have been staring at that bar every day for the past five years, wondering where I went wrong with Griffin. If I had raised him differently, or seen him earlier for what he was, if Evie would still – but never mind.' Professor Lovell's voice hardened. 'Now it weighs on your conscience. Keep it, Robin Swift. Carry it in your front pocket. Pull it out whenever you begin to doubt, and let it remind you which side are the villains.'

He motioned for Robin to leave the office. Robin stumbled down the stairs, the silver clutched tight in his fingers, dazed and quite sure he'd pushed his entire world off course. Only he hadn't the faintest clue whether he'd done the right thing, what right and wrong meant at all, or how the pieces might now fall.

INTERLUDE

Ramy

Ramiz Rafi Mirza had always been a clever boy. He had a prodigious memory, the gift of the gab. He soaked up languages like a sponge, and he had an uncanny ear for rhythm and sound. He did not merely repeat the phrases he absorbed; he uttered them in such precise imitation of the original speaker, investing his words with all their intended emotion, it was like he momentarily became them. In another life, he would have been destined for the stage. He had that ineffable skill, of making simple words sing.

Ramy was brilliant, and he had ample opportunity to show off. The Mirza family had navigated the vicissitudes of that era with great fortune. Although they were among the Muslim families who had lost land and holdings after the Permanent Settlement, the Mirzas had found steady, if not very lucrative, employment in the household of one Mr Horace Hayman Wilson, secretary of the Asiatic Society of Bengal in Calcutta. Sir Horace had a keen interest in Indian languages and literatures, and he took great delight in conversing with Ramy's father, who had been well educated in Arabic, Persian, and Urdu.

So Ramy grew up among the elite English families of Calcutta's white town, among porticoed and colonnaded houses built in European styles and shops catering exclusively to a European clientele. Wilson took an early interest in his education, and while other boys his age were still playing in the streets, Ramy was auditing classes at the Mohammedan College of Calcutta, where he learned arithmetic, theology, and philosophy. Arabic, Persian, and Urdu he studied with his father. Latin and Greek he learned from tutors hired by Wilson. English he absorbed from the world around him.

In the Wilson household, they called him the little professor. Blessed Ramy, dazzling Ramy. He had no idea what the purpose was of anything he studied, only that it delighted the adults so when he mastered it all. Often, he performed tricks for the guests Sir Horace had over to his sitting room. They would show him a series of playing cards, and he'd repeat with perfect accuracy the suit and number of the cards in the order in which they'd appeared. They would read out whole passages or poems in Spanish or Italian and he, not understanding a word of what was said, would recite it back, intonations and all.

He once took pride in this. He liked hearing the guests' shouts of wonder, liked the way they ruffled his hair and pressed sweets into his palm before they bade him scamper off to the kitchens. He had no understanding of class then, or of race. He thought it was all a game. He did not see his father watching from around the corner, eyebrows knitted with worry. He did not know that impressing a white man could be as dangerous as provoking one.

One afternoon when he was twelve years old, Wilson's guests summoned him during a heated debate.

'Ramy.' The man who waved him over was Mr Trevelyan, a frequent visitor, a man with prodigious sideburns and a dry, wolflike smile. 'Come here.'

'Oh, leave him be,' said Sir Horace.

'I'm proving a point.' Mr Trevelyan beckoned with one hand. 'Ramy, if you please.'

Sir Horace did not tell Ramy not to, so Ramy hurried to Mr Trevelyan's side and stood straight, hands clasped behind his back like a little soldier. He'd learned that English guests adored this stance; they found it precious. 'Yes, sir?'

'Count to ten in English,' said Mr Trevelyan.

Ramy obliged. Mr Trevelyan knew perfectly well he could do this; the performance was for the other gentlemen present.

'Now in Latin,' said Mr Trevelyan, and when Ramy had accomplished that, 'Now in Greek.'

Ramy complied. Gratified chuckles around the room. Ramy decided to test his luck. 'Little numbers are for little children,' he said in perfect English. 'If you'd like to converse about algebra, pick a language and we'll do that too.'

Charmed chuckles. Ramy grinned, rocking back and forth on his feet, waiting for the inevitable press of candy or coin.

Mr Trevelyan turned back to the other guests. 'Consider this boy and his father. Both of similar ability, both of a similar background and education. The father begins with even more of an advantage, I would say, as *his* father, I'm told, belonged to a wealthier merchant class. But so fortunes rise and fall. Despite his natural talents, Mr Mirza here can attain no better than a posting as a domestic servant. Don't you agree, Mr Mirza?'

Ramy saw the most peculiar expression then on his father's face. He looked as if he were holding something in, as if he'd swallowed a very bitter seed but was unable to spit it out.

Suddenly this game did not seem such fun. He felt nervous now for showing off, but couldn't quite put his finger on why.

'Come now, Mr Mirza,' said Mr Trevelyan. 'You can't claim that you *wanted* to be a footman.'

Mr Mirza gave a nervous chuckle. 'It's a great honour to serve Sir Horace Wilson.'

'Oh, come off it – no need to be polite, we all know how he farts.'

Ramy stared at his father; the man he still thought was as tall as a mountain, the man who had taught him all his scripts: Roman, Arabic, and Nastaliq. The man who taught him salah. The man who taught him the meaning of respect. His hafiz.

Mr Mirza nodded and smiled. 'Yes. That's right, Mr Trevelyan, sir. Of course, I'd rather be in your position.'

'Well, there you go,' said Mr Trevelyan. 'You see, Horace, these people have ambitions. They have the intellect, and the desire to self-govern, as so they should.* And it's your educational policies that

---

* Ramy was, though he did not know it, then at the centre of a debate between the Orientalists, including Sir Horace Wilson, who favoured teaching Sanskrit and Arabic to Indian students, and the Anglicists, including Mr Trevelyan, who believed Indian students of promise ought to be taught English.

This debate would come down firmly on the side of the Anglicists, best represented by Lord Thomas Macaulay's infamous February 1835 'Minute on Education': 'We must at present do our best to form a class who may be interpreters between us and the millions whom we govern – a class of persons Indian in blood and colour, but English in tastes, in opinions, in morals, and in intellect.'

are keeping them down. India simply has no languages for *statecraft*. Your poems and epics are all very interesting, to be sure, but on the matters of administration—'

The room exploded again into clamorous debate. Ramy was forgotten. He glanced at Wilson, still hoping for his reward, but his father cast him a sharp look and shook his head.

Ramy was a clever boy. He knew to make himself scarce.

Two years later, in 1833, Sir Horace Wilson left Calcutta to take on the position of the first Chair of Sanskrit at Oxford University.* Mr and Mrs Mirza knew better than to protest when Wilson proposed to bring their son with him to England, and Ramy did not begrudge his parents for not fighting to keep him at their side. (He knew, by then, how dangerous it was to defy a white man.)

'My staff will raise him up in Yorkshire,' Wilson explained. 'I will visit him when I can take leave from the university. Then, when he's grown, I'll have him enrolled at University College. Charles Trevelyan might be right, and English might be the path forward for the natives, but there's value yet in Indian languages where scholars are concerned. English is good enough for those chaps in civil administration, but we need our real geniuses studying Persian and Arabic, don't we? Someone's got to keep the ancient traditions alive.'

Ramy's family bid him farewell at the docks. He hadn't packed much; he would outgrow any clothes he brought in half a year.

His mother clasped the sides of his face and kissed him on the forehead. 'Make sure to write. Once a month – no, once a week – and make sure to pray—'

'Yes, Amma.'

His sisters clung to his jacket. 'Will you send presents?' they asked. 'Will you meet the King?'

'Yes,' he said. 'And no, I don't care to.'

His father stood a little way back, observing his wife and children, blinking hard as if trying to commit everything to memory. At last,

---

* Wilson's election to this position had raised something of a controversy. He had been in heated competition with Reverend W.H. Mill for election, and Reverend Mill's supporters spread the rumour that Wilson had insufficient character for the job, as he had eight illegitimate children. Wilson's supporters defended him on the grounds that in fact, he had only two.

when the boarding call sounded, he hugged his son to his chest and whispered, '*Allah hafiz.*' Write to your mother.'

'Yes, Abbu.'

'Forget not who you are, Ramiz.'

'Yes, Abbu.'

Ramy was fourteen then, and old enough to understand the meaning of pride. Ramy intended to do more than remember. For he understood now why his father had smiled that day in the sitting room – not out of weakness or submission, and not out of fear of reprisal. He'd been playing a part. He'd been showing Ramy how it was done.

Lie, Ramiz. This was the lesson, the most important lesson he'd ever been taught. *Hide, Ramiz. Show the world what they want; contort yourself into the image they want to see, because seizing control of the story is how you in turn control them. Hide your faith, hide your prayers, for Allah will still know your heart.*

And what an act Ramy put on. He had no trouble navigating English high society – Calcutta had its fair share of English taverns, music halls, and theatres, and what he saw in Yorkshire was no more than an expansion of the elite microcosm he'd grown up in. He thickened and thinned his accent depending on his audience. He learned all the fanciful notions the English held about his people, elaborated on them like an expert playwright, and spat them back out. He knew when to play a lascar, a houseboy, a prince. He learned when to flatter and when to engage in self-deprecation. He could have written a thesis on white pride, on white curiosity. He knew how to make himself an object of fascination while neutralizing himself as a threat. He fine-tuned the greatest of all tricks, which was to swindle an Englishman into looking at him with respect.

He grew so good at this that he almost began to lose himself in the artifice. A dangerous trap indeed, for a player to believe his own stories, to be blinded by the applause. He could envision himself as a postgraduate fellow, dripping with distinctions and awards. A richly paid solicitor on Legal. A highly acclaimed spontaneous interpreter, sailing back and forth between London and Calcutta, bringing riches and gifts for his family every time he returned.

And this scared him sometimes, how easily he danced around Oxford,

---

* 'Goodbye; may God be your protector.'

how attainable this imagined future seemed. Outside, he dazzled. Inside, he felt like a fraud, a traitor. And he was just starting to despair, to wonder if all he would ever accomplish was to become a lackey of empire as Wilson had intended, for the avenues of anticolonial resistance seemed so few, and so hopeless.

Until his third year, when Anthony Ribben appeared back from the dead and asked, 'Will you join us?'

And Ramy, without hesitating, looked him in the eyes and said, 'Yes.'

CHAPTER SIXTEEN

———— ⊶∞⊷ ————

It appears quite certain that the Chinese, a money-making and money-loving people, are as much addicted to trade, and as anxious as any nation on earth to court a commercial intercourse with strangers.

JOHN CRAWFURD, 'Chinese Empire and Trade'

Morning came. Robin rose, washed, and dressed for class. He met Ramy outside the house. Neither said a word; they walked in silence to the tower door, which, despite Robin's sudden fear, opened to let them in. They were late; Professor Craft was already lecturing when they took their seats. Letty shot them an irritated glare. Victoire gave Robin a nod, her face inscrutable. Professor Craft continued as if she hadn't seen them; this was how she always dealt with tardiness. They pulled out their pens and began taking down notes on Tacitus and his thorny ablative absolutes.

The room seemed at once both mundane and heartbreakingly beautiful: the morning light streaming through stained-glass windows, casting colourful patterns on the polished wooden desks; the clean scratch of chalk against the blackboard; and the sweet, woody smell of old books. A dream; this was an impossible dream, this fragile, lovely world in which, for the price of his convictions, he had been allowed to remain.

That afternoon they received notices in their pidges to prepare to depart for Canton by way of London by the eleventh of October – the day after next. They would spend three weeks in China – two in Canton, and one in Macau – and then stop in Mauritius for ten days on the way home.

Your destinations are temperate, but the sea voyage can be chilly, read the notice. *Bring a thick coat.*

'Isn't this a bit early?' asked Letty. 'I thought we weren't going until after our exams.'

'It explains here.' Ramy tapped the bottom of the page. 'Special circumstances in Canton – they're short on Chinese translators and want Babblers to fill in the gap, so they've pushed our voyage up ahead.'

'Well, that's exciting!' Letty beamed. 'It'll be our first chance to go out in the world and *do* something.'

Robin, Ramy, and Victoire exchanged glances with one another. They all shared the same suspicion – that this sudden departure was somehow linked to Friday night. But they couldn't know what that meant for Ramy's and Victoire's presumed innocence, or what this voyage held in store for them all.

The final day before they left was torture. The only one among them who felt any excitement was Letty, who took it upon herself to march into their rooms that night and make sure their trunks were properly packed. 'You don't realize how cold it gets at sea in the mornings,' she said, folding Ramy's shirts into a neat pile on his bed. 'You'll need more than just a linen shirt, Ramy, you'll want two layers at least.'

'Please, Letitia.' Ramy swatted her hand away before she could get at his socks. 'We've all been at sea before.'

'Well, I've travelled regularly,' she said, ignoring him. 'I ought to know. And we should keep a little bag of remedies – sleeping tinctures, ginger – I'm not sure there's time to run to a shop, we might have to do so in London—'

'It's a long time on a little ship,' snapped Ramy. 'It's not the Crusades.'

Letty turned stiffly to sort through Robin's trunk. Victoire cast Robin and Ramy a helpless look. They couldn't speak freely in Letty's presence, so they could only sit simmering in anxiety. The same unanswered questions bedevilled them all. What was happening? Had they been forgiven, or was the axe still waiting to drop? Would they naively board the ship to Canton, only to be abandoned on the other side?

Most importantly – how was it possible they'd been recruited separately to the Hermes Society without knowledge of the others? Ramy and Victoire at least had some excuse – they were new to Hermes; they might have been too frightened by the society's demands for silence to say anything to Robin yet. But Robin had known about Hermes for three years now, and he'd never spoken of it once, not even to Ramy. He'd done a marvellous job hiding his greatest secret from friends who, he'd proclaimed, owned his heart.

This, Robin suspected, had greatly rattled Ramy. After they'd walked the girls north to their lodgings that night, Robin tried to broach the subject, but Ramy shook his head. 'Not now, Birdie.'

Robin's heart ached. 'But I only wanted to explain—'

'Then I think we ought to wait for Victoire,' Ramy said curtly. 'Don't you?'

They headed to London the next afternoon with Professor Lovell, who was to be their supervisor throughout the voyage. The trip was, thankfully, much shorter than the ten-hour stagecoach ride that had brought Robin to Oxford three years ago. The railway line between Oxford and Paddington Station had finally been completed over the previous summer, its opening commemorated with the installation of silver bars under the platform of the newly constructed Oxford Station,* and so the journey took them only an hour and a half, during which Robin managed not to meet Professor Lovell's eyes once.

Their ship did not depart until tomorrow; they would lodge overnight at an inn on New Bond Street. Letty insisted they go out and explore London for a bit, so they ended up going to see the sitting room show of someone who called herself Princess Caraboo. Princess Caraboo was notorious among Babel students. Once a humble cobbler's daughter, she had persuaded several people into believing she was exotic royalty from the island of Javasu. But it was now nearly a decade since Princess Caraboo had been unmasked as Mary Willcocks of North Devon, and her show – which consisted of a strange hopping dance, several very emphatic utterances in a made-up tongue, and prayers to a god she called Allah-Tallah (here Ramy wrinkled his nose), came off as more

---

* The proliferation of Britain's railways had happened very quickly after the invention of silver-powered steam engines. The thirty-five-mile Liverpool-to-Manchester line, built in 1830, was the first railway built for general use, and nearly seven thousand miles of track had been laid around England since. The line from Oxford to London would have been built much sooner, but Oxford's professors delayed it for nearly four years on the grounds that such easy access to the temptations of the capital would wreak moral havoc on the young, naive gentlemen left in their care. And because of the noise.

pathetic than funny. The display put a bad taste in their mouths; they left early and returned to the inn, tired and laconic.

The next morning, they boarded an East India Company clipper named the *Merope* heading straight for Canton. These ships were built for speed, for they had to ferry perishable goods back and forth as quickly as possible, and were thus fitted out with state-of-the-art silver bars to hasten their voyage. Robin vaguely remembered that his first journey from Canton to London, ten years ago, had taken close to four months. These clippers could make that journey a mere six weeks.

'Excited?' Letty asked him as the *Merope* made its way out from the Port of London over the Thames towards open water.

Robin wasn't sure. He'd felt funny ever since they'd boarded, though he couldn't quite give a name to his discomfort. It didn't seem real that he was headed back. Ten years ago he'd been thrilled as he sailed towards London, head spinning with dreams of the world on the other side of the ocean. This time, he thought he knew what to expect. That scared him. He imagined his homecoming with a dreadful anticipation; the fear of not knowing one's own mother in a crowd. Would he recognize what he saw? Would he remember it at all? At the same time, the prospect of seeing Canton again seemed so sudden and unbelievable; he found himself with the strange conviction that by the time they reached it, it would have disappeared clean off the globe.

Still more frightening was the possibility that once he arrived, he'd be made to stay; that Lovell had lied and this whole trip was contrived to get him out of England; that he would be exiled from Oxford, and all that he knew, forever.

Meanwhile, there were six weeks at sea to suffer through. These proved torturous from the start. Ramy and Victoire were like dead men walking, pale-faced and jumpy, flinching at the slightest noises, and unable to engage in the simplest small talk without assuming expressions of utter terror. Neither of them had been punished by the university. Neither of them had even been called in for questioning. But surely, Robin thought, Professor Lovell at least suspected their involvement. The guilt was written all over their faces. How much, then, did Babel know? How much did Hermes know? And what had happened to Griffin's safe room?

Robin wanted nothing more than to discuss things with Ramy and Victoire, but they never had the opportunity. Letty was always there.

Even at night, when they retreated into their separate cabins, there was no chance that Victoire could sneak away to join the boys without Letty growing suspicious. They had no choice but to pretend everything was normal, but they were dreadful at this. They were all clammy, fidgety, and irritable. None of them could drum up enthusiasm for what ought to have been the most exciting chapter of their careers. And they couldn't make conversation about anything else; none of their old jokes or inconsequential debates came easily to mind, and whenever they did, they sounded heavy and forced. Letty – pushy, chatty, and oblivious – was grating on them all, and though they tried to conceal their irritation, for it wasn't her fault, they couldn't help snapping at her when she asked their thoughts on Cantonese cuisine for the dozenth time.

Finally she caught wind that something was going on. Three nights in, after Professor Lovell had departed the mess, she slammed down her fork at dinner and demanded, 'What is wrong with everyone?'

Ramy gave her a wooden stare. 'I don't know what you mean.'

'Don't pretend,' Letty snapped. 'You're all acting bizarre. You won't touch your food, you're mangling your lessons – I don't think you've even touched your phrasebook, Ramy, which is funny because you've been saying for months that you bet you could imitate a better Chinese accent than Robin—'

'We're seasick,' Victoire blurted. 'All right? Not all of us grew up summering up and down the Mediterranean like you.'

'And I suppose you were seasick in London, too?' Letty asked archly.

'No, just tired of your voice,' Ramy said viciously.

Letty reeled.

Robin pushed his chair back and stood. 'I need air.'

Victoire called after him, but he pretended not to hear. He felt guilty abandoning her and Ramy to Letty, for fleeing the catastrophic fallout, but he couldn't bear to be at that table for another moment. He felt very hot and agitated, as if a thousand ants were crawling around under his clothes. If he didn't get away, walk around, move, then he was sure he would explode.

Outside, it was cold and quickly turning dark. The deck was empty except for Professor Lovell, who was having a smoke by the prow. Robin almost turned back around when he saw him – they had not uttered a word to each other except for pleasantries since the morning after he'd been caught – but Professor Lovell had already seen him. He lowered his pipe and beckoned Robin to join him. Heart pounding, Robin approached.

'I remember the last time you made this voyage.' Professor Lovell nodded at the black, rolling waves. 'You were so small.'

Robin didn't know how to respond, so he merely stared at him, waiting for him to continue. To his great surprise, Professor Lovell reached out then and placed a hand on Robin's shoulder. But the touch felt awkward, forced; the angles off, the pressure too heavy. They stood, strained and baffled, like two actors before a daguerreotype, holding their positions just until the light flashed.

'I believe in fresh starts,' said Professor Lovell. He seemed to have rehearsed these words; they came out as stilted and awkward as his touch. 'What I mean to say, Robin, is that you're very talented. We'd be sorry to lose you.'

'Thank you,' was all Robin said, for he still had no idea where this was going.

Professor Lovell cleared his throat, then waved his pipe around a bit before he spoke, as if coaxing his own words out of his chest. 'Anyhow, what I really wish to say is – which I perhaps ought to have said before – I can understand if you were feeling . . . disappointed by me.'

Robin blinked. 'Sir?'

'I should have been more sympathetic to your situation.' Professor Lovell glanced back out at the ocean. He seemed to have trouble looking Robin in the eye and speaking at the same time. 'Growing up outside your country, leaving everything you knew behind, adapting to a new environment where I'm sure you received – well, less than the amount of care and affection you likely needed . . . Those were all things that affected Griffin as well, and I can't say I've handled things better the second time. You are responsible for your own poor decisions, but I confess I do in part blame myself.'

He cleared his throat again. 'I'd like for us to start anew. A clean slate for you, a renewed commitment on my part to be a better guardian. We'll pretend the past few days never happened. We'll put the Hermes Society, and Griffin, behind us. We'll think only of the future, and all the glorious and brilliant things you will achieve at Babel. Is that fair?'

Robin was momentarily struck dumb. To be honest, this was not a very large concession. Professor Lovell had only apologized for being, occasionally, somewhat distant. He hadn't apologized for refusing to claim Robin as a son. He hadn't apologized for letting his mother die.

Still, he'd made a greater acknowledgment of Robin's feelings than he'd ever done, and for the first time since they'd boarded the *Merope*, Robin felt that he could breathe.

'Yes, sir,' Robin murmured, for there was nothing else to say.

'Very good, then.' Professor Lovell patted him on the shoulder, a gesture so awkward that Robin cringed, and headed past him for the stairs. 'Good night.'

Robin turned back to the waves. He took another breath and closed his eyes, trying to imagine how he might feel if he really could erase the past week. He'd be exhilarated, wouldn't he? He'd be gazing over the horizon, hurtling into the future he'd been training for. And what an exciting future – a successful Canton trip, a gruelling fourth year, and then graduation into a post at the Foreign Office or a fellowship in the tower. Repeat voyages to Canton, Macau, and Peking. A long and glorious career translating on behalf of the Crown. There were so very few qualified Sinologists in England. He could be so many firsts. He could chart so much territory.

Shouldn't he want it? Shouldn't that thrill him?

He could still have it. That was what Professor Lovell had been trying to tell him – that history was malleable, that all that mattered were decisions of the present. That they could bury Griffin and the Hermes Society into the recesses of the untouched past – he wouldn't even need to betray them, simply ignore them – just like they'd buried everything else they'd agreed was better left unmentioned.

Robin opened his eyes, stared out over the rolling waves until he lost focus, until he was staring at nothing at all, and tried to convince himself that if he was not happy, he was at least content.

It was a week into the voyage before Robin, Ramy, and Victoire had a private moment to themselves. Halfway through their morning stroll, Letty went back below deck, claiming an upset stomach. Victoire offered half-heartedly to go with her, but Letty waved her off – she was still annoyed with them all, and clearly wanted to be alone.

'All right.' Victoire stepped closer to Robin and Ramy as soon as Letty had gone, closing off the gap made by her absence so that the three of them stood tight, an impenetrable silo against the wind. 'What in God's name—'

They all started talking at once.

'Why didn't—'

'Do you think Lovell—'

'When did you first—'

They fell silent. Victoire tried again. 'So who recruited you?' she asked Robin. 'It wouldn't have been Anthony, he would have told us.'

'But isn't Anthony—'

'No, he's very much alive,' said Ramy. 'Faked his death abroad. But answer the question, Birdie.'

'Griffin,' Robin said, still reeling from this revelation. 'I told you. Griffin Lovell.'

'Who's that?' Victoire asked, at the same time that Ramy said, '*Lovell?*'

'A former Babel student. I think he's also – I mean, he said he's my half-brother. He looks just like me, we think Lovell – I mean, our father—' Robin was tripping over his words. The Chinese character 布 meant both 'cloth' and 'to relate, to tell'. The truth was embroidered on a cloth tapestry, spread out to display its contents. But Robin, coming clean to his friends at last, had no idea where to start. The image he displayed was a jumbled and confused one, warped no matter how he told it by its complexity. 'He left Babel several years ago, and then went underground right around Evie Brooke's – I mean, ah, I think he killed Evie Brooke.'

'Good heavens,' Victoire said. 'Really? Why?'

'Because she caught him on Hermes business,' said Robin. 'I didn't know until Professor Lovell told me.'

'And you believe him?' asked Ramy.

'Yes,' said Robin. 'Yes, I think Griffin would – Griffin is absolutely the kind of person who would have . . .' He shook his head. 'Listen, the important thing is that Lovell thinks I was acting alone. Has he talked to either one of you?'

'Not me,' said Victoire.

'Nor I,' said Ramy. 'No one's approached us at all.'

'That's good!' Robin exclaimed. 'Isn't it?'

There was an awkward silence. Ramy and Victoire did not look half as relieved as Robin expected.

'That's good?' Ramy said finally. 'That's all you've got to say?'

'What do you mean?' asked Robin.

'What do you think I mean?' demanded Ramy. 'Don't avoid the subject. How long were you with Hermes?'

There was nothing to do but be honest. 'Since I started here. Since the very first week.'

'Are you joking?'

Victoire touched his arm. 'Ramy, don't—'

'Don't tell me that doesn't infuriate you,' Ramy snapped at her. 'That's three years. Three years he never told us what he was up to.'

'Hold on,' said Robin. 'Are you angry with *me*?'

'Very good, Birdie, you noticed.'

'I don't understand – Ramy, what did I do wrong?'

Victoire sighed and glanced out over the water. Ramy gave him a hard glare, and then burst out, 'Why didn't you just *ask* me?'

Robin was stunned by his vehemence. 'Are you serious?'

'You'd known Griffin for years,' said Ramy. '*Years*. And you never thought to tell us about it? You never thought we might like to join up as well?'

Robin could not believe how unfair this was. 'But you never told *me*—'

'I wanted to,' said Ramy.

'We were going to,' said Victoire. 'We begged Anthony, we almost let it slip so many times – he kept telling us not to, but we decided we would break it to you ourselves, we were going to do it that Sunday—'

'But you didn't even ask Griffin, did you?' Ramy demanded. 'Three years. Lord, Birdie.'

'I was trying to protect you,' Robin said helplessly.

Ramy scoffed. 'From what? Precisely the community we wanted?'

'I didn't want to put you at risk—'

'Why didn't you let me decide that for myself?'

'Because I knew you'd say yes,' Robin said. 'Because you'd join up with them on the spot and abdicate everything at Babel, everything you've worked for—'

'Everything I've worked for is *this*!' Ramy exclaimed. 'What, you think I came to Babel because I want to be a translator for the Queen? Birdie, I hate it in this country. I hate the way they look at me, I hate being passed around at their wine parties like an animal on display. I hate knowing that my very presence at Oxford is a betrayal of my race and religion, because I'm becoming just that class of person Macaulay hoped to create. I've been waiting for an opportunity like Hermes since I got here—'

'But that's just it,' said Robin. 'That's precisely why it was too risky for you—'

'And it's not for you?'

'No,' Robin said, suddenly angry. 'It wasn't.'

He didn't have to say why. Robin, whose father was on the faculty, who could pass for white under the right lighting, at the right angles, was shielded in a way Ramy and Victoire were not. If Ramy or Victoire had faced the police that night, they wouldn't have been on this ship, they would have been behind bars, or worse.

Ramy's throat pulsed. 'Damn it, Robin.'

'I'm sure it wasn't easy,' Victoire said, trying valiantly to broker a peace. 'They're so strict with their secrecy, you remember—'

'Yes, but we know each other.' Ramy shot Robin a glare. 'Or at least I thought we did.'

'Hermes is messy,' Robin insisted. 'They've ignored my warnings, they hang their members out to dry, and it wouldn't have done you any good to be sent down your first year—'

'I would have been careful,' Ramy scoffed. 'I'm not like you, I'm not scared of my own shadow—'

'But you're not careful,' Robin said, exasperated. So they were trading insults now. So they were being frank now. 'You were caught, weren't you? You're impulsive, you don't *think* – the moment anyone insults your pride you lash out—'

'Then what about Victoire?'

'Victoire's . . .' Robin trailed off. He had no defence. He hadn't told Victoire about Hermes because he'd assumed she had too much to lose, but there was no good way to say this out loud, or to justify its logic.

She knew what he meant. She would not meet his pleading look. 'Thank God for Anthony,' was all she said.

'I've just one more question,' Ramy said abruptly. He was really, truly furious, Robin realized. This was not merely a burst of Ramy-esque passion. This was something they perhaps could not come back from. 'What did you say to make it go away? What'd you give up?'

Robin couldn't lie to Ramy's face. He wanted to; he was so afraid of the truth, and of the way Ramy would look at him when he heard it, but this he could not hide. It would rip him apart. 'He wanted information.'

'And so?'

'So I gave him information.'

Victoire touched a hand to her mouth. 'Everything?'

'Just what I knew,' Robin said. 'Which wasn't much, Griffin made sure of it – I never even knew what he did with the books I took out for him. All I told Lovell about was one safe room at St Aldate's.'

It didn't help. She still looked at him as if he'd kicked a puppy.

'Are you mad?' Ramy asked.

'It didn't matter,' Robin insisted. 'Griffin's never there, he told me himself – and I bet they haven't even caught him, he's so incredibly paranoid; I bet he's already out of the country by now.'

Ramy shook his head in amazement. 'But you still betrayed them.'

This was profoundly unfair, Robin thought. He'd saved them – he'd done the only thing he could think of to minimize the damage – which was more than Hermes had ever done for him. Why was he now under siege? 'I was only trying to save you—'

Ramy was unmoved. 'You were saving yourself.'

'Look,' Robin snapped. 'I don't have a family. I have a contract, a guardian, and a house in Canton full of dead relatives that for all I know could still be rotting in their beds. That's what I'm sailing home to. You have Calcutta. Without Babel, I have nothing.'

Ramy crossed his arms and set his jaw.

Victoire cast Robin a sympathetic look, but said nothing in his defence.

'I'm not a traitor,' Robin pleaded. 'I'm just trying to survive.'

'Survival's not that difficult, Birdie.' Ramy's eyes were very hard. 'But you've got to maintain some dignity while you're at it.'

The rest of the voyage was decidedly miserable. Ramy, it seemed, had said all he wanted to say. He and Robin passed all the hours they spent in their shared cabin in desperately uncomfortable silence. Mealtimes weren't much better. Victoire was polite but distant; there was little she could say in Letty's presence, and she didn't make much effort to seek Robin out otherwise. And Letty was still angry with all of them, which made small talk nigh impossible.

Things would have been better if they had had a single other soul for company, but they were the only passengers on a trade ship where the sailors seemed interested in anything but befriending Oxford scholars, whom they considered an unwanted and ill-timed burden. Robin spent most of his days either alone above deck or alone in his cabin. Under any other circumstances, the voyage would have been a fascinating chance to examine the unique linguistics of nautical environments, which blended the necessary multilingualism brought about by foreign crews and foreign destinations with the highly technical vocabulary of seacraft. What was a banian day? What was marling? Was the anchor attached to the better end, or the bitter end? Normally he would have delighted in finding out. But he was busy sulking, still both baffled and resentful at how he'd lost his friends in the process of trying to save them.

Letty, poor thing, was the most confused of all. The rest of them at least understood the cause for the hostilities. Letty hadn't a clue what was going on. She was the only innocent here, unfairly caught in the crossfire. All she knew was that things were wrong and sour, and she was driving herself up the wall trying to figure out what the reason was. Someone else might have grown withdrawn and sullen, resentful at being shut out by their closest friends. But Letty was as pigheaded as ever, determined to resolve problems through brute force. When none of them would give her a concrete answer to the question 'What's happened?' she decided to try conquering them one by one, to pry out their secrets through oversolicitous kindness.

But this had the opposite of her intended effect. Ramy began leaving the room every time she came in. Victoire, who as Letty's roommate could not escape her, started showing up at breakfast looking haggard and exasperated. When Letty asked her for the salt, Victoire snapped so viciously at her to get it herself that Letty reeled back, wounded.

Undaunted, she began broaching startlingly personal topics every time she was alone with one of them, like a dentist prodding teeth to see where it hurt most, to find what needed fixing.

'It can't be easy,' she said to Robin one day. 'You and him.'

Robin, who thought at first she was talking about Ramy, stiffened. 'I don't – how do you mean?'

'It's just so obvious,' she said. 'I mean, you look so much like him. Everyone can see it, it's not like anyone suspects otherwise.'

She meant Professor Lovell, Robin realized. Not Ramy. He was so relieved that he found himself engaging in the conversation. 'It's a strange arrangement,' he admitted. 'Only I've grown so used to it that I've stopped wondering why it isn't otherwise.'

'Why won't he publicly acknowledge you?' she asked. 'Is it because of his family, do you think? The wife?'

'Perhaps,' he said. 'But I'm really not bothered. I wouldn't know what to do if he did declare himself my father, to be honest. I'm not sure I want to be a Lovell.'

'But doesn't it kill you?'

'Why would it?'

'Well, my father—' she started, then broke off and coughed primly. 'I mean. You all know. My father won't speak to me, hasn't looked me in the eyes and spoken to me after Lincoln, and . . . I just wanted to say, I know a bit what it's like. That's all.'

'I'm sorry, Letty.' He patted her hand and immediately felt guilty for doing it; it seemed so fake.

But she took the gesture at face value. She, too, must have been starved for familiar contact, for some indication that her friends still liked her. 'And I just wanted to say, I'm here for you.' She took his hand in hers. 'I hope this isn't too forward, but it's just that I've noticed, he's not treating you the same, not the way he used to. He won't look you in the eyes, and he won't speak to you directly. And I don't know what happened, but it's not right, and it's very unfair what he's done to you. And I want you to know that if you want to talk, Birdie, I'm here.'

She never called him Birdie. *That's Ramy's word*, Robin almost uttered, before realizing that would be the absolute worst thing to say. He tried to remind himself to be kind. She was, after all, only attempting her version of comfort. Letty was bull-headed and overbearing, but she did care.

'Thank you.' He gave her fingers a squeeze, hoping that if he did not elaborate, then this might force the end of the conversation. 'I appreciate that.'

At least there was work to distract. Babel's practice of sending entire cohorts, all of whom specialized in different languages, on the same graduation voyages was a testament to the reach and connectedness of the British trading companies. The colonial trade had its claws in dozens of countries across the world, and its labour, consumers, and producers spoke scores of tongues. During the voyage, Ramy was often asked to translate for the Urdu- and Bengali-speaking lascars; never mind that his Bengali was now rudimentary at best. Letty and Victoire were put to work looking over shipping manifests for their next leg to Mauritius, and translating stolen correspondences from French missionaries and French trading companies out of China – the Napoleonic Wars had ended, but the competition for empire had not.

Every afternoon, Professor Lovell tutored Ramy, Letty, and Victoire in Mandarin from two to five. No one expected they would be fluent by the time they docked in Canton, but the point was to force-feed them enough vocabulary that they would understand basic salutations, directions, and common nouns. There was also, Professor Lovell argued, a great pedagogical benefit to learning a wholly new language in a very short amount of time; it forced the mind to stretch and build rapid connections, to contrast unfamiliar language structures with what one already knew.

'Chinese is awful,' Victoire complained to Robin one night after class. 'There are no conjugations, no tenses, no declensions – how do you ever know the meaning of a sentence? And don't get me started on tones. I simply can't hear them. Perhaps I'm just not very musical, but I really can't tell the difference. I'm starting to think they're a hoax.'

'It doesn't matter,' Robin assured her. He was mostly glad she was talking to him at all. After three weeks Ramy had finally deigned to exchange basic civilities, but Victoire – though she still held him at arm's length – had forgiven him enough to speak to him like a friend. 'They don't speak Mandarin in Canton anyway. You'd need Cantonese to actually get around.'

'And Lovell doesn't speak it?'

'No,' Robin said. 'No, that's why he needs me.'

In the evenings, Professor Lovell primed them for the purpose of their mission in Canton. They were going to help negotiate on behalf of several private trading companies, foremost among them Jardine, Matheson & Company. This would be more difficult than it sounded, for trade relations with the Qing court had been marked by mutual misunderstanding and suspicion since the end of the past century. The Chinese, wary of foreign influences, preferred to keep the British contained with other foreign traders at Canton and Macau. But British merchants wanted free trade – open ports, market access past the islands, and the lifting of restrictions on particular imports such as opium.

The three previous attempts by the British to negotiate broader trading rights had ended in abject failure. In 1793, the Macartney embassy became a global punchline when Lord George Macartney refused to kowtow to the Qianlong Emperor and came away with nothing. The Amherst embassy of 1816 went very much the same way when Lord William Amherst similarly refused to kowtow to the Jiaqing Emperor and was subsequently refused admission to Peking at all. There was also, of course, the disastrous Napier affair of 1834, which climaxed in a pointless exchange of cannon fire and Lord William Napier's ignoble death of fever in Macau.

Theirs would be the fourth such delegation. 'It'll be different this time,' vowed Professor Lovell, 'because at last they've called on Babel translators to lead the talks. No more fiascoes of cultural miscommunication.'

'Had they not consulted you before?' Letty asked. 'That's quite amazing.'

'You'd be surprised how often traders think they shouldn't need our help,' said Professor Lovell. 'They tend to assume everyone should naturally just learn to speak and behave like the English. They've done a fairly good job at provoking local animosity with that attitude, if the Canton papers aren't exaggerating. Expect some less-than-friendly natives.'

They all had a good idea of the kind of tension they would see in China. They'd read more and more coverage of Canton in London's newspapers of late, which mostly reported the kinds of ignominies British merchants were suffering at the hands of brutal local barbarians. Chinese forces, according to *The Times*, were intimidating merchants, attempting to expel them from their homes and factories, and publishing insulting things about them in their own press.

Professor Lovell opined strongly that, though the traders could have been more delicate, such heightened tensions were fundamentally the fault of the Chinese.

'The problem is that the Chinese have convinced themselves that they're the most superior nation in the world,' he said. 'They insist on using the word *yi* to describe Europeans in their official memos, though we've asked them time and time again to use something more respectful, as *yi* is a designation for barbarians. And they take this attitude into all trade and legal negotiations. They recognize no laws except their own, and they don't regard foreign trade as an opportunity, but as a pesky incursion to be dealt with.'

'You'd be in favour of violence, then?' Letty asked.

'It might be the best thing for them,' said Professor Lovell with surprising vehemence. 'It'd do well to teach them a lesson. China is a nation of semi-barbarous people in the grips of backward Manchu rulers, and it would do them good to be forcibly opened to commercial enterprise and progress. No, I wouldn't oppose a bit of a shake-up. Sometimes a crying child must be spanked.'

Here Ramy glanced sideways at Robin, who looked away. What more was there to say?

Six weeks at last came to an end. Professor Lovell informed them at dinner one night that they could expect to dock at Canton by noon the next day. Prior to disembarking, Victoire and Letty were requested to bind their chests and to clip their hair, which they'd grown long during their years as upperclassmen, above their ears.

'The Chinese are strict about barring foreign women in Canton,' explained Professor Lovell. 'They don't like it when traders bring their families in; it makes it seem like they're here to stay.'

'Surely they don't actually enforce that,' protested Letty. 'What about the wives? And the maidservants?'

'The expats here hire local servants, and they keep their wives in Macau. They're quite serious about enforcing these laws. The last time a British man tried to bring his wife to Canton – William Baynes, I believe it was – the local authorities threatened to send in soldiers to remove her.* Anyhow, it's for your own benefit. The Chinese treat women very badly. They have no conception of chivalry. They hold their women in low esteem and, in some cases, don't even permit them to leave the house. You'll be better off if they think you're young men. You'll learn that Chinese society remains quite backwards and unjust.'

'I wonder what that's like,' Victoire said drily, accepting the cap.

The next morning they spent the sunrise hour above deck, milling about the prow, occasionally leaning over the railing as if those inches of difference would help them spot what navigational science claimed they were fast approaching. The thick dawn mists had just given way to blue sky when the horizon revealed a thin strip of green and grey. Slowly this acquired detail, like a dream materializing; the blurred colours became a

---

* Baynes ended up placing a cannon in front of the English Factory to keep the Chinese from seizing his wife, and it was all very exciting for a fortnight until the lady was at last peaceably persuaded to leave.

coast, became a silhouette of buildings behind a mass of ships docking at the tiny point where the Middle Kingdom encountered the world.

For the first time in a decade, Robin found himself gazing at the shores of his motherland.

'What are you thinking?' Ramy asked him quietly.

This was the first time they'd spoken directly to each other in weeks. It was not a truce – Ramy still refused to look him in the eyes. But it was an opening, a grudging acknowledgment that despite everything, Ramy still cared, and for that Robin was grateful.

'I'm thinking about the Chinese character for dawn,' he said truthfully. He couldn't let himself dwell on the larger magnitude of it all. His thoughts threatened to spiral to places he feared he could not control unless he brought them down to the familiar distraction of language. '*Dàn*. It looks like this.' He drew the character in the air: 旦. 'Up top is the radical for the sun – *rì*.' He drew 日. 'And under that, a line. And I'm just thinking about how it's beautiful because it's so simple. It's the most direct use of pictography, see. Because dawn is just the sun coming up over the horizon.'

CHAPTER SEVENTEEN

Quae caret ora cruore nostro?
What coast knows not our blood?

HORACE, *Odes*

A year ago, after overhearing Colin and the Sharp brothers loudly discussing it in the common room, Robin had gone alone to London over a weekend to see the celebrated Afong Moy. Advertised as the 'Chinese Lady', Afong Moy had been brought out of China by a pair of American traders who'd initially hoped to use an Oriental lady to showcase goods acquired overseas, but who quickly realized they could instead make a fortune exhibiting her person across the eastern seaboard. This was her first tour to England.

Robin had read somewhere that she was also from Canton. He wasn't sure what he'd hoped for other than a glimpse of, perhaps a moment of connection with, someone who shared his motherland. His ticket granted him admission to a garish stage room advertised as a 'Chinese Saloon', decorated with randomly placed ceramics, shoddy imitations of Chinese paintings, and a suffocating quantity of gold and red damask illuminated by cheap paper lanterns. The Chinese Lady herself was seated on a chair at the front of the room. She wore a blue silk buttoned shirt, and her feet, bound conspicuously in linen, were propped up on a small cushion before her. She looked very small. The pamphlet he'd been handed at the ticket booth claimed she was somewhere in her twenties, but she could have easily been as young as twelve.

The room was loud and packed with an audience of mostly men. They hushed when, slowly, she reached down to unbind her feet.

The story of her feet was also explained in the pamphlet. Like many young Chinese women, Afong Moy's feet had been broken and bound when she was young to restrict their growth and to leave them curved in an unnatural arch that gave her a tottering, unstable gait. As she walked across the stage, the men around Robin pushed forward, trying to get a closer look. But Robin could not understand the appeal. The sight of her feet seemed neither erotic nor fascinating, but rather a great invasion of intimacy. Standing there, watching her, he felt as embarrassed as if she'd just pulled down her trousers before him.

Afong May returned to her chair. Her eyes locked suddenly on Robin's; she seemed to have scanned the room and found kinship in his face. Cheeks flushing, he averted his eyes. When she started to sing – a lilting, haunting melody that he did not recognize and could not understand – he pushed his way through the crowd and left the room.

Apart from Griffin, he had not seen any Chinese people since.

As they sailed inland, he noticed that Letty kept looking at his face, then at the dockworkers' faces, as if comparing them. Perhaps she was trying to determine precisely how Chinese he looked, or to see if he was experiencing some great emotional catharsis. But nothing stirred in his chest. Standing on the deck, minutes from stepping foot in his motherland after a lifetime away, all Robin felt was empty.

They made anchor and disembarked at Whampoa, where they boarded smaller boats to continue up Canton's riverfront. Here, the city became a wash of noise, of the ongoing rumbling and humming of gongs, firecrackers, and shouting boatmen moving their craft up and down the river. It was unbearably loud. Robin did not remember such a din from his childhood; either Canton had grown much busier, or his ears had grown unaccustomed to its sounds.

They stepped ashore at Jackass Point, where they were met by Mr Baylis, their liaison with Jardine, Matheson & Co. Mr Baylis was a short, well-dressed man with dark, clever eyes who spoke with astonishing animation. 'You couldn't have arrived at a better time,' he said, pumping Professor Lovell's hand, then Robin's, and then Ramy's. The girls he ignored. 'It's a disaster here – the Chinese are getting bolder and bolder by the day. They've broken up the distribution rings – they bombed one of the fast crabs to bits in the harbour just the other day, thank God no one was on board – and the crackdowns will make trade impossible if this keeps up.'

'What about the European smuggling boats?' asked Professor Lovell as they walked.

'That was a workaround, but only for a bit. Then the Viceroy started sending his people door to door on house searches. The whole city's terrified. You'll scare a man off just by mentioning the name of the drug. It's all the fault of that new Imperial Commissioner the Emperor has sent down. Lin Zexu. You'll meet him soon; he's the one we'll have to deal with.' Mr Baylis spoke so quickly as they walked that Robin was astonished he never ran out of breath. 'So he comes in and demands the immediate surrender of all opium brought to China. This was last March. Of course we said no, so he suspended trade and told us we're not to leave the Factories until we're ready to play by the rules. Can you imagine? He put us under siege.'

'A siege?' Professor Lovell repeated, looking mildly concerned.

'Oh, well, it really wasn't so bad. The Chinese staff went home, which was a trial – I had to do my own washing, and that was a disaster – but otherwise we generally kept our spirits high. Really the only harms were overfeeding and lack of exercise.' Mr Baylis gave a short, nasty laugh. 'Happily that's over with, and now we can stroll around outside as we wish, no harm done. But there must be penalties, Richard. They've got to learn they can't get away with this. Ah – here we are, ladies and gents, here is your home from home.'

Past the southwestern suburbs they came upon a row of thirteen buildings in a line, all visibly Western in design, replete with recessed verandahs, neoclassical ornaments, and European flags. These looked so jarring against the rest of Canton that it seemed as if some giant had dug up a neat strip of France or England and dropped it wholesale onto the city's edge. These were the Factories, explained Mr Baylis, named not because they were centres of production, but because they were the residences of the factors – the agents of trade. Merchants, missionaries, government officials, and soldiers lived here during trading season.

'Lovely, aren't they?' said Mr Baylis. 'Quite like a handful of diamonds on top of a heap of old rubbish.'

They were to stay at the New English Factory. Mr Baylis led them quickly through the ground-floor warehouse, past the social room and dining room to the visiting chambers on the upper floors. There were also, he pointed out, a well-stocked library, several rooftop terraces, and even a garden facing the riverside.

'Now, they're very strict about keeping foreigners within the foreign enclave, so don't go exploring by yourselves,' Mr Baylis warned. 'Stay within the Factories. There's a corner in the Imperial Factory – that's number three – where Markwick & Lane sell all sorts of European goods you might need, though they haven't got many books apart from nautical charts. Those flower boats are strictly off limits, do you hear me? Our merchant friends can arrange for some women of a more discreet temperament to visit in the evenings if you need some company – no?'

Ramy's ears had gone bright red. 'We'll be fine, sir.'

Mr Baylis chuckled. 'Suit yourself. You'll be staying just down this hall.'

Robin and Ramy's room was quite gloomy. The walls, which must have originally been painted dark green, were now nearly black. The girls' room was as dark, and considerably smaller; there was barely space to walk between the single bed and the wall. It also had no windows. Robin could not see how they were possibly expected to live there for two weeks.

'Technically this is a storage unit, but we couldn't have you too close to the gentlemen.' Mr Baylis at least made an effort to sound apologetic. 'You understand.'

'Of course,' Letty said, pushing her trunk into the room. 'Thank you for your accommodations.'

After putting down their things, they congregated in the dining room, which was furnished with one very large table capable of seating at least twenty-five. Over the middle of the table was suspended an immense fan made of a cloth sail stretched over a wooden frame, which was kept in constant motion by a coolie servant who pulled and slackened it without pause throughout the dinner service. Robin found it quite distracting – he felt an odd pang of guilt every time he met the servant's eyes – but the other residents of the factory seemed to find the coolie invisible.

Dinner that night was one of the most ghastly and uncomfortable affairs Robin had ever endured. The men at the table included both Jardine & Matheson employees and a number of representatives from other shipping companies – Magniac & Co., J. Scott & Co., and others whose names Robin promptly forgot. They were all white men who seemed cut from precisely the same cloth as Mr Baylis – superficially charming and talkative men who, despite their clean-cut attire, seemed to exude an air of intangible dirtiness. Apart from businessmen there was Reverend Karl Gützlaff, a German-born missionary who apparently did more interpreting for the shipping companies than conversion of Chinese souls. Reverend Gützlaff proudly informed them that he was also a member of the Society for the Diffusion of Useful Knowledge in China,* and was currently writing a series of articles for a Chinese-language magazine to teach the Chinese about the difficult Western concept of free trade.

'We're delighted to have you working with us,' said Mr Baylis to Robin as the first course – a bland gingery soup – was served. 'It's so hard to find good Chinese translators that can string together a full sentence in English. The Western-trained ones are much better. You'll be interpreting for me during my audience with the Commissioner on Thursday.'

'I am?' Robin was startled. 'Why me?' This was a fair question, he thought; he'd never interpreted professionally before, and it seemed odd to choose him for an audience with the greatest authority in Canton. 'Why not Reverend Gützlaff? Or Professor Lovell?'

'Because we are Caucasian men,' Professor Lovell said wryly. 'And therefore, barbarians.'

'And they won't speak to barbarians, of course,' said Mr Baylis.

'Karl looks rather Chinese, though,' said Professor Lovell. 'Aren't they still convinced you're at least part Oriental?'

'Only when I introduce myself as Ai Han Zhe,'† said Reverend Gützlaff. 'Though I think Commissioner Lin will not be too enamoured with the title.'

The company men all chuckled, though Robin couldn't see what was

---

* This society, founded in November 1834, was created with the goal of inducing the Qing Empire to become more open to Western traders and missionaries through deploying 'intellectual artillery'. It was inspired by the London Society, which generously elevated the poor and dissuaded political radicalism through the gift of education.

† Reverend Gützlaff indeed often went by the name Ai Han Zhe, which translates as 'One who loves the Chinese'. This moniker was not ironic; Gützlaff really did see himself as the champion of the Chinese people, whom he referred to in correspondence as kind, friendly, open, and intellectually curious people who unfortunately happened to be under the 'thralldom of Satan'. That he could reconcile this attitude with his support for the opium trade remains an interesting contradiction.

so funny. A certain smugness underwrote this entire exchange, an air of brotherly fraternity, of shared access to some long-running joke the rest of them didn't understand. It reminded Robin of Professor Lovell's gatherings in Hampstead, as he'd never been able to tell what the joke was back then either, or what the men had to be so satisfied about.

No one was drinking much of their soup. Servants cleared their bowls away and replaced them with both the main course and dessert at once. The main course was potatoes with some sort of grey, sauce-covered lump – either beef or pork, Robin couldn't tell. Dessert was even more mysterious, a violently orange thing that looked a bit like a sponge.

'What's this?' Ramy asked, prodding his dessert.

Victoire sliced off a piece with her fork and examined it. 'It's sticky toffee pudding, I think.'

'It's orange,' said Robin.

'It's burnt.' Letty licked her thumb. 'And it's made with carrots, I think?'

The other guests were chuckling again.

'The kitchen staff are all Chinks,' explained Mr Baylis. 'They've never been to England. We keep describing the foods we'd like, and of course they have no idea how it tastes or how to make it, but it's still funny to see them try. Afternoon tea is better. They understand the point of sweet treats, and we've got our own English cows here to supply the milk.'

'I don't understand,' said Robin. 'Why don't you just have them cook Cantonese dishes?'

'Because English cuisine reminds one of home,' said Reverend Gützlaff. 'One appreciates such creature comforts on faraway journeys.'

'But it tastes like rubbish,' said Ramy.

'And nothing could be more English,' said Reverend Gützlaff, cutting vigorously into his grey meat.

'Anyhow,' said Mr Baylis, 'the Commissioner is going to be devilishly difficult to work with. Rumours are he's very strict, extremely uptight. He thinks Canton is a cesspool of corruption, and that all Western traders are nefarious villains intent on swindling his government.'

'Astute one, that,' said Reverend Gützlaff, to more self-satisfied chuckles.

'I do prefer when they underestimate us,' Mr Baylis agreed. 'Now, Robin Swift, the issue at hand is the opium bond, which would make all foreign ships assume responsibility before Chinese law for any opium they may smuggle in. It used to be that this ban existed on paper only. We'd dock our ships at – how shall we call them? – *outer anchorages*, like Lintin and Camsingmoon and such, where we'd distribute cargo for resale with local partners. But that's all changed under Commissioner Lin. His arrival, as I've told you, was quite the shake-up. Captain Elliot – good man, but he's a coward where it matters – defused the situation by letting them confiscate all the opium we had in our possession.' Here Mr Baylis clutched his chest as if physically pained. 'Over twenty thousand chests. Do you know how much that's worth? Nearly two and a half million pounds. That's unjust seizure of British property, I tell you. Surely that's grounds for war. Captain Elliot thinks he saved us from starvation and violence, but he's only shown the Chinese that they can walk all over us.' Mr Baylis pointed his fork at Robin. 'So that's what we'll need you for. Richard's caught you up on what we want in this round of negotiations, yes?'

'I've read through the proposal drafts,' Robin said. 'But I'm a bit confused on the priorities ...'

'Yes?'

'Well, it seems the ultimatum on opium is a bit extreme,' said Robin. 'I don't see why you couldn't break it into some more piecemeal deals. I mean, certainly you could still negotiate on all the other exports—'

'There are no other exports,' said Mr Baylis. 'None that matter.'

'It just seems that the Chinese have a rather good point,' Robin said helplessly. 'Given it's such a harmful drug.'

'Don't be ridiculous.' Mr Baylis smiled a wide, practised smile. 'Smoking opium is the safest and most gentleman-like speculation I am aware of.'

This was such an obvious lie that Robin blinked at him, astounded. 'The Chinese memorandums call it one of the greatest vices ever to plague their country.'

'Oh, opium's not as harmful as all that,' said Reverend Gützlaff. 'Indeed, it's prescribed as laudanum in Britain all the time. Little old ladies regularly use it to go to sleep. It's no more a vice than tobacco or brandy. I often recommend it to members of my congregation.'

'But isn't pipe opium a great deal stronger?' Ramy cut in. 'It really doesn't seem like sleep aids are the issue here.'

'That's missing the point,' said Mr Baylis with a touch of impatience. 'The point is free trade between nations. We're all liberals, aren't we?

There should be no restrictions between those who have goods and those who want to purchase them. That's justice.'

'A curious defence,' said Ramy, 'to justify a vice with virtue.'

Mr Baylis scoffed. 'Oh, the Qing Emperor doesn't care about *vices*. He's stingy about his silver, that's all. But trade only works when there's give and take, and currently we're sitting at a deficit. There's nothing we have that those Chinamen want, apparently, except opium. They can't get enough of the stuff. They'll pay anything for it. And if I had my way, every man, woman, and child in this country would be puffing opium smoke until they couldn't think straight.'

He concluded by slamming his hand against the table. The noise was perhaps louder than he intended; it cracked like a gunshot. Victoire and Letty flinched back. Ramy looked too amazed to reply.

'But that's cruel,' said Robin. 'That's – that's terribly cruel.'

'It's their free choice, isn't it?' Mr Baylis said. 'You can't fault business. Chinamen are simply filthy, lazy, and easily addicted. And you certainly can't blame England for the foibles of an inferior race. Not where there's money to be made.'

'Mr Baylis.' Robin's fingers tingled with a strange and urgent energy; he didn't know whether he wanted to bolt or to hit the man. 'Mr Baylis, *I'm* a Chinaman.'

Mr Baylis, for once, fell silent. His eyes roved over Robin's face, as if trying to detect the truth of this statement in his features. Then, to Robin's great surprise, he burst out laughing.

'No, you're not.' He leaned back and clasped his hands over his chest, still guffawing. 'Good Lord. That's hilarious. No, you're not.'

Professor Lovell said nothing.

Translation work began promptly the next day. Good linguists were always in heavy demand at Canton, and were pulled in a dozen different directions whenever they did show up. Western traders did not like using the government-licensed native Chinese linguists because their language skills were so often subpar.

'Forget English,' complained Mr Baylis to Professor Lovell, 'half of them aren't even fluent in Mandarin. And you can't trust them to represent your interests besides. You can always tell when they're not giving you the truth – I once had a man lie to my face about the customs rates when the Arabic numerals were right there.'

The trading companies occasionally employed Westerners fluent in Chinese, but they were hard to find. Officially, teaching Chinese to a foreigner was a crime punishable by death. Now, as China's borders were slightly more porous, this law was impossible to enforce, but it did mean skilled translators were often missionaries like Reverend Gützlaff with little spare time. The upshot was that people like Robin and Professor Lovell were worth their weight in gold. Ramy, Letty, and Victoire, poor things, would be shuttled from factory to factory all day doing silver-work maintenance, but Robin and Professor Lovell's itineraries were crammed with meetings starting from eight in the morning.

Promptly after breakfast, Robin accompanied Mr Baylis to the harbour to go over shipping manifests with Chinese customs officials. The customs office had supplied their own translator, a reedy, bespectacled man named Meng who uttered each English word with slow, timid deliberateness, as if terrified of mispronouncing anything.

'We will now go over the inventory,' he told Robin. His deferential, upwards-trailing tone made it sound as if he were asking a question; Robin could not tell if he was asking him for permission or not.

'Er – yes.' He cleared his throat, then enunciated in his best Mandarin, 'Proceed.'

Meng began reading off the inventory list, glancing up after every item so that Mr Baylis could confirm in which boxes those goods had been stored. 'One hundred twenty-five pounds copper. Seventy-eight pounds ginseng crude. Twenty-four boxes be . . . beetle—'

'Betel nuts,' corrected Mr Baylis.

'Betel?'

'You know, betel,' said Mr Baylis. 'Or areca nuts, if you will. For chewing.' He pointed to his jaw and mimed the act. 'No?'

Meng, still baffled, looked to Robin for help. Robin swiftly translated into Chinese, and Meng nodded. 'Beetle nuts.'

'Oh, enough of this,' snapped Mr Baylis. 'Let Robin do it – you can translate the whole list, can't you, Robin? It would save us a good deal of time. They're hopeless, I told you, all of them – a whole country, and not a single competent English speaker among them.'

Meng seemed to understand this perfectly. He cast Robin a scathing look, and Robin bent his head over the manifest to avoid his eye.

*   *   *

It went on like this all morning: Mr Baylis met with a procession of Chinese agents, all of whom he treated with incredible rudeness, and then looked to Robin as if expecting him to translate not only his words but his utter contempt for his interlocutors.

By the time they adjourned for lunch, Robin had developed a painful, throbbing headache. He could not take another moment of Mr Baylis's company. Even supper, which was served back in the English Factory, was no respite; Mr Baylis spent the whole time recounting silly claims the customs officials had made, and kept casting his stories in a way that made Robin sound like he'd verbally slapped the Chinese at every turn. Ramy, Victoire, and Letty looked very confused. Robin scarcely spoke. He scarfed down his food – this time a more tolerable, if flavour-less, dish of beef over rice – and then announced that he was heading back out.

'Where are you going?' asked Mr Baylis.

'I want to go and see the city.' Robin's irritation made him bold. 'We're done for the day, aren't we?'

'Foreigners aren't allowed in the city,' said Mr Baylis.

'I'm not a foreigner. I was born here.'

Mr Baylis had no rejoinder. Robin took his silence as assent. He snatched up his coat and strode towards the door.

Ramy hurried after him. 'Suppose I come with you?'

Please, Robin almost said, but hesitated. 'I'm not sure if you can.'

Robin saw Victoire and Letty glancing their way. Letty made as if to rise, but Victoire put an arm on her shoulder.

'I'll be fine,' said Ramy, pulling on his coat. 'I'll be with you.'

They walked out the front door and down the length of the Thirteen Factories. When they crossed from the foreign enclave into the Canton-ese suburbs, no one stopped them; no one seized them by the arm and insisted they return to where they belonged. Even Ramy's face attracted no peculiar comment; Indian lascars were a common sight in Canton, and they attracted less attention than white foreigners. It was, strangely, a complete reversal of their situation in England.

Robin led them through the streets of downtown Canton at random. He didn't know what he was looking for. Childhood haunts? Familiar landmarks? He had no destination in mind; no place he thought would bring catharsis. All he felt was a deep urgency, a need to walk over as much territory as he could before the sun went down.

'Does it feel like home?' Ramy asked – lightly, neutrally, as if tiptoeing on eggshells.

'Not in the least,' Robin said. He felt so deeply confused. 'This is – I'm not sure what this is.'

Canton was wildly different from the way he'd left it. The construction on the docks, which had been going on since Robin could remember, had exploded into entire complexes of new buildings – warehouses, company offices, inns, restaurants, and teahouses. But what else had he expected? Canton had always been a shifting, dynamic city, sucking in what the sea delivered and digesting it all into its own peculiar hybridity. How could he ever assume it might remain rooted in the past?

Still, this transformation felt like a betrayal. It felt like the city had closed off any possible path home.

'Where did you used to live?' Ramy asked, still in that careful, gentle tone, as if Robin were a basket of emotions threatening to spill.

'One of the shanty towns.' Robin looked around. 'Not too far from here, I think.'

'Do you want to go?'

Robin thought of that dry, stuffy house; the stink of diarrhoea and decomposing bodies. It was the last place in the world he wanted to visit again. But it seemed even worse not to have a look. 'I'm not sure I can find it. But we can try.'

Eventually Robin found his way back to his old home – not by following the streets, which had now become wholly unfamiliar, but by walking until the distance between the docks, the river, and the setting sun felt familiar. Yes, this was where home should have been – he remembered the curve of the riverfront, as well as the rickshaw lot on the opposite bank.

'Is this it?' asked Ramy. 'It's all shops.'

The street didn't resemble anything he remembered. His family house had disappeared off the face of the planet. He couldn't even tell where its foundations lay – they could have been beneath the tea shop in front of them, or the company office to its left, or the lavishly ornamented shop near the end of the street with a sign that read, in garish red paint: *huā yān guǎn*. Flower-smoke shop. An opium den.

Robin strode towards it.

'Where are you going?' Ramy hurried behind him. 'What's that?'

'It's where all the opium goes. They come here to smoke it.' Robin felt a sudden unbearable curiosity. His gaze darted around the shopfront, trying to memorize every detail of it – the large paper lanterns, the lacquered exterior, the girls in face paint and long skirts beckoning from the shopfront. They beamed at him, extending their arms like dancers as he approached.

'Hello, mister,' they cooed in Cantonese. 'Won't you come in for some fun?'

'Good heavens,' said Ramy. 'Come away from there.'

'One moment.' Robin felt compelled by some fierce, twisted desire to know, the same vicious urge that compelled one to prod at a sore, just to see how badly it could hurt. 'I just want to have a look around.'

Inside, the smell hit him like a wall. It was cloying, sickly, and sugar-sweet, both repulsive and enticing at once.

'Welcome, sir.' A hostess materialized around Robin's arm. She smiled wide as she took in his expression. 'Is this your first time?'

'I don't—' Suddenly the words failed Robin. He could understand Cantonese, but he couldn't speak it.

'Would you like to try?' The hostess held out a pipe towards him. It was already lit; the pot glowed with gently burning opium, and a small trickle of smoke unfurled from the tip. 'Your first on the house, mister.'

'What's she saying?' Ramy asked. 'Birdie, don't touch that.'

'Look how much fun they're having.' The hostess gestured around the sitting room. 'Won't you have a taste?'

The den was filled with men. Robin hadn't noticed them before, it was so dark, but now he saw that there were at least a dozen opium smokers sprawled over low couches in various states of undress. Some fondled girls perched atop their laps, some listlessly played a gambling game, and some lay alone in a stupor, mouths half-open and eyes half-closed, staring out at nothing.

Your uncle couldn't stay away from those dens. The sight prompted words he hadn't recalled in a decade, words in his mother's voice, words she'd sighed throughout his childhood. *We used to be rich, darling. Look at us now.*

He thought of his mother reminiscing bitterly about the gardens she used to tend and the dresses she used to wear before his uncle frittered their family fortune away in an opium den like this. He imagined his mother, young and desperate, eager to do anything for the foreign man who promised her coin, who used and abused her and left her with an

English maid and a bewildering set of instructions to raise their child, her child, in a language she couldn't speak herself. Robin was birthed by choices produced from poverty, poverty produced from this.

'A draught, mister?'

Before he registered what he was doing, the pipe was in his mouth – he was breathing in, the hostess was smiling wider, saying something he didn't understand, and everything was sweet and dizzy and lovely and awful all at once. He coughed, then sucked in hard again; he had to see how addictive this stuff was, if it really could make one sacrifice all else.

'Fine.' Ramy gripped his arm. 'That's enough, let's go.'

They walked briskly back through the city, this time with Ramy in the lead. Robin didn't speak a word. He couldn't tell how much those few draughts of opium had affected him, whether he was only imagining his symptoms. Once, out of curiosity, he had thumbed through a copy of De Quincey's *Confessions of an English Opium-Eater*, which described the effect of opium as communicating 'serenity and equipoise' to all the faculties, of 'greatly invigorating' one's self-possession, and of giving 'an expansion to the heart'. But he felt none of those things. The only words he would use to describe himself now were 'not quite right'; he felt vaguely nauseated, his head swam, his heart beat too fast, and his body moved far too slowly.

'You all right?' Ramy asked after a while.

'I'm drowning,' Robin mumbled.

'No, you're not,' said Ramy. 'You're only being hysterical. We'll get back to the Factories, and you'll drink a nice tall glass of water—'

'It's called *yánghuò*,'* said Robin. 'That's what she called the opium. *Yáng* means "foreign", *huò* means "goods". *Yánghuò* means "foreign goods". That's how they refer to everything here. *Yáng* people. *Yáng* guilds. *Yánghuòre* – an obsession with foreign goods, with opium. And that's me. That's coming from me. I'm *yáng*.'

They paused over a bridge, beneath which fishermen and sampans went back and forth. The din of it, the cacophony of a language he'd spent so much time away from and now had to focus on to decipher, made Robin want to press his hands against his ears, to block out a soundscape that should have but did not feel like home.

'I'm sorry I didn't tell you,' he said. 'About Hermes.'

---

* 洋货.

Ramy sighed. 'Birdie, not now.'

'I should have told you,' Robin insisted. 'I should have, and I didn't, because somehow I still had it all split in my head, and I never put the two pieces together because I just didn't see ... I just – I don't know how I didn't see.'

Ramy regarded him in silence for a long moment, and then stepped closer so that they were standing side by side, gazing out over the water.

'You know,' he said quietly, 'Sir Horace Wilson, my guardian, once took me to one of the opium fields he'd invested in. In West Bengal. I don't think I ever told you about it. That's where the bulk of this stuff is grown – in Bengal, Bihar, and Patna. Sir Horace owned a share in one of the plantations. He was so proud; he thought this was the future of the colonial trade. He made me shake hands with his fieldworkers. He told them that someday, I might be their supervisor. This stuff changed everything, he said. This corrected the trade deficit.

'I don't think I'll ever forget what I saw.' He rested his elbows against the bridge and sighed. 'Rows and rows of flowers. A whole ocean of them. They're such bright scarlet that the fields look wrong, like the land itself is bleeding. It's all grown in the countryside. Then it gets packed and transported to Calcutta, where it's handed off to private merchants who bring it straight here. The two most popular opium brands here are called Patna and Malwa. Both regions in India. From my home straight to yours, Birdie. Isn't that funny?' Ramy glanced sideways at him. 'The British are turning my homeland into a narco-military state to pump drugs into yours. That's how this empire connects us.'

Robin saw a great spider's web in his mind then. Cotton from India to Britain, opium from India to China, silver becoming tea and porcelain in China, and everything flowing back to Britain. It sounded so abstract – just categories of use, exchange, and value – until it wasn't; until you realized the web you lived in and the exploitations your lifestyle demanded, until you saw looming above it all the spectre of colonial labour and colonial pain.

'It's sick,' he whispered. 'It's sick, it's so sick ...'

'But it's just trade,' said Ramy. 'Everyone benefits; everyone profits, even if it's only one country that profits a good deal more. Continuous gains – that's the logic, isn't it? So why would we ever try to break out? The point is, Birdie, I think I understand why you didn't see. Almost no one does.'

Free trade. This was always the British line of argument – free trade, free competition, an equal playing field for all. Only it never ended up that way, did it? What 'free trade' really meant was British imperial dominance, for what was free about a trade that relied on a massive build-up of naval power to secure maritime access? When mere trading companies could wage war, assess taxes, and administer civil and criminal justice?

Griffin was right to be angry, thought Robin, but he was wrong to think he could do anything about it. These trade networks were carved in stone. Nothing was pushing this arrangement off its course; there were too many private interests, too much money at stake. They could see where it was going, but the people who had the power to do anything about it had been placed in positions where they would profit, and the people who suffered most had no power at all.

'It was so easy to forget,' he said. 'The cards it's built on, I mean – because when you're at Oxford, in the tower, they're just words, just ideas. But the world's so much bigger than I thought—'

'It's just as big as we thought,' Ramy said. 'It's just that we forgot the rest of it mattered. We got so good at refusing to see what was right in front of us.'

'But now I've seen it,' said Robin, 'or at least understand it a bit better, and it's tearing me apart, Ramy, and I don't even understand why. It's not as if – as if—'

As if what? As if he'd seen anything properly horrible? As if he'd seen the slave plantations in the West Indies at the height of their cruelty, or the starved bodies in India, victims of utterly avoidable famines, or the slaughtered natives of the New World? All he'd seen was one opium den – but that was enough to act as synecdoche for the awful, undeniable rest.

He leaned over the side of the bridge, wondering how it might feel if he just toppled over the edge.

'Are you going to jump, Birdie?' Ramy asked.

'It just doesn't feel . . .' Robin took a deep breath. 'It doesn't feel like we have the right to be alive.'

Ramy sounded very calm. 'Do you mean that?'

'No, I don't, I just . . .' Robin squeezed his eyes shut. His thoughts were so jumbled; he had no idea how to convey what he meant, and all he could grasp at were memories, passing references. 'Did you ever read *Gulliver's*

Travels? I read it all the time, when I lived here – I read it so often I nearly memorized it. And there's this chapter where Gulliver winds up on a land ruled by horses, who call themselves the Houyhnhnms, and where the humans are savage, idiot slaves called Yahoos. They're swapped. And Gulliver gets so used to living with his Houyhnhnm master, gets so convinced of Houyhnhnm superiority, that when he gets home, he's horrified by his fellow humans. He thinks they're imbeciles. He can't stand to be around them. And that's how this . . . that's . . .' Robin rocked back and forth over the bridge. He felt like no matter how hard he breathed, he could not get enough air. 'Do you know what I mean?'

'I do,' Ramy said gently. 'But it does no one any good for us to get into histrionics about it. So step down, Birdie, and let's go and have that glass of water.'

The next morning Robin accompanied Mr Baylis to the downtown government office for their audience with Imperial High Commissioner Lin Zexu.

'This Lin fellow is smarter than the rest,' said Mr Baylis as they walked. 'Nigh incorruptible. In the southeast, they call him Lin Qingtian* – clear as the heavens, he's so impervious to bribes.'

Robin said nothing. He had decided to suffer through the rest of his duties in Canton by doing the bare minimum required of him, and this did not involve egging on Mr Baylis's racist diatribes.

Mr Baylis did not appear to notice. 'Now, be on your toes. The Chinese are a devilishly tricky sort – duplicitous by nature, and all that. Always saying one thing when they mean quite the opposite. Careful you don't let them get the better of you.'

'I'll stay sharp,' Robin said shortly.

By Mr Baylis's account, one would imagine Commissioner Lin was nine-foot tall, had eyes that could shoot fire and trickster's horns. In person, the Commissioner was a mild-mannered, gentle-featured man of average height and build. His person was entirely nondescript save for his eyes, which seemed unusually bright and perceptive. He had with him his own interpreter, a young Chinese man who introduced himself as William Botelho, and who, to Robin's surprise, had studied English in the United States.

---

* 晴天, *qīngtiān*; *qīng* meaning 'clear', *tiān* meaning 'the skies or heavens'.

'Welcome, Mr Baylis,' said Commissioner Lin as William swiftly translated into English. 'I'm told you have some thoughts you would like to share with me.'

'The issue, as you know, is the opium trade,' said Mr Baylis. 'It is the opinion of Mr Jardine and Mr Matheson that it would benefit both your people and ours if their agents could legally sell opium along the coast in Canton without interference. They'd appreciate an official apology for the inhospitable treatment their trading agents received earlier this year. And it seems only just that the twenty thousand chests of opium that were seized a few months ago are returned to us, or at least monetary compensation equivalent to their market value.'

For the first few moments Commissioner Lin only listened, blinking, as Robin continued to rattle off Mr Baylis's list of demands. Robin tried not to convey Mr Baylis's tone, which was loud and patronizing, but to instead deliver them in as flat and emotionless a manner as he could manage. Still, his ears reddened in embarrassment; this did not feel like a dialogue but a lecture, the sort one might give a dim child.

Mr Baylis did not seem baffled by Commissioner Lin's lack of response; when his words met with silence, he merely continued: 'Misters Jardine and Matheson would also like to say that the Qing Emperor ought to realize his government's exclusive trade policies do not benefit the Chinese. Your own people, in fact, resent your trade barriers, which they believe do not represent their interests. They would much rather enjoy free association with foreigners, for that gives them too an opportunity to seek wealth. Free trade is, after all, the secret to national prosperity – and believe me, your people could do with reading some Adam Smith.'

Finally, Commissioner Lin spoke. 'We know this.' William Botelho swiftly translated. It was an odd conversation, conveyed through four people, none of whom spoke directly to the person he was listening to. 'These are the precise terms in the many letters delivered from Misters Jardine and Matheson, no? Have you come to say anything new?'

Robin looked expectantly to Mr Baylis. Mr Baylis faltered briefly. 'Well – no, but it bears repeating in person—'

Commissioner Lin clasped his hands behind his back, then asked, 'Mr Baylis, is it not true that in your own country, opium is prohibited with the utmost strictness and severity?' He paused to let William translate.

'Well, yes,' said Mr Baylis, 'but the question is trade, not Britain's domestic restrictions—'

'And,' continued Commissioner Lin, 'does not the sanction against your own civilians' use of opium prove that you know full well how harmful it is to mankind? We should like to ask, has China ever sent forth a noxious article from its soil? Have we ever sold you anything save for that which is beneficial, that which your country has great demand for? Is your argument now that the opium trade is, in fact, good for us?'

'The debate,' insisted Mr Baylis, 'is about economics. I once had an admiral seize my ship and search it for opium. When I explained to him I had none, as I follow the laws set by the Qing Emperor, he professed disappointment. He was hoping to purchase it wholesale and redistribute it himself, you see. Which proves the Chinese have much to profit from this trade as well—'

'You are still avoiding the question of who smokes the opium,' said Commissioner Lin.

Mr Baylis gave an exasperated sigh. 'Robin, tell him—'

'I will reiterate to you what we wrote to your Queen Victoria,' said Commissioner Lin. 'Those who wish to trade with our celestial empire must obey the laws set down by the Emperor. And the Emperor's new law, about to be put into force, reads that any foreigners bringing opium into China with designs to sell it will be decapitated, and all property on board the ship will be confiscated.'

'But you can't do that,' Mr Baylis blustered. 'Those are British citizens you're talking about. That's British property.'

'Not when they choose to be criminals.' Here William Botelho mirrored Commissioner Lin's cool disdain with exact precision, down to the slightest arch of his eyebrow. Robin was impressed.

'Now look here,' said Mr Baylis. 'The British don't fall under your jurisdiction, Commissioner. You haven't got any real authority.'

'I am aware that you believe your interests will always supersede our laws,' said Commissioner Lin. 'Yet we stand inside Chinese territory. And so I will remind you, and your masters, that we will enforce our laws as we see fit.'

'Then you know we'll have to defend our citizens as we see fit.'

Robin was so amazed Mr Baylis had spoken these words out loud that he forgot to translate. There was an awkward pause. At last, William

Botelho murmured Mr Baylis's meaning in Chinese to Commissioner Lin.

Commissioner Lin was utterly unfazed. 'Is this a threat, Mr Baylis?'

Mr Baylis opened his mouth, seemed to think better of it, and then closed it. Irritated as he was, he'd apparently realized that as much as he loved verbally berating the Chinese, he still couldn't issue a declaration of war without his government's backing.

All four parties regarded each other in silence.

Then abruptly, Commissioner Lin nodded to Robin. 'I would like a private conversation with your assistant.'

'Him? He hasn't any company authority,' Robin translated automatically on Mr Baylis's behalf. 'He's just the interpreter.'

'I mean only for a casual conversation,' said Commissioner Lin.

'I – but he's not permitted to speak on my behalf.'

'I don't need him to. In fact, I rather think we've said all that needs to be said to each other,' said Commissioner Lin. 'Don't you?'

Robin allowed himself the simple pleasure of watching Mr Baylis's shock turn to indignation. He considered translating his stuttered protests, but decided on silence when it became clear none of it was coherent. At last Mr Baylis, for lack of any better option, allowed himself to be escorted out of the room.

'You too,' Commissioner Lin told William Botelho, who obeyed without comment.

Then they were alone. Commissioner Lin gazed at him for a long, silent moment. Robin blinked, unable to sustain eye contact; he felt certain he was being searched, and this made him feel both inadequate and desperately uncomfortable.

'What is your name?' Commissioner Lin asked quietly.

'Robin Swift,' Robin said, then blinked, confused. The Anglophone name seemed incongruous for a conversation held in Chinese. His other name, his first name, had not been used for so long that it hadn't crossed his mind to say it.

'I mean—' But he was too embarrassed to continue.

Commissioner Lin's gaze was curious, unmoving. 'Where are you from?'

'Here, in fact,' said Robin, grateful for a question he could easily answer. 'Though I left when I was very young. And I haven't been back in a long time.'

'How interesting. Why did you leave?'

'My mother died of cholera, and a professor at Oxford became my guardian.'

'You belong to their school, then? The Translation Institute?'

'I do. It's the reason why I left for England. I've studied my whole life to be a translator.'

'A very honourable profession,' said Commissioner Lin. 'Many of my countrymen look down on learning barbarian tongues. But I've commissioned quite a few translation projects since I assumed power here. You must know the barbarians to control the barbarians, don't you think?'

Something about the man compelled Robin to speak frankly. 'That's rather the same attitude they have about you.'

To his relief, Commissioner Lin laughed. This emboldened Robin. 'May I ask you something?'

'Go ahead.'

'Why do you call them *yi*? You must know that they hate it.'

'But all it means is "foreign",' said Commissioner Lin. 'They are the ones who insisted on its connotations. They create the insult for themselves.'

'Then wouldn't it be easier just to say *yáng*?'

'Would you let someone come in and tell you what words in your own language mean? We have words to use when we wish to insult. They should feel lucky *guǐ** is not more prevalent.'

Robin chuckled. 'Fair enough.'

'Now I would like you to be frank with me,' said Commissioner Lin. 'Is there any point to negotiating this subject? If we swallowed our pride, if we bent the knee – would this mediate things whatsoever?'

Robin wanted to say yes. He wished he could claim that yes, of course, there was yet space to negotiate – that Britain and China, both being nations led by rational, enlightened people, could certainly find a middle ground without resorting to hostilities. But he knew this was not true. He knew Baylis, Jardine, and Matheson had no intention of compromising with the Chinese. Compromise required some acknowledgment that the other party deserved equal moral standing. But to the British, he'd learned, the Chinese were like animals.

---

* *Guǐ* (鬼) can mean 'ghost' or 'demon'; in this context, it is most commonly translated as 'foreign devil'.

'No,' he said. 'They want what they want, and they won't settle for anything less. They don't respect you, or your government. You are obstacles to be resolved, one way or another.'

'Disappointing. For all their talk of rights and dignity.'

'I think those principles only apply to those they find human.'

Commissioner Lin nodded. He seemed to have decided something; his features set with resolve. 'Then there's no need to waste words, is there?'

Only when Commissioner Lin turned his back to him did Robin realize he had been dismissed.

Unsure what to do, he gave an awkward, perfunctory bow and left the room. Mr Baylis was waiting in the corridor, looking disgruntled.

'Anything?' he demanded as servants escorted them out of the hall.

'Nothing,' Robin said. He felt slightly dizzy. The audience had ended so abruptly that he didn't know what to make of it. He'd been so focused on the mechanics of translation, on conveying Mr Baylis's precise meanings, word for word, that he'd failed to grasp the shift in the conversation. He sensed something momentous had just occurred, but he wasn't sure of what, nor his role in it. He kept going over the negotiation in his head, wondering if he'd made some disastrous mistake. But it had all been so civil. They had only reiterated positions well established on paper, had they not? 'He seemed to have considered the matter settled.'

Mr Baylis hurried immediately to the upstairs offices upon their return to the English Factory, leaving Robin alone in the lobby. He wasn't sure what to do with himself. He was supposed to have been out interpreting all afternoon, but Mr Baylis had absconded without any parting instructions. He waited in the lobby for a few minutes, then at last made his way to the sitting room, assuming it would be best to stay in a public area in case Mr Baylis decided he still needed him. Ramy, Letty, and Victoire sat at a table playing a game of cards.

Robin took the empty seat beside Ramy. 'Don't you have silver to polish?'

'Finished early.' Ramy dealt him a hand. 'Gets a bit boring here when you can't speak the language, to be honest. We're thinking we might take a boat trip to see the Fa Ti river gardens later when we're allowed. How was the meeting with the Commissioner?'

'Strange,' said Robin. 'We didn't get anywhere. He seemed very interested in me, though.'

'Because he can't figure out why a Chinese interpreter is working for the enemy?'

'I suppose,' Robin said. He couldn't shake a sense of foreboding, as if watching a gathering storm, waiting for the skies to split. The mood in the sitting room seemed too light-hearted, too tranquil. 'How are you all? You think they'll give you anything more interesting to do?'

'Not likely.' Victoire yawned. 'We're abandoned children. Mama and Papa are too busy wrecking economies to deal with us.'

'Good Lord.' Suddenly Letty stood. Her eyes were fixed, wide and horrified, on the window, where she pointed. 'Look – what in God's name—'

A great fire roared on the opposite bank. But the burn, they saw when they rushed to the window, was a controlled burn; it only seemed catastrophic because of the billowing flames and smoke. When Robin squinted, he saw that the flames were contained at their source to a pile of chests loaded on deep-bellied boats that had been pushed out to the shallows. A few seconds later he smelled their contents: a sickly sweet scent carried by wind across the coast through the windows of the English Factory.

Opium. Commissioner Lin was burning the opium.

'Robin.' Professor Lovell stormed into the room, followed closely by Mr Baylis. Both looked furious; Professor Lovell's face in particular was twisted with a rage Robin had never seen on him. 'What did you do?'

'I – what?' Robin looked from Professor Lovell to the window, baffled. 'I don't understand—'

'What did you say?' Professor Lovell repeated, shaking Robin by the collar. '*What did you tell him?*'

It was the first time Professor Lovell had laid hands on him since that day in the library. Robin didn't know what Professor Lovell might do now – the look in his eyes was beastly, wholly unrecognizable. *Please*, Robin thought wildly. *Please, hurt me, hit me, because then we'll know. Then there won't be any question.* But the spell passed as quickly as it came. Professor Lovell let go of Robin, blinking, as if coming back to himself. He took a step back and dusted off the front of his jacket.

Around them Ramy and Victoire stood tense, both crouching as if to spring between them.

'Excuse me, I simply—' Professor Lovell cleared his throat. 'Get your things and meet me outside. All of you. The *Hellas* is waiting in the bay.'

'But aren't we headed to Macau next?' Letty asked. 'Our notices said—'

'The situation's changed,' Professor Lovell said curtly. 'We've booked early passage back to England. Go.'

CHAPTER EIGHTEEN

*It were too much to expect that they will not require a further
demonstration of force on a larger scale before being brought to
their senses.*

JAMES MATHESON, letter to John Purvis

The *Hellas* departed Pearl Bay with impressive haste. Within fifteen
minutes of their boarding, the ropes were cut, the anchors pulled,
and the sails unfurled. They darted out of the harbour, chased by billowing smoke that seemed to engulf the whole of the city.

The crew, who had not been told until boarding that they would be
responsible for the room and board of five additional passengers, were
curt and annoyed. The *Hellas* was not a passenger ship, and its quarters
were already cramped. Ramy and Robin were told to bunk with the
sailors, but the girls were afforded a private cabin, which they shared
with the only other civilian on board – a woman named Jemima Smythe,
a Christian missionary from America who'd tried to sneak into the
mainland but was caught trying to ford the river into Canton's suburbs.

'Do you know what all the fuss is?' She kept asking this as they sat
hunched together in the mess. 'Was it an accident, or did the Chinese do
it on purpose? Will it be open war now, do you think?' The last question
she kept repeating excitedly at intervals, despite their exasperated assurances that they did not know. At last she changed the subject to what
they'd been doing in Canton, and how they'd passed their days in the
English Factory. 'There are quite a few reverends under that roof, aren't
there? What did you do for your Sunday services?' She stared inquir-
ingly at Ramy. 'Do you go to Sunday services?'

'Of course.' Ramy did not miss a beat. 'I go because I'm forced, where
I mumble apologies to Allah whenever possible.'

'He's joking,' Letty said quickly before the horrified Miss Smythe could begin trying to convert him. 'He's Christian, of course – we all had to subscribe to the Thirty-Nine Articles at Oxford matriculation.'*

'I'm very glad for you,' Miss Smythe said sincerely. 'Will you be spreading the gospel back home as well?'

'Home is Oxford,' Ramy said, blinking innocently. *God help us*, thought Robin, *he's snapped*. 'Do you mean that Oxford is full of heathens? Good heavens. Has anyone told them?'

At last Miss Smythe grew tired of them and wandered above deck to say her prayers, or whatever it was that missionaries did. Robin, Letty, Ramy, and Victoire huddled around the table, fidgeting like naughty schoolchildren awaiting punishment. Professor Lovell was nowhere to be seen; the moment they'd boarded, he'd gone off to speak to the captain. Still, no one had told them what was going on, or what would happen next.

'What *did* you say to the Commissioner?' Victoire asked quietly.

'The truth,' said Robin. 'All I told him was the truth.'

'But surely *something* set him off—'

Professor Lovell appeared at the door. They fell silent.

'Robin,' he said. 'Let's have a chat.'

He did not wait for Robin's answer before he turned and headed down the passage. Reluctantly, Robin stood.

Ramy touched his arm. 'Are you all right?'

'I'm fine.' Robin hoped they could not tell how quickly his heart was beating, or how loudly the blood thundered through his ears. He did not want to follow Professor Lovell; he wanted to hide and stall, to sit in the corner of the mess with his head buried in his arms. But this confrontation had been a long time coming. The fragile truce struck on the morning of his arrest was never sustainable. They'd been lying

---

* This was true, though Ramy did so only because he would not have been allowed to matriculate otherwise.

Religion had always been a point of contention between the four of them. Though they were all mandated by the college to attend Sunday services, only Letty and Victoire did so willingly; Ramy, of course, resented every minute, and Robin had been raised by Professor Lovell to be a devout atheist. 'Christianity is barbaric,' Professor Lovell opined. 'It's all self-flagellation, professed repression, and bloody, superstitious rituals as dress-up for doing whatever one wants. Go to church, if they make you, but take it as a chance to practise your recitations under your breath.'

to themselves for too long, he and his father. Things could not remain buried, hidden, and wilfully ignored forever. Sooner or later, things had to come to a head.

'I'm curious.' Professor Lovell was sitting behind a desk, paging idly through a dictionary when Robin at last made his way to his cabin. 'Do you know the value of those chests burned in the harbour?'

Robin stepped inside and closed the door behind him. His knees trembled. He could have been eleven again, caught for reading fiction when he shouldn't have been, cringing from the impending blow. But he was not a child anymore. He tried his very best to keep his voice from wobbling. 'Sir, I don't know what happened with the Commissioner, but it's not—'

'Over two million pounds,' said Professor Lovell. 'You heard Mr Baylis. Two million, much of which William Jardine and James Matheson are now personally responsible for.'

'He'd made up his mind,' said Robin. 'He'd made it up before he even met with us. There was nothing I could say—'

'Your job was not difficult. Be a mouthpiece for Harold Baylis. Present a friendly face to the Chinese. Smooth things over. I thought we were clear on your priorities here, no? What did you say to Commissioner Lin?'

'I don't know what you think I did,' said Robin, frustrated. 'But what happened at the docks wasn't because of me.'

'Did you suggest he should destroy the opium?'

'Of course not.'

'Did you intimate anything else to him about Jardine and Matheson? Did you, perhaps, usurp Harold in any way? You're sure there was nothing untoward about how you conducted yourself?'

'I did what I was told,' Robin insisted. 'I don't like Mr Baylis, no, but as far as how I represented the company—'

'For once, Robin, please try to simply say what you mean,' said Professor Lovell. 'Be honest. Whatever you're doing now, it's embarrassing.'

'I – all right, then.' Robin folded his arms. He had nothing to apologize for, nothing more to hide. Ramy and Victoire were safe; he had nothing to lose. No more bowing, no more silence. 'Fine. Let's be honest with each other. I don't agree with what Jardine & Matheson is doing in Canton. It's wrong, it disgusts me—'

Professor Lovell shook his head. 'For heaven's sake, it's just a market. Don't be childish.'

'It's a sovereign nation.'

'It is a nation mired in superstition and antiquity, devoid of the rule of law, hopelessly behind the West on every possible register. It is a nation of semi-barbarous, incorrigibly backwards fools—'

'It's a nation of *people*,' Robin snapped. 'People you're poisoning, whose lives you're ruining. And if the question is whether I'll keep facilitating that project, then it's no – I won't come back to Canton again, not for the traders, and not for anything remotely related to opium. I'll do research at Babel, I'll do translations, but I won't do that. You can't make me.'

He was breathing very hard when he finished. Professor Lovell's expression had not changed. He watched Robin for a long moment, eyelids half-closed, tapping his fingers against his desk as if it were a piano.

'You know what astounds me?' His voice had grown very soft. 'How utterly ungrateful one can be.'

This line of argument again. Robin could have kicked something. Always this, the argument from bondage, as if his loyalties were shackled by privilege he had not asked for and did not choose to receive. Did he owe Oxford his life, just because he had drunk champagne within its cloisters? Did he owe Babel his loyalty because he had once believed its lies?

'This wasn't for me,' he said. 'I didn't ask for it. It was all for you, because you wanted a Chinese pupil, because you wanted someone who was fluent—'

'You resent me, then?' asked Professor Lovell. 'For giving you a life? For giving you opportunities you couldn't have dreamed of?' He sneered. 'Yes, Robin, I took you from your home. From the squalor and disease and hunger. What do you want? An apology?'

What he wanted, Robin thought, was for Professor Lovell to admit what he'd done. That it was unnatural, this entire arrangement; that children were not stock to be experimented on, judged for their blood, spirited away from their homeland in service of Crown and country. That Robin was more than a talking dictionary, and that his motherland was more than a fat golden goose. But he knew these were acknowledgments that Professor Lovell would never make. The truth between them was not buried because it was painful, but because it was inconvenient, and because Professor Lovell simply refused to address it.

It was so obvious now that he was not, and could never be, a person in his father's eyes. No, personhood demanded the blood purity of the European man, the racial status that would make him Professor Lovell's equal. Little Dick and Philippa were persons. Robin Swift was an asset, and assets should be undyingly grateful that they were treated well at all.

There could be no resolution here. But at least Robin would have the truth about something.

'Who was my mother to you?' he asked.

This, at least, seemed to rattle the professor, if only for the briefest moment. 'We are not here to discuss your mother.'

'You killed her. And you didn't even bother to bury her.'

'Don't be absurd. It was the Asiatic Cholera that killed her—'

'You were in Macau for two weeks before she died. Mrs Piper told me. You knew the plague was spreading, you know you could have saved her—'

'Heavens, Robin, she was just some Chink.'

'But I'm just some Chink, Professor. I'm also her son.' Robin felt a fierce urge to cry. He forced it down. Hurt never garnered sympathy from his father. But anger, perhaps, might spark fear. 'Did you think you'd washed that part out of me?'

He had become so good at holding two truths in his head at once. That he was an Englishman and not. That Professor Lovell was his father and not. That the Chinese were a stupid, backwards people, and that he was also one of them. That he hated Babel, and wanted to live forever in its embrace. He had danced for years on the razor's edge of these truths, had remained there as a means of survival, a way to cope, unable to accept either side fully because an unflinching examination of the truth was so frightening that the contradictions threatened to break him.

But he could not go on like this. He could not exist a split man, his psyche constantly erasing and re-erasing the truth. He felt a great pressure in the back of his mind. He felt like he would quite literally burst, unless he stopped being double. Unless he chose.

'Did you think,' said Robin, 'that enough time in England would make me just like you?'

Professor Lovell cocked his head. 'You know, I once thought that having offspring was a kind of translation of its own. Especially when the parents are of such vastly different stock. One is curious to see what ends up coming through.' His face underwent the strangest transformation as he spoke. His eyes grew larger and larger until they were frighteningly bulbous; his condescending sneer grew more pronounced, and his lips drew back to reveal teeth. It was meant, perhaps, as a look of exaggerated disgust, but it appeared more to Robin as if a mask of civility had been stripped away. It was the ugliest expression he had ever seen his father wear. 'I'd hoped to raise you to avoid the failings of your brother. I hoped to instill you with a more civilized sense of ethics. *Quo semel est imbuta recens, servabit odorem testa diu,*[*] and all that. I hoped I might develop you into a more elevated cask. But for all your education, there is no raising you from that base, original stock, is there?'

'You're a monster,' Robin said, amazed.

'I haven't the time for this.' Professor Lovell flipped the dictionary shut. 'It's clear bringing you to Canton was the wrong idea. I had hoped it might remind you how lucky you were, but all it's done is confuse you.'

'I'm not confused—'

'We'll re-evaluate your position at Babel when we return.' Professor Lovell gestured towards the door. 'For now, I think, you ought to take some time to reflect. Imagine spending the rest of your life in Newgate, Robin. You can rail against the evils of commerce all you like, if you do it in a prison cell. Would you prefer that?'

Robin's hands formed fists. 'Say her name.'

Professor Lovell's eyebrow twitched. He gestured again to the door. 'That will be all.'

'Say her name, you coward.'

'*Robin.*'

This was a warning. This was where his father drew the line. Everything Robin had done until now might still be forgiven, if he only backed down; if he only made his apologies, bent to authority, and returned to naive, ignorant luxury.

But Robin had been bending for so long. And even a gilded cage was still a cage.

He stepped forward. 'Father, *say her name.*'

Professor Lovell pushed his chair back and stood.

---

[*] Horace, on the education of youths to ward off corruption. 'A cask will long retain the flavour of that with which it was first filled.'

The origins of the word *anger* were tied closely to physical suffering. *Anger* was first an 'affliction', as meant by the Old Icelandic *angr*, and then a 'painful, cruel, narrow' state, as meant by the Old English *enge*, which in turn came from the Latin *angor*, which meant 'strangling, anguish, distress'. Anger was a chokehold. Anger did not empower you. It sat on your chest; it squeezed your ribs until you felt trapped, suffocated, out of options. Anger simmered, then exploded. Anger was constriction, and the consequent rage a desperate attempt to breathe.

And *rage*, of course, came from madness.*

Afterwards, Robin wondered often if Professor Lovell had seen something in his eyes, a fire he hadn't known his son possessed, and whether that – his startled realization that his linguistic experiment had developed a will of his own – had prompted Robin in turn to act. He would try desperately to justify what he'd done as self-defence, but such justification would rely on details he could hardly remember, details he wasn't sure whether he'd made up to convince himself he had not really murdered his father in cold blood.

Over and over again he would ask himself who had moved first, and this would torture him for the rest of his days, for he truly did not know.

This he knew:

Professor Lovell stood abruptly. His hand went to his pocket. And Robin, either mirroring or provoking him, did the same. He reached for his front pocket, where he kept the bar that had killed Eveline Brooke. He was not imagining what the bar might do – of this he was certain. He spoke the match-pair because they were the only words that came to mind to describe this moment, its immensity. He thought of Professor Lovell's poker cracking over and over against his ribs as he lay curled on the library floor, too startled and confused to cry out. He thought of Griffin, poor Griffin, spirited to England at a younger age than he'd been; chewed up and thrown away because he didn't remember enough of his native tongue. He thought of the listless men in the opium den. He thought of his mother.

He was not thinking of how the bar would claw apart his father's chest. Some part of him must have known, of course, because words only activated the bars if you meant them. If you only uttered the syllables, they had no effect. And when he saw the character in his mind, saw the

---

* From the Latin *rabere*: 'to rave, to be mad'.

grooves etched in shining silver, and spoke the word and its translation out loud, he must have thought of what it would do.

Bào: to explode, to burst forth with what could no longer be contained.

But it was not until Professor Lovell fell to the floor, until the heady, salty scent of blood filled the air, that Robin realized what he'd done.

He dropped to his knees. 'Sir?'

Professor Lovell did not stir.

'Father?' He grasped Professor Lovell's shoulders. Hot, wet blood spilled over his fingers. It would not stop; it was everywhere, an endless fountain gushing out of that ruin of a chest.

'*Diē?*'

He did not know what made him say it, the word for *father*. Perhaps he thought it would stun Professor Lovell, that the shock alone would bring him back to life, that he could yank his father's soul back to his body by naming the one thing that they had never named. But Professor Lovell was limp, gone, and no matter how hard Robin shook him the blood would not stop pouring.

'*Diē,*' he said again. Then a laugh escaped his throat; hysterical, helpless, because it was so very funny, so apt that the romanization of *father* contained the same letters for death in English. And Professor Lovell was so clearly, incontrovertibly dead. There was no walking back from this. There could be no more pretending.

'Robin?'

Someone banged at the door. Dazed, without thinking, Robin stood and unlatched it. Ramy, Letty, and Victoire came tumbling in, a babble of voices – 'Oh, Robin, are you—'; 'What's happening—'; 'We heard shouting, we thought—'

Then they saw the body and the blood. Letty let out a muffled shriek. Victoire's hands flew to her mouth. Ramy blinked several times, then uttered, very softly, 'Oh.'

Letty asked, very faintly, 'Is he . . . ?'

'Yes,' Robin whispered.

The cabin went very silent. Robin's ears were ringing; he brought his hands to his head, then immediately lowered them, for they were bright scarlet and dripping.

'What happened . . . ?' Victoire ventured.

'We quarrelled.' Robin could barely get the words out. He was struggling now to breathe. Black pressed in at the edges of his vision. His knees felt very weak, and he wanted badly to sit down, only the floor was drenched in a spreading pool of blood. 'We quarrelled, and . . .'

'Don't look,' Ramy instructed.

No one obeyed. They all stood frozen in place, gazes locked on Professor Lovell's still form as Ramy knelt beside him and held two fingers against his neck. A long moment passed. Ramy murmured a prayer under his breath – *'Inna lillahi wa inna ilayhi Raji'un'* – and then moved his hands over Professor Lovell's eyelids to push them closed.

He exhaled very slowly, pressed his hands against his knees for a moment, then stood up. 'What now?'

BOOK IV

ROYAL INSTITUTE OF TRANSLATION
UNIVERSITY OF OXFORD

Chapter Nineteen

―∞∞∞―

'There is, first of all,' I said, 'the greatest lie about the things of greatest concernment, which was no pretty invention of him who told how Uranus did what Hesiod says he did to Cronos, and how Cronos in turn took his revenge; and then there are the doings and sufferings of Cronos at the hands of his son. Even if they were true I should not think that they ought to be thus lightly told to thoughtless young persons.'

PLATO, *Republic*, trans. Paul Shorey

'Keep him in the cabin,' Victoire said with amazing composure, though the words that came out of her mouth were quite mad. 'We'll just . . . roll him up in those sheets and keep him out of sight until we get back to England—'

'We can't keep a body concealed for six weeks,' Letty shrilled.

'Why not?'

'It'll rot!'

'Fair that,' said Ramy. 'Sailors smell bad, but they don't smell that bad.'

Robin was stunned that their first instinct was to discuss how to hide the body. It didn't change the fact that he'd just killed his father, or that he'd possibly implicated all of them in the murder, or that scarlet streaked the walls, the floor, his neck, and his hands. But they were talking as if this were only a matter to be fixed – a thorny translation that could be resolved, if they could only find the right turn of phrase.

'All right, look – here's what we'll do.' Victoire pushed her palms against her temples and took a deep breath. 'We'll get rid of the body somehow. I don't know how, we'll figure out a way. Then when we dock—'

'How do we tell the crew to leave him alone for six *weeks*?' Letty demanded.

'Nine weeks,' said Victoire.

'What?'

'This isn't one of the fast clippers,' said Victoire. 'It'll take nine weeks.'

Letty pressed her palms against her eyes. 'For the love of God.'

'How's this?' asked Victoire. 'We'll tell them he's got some contagion. I don't know, some – some scary disease – Robin, you come up with something exotic and disgusting that will scare them off. Say it's something he picked up in the slums and they'll all be too scared to come in.'

There was a brief silence. This was, they all had to admit, rather good logic; or at least, it was not immediately evident this was nonsense.

'Fine.' Ramy had begun pacing back and forth across the small stretch of wooden floorboards that weren't covered with blood. 'Oh, heavens – Allah forgive us.' He rubbed at his eyes. 'Fine, yes, that could work. Suppose we keep this a secret until we're back in London. What then?'

'Easy,' said Victoire. 'We'll say he died during the journey. During his sleep, perhaps. Only we can't have the ship's doctor coming to do an autopsy, because the risk of contamination is too great. We'll ask for a coffin, which we'll stuff a bunch of – I don't know, books rolled up in clothes – and then we'll carry it off and get rid of it.'

'That's insane,' said Letty. 'That's absolutely insane.'

'Do you have a better idea?' Victoire inquired.

Letty was silent for a moment. Robin was absolutely sure she would insist they turn themselves in, but then she threw up her hands and said, 'We could just tip him overboard in broad daylight, say he accidentally drowned, and then they'll all have seen him die so we won't seem suspicious—'

'Oh, and that's not suspicious?' asked Ramy. 'We'll just drag this bloody corpse up above deck, pretend it's walking on its own, and then hurl it into the waves where anyone can see that gaping hole where his heart should be? That's how we prove our innocence? Have some *creativity*, Letty, we've got to play this right—'

At last Robin found his tongue. 'No. No, this is mad, I can't let – You all can't—' He kept tripping over his words. He took a deep breath, stilled his tongue. 'I did this. I'll tell the captain, I'll turn myself in, and that's it.'

Ramy scoffed. 'Well, that's out of the question.'

'Don't be an idiot,' said Robin. 'You'll be implicated if—'

'We're all implicated regardless,' said Victoire. 'We're all foreigners returning from a foreign country on a ship with a dead white man.' This statement excluded Letty, but no one corrected her. 'There is no world in which you go to prison and the rest of us walk free. You see this, right? Either we protect you, or we damn ourselves.'

'That's right,' Ramy said firmly. 'And none of us are letting you go to prison, Birdie. We'll all keep our silence, all right?'

Only Letty hadn't spoken. Victoire nudged her. 'Letty?'

Letty had turned so pale she matched the bloodless corpse on the floor. 'I . . . yes. All right.'

'You can go, Letty,' said Robin. 'You don't have to hear—'

'No, I want to be here,' said Letty. 'I want to know what happens next. I can't just let you all . . . No.' She squeezed her eyes shut and shook her head, then reopened her eyes and announced very slowly, as if she'd just come to the decision, 'I'm in this. With you. All of you.'

'Good,' Ramy said briskly. He wiped his hands on his trousers, then resumed his pacing. 'Now, here's what I'm thinking. We aren't supposed to be on this packet. We were originally scheduled to return on the fourth, remember? No one's expecting us back before then, which means nobody will be looking for him when we disembark.'

'Right.' Victoire nodded, then picked up his train of thought. It was quite frightening, watching the two of them. They grew more confident as they spoke. It was as if they were simply collaborating on a group translation, playing off each other's brilliance. 'It's clear the easiest way to get caught is for someone to glimpse the body. So our first priority, as I said, should be to get rid of it as soon as possible – as soon as it's dark outside. Then, for the rest of the voyage, we'll tell everyone he's ill. No one's more afraid of foreign diseases than sailors, isn't that right? The moment we let slip that he's down with something that they might catch, I guarantee you no one will approach that door for weeks. Which means all we've got to worry about is getting him into the water.'

'Well, and cleaning up all this blood,' said Ramy.

Madness, Robin thought. This was madness, and he couldn't understand why no one was laughing, why everyone seemed to be very seriously contemplating the idea of dragging their professor's body up two flights of stairs and hurling it into the sea. They were all past the point of incredulity. The shock had worn off, and the surreal had become the practical. They were speaking not in terms of ethics, but of logistics, and this made Robin feel as if they'd stepped into an upside-down world where nothing made sense, and no one had a single problem with it but him.

'Robin?' Ramy asked.

Robin blinked. They were all looking at him with very concerned expressions. He gathered this was not the first time he'd been addressed. 'I'm sorry – what?'

'What do you think?' Victoire asked gently. 'We're going to drop him overboard, all right?'

'I – well, I suppose that works, I just . . .' He shook his head. There was a very loud ringing in his ears, and it made it hard for him to collect his thoughts. 'Sorry, I just . . . aren't any of you going to ask me why?'

Blank stares all around.

'It's just – you're all signed up to help me conceal a murder?' Robin couldn't help all his statements becoming questions. The whole world right then seemed like one great, unanswerable question. 'And you're not even going to ask how, or why?'

Ramy and Victoire exchanged a look. But it was Letty who answered first. 'I think we all understand why.' Her throat pulsed. He could not decipher the expression on her face – it was something he'd never seen on her before, some strange mixture of pity and resolve. 'And to be honest, Robin, I think the less we say about it the better.'

Cleaning up the cabin went faster than Robin had feared. Letty secured a mop and bucket from the crew by claiming she'd vomited from seasickness, and the rest of them contributed several articles of clothing to soak up the bloody water.

Then there was the matter of disposal. They decided that shoving Professor Lovell in a trunk was their best chance at getting his body to the upper deck unquestioned. The migration upstairs was a game of bated breaths and progress in inches. Victoire would dart forward every few seconds, check to make sure there was no one in sight, and then motion frantically for Robin and Ramy to drag the trunk up another few steps. Letty kept guard on the top deck, feigning a nighttime stroll for some fresh air.

Somehow they got the trunk to the edge of the railing without attracting suspicion.

'All right.' Robin slid the lid off the trunk. Originally they'd considered throwing the whole trunk away, but Victoire had astutely pointed out that wood would float. He was afraid to look down; he wanted, if possible, to do this without looking at his father's face. 'Quickly, before anyone sees—'

'Hold on,' said Ramy. 'We have to weight it down, otherwise it'll bob around.'

Robin had a sudden vision of Professor Lovell's body floating in the wake of the ship, attracting a crowd of sailors and seagulls. He fought a wave of nausea. 'Why didn't you say so before?'

'I was a bit panicked, all right?'

'But you seemed so calm—'

'I'm good in emergencies, Birdie, but I'm not God.'

Robin's eyes darted around the deck, searching for anything that might serve as an anchor – oars, wooden buckets, spare planks – damn it, why was everything on a ship designed to float?

At last he found a pile of rope knotted through with what looked like weights. He prayed it wasn't needed for anything important and dragged it over to the trunk. Securing the rope around Professor Lovell was a nightmare. His heavy, stiffening limbs did not move easily; the corpse seemed in fact to be actively resisting them. The rope, horrifically, snagged on exposed and jagged ribs. Robin's hands, sweaty with fear, kept slipping; several agonizing minutes passed before they got the rope snugly around the professor's arms and legs. Robin wanted to tie a quick knot and be done with it, but Ramy was adamant they take their time; he didn't want the ropes to disentangle as soon as the body hit the water.

'All right,' Ramy whispered at last, yanking at the rope. 'That should do it.'

They each took an end of the corpse – Robin the shoulders, and Ramy the feet – and hoisted it out of the trunk.

'One,' Ramy whispered. 'Two . . .'

On the third swing, they lifted Professor Lovell's body over the railing and let go. It seemed an eternity before they heard the splash.

Ramy bent over the railing, scrutinizing the dark waves.

'It's gone,' he said at last. 'He's not coming up.'

Robin couldn't speak. He staggered several steps back and vomited onto the deck.

Now, Ramy instructed, they simply went back to their bunks and acted normal for the rest of the voyage. Simple, in theory. But of all the places

to commit a murder, a ship midvoyage had to be one of the worst. A
killer on the street could at least drop his weapon and flee the city. But
they were stuck for two more months at the scene of the crime, two
months during which they had to maintain the fiction that they had not
blown a man's chest apart and dumped his body into the ocean.

They tried to keep up appearances. They took their daily strolls around
the deck, they entertained Miss Smythe and her tiresome inquiries, and
they appeared for meals in the mess, thrice a day on the clock, trying
their best to work up an appetite.

'He's just feeling under the weather,' Ramy answered when the cook
asked why he hadn't seen Professor Lovell for several days. 'He says he's
not very hungry – some kind of stomach affliction – but we'll bring him
something to eat later.'

'Did he say what's precisely the matter?' The cook was a smiling and
gregarious man; Robin couldn't tell if he was prying or just being friendly.

'Oh, it's a whole host of minor symptoms,' Ramy lied smoothly. 'He's
complained of a headache, some congestion, but it's mostly nausea. He
gets dizzy if he stands up for too long, so he's spending most of his days
in bed. Sleeping quite a lot. Could be seasickness, although he didn't
have any problems with it on the way over.'

'Interesting.' The cook rubbed his beard for a moment, then turned on
his heel. 'You wait right here.'

He strode out of the mess at a fast clip. They stared at the door,
stricken. Had he grown suspicious? Was he alerting the captain? Was he
checking on Professor Lovell's cabin to confirm their story?

'So,' Ramy muttered, 'do we run now, or . . . ?'

'And go where?' Victoire hissed. 'We're in the middle of an ocean!'

'We could beat him to Lovell's cabin, perhaps—'

'But there's nothing there, there's nothing we can do—'

'Shush.' Letty nodded over her shoulder. The cook was already striding
back into the mess, holding a small brown sachet in one hand.

'Candied ginger.' He offered it to Robin. 'Good for upset stomachs.
You scholars always forget to bring your own.'

'Thank you.' Heart hammering, Robin took the sachet. He tried his
best to keep his voice level. 'I'm sure he'll be very grateful.'

Luckily, none of the rest of the crew ever questioned Professor Lovell's
whereabouts. The sailors were none too fascinated by the daily dealings
of scholars they'd been paid a pittance to transport; they were more than

happy to pretend they did not exist at all. Miss Smythe was a different story. She was, likely out of sheer boredom, desperately persistent in making herself useful. She asked incessantly about Professor Lovell's fever, the sound of his cough, and colour and composition of his stool. 'I've seen my share of tropical diseases,' she said. 'Whatever he's got, I've surely seen it in among the locals. Just let me have a look at him, I'll get him fixed right up.'

Somehow they convinced her that Professor Lovell was both highly contagious and painfully shy. ('He won't be alone with an unmarried woman,' Letty vowed solemnly. 'He'll be furious if we let you in there.') Still, Miss Smythe insisted that they join her in a daily prayer for his health, during which it took Robin all he had not to retch from guilt.

The days were terribly long. Time crawled when every second contained a horrible contingency, the question *will we get away?* Robin was constantly sick. His nausea was wholly different from the roiling unease of seasickness; it was a vicious mass of guilt gnawing at his stomach and clawing at his throat, a poisonous weight that made it hard to breathe. Trying to relax or to distract himself was no help; it was when he slipped up and lost his guard that the sickness redoubled. Then the buzzing in his ears grew louder and louder and black seeped into the edges of his vision, reducing the world to a blurry pinprick.

Behaving like a person demanded tremendous focus. Sometimes the most he could do was to remember to breathe, hard and even. He had to scream a mantra in his mind – *it's all right, it's all right, you're all right, they don't know, they think you're just a student and they think he's just sick* – but even that mantra threatened to spin out of control; if he relaxed his focus for just one second, it morphed to the truth – *you killed him, you blew a hole in his chest and his blood's all over the books, all over your hands, slick, wet, warm—*

He was scared of his subconscious; of letting it wander. He could dwell on nothing. Every thought that passed through his mind spiralled into a chaotic jumble of guilt and horror; always solidified into the same bleak refrain:

I have killed my father.
I have killed my father.
I have killed my father.

He tortured himself with imagining what might happen to them if they were caught. He projected the scenes so vividly they felt like memories – the short and damning trial, the disgusted looks from the jurors; the manacles around their wrists and, if not the gallows, then the long, crowded, miserable journey to a penal colony in Australia.

What he couldn't wrap his mind around was what a truly fleeting moment the actual killing had been – no more than a split second of impulsive hatred, a single uttered phrase, a single throw. The Analects of Confucius made the claim *sìbùjíshé*,* that even a four-horse chariot could not catch a word once uttered, that the spoken word was irrevocable. But this seemed like a great trick of time. It did not seem fair that such a minuscule action could have such reverberating consequences. Something that broke not only his world but Ramy's, Letty's, and Victoire's should have taken minutes at least, it seemed; should have required repeated effort. The truth of the murder would have made more sense had he stood over his father's body with a blunt axe, bringing it down over and over into his skull and chest until blood sprayed across both their faces. Something brutal, something sustained, a true manifestation of monstrous intent.

But that did not describe what had happened at all. It had not been vicious. It had not taken effort. It was all over so fast, he hadn't even had time to deliberate. He couldn't remember acting at all. Could you intend a murder if you couldn't remember wanting it?

But what kind of question was that? What was the blasted point of sorting through whether he'd desired his father's death or not, when his ruined corpse was incontrovertibly, irreversibly sinking to the bottom of the ocean?

The nights were far worse than the days. At least the days offered the temporary distractions of the outdoors, the rolling ocean and spraying mists. At night, confined to his hammock, there was only the unforgiving dark. Nights meant sweat-drenched sheets, chills, and shakes, and not even the privacy to moan and scream out loud. Robin lay with his knees curled up to his chest, muffling his frantic breathing with both hands. When he managed snatches of sleep, his dreams were fragmented and horrifyingly vivid, revisiting every beat of that final conversation until the devastating finale. But the details kept changing. What were the last words Professor Lovell had said? How had he looked at Robin? Had

---

* 駟不及舌.

he really stepped closer? Who had moved first? Was it self-defence, or was it a preemptive strike? Was there a difference? He wrecked his own memory. Awake and asleep, he examined the same moment from a thousand different angles until he truly no longer knew what had happened.

He wanted all thoughts to stop. He wanted to disappear. At night, the black, endless waves seemed like utopia, and he wanted nothing more than to hurl himself over the side, to let the ocean swallow him and his guilt into its obliterating depths. But that would only condemn the others. How would that look, one student drowned and their professor killed? No excuses, however creative, however true, could extricate them from that.

But if death was not an option, perhaps punishment still was. 'I have to confess,' he whispered to Ramy one sleepless night. 'That's the only way, we have to end it—'

'Don't be an idiot,' said Ramy.

He scrambled madly out of his hammock. 'I mean it, I'm going to the captain—'

Ramy jumped up and caught him in the passageway. 'Birdie, get back in there.'

Robin tried to push past Ramy for the stairs. Ramy promptly slapped him across the face. Somehow this calmed him, if only due to shock – the blinding white pain wiped everything from his mind, just for a few seconds, just long enough to still his racing heart.

'We are all implicated now,' Ramy hissed. 'We cleaned that room. We hid the body for you. To protect *you*. We've all lied a dozen times now; we are accessories in this crime, and if you go to the hangman, you doom us all. Do you understand?'

Chastened, he hung his head and nodded.

'Good,' said Ramy. 'Now back to bed.'

The only silver lining to this whole grotesque affair was that he and Ramy were finally reconciled. The act of murder had bridged the gap between them, had blown Ramy's accusations of complicity and cowardice out of the water. It didn't matter that it had been an accident, or that Robin would take it back immediately if he could. Ramy no longer had any ideological grounds to resent him, for between them, only one of them had killed a colonizer. They were co-conspirators now, and this brought them closer than they ever had been. Ramy took on the role of comforter and counsellor, witness to his confessions. Robin didn't know why he thought speaking his thoughts might make anything better, for saying any of it out loud only served to make him more confused, but he was desperately grateful that Ramy was at least there to listen.

'Do you think I'm evil?' he asked.

'Don't be ridiculous.'

'You've been saying that a lot.'

'You've been ridiculous a lot. But you're not evil.'

'But I'm a murderer,' he said, then said it again, because the words were so absurd that the very act of forming the vowels felt bizarre. 'I took a life. With full deliberation, with full intent – I knew what the bar would do to him and I threw it, and I watched it break his body, and in the moment before I regretted it, I was satisfied with what I had done. It wasn't an accident. It doesn't matter how much I wish I could take it back now – I wanted him dead, and I killed him.' He took a shuddering breath. 'Am I – what kind of person do you have to be to do that? A villain. A blackhearted wretch. How else does that happen, Ramy? There's no in-between. There's no rule under which this is forgivable, is there?'

Ramy sighed. 'Whoever takes a life – it will be as if they killed all humanity. So says the Qu'ran.'

'Thanks,' Robin muttered. 'That's comforting.'

'But the Qu'ran also speaks of Allah's infinite mercy.' Ramy was quiet for a moment. 'And I think . . . well, Professor Lovell was a very bad man, wasn't he? You acted in self-defence, didn't you? And the things he did to you, to your brother, to your mothers . . . perhaps he did deserve to die. Perhaps the fact that you killed him first prevented unforetold harm from coming to others. But that's really not your decision to make. That's God's.'

'Then what do I do?' Robin asked miserably. 'What do I *do?*'

'There's nothing you can do,' said Ramy. 'He's dead, you killed him, and there's nothing you can do to change that except pray to God for forgiveness.' He paused, tapping his fingers against his knee. 'But the question now is how to protect Victoire and Letty. And your turning yourself in doesn't do that, Birdie. Neither does your torturing yourself about your worth as a human being. Lovell's dead, and you're alive, and perhaps that's what God willed. And that's as much comfort as I can offer.'

The four of them took turns losing their minds. There was an unspoken rule to this game: one of them was allowed to break down at a time, but not all of them at once, for the duty of the saner heads was to talk the mad one down.

Ramy's favourite way of panicking was to voice all his anxieties in extravagant, incredibly specific detail. 'Someone will go to his cabin,' he declared. 'They'll need to ask him a question – something inane, something about the arrival date or about payment for passage. Only he won't be there, and they'll ask us about it, and finally somebody will get suspicious and they'll search the whole ship, and we'll pretend we've no idea where he's gone either and they won't believe us, and then they'll find the bloodstains—'

'Please,' Victoire said. 'Please, for the love of God, stop.'

'Then they'll send us to Newgate,' Ramy continued, intoning grandly as if narrating an epic poem, 'and St Sepulchre's bell will ring twelve times, and a great crowd will gather outside, and the next morning we'll be hanged, one by one . . .'

The only way to get Ramy to stop was to let him finishing narrating the entire sick fantasy, which he always did, with more and more ludicrous descriptions of their executions every time. They actually brought Robin some relief – it was relaxing, in a way, to imagine the very worst that could happen, since it took the terror out of the unknown. But it only ever set Victoire off. Whenever these conversations occurred, she'd be unable to sleep. Then it would be her turn to lose her head, and she'd nudge them awake at four in the morning, whispering that she felt bad about keeping Letty up, and they would have to sit above deck with her, whispering inane stories about whatever came to mind – birdsong, Beethoven, departmental gossip – until the gentle reprieve of dawn.

Letty's bad spells were the hardest to deal with. For Letty, alone among them, did not understand why Ramy and Victoire had come so readily to Robin's defence. She assumed they'd protected Robin because they were friends. The one motive she understood was that she'd seen Professor Lovell seize Robin's collar in Canton, and abusive fathers was something she and Robin had in common.

But since she saw Professor Lovell's death as an isolated incident, not the tip of an iceberg, she was constantly trying to fix their situation. 'There have to be ways to come clean,' she kept saying. 'We can say Professor Lovell was hurting Robin, that it was self-defence? That he'd lost his mind from stress, that he began it all, and that Robin was only trying to get away? We'd all testify, it's all true, they'd have to acquit him – Robin, what do you think?'

'But that's not what happened,' said Robin.

'But you could *say* it's what happened—'

'It won't work,' Ramy insisted. 'It's too dangerous, and more, it's a risk we absolutely don't need to take.'

How could they tell her she was being delusional? That it was insane to imagine that the British legal system was truly neutral, that they would receive a fair trial, that people who looked like Robin, Ramy, and Victoire might kill a white Oxford professor, throw his body overboard, lie about it for weeks, and then walk away unscathed? That the fact that she clearly believed all this was only evidence of the starkly different worlds they lived in?

But since they couldn't tell her the truth, Letty was undeterred. 'I've got a new idea,' she announced after they shot down her self-defence proposal. 'So, as you all probably know, my father's quite an important man—'

'No,' said Ramy.

'Just let me finish. My father was rather influential in his time—'

'Your father's a retired admiral, put out to pasture—'

'But he still knows people,' Letty insisted. 'He could call in some favours—'

'What kind of favours?' demanded Ramy. '"Hello, Judge Blathers, here's the thing – my daughter and her dirty foreign friends have had their professor killed – a man crucial to the Empire, both financially and diplomatically – so when they're up for trial I'll need you to just go ahead and proclaim them innocent—"'

'It doesn't have to be like that,' Letty snapped. 'What I'm saying is, if we tell him what happened and explain it's an accident—'

'An *accident*?' Ramy repeated. 'Have you covered up accidents before? Do they just look the other way when rich white girls kill people? Is that how it works, Letty? Besides, aren't you on the outs with the admiral?'

Letty's nostrils flared. 'I'm only trying to help.'

'We know,' Robin said quickly, desperate to diffuse the tension. 'And I'm grateful, truly. But Ramy's right. I think it's best that we keep all this quiet.'

Letty, glaring stiffly at the wall, said nothing.

Somehow they made it back to England. Two months passed and one morning they woke up to London on the horizon, shrouded in its familiar gloomy greys.

Feigning Professor Lovell's illness throughout the journey had turned out to be simpler than even Victoire had expected; it was apparently very easy to convince an entire ship that an Oxford professor had a remarkably weak constitution. Jemima Smythe, for all her efforts, had finally grown tired of her clammed-up company, and made no efforts to draw out their parting. The sailors said hardly as much as a word of farewell when they disembarked. No one paid much attention to four travel-worn students making their way through the Legal Quays, not when there were goods to unload and pay to collect.

'We sent the professor on ahead to see a physician,' Letty told the captain when they passed him on the docks. 'He said – ah, to say thank you for a smooth trip.'

The captain looked slightly puzzled by these words, but shrugged and waved them off.

'A smooth trip?' Ramy muttered. '*A smooth trip?*'

'I couldn't think of anything else to say!'

'Be quiet and walk,' Victoire hissed.

Robin was sure that everything they did screamed *Murderers!* as they lugged their trunks down the planks. Any moment now, he thought dizzily; one more step, and there it would be – a suspicious look, a flurry of footsteps, a call of 'Hey there! You, stop!' Surely they would not let them escape the *Hellas* so easily.

On shore, just twelve feet away, was England, was asylum, was freedom. Once they reached that shore, once they disappeared into the crowd, they would be free. But that was impossible, surely – the links connecting them to that bloody room could not be so easily severed. Could they?

The boardwalk gave way to solid land. Robin glimpsed over his shoulder. No one had followed them. No one was even looking their way.

They boarded an omnibus to north London, from which they hailed a cab to Hampstead. They'd agreed without much debate that they would first spend the night at Professor Lovell's Hampstead residence upon arrival – they had got in too late to catch any trains to Oxford, and Robin knew both that Mrs Piper would still be in Jericho and that the spare key to the estate was hidden under the Ming flowerpot in the garden. The next morning they would board a train to Paddington and return to school as planned.

During the voyage it had crossed all their minds that there remained one obvious option – running, dropping everything and fleeing the continent; climbing onto a packet bound for America or Australia, or returning to the countries from which they'd been plucked.

'We could escape to the New World,' Ramy proposed. 'Go to Canada.'

'You don't even speak French,' Letty said.

'It's French, Letty.' Ramy rolled his eyes. 'Latin's flimsiest daughter. How hard could it be?'

'We'd have to find work,' Victoire pointed out. 'We won't have our stipends anymore; how would we live?'

This was a good point, and one they'd somehow overlooked. Years of receiving a reliable stipend had made them forget that they only ever had enough to live on for several months; outside Oxford, in a place where their lodgings and meals were no longer provided, they would have nothing.

'Well, how do other people find employment?' Ramy had asked. 'I suppose you just go up to a shop and answer an advertisement?'

'You have to have been an apprentice,' Letty had said. 'There's a training period, I think, though that costs money—'

'Then how does one find a tradesman to take them on?'

'I don't know,' Letty had said, frustrated. 'How would I know? I've no idea.'

No, there was never any real possibility they would leave the university. Despite everything, despite the very real risk that if they went back to Oxford then they'd be arrested, investigated, and thrown in prison or hanged, they couldn't conceive of a life not tied to the university. For they had nothing else. They had no skills; they had not the strength nor the temperament for manual labour, and they did not have the connections to find employment. Most importantly, they didn't know how to live. None of them had the faintest idea how much it would cost to rent rooms, acquire a week's worth of groceries, or set oneself up in a town that was not the university. Until now, all of that had been taken care of for them. In Hampstead, there had been Mrs Piper, and at Oxford, there were the scouts and bedmakers. Robin, indeed, would have been hard-pressed to explain how exactly one did the laundry.

When it came down to it, they simply could not think of themselves as anything else but students, couldn't imagine a world where they did not belong to Babel. Babel was all they knew. Babel was home. And though he knew it was stupid, Robin suspected he wasn't the only one who believed deep down that, despite everything, there was a world where once this trouble ended, once all necessary arrangements had been made and things were swept under the rug, he might still return to his room on Magpie Lane, might wake up to gentle birdsong and warm sunlight streaming through the narrow window, and once again spend his days poring over nothing but dead languages.

CHAPTER TWENTY

To the assistance and information which you and Mr Jardine so handsomely afforded to us it was mainly owing that we were able to give our affairs naval, military and diplomatic, in China those detailed instructions which have led to these satisfactory results.

FOREIGN SECRETARY PALMERSTON,
letter to John Abel Smith

It was raining hard when they climbed out of the cab in Hampstead. They found Professor Lovell's house more by sheer luck than anything else. Robin had thought he'd easily remember the route, but three years away had done more to his memory than he'd realized, and the hammering sheets of rain made every residence look the same: wet, blockish, surrounded by slick, dripping foliage. By the time they finally found the brick-and-white-stucco house, they were sopping wet and trembling.

'Hold on.' Victoire pulled Ramy back just as he started for the door. 'Shouldn't we go round the back? In case someone sees us?'

'If they see us then they see us, it's not a crime to be in Hampstead—'

'It is if it's obvious you don't live here—'

'Hello there!'

They all turned their heads at once like startled kittens. A woman waved to them from the doorstep of the house across the street. 'Hello,' she called again. 'Are you looking for the professor?'

They glanced at each other, panicked; they had not discussed an answer for this occasion. They had wanted to avoid all association with a man whose absence would soon garner considerable interest. But how else could they justify their presence in Hampstead?

'We are,' Robin said quickly, before their silence became suspicious. 'We're his students. We're just back from overseas – he told us to meet him here when we returned, only it's getting late and no one's at the door.'

'He's probably at the university.' The woman's expression was actually quite friendly; she'd only seemed hostile because she'd been shouting over the rain. 'He's only here a few weeks of the year. Stay right there.'

She turned and hurried back inside her house. The door slammed shut behind her.

'Damn it,' Ramy muttered. 'What are you doing?'

'I thought it'd be better to stick close to the truth—'

'A bit *too* close to the truth, don't you think? What happens if someone questions her?'

'What do you want to do, then, run?'

But the woman had already popped back outside. She rushed across the street towards them, shielding off the rain with an elbow. She extended her palm to Robin.

'Here you are.' She opened her fingers, revealing a key. 'That's his spare. He's so scatterbrained – they asked me to keep one on hand for when he loses his. You poor things.'

'Thank you,' Robin said, stunned by their good fortune. Then a memory struck him, and he took a wild guess. 'You're Mrs Clemens, aren't you?'

She beamed. 'I certainly am!'

'Right, that's right – he said to ask you if we couldn't find the key. Only we couldn't figure out what house you were in.'

'A good thing I was watching the rain, then.' She had a broad, friendly smile; any suspicion, if it ever was there, had disappeared from her face. 'I like to face the outside when I play my pianoforte. The world informs my music.'

'Right,' he said again, too giddy with relief to process this statement. 'Well, thanks very much.'

'Oh, it's nothing. Call if you need anything.' She nodded first to Robin, and then to Letty – she seemed not to even see Ramy or Victoire, for which Robin supposed they could only be grateful – and headed back across the street.

'How on earth did you know?' Victoire muttered.

'Mrs Piper wrote about her,' said Robin as he dragged his trunk up through the front garden. 'Said a new family's moved in, and that the wife is a lonely and eccentric type. I think she comes here most afternoons for tea when the professor is here.'

'Well, thank God you write to your housekeeper,' said Letty.

'Truly,' said Robin, and unlocked the door.

Robin had not been back to the house in Hampstead since he'd left for Oxford, and it seemed greatly changed in his absence. It was a good deal smaller than he'd remembered, or perhaps he'd just grown taller. The staircase was not such an endless spiral, and the high ceilings did not induce such a heavy sense of solitude. It was very dim inside; all the curtains were drawn, and sheets pulled over the furniture to protect it from dust. They groped around in the dark for a bit – Mrs Piper had always lit the lamps and candles, and Robin hadn't a clue where she kept the matches. At last Victoire found some flint and candlesticks in the parlour, and from there they managed to light the fireplace.

'Say, Birdie,' said Ramy. 'What's all this . . . stuff?'

He meant the chinoiserie. Robin glanced around. The parlour was filled with painted fans, hanging scrolls, and porcelain vases, sculptures, and teapots. The effect was a garish re-creation of a Canton teahouse juxtaposed upon a base of English furniture. Had these always been there? Robin didn't know how he had failed to notice as a child. Perhaps, fresh from Canton, he had not found the separation of two worlds so obvious; perhaps it was only now, after a full immersion in the most English of universities, that he'd developed a sharper sense of the foreign and the exotic.

'I suppose he was a collector,' said Robin. 'Oh, I do remember now – he loved telling his guests about his acquisitions, where they'd come from and their particular histories. He was quite proud.'

'How strange,' said Ramy. 'To love the stuff and the language, but to hate the country.'

'Not as odd as you'd think,' said Victoire. 'There are people, after all, and then there are things.'

An expedition to the kitchens turned up nothing to eat. Mrs Piper wouldn't have stocked provisions while she was still at the Oxford house. The Hampstead house had a persistent rat problem, Robin recalled, never resolved because Professor Lovell abhorred cats, and Mrs Piper hated leaving perishables at their mercy. Ramy found a tin of ground coffee and a jar of salt, but no sugar. They made and drank the coffee anyway. It only sharpened their hunger, but at least it kept them alert.

They had just washed and dried their empty mugs – Robin didn't know why they were cleaning up when the owner of this place would never come home, but it still felt wrong to leave a mess – when they heard a sharp knock at the door. They all jumped. The knocker paused, then rapped again firmly, thrice in succession.

Ramy sprang up and reached for the fire poker.

'What are you doing?' Letty hissed.

'Well, assuming they come in—'

'Just don't open the door, we'll pretend no one's here—'

'But all the lights are on, you dolt—'

'Then look out the window first—'

'No, then they'll see us—'

'Hello?' The knocker called through the door. 'Can you hear me?'

They sagged with relief. It was only Mrs Clemens.

'I'll get it.' Robin stood and shot Ramy a glare. 'Put that away.'

Their kindly neighbour stood sopping wet on the doorstep, carrying a flimsy, ineffective umbrella in one hand and a covered basket in the other. 'I noticed you hadn't brought provisions. He always leaves the pantry empty when he's gone – rat problem.'

'I . . . I see.' Mrs Clemens was very chatty. Robin hoped she did not want to come in.

When he said nothing else, she held the basket out towards him. 'I've just asked my girl Fanny to cobble together what we had on hand. There's some wine, a hard and a soft cheese, this morning's bread – crusty, I'm afraid – and some olives and sardines. If you want bread fresh baked, you'll have to try again in the morning, but let me know if you do want to come over so I can have Fanny send for more fresh butter, we're nearly out.'

'Thank you,' Robin said, rather astounded by this generosity. 'That's very kind of you.'

'Of course,' Mrs Clemens said promptly. 'Can you tell me when the professor will be back? I need to have a word with him about his hedges.'

Robin blanked. 'I . . . don't know.'

'Didn't you say you'd come up ahead of him?'

Robin wasn't sure what to say. He felt vaguely that the less of an oral trail they left, the better – he'd already told the captain that Professor Lovell had gone ahead of them, and they intended to tell the Babel faculty that Professor Lovell was still in Hampstead, so it might be very dangerous should Mrs Clemens present a different account entirely. But who was going to question all three parties? If the police had got that far, wouldn't the four of them already be detained?

Letty came to his rescue. 'Could be as soon as Monday,' she said, nudging him aside. 'But we heard at the docks that his ship might be delayed – bad weather over the Atlantic, you know – so it could be weeks still.'

'How inconvenient,' said Mrs Clemens. 'Will you be staying as long, then?'

'Oh, no, we're heading back to school tomorrow. We'll leave a note on the dining room table before we go.'

'Very prudent. Well, good night,' Mrs Clemens said cheerfully, and went back out into the rain.

They devoured the cheese and olives in seconds. The bread was hard and took some chewing, which slowed them down, but in minutes that was gone as well. Then they eyed the wine bottle with great longing, caught between knowing they should stay on their guard and wanting desperately to be drunk, until Ramy took responsibility and hid it in the pantry.

By then it was half past eleven. At Oxford, all of them would be awake for hours yet, poring over their assignments or laughing in each other's rooms. But they were all exhausted, and too scared to part ways to separate bedrooms, so they searched the house for all the blankets and pillows they could find and piled them in the sitting room.

They decided to sleep in shifts, with one person always awake to keep watch. None of them really believed that the police might come crashing through the doors – and never mind that there was little they could do about it if that did happen – but it felt good to be at least minimally prudent.

Robin volunteered to go first. At first none of them could keep still, all jittery from coffee and nerves, but soon fatigue got the better of them, and in minutes their murmured anxieties gave way to deep, even breathing. Letty and Victoire were slumped together on the couch, Victoire's head on Letty's arm. Ramy slept on the floor beside Robin, body curled around the couch like protective parenthesis. The sight of them all together made Robin's chest ache.

He waited half an hour, watching their chests rise and fall, before he dared to stand up. He reasoned it was safe to leave his post. If anything happened, he'd hear it across the house – the rain had now eased to a light patter, and the house was otherwise deathly silent. Holding his breath, he tiptoed out of the sitting room and up the stairs to Professor Lovell's office.

It was just as cramped and messy as he remembered. At Oxford, Professor Lovell kept his office in some semblance of order, but at home he let his things devolve to a state of managed chaos. Loose papers lay strewn across the floor; books were stacked in piles around the shelves, some lying open, some shut around pens crammed inside to mark the pages.

Robin picked his way across the room to Professor Lovell's desk. He'd never stood behind it; he'd only ever sat across it, hands clasped nervously in his lap. The desk seemed unrecognizable from the other side. A framed painting was propped upright on the right corner – no, not a painting, a daguerreotype. Robin tried not to look closely, but he couldn't help but glimpse the outline of a dark-haired woman and two children. He turned the frame down.

He flipped through the loose papers on the desk. They were nothing interesting – notes on Tang dynasty poems and oracle bone inscriptions, both research projects Robin had known Professor Lovell was pursuing at Oxford. He tried the drawer on the right. He expected it to be locked, but it slid open with no trouble. Stashed inside were sheafs and sheafs of letters. He pulled them out and held them up to the lamplight one by one, unsure what he was looking for, or even what he expected to see.

He only wanted a picture of the man. He only wanted to know who his father was.

Most of Professor Lovell's correspondence was with Babel faculty and representatives of the various trading companies – a handful with the East India Company, more from representatives with Magniac & Co., but the lion's share were from men at Jardine & Matheson. These were quite interesting. He read faster and faster as he made his way through the pile, skimming over opening niceties for critical phrases buried in the middle paragraphs——

. . . Gützlaff's blockade might work . . . would only take thirteen warships, though the question is the time and expense . . . Simple show of force . . . Lindsay wants to embarrass them with a diplomatic withdrawal, but surely this endangers the sole customs agents left behind . . . bring them to the edge and they will back down . . . can't be hard to decimate a fleet run by sailors who don't even know what steamers are . . .

Robin exhaled slowly and sat back in the chair.

Two things were clear. First, there was no ambiguity what these documents were. A letter from Reverend Gützlaff from four months ago contained a detailed sketch of Canton's main docks. On the other side was a list of all the known ships in the Chinese navy. These were not hypotheticals of Britain's China policy. These were war plans. These letters included thorough accounts of the Qing government's coastal defences, reports detailing the number of junks defending the naval stations, the number and placement of forts on the surrounding islands, and even the precise number of troops stationed at each.

Second, Professor Lovell's voice emerged as one of the most hawkish among his interlocutors. Initially, Robin had conceived a silly, baseless hope that perhaps this war was not Professor Lovell's idea, and that perhaps he had been urging them to stop. But Professor Lovell was quite vocal, not only on the many benefits of such a war (including the vast linguistic resources that would then be at his disposal), but about the ease with which the 'Chinese, languid and lazy, with an army without one iota of bravery or discipline, might be defeated'. His father had not simply been a scholar caught up in trade hostilities. He had helped design them. One unsent missive, written in Professor Lovell's neat, tiny hand and addressed to Lord Palmerston, read:

> *The Chinese fleet consists of outdated junks whose cannons are too small to aim effectively. The Chinese have only one ship worthy of combat against our fleet, the merchantman the Cambridge, purchased from the Americans, but they have no sailors that can handle her. Our agents report she sits idle in the bay. We will make short work of her with the Nemesis.*

Robin's heart was beating very quickly. He felt seized by a sudden urge to discover all he could, to determine the full extent of this conspiracy. He read frantically through the stack; when the letters ran out, he pulled another pile of correspondence from the left drawer. It revealed much of the same. The desirability of war was never a question, only its timing, and the difficulty of persuading Parliament to act. But some of these letters dated as far back as 1837. How had Jardine, Matheson, and Lovell known negotiations in Canton would break out in hostilities more than two years ago?

But that was obvious. They'd known because this was their intent all along. They wanted hostilities because they wanted silver, and without some miraculous change in the Qing Emperor's mind, the only way to get that was to turn their guns on China. They'd planned on war before they had even set sail. They'd never meant to negotiate with Commissioner Lin in good faith. Those talks were merely a pretext for hostilities. Those men had funded Professor Lovell's trip to Canton as a final expedition before they introduced the bill to Parliament. These men were relying on Professor Lovell to help them win a short, brutal, efficient war.

What would happen when they learned Professor Lovell was never coming back?

'What's that?'

Robin glanced up. Ramy stood in the doorway, yawning.

'You've got an hour left before your turn,' Robin said.

'Couldn't sleep. And these shifts are nonsense anyway, no one's coming for us tonight.' Ramy joined Robin behind Professor Lovell's desk. 'Digging around, are we?'

'Look.' Robin tapped the letters. 'Read these.'

Ramy picked up a letter from the top of the pile, skimmed it, and then sat down across from Robin to take a closer look at the rest. 'Good heavens.'

'They're war plans,' said Robin. 'Everyone's in on it, everyone we met in Canton – look, here are letters from Reverends Morrison and Gützlaff – they've been using their covers as missionaries to spy on the Qing military. Gützlaff's even been bribing informants to tell him particulars of Chinese troop deployment, which influential Chinese traders are against the British, and even which pawnshops would be good places to raid.'

'Gützlaff?' Ramy snorted. 'Really? I didn't know that German had it in him.'

'There are also pamphlets to whip up public support for the war – look, here Matheson calls the Chinese "a people characterized by a marvellous degree of imbecility, avarice, conceit, and obstinacy". And here someone called Goddard writes that deploying warships would be a "tranquil and judicious visit". Imagine. *A tranquil and judicious visit.* What a way to describe a violent invasion.'

'Incredible.' Ramy's eyes roved up and down the documents as he flipped through with increasing speed. 'Makes you wonder why they sent us in the first place.'

'Because they still needed a pretext,' said Robin. It was falling into place now. It was all so clear, so ridiculously simple that he wanted to kick himself for not seeing it earlier. 'Because they still needed something to take to Parliament to prove the only way they were going to get what they wanted was by sheer force. They wanted Baylis to humiliate Lin, not compromise with him. They wanted to bait Lin into declaring hostilities first.'

Ramy snorted. 'Only they didn't count on Lin blowing up all that opium in the harbour.'

'No,' said Robin. 'But I suppose they're getting the just cause they wanted anyway.'

'There you are,' said Victoire.

They both jumped, startled.

'Who's watching the door?' asked Robin.

'It'll be fine, no one's breaking in at three in the morning. And Letty's out like a log.' Victoire crossed the room and peered down at the stack of letters. 'What are these?'

Ramy gestured for her to sit. 'You'll see.'

Victoire, like Ramy, started reading faster and faster when she realized what she was looking at. 'Oh, goodness.' She touched her fingers to her lips. 'So you think – so they never even—'

'Right,' said Robin. 'It was all for show. We weren't meant to negotiate peace at all.'

She gave the papers a helpless shake. 'Then what do we do with this?'

'What do you mean?' Robin asked.

She shot him a puzzled look. 'These are war plans.'

'And we're students,' he replied. 'What *can* we do?'

There was a long silence.

'Oh, Birdie.' Ramy sighed. 'What are we even doing here? What do we think we're running back to?'

Oxford was the answer. Oxford, which was what they'd all agreed on, because when they'd been trapped on the *Hellas*, their professor's corpse sinking into the depths of the ocean behind them, the promise of a return to the normal and familiar was what kept them calm, a shared delusion of stability that kept them from going mad. All their planning had always stopped at their safe arrival in England. But they couldn't keep skirting the issue, couldn't keep up the blind and ridiculous faith that if they just got back to Oxford, then everything would be all right.

There was no going back. They all knew it. There was no pretending anymore, no hiding in their supposedly safe corner of the world while unimaginable cruelty and exploitation carried on beyond. There was only the vast, frightening web of the colonial empire, and the demands of justice to resist it.

'Then what?' asked Robin. 'Where do we go?'

'Well,' said Victoire, 'the Hermes Society.'

It seemed so obvious when she said it. Only Hermes might know what to do with this. The Hermes Society, which Robin had betrayed, which might not even be willing to take them back, was the only entity they'd encountered that had ever professed to bother with the problem of colonialism. Here was a way out, a rare and undeserved second chance to make good on wrong choices – if only they could find Hermes before the police found them.

'We're agreed, then?' Victoire glanced back and forth between them. 'Oxford, then Hermes – and then whatever Hermes needs of us, yes?'

'Yes,' Ramy said firmly.

'No,' said Robin. 'No, this is madness. I've got to turn myself in, I need to go to the police as soon as I can—'

Ramy scoffed. 'We've been over this, over and over and over. You turn yourself in and what? Forget that Jardine and Matheson are trying to start a war? This is bigger than us now, Birdie. Bigger than you. You've got obligations.'

'But that's just it,' Robin insisted. 'If I turn myself in, that takes the heat off the two of you. It disentangles this opium war from the murder, don't you see? It frees you up—'

'Stop it,' said Victoire. 'We won't let you.'

'Course we won't,' said Ramy. 'Besides, that's selfish – you don't get to take the easy way out.'

'How is that the *easy*—'

'You want to do the right thing,' said Ramy, bullish. 'You always do. But you think the right thing is martyrdom. You think if you suffer enough for whatever sins you've committed, then you're absolved.'

'I do *not*—'

'That's why you took the fall for us that night. Every time you come up against something difficult, you just want to make it go away, and you think the way to do that is self-flagellation. You're obsessed with punishment. But that's not how this works, Birdie. You going to prison fixes nothing. You hanging from the gallows fixes nothing. The world's still broken. A war's still coming. The only way to properly make amends is to stop it, which you don't want to do, because really what this is about is your being afraid.'

Robin thought this was supremely unfair. 'I was only trying to save you that night.'

'You were trying to let yourself off the hook,' Ramy said, not unkindly. 'But all sacrifice does is make you feel better. It doesn't help the rest of us, so it's an ultimately meaningless gesture. Now, if you're finished with grand attempts at martyrdom, I think we should discuss . . .'

He trailed off. Victoire and Ramy followed his gaze to the door, where Letty stood, hands clutched against her chest. None of them knew how long she'd been there. Her face had gone very pale, save for two blotches of colour high on her cheeks.

'Oh,' said Ramy. 'We thought you were asleep.'

Letty's throat pulsed. She looked about to burst into sobs. 'What,' she asked in a tremulous whisper, 'is the Hermes Society?'

'But I don't understand.'

Letty had been repeating this for the last ten minutes at regular intervals. It didn't matter how they explained it – the necessity of the Hermes Society, and the myriad reasons why such an organization had to exist in the shadows – she kept shaking her head, her eyes blank and uncomprehending. She didn't seem outraged or upset so much as truly baffled, as if they were trying to convince her that the sky was green. 'I don't understand. Weren't you happy at Babel?'

'Happy?' Ramy repeated. 'I suppose no one's ever asked you if your skin's been washed with walnut juice.'

'Oh, Ramy, do they really?' Her eyes widened. 'But I never heard – but your skin is lovely—'

'Or said you weren't allowed in a shop, for reasons unclear,' Ramy continued. 'Or cut a wide circle around you on the pavement as if you had fleas.'

'But that's just Oxfordians being stupid and provincial,' said Letty, 'it doesn't mean—'

'I know you don't see it,' said Ramy. 'And I don't expect you to, that's not your lot in life. But it's not really about whether we were happy at Babel. It's about what our conscience demands.'

'But Babel gave you everything.' Letty seemed unable to move past this point. 'You had everything you wanted, you had such *privileges*—'

'Not enough to make us forget where we're from.'

'But the scholarships – I mean, without those scholarships all of you would have been – I don't understand—'

'You've made that abundantly clear,' Ramy snapped. 'You're a proper little princess, aren't you? Big estate in Brighton, summers in Toulouse, porcelain china on your shelves and Assam in your teacups? How could you understand? Your people reap the fruits of the Empire. Ours don't. So shut up, Letty, and just listen to what we're trying to tell you. It's not right what they're doing to our countries.' His voice grew louder, harder. 'And it's not right that I'm trained to use my languages for their benefit, to translate laws and texts to facilitate their rule, when there are people in India and China and Haiti and all over the Empire and the world who are hungry and starving because the British would rather put silver in their hats and harpsichords than anywhere it could do some good.'

Letty took this better than Robin thought she would. She sat in silence for a moment, blinking, her eyes huge. Then her brows furrowed, and she asked, 'But . . . but if inequality is the issue, then couldn't you have gone through the university? There are all sorts of aid programmes, missionary groups. There's *philanthropy*, you know, why couldn't we just go to the colonial governments and—'

'That's a bit difficult when the whole point of the institution is preserving the Empire,' said Victoire. 'Babel doesn't do anything that doesn't benefit itself.'

'But that's not true,' said Letty. 'They contribute to charity all the time, I know, Professor Leblanc was leading research into London's waterworks so that the tenement housing wouldn't be so diseased, and there are humanitarian societies all over the globe—'*

---

* Here Letty was referring to the establishment of humanitarian societies for the protection of Indigenous peoples in British territories, such as the evangelical authors of the 1837 'Report of the Parliamentary Select Committee on Aboriginal Tribes', which, though recognizing British presence had been a 'source of many calamities to uncivilized nations', recommended the continued expansion of white settlement and spread of British missionaries in Australia and New Zealand in the name of a holy 'civilizing mission'. The Aborigines, they argued, would not suffer so greatly if only they learned to dress, talk, and behave like proper Christians. The great contradiction, of course, is that there is no such thing as humane colonization. The contribution of Babel to such a mission, meanwhile, was to supply English teaching materials to missionary schools and to translate English property laws to peoples displaced by colonial settlement.

'Did you know that Babel sells bars to slave traders?' Victoire interrupted.

Letty blinked at her. 'What?'

'*Capitale*,' Victoire said. 'The Latin *capitale*, derived from *caput*, becomes the Old French *chatel*, which in English becomes *chattel*. Livestock and property become wealth. They write that on the bars, daisy-chain it with the word *cattle*, and then they fix those bars to iron chains so that slaves can't escape. You know how? It makes them docile. Like animals.'

'But that's . . .' Letty was blinking very rapidly now, as if trying to force a mote of dust from her eye. 'But, Victoire love, the slave trade was abolished in 1807.'*

'And you think they just stopped?' Victoire made a noise that was half laugh, half sob. 'You don't think we sell bars to America? You think British manufacturers don't still profit from shackles and irons? You don't think there are people who still keep slaves in England who simply manage to hide it well?'

'But Babel scholars wouldn't—'

'That's exactly the kind of thing Babel scholars do,' Victoire said viciously. 'I should know. It's the kind of thing our supervisor was working on. Every time I met with Leblanc he'd change the subject to his precious chattel bars. He said he thought I might have special insight. He even asked once if I would put them on. He said he wanted to make sure it worked on Negroes.'

'Why didn't you tell me?'

'Letty, I tried.' Victoire's voice broke. There was such pain in her eyes.

---

* This is a great lie, and one that white Britons are happy to believe. Victoire's following argument notwithstanding, slavery continued in India under the East India Company for a long time after. Indeed, slavery in India was specifically exempt from the Slave Emancipation Act of 1833. Despite early abolitionists' belief that India under the EIC was a country of free labour, the EIC was complicit in, directly profited from, and in many cases encouraged a range of types of bondage, including forced plantation labour, domestic labour, and indentured servitude. The refusal to call such practices slavery simply because they did not match precisely the transatlantic plantation model of slavery was a profound act of semantic blindness.

But the British, after all, were astoundingly good at holding contradictions in their head. Sir William Jones, a virulent abolitionist, at the same time admitted of his own household, 'I have slaves that I rescued from death and misery, but consider them as servants.'

And it made Robin deeply ashamed, for only now did he see the cruel pattern of their friendship. Robin had always had Ramy. But at the end of the day, when they parted ways, Victoire only had Letty, who professed always to love her, to absolutely adore her, but who failed to hear anything she was saying if it didn't comport with how she already saw the world.

And where were he and Ramy? Looking away, failing to notice, hoping secretly the girls would simply stop bickering and move on. Occasionally Ramy made jabs at Letty, but only for his own satisfaction. Never had either of them paused to consider how deeply alone Victoire had to have felt, all this time.

'You didn't care,' Victoire continued. 'Letty, you don't even care that our landlady doesn't let me use the indoor bathroom—'

'What? That's ridiculous, I would have noticed—'

'No,' said Victoire. 'You didn't. You never did, Letty, and that's the point. And we're asking you now to finally, please, *hear* what we're trying to tell you. Please believe us.'

Letty, Robin thought, was close to a breaking point. She was running out of arguments. She had the look of a dog backed into a corner. But her eyes darted around, desperately seeking an escape. She would find any flimsy excuse, accept any convoluted alternative logic before she let go of her illusions.

He knew, because not so long ago, he'd done the same.

'So there's a war,' she said after a pause. 'You're absolutely sure there's going to be a war.'

Robin sighed. 'Yes, Letty.'

'And it's absolutely Babel's doing.'

'You can read the letters yourself.'

'And what's – what's the Hermes Society going to do about it?'

'We don't know,' said Robin. 'But they're the only ones who *can* do something about it. We'll bring them these documents, we'll tell them all we know—'

'But why?' Letty persisted. 'Why involve them? We should just do this ourselves. We should make pamphlets, we should go to Parliament – there are a thousand options we've got other than going through some . . . some secret ring of thieves. This degree of collusion, of corruption – if the public just knew, they wouldn't possibly be for it, I'm certain. But operating underground, stealing from the university – that only hurts your cause, doesn't it? Why can't you simply go public?'

They were silent for a moment, all of them wondering who would tell Letty first.

Victoire shouldered the task. 'I wonder,' she said, very slowly, 'if you've ever read any of the abolition literature published before Parliament finally outlawed slavery.'

Letty frowned. 'I don't see how ...'

'The Quakers presented the first antislavery petition to Parliament in 1783,' said Victoire. 'Equiano published his memoir in 1789. Add that to the countless slave stories the abolitionists were telling the British public – stories of the cruellest, most awful tortures you can inflict on a fellow human. Because the mere fact that Black people were denied their freedom was not enough. They needed to see how grotesque it was. And even then, it took them decades to finally outlaw the trade. And that's *slavery*. Compared to that, a war in Canton over trade rights is going to look like nothing. It's not romantic. There are no novelists penning sagas about the effects of opium addiction on Chinese families. If Parliament votes to force Canton's ports open, it's going to look like free trade working as it should. So don't tell me that the British public, if they knew, would do anything at all.'

'But this is war,' said Letty. 'Surely that's different, surely that'll provoke outrage—'

'What you don't understand,' said Ramy, 'is how much people like you will excuse if it just means they can get tea and coffee on their breakfast tables. They don't care, Letty. They just don't care.'

Letty was quiet for a long time. She looked pitiful, stricken and frail, as if she'd just been informed of a death in the family. She loosed a long, shaky breath and cast her eyes about each one of them in turn. 'I see why you never told me.'

'Oh, Letty.' Victoire hesitated, then reached out and put her hand on Letty's shoulder. 'It wasn't like that.'

But she stopped there. It was clear Victoire could not think of anything more reassuring to say. There was nothing more to say at all, except the truth, which was that of course they wouldn't have trusted her. That for all their history, for all their declarations of eternal friendship, they had no way of knowing which side she would take.

'Our minds are made up,' Victoire said gently, but firmly. 'We're taking this to Hermes, as soon as we arrive in Oxford. And you don't have to go with us – we can't force you to take that risk; we know you've suffered so much already. But if you're not with us, then we ask you at least to keep our secrets.'

'What do you mean?' Letty cried. 'Of course I'm with you. You're my friends, I'm with you until the end.'

Then she flung her arms around Victoire and began to weep stormily. Victoire stiffened, looking baffled, but after a moment she raised her arms and cautiously hugged Letty back.

'I'm sorry.' Letty sniffled between sobs. 'I'm sorry, I'm so sorry . . .'

Ramy and Robin watched, unsure what to make of this. On someone else it would have been performative, sickening even, but with Letty, they knew it was not a charade. Letty could not cry on command; she could not even fake basic emotions on command. She was too stiff, too transparent; they knew she was unable to act in any way other than how she felt. So it did feel cathartic, seeing her break down like this, knowing that at last she understood how they all felt. It was a relief to see that in her they still had an ally.

Still, something did not seem right, and Robin could tell from Victoire's and Ramy's faces that they thought so too. It took him a moment to realize what it was that grated on him, and when he did, it would bother him constantly, now and thereafter; it would seem a great paradox, the fact that after everything they had told Letty, all the pain they had shared, she was the one who needed comfort.

CHAPTER TWENTY-ONE

O ye spires of Oxford! Domes and towers!
Gardens and groves! Your presence overpowers
The soberness of reason

WILLIAM WORDSWORTH,
'Oxford, May 30, 1820'

Their return to Oxford the next morning quickly spiralled into a comedy of errors, much of which could have been avoided if they hadn't been too exhausted or hungry or irritated with each other to communicate. Their purses were running low, so they spent an hour arguing over whether it was prudent to borrow Mrs Clemens's carriage to Paddington Station until they gave up and forked over the fare for cabs. But cabs in Hampstead were hard to come by on Sunday mornings, which meant they didn't reach the station until ten minutes after the Oxford train had departed. The next train was fully booked, and the one after that was delayed by a cow that had wandered onto the tracks, which meant they would not arrive at Oxford until after midnight.

A whole day, wasted.

They whiled away the hours in London, migrating from coffeehouse to coffeehouse so as not to attract suspicion, growing ever more twitchy and paranoid from the absurd amounts of coffee and sweets they bought to justify keeping their tables. Every now and then one of them would bring up Professor Lovell, or Hermes, only to be shushed viciously by the others; they didn't know who could be listening, and the whole of London felt full of hostile eavesdroppers. It felt bad to be shushed, but no one had the heart for lighter conversation, and so none of them were speaking to each other by the time they dragged their trunks onto the crowded late train.

They passed the ride in resentful silence. They were ten minutes out from Oxford Station when Letty suddenly sat up and began hyperventilating.

'Oh God,' she whispered. 'Oh God, oh God, oh God—'

She was attracting looks. Letty grabbed at Ramy's shoulder in some appeal for comfort, but Ramy, impatient, jerked his arm from her grasp. 'Letty, *shut up.*'

That was cruel, but Robin sympathized. Letty was wearing on him as well; she'd spent most of the day in hysterics, and he was sick of it. All of their nerves were shot, he thought nastily, and Letty should just chin up and keep it together like the rest of them.

Astounded, Letty fell silent.

At last, their train creaked into Oxford Station. Yawning and shivering, they lugged their trunks over bumpy cobblestones for the twenty minutes it took to walk back to the college – the girls would come to the porter's lodge first to call a cab, they'd decided; it was too dark to walk so far up north alone. At last the austere stone face of University College emerged from the dark, and Robin felt a sharp pang of nostalgia at the sight of this magical and tainted place which, despite everything, still felt like home.

'Hey there!' It was the head porter, Billings, swinging a lantern before him. He looked them up and down and, upon recognition, cast them a broad smile. 'Back from the Orient at last, are you?'

Robin wondered how they looked under the lamplight – panicked, ragged, and sweaty in yesterday's clothes. Their exhaustion must have been obvious, for Billings's expression changed to one of pity. 'Oh, you poor dears.' He turned and waved for them to follow. 'Come with me.'

Fifteen minutes later they were seated around a table in the hall, huddled over cups of strong black tea while Billings fussed around in the kitchen. They'd protested they didn't want to put him out of the way, but he'd insisted on cooking them a proper fry-up. Soon he emerged with plates of sizzling eggs, sausages, potatoes, and toast.

'And something to lift the spirits.' Billings set four mugs down in front of them. 'Just some brandy and water. You're not the first Babblers I've seen back from abroad. That's always done the trick.'

The smell of food reminded them they were ravenous. They fell on the spread like wolves, chewing in frantic silence as Billings sat watching them, amused.

'So,' he said, 'tell me about this exciting voyage, eh? Canton and Mauritius, was it? Did they feed you anything funny? See any local ceremonies?'

They glanced at each other, unsure of what to say. Letty began to cry.

'Oh, come now.' Billings nudged the mug of brandy closer to her. 'It can't have been that bad.'

Letty shook her head. She bit her lip, but a whining noise burst out. It was not a mere sniffle but a stormy, full-body cry. She clamped her hands over her face and sobbed heartily, shoulders quaking, incoherent words leaking through her fingers.

'She was homesick,' Victoire said lamely. 'She was, ah, quite homesick.'

Billings reached out to pat Letty's shoulder. 'All's well, child. You're back home, you're safe.'

He went out to wake the driver. Ten minutes later a cab pulled up to the hall, and the girls were off to their lodgings. Robin and Ramy dragged their trunks down to Magpie Lane and said their goodnights. Robin felt a fleeting anxiety when Ramy disappeared through the door into his room – he had grown used to Ramy's company during all those nights on the voyage, and he was scared of being on his own for the first time in weeks, with no other voice to soften the dark.

But when he closed his own door behind him, he was surprised by how normal everything felt. His desk, bed, and bookshelves were exactly as he'd left them. Nothing had changed in his absence. The translation of the *Shanhaijing* he'd been working on for Professor Chakravarti still sat on his desk, half-finished in the middle of a sentence. The scout must have been in recently, because there wasn't a speck of dust in sight. As he sat down on his lumpy mattress and breathed in the familiar, comforting scent of old books and mildew, Robin felt that if he only lay back and closed his eyes, he could get up in the morning and head to class like nothing had ever happened.

He woke to the sight of Ramy looming above him. 'Good God.' He bolted upright, breathing hard. 'Don't do that.'

'You really should start locking your door.' Ramy handed him a cup. 'Now that we're – you know. Tea?'

'Thanks.' He took the cup in both hands and sipped. It was their favourite blend of Assam, dark and heady and strong. For just a bliss-ful moment there, sunlight streaming through the window and birds chirping softly outside, all that had transpired in Canton seemed like a terrible dream before cold, twisting memory sank in. He sighed. 'What's going on?'

'The girls are here,' said Ramy. 'Time to get up.'

'Here?'

'In my sitting room. Come on.'

Robin washed his face and dressed. Across the hall, Victoire and Letty sat-perched on Ramy's sofa as Ramy passed around tea, a burlap sack of scones, and a small pot of clotted cream. 'I assumed no one felt like going to hall, so that's breakfast.'

'These are very good,' Victoire said, looking surprised. 'Where—'

'Vaults, just before they opened. They always have yesterday's scones out for a fraction of the price.' Ramy had no knife, so he scraped his scone directly against the cream. 'Good, right?'

Robin sat down opposite the girls. 'How'd you two sleep?'

'All well, considered,' said Letty. 'Feels strange to be back.'

'It's too comfortable,' Victoire agreed. 'It feels like the world should be different now, but it's . . . not.'

That was how Robin felt too. It seemed wrong to be back among his creature comforts, to sit on Ramy's sofa and have their favourite tea with scones from their favourite café. Their situation did not feel commensurate to the stakes. The stakes, rather, seemed to demand that the world be on fire.

'So, listen.' Ramy took a seat beside Robin. 'We can't just wait around. Every passing second is one that we're not in prison, and so we've got to use them. We've got to find Hermes. Birdie, how do you contact Griffin?'

'I can't,' said Robin. 'Griffin was very adamant about that. He knew how to find me, but I didn't have any ways to reach him. That's how it always worked.'

'Anthony was the same,' Victoire said. 'Although – he did show us several drop points, places where we left things for him. Suppose we went and left messages there—'

'How often does he check them, though?' Letty asked. 'Will he even check if he's not expecting anything?'

'I don't know,' said Victoire, frustrated. 'But it's our only option.'

'I do think they'll be looking out for us,' said Robin. 'After what happened that night we were caught – I mean, there are too many loose ends, and now we're all back I assume they'll want to be in touch.'

He could tell from their expressions that this was no great reassurance. Hermes was finicky, unpredictable. Hermes might come knocking in the next hour, or they could go silent for six months.

'How much time do we have, anyway?' Ramy asked after a pause. 'I mean, how long before they realize dear old Richard isn't coming back?'

None of them could know for sure. Term was not due to start for another week, at which point it would be very suspicious that Professor Lovell had not returned to teach. But suppose the other professors had expected them all back earlier?

'Well, who's in regular contact with him?' asked Letty. 'We'll have to tell some kind of story to the faculty, of course—'

'And there's Mrs Piper,' said Robin. 'His housekeeper in Jericho – she'll be wondering where he is, I've got to call on her as well.'

'Here's an idea,' said Victoire. 'We could go to his office and look through his correspondence, see if there are any appointments he was due to keep – or even forge some replies if that buys us a little time.'

'To be clear,' said Letty, 'you think we ought to break into the office of the man whose murder we covered up and rifle through his things, all while hoping no one catches us?'

'The time to do it would be now,' Victoire pointed out. 'While no one knows we did it.'

'How do you know they don't already?' Letty's voice rose in pitch. 'How do you know we won't be clapped in irons the moment we walk into the tower?'

'Holy God,' Robin muttered. Suddenly it seemed absurd that they were having this conversation, that they were even in Oxford at all. 'Why *did* we come back?'

'We should go to Calcutta,' Ramy declared abruptly. 'Come on, let's escape to Liverpool, we can book a passage from there—'

Letty's nose wrinkled. 'Why Calcutta?'

'It's safe there, I've got parents who can shield us, there's space in the attic—'

'I'm not spending the rest of my life hiding in your parents' attic!'

'It would only be *temporary*—'

'Everyone calm down.' Victoire so seldom raised her voice, it hushed them at once. 'It's like – like an assignment, you understand? We only need a plan. We only have to break this down into component parts, finish them, and we'll be fine.' She lifted two fingers. 'Now, it seems there are two things we need to do. Task one: get in touch with the Hermes Society. Task two: accumulate as much information as we can so when we do reach Hermes, they'll be able to do something with it.'

'You forgot task three,' Letty said. 'Don't get caught.'

'Well, that goes without saying.'

'How exposed are we?' asked Ramy. 'I mean, if you think about it, we're even safer here than we were on the ship. Bodies can't talk, and he's not going to wash up anywhere. Seems to me that if we all keep quiet, we're fine, aren't we?'

'But they'll start asking questions,' said Letty. 'I mean, obviously, at some point, someone's going to notice Professor Lovell's not answering any letters.'

'So we keep telling them the same thing,' said Victoire. 'He's holed up in his house, he's grievously ill, which is why he's not answering letters or taking visitors, and he told us to come back without him. That's the whole story. Keep it simple, don't embellish details. If we all give the same account, then no one will get suspicious. And if we come off as nervous, it's because we're concerned for our dear professor. Yes?'

No one challenged her. They were all hanging on her every word. The world had stopped spinning out of control; all that mattered was what Victoire said next.

She continued. 'What I think, though, is that the more sitting around we do – that is, the more cautiously we behave – the more suspicious we look. We can't hide away and keep out of sight. We're Babel students. We're busy. We're fourth years losing our minds from all the work we've been assigned. We don't have to pretend we're not mad, because students here are always mad, but we've got to pretend we're mad for the right reasons.'

Somehow, this made complete and utter sense.

Victoire pointed at Robin. 'You get the housekeeper sorted, then go and get Professor Lovell's correspondence. Ramy and I will go to Anthony's drop points and leave as many encrypted messages as we can. Letty, you'll go about your daily routine and give the impression that everything is perfectly fine. If people ask you about Canton, start spreading the story about the professor's illness. We'll all meet back here tonight, and hope to God nothing goes wrong.' She took a deep breath and looked around, nodding as if trying to convince herself. 'We're going to make it through this, all right? We just can't lose our heads.'

But this, Robin thought, was a foregone conclusion.

One by one they dispersed from Magpie Lane. Robin had hoped that Mrs Piper would not be at home in Jericho, that he could get away with simply leaving a message in the letterbox, but he'd barely knocked before she threw the door open with a wide smile. 'Robin, dear!'

She hugged him tight. She smelled of warm bread. Robin's sinuses stung, threatening tears. He broke away and rubbed at his nose, trying to pass it off as a sneeze.

'You look thin.' She patted his cheeks. 'Didn't they feed you in Canton? Or had you lost your taste for Chinese food?'

'Canton was fine,' he said weakly. 'It's the voyages where food's scarce.'

'Shame on them. You're only kids, still.' She stepped back and glanced around. 'Is the professor back too, then?'

'He won't be back for a bit, actually.' Robin's voice wobbled. He cleared his throat and tried again. He'd never lied to Mrs Piper before, and it felt much worse than he'd expected. 'He – well, he fell badly ill on the return voyage.'

'My word, really?'

'And he didn't feel up to the journey back to Oxford, and was worried about transmitting it besides, so he's quarantining himself in Hampstead for now.'

'All on his own?' Mrs Piper looked alarmed. 'That fool, he should have written. I should head down tonight, Lord knows the man can't even make himself tea—'

'Please don't,' Robin blurted. 'Erm – I mean, what he's got is very contagious. It spreads through the air in particles when he coughs or speaks. We couldn't even be in the same cabin with him on the ship. He's trying to see as few people as possible. But he's being taken care of. We had a doctor in to look at him—'

'Which one? Smith? Hastings?'

He tried to remember the name of the doctor who'd come to treat him when he caught influenza as a child. 'Erm – Hastings?'

'Good,' said Mrs Piper. 'I always thought Smith was a quack. I had this terrible fever several years back, and he diagnosed it as simple hysterics. Hysterics! I couldn't even keep broth down, and he thought I was making it all up.'

Robin took a steadying breath. 'I'm sure Dr Hastings will take good care of him.'

'Oh, sure, he'll be back here demanding his sultana scones by the weekend.' Mrs Piper smiled broadly. It was clearly fake; it did not quite reach her eyes, but she seemed determined to cheer him up. 'Well, I can look after you, at least. Can I make you some lunch?'

'Oh, no,' he said quickly. 'I can't stay, there's – I've got to go and tell the other professors. They don't know yet, you see.'

'You won't even stay for tea?'

He wanted to. He wanted so badly to sit at her table, to listen to her rambling stories and feel, just for a fleeting moment, the warm comfort and safety of his childhood. But he knew he wouldn't last five minutes, much less the time it would take to pour, steep, and sip a cup of Darjeeling. If he stayed, if he stepped inside that house, he would break down completely.

'Robin?' Mrs Piper examined his face, concerned. 'Dear, you look so upset.'

'It's just—' Tears blurred his eyes; he could not hold them back. His voice cracked. 'I'm just so scared.'

'Oh, dear.' She wrapped her arms around him. Robin hugged her back, shoulders shaking with suppressed sobs. For the first time he realized he might never see her again – indeed, he hadn't spared a second thought about what might happen to her when it became known Professor Lovell was dead.

'Mrs Piper, I was wondering . . .' He untangled himself and took a step back. He felt wretched with guilt. 'Are you . . . have you got family or something? Some other place to go?'

She looked confused. 'How do you mean?'

'If Professor Lovell doesn't make it,' he said. 'I'm just wondering – because if he doesn't pull through, then you won't have—'

'Oh. Dear boy.' Her eyes grew leaky. 'Don't you worry about me. I've got a niece and brother in Edinburgh – there's no love lost there, but they'll have to take me in if I come knocking. But it won't come to that. Richard has caught his share of foreign diseases before. He'll be back here for your monthly dinners in no time, and I'll treat you both to a whole roasted goose when he is.' She squeezed his shoulders. 'You just focus on your studies, won't you? Do good work, and don't worry about the rest.'

He was never going to see her again. No matter how things fell out, this at least seemed certain. Robin fixed his eyes on her gentle smile, trying to memorize this moment. 'I'll do my best, Mrs Piper. Goodbye.'

He had to compose himself for a moment on the street before he could summon the nerve to walk into the tower.

The faculty offices were on the seventh floor. Robin waited in the stairwell until he was sure the hallway was empty before he darted forth and slid Professor Lovell's key into the lock. The correspondence in the office was much the same as he'd found in Hampstead: letters to Jardine, Matheson, Gützlaff, and others on war plans for the coming invasion. He shuffled some into a pile and stuffed them into his jacket. He didn't have the faintest clue what Hermes might do with them, but some proof, he assumed, was better than none.

He'd just locked the door behind him when he heard voices from Professor Playfair's office. The first belonged to a woman, demanding and loud. 'He's missed three consecutive payments, and I haven't been in touch with him in months—'

'Richard is a very busy man,' said Professor Playfair. 'And he's still overseas on the annual fourth years' trip, which I'm sure he told you—'

'He did not,' said the woman. 'You know he's terrible about such things, we never know where he's going. He doesn't write, doesn't even telegraph, he sends nothing for the children. You know, they're starting to forget they have a father.'

Heart pounding, Robin crept to the corner of the hallway, remaining just within earshot. The staircase was just a few feet behind him. If the door opened, he could flee to the sixth floor before anyone saw him.

'That must be, ah, very difficult,' Professor Playfair said awkwardly. 'Though I must say this isn't a subject on which Richard and I converse frequently. You'd be better off taking it up directly with him—'

'When's he expected back?'

'Next week. Though there's been some trouble in Canton, I've heard, so it may be a few days earlier. But I truly don't know, Mrs Lovell – I'll send word when we hear anything, but for now we know as little as you do.'

The door opened. Robin tensed to flee, but morbid curiosity kept him bolted in place. He peeked out from around the corner. He wanted to see, to know for certain.

A tall, thin woman with grey-streaked hair stepped into the hallway. With her were two small children. The older one, a girl, looked about ten and had clearly been crying, though she concealed her sobs in one fist while she clenched her mother's hand in the other. The younger child, a boy, was much smaller – perhaps only five or six. He tottered out into the hallway as Mrs Lovell said her goodbyes to Professor Playfair.

Robin's breath caught in his throat. He found himself leaning further out into the hallway, unable to look away. The boy looked so much like himself, like Griffin. His eyes were the same light brown, his hair similarly dark, though it curled more than either of theirs.

The boy met his eyes. Then, to Robin's horror, he opened his mouth and uttered in a high, clear voice, 'Papa.'

Robin turned and fled.

'What was that?' Mrs Lovell's voice carried over towards the staircase. 'Dick, what did you say?'

Professor Lovell's son babbled something in response, but Robin was flying too quickly down the stairs to hear.

'Bloody hell,' said Ramy. 'I didn't know Professor Lovell even had a family.'

'I told you he had an estate in Yorkshire!'

'I thought you were making that up,' said Ramy. 'I've never seen him take a vacation once. He's just not – not a family man. How'd he stay home long enough to conceive?'

'The issue is, they exist and they're worried,' said Robin. 'He's apparently been missing payments to his estate. And now Playfair knows something's wrong.'

'Suppose we paid them off?' asked Victoire. 'Forged his handwriting and sent the money ourselves, I mean. How much does it take to maintain a household for a month?'

'If it's just the three of them?' Letty thought for a moment. 'Only about ten pounds.'

Victoire blanched. Ramy sighed and rubbed at his temples. Robin reached to pour himself a glass of brandy.

The mood that night was decidedly glum. Other than the stack of letters Robin had found in Professor Lovell's office, the day had yielded nothing. The Hermes Society had remained silent. Robin's window was empty. Victoire and Ramy had been to each of Anthony's old drop points – a loose brick behind the Christ Church cathedral, a hidden bench in the Botanic Garden, an overturned and rarely used punt on the bank of the Cherwell – but none showed signs of recent visitation. They'd even walked back and forth in front of the Twisted Root for the better part of an hour, hoping Griffin might spot them lurking, but succeeded only in drawing looks from the patrons.

At least nothing disastrous had happened – no breakdowns, no ominous encounters with the Oxford police. Letty had begun hyperventilating again in the Buttery during lunch, or so Robin heard, but Victoire had slapped her on the back and pretended she'd merely choked on a grape. (Letty, Robin thought unkindly, was not helping the general feminist case that women were not nervous, pea-brained hysterics.)

They were safe, perhaps, for now. Yet they could not help feeling like sitting ducks. The clock was running out on them; too many people were growing suspicious, and their luck would not hold forever. But where else could they go? If they ran, then the Hermes Society had no way of finding them. They were trapped by obligation.

'Oh, hell,' said Ramy. He was going through the stacks of correspondence he'd retrieved from their pidges, sorting out the meaningless pamphlets from everything important. 'I forgot.'

'What?' asked Letty.

'The faculty party.' Ramy waved a thick cream-coloured invitation card at them. 'The damn faculty party, it's this Friday.'

'Well of course we're not going,' said Robin.

'We can't not go,' said Ramy. 'It's the faculty party.'

Every year just before the start of Hilary, the Royal Institute of Translation put on a garden party in the University College grounds for faculty, students, and graduate fellows. They'd been to three by now. They were long, unremarkable events; like at all Oxford functions, the food was barely passable and the speeches were long. What Robin couldn't understand was why Ramy was making such a big deal of it.

'So what?' asked Victoire.

'So everyone goes,' said Ramy. 'It's mandatory. They all know we're back by now – we ran into Professor Craft outside the Rad Cam this morning, and plenty of people saw Letty in the Buttery. We have to keep up appearances.'

Robin could not imagine anything more horrifying than eating hors d'oeuvres in the company of Babel faculty.

'Are you mad?' Victoire demanded. 'Those things are endless; we'll never make it through.'

'It's only a party,' said Ramy.

'Three courses? Wine? *Speeches?* Letty's barely keeping it together as it is, and you want to plant her by Craft and Playfair and expect her to talk about what a lovely time she had in Canton for over three hours?'

'I'll be all right,' Letty said weakly, convincing no one.

'They'll start asking questions if we're not there—'

'And they won't ask questions when Letty vomits all over the centrepiece?'

'She can pretend she has food poisoning,' said Ramy. 'We can pretend she's been sick since this morning, which explains why she's all pale and clammy, and why she had a fit in the Buttery. But can you really argue that's more suspicious than all four of us failing to show up at all?'

Robin glanced to Victoire, hoping she had a counter-argument. But she was looking to him, expecting the same.

'The party buys time,' Ramy said firmly. 'If we can just manage not to seem like total lunatics, we buy ourselves a day. Or two. That's it. More time. That's the only factor that matters.'

Friday turned out to be an unseasonably hot day. It began with a typical January morning chill, but by midafternoon the sun had burned through the cloud cover and was shining in full force. They'd all overestimated the cold when they got dressed, but once in the courtyard they could not easily remove their wool undershirts, which meant they had no choice but to sweat.

That year's garden party was the most extravagant Babel had ever put on. The faculty was swimming in coin after a visit by the Russian Archduke Alexander to the university the previous May; the archduke, who had been so impressed by the wit and skill of his spontaneous interpreters at the reception, had made Babel a gift of one thousand pounds for discretionary funding. The professors had put that to lavish, if ill-considered, use. A string quartet played lustily in the middle of the quadrangle, though everyone veered away from them because the noise made conversation impossible. Half a dozen peacocks, reportedly imported from London Zoo, wandered around the green, harassing anyone dressed in bright colours. Three long, tented tables of food and drink occupied the centre of the green. The offerings included finger sandwiches, small pies, a grotesque variety of chocolates, and seven different flavours of ice cream.

Babel scholars milled around holding rapidly warming glasses of wine, making tepid and petty conversation. Like all faculties at Oxford, the Translation Institute was rife with internal rivalries and jealousies over funding and appointments, a problem exacerbated by the fact that each regional specialist thought their language was more rich, more poetic, more literary, and more fertile for silver-working than others. Babel's departmental prejudices were just as arbitrary as they were confusing. The Romanticists enjoyed most of the literary prestige,* though Arabic and Chinese were highly prized mostly by virtue of how foreign and different they were, while languages closer to home like Gaelic and Welsh had almost no respect at all. This made small talk very dangerous; it was very easy to give offence if one displayed either too much or too little enthusiasm about one's research. Walking around in the midst of it all was Reverend Doctor Frederick Charles Plumptre, Master of the College, and it was understood at some point that each of them would have to shake his hand, pretend that they believed he remembered them when it was obvious he hadn't a clue what their names were, and suffer a painfully banal conversation about where they were from and what they studied before he let them go.

All this for three unbearable hours, for no one could leave before the banquet was over. The seating charts were made; their absences would be noticed. They had to stay until the sun had set, until all the toasts had been given, and until all the scholars present had had enough of pretending to enjoy socializing for a lifetime.

This is a disaster, Robin thought, glancing around. They would have been better off not showing up. None of them had their wits about them. He watched a graduate fellow ask Victoire a question three times before

---

* The poor Germanists always lost to the Romance linguists in these verbal spars, for they had to deal with hearing the words of their own King Frederick II of Prussia thrown back at them. Frederick was so cowed by the literary dominance of French that he wrote in 1780 an essay, in French, criticizing his native German for sounding half-barbarous, unrefined, and unpleasing to the ear. He then proposed to improve the sound of German by adding -*a* as the final syllable to a great quantity of verbs to make them sound more Italian.

she finally registered his presence. Letty was standing in the corner, gulping down glass after glass of cold water as sweat dripped down her forehead. Ramy was faring the best, holding court with a gaggle of first years regaling him with questions about his voyage, but as Robin walked past him, he heard Ramy burst out in such an abrupt, hysterical peal of laughter that he nearly flinched back with fright.

Robin felt dizzy as he looked out over the crowded lawn. This was madness, he thought, sheer madness that he should be standing here among the faculty, holding a wineglass, concealing the truth that he'd killed one of their number. He wandered towards the buffet tables and filled a small plate with hors d'oeuvres, just to have something to do, but the thought of putting any of the rapidly spoiling tarts in his mouth was nauseating.

'Feeling all right?'

He jumped and turned. It was Professors De Vreese and Playfair. They stood on either side of him like prison guards. Robin blinked rapidly, trying to arrange his features into something like a neutral smile. 'Professors. Sirs.'

'You're sweating buckets.' Professor Playfair scrutinized his face, looking concerned. 'And you've got enormous shadows under your eyes, Swift. Have you been sleeping?'

'Time lag,' Robin blurted. 'We didn't – erm, we didn't adjust our sleeping schedules on the return voyage as well as we should have. And besides we're exhausted with, erm, with preterm reading.'

To his astonishment, Professor Playfair nodded in sympathy. 'Ah, well. You know what they say. *Student* from *studere*, meaning "painstaking, dedicated application". If you don't feel like a nail struck constantly by a hammer, you're doing it wrong.'

'Indeed,' said Robin. His strategy, he'd decided, was to come off as so boring that they lost interest and wandered off.

'Did you have a good trip?' inquired Professor De Vreese.

'It was—' Robin cleared his throat. 'It was more than we bargained for, we think. We're all very glad to be back.'

'Don't I know it. Those overseas affairs can be exhausting.' Professor Playfair nodded to the plate in Robin's hand. 'Ah, I see you've found my inventions. Go on, have a bite.'

Robin, feeling pressured, bit into a tart.

'Good, isn't it?' Professor Playfair watched him as he chewed. 'Yes, it's silver-enhanced. A fanciful little match-pair that I came up with on vacation in Rome. *Pomodoro* is a rather fanciful description for a tomato, you see – it literally means "apple of gold". Now add the French intermediary, *pomme d'amour*, and you get a richness that the English doesn't . . .'

Robin chewed, trying to look appreciative. All he could register was how slimy it was; how the salty juices bursting in his mouth made him think of blood and corpses.

'You have *pretoogjes*,' Professor De Vreese observed.

'I'm sorry?'

'*Pretoogjes.*' Professor De Vreese gestured at his face. 'Fun eyes. A Dutch word. Twinkling eyes, shifting eyes. We use it to describe children who are up to no good.'

Robin had not the faintest idea what he was supposed to say in response to this. 'I . . . how interesting.'

'I think I'll go and say hello to the Master now,' said Professor De Vreese as if Robin hadn't spoken. 'Welcome back, Swift. Enjoy the party.'

'So.' Professor Playfair handed Robin a glass of claret. 'Do you have any idea when Professor Lovell is back from London?'

'I don't know.' Robin took a sip, doing his best to collect himself before he answered. 'You've probably heard he's holed up with something he contracted in Canton. He looked in a bad state when we left him, I'm not sure if he'll even be back for the term.'

'Interesting,' said Professor Playfair. 'It's quite fortunate it didn't spread to any of you.'

'Oh, well – we took precautions when he started feeling out of sorts. Quarantine, face cloths, all of that – you know.'

'Come now, Mr Swift.' Professor Playfair's voice became stern. 'I know he's not ill. I've sent three messengers to London since you lot have been back, and they've all reported the Hampstead house is presently empty.'

'Really?' Robin's ears began to buzz. What was he supposed to do now? Was there any point in trying to maintain the lie? Should he just cut and run? 'How very odd, that's – I don't know why he would . . .'

Professor Playfair took a step closer and bent his head conspiratorially towards Robin's ear. 'You know,' he whispered, 'our friends at Hermes would like very much to know where he is.'

Robin nearly spat out his claret. His throat caught the wine before he made a mess, but he then swallowed it up the wrong channel. Professor

Playfair stood by calmly as he choked and gasped, spilling both his plate and glass in the process.

'Quite all right, Swift?'

Robin's eyes watered. 'What did you—'

'I'm with Hermes,' Professor Playfair murmured pleasantly, eyes fixed on the string quartet. 'Whatever you're hiding, you're safe telling me.'

Robin had no idea what to make of this. Certainly he felt no relief. *Trust no one* – Griffin had all but engraved this lesson in his bones. Professor Playfair could be easily lying – and this would be the simplest trick, too, if his goal was to coax Robin into spilling everything that he knew. Or Professor Playfair could be the ally, the saviour they'd been waiting for. He felt a pang of residual frustration. If only Griffin had ever told him more, if only Griffin hadn't been so happy to leave him in the dark, cut off from others, and so utterly helpless.

He had no useful information to act on, only a gut instinct that something was badly wrong. 'Thank the Lord,' he said, mirroring Professor Playfair's covert murmur. 'So you know about Griffin's Canton plot?'

'Of course,' Professor Playfair said, just a bit too eagerly. 'Did it work?'

Robin paused. He had to play this next part very carefully. He had to reel out just enough to keep Professor Playfair on the line, curious but not quite ready to pounce. And he needed time – at least enough time to gather the others and run.

Professor Playfair slung his arm around Robin's shoulders, drawing him in close. 'Why don't you and I go and have a chat?'

'Not here.' Robin's eyes darted around the quad. Letty and Victoire were both staring at him over their shoulders. He blinked hard, glanced pointedly at the front exit, then back at them. 'Not in front of the faculty, you never know who's listening.'

'Of course,' said Professor Playfair.

'The tunnels,' said Robin, before Professor Playfair could suggest that they leave the party right then. 'I'm meeting Griffin and the others tonight at the Taylorian tunnels at midnight, why don't you come? I've got . . . I've got all those documents they've been waiting for.'

It worked. Professor Playfair let go of Robin's shoulders and stepped away.

'Very well.' His eyes shone with glee; he looked one step away from rubbing his hands together like a villain on a stage. 'Good work, Swift.'

Robin nodded, and only barely managed to keep a straight face until

Professor Playfair moved on to chat with Professor Chakravarti across the green.

Then it took everything he had not to break into a run. He scanned the quad for Ramy, who was trapped in a conversation with Reverend Doctor Plumptre. Robin blinked frantically at him. Immediately Ramy spilled his wineglass all over his own front, exclaimed loudly in dismay, made his excuses, and beelined through the garden towards Robin.

'Playfair knows,' Robin told him.

'What?' Ramy glanced around. 'Are you sure—'

'We have to go.' To his relief, Robin saw that Victoire and Letty were already moving towards the front gate. He wanted to follow, but too many faculty stood between them; he and Ramy would have to go out the back, by the kitchens. 'Come on.'

'How—'

'Later.' Robin hazarded a glimpse over his shoulder just before they left the garden. His stomach twisted – Playfair was saying something to Professor De Vreese, their heads bent close together. De Vreese glanced up and looked straight into Robin's eyes. Robin looked away. 'Just – come on.'

Victoire and Letty rushed towards them the moment they stepped outside.

'What's happened?' Letty breathed. 'Why—'

'Not here,' Robin said. 'Walk.'

They marched at a hasty pace down Kybald Street, then turned right onto Magpie Lane.

'Playfair's onto us,' said Robin. 'We're done.'

'How do you know?' Letty asked. 'What did he say? Did you tell him?'

'Of course not,' Robin said. 'But he pretended he was with Hermes, tried to get me to confess everything—'

'How do you know he's not?'

'Because I lied,' said Robin. 'And he fell for it. He hasn't a clue what Hermes does, he was fishing for information.'

'Then what are we doing?' Victoire asked suddenly. 'Good God, *where are we going?*'

They had, Robin realized, been walking without purpose. They were headed now for High Street, but what would they do there? If Professor Playfair called for the police, they'd be spotted in seconds. They couldn't go back into Number 4; they'd be trapped. But they had no money on their persons, and no means to pay the fare to anywhere else.

'There you are.'

They all flinched backwards in fright.

Anthony Ribben stepped out onto the main road and looked them over, counting them with one finger like they were ducklings. 'You're all here? Excellent. Come with me.'

CHAPTER TWENTY-TWO

This group is remarkable, although it has vanished in the invisible depths which are behind us.

> VICTOR HUGO, *Les Misérables*,
> trans. Frederic Charles Lascelles Wraxall

Their shock was fleeting. Anthony broke into a run, and they followed without question. But instead of doubling back on Magpie Lane all the way to Merton Street, from where they might escape out towards Christ Church meadow, he took them back onto Kybald towards the college.

'What are you doing?' Ramy panted. 'That's where everyone—'

'Just hurry,' Anthony hissed.

They obeyed. It was wonderful to have someone tell them what to do. Anthony led them through the doors behind the kitchen, past the Old Library, and straight into the hall. On the other side of the wall, the garden party was still going on in full force; they could hear string instruments and voices through the stone.

'In here.' Anthony waved them into the chapel.

They darted in and shut the heavy wooden doors behind them. Outside service hours, the chapel felt strange: unearthly, silent. The air inside was repressively still. Apart from their panting, the only movement was the dust motes floating in the prisms of light streaming through the windows.

Anthony stopped before the memorial frieze of Sir William Jones.

'What are you—' Letty began.

'Hush.' Anthony reached towards the epigram, which read, *He formed a digest of Hindu and Mohammedan Laws.* He touched a succession of letters in turn, which sank slightly back into the stone when pushed. *G, O, R . . .*

Ramy snickered. Anthony touched a final letter in the much longer Latin inscription above the frieze, a rambling celebration of William Jones's life and accomplishments. *B.*

Gorasahib.*

There was a scraping noise, then a whoosh of cold air. The frieze popped several inches out from the wall. Anthony pushed his fingers into the crack at the bottom edge and slid the panel upwards to reveal a pitch-black hole in the wall. 'Get in.'

One by one, they helped each other inside. The tunnel turned out to be much wider than it appeared from the outside. They only had to crawl on their hands and knees for several seconds before the shaft emptied into a larger corridor. Robin could just feel the damp earth skimming the top of his head when he stood, though Ramy exclaimed when his head bumped against the ceiling.

'Hush,' Anthony grunted again as he pulled the door down behind them. 'The walls are thin.'

The frieze slid back into place with a thud. The light in the passage disappeared. They groped their way forward, cursing as they stumbled against each other.

'Ah, sorry.' Anthony struck a match, and a flame materialized in his palm. Now they could see that several yards in, the cramped shaft expanded outwards into something more like a hallway. 'There we go. Keep going, there's a long walk ahead.'

'Where—' Letty began, but Anthony shook his head, lifted a finger to his lips, and pointed to the walls.

The tunnel widened more and more as they walked. The branch leading to the Univ chapel was apparently a new addition, for the passage where they walked now seemed much larger and older. Dried mud gave way to brick walls, and at several junctures, Robin saw sconces affixed to the upper corners. The dark should have felt claustrophobic, but in fact

---

* *Gora* – 'white, pale', in reference to skin colour. *Sahib* – a salutation of respect. Put together, with the right tone of sarcasm and vehemence, it means something else altogether. Let it not be forgotten that, though Jones professed a great love and admiration for Indian languages throughout his career, he initially turned his scholarly attentions to Sanskrit because he suspected indigenous translators of being dishonest and unreliable.

it felt comforting. Swallowed in the belly of the earth, truly hidden from view for the first time since their return voyage, they all found that they could finally breathe.

After several minutes of silence, Ramy asked, 'How long's that been there?'

'Only a few decades, actually,' said Anthony. 'The tunnels have been here forever – they aren't a Hermes project, we only took advantage of them – but that entryway is new. Lady Jones had the frieze installed not too many years ago, but we got in fast before construction work was done. Don't worry, no one else knows. Is everyone all right?'

'We're okay,' said Robin. 'But, Anthony, there's something you have to—'

'I imagine there's quite a lot you need to tell me,' said Anthony. 'Why don't we start with what you've done with Professor Lovell? Is he dead? The faculty seem to think so.'

'Robin killed him,' Ramy said cheerily.

Anthony turned to glance at Robin over his shoulder. 'Oh, really?'

'It was an accident,' Robin insisted. 'We were quarrelling, and he – I don't know, I suddenly . . . I mean, I did use this match-pair, only I didn't know I was doing it until it was over—'

'What's more important is the war on China,' said Victoire. 'We've been trying to find you, to tell you. They're planning an invasion—'

'We know,' said Anthony.

'You do?' asked Robin.

'Griffin's been afraid of this for a while. We've kept an eye on Jardine and Matheson, been tracking developments in the Factories. Though it's never got this bad before. Up until now it was all noise. But they'll really go to war, you think?'

'I've got papers—' Robin reached for his breast pocket as if they were still stowed within his jacket, and then cursed. 'Damn it, they're all in my room—'

'What do they say?'

'They're letters, correspondence between Lovell and Jardine and Matheson both – and Palmerston, and Gützlaff, the whole lot of them – oh, but I left them on Magpie Lane—'

'What do they *say*?'

'They're war plans,' said Robin, flustered. 'They're plans that have been months, years in the making—'

'They're evidence of direct collusion?' Anthony pressed.

'Yes, they indicate that the negotiations were never in good faith, that the last round was only a pretext—'

'Good,' said Anthony. 'That's very good. We can work with that. We'll send someone over to retrieve them. You're in Griffin's old room, correct? Number seven?'

'I – yes.'

'Very good. I'll have that sorted. In the meantime, I suggest you all calm down.' He paused, turned around, and gave them a warm smile. After the week they'd just had, the sight of Anthony's face in the soft candlelight made Robin want to cry with relief. 'You're in safe hands now. I agree it's quite dire, but we can't solve anything in this tunnel. You've done very well, and I imagine you're quite scared, but you can relax now. The grown-ups are here.'

The underground passage turned out to be quite long. Robin lost track of how far they walked; it had to be nearly a mile. He wondered how vast the network was – now and then they passed a split in the tunnel or a door embedded in the wall, suggesting more hidden entrances across the university, but Anthony shepherded them along without comment. These were, Robin assumed, among Hermes's many secrets.

At last, the passage narrowed again until there was only space to walk in single file. Anthony took the lead, holding the candle high above his head like a beacon. Letty followed just behind him.

'Why you?' she asked quietly. Robin couldn't tell if she meant to be discreet, but the tunnel was so narrow, her voice carried to the back of the line.

'Whatever do you mean?' murmured Anthony.

'You loved it at Babel,' said Letty. 'I remember, you gave us our orientation tour. You adored it there, and they adored you.'

'That's true,' said Anthony. 'Babel treated me better than anyone ever had.'

'Then why—'

'She thinks it's about personal happiness,' Ramy interjected. 'But Letty, we've told you, it doesn't matter how happy we were personally, it's about the broader injustice—'

'That's not what I meant, Ramy, I only—'

'Let me try to explain,' Anthony said gently. 'On the eve of abolition throughout the colonies, my master decided he wanted to pack up and return to America. I wouldn't be free there, you see. He could keep me in his household and call me his. This man had labelled himself an abolitionist. He'd decried the general trade for years; he just seemed to think our relationship was special. But when the proposals he'd publicly supported became law, he decided he really couldn't bear the sacrifice of losing me. So I went on the run and sought refuge at Oxford. The college took me in and hid me until I was legally declared a free man – not because they care much about abolition either, but because the professors at Babel knew my worth. And they knew if I were sent back to America, they would lose me to Harvard or Princeton.'

Robin couldn't see Letty's face in the darkness, but he could hear her breathing growing shallower. He wondered if she was about to cry again.

'There are no kind masters, Letty,' Anthony continued. 'It doesn't matter how lenient, how gracious, how invested in your education they make out to be. Masters are masters in the end.'

'But you don't really believe that about Babel,' Letty whispered. 'Do you? It's just not the same – they weren't *enslaving* you – I mean, Christ, you had a *fellowship*—'

'Do you know what Equiano's master told him when he was manumitted?' Anthony asked mildly. 'He told him that in a short time, he'd have slaves of his own.'

At last, the tunnel ended in a set of steps covered with a wooden board, sunlight streaming in through the slats. Anthony pressed his ears to the slats, waited a moment, then unlocked the board and pushed. 'Come on up.'

They emerged in a sunny yard facing an old one-storey brick building half-hidden behind a mass of overgrown shrubbery. They couldn't have strayed too far from the town centre – they were only two miles out at most – but Robin had never seen this building before. Its doors looked rusted shut, and its walls were nearly swallowed by ivy, as if someone had built this place and then abandoned it decades ago.

'Welcome to the Old Library.' Anthony helped them out of the tunnel. 'Durham College built this place in the fourteenth century as an overflow room for old books, then forgot about it when they secured funding to build a new library closer to the centre of town.'

'Just the Old Library?' asked Victoire. 'No other name?'

'None that we use. A name would mark its importance, and we want it unnoticed and forgotten – something you skim over when you see it in the records, something easily confused for something else.' Anthony spread his palm against the rusted door, murmured something under his breath, and then pushed. The door screeched open. 'Come on in.'

Like Babel, the Old Library was much larger on the inside than its exterior suggested. From the outside, it looked as if it could contain a single lecture hall at most. Its interior, meanwhile, could have been the ground floor of the Radcliffe Library. Wooden bookshelves radiated from the centre, and more lined walls which looked, magically and contradictorily, circular. All the shelves were meticulously labelled, and a long yellowed parchment listing the classification system hung from the opposite wall. Near the front was a shelf boasting new arrivals, on which Robin recognized a few of the titles he'd snuck out for Griffin over the past few years. They'd all had their Babel serial numbers scratched out.

'We don't like their categorization system,' explained Anthony. 'It only makes sense in Roman characters, but not every language is so easily Romanized, is it?' He pointed to a mat near the door. 'Wipe your shoes off, we don't like tracking mud between the shelves. And there's a stand over there for your coats.'

A rusted iron kettle hung inexplicably from the top rung of the coat stand. Robin reached towards it, curious, but Anthony said sharply, 'Leave that alone.'

'Sorry – what's it for?'

'Not tea, clearly.' Anthony swung the kettle towards them to reveal the bottom, which displayed a familiar glint of silver. 'It's a security system. It whistles when someone we don't know gets near the library.'

'With what match-pair?'

'Wouldn't you like to know?' Anthony winked. 'We do security like Babel does. Everyone devises their own traps, and we don't tell the others how it's done. The best thing we have set up is the glamour – it keeps sound from escaping the building, which means no passerby can eavesdrop on our conversations.'

'But this place is massive,' said Ramy. 'I mean, you're not invisible – how on earth do you stay hidden?'

'Oldest trick in the world. We're hidden in plain sight.' Anthony led them further into the library. 'When Durham went extinct in the mid-sixteenth century and Trinity took over its property, they overlooked the supplemental library in the deed transfer. The only things listed in that library on the catalogue were materials no one had used for decades, and which have more accessible duplicates in the Bodleian. So now we live on the edge of bureaucracy – everyone who walks past knows this is a storage library, but everyone assumes it belongs to some other, poorer college. These colleges are all too rich, you see. It makes them lose track of their holdings.'

'Ah, you found the undergraduates!'

Figures emerged from within the shelves. Robin recognized them all – they were all former students or current graduate fellows he'd seen lurking around the tower. He supposed this shouldn't have come as a surprise. There were Vimal Srinivasan, Cathy O'Nell, and Ilse Dejima, who gave them a small wave as she approached.

'Heard you'd had a bad week.' She was much friendlier now than she'd ever been at the tower. 'Welcome to Chez Hermes. You're just in time for dinner.'

'I didn't realize there were so many of you,' said Ramy. 'Who else here has faked their death?'

Anthony chuckled. 'I'm the only ghost in residence at Oxford. We have a few others overseas – Vaibhav and Frédérique, you might have heard of them – they faked drowning on a clipper back from Bombay and they've been operating from India since. Lisette simply announced she was leaving for home to get married, and all the Babel faculty were too disappointed in her to follow up on her story. Obviously, Vimal, Cathy, and Ilse are still at Babel. Easier for them to siphon out resources.'

'Then why'd you leave?' asked Robin.

'Someone needs to be in the Old Library full time. In any case, I'd got tired of the campus life, so I faked my death in Barbados, bought a passage on the next packet home, and made my way back to Oxford unnoticed.' Anthony winked at Robin. 'I thought you had me that day at the bookshop. I didn't dare leave the Old Library for a week. Come on, let me show you the rest.'

A quick tour of the workspaces past the shelves revealed a number of ongoing projects, which Anthony introduced with pride. These included the compilation of dictionaries between regional languages ('We lose a lot by assuming everything must first come through English'), non-English silver match-pairs ('Same principle – Babel won't fund match-pairs that don't translate into English since all of its bars are for use by the British. But that's like painting with only one colour, or playing only one note on a piano.'), and critiques of existing English translations of religious texts and literary classics ('Well – you know my opinion on literature in general, but something has to keep Vimal occupied.') The Hermes Society was not only a hotbed of Robin Hoods, as Griffin had led Robin to believe; it was also a research centre in its own right, though its projects had to be done in secret, with scant and stolen resources.*

'What are you going to do with all this?' asked Victoire. 'You can't publish, surely.'

'We've got partners at a few other translation centres,' said Vimal. 'We ship them work for review, sometimes.'

'There are other translation centres?' asked Robin.

'Of course,' said Anthony. 'It's only recently that Babel achieved pre-eminence in linguistics and philology. It was the French who ran the show for most of the eighteenth century, and then the German Romanticists had their heyday for a bit. The difference now is that we have silver to spare, and they don't.'†

'They're fickle allies, though,' said Vimal. 'They're helpful insofar as

---

* Other projects included, among others:
1. A comparative analysis of the quantity of footnotes added to translations of European texts versus non-European texts. Non-European texts, Griffin found, tended to be loaded down with an astonishing amount of explanatory context, to the effect that the text was never read as a work on its own, but always through the guided lens of the (white, European) translator.
2. An inquiry into the silver-working potential of words originating in cants and cryptolects.
3. Plans for the theft and subsequent return to Egypt of the Rosetta Stone.

† The Hermes Society also had connections with translation centres at universities in America, but these were even more repressive and dangerous than Oxford. For one, they were founded by slave owners, built and maintained with slave labour, and their endowments were sustained by the slave trade. For another, these American universities since their founding were preoccupied with the project of evangelizing, eradicating, and erasing Natives; the Indian College, founded 1655 at Harvard University, promised free tuition and housing to Native students who were required in turn to speak only in Latin and Greek, convert to Christianity, and either assimilate into white society or return to their villages to evangelize English culture and religion. A similar programme at the College of William and Mary was described by their president, Lyon G. Tyler, as a prison where Native children 'served as so many hostages for the good behaviour of the rest'.

they, too, hate the British, but they've no real commitment towards global liberation. Really, all this research is just gambling on the future. We can't make good use of it yet. We haven't got the reach or the resources. So it's all we can do to produce the knowledge, write it down, and hope one day there exists a state that can put all this to proper, altruistic use.'

At the other end of the library, the back wall resembled the aftermath of several mortar explosions, charred and cratered across the centre. Underneath, two equally charred tables stood side by side, both somehow upright despite their blackened, shrivelled legs.

'Right,' said Anthony. 'So that's our silver-work and, er, munitions workshop.'

'Did that happen over time, or all at once?' Victoire asked drily.

'That's entirely Griffin's fault,' said Vimal. 'Doesn't seem to think gunpowder is an outdoor activity.'

The intact portion of the back wall was covered with a massive map of the world, dotted with differently coloured pins attached by strings to notes covered in dense, tiny handwriting. Robin wandered closer, curious.

'That's a group project.' Cathy joined him before the map. 'We add to it little by little when we get back from overseas.'

'Do all of these pins represent languages?'

'We think they do. We're trying to track the number of languages still spoken around the world, and where they're dying out. And there are a good deal of languages which are dying, you know. A great extinction event began the day Christopher Columbus set foot in the New World. Spanish, Portuguese, French, English – they've been edging out regional languages and dialects like cuckoo chicks. I think it's not inconceivable that one day, most of the world will speak only English.' She sighed, looking up at the map. 'I was born a generation too late. It's not so long ago that I might have grown up around Gaelic.'

'But that would destroy silver-working,' said Robin. 'Wouldn't it? It'd collapse the linguistic landscape. There would be nothing to translate. No differences to distort.'

'But that's the great contradiction of colonialism.' Cathy uttered this like a simple matter of fact. 'It's built to destroy that which it prizes most.'

'Come on, you two.' Anthony waved them over to a doorway, which led to a small reading room that had been converted into a dining room. 'Let's eat.'

The offerings at dinner were global – a vegetable curry, a platter of boiled potatoes, a fried fish dish that tasted startlingly similar to a kind Robin had once eaten in Canton, and a flat, chewy bread that paired well with everything else. The eight of them sat around a very fine ornamented table that looked incongruous against the plain wooden panels. There weren't enough chairs for all of them, so Anthony and Ilse had dragged over benches and sitting stools from around the library. None of the tableware matched, nor the silverware. Flames burned merrily from a fireplace in the corner, heating the room unevenly so that Robin's left side dripped sweat while his right side felt chilly. The whole scene was quintessentially collegial.

'Is it just you lot?' Robin asked.

'What do you mean?' asked Vimal.

'Well, you're . . . ' Robin gestured around the table. 'You're all very young.'

'Necessarily,' said Anthony. 'It's dangerous business.'

'But aren't there – I don't know—'

'Proper adults? Reinforcements?' Anthony nodded. 'Some, yes. They're scattered across the globe. I don't know who they all are – not one of us knows exhaustively who they all are, and that's intentional. There are probably even Hermes associates at Babel I'm still not aware of, though whoever they are, I hope they start making a bit more of an effort.'

'That, and attrition's a problem,' said Ilse. 'Take Burma.'

'What happened in Burma?' asked Robin.

'Sterling Jones happened,' Anthony said tightly, but did not elaborate.

This seemed a sensitive topic. For a moment, everyone stared at their food.

Robin thought of the two thieves he'd met his first night at Oxford, the young woman and the blond-haired man, neither of whom he'd ever seen again. He did not venture to ask. He knew the answer: attrition.

'But how do you get anything done?' asked Ramy. 'That is, if you don't even know who your allies are?'

'Well, it's not so different from Oxford bureaucracy,' Anthony said. 'The university, the colleges, and the faculties never seem to agree on who's in charge of what, but they get things done, don't they?'

'*Langue de bœuf sauce Madère*,' Cathy announced, setting a heavy pot in the centre of the table. 'Beef tongue in Madeira sauce.'

'Cathy loves to serve tongue,' Vimal informed them. 'She thinks it's funny.'

'She's creating a dictionary of tongues,' said Anthony. 'Boiled tongue, pickled tongue, dried tongue, smoked—'

'Shush.' Cathy slid onto the bench in between them. 'Tongue's my favourite cut.'

'It's the cheapest cut,' said Ilse.

'It's disgusting,' said Anthony.

Cathy flung a potato at him. 'Fill up on these, then.'

'Ah, *pommes de terre à l'anglaise*.' Anthony speared a potato with his fork. 'You know why the French called boiled potatoes à l'anglaise? Because they think boiling things is boring, Cathy, just like all of English cooking is deathly boring—'

'Then don't eat them, Anthony.'

'Roast them,' Anthony persisted. 'Braise them with butter, or bake them with a cheese – just don't be so *English*.'

Watching them, Robin felt a sharp prickle at the base of his nose. He felt the same as he had the night of the commemoration ball, dancing on the tables under the fairy lights. How magical, he thought; how impossible, that a place like this could exist, a distillation of all that Babel promised. He felt he'd been looking for a place like this all his life, and still he'd betrayed it.

To his horror, he began to cry.

'Oh, there, there.' Cathy patted him on the shoulder. 'You're safe, Robin. You're with friends.'

'I'm sorry,' he said miserably.

'It's all right.' Cathy did not ask him what he was apologizing for. 'You're here now. That's what matters.'

Three sudden, violent raps sounded at the door. Robin flinched, dropping his fork, but none of the postgraduates looked alarmed.

'That'll be Griffin,' Anthony said cheerfully. 'He forgets the passcodes whenever we change them, so he beats out a rhythm instead.'

'He's come too late for dinner,' Cathy said, annoyed.

'Well, make him up a plate.'

'*Please*.'

'Please, Cathy.' Anthony stood up. 'The rest of you, into the Reading Room.'

Robin's heart hammered as he filed out of the dining room with the others. He suddenly felt very nervous. He didn't want to see his brother. The world had turned upside down since they'd last spoken, and he was terrified of what Griffin had to say about it.

Griffin strode through the door looking lean, haggard, and as travel-weary as ever. Robin scrutinized his brother as he shrugged off his ratty black coat. He seemed like an utter stranger, now that Robin knew what he had done. Each of his features told a new story; those lean, capable hands; those sharp, darting eyes – were those the traits of a murderer? How had he felt when he threw a silver bar at Evie Brooke, knowing full well it would rip her chest apart? Had he laughed when she died, the way he did upon seeing Robin now?

'Hello, brother.' Griffin smiled his wolf's smile and reached out to clasp Robin's hand. 'I heard you killed dear old Pa.'

It was an accident, Robin wanted to say, but the words stuck in his throat. They had never rung true before; he could not bring himself to speak them now.

'Well done,' said Griffin. 'I never thought you had it in you.'

Robin had no response. He found it hard to breathe. He had the strangest urge to sock Griffin in the face.

Griffin, indifferent, gestured towards the Reading Room. 'Shall we get to work?'

'The task, as we see it, is to convince Parliament and the British public that it would be against their best interests to take Britain to war against China,' said Anthony.

'The opium-burning disaster has brought everything to a head,' said Griffin. 'Commissioner Lin has issued a proclamation banning English trade from Canton entirely. Jardine & Matheson, meanwhile, have taken those hostilities as justification for war. They're saying England must act now to defend her honour, or face humiliation in the East forever. Nice way to ruffle some nationalist feathers. The House of Lords began debating a military expedition last week.'

But a vote had not yet come to pass. The lords of Parliament were still hesitant, uncertain about throwing the country's resources at such a distant and unprecedented endeavour. The issue at hand, however, was silver. Defeating China would give the British Empire access to the greatest reserve of silver in the world, silver that would make their warships sail faster, their guns shoot further and more precisely. If

Parliament did choose war, the future of the colonized world was unimaginable. Britain, flush with China's riches, could enact any number of agendas towards Africa, Asia, and South America that until now had remained pipe dreams.

'But we can't do anything about those plots right now,' said Griffin. 'And we can't think on the scale of a global revolution, because it's impossible. We don't have the numbers. What we must focus on now, before we can turn to anything else, is stopping the invasion of Canton. If England wins – for she absolutely will win, there's no question – she obtains a near infinite supply of silver for the foreseeable future. If she doesn't, her silver supply dries up, and her imperial capacities shrink considerably. That's it. Everything else is inconsequential.'

He rapped the blackboard, on which names of various lords were sorted into different columns. 'The House of Commons hasn't voted yet. It's still an open debate. There's a strong antiwar faction, headed by Sir James Graham, Viscount Mahon, and William Gladstone. And Gladstone's a very good man to have on our side – he hates opium more than anyone; he's got a sister who's addicted to laudanum, I think.'

'But there are internal politics at play too,' Cathy explained. 'The Melbourne ministry's facing a political crisis at home. The Whigs have just barely survived a vote of no confidence, so now they're walking an impossible tightrope between the Conservatives and Radicals, exacerbated by the fact that they've been weak in foreign trade in Mexico, Argentina, and Arabia—'

'I'm sorry,' said Ramy. 'What, now?'

Cathy waved her hand impatiently. 'The bottom line is, the Radicals and their northern constituencies need a healthy overseas trade, and the Whigs need to keep their support to counterbalance the Tories. A show of force regarding the Opium Crisis is precisely the way to do that. It'll be a tight vote either way, though.'

Anthony nodded at the board. 'Our mission now, then, is to swing enough votes that the war proposal's shot down.'

'Just to be clear,' Ramy said slowly, 'your plan right now is to become *lobbyists*?'

'Indeed,' said Anthony. 'We'll have to convince them that war is against the best interests of their constituents. Now, that's a tricky argument to make, because it affects different classes differently. Obviously, siphoning all the silver out of China will be a massive boon to anyone who's already got money. But there's also an existing movement that believes that increased silver use is the worst thing that could happen to labourers. A silver-enhanced loom puts a dozen weavers out of work; that's why they're always striking. That's a decent argument for a Radical to vote no.'

'So you're just targeting the House of Lords?' asked Robin. 'Not the general public?'

'Good question,' said Anthony. 'The lords are the decision-makers, yes, but a certain amount of pressure from the press and public can sway those still on the fence. The trick is how to get the average Londoner worked up over a war they're not likely to have ever heard of.'

'Appeal to their human nature and sympathy for the oppressed,' said Letty.

'Ha,' said Ramy. 'Ha, ha, ha.'

'It simply seems to me that all this aggression is quite pre-emptive,' Letty insisted. 'I mean, you haven't even tried making your case to the public. Have you ever considered you might better make your point by being nice?'

'*Nice* comes from the Latin word for "stupid",'* said Griffin. 'We do not want to be nice.'

'But public opinion on China *is* malleable,' Anthony intervened. 'Most Londoners oppose the opium trade to begin with, and there's quite a lot of sympathetic coverage for Commissioner Lin in the newspapers. You can get pretty far with moralists and religious conservatives in this country. The question there is how to get them sufficiently bothered about it to exert pressure on Parliament. Unpopular wars have been fought over less.'

'In terms of sparking public outcry, we've had one idea,' said Griffin. 'The match-pair *polemic* and the Greek root *polemikós*, which of course, means—'

'War,' said Ramy.

'Correct.'

'So you've got a war of ideas.' Ramy frowned. 'What does the match-pair do?'

'That's a work in progress; we're still fiddling around with it. If we

---

* This is true. *Nice* comes to us by way of the Old French *nice* ('weak, clumsy, silly'), from the Latin *nescius* ('ignorant, not knowing').

can just connect that semantic warp with the right medium, we might get somewhere. But the point is, we can't achieve anything until more people understand where we're coming from. Most of the British don't understand there's a fight to be had at all. For them, this war is something imaginary – something that could only benefit them, something they don't have to look at or worry over. They don't know the cruelty involved, or the continued violence it will enable. They don't know what opium does to people.'

'You won't get anywhere with that argument,' said Robin.

'Why not?'

'Because they don't care,' said Robin. 'It's a war happening in a foreign land that they can't even imagine. It's too distant for them to care.'

'What makes you so sure of that?' asked Cathy.

'Because I didn't,' said Robin. 'I didn't, even though I'd been told time and time again how awful things were. It took witnessing it happening, in person, for me to realize all the abstractions were real. And even then, I tried my very hardest to look away. It's hard to accept what you don't want to see.'

There was a brief silence.

'Well then,' Anthony said, with forced cheer, 'we'll have to get creative with our persuasions, won't we?'

So that was the goal of the night: to shift the engines of history onto a different track. Things were not as helpless as they seemed. The Hermes Society had several plans already in motion, most including various forms of bribery and blackmail, and one including the destruction of a shipyard in Glasgow.

'The vote for war hinges on Parliament's belief that it'll be easily won,' Griffin explained. 'And technically, yes, our ships could blow Canton's navy out of the water. But they run on silver to work. A few months ago, Thomas Peacock—'

'Oh,' Ramy made a face. 'Him.'*

'Indeed. He's a rabid enthusiast of steam technology, and he put in an order for six iron steamboats at the shipbuilders Laird's. William

---

* Thomas Love Peacock, essayist, poet, and friend of Percy Bysshe Shelley, had also enjoyed a long career in India as an official with the East India Company. He was, in that year, the Chief Examiner of Indian Correspondence.

Laird and Son, that is – they're based in Glasgow. These ships are more frightening than anything the waters of Asia have ever seen. They've got Congreve rockets, and their shallow draught and steam power make them more mobile than anything in the Chinese fleet. If Parliament votes yes, at least one of them is heading straight to Canton.'

'So I assume you're going to Glasgow,' said Robin.

'First thing tomorrow morning,' said Griffin. 'It'll take ten hours by train. But I expect Parliament will hear within the day once I'm there.'

He did not elaborate on precisely what he would do in Glasgow, though Robin did not doubt his brother was capable of demolishing an entire shipyard.

'Well, that sounds much more effective,' Ramy said happily. 'Why aren't we putting all of our efforts into sabotage?'

'Because we're scholars, not soldiers,' said Anthony. 'The shipyard's one thing, but we're not going to take on the entire British Navy. We've got to leverage influence where we can. Leave the violent theatrics to Griffin—'

Griffin bristled. 'They aren't mere *theatrics*—'

'The violent high jinks,' Anthony amended, though Griffin bristled at that too. 'And let's focus on how to sway the vote in London.'

So they went back to the blackboard. A war for the fate of the world could not be won overnight – this they all knew in theory – but they could not bring themselves to stop and go to sleep. Every passing hour brought new ideas and tactics, though as the hours dragged far past midnight, their thoughts began to lose some coherence. Suppose they ensnared Lord Palmerston in a prostitution scandal by sending in Letty and Cathy to seduce him in disguise. Suppose they convinced the British public that the country China did not actually exist and was in fact an elaborate hoax by Marco Polo. At some point, they dissolved into helpless laughter as Griffin described in intricate detail a plot to kidnap Queen Victoria in the gardens of Buckingham Palace under the guise of an underground Chinese crime ring and hold her hostage in Trafalgar Square.

Theirs was a harrowing and impossible mission, yes, but Robin also found a certain exhilarating pleasure in this work. This creative prob-lem-solving, this breaking up of a momentous mission into a dozen small tasks which, combined with enormous luck and possibly divine intervention, might carry them to victory – it all reminded him of how it felt to be in the library working on a thorny translation at four in the morning, laughing hysterically because they were so unbelievably tired but somehow thrumming with energy because it was such a thrill when a solution inevitably coalesced from their mess of scrawled notes and wild brainstorming.

Defying empire, it turned out, was fun.

For some reason they kept coming back to the *polemikós* match-pair, perhaps because it did in fact seem like they were fighting a war of ideas, a battle for Britain's soul. Discursive metaphors, Letty observed, revolved around war imagery rather often. 'Think about it,' she said. 'Their stance is indefensible. We must attack their weak points. We must shoot down their premises.'

'We do that in French too,' said Victoire. '*Cheval de bataille.*'*

'Warhorse,' Letty said, smiling.

'Well then,' said Griffin, 'as long as we're talking about military solutions, I still think we should go with Operation Divine Fury.'

'What's Operation Divine Fury?' asked Ramy.

'Never mind,' said Anthony. 'It's a stupid name, and a stupider idea.'

'*When God saw this, He did not permit them, but smote them with blindness and confusion of speech, and rendered them as thou seest,*'[†] Griffin said grandly. 'Look, it's a good idea. If we could just take out the tower—'

'With what, Griffin?' Anthony asked, exasperated. 'With what army?'

'We don't need an army,' said Griffin. 'They're scholars, not soldiers. You take a gun in there, wave it around and shout for a bit, and you've taken the whole tower hostage. And then you've taken the whole country hostage. Babel is the crux, Anthony; it's the source of all the Empire's power. We've only got to seize it.'

Robin stared at him, alarmed. In Chinese, the phrase *huǒyàowèi*[‡] meant literally 'the taste of gunpowder'; figuratively, 'belligerence, combativeness'. His brother smelled of gunpowder. He reeked of violence.

---

* Meaning one's favourite trope or favourite line of argument.

† This is not a quotation from the Book of Genesis, which recounts the scattering of languages at Babel in much tamer terms. It is rather from the Third Apocalypse of Baruch, falsely attributed to the scribe Baruch ben Neriah. Griffin, in a fit of disillusionment, had briefly pursued a project recounting various versions of the fall of Babel.

‡ 火藥味.

'Wait,' said Letty. 'You want to storm the tower?'

'I want to *occupy* the tower. It wouldn't be so very difficult.' Griffin shrugged. 'And it's a more direct solution to our problems, isn't it? I've been trying to convince these fellows, but they're too scared to pull it off.'

'What would you need to pull it off?' Victoire inquired.

'Now that's the right question.' Griffin beamed. 'Rope, two guns, perhaps not even that – some knives, at least—'

'Guns?' Letty repeated. '*Knives?*'

'They're just for intimidation, darling, we wouldn't actually hurt anyone.'

Letty reeled. 'Do you *honestly*—'

'Don't worry.' Cathy glared at Griffin. 'We've made our thoughts on this quite clear.'

'But think of what would happen,' Griffin insisted. 'What does this country do without enchanted silver? Without the people to maintain it? Steam power, gone. Perpetual lamps, gone. Building reinforcements, gone. The roads would deteriorate, the carriages would malfunction – forget Oxford, the whole of England would fall apart in months. They'd be brought to their knees. Paralysed.'

'And dozens of innocent people would die,' said Anthony. 'We are not entertaining this.'

'Fine.' Griffin sat back and folded his arms. 'Have it your way. Let's be lobbyists.'

They adjourned at three in the morning. Anthony showed them to a sink at the back of the library where they could wash – 'No tub, sorry, so you'll have to soap your armpits standing up – ' and then pulled a stack of quilts and pillows from a cupboard.

'We only have three cots,' he said apologetically. 'We don't often all spend the night here. Ladies, why don't you follow Ilse to the Reading Room – and gents, you can bunk on your own between the stacks. Creates a bit of privacy.'

Robin was so exhausted then that a space of hardwood between the shelves sounded wonderful. It felt as if he had been awake for one long day ever since their arrival in Oxford; that he had experienced enough for one lifetime. He accepted a quilt from Anthony and made his way towards the stacks, but Griffin materialized by his side before he could settle down. 'Have a moment?'

'You're not going to sleep?' Robin asked. Griffin was fully dressed, buttoned up in that black overcoat.

'No, I'm heading out early,' said Griffin. 'There's no direct line to Glasgow – I'll ride into London, then take the first train in the morning. Come out to the yard with me.'

'Why?'

Griffin patted the gun at his belt. 'I'm going to show you how to fire this.'

Robin hugged the quilt closer to his chest. 'Absolutely not.'

'Then you're going to watch me fire a gun,' said Griffin. 'I think we're long overdue for a chat, don't you?'

Robin sighed, set the quilt down, and followed Griffin out the door. The yard was very bright under the full moon. Griffin must have used it for shooting practice often, for Robin could see that the trees across the yard were riddled with bullet holes.

'Aren't you afraid someone will hear?'

'This whole area's protected by the glamour,' said Griffin. 'Very clever work. No one can see or hear much who doesn't already know we're here. Do you know anything about guns?'

'Not even a little bit.'

'Well, it's never too late to learn.' Griffin placed the gun in Robin's hands. Like silver bars, it was heavier than it looked, and very cool to the touch. There was a certain inarguable elegance to the curve of the wooden handle, how easily it fitted into his hand. Still, Robin felt a wave of revulsion as he held it. It felt mean, like the metal was trying to bite him. He wanted very much to fling it to the ground, but was afraid of accidentally setting it off.

'This is a pepperbox revolver,' said Griffin. 'Very popular with civilians. It uses a caplock mechanism, which means it can fire when it's wet – don't look down the barrel, you idiot, never look straight down the barrel. Try aiming it.'

'I don't see the point,' said Robin. 'I'm never going to fire this.'

'It doesn't matter that you'll fire it. It matters that someone thinks you will. You see, my colleagues in there are still holding on to this unbelievable faith in human goodness.' Griffin cocked the gun and pointed it at a birch tree across the yard. 'But I'm a sceptic. I think decolonization must be a violent process.'

He pulled the trigger. The blast was very loud. Robin jumped back, but Griffin was unfazed. 'It's not double action,' he said, adjusting the barrels. 'You've got to cock the hammer after each shot.'

His aim was quite good. Robin squinted and saw a notch in the centre of the birch that hadn't been there before.

'See, a gun changes everything. It's not just about the impact, it's about what it signals.' Griffin ran his fingers over the barrel, then spun around to point the gun at Robin.

Robin jumped back. 'Jesus—'

'Scary, isn't it? Think, why is this more frightening than a knife?' Griffin did not move his arm. 'It says I'm willing to kill you, and all I have to do is pull this trigger. I can kill at a distance, without effort. A gun takes all the hard work out of murder and makes it elegant. It shrinks the distance between resolve and action, you see?'

'Have you ever shot at someone?' Robin asked.

'Of course.'

'Did you hit them?'

Griffin didn't answer the question. 'You have to understand where I've been. It's not all libraries and debating theatres out there, brother. Things look different on a battlefield.'

'Is Babel a battlefield?' Robin asked. 'Was Evie Brooke an enemy combatant?'

Griffin lowered the gun. 'So that's what we're hung up on?'

'You killed an innocent girl.'

'Innocent? Is that what our father told you? That I killed Evie in cold blood?'

'I've seen that bar,' said Robin. 'It's in my pocket, Griffin.'

'Evie wasn't some innocent bystander,' Griffin sneered. 'We'd been trying to recruit her for months. It was tricky, see, because she and Sterling Jones were so close, but if either of them had a conscience it was bound to be her. Or so we thought. I spent months and months talking things over with her at the Twisted Root until one night she decided she was ready, she was in. Only it was all a set-up – she'd been talking to the constables and the professors the whole time, and they'd hatched this plan to catch me in the act.

'She was a brilliant actor, you see. She had this way of looking at you, eyes wide, nodding like you had all of her sympathy. Of course, I didn't know it was all a performance. I thought I'd made an ally – I was thrilled when she seemed to be coming around – and with everyone we lost in

Burma, I felt very alone. And Evie was so clever about it. Asked all these questions, far more than you did – made it sound like she just wanted to know because she was so thrilled to join the cause, because she wanted to learn all the ways she could help.'

'Then how'd you find out?'

'Well, she wasn't that clever. If she were smarter, she wouldn't have dropped her cover until she was safe.'

'But she told you.' Robin's stomach twisted. 'She wanted to gloat.'

'She smiled at me,' said Griffin. 'When the siren sounded, she grinned at me and told me it was all over. And so I killed her. I didn't mean to. You won't believe me, but it's the truth. I meant to frighten her. But I was angry and scared – and Evie was vicious, you know. If I'd given her an opening, I still think she might have hurt me first.'

'Do you really believe that?' Robin whispered. 'Or is it a lie you conjure so you can sleep at night?'

'I sleep just fine.' Griffin sneered. 'But you need your lies, don't you? Let me guess – you're telling yourself it was an accident? That you didn't mean it?'

'I didn't,' Robin insisted. 'It just *happened* – and it wasn't on purpose, I never wanted—'

'Don't,' said Griffin. 'Don't hide, don't pretend – that's so cowardly. Say how you feel. It felt good, admit it. The sheer power felt so good—'

'I'd take it all back if I could,' Robin insisted. He didn't know why it felt so important that Griffin believe him, but this seemed like the last line he had to hold, the last truth he had to maintain about his identity. Otherwise he didn't recognize himself. 'I wish he'd lived—'

'You don't mean that. He deserved what he got.'

'He didn't deserve to die.'

'Our father,' Griffin said loudly, 'was a cruel, selfish man who thought anyone who wasn't white and English was less than human. Our father destroyed my mother's life, and let yours perish. Our father is one of the principal engineers of a war on our motherland. If he'd come back from Canton alive, Parliament wouldn't be debating right now. They'd have voted already. You've bought us days, perhaps weeks. So what if you're a killer, brother? The world's better off without the professor in it. Stop shrivelling under the weight of your conscience and take the damned credit.' He turned the gun around and offered it handle-first to Robin. 'Take it.'

'I said no.'

'You still don't understand.' Impatiently, Griffin grabbed Robin's fingers and forced them around the handle. 'We've moved out of the realm of ideas now, brother. We're at war.'

'But if this is a war, then you've lost.' Still Robin refused to take the gun. 'There's no way you win on the battlefield. Your ranks are what, a couple dozen? At most? And you're going to take on the entire British Army?'

'Oh, but that's where you're wrong,' said Griffin. 'The thing about violence, see, is that the Empire has a lot more to lose than we do. Violence disrupts the extractive economy. You wreak havoc on one supply line, and there's a dip in prices across the Atlantic. Their entire system of trade is high-strung and vulnerable to shocks because they've made it thus, because the rapacious greed of capitalism is punishing. It's why slave revolts succeed. They can't fire on their own source of labour – it'd be like killing their own golden geese.

'But if the system is so fragile, why do we so easily accept the colonial situation? Why do we think it's inevitable? Why doesn't Man Friday ever get himself a rifle, or slit Robinson Crusoe's neck in the night? The problem is that we're always living like we've lost. We're all living like *you*. We see their guns, their silver-work, and their ships, and we think it's already over for us. We don't stop to consider how even the playing field actually might be. And we never consider what things would look like if we took the gun.' Once again, Griffin offered the gun to Robin. 'Careful, it's front-heavy.'

This time Robin accepted it. He aimed it experimentally at the trees. The barrel did, indeed, tip downwards; he tilted his hand up against his wrist to keep it level.

'Violence shows them how much we're willing to give up,' said Griffin. 'Violence is the only language they understand, because their system of extraction is inherently violent. Violence shocks the system. And the system cannot survive the shock. You have no idea what you're capable of, truly. You can't imagine how the world might shift unless you pull the trigger.' Griffin pointed at the middle birch. 'Pull the trigger, kid.'

Robin obeyed. The bang split his ears; he nearly dropped the gun. He was sure he had not aimed true. He had not been prepared for the force of the kickback, and his arm trembled from wrist to shoulder. The birch was untouched. The bullet had flown pointlessly into the dark.

But he had to admit that Griffin was right – the rush of that moment, the explosion of force contained within its hands, the sheer power he could trigger with just a twitch of his finger – it felt good.

CHAPTER TWENTY-THREE

Oh those white people have small hearts who can only feel for themselves.

MARY PRINCE, *The History of Mary Prince*

Robin couldn't fall asleep after Griffin left for Glasgow. He sat in the dark, thrumming with nervous energy. He felt a breathless vertigo, the sensation of looking out over a steep cliff the moment before he jumped. The whole world was on the verge of some cataclysmic shift, it seemed, and he could only cling on to what was around him as they all hurtled towards the breaking point.

An hour later the Old Library began to stir. Just as the clock struck seven, a symphony of birdsong echoed through the stacks. The noise was too loud to be coming from outside; rather, it sounded as if a whole flock of birds was perched invisibly among the books.

'What is that?' Ramy asked, rubbing his eyes. 'Have you got a menagerie in a cupboard out the back?'

'It's coming from here.' Anthony showed them a wooden grandfather clock decorated with carved songbirds around the edges. 'A gift from one of our Swedish associates. She translated *gökatta* to "rising at dawn", only in Swedish, *gökatta* has the particular meaning of waking up early to listen to the birds sing. There's some music box mechanism inside, but the silver really imitates true birdsong. It's lovely, isn't it?'

'Could be a little quieter,' said Ramy.

'Ah, ours is a prototype. It's getting old. You can get these in London boutiques now, you know. They're very popular, the wealthy love them.'

One by one they took their turns at washing themselves with cold water in the sink. Then they joined the girls in the Reading Room around yesterday's clustered notes to resume their work.

Letty looked as if she hadn't slept a wink either. She had great dark shadows under her eyes, and she hugged her arms miserably against her chest as she yawned.

'Are you all right?' Robin asked.

'It feels rather as if I'm dreaming.' She blinked around the room, her gaze unfocused. 'Everything's upside down. Everything's backwards.'

Fair enough, Robin thought. Letty was holding up rather well, all considered. He didn't know how to politely phrase what he wanted to say next, so he asked obliquely, 'What do you think?'

'About what, Robin?' she asked, exasperated. 'The murder we're covering up, the fall of the British Empire, or the fact that we're fugitives now for the rest of our lives?'

'All of it, I suppose.'

'Justice is exhausting.' She rubbed her temples. 'That's what I think.'

Cathy brought out a steaming pot of black tea, and they held their mugs forth in gratitude. Vimal stumbled yawning from the bathroom towards the kitchen. A few minutes later, the wonderful aroma of a fry-up seeped up through the Reading Room. 'Masala eggs,' he announced, heaping scrambled eggs in a tomatoey mess onto their plates. 'There's toast coming.'

'Vimal,' Cathy groaned. 'I could marry you.'

They wolfed down their food in fast, mechanical silence. Minutes later the table was cleared, the dirty plates returned to the kitchenette. The front door screeched open. It was Ilse, back from the city centre with that morning's newspapers.

'Any word on the debates?' Anthony asked.

'They're still at loggerheads,' she said. 'So we have some time yet. The Whigs are shaky on their numbers, and they won't hold a vote until they're confident. But we still want those pamphlets in London today or tomorrow. Get someone on the noon train, then get them printed on Fleet Street.'

'Do we still know anyone in Fleet Street?' Vimal asked.

'Yes, Theresa's still at the *Standard*. They go to print on Fridays. I can get in and use the machines, I'm sure, if you have something for me by tonight.' She pulled a crumpled newspaper out of her messenger bag and slid it across the table. 'Here's the latest from London, by the way. Thought you'd like to see it.'

Robin craned his neck to read the upside-down text.

OXFORD PROFESSOR MURDERED IN CANTON, it read. PERPETRATORS IN CONSPIRACY WITH CHINESE LOBBYISTS.

'Well.' He blinked. 'I guess that's got most of the details right.'

Ramy flipped the paper open. 'Oh, look. It's got drawings of our faces.'

'That doesn't look like you,' said Victoire.

'No, they haven't quite captured my nose,' Ramy agreed. 'And they've made Robin's eyes very small.'

'Have they printed this in Oxford, too?' Anthony asked Ilse.

'Surprisingly, no. They've kept it all quiet.'

'Interesting. Well, London's still cancelled for you lot,' said Anthony. They all began protesting at once, but he held up a hand. 'Don't be mad. It's too dangerous, we're not risking it. You're hiding out in the Old Library until this is over. You can't be recognized.'

'Neither can you,' Ramy retorted.

'They think I'm dead. They think you're a murderer. Those are very different things. No one's printing my face in the papers.'

'But I want to be out there,' Ramy said, unhappy. 'I want to do something, I want to help—'

'You can help by not getting yourself thrown in gaol. This isn't open war, as much as dear Griffin would like to pretend it is. These matters demand finesse.' Anthony pointed to the blackboard. 'Focus on the agenda. Let's pick up where we left off. I think we tabled the issue of Lord Arsenault last night. Letty?'

Letty took a long draught of her tea, closed her eyes, then seemed to pull herself together. 'Yes. I believe Lord Arsenault and my father are on rather good terms. I could write to him, try to set up a meeting—'

'You don't think your father's going to be distracted by the news that you're a murderer?' asked Robin.

'It doesn't name Letty as a perpetrator.' Victoire scanned the column. 'It's only the three of us. She's not mentioned here at all.'

There was a brief, awkward silence.

'No, that's very good for us,' Anthony said smoothly. 'Gives us some freedom of movement. Now you start writing to your father, Letty, and the rest of you get to your assignments.'

One by one they filtered out of the Reading Room to carry out their designated tasks. Ilse set off to Babel to retrieve further news on developments in London. Cathy and Vimal went to the workshop to tinker with match-pairs using *polemikós*. Ramy and Victoire were put to work writing letters to prominent Radical leaders by impersonating white, middle-aged Radical supporters. Robin sat with Anthony in the Reading Room, pulling the most damning evidence of collusion from Professor Lovell's letters as quotations for short, inflammatory pamphlets. Their hope was that such evidence might prove scandalous enough to get picked up by the London papers.

'Be careful with your language,' Anthony told him. 'You'll want to avoid rhetoric about anticolonialism and respecting national sovereignty. Use terms like *scandal, collusion, corruption, lack of transparency*, and whatnot. Cast things in terms that the average Londoner will get worked up about, and don't make it an issue of race.'

'You want me to translate things for white people,' said Robin.

'Precisely.'

They worked in comfortable silence for about an hour, until Robin's hand grew too sore to continue. He sat back, cradling a mug of tea in silence, until it seemed as if Anthony had reached the end of a paragraph. 'Anthony, can I ask you something?'

Anthony put down his pen. 'What's on your mind?'

'Do you honestly think this will work?' Robin nodded to the stack of draft pamphlets. 'Winning in the realm of public opinion, I mean.'

Anthony leaned back and flexed his fingers. 'I see your brother's got to you.'

'Griffin spent last night teaching me how to use a gun,' said Robin. 'He thinks revolution's impossible without violent insurrection. And he's quite persuasive.'

Anthony thought for a while, nodding, tapping his pen against the inkwell. 'Your brother likes to call me naive.'

'That's not what I—'

'I know, I know. I only mean to say that I'm not as soft as Griffin thinks. Let me remind you that I came to this country before they'd decided I could no longer be legally called a slave. I've lived most of my life in a country that is deeply confused on whether I fully count as human. Trust me, I am no jolly optimist on the ethical qualms of white Britain.'

'But I suppose they did come around on abolition,' said Robin. 'Eventually.'

Anthony laughed gently. 'Do you think abolition was a matter of ethics? No, abolition gained popularity because the British, after losing America, decided that India was going to be their new golden goose. But cotton, indigo, and sugar from India weren't going to dominate the market unless France could be edged out, and France would not be edged out, you see, as long as the British slave trade was making the West Indies so very profitable for them.'

'But—'

'But nothing. The abolitionist movement you know is a load of pomp. Rhetoric only. Pitt first raised the motion because he saw the need to cut off the slave trade to France. And Parliament got on board with the abolitionists because they were so very afraid of Black insurrection in the West Indies.'

'So you think it's purely risk and economics.'

'Well, not necessarily. You brother likes to argue that the Jamaican slave revolt, failed though it was, is what impelled the British to legislate abolition. He's right, but only half right. See, the revolt won British sympathy because the leaders were part of the Baptist church, and when it failed, proslavery whites in Jamaica started destroying chapels and threatening missionaries. Those Baptists went back to England and drummed up support on the grounds of religion, not natural rights. My point being, abolition happened because white people found reasons to care – whether those be economic or religious. You just have to make them think they came up with the idea themselves. You can't appeal to their inner goodness. I have never met an Englishman I trusted to do the right thing out of sympathy.'

'Well,' said Robin, 'there's Letty.'

'Yes,' said Anthony after a pause. 'I suppose there's Letty. But she's a rare case, isn't she?'

'Then what's our path forward?' asked Robin. 'Then what's the point of any of this?'

'The point is to build a coalition,' said Anthony. 'And it needs to include unlikely sympathizers. We can siphon as many resources from Babel as we want, but it still won't be enough to budge such firmly entrenched levers of power as the likes of Jardine and Matheson. If we are to turn the tides of history, we need some of these men – the same men who find no issue in selling me and my kind at auction – to become our allies. We need to convince them that a global British expansion, founded on pyramids of silver, is not in their own best interest. Because their own interest is the only logic they'll listen to. Not justice, not human dignity, not the liberal freedoms they so profess to value. Profit.'

'You may as well convince them to walk the streets naked.'

'Ha. No, the seeds for a coalition are there. The time's ripe for a revolution in England, you know. The whole of Europe has been feverish for reform for decades; they caught it from the French. We must simply make this a war of class instead of race. And this is, indeed, an issue of class. It seems like a debate over opium and China, but the Chinese aren't the only ones who stand to lose, are they? It's all related. The silver industrial revolution is one of the greatest drivers of inequality, pollution, and unemployment in this country. The fate of a poor family in Canton is in fact intricately tied to the fate of an out-of-work weaver from Yorkshire. Neither benefits from the expansion of empire. Both only get poorer as the companies get richer. So if they could only form an alliance . . . '

Anthony wove his fingers together. 'But that's the problem, you see. No one's focused on how we're all connected. We only think about how we suffer, individually. The poor and middle-class of this country don't realize they have more in common with us than they do with Westminster.'

'There's a Chinese idiom that catches the gist,' said Robin. '*Tùsǐhúbēi.*[*] The rabbit dies, and the fox grieves, for they're animals of a kind.'

'Precisely,' said Anthony. 'Only we've got to convince them we're not their prey. That there's a hunter in the forest, and we're all in danger.'

Robin glanced down at the pamphlets. They seemed so inadequate just then; just words, just ink scrawls on flimsy white paper. 'And you truly think you can convince them so?'

'We have to.' Anthony flexed his fingers once more, then picked up his pen and resumed flipping through Professor Lovell's letters. 'I don't see any other way out.'

Robin wondered then how much of Anthony's life had been spent carefully translating himself to white people, how much of his genial, affable polish was an artful construction to fit a particular idea of a Black man in white England and to afford himself maximum access within an institution like Babel. And he wondered if there would ever be a day that came when all this was unnecessary, when white people would look at him and Anthony and simply listen, when their words would have worth and value because they were uttered, when they would not have

---

* 兔死狐悲.

to hide who they were, when they wouldn't have to go through endless distortions just to be understood.

At noon they regrouped in the Reading Room for lunch. Cathy and Vimal were quite excited with what they'd done with the *polemikós* match-pair, which, true to Griffin's predictions, caused pamphlets to fly about and continue flapping around bystanders if thrown into the air. Vimal had supplemented this with the Latin origin of the word *discuss*: *discutere* could mean 'to scatter', or 'to disperse'.

'Suppose we apply both bars to a stack of printed pamphlets,' he said. 'They'd fly all over London, wind or no. How's that for getting people's attention?'

Gradually, the ideas that had seemed so ridiculous last night, those chaotic scribblings of sleep-deprived minds, coalesced into a rather impressive plan of action. Anthony summed up their numerous endeavours on the blackboard. Over the next few days, weeks if necessary, the Hermes Society would try to influence the debates in any way they could. Ilse's connection on Fleet Street would soon publish a hit piece on how William Jardine, who'd stirred up all this mess in the first place, was whiling away his days at a spa town in Cheltenham. Vimal and Cathy, through several more respectable white intermediaries, would try to convince waffling Whigs that restoring good relations with China would at least keep open avenues trading legal goods, such as teas and rhubarbs. Then there were Griffin's efforts in Glasgow, as well as the pamphlets about to fly all over London. Through blackmail, lobbying, and public pressure, Anthony concluded, they might make up enough votes to defeat the war motion.

'This could work,' Ilse said, blinking at the blackboard as if surprised.

'It *could* work,' Vimal agreed. 'Bloody hell.'

'Are you sure we can't come with you?' Ramy asked.

Anthony gave him a sympathetic pat on the shoulder. 'You've done your part. You've been very brave, all of you. But it's time to leave things to the professionals.'

'You've barely got five years on us,' said Robin. 'How does that make you a professional?'

'I don't know,' said Anthony. 'It just does.'

'And we're supposed to just wait without knowing anything?' Letty asked. 'We can't even get the papers here.'

'We'll all be back after the vote,' said Anthony. 'And we'll come back occasionally to check on you – every other day, if you're that nervous.'

'But what if something happens?' Letty persisted. 'What if you need our help? What if we need *your* help?'

The graduate fellows all exchanged glances with each other. It looked like they were having a silent conversation – a repeat, Robin guessed, of a conversation they'd had many times before, for it was clear what everyone's position was. Anthony raised his eyebrows. Cathy and Vimal both nodded. Ilse, lips pursed, seemed reluctant, but at last she sighed and shrugged.

'Go ahead,' she said.

'Griffin would say no,' said Anthony.

'Well,' said Cathy, 'Griffin's not here.'

Anthony stood up, disappeared for a moment into the stacks, and returned bearing a sealed envelope. 'This,' he said, placing it down on the table, 'contains the contact information for a dozen Hermes associates across the globe.'

Robin was astonished. 'You're sure you should be showing us that?'

'No,' said Anthony. 'We really shouldn't. I see Griffin's paranoia has rubbed off on you, and that's not a bad thing. But suppose you lot are the only ones left. There are no names or addresses here – only drop points and contact instructions. If you end up on your own, you'll have at least some means to keep Hermes alive.'

'You're talking like you might not come back,' said Victoire.

'Well, there's a non-zero chance we don't, isn't there?'

The library felt silent.

Suddenly Robin felt so young, so childish. It had seemed like such a fun game, plotting into the deep hours with the Hermes Society, playing around with his older brother's gun. Their situation was so bizarre, and the conditions of victory so unimaginable, it had felt more like an exercise than real life. It sank in now that the forces they were playing with were actually quite terrifying, that the trading companies and political lobbies they were attempting to manipulate were not the laughable bogeymen they'd made them out to be but incredibly powerful organizations with deep, entrenched interests in the colonial trade, interests they would murder to protect.

'But you'll be all right,' said Ramy. 'Won't you? Babel's never caught you before—'

'They've caught us many times,' Anthony said gently. 'Hence the paranoia.'

'Hence the attrition,' Vimal said as he slid a pistol into his belt. 'We know the risks.'

'But you'll be safe here even if we're compromised,' Cathy reassured them. 'We won't give you up.'

Ilse nodded. 'We'll bite our tongues and suffocate first.'

'I'm sorry.' Letty stood up abruptly. She looked very pale; she touched her fingers to her mouth, as if she might vomit. 'I just – I just need some air.'

'Do you want some water?' Victoire asked, concerned.

'No, I'll be fine.' Letty bustled past their crowded chairs to the door. 'I just need to breathe for a moment, if that's all right.'

Anthony pointed. 'The yard is that way.'

'I think I'll take a stroll round the front,' said Letty. 'The yard feels a bit . . . a bit penned in.'

'Keep to the block, then,' said Anthony. 'Don't be seen.'

'Yes – yes, of course.' Letty seemed quite distressed; her breath came in such quick, shallow bursts that Robin was worried she might faint. Ramy pushed his chair back to give her space to break free. Letty paused by the doorway and glanced over her shoulder – her eyes lingered on Robin, and she seemed on the verge of saying something – but then she pursed her lips and hurried out the door.

In the last minutes before the postgraduates left, Anthony went over housekeeping matters with Robin, Ramy, and Victoire. The kitchenette stocked enough provisions to last a week, and longer if they were happy with gruel and salt-cured fish. Fresh drinking water was trickier to acquire – the Old Library did receive its water supply from the city pumps, but they couldn't run the taps too late at night or for too long at any time, since drainage elsewhere might draw attention. Otherwise, there were more than enough books in the library to keep them occupied, though they had strict orders not to mess with any ongoing projects in the workshop.

'And try to stay inside as much as you can,' Anthony said as he finished packing his bag. 'You can take turns in the yard if you like, but keep your voices down – the glamour acts up every now and then. If you must get some fresh air, do it after sunset. If you get scared, there's a rifle in that broom cupboard – I do hope you'll never have to do it, but if you do, can any of you—'

'I can manage,' said Robin. 'I think. It's the same principle as a pistol, right?'

'It's close enough.' Anthony laced up his boots. 'Fiddle with it in your spare time; the weighting's a bit different. As for comfort, you'll find soaps and things in the bathroom cabinet. Make sure you rake the ashes out of the fireplace every morning, or it'll get stuffy. Oh – we used to have a laundry tub, but Griffin destroyed it messing around with pipe bombs. You can go a few days without changing, can't you?'

Ramy snorted. 'That's a question for Letty.'

There was a pause. Then Anthony asked, 'Where is Letty?'

Robin glanced at the clock. He had not noticed the time slipping away; it was nearly a half hour since Letty stepped out of the house.

Victoire stood. 'Perhaps I should—'

Something shrieked near the front door. The sound was so sharp and raw, so like a human scream, that it took Robin a moment to realize it was the kettle.

'Damn it.' Anthony pulled the rifle down. 'Into the yard, quick, all of you—'

But it was too late. The shrieking grew louder and louder, until the walls to the library seemed to vibrate. Seconds later the front door crashed inwards, and Oxford policemen poured inside.

'Hands up!' someone shouted.

The postgraduates seemed to have drilled for this. Cathy and Vimal ran in from the workshop, each holding silver bars in hand. Ilse threw her weight at a towering shelf; it toppled forward, starting a chain reaction that collapsed the path in front of the police. Ramy started forward to help, but Anthony shouted, 'No, hide – the Reading Room—'

They stumbled back. Anthony kicked the door shut behind them. Outside they heard booms and crashes – Anthony shouted something that sounded like 'The beacon', and Cathy screamed something in response – the postgraduates were fighting, fighting to defend them.

But what was the point? The Reading Room was a dead end. There were no other doors, no windows. They could only huddle behind the table, flinching at the gunshots outside. Ramy made a noise about barricading the door, but the moment they moved to push the chairs forward, the door swung open.

Letty stood in the frame. She held a revolver.

'Letty?' Victoire asked in disbelief. 'Letty, what are you doing?'

Robin felt a very brief, naive swell of relief before it became very clear Letty was not here to rescue them. She lifted the revolver, aimed at each one of them in turn. She seemed quite practised with the gun. Her arm did not tremble beneath its weight. And the sight was so absurd – their Letty, their prim English rose, wielding a weapon with such calm, deadly precision – that he wondered for a moment if he was hallucinating.

But then he remembered: Letty was an admiral's daughter. Of course she knew how to shoot.

'Put your hands above your heads,' she said. Her voice was high and clear, like polished crystal. She sounded like an utter stranger. 'They won't hurt anyone, as long as you come quietly. If you don't resist. They've killed the rest, but they'll take you alive. Unhurt.'

Victoire eyed the envelope on the table, and then the crackling fireplace.

Letty followed her gaze. 'I wouldn't do that.'

Victoire and Letty stood glaring at each other, breathing hard, just for a moment.

Several things happened at once. Victoire lunged for the envelope. Letty whipped the gun around. By instinct, Robin rushed towards her – he didn't know what he intended, only that he was sure Letty would hurt Victoire – but just as he approached her, Ramy shoved him to the side. He fell forward, tripping against a table leg—

And then Letty broke the world.

A click; a bang.

Ramy collapsed. Victoire screamed.

'No—' Robin dropped to his knees. Ramy was limp, unmoving; he struggled to turn him over onto his back. 'No, Ramy, please—' For a moment he thought Ramy was pretending, for how was this possible? He'd been upright, moving and alive, just a second ago. The world could not end so abruptly; death could not be so swift. Robin patted Ramy's cheek, his neck, anything he could to provoke a reaction, but it was no use, his eyes would not open – *why wouldn't they open?* Surely this was a joke; he couldn't see any blood – but then he spotted it, a tiny red dot over Ramy's heart that rapidly blossomed outwards until it soaked through his shirt, his coat, through everything.

Victoire stepped back from the fireplace. The papers crackled inside the flames, blackening to ash. Letty made no move to retrieve them. She stood stunned, eyes wide, the revolver hanging limply at her side.

No one moved. They were all staring at Ramy, who was undeniably, irreversibly still.

'I didn't . . . ' Letty touched her fingers to her mouth. She'd lost her cool. Now her voice was very shrill and high, like a little girl's. 'Oh, my God . . .'

'Oh, Letty.' Victoire moaned softly. 'What have you *done*?'

Robin lowered Ramy to the floor and stood.

One day Robin would ask himself how his shock had turned so easily to rage; why his first reaction was not disbelief at this betrayal but black, consuming hatred. And the answer would elude and disturb him, for it tiptoed around a complicated tangle of love and jealousy that ensnared them all, for which they had no name or explanation, a truth they'd only been starting to wake up to and now, after this, would never acknowledge.

But just then, all he knew was red blurring out the edges of his vision, crowding out everything but Letty. He knew now how it felt to truly want a person dead, to want to tear them apart limb by limb, to hear them scream, to make them hurt. He understood now how murder felt, how rage felt, for this was it, the intent to kill he ought to have felt when he killed his father.

He lunged at her.

'Don't,' Victoire cried. 'She's—'

Letty turned and fled. Robin rushed after her just as she retreated behind a mass of constables. He pushed against them; he didn't care about the danger, the truncheons and guns; he only wanted to get through to her, wanted to wring the life from her neck, to tear the white bitch to pieces.

Strong arms wrenched him back. He felt a blunt force against the small of his back. He stumbled. He heard Victoire screaming but couldn't see her past the tangle of constables. Someone threw a cloth bag over his head. He flailed violently; his arm struck something solid, and the pressure against his back let up so slightly, but then something hard connected against his cheekbone, and the explosion of pain was so blinding it made him go limp. Someone cuffed his hands behind his back. Two sets of hands gripped his arms, hoisted him up, and dragged him out of the Reading Room.

The struggle was over. The Old Library was quiet. He shook his head frantically, trying to shake the bag off, but all he caught were glimpses of overturned shelves and blackened carpet before someone yanked the bag tighter over his head. He saw nothing of Vimal, Anthony, Ilse, or Cathy. He could no longer hear Victoire's screaming.

'Victoire?' he gasped, terrified. 'Victoire?'

'Quiet,' said a deep voice.

'Victoire!' he shouted. 'Where—'

'*Quiet*, you.' Someone pulled the hood away just long enough to stuff a rag in his mouth. Then he was plunged back into darkness. He saw nothing, heard nothing; just bleak, awful silence as they pulled him out of the ruins of the Old Library and into a waiting cab.

CHAPTER TWENTY-FOUR

Thou was not born for death, immortal Bird!
No hungry generations tread thee down.

JOHN KEATS, 'Ode to a Nightingale'

B umpy cobblestones, painful jostles. *Get out, walk.* He obeyed,
unthinking. They pulled him from the carriage, tossed him in a
cell, and left him to his thoughts.

Hours or days might have passed. He couldn't tell – he had no sense
of time. He was not in his body, not in this cell; he curled miserably on
the stone tiles and left the bruised and aching present behind. He was
in the Old Library, helpless, watching over and over as Ramy jerked and
lurched forward like someone had kicked him between the shoulder
blades, as Ramy lay limp in his arms, as Ramy, despite everything he
tried, did not stir again.

Ramy was dead.

Letty had betrayed them, Hermes had fallen, and Ramy was dead.

Ramy was dead.

Grief suffocated. Grief paralysed. Grief was a cruel, heavy boot
pressed so hard against his chest that he could not breathe. Grief took
him out of his body, made his injuries theoretical. He was bleeding,
but he didn't know where from. He ached all over from the handcuffs
digging into his wrists, from the hard stone floor against his limbs, from
the way the police had flung him down as if trying to break all of his
bones. He registered these hurts as factual, but he could not really feel
them; he couldn't feel anything other than the singular, blinding pain
of Ramy's loss. And he did not want to feel anything else, did not want
to sink into his body and register its hurts, because that physical pain

would mean he was alive, and because being alive meant that he had to move forward. But he could not go on. Not from this.

He was stuck in the past. He revisited that memory a thousand times, the same way he had revisited his father's death. Only this time instead of convincing himself he had not intended to kill, he tried to convince himself of the possibility Ramy was alive. Had he really watched Ramy die? Or had he only heard the gunshot, seen the burst of blood and the fall? Was there breath left in Ramy's lungs, life left in his eyes? It seemed so unfair. No, it seemed impossible that Ramy could just leave this world so abruptly, that he could be so alive one moment and so still the next. It seemed to defy the laws of physics that Ramiz Rafi Mirza could be silenced by something so tiny as a bullet.

And, certainly, Letty could not have been aiming for his heart. That was also impossible. She loved him, she loved him almost like Robin loved him – she'd told him so, he remembered, and if that were true, then how could she look into Ramy's eyes and shoot to kill?

Which meant Ramy might still be alive, might have survived against all odds, might have dragged himself from the carnage of the Old Library and found himself somewhere to hide, might yet recover if only someone found him in time, stanched the wound in time. Unlikely, but perhaps, perhaps, perhaps . . .

Perhaps when Robin escaped this place, when they were reunited, they'd laugh so hard over this whole thing that their ribs hurt.

He hoped. He hoped until hope became its own form of torture. The original meaning of *hope* was 'to desire', and Robin wanted with every ounce of his being a world that no longer was. He hoped until he thought he was going mad, until he started hearing fragments of his thoughts as if spoken outside of him, low, gruff words that echoed around the stone.

I wish—

I regret—

And then a flurry of confessions that weren't his.

I wish I'd loved her better.

I wish I'd never touched that knife.

This wasn't his imagination. He lifted his throbbing head, his cheek sticky with blood and tears. He glanced around, astonished. The stones were talking, whispering a thousand different testimonies, each too drowned out by the next for him to make out anything but passing phrases.

If only, they said.

It isn't fair, they said.

I deserve this, they said.

And yet, amidst of all that despair:

I hope—

I hope—

I hope against hope—

Wincing, he stood up, pressed his face against the stone, and inched down the wall until he found the telltale glint of silver. The bar was inscribed with a classic Greek to Latin to English daisy-chain. The Greek *epitaphion* meant 'a funeral oration' – something spoken, something meant to be heard; the Latin *epitaphium*, similarly, referred to a eulogy. It was only the modern English epitaph that referred to something written and silent. The distorted translation gave voices to the written. He was surrounded by the confessions of the dead.

He sank down and clutched his head in his hands.

What a uniquely terrible torture. What genius had thought this up? The point was, surely, to inundate him with the despair of every other poor soul who had been imprisoned here, to fill him with such unfathomable sadness that, when questioned, he would give up anyone and anything to make it stop.

But these whispers were redundant. They did not darken his thoughts; they merely echoed them. Ramy was dead; Hermes was lost. The world could not go on. The future was only a vast expanse of black, and the only thing that gave him a shred of hope was the promise that someday, all this would end.

The door opened. Robin jerked awake, startled by the creaking hinges. In walked a graceful young man, blond hair gathered into a knot just above his neck.

'Hello, Robin Swift,' he said. His voice was gentle, musical. 'Do you remember me?'

Of course not, Robin almost said, but then the man walked closer, and the words died on his tongue. He wore the same features as the likeness in the frieze in the University College chapel: the same straight, aristocratic nose and intelligent, deep-set eyes. Robin had seen this face just once, over three years ago, in Professor Lovell's dining room. He'd never forget it.

'You're Sterling.' Brilliant, famed Sterling Jones, nephew of Sir William Jones, the greatest translator of the age. His appearance here was so unexpected that for a moment Robin could only blink at him. 'Why—'

'Why am I here?' Sterling laughed. Even his laughter was graceful. 'I couldn't miss it. Not after they told me they'd caught Griffin Lovell's little brother.'

Sterling drew two chairs into the room and sat down opposite Robin, crossing his legs at the knees. He tugged his jacket down to straighten it, then cocked his head at Robin. 'My word. You've really grown alike. You're a bit easier on the eye, though. Griffin was all sneers and hackles. Like a wet dog.' He placed his hands on his knees and leaned forward. 'So you killed your father, did you? You don't look like a killer.'

'And you don't look like a county policeman,' said Robin.

But even as he said this, the last false binary he'd constructed in his head – the one between scholars and the blades of empire – fell away. He recalled Griffin's words. He recalled his father's letters. Slave traders and soldiers. Ready killers, all of them.

'You are so like your brother.' Sterling shook his head. 'What's the Chinese expression? Badgers of the same mound, or jackals of the same tribe? Cheeky, impudent, and so unbearably self-righteous.' He folded his arms over his chest and leaned back, appraising him. 'Help me understand. I could never figure this out with Griffin. Simply – *why*? You got everything you could possibly want. You'll never have to work a day in your life – not real work, anyhow; it doesn't count when it's scholarship. You're swimming in riches.'

'My countrymen aren't,' said Robin.

'But you aren't your countrymen!' exclaimed Sterling. 'You are the exception. You are the lucky one, the elevated. Or do you really find more in common with those poor fools in Canton than your fellow Oxfordians?'

'I do,' said Robin. 'Your country reminds me every day that I do.'

'Is that the problem, then? Some white Brits weren't very nice to you?'

Robin saw no point in arguing further. It had been foolish to play along at all. Sterling Jones was just the same as Letty, except without the shallow sympathy of purported friendship. They both thought this was a matter of individual fortunes instead of systematic oppression, and neither could see outside the perspective of people who looked and spoke just like them.

'Oh, don't tell me.' Sterling sighed. 'You've formed the half-baked idea that empire is somehow a bad thing, haven't you?'

'You know what they do is wrong,' Robin said tiredly. Enough with the euphemisms; he simply could not, would not believe that intelligent men like Sterling Jones, Professor Lovell, and Mr Baylis really believed their flimsy excuses were anything but that. Only men like them could justify the exploitation of other peoples and countries with clever rhetoric, verbal ripostes, and convoluted philosophical reasoning. Only men like them thought this was still a matter of debate. 'You know.'

'Suppose you have your way,' said Sterling, conceding nothing. 'Suppose we don't go to war, and Canton keeps all of its silver. What do you think they're doing with it?'

'Perhaps,' said Robin, 'they'll spend it.'

Sterling scoffed. 'This world belongs to those who grasp. You and I both know that, that's how we got to Babel. Meanwhile your motherland is ruled by indolent, lazy aristocrats who are terrified by the very mention of a railroad.'

'One thing we have in common.'

'Very funny, Robin Swift. Do you think England should be punished, then, for daring to use those natural gifts given to us by God? Shall we leave the East in the hands of corrupt denigrates who would squander their riches on silks and concubines?' Sterling leaned forward. His blue eyes glittered. 'Or shall we *lead*? Britain hurtles towards a vast, glowing future. You could be part of that future. Why throw it all away?'

Robin said nothing. There was no point; this was not a dialogue in good faith. Sterling wanted nothing but conversion.

Sterling threw his hands in the air. 'What about this is so difficult to understand, Swift? Why fight the current? Why this absurd impulse to bite the hand that feeds you?'

'The university doesn't own me.'

'Bah. The university gave you everything.'

'The university ripped us from our homes and made us believe that our futures could only consist of serving the Crown,' said Robin. 'The university tells us we are special, chosen, selected, when really we are severed from our motherlands and raised within spitting distance of a class we can never truly become a part of. The university turned us against our own and made us believe our only options were complicity or the streets. That was no favour, Sterling. It was cruelty. Don't ask me to love my master.'

Sterling glared at him. He was breathing very hard. It was the strangest thing, Robin thought, how much he'd worked himself up. His cheeks were flushed, and his forehead was beginning to shine with sweat. Why, he wondered, did white people get so very upset when anyone disagreed with them?

'Your friend Miss Price warned me you'd become a bit of a fanatic.'

This was quite nakedly bait. Robin held his tongue.

'Go on,' Sterling sneered. 'Don't you want to ask about her? Don't you want to know why?'

'I know why. Your sort is predictable.'

Anger twisted over Sterling's face. He stood up and dragged his chair closer until their knees nearly touched.

'We have ways of extricating the truth. The word *soothe* derives from a Proto-Germanic root that means "truth". We daisy-chain it with the Swedish *sand*. It lulls you, lets you put your guard down, comforts you until you're singing.' Sterling leaned forward. 'But I've always found that one quite boring.

'Do you know where the word *agony* comes from?' He fished inside his coat pocket, then pulled out a pair of silver handcuffs, which he laid across his knees. 'Greek, by way of Latin and later, Old French. The Greek *agōnia* means a contest – originally, a sports gathering between athletes. It gained the connotation of suffering much later. But I'm translating from English back into the Greek, so the bar knows to induce suffering, not remove it. Clever, no?'

He gave the cuffs a satisfied smile. There was no malice in that smile – only a gleeful triumph that ancient languages could be hacked apart and reworked for his intended purpose. 'It took some experimenting before we got it right, but we've now perfected the effect. It'll hurt, Robin Swift. It'll hurt like hell. I've tried it before, just out of curiosity. It's not a surface-level pain, see; it's not like being stabbed with a blade, or even like being burned by flames. It's inside you. Like your wrists are shatter-ing, over and over again, only there's no upper limit to the agony, because physically, you're fine – it's all in your head. It's quite awful. You'll strain against it, of course. The body can't help it, not against pain like that. But every time you struggle, the pain will double, and double again. Would you like to see for yourself?'

I'm tired, thought Robin; *I'm so tired; I would rather you shoot me in the head.*

'Here, let me.' Sterling rose, then knelt down behind him. 'Try this.'

He snapped the cuffs shut. Robin screamed. He could not help it. He'd wanted to keep silent, to refuse Sterling the satisfaction, but the pain was so overwhelming he had no control, no sense of his body at all except for the pain, which was far worse than Sterling had described. It did not feel like his wrists were breaking. It felt as if someone were hammering thick iron spikes into his bones, straight into the marrow, and every time he writhed, flailing to break free, the pain intensified.

Control, said a voice inside his head, a voice that sounded like Griffin. *Control yourself, stop, it'll hurt less—*

But the pain only grew. Sterling hadn't lied; there was no limit. Every time he thought that this was it, that if he suffered one more moment of this then he would die, it somehow amplified. He had not known human flesh could feel such pain.

Control, said Griffin again.

Then another voice, horribly familiar: *That's one good thing about you. When you're beaten, you don't cry.*

Restraint. Repression. Had he not practised this his entire life? *Let the pain slide off you like raindrops, without acknowledgment, without reaction, because to pretend it is not happening is the only way to survive.*

Sweat dripped down his forehead. He fought to push past the blinding agony, to gain a sense of his arms and hold them still. It was the most difficult thing he'd ever done; it felt like he was forcing his own wrists under a hammer.

But the pain subsided. Robin slumped forward, gasping.

'Impressive,' said Sterling. 'See how long you can keep that up. Meanwhile, I've got something else to show you.' He pulled another bar out from his pocket and held it down over Robin's face. The left side read: φρήν. 'I don't suppose you did Ancient Greek? Griffin's was very poor, but I'm told you're the better student. You'll know what *phren* refers to, then – the seat of intellect and emotion. Only the Greeks didn't think it resided in the mind. Homer, for instance, describes the *phren* as being located in the chest.' He placed the bar into Robin's front pocket. 'Imagine what this does, then.'

He drew back his fist and slammed it against Robin's sternum.

The physical torture was not so bad – more of a hard pressure than acute pain. But the moment Sterling's knuckles touched his chest, Robin's mind exploded: feelings and memories flooded to the fore, everything he'd hidden, everything he feared and dreaded, all the truths he dared not acknowledge. He was a babbling idiot, he had no idea what he was saying; words in Chinese and English both spilled out of him without reason or order. *Ramy*, he said, or thought, he didn't know; *Ramy, Ramy, my fault, father, my father – my father, my mother, three people I have witnessed die and not once could I lift a finger to help—*

Vaguely he was aware of Sterling urging him along, trying to guide his fount of babble. 'Hermes,' Sterling kept saying. 'Tell me about Hermes.'

'Kill me,' he gasped. He meant it; he'd never wanted anything more in the world. A mind was not meant to feel this much. Only death would silence the chorus. 'Holy God, *kill me—*'

'Oh, no, Robin Swift. You don't get off that easily. We don't want you dead; that defies the point.' Sterling pulled a watch out of his pocket, examined it, and then cocked his ear towards the door as if listening for something. Seconds later, Robin heard Victoire scream. 'Can't say the same for her.'

Robin gathered his legs beneath him and launched himself at Sterling's waist. Sterling stepped to the side. Robin crashed to the ground, his cheek slamming painfully against stone. His wrists pulled against the cuffs, and his arms once again exploded into pain that did not stop until he curled in on himself, gasping, pouring every ounce of his focus into keeping still.

'Here's how it works.' Sterling dangled the watch chain over Robin's eyes. 'Tell me everything you know about the Hermes Society, and all of this stops. I'll remove the cuffs, and I'll set your friend free. Everything will be all right.'

Robin glared at him, panting.

'Tell me, and this stops,' said Sterling once more.

The Old Library was gone. Ramy was dead. Anthony, Cathy, Vimal, and Ilse – all likely dead. *They've killed the rest*, Letty had said. What else was there to give up?

There's Griffin, spoke a voice. *There are those who were in the envelope, there are countless others you don't know about.* And that was the point – he didn't know who was still out there or what they were doing, and he could not risk revealing anything that put them in danger. He'd made that mistake once before; he could not fail Hermes again.

'Tell me or we'll shoot the girl.' Sterling dangled his pocket watch over Robin's face. 'In one minute, at half past the hour, they're going to put a bullet in her skull. Unless I tell them to stop.'

'You're lying,' Robin gasped.

'I am not. Fifty seconds.'

'You wouldn't.'

'We only need one of you alive, and she's more stubborn to work with.' Sterling shook the watch again. 'Forty seconds.'

It was a bluff. It had to be a bluff; they couldn't possibly have timed things so precisely. And they ought to want them both alive – two sources of information were better than one, weren't they?

'Twenty seconds.'

He thought frantically for a passable lie, anything to make the time stop. 'There are other schools,' he breathed, 'there are contacts at other schools, stop—'

'Ah.' Sterling put away the pocket watch. 'Time's up.'

Down the hall, Victoire screamed. Robin heard a gunshot. The scream broke off.

'Thank heavens,' said Sterling. 'What a screech.'

Robin threw himself at Sterling's legs. This time it worked; he'd caught Sterling by surprise. They crashed to the floor, Robin above Sterling, cuffed hands above his head. He brought his fists down onto Sterling's forehead, his shoulders, anywhere he could reach.

'Agony,' Sterling gasped. '*Agōnia.*'

The pain in Robin's wrists redoubled. He couldn't see. He couldn't breathe. Sterling struggled out from beneath him. He toppled sideways, choking. Tears streamed down his cheeks. Sterling stood over him for a moment, breathing hard. Then he drew his boot back and aimed a vicious kick at Robin's sternum.

Pain; white-hot, blinding pain. Robin could perceive nothing else. He didn't have the breath to scream. He had no bodily control at all, no dignity; his eyes were blank, his mouth slack, leaking drool onto the floor.

'Good Lord.' Sterling adjusted his necktie as he straightened up. 'Richard was right. Animals, the lot of you.'

*   *   *

Then Robin was alone again. Sterling did not say when he would return, or what would happen to Robin next. There was only the vast expanse of time and the black grief that engulfed it. He wept until he was hollow. He screamed until it hurt to breathe.

Sometimes the waves of pain subsided ever so slightly and he thought he could organize his thoughts, take stock of his situation, ponder his next move. What came next? Was victory on the table any longer, or was there only survival? But Ramy and Victoire permeated everything. Every time he saw the slightest glimpse of the future, he remembered they would not be in it, and then the tears flowed again, and the suffocating boot of grief came down again on his chest.

He considered dying. It would not be so hard; he needed only to strike his head against stone with enough effort or figure out some way to strangle himself with his cuffs. The pain of it did not frighten him. His whole body felt numb; it seemed impossible that he might feel anything ever again except the overwhelming sense of drowning – and perhaps, he thought, death was the only way to break the surface.

He might not have to do it himself. When they'd wrung everything they could from his mind, wouldn't they try him in court and then hang him? In his youth he had once glimpsed a hanging at Newcastle; he'd seen the crowd gathered around the gallows during one of his jaunts around the city and, not knowing what he was seeing, drawn closer to the crush. There had been three men standing in a line on the platform. He remembered the whack of the panel giving way, the abrupt snap of their necks. He remembered hearing someone mutter their disappointment that the victims had not kicked.

Death by hanging might be quick – perhaps even easy, painless. He felt guilty for even considering it – *that's selfish*, Ramy had said, *you don't get to take the easy way out.*

But what in God's name was he still alive for? Robin could not see how anything he did from now on mattered. His despair was total. They had lost, they had lost with such crushing completeness, and there was nothing left. If he clung to life for the days or weeks he had left, it was solely for Ramy's sake, because he did not deserve what was easy.

Time crept on. Robin drifted between waking and sleep. Pain and grief made it impossible to truly rest. But he was tired, so tired, and his thoughts spiralled, became vivid, nightmarish memories. He was on the *Hellas* again, speaking the words that set all this in motion; he was staring down at his father, watching blood bubble over that ruin of a chest. And it was such a perfect tragedy, wasn't it? An age-old story, parricide. The Greeks loved parricide, Mr Chester had been fond of saying; they loved it for its infinite narrative potential, its invocations of legacy, pride, honour, and dominance. They loved the way it struck every possible emotion because it so deviously inverted the most basic tenet of human existence. One being creates another, moulds and influences it in its own image. The son becomes, then replaces, the father; Kronos destroys Ouranos, Zeus destroys Kronos and, eventually, becomes him. But Robin had never envied his father, never wanted anything of his except his recognition, and he hated to see himself reflected in that cold, dead face. No, not dead – reanimated, haunting; Professor Lovell leered at him, and behind him, opium burned on Canton's shores, hot and booming and sweet.

'Get up,' said Professor Lovell. '*Get up.*'

Robin jerked awake. His father's face became his brother's. Griffin loomed above him, covered in soot. Behind him, the cell door was in pieces.

Robin stared. 'How—'

Griffin brandished a silver bar. 'Same old trick. *Wúxíng.*'

'I thought it couldn't work for you.'

'Funniest thing, isn't it? Sit up.' Griffin knelt down behind him and set to work on Robin's cuffs. 'Once you said it for the first time, I finally got it. Like I've been waiting for someone to say those words my whole life. Christ, kid, who did this to you?'

'Sterling Jones.'

'Of course. Bastard.' He fiddled a moment with the lock. Metal dug into Robin's wrists. Robin winced, trying his hardest not to move.

'Ah, damn it.' Griffin rummaged around in his bag and pulled out a large pair of shears. 'I'm cutting through, hold still.' Robin felt an agonizing, intense pressure – and then nothing. His hands sprang free – still cuffed, but no longer bolted together.

The pain vanished. He sagged from the reprieve. 'I thought you were in Glasgow.'

'I was fifty miles out when I got word. Then I jumped out, waited, and hopped onto the first train I could coming back.'

'Got word?'

'We have our ways.' Robin noticed then that Griffin's right hand shone mottled pale, red, and angry. It looked like a burn scar. 'Anthony didn't elaborate, he only sent an emergency signal, but I reckoned it was bad. Then all the rumours from the tower said they'd hauled you lot here, so I skipped the Old Library – would have been dangerous, regardless – and came here. Good bet. Where is Anthony?'

'He's dead,' said Robin.

'I see.' Something rippled across Griffin's face, but he blinked, and his features resumed their calm. 'And the rest—?'

'I think they're all dead.' Robin felt wretched; he could not meet Griffin's eyes. 'Cathy, Vimal, Ilse – everyone in the house – I didn't see them fall, but I heard the shooting, and then I didn't see them again.'

'No other survivors?'

'There's Victoire. I know they brought Victoire, but—'

'Where is she?'

'I don't know,' Robin said miserably. She could be lying dead in her cell. They could have already dragged her body outside, dumped it in a shallow grave. He couldn't speak the words to explain; that would shatter him.

'Then let's look.' Griffin grabbed his shoulders and gave him a hard shake. 'Your legs are fine, aren't they? Come, get up.'

The hallway was miraculously empty. Robin glanced left and right, baffled. 'Where are all the guards?'

'Got rid of them.' Griffin tapped another bar in his belt. 'A daisy-chain riff on the word *explode*. The Latin *explōdere* is a theatre term – it refers to driving an actor off the stage by clapping one's hands. From there we get the Old English meaning "to reject or drive away with loud noise". It's not until the modern English that we get a detonation.' He looked very pleased with himself. 'My Latin's better than my Chinese.'

'So that didn't destroy the door?'

'No, it only makes a sound so awful it drives all listeners away. I got them all running to the second floor, and then I crept up here and locked the doors behind me.'

'Then what made that hole?'

'Just black powder.' Griffin hauled Robin along. 'Can't rely on silver for everything. You scholars always forget that.'

They searched every cell in the hall for Victoire. Most were empty, and Robin felt a growing dread as they moved down the doors. He did not want to look; he did not want to see the blood-streaked floor – or worse, her limp body lying where they'd left it, a bullet wound through her head.

'Here,' Griffin called from the end of the hallway. He banged on the door. 'Wake up, dear.'

Robin nearly collapsed with relief when he heard Victoire's muffled response. 'Who's that?'

'Can you walk?' Griffin asked.

This time Victoire's voice was clearer; she must have approached the door. 'Yes.'

'Are you hurt?'

'No, I'm all right.' Victoire sounded confused. 'Robin, is that—?'

'It's Griffin. Robin's here too. Don't fret, we're going to get you out.' Griffin reached into his pocket and pulled out what looked like an improvised hand grenade – a ceramic sphere a quarter the size of a cricket ball with a fuse sticking out one end.

It seemed rather small to Robin. 'Can that blow through iron?'

'Doesn't have to. The door's made of wood.' Griffin raised his voice. 'Victoire, get against the far corner and put your head between your arms and knees. Ready?'

Victoire yelled her assent. Griffin placed the grenade at the corner of the door, lit it with a match, and hastily dragged Robin several paces down the hall. The bang came seconds later.

Robin waved the smoke from his face, coughing. The door hadn't blasted apart – any explosion that large would have surely killed Victoire. But it had made a hole at the bottom just large enough for a child to crawl through. Griffin kicked at the charred wood until several large pieces fell away. 'Victoire, can you—'

She crawled out, coughing. Griffin and Robin seized her by each arm and pulled her through the rest of the way. When at last she slid free, she clambered to her knees and threw her arms around Robin. 'I thought—'

'Me too,' he murmured, hugging her tight. She was, thank God, largely unharmed. Her wrists were somewhat chafed, but free of cuffs, and there was no blood on her, no gaping bullet wounds. Sterling had been bluffing.

'They said they'd shot you.' She pressed against his chest, shaking. 'Oh, Robin, I heard a gunshot—'

'Did you—?' He couldn't finish the question. Immediately he regretted asking; he didn't want to know.

'No,' she whispered. 'I'm sorry, I thought – since they had us anyhow, I thought . . .' Her voice broke; she looked away.

He knew what she meant. She had chosen to let him die. This did not hurt as much as it should have. Rather, it clarified things; the stakes before them, the insignificance of their lives against the cause they'd chosen. He saw her begin to apologize, and then catch herself – good, he thought; she had nothing to be sorry for, for between them only one had refused to break.

'Which way is the door?' Victoire asked.

'Four floors down,' said Griffin. 'The guards are all trapped in the stairwell, but they'll break through soon.'

Robin glanced out of the window at the end of the hall. They were quite far up, he realized. He'd thought they were in the city gaol on Gloucester Green, but that building was only two storeys high. The ground looked so far away from where they stood. 'Where are we?'

'Oxford Castle,' said Griffin, pulling a rope out from his satchel. 'North tower.'

'There's not another staircase?'

'None.' Griffin nodded to the window. 'Break the glass with your elbow. We're climbing.'

Griffin descended first, then Victoire, and then Robin. Climbing down was far harder than Griffin made it look; Robin slid too quickly down the last ten feet as his arms gave out, and the rope left searing burns on his palms. Outside, it was apparent Griffin had caused much more than a simple diversion. The entire north front of Oxford Castle was ablaze, and flames and smoke were quickly spreading through the building.

Had Griffin done this all himself? Robin glanced sideways at his brother, and it was like seeing a stranger. Griffin became new in his imagination every time he encountered him, and this version was most frightening, this hard, sharp-edged man who shot and killed and burned without flinching. It was the first time he'd ever connected his brother's abstract commitments to violence with its material effects. And they were awesome. Robin didn't know if he feared him, or admired his sheer ability.

Griffin tossed them two plain black cloaks from his satchel – from a distance, they'd look vaguely like the constables' cloaks – then shepherded them along the side of the castle towards the main street. 'Move quickly and don't look behind you,' he muttered. 'They're all distracted – be calm, be fast, we'll be out of here just fine.'

And for a moment, it did seem like escape really could be that easy. The whole of the castle square looked deserted; all sentries were preoccupied with the flames and the high stone walls cast plenty of shadows in which to hide.

Only one figure stood between them and the gate.

'*Explōdere.*' Sterling Jones lurched towards them. His hair was burned, his princely face scratched and bloody. 'Clever. Didn't think you had the Latin to pull it off.'

Griffin put a hand out before Robin and Victoire as if shielding them from a charging beast. 'Hello, Sterling.'

'I see you've reached new heights of destruction.' Sterling gestured vaguely at the castle. In the dim lamplight, with blood coating his pale hair and white-grey dust all over his coat, he looked quite deranged. 'Wasn't enough for you to kill Evie?'

'Evie chose her fate,' Griffin snarled.

'Bold words from a killer.'

'*I'm* the killer? After Burma?'

'She was unarmed—'

'She knew what she'd done. So do you.'

There was history here, Robin saw. Something beyond belonging to the same cohort. Griffin and Sterling spoke with the intimacy of old friends caught in some complicated tangle of love and hatred to which he was not privy, something that had brewed over many years. He didn't know their story, but it was obvious that Griffin and Sterling had been anticipating this confrontation for quite some time.

Sterling raised his gun. 'I'd put your hands up now.'

'Three targets,' said Griffin said. 'One gun. Who are you aiming at, Sterling?'

Sterling had to realize he was outnumbered. He seemed not to care. 'Oh, I think you know.'

It was over so quickly Robin hardly registered what was happening. Griffin whipped out his revolver. Sterling pointed his gun at Griffin's chest. They must have pulled their triggers simultaneously, for the noise that split the night sounded like a single shot. They both collapsed at once.

Victoire screamed. Robin dropped to his knees, pulling at Griffin's coat, patting frantically at his chest until he found the wet, growing patch of blood over his left shoulder. Shoulder wounds were not fatal, were they? Robin tried to remember what little he'd gleaned from adventure stories – one might bleed to death, but not if they got help in time, not if someone stanched the bleeding long enough to bind the wound, or stitch it, or whatever it was doctors did to fix a bullet through the shoulder—

'Pocket,' Griffin gasped. 'Front pocket—'

Robin rooted through his front pocket and pulled out a thin silver bar.

'Try that – I wrote it, don't know if it'll—'

Robin read the bar, then pressed it against his brother's shoulder. '*Xiū,*' he whispered. 'Heal.'

修. To fix. Not merely to heal, but to repair, to patch over the damage; undo the wound with brute, mechanical reparation. The distortion was subtle, but it was there, it could work. And something was happening – he felt it under his hand, the knitting together of broken flesh, a crackling noise of bone regrowing. But the blood wouldn't stop; it spilled over his hands, coating the bar, coating the silver. Something was wrong – the flesh was moving but it wouldn't patch together; the bullet was in the way, and it was too deep for him to prise out. 'No,' Robin begged. 'No, please—' Not again; not thrice; how many times was he doomed to bend over a dying body, watching a life slip away, helpless to snatch it back?

Griffin writhed beneath him, face contorted with pain. 'Stop,' he begged. 'Stop, just let it—'

'Someone's coming,' said Victoire.

Robin felt paralysed. 'Griffin—'

'Go.' Griffin's face had turned paper-white, almost green. χλωρός, Robin thought stupidly; it was the only thing his mind could process, a memory of a frivolous debate over the translation of colour. He found himself remembering in detail how Professor Craft had questioned why they kept translating χλωρός as 'green', when Homer had also applied it to fresh twigs, to honey, to faces pale with fright. Was the bard merely blind, then? No. Perhaps, proposed Professor Craft, it was simply the colour of fresh nature, of verdant life – but that could not be right, for the sickly green of Griffin's body was nothing but the onset of death.

'I'm trying—'

'No, Robin, listen.' Griffin spasmed in pain; Robin held him tight, unable to do anything more. 'There's more than you think. Hermes – the safe room, Victoire knows where, she knows what to do – and in my satchel, *wúxíng*, there's—'

'They're coming,' Victoire urged. 'Robin, the constables, they'll see us—'

Griffin pushed him away. 'Go, run—'

'No.' Robin slid his arms under Griffin's torso. But Griffin was so heavy, and his own arms so weak. Blood spilled all over his hands. The smell of it, salty; his vision went fuzzy. He tried pulling his brother upright. They lurched to the side.

Griffin moaned. 'Stop ...'

'Robin.' Victoire grasped his arm. 'Please, we have to hide—'

Robin reached into the satchel, dug around until he felt the cold burn of silver. '*Wúxíng*,' he whispered. '*Invisible*.'

Robin and Victoire flickered, then disappeared just as three constables came running down the square.

'Christ,' someone said. 'It's Sterling Jones.'

'Dead?'

'He's not moving.'

'This one's still alive.' Someone bent over Griffin's body. A rustle of fabric – a gun drawn. A sharp, surprised laugh; a half-hearted utterance, 'Don't – he's—'

The click of a trigger.

'No,' Robin almost shouted, but Victoire clamped a hand over his mouth.

The shot boomed like a cannon. Griffin convulsed and lay still. Robin doubled over, screaming, but there was no sound to his anguish, no shape to his pain; he was incorporeal, voiceless, and though he suffered the kind of shattering grief that demanded shrieking, beating, a ripping of the world – and if not the world, then himself – he could not move; until the square was clear, all he could do was wait, and watch.

When at last the guards had gone, Griffin's body had turned a ghastly white. His eyes were open, glassy. Robin pressed his fingers against his neck, looking for a pulse and knowing he'd find none; the blast had been so direct, from such a short range.

Victoire stood over him. 'Is he—'

'Yes.'

'Then we have to go,' she said, fingers closing around his wrist. 'Robin, we don't know when they'll be back.'

He stood. What an awful tableau, he thought. Griffin's and Sterling's bodies lay adjacent on the ground, blood pooling beneath each one, running together under the rain. Some kind of love story had concluded on this square – some vicious triangle of desire, resentment, jealousy, and hatred had opened with Evie's death and closed with Griffin's. Its details were murky, would never be known to Robin in full;* all he knew, with certainty, was that this was not the first time Griffin and Sterling had tried to kill each other, only the first time one of them had succeeded. But all the principal characters were dead now, and the circle was closed.

'Let's go,' Victoire urged again. 'Robin, there's not much time.'

It felt so wrong to leave them like this. Robin wanted at least to pull his brother's body away, to lay it somewhere quiet and private, to close his eyes and place his hands over his chest. But there was only time now to run, to put the scene of the massacre behind.

---

* He would never know, for instance, that there was a time when Griffin, Sterling, Anthony, and Evie had thought of themselves as a cohort as eternally bonded as Robin's did; or that Griffin and Sterling had quarrelled once over Evie, bright and vibrant and brilliant and beautiful Evie, or that Griffin truly hadn't meant it when he'd killed her. In his retellings of that night, Griffin made himself out to be a calm and deliberate murderer. But the truth was that, like Robin, he'd acted without thinking, from anger, from fear, but not from malice; he did not even really believe it would work, for silver responded only sporadically to his command, and he didn't know what he'd done until Evie was bleeding out on the floor. Nor would he ever know that Griffin, unlike Robin, had no cohort to lean on after his act, no one to help him absorb the shock of this violence. And so he'd swallowed it, curled in around it, made it a part of himself – and while for others this might have been the first step on the road to madness, Griffin Lovell had instead whittled this capacity to kill into a sharp and necessary weapon.

Chapter Twenty-Five

And I alone am left of all that lived,
Pent in this narrow, horrible conviction.

THOMAS LOVELL BEDDOES,
Death's Jest-Book

Robin did not remember how they escaped unnoticed from Oxford Castle. His mind had fled with Griffin's death; he could not make decisions; he could hardly register where he was. The most he could do was to put one foot in front of the other, blindly following Victoire wherever she led them: into forests, through bushes and brambles, down a riverbank where they waited, huddled together in the mud, as dogs raced past, barking; then up onto a winding back road into the centre of town. Only when they were back among familiar surroundings, nearly in the shadows of Babel and the Radcliffe Library, did he find the self-possession to take stock of where they were going.

'Isn't this a bit close?' he asked. 'Shouldn't we try the canal . . . ?'

'Not the canal,' whispered Victoire. 'It'll take us right to the police station.'

'But why aren't we heading to the Cotswolds?' He didn't know why his mind had seized upon the Cotswold Hills, northwest of Oxford, filled with rolling empty plains and forests. They just seemed like the natural place to flee to. Perhaps he'd read it in a penny dreadful once, and had assumed the Cotswolds were a place for fugitives ever since. Certainly they seemed better than the heart of Oxford.

'They'll be looking for us in the Cotswolds,' said Victoire. 'They'll be expecting us to run, they'll have dogs combing the woods. But there's a safe house near the city centre—'

'No, we can't – I gave that one up; Lovell knew, and so Playfair must too—'

'There's another. Anthony showed me – right near the Radcliffe Library, there's a tunnel entrance at the back of Vaults. Just follow me.'

Robin could hear dogs barking in the distance as they approached the Radcliffe quadrangle. The police must have launched a city-wide manhunt; surely there were men and dogs trawling every street for them. Yet suddenly, absurdly, he felt no urgency to flee. They had Griffin's *wúxíng* bar in hand; they could disappear at any moment.

And Oxford at night was still so serene, still seemed like a place where they were safe, where arrest was impossible. It still looked like a city carved out of the past; of ancient spires, pinnacles, and turrets; of soft moonlight on old stones and worn, cobbled roads. Its buildings were still so reassuringly heavy, solid, ancient and eternal. The lights that shone through arched windows still promised warmth, old books, and hot tea within; still suggested an idyllic scholar's life, where ideas were abstract entertainments that could be bandied about without consequences.

But the dream was shattered. That dream had always been founded on a lie. None of them had ever stood a chance of truly belonging here, for Oxford wanted only one kind of scholar, the kind born and bred to cycle through posts of power it had created for itself. Everyone else it chewed up and discarded. These towering edifices were built with coin from the sale of slaves, and the silver that kept them running came blood-stained from the mines of Potosí. It was smelted in choking forges where native labourers were paid a pittance, before making its way on ships across the Atlantic to where it was shaped by translators ripped from their countries, stolen to this faraway land and never truly allowed to go home.

He'd been so foolish ever to think he could build a life here. There was no straddling the line; he knew that now. No stepping back and forth between two worlds, no seeing and not seeing, no holding a hand over one eye or the other like a child playing a game. You were either a part of this institution, one of the bricks that held it up, or you weren't.

Victoire's fingers wound around his.

'There's no redeeming it, is there?' he asked.

She squeezed his hand. 'No.'

Their mistake had been so obvious. They had assumed that Oxford might not betray them. Their dependence on Babel was ingrained, unconscious. On some level, they had still believed that the university, and their status as its scholars, might protect them. They had assumed, in spite of every indication otherwise, that those with the most to gain from the Empire's continued expansion might find it within themselves to do the right thing.

Pamphlets. They'd thought they could win this with pamphlets.

He almost laughed at the absurdity. Power did not lie in the tip of a pen. Power did not work against its own interests. Power could only be brought to heel by acts of defiance it could not ignore. With brute, unflinching force. With violence.

'I think Griffin was right,' Robin murmured. 'It had to be the tower all along. We have to take the tower.'

'Hm.' Victoire's lip curled up; her fingers tightened around his. 'How do you want to do that?'

'He said it would be easy. He said they were scholars, not soldiers. He said all you'd need was a gun. Perhaps a knife.'

She laughed bitterly. 'I believe it.'

It was only an idea, a wish more than anything, but it was a beginning. And it took root and grew inside them, unfurled until it became less a ludicrous fantasy and more a question of logistics, of how and when.

Across the town students were fast asleep. Next to them, tomes by Plato and Locke and Montesquieu waited to be read, discussed, gesticulated about; theoretical rights like freedom and liberty would be debated between those who already enjoyed them, stale concepts that, upon their readers' graduation ceremonies, would promptly be forgotten. That life, and all of its preoccupations, seemed insane to him now; he could not believe there was ever a time when his greatest concerns were what colour neckties to order from Randall's, or what insults to shout at houseboats hogging the river during rowing practice. It was all such frippery, fluff, trivial distractions built over a foundation of ongoing, unimaginable cruelty.

Robin gazed at the curve of Babel against the moonlight, at the faint silver glow cast off by its many reinforcements. He had a sudden, very clear vision of the tower in ruins. He wanted it to shatter. He wanted it to, for once, feel the pain that had made possible its rarefied existence. 'I want it to crumble.'

Victoire's throat pulsed, and he knew she was thinking of Anthony, of gunshots, of the wreckage of the Old Library. 'I want it to burn.'

BOOK V

ROYAL INSTITUTE OF TRANSLATION
UNIVERSITY OF OXFORD

INTERLUDE

Letty

Letitia Price was not a wicked person.

Harsh, perhaps. Cold, blunt, severe: all the words one might use to describe a girl who demanded from the world the same things a man would. But only because severity was the only way to make people take her seriously, because it was better to be feared and disliked than to be considered a sweet, pretty, stupid pet; and because academia respected steel, could tolerate cruelty, but could never accept weakness.

Letty had fought and clawed for everything she had. Oh, one wouldn't know it from looking at her, this fair English rose, this admiral's daughter raised on a Brighton estate with half a dozen servants at hand and two hundred pounds per annum to whoever married her. *Letitia Price has everything*, said the ugly jealous girls at London balls. But Letty was born second after a boy, Lincoln, the apple of her father's eye. Meanwhile her father, the admiral, could barely stand to look at her, for when he did all he saw was a shadow of the frail and late Mrs Amelia Price, killed by childbirth in a room humid with blood that smelled like the ocean.

'I certainly don't blame you,' he told her, late one night, after too much wine. 'But you'll understand, Letitia, if I'd rather you made yourself scarce in my presence.'

Lincoln was meant for Oxford, Letty for an early marriage. Lincoln received the rotation of tutors, all recent Oxford graduates who hadn't landed a parish elsewhere; the fancy pens, creamy stationery, and thick, glossy books on birthdays and Christmases. As for Letty – well, her father's opinion on women's literacy was that they needed only to be able to sign the marriage certificate.

But it was Letty who had the talent for languages, who absorbed Greek and Latin as easily as she did English. She learned from reading on her own, and from sitting with her ear pressed to the door during Lincoln's tutoring sessions. Her formidable mind retained information like a steel trap. She held grammar rules the way other women held grudges. She approached language with a determined, mathematical rigour, and she broke down the thorniest of Latin constructions through sheer force of will. It was Letty who drilled her brother late at night when he couldn't remember his vocabulary lists, who finished his translations and corrected his compositions when he got bored and went off to ride or hunt or whatever it was boys did outdoors.

If their roles had been switched, she would have been hailed as a genius. She would have been the next Sir William Jones.

But this was not in her stars. She tried to be happy for Lincoln, to project her hopes and dreams onto her brother like so many women of that era did. If Lincoln became an Oxford don, then perhaps she might become his secretary. But his mind was simply a brick wall. He hated his lessons; he despised his tutors. He thought his readings boring. All he ever wanted was to be outdoors; he could not sit still in front of a book for more than a minute before he began to fidget. And she simply couldn't understand him, why someone with such opportunities would reject the chance to *use* them.

'If I were at Oxford I would read until my eyes bled,' she told him.

'If you were at Oxford,' said Lincoln, 'the world would know to tremble.'

She loved her brother, she did. But she could not stand his ingratitude, the way he scorned all the gifts he'd been given by the world. And it felt like justice, almost, when it turned out that Oxford suited Lincoln very badly. His tutors at Balliol wrote to Admiral Price with complaints of drinking, gambling, staying out past curfew. Lincoln wrote home asking for money. His letters to Letty were brief, tantalizing, offering glimpses of a world he clearly did not appreciate – *classes a snooze, don't bother to go – not during rowing season, anyhow, you should come up and see us at Bumps next spring*. In the beginning, Admiral Price wrote this off as natural, as growing pains. Young men, living away from home for the first time, always took some time to adjust – and why shouldn't they sow their wild oats? Lincoln would pick up his books, in time.

But things only got worse. Lincoln's marks never improved. The letters from his tutors were less patient now, more threatening. When Lincoln came home for holidays during his third year, something had changed. A rot had set in, Letty saw. Something permanent, dark. Her brother's face was puffy, his speech slow, biting, and bitter. He said scarcely a word to either of them all vacation. Afternoons he spent alone in his room, working steadily through a bottle of scotch. Evenings he either went out and didn't come back until the early hours, or he quarrelled with his father, and though the two of them locked the door to the study, their angry voices pierced every room in the house. *You're a disgrace*, said Admiral Price. *I hate it there*, said Lincoln. *I'm not happy. And it's your dream, not mine.*

At last Letty decided to confront him. When Lincoln left the study that night, she was in the hallway, waiting.

'What are you looking at?' he leered. 'Here to gloat?'

'You're breaking his heart,' she said.

'You don't care about his heart. You're jealous.'

'Of course I'm jealous. You have everything. *Everything*, Lincoln. And I don't understand what's impelled you to squander it. If your friends are a drag, cut them off. If the courses are difficult, I'll help you – I'll come with you, I'll look over every paper you write—'

But he was swaying, eyes unfocused, barely listening to her. 'Go and bring me a brandy.'

'Lincoln, *what is wrong with you?*'

'Oh, don't you judge me.' His lip curled. 'Righteous Letty, brilliant Letty, should have been at Oxford except for the gap between her legs—'

'You disgust me.'

Lincoln only laughed and turned away.

'Don't come home,' she shouted after him. 'You're better off gone. You're better off dead.'

The next morning a constable knocked at their door and asked if this was the residence of Admiral Price, and if he would come with them, please, to identify a body. The driver never saw him, they said. Didn't even know he was under the cart until this morning, when the horses had a fright. It was dark, it was raining, and Lincoln had been drunk, traipsing across the road – the admiral could sue, as was his right, but they doubted the court would be on his side. It was an accident.

After this, Letty would always fear and marvel at the power of a single word. She did not need silver bars to prove how saying something could make it true.

While her father prepared for the funeral, Letty wrote to Lincoln's tutors. She included some compositions of her own.

Once admitted, she still suffered a thousand and one humiliations at Oxford. Professors talked down to her as if she were stupid. Clerks kept trying to glance through her shirt. She had an infuriatingly long walk to every class because the faculty forced women to live in a building nearly two miles north, where the landlady seemed to confuse her tenants with housemaids and yelled if they refused to do the sweeping. Scholars would reach past her at faculty parties to shake Robin's or Ramy's hand; if she spoke up, they pretended she did not exist. If Ramy corrected a professor, he was bold and brilliant; if Letty did the same she was aggravating. If she wanted to take a book out of the Bodleian, she needed Ramy or Robin present to give permission. If she wanted to get around in the dark, alone and unafraid, she had to dress and walk like a man.

None of this came as a surprise. She was, after all, a woman scholar in a country whose word for madness derived from the word for a womb. It was infuriating. Her friends were always going on about the discrimination they faced as foreigners, but why didn't anyone care that Oxford was equally cruel to women?

But in spite of all that, look at them – they were here, they were thriving, defying the odds. They'd got into the castle. They had a place here, where they could transcend their birth. They had, if they seized it, the opportunity to become some of the lauded exceptions. And why would they be anything but unfailingly, desperately grateful?

But suddenly, after Canton, they were all speaking in a language that she couldn't understand. Suddenly Letty was on the outside, and she couldn't bear it. She couldn't seem to crack the code, no matter how she tried, because every time she asked, the response was always *Isn't it obvious, Letty? Don't you see?* No, she *didn't* see. She found their principles absurd, the height of foolishness. She thought the Empire inevitable. The future immutable. And resistance pointless.

Their convictions baffled her – why, she wondered, would you dash yourself against a brick wall?

Still, she'd helped them, protected them, and kept their secrets. She loved them. She would have killed for them. And she tried not to believe the worst things about them, the things her upbringing would have had her think. They were not savages. They were not lesser, not soft-minded ingrates. They were only – sadly, dreadfully – misguided.

But oh, how she hated to see them making the same mistakes that Lincoln had.

Why could they not see how fortunate they were? To be allowed into these hallowed halls, to be lifted from their squalid upbringings into the dazzling heights of the Royal Institute of Translation! All of them had fought tooth and nail to win a seat in a classroom at Oxford. She was dazzled by her luck every day she sat in the Bodleian, thumbing through books that, without her Translator's Privileges, she could not have requested from the stacks. Letty had defied fate to get here; they all had.

So why wasn't that enough? They'd beaten the system. Why in God's name did they want so badly to break it as well? Why bite the hand that fed you? Why throw it all away?

But there are larger things at stake, they told her (condescending, patronizing; as if she were an infant, as if she knew nothing at all). *It's a matter of global injustice, Letty. The plunder of the rest of the world.*

She tried again to put aside her prejudices, to keep an open mind, to learn what it was that bothered them so. Time and time again she found her ethics questioned, and she reiterated her positions, as if proving she was not indeed a bad person. Of course she did not support this war. Of course she was against all kinds of prejudice and exploitation. Of course she sided with the abolitionists.

Of course she could support lobbying for change, as long as it was peaceful, respectable, civilized.

But then they were talking about blackmail. About kidnapping, rioting, blowing up a shipyard. This was vindictive, violent, awful. And she couldn't bear it – watching that horrible Griffin Lovell speak, that delighted glimmer in his eyes, and watching Ramy, her Ramy, nodding along. She could not believe it, what he'd become. What they'd all become.

Was it not awful enough that they'd covered up a murder? Did she have to be complicit in several more?

It was like waking up, like being doused with cold water. What was she doing here? What was she *entertaining*? This was no noble fight, only a shared delusion.

There was no future down this path. She saw this now. She'd been duped, strung along in this sickening charade, but this ended in only two ways: prison or the hangman. She was the only one there who wasn't too mad to see it. And though it killed her, she had to act with resolve – for if she could not save her friends, she had at least to save herself.

CHAPTER TWENTY-SIX

—⊗⊗⊗—

Colonialism is not a machine capable of thinking, a body endowed with reason. It is naked violence and only gives in when confronted with greater violence.

FRANTZ FANON, *The Wretched of the Earth*,
trans. Richard Philcox

A hidden door by the Vaults & Garden supply cellar revealed a cramped dirt tunnel, just large enough for them to wriggle through on their hands and knees. It felt endless. They inched forth, groping blindly. Robin wished for a light, but they had no candle, no kindling or flint; they could only trust in Anthony's word and crawl, their shallow breaths echoing around them. At last, the ceiling of the tunnel sloped upwards, and a rush of cool air bathed their clammy skin. They pawed the earthen wall until they found a door, and then a handle; this they pushed open to find a small, low-ceilinged room, illuminated by moon-light seeping through a tiny grate above.

They stepped inside and blinked around.

Someone had been here recently. A loaf of bread sat on the desk, still so fresh that it was soft to the touch, and a half-melted candle beside it. Victoire rooted in the drawers until she found a box of matches, and then held the lit candle up to the room. 'So this is where Griffin hid.'

The safe room felt uncannily familiar to Robin, though it took him a moment to realize why. The room's layout – the desk beneath the grated window, the cot tucked neatly in the corner, the double bookshelves on the opposite wall – was a precise match of the dormitories on Magpie Lane. Here below Oxford, Griffin – consciously or not – had tried to re-create his college days.

'Do you think we're safe here for the night?' Robin asked. 'I mean –
do you think—'

'It doesn't look disturbed.' Victoire sat down gingerly on the edge of
the cot. 'I think if they knew, they would have torn this place apart.'

'I think you're right.' He sat down beside her. Only now did he feel
the exhaustion, seeping up his legs and into his chest. All the adrenaline
of their escape had ebbed, now that they were safe, hidden in the belly
of the earth. He wanted to keel over and never wake up.

Victoire leaned over to the side of the cot, where a barrel of what
looked like fresh water stood. She poured some over a bunched-up shirt,
then handed it to Robin. 'Wipe.'

'What?'

'There's blood,' she said softly. 'There's blood all over you.'

He glanced up and looked at her, properly, for the first time since
their escape. 'There's blood all over *you*.'

They sat side by side and cleaned themselves in silence. They were covered
in an astonishing amount of grime; they went through one shirt each, and
then another. Somehow, Griffin's blood had got not only on Robin's hands
and arms but also across his cheeks, behind his ears, and up in the hollows
where his neck met his ears, caked under layers of dust and dirt.

They took turns wiping at each other's faces. The simple, tactile act felt
good; it gave them something to focus on, distracted from all the words
that hung heavy and unsaid. It felt good not trying to give them voice.
They could not articulate them anyhow; they were not discrete thoughts
but black, suffocating clouds. They were both thinking of Ramy and
Griffin and Anthony and everyone else who'd been abruptly, brutally
torn from this world. But they could not touch that abyss of grief. It was
too early yet to give it a name, to shape and tame it with words, and any
attempt would crush them. They could only wipe the blood from their
skin and try to keep breathing.

At last, they dropped the dirty rags on the floor and leaned back
against the wall, against each other. The damp air was cold, and there
was no fireplace. They sat close, pulling the flimsy blanket tight around
their shoulders. It was a long while before either of them spoke.

'What do you suppose we do now?' asked Victoire.

Such a heavy question, uttered in such a small voice. What *could* they
do now? They had spoken of making Babel burn, but how in God's
name was that in their power? The Old Library was destroyed. Their

friends were dead. Everyone bolder and better than them was dead. But the two of them were still here, and it was their duty to ensure their friends had not died in vain.

'Griffin said you would know what to do,' said Robin. 'What did he mean?'

'Only that we'd find allies,' Victoire whispered. 'That we had more friends than we knew, if we could just get to the safe room.'

'We're here.' Robin gestured pointlessly about. 'It's empty.'

Victoire stood. 'Oh, don't be like that.'

They began searching the room for clues. Victoire took the cabinet, Robin the desk. Inside the desk drawers were stacks upon stacks of Griffin's notes and letters. These he held up to the flickering candle, squinting. It made Robin's chest ache to read Griffin's handwriting in English – a cramped, spidered style that looked so similar to Robin's own, and to their father's. These letters, all these narrow, bold, and crowded lines, spoke of a frenetic but meticulous writer, were a glimpse into a version of Griffin that Robin had never known.

And Griffin's network had been so much vaster than he'd suspected. He saw correspondence addressed to recipients in Boston, in New York, in Cairo, in Singapore. But the names were always coded, always obvious literary references like 'Mr Pickwick' and 'King Ahab' or names so generically English like 'Mr Brown' and 'Mr Pink' that they could not possibly be real.

'Hm.' Victoire held a small square of paper up to her eyes, frowning.

'What's that?'

'It's a letter. Addressed to you.'

'Can I see?'

She hesitated a moment before handing it over. The envelope was thin and sealed. There on the back was his name, *Robin Swift*, dashed out in Griffin's forceful scrawl. But when had he found the time to write this? It couldn't have been after Anthony brought them to Hermes; Griffin hadn't known where they were back then. It could only have been written after Robin had cut ties with Hermes, after Robin had declared he wanted nothing to do with him.

'Are you going to read it?' Victoire asked.

'I – I don't think I can.' He passed it back to her. He felt terrified of the contents; it made his breath quicken to even hold it in his hand. He could not face his brother's judgment. Not now. 'Will you keep it for me?'

'What if it's something that can help?'

'I don't think it is,' said Robin. 'I think ... it has to be something else. Please, Victoire – you can read it later, if you want, but I can't look at it right now.'

She hesitated, then folded it into her inner pocket. 'Of course.'

They resumed rooting through Griffin's belongings. Apart from letters, Griffin had kept an impressive array of weapons – knives, garrotes, a number of silver bars, and at least three pistols. Robin refused to touch them; Victoire surveyed the collection, fingers skimming the barrels, before selecting one and tucking it into her belt.

'Do you know how to use that?' he asked.

'Yes,' she said, 'Anthony taught me.'

'Wondrous girl, you. Full of surprises.'

She snorted. 'Oh, you just weren't paying attention.'

But there was no list of contacts, no clues to other safe houses or possible allies. Griffin had shrouded everything in code, had created a network so invisible that, upon his death, it could never be reconstructed.

'What's that?' Victoire pointed.

Up on top of the bookshelf, pushed so far back it was nearly hidden, was a lamp.

Robin reached for it, hoping wildly – yes, there it was, the familiar glint of silver embedded in the bottom. *The beacon*, Anthony had yelled. He thought of the burn on Griffin's hand, of how Griffin had known, even miles away, that something awful had happened.

He turned it over, squinting. 燎. *Liáo.*

Griffin had made this. *Liáo*, in Mandarin, could mean 'to burn' or 'to illuminate'. It could also refer to a signal lamp. There was a second, smaller silver bar inscribed above the first. *Bēacen*, it read. It looked like Latin, but Robin, raking his memory, couldn't come up with its precise meaning or origin. Germanic, perhaps?[*]

---

[*] This supplementary silver bar is one of the rare Old English–to-English match-pairs, created by a Hermes scholar, John Fugues, who participated in a project in the 1780s where scholars locked themselves in a castle and spoke only Old English to each other for three months. (Such experiments have not been repeated since, though not for lack of funding; Babel was simply unable to find volunteers willing to undergo the same extreme isolation, compounded by the inability to properly express oneself to others.) The Old English *bēacen* refers to audible signals, portents, and signs – instead of the rather flat English meaning, which just refers to a great signal of fire.

Still, he could guess vaguely at the function of the lamp. This was how Hermes communicated. They sent signals through fire.

'How do you think it works?' asked Victoire.

'Perhaps they're all linked, somehow.' He passed it to her. 'That's how Griffin knew we were in trouble – he must have been carrying one on his person.'

'But who else has one of these?' She turned it over in her hands, ran her fingers over the shrivelled wick. 'Who do you think is on the other side?'

'Friends, I hope. What do you think we should tell them?'

She thought for a moment. 'A call to arms.'

He glanced at her. 'We're really doing this?'

'I don't see what other choice we have.'

'You know, there's a Chinese idiom that goes *sǐ zhū bú pà kāi shuǐ tàng.*[*] Dead pigs don't fear scalding water.'

She gave him a wan smile. 'In for a penny, in for a pound.'

'We're dead men walking.'

'But that's what makes us frightening.' She set the lamp down between them. 'We've nothing left to lose.'

They rummaged through the desk for pen and paper, then set about composing their message. The remaining oil in the lamp looked dangerously low; the wick was burnt down to a stub. Their message would have to be as succinct and unambiguous as possible. There could be no questioning what they meant. When they'd agreed on what to say, Victoire held the candle to the lamp. There was a tentative flicker, then a sudden whoosh, until flames over a foot tall leapt and danced before their eyes.

They weren't sure about the mechanics of the beacon. Robin had spoken the Mandarin match-pair out loud, but they could only hope that the second, mysterious match-pair was designed to endure in effect. They'd come up with an exhaustive list of every method they could think to try. They recited the message into the flame. They clapped it in Morse code. They repeated the code, this time by thrusting a metal rod through the flame, so it flickered with every dot and dash. Finally, as the oil began sputtering, they fed the paper into the lamp.

The effect was immediate. The fire tripled in size; long tongues lashed outwards and then back in around the paper, like some demonic creature

---

* 死豬不怕開水燙.

devouring their words. The paper did not burn or crumple; it simply vanished. A moment later, the oil ran out, the flames sputtered to nothing, and the room dimmed.

'You think that did it?' Victoire asked.

'I don't know. I don't know if anyone's even listening.' Robin set the lamp down. He felt unbearably tired, his limbs like lead. He did not know what they'd just set into motion. Part of him never wanted to find out, wanted to curl up in this cool, dark space and disappear. He had a duty, he knew, to finish the job, and when tomorrow came, he would summon what strength he had left to face it. But for now, he wanted to sleep like the dead. 'I suppose we'll see.'

At daybreak they sneaked across town to the Old Library. Dozens of policemen stood stationed around the building – perhaps they were lying in wait, to see if anyone was foolish enough to return. Robin and Victoire crept forth cautiously from the forest behind the yard. This was stupid, yes, but they could not resist the urge to tally the damage. They'd hoped they might have a chance to creep inside and retrieve some supplies, but the police presence was too thick for them to pull it off.

So instead they came to stand witness, for, despite the risks, someone had to remember the sight of the betrayal. Someone had to register the loss.

The Old Library was utterly destroyed. The whole back had been blown away, a gaping wound exposing the library's naked insides in a way that felt cruel and humiliating. The shelves were half-bare. What books had not been burnt in the explosions were stacked up in wheelbarrows all around the building to be carted away, Robin assumed, for analysis by Babel's own scholars. He doubted most of that work would ever see the light of day.

All that wonderful, original research, hidden away in the imperial archives for fear of what it could inspire.

Only when he crept closer did he see that bodies still lay in the rubble. He saw a pale arm, half-buried beneath fallen bricks. He saw a shoe buckle attached to a charred shin. Near the side of the Old Library he saw a mass of hair, black, dust-covered. He turned away before he could glimpse the face beneath.

'They haven't cleared the bodies.' He felt dizzy.

Victoire touched a hand to her mouth. 'Oh, dear God.'

'They haven't cleared the bodies—'

He stood up. He didn't know what he meant to do – pull them into the forest one by one? Dig their graves right by the library? Place a cloth, at least, over their open, staring eyes? He didn't know, only it felt so wrong to leave them there, exposed and vulnerable.

But Victoire was already pulling him back behind the trees. 'We can't, you know we can't—'

'They're just lying there – Anthony, Vimal, *Ramy*—'

They hadn't carted them to the morgue. Hadn't even covered them. They'd simply left the dead where they'd fallen, bleeding across the bricks and pages, were simply stepping around them on their way to excavate the library. Was this their petty revenge, retribution for a lifetime of inconvenience? Or did they simply not care?

The world has to break, he thought. *Someone has to answer for this. Someone has to bleed.* But Victoire yanked him down the way they'd come, and her vicelike grip was the only thing that kept him from racing into the fray.

'There's nothing here for us,' she whispered. 'It's time, Robin. We've got to go.'

They'd chosen a good day for revolution.

It was the first day of term, and one of the rare days in Oxford when the weather was deceitfully marvellous; when its warmth promised more sunshine and joy than the relentless rain and sleet Hilary inevitably brought. Everything was clear blue skies and zesty hints of spring winds. Everyone would be inside today – faculty, graduate fellows, and students – and the tower lobby would be empty of clients, for this year Babel was closed for reshelving and renovations during the first week of the term. No civilians would be caught in the crossfire.

The question, then, was how to get into the tower.

They could not simply stroll up to the front door and go in. Their faces were plastered on newspapers all over London; certainly some of the scholars knew, even if the whole thing had been covered up in Oxford. The front door was still manned with half a dozen police. And by now, certainly, Professor Playfair had destroyed the blood vials that marked their belonging.

Still, they had three advantages at their disposal: Griffin's *explōdere* distraction, the invisibility bar, and the fact that the wards around the door were designed to keep materials in, not out. This latter fact was only a theory, but a strong one. As far as they knew, the wards had only ever activated upon exit, not upon entrance. Thieves had always got in fine, so far as someone held the door open; it was leaving that was trouble.*

And if they did what they set out to do here today, they would not leave the tower for a very long time.

Victoire took a deep breath. 'Ready?'

There was no other way. They had racked their brains all night and come up short. Nothing to do now but act.

Robin nodded.

'*Explōdere,*' he whispered, and flung Griffin's bar across the green.

The air shattered. The bar was harmless, Robin knew in theory, but still its noise was dreadful, was the sound of cities breaking, pyramids collapsing. He felt an instinct to scarper, to find safety, and though he knew it was only the silver manifesting on his mind, he had to overcome every impulse not to run in the other direction.

'Let's go,' Victoire insisted, jerking at his arm.

As expected, the police had gone across the green; the door was swinging shut behind a handful of scholars. Robin and Victoire dashed up the pavement, around the seal, and pushed their way in behind them. Robin held his breath as they stepped over the threshold, but no sirens went off; no traps were sprung. They were in; they were safe.

The lobby felt more crowded than usual. Had their message been seen, then? Had some of these people come to answer their call? He had no way of knowing who was with Hermes and who wasn't; everyone who met his gaze gave him the same disinterested, polite nod before moving on with their business. It all felt so absurdly normal. Did no one here know the world had broken?

Across the rotunda Professor Playfair leaned against the second-floor balcony, chatting with Professor Chakravarti. Professor Chakravarti

---

* This loophole was, in fact, deliberate. In its early days, the tower viciously attacked entrants and escapees alike, but the wards were imprecise, and the number of wrongful maimings escalated until the city government insisted there had to be some sort of due process. Professor Playfair's response was to catch thieves only upon departure, when the incriminating evidence would be in their pockets or strewn across the cobblestones around them.

must have made a joke, for Professor Playfair laughed, shook his head, and looked out over the lobby. He met Robin's gaze. His eyes bulged.

Robin jumped up onto a table in the centre of the lobby just as Professor Playfair rushed to the staircase.

'Listen to me!' he shouted.

The bustling tower paid him no heed. Victoire climbed up next to him, wielding the ceremonial bell Professor Playfair used to announce exam results. She raised it over her head and gave it three furious shakes. The tower fell silent.

'Thank you,' said Robin. 'Ah. So. I've got to say something.' His mind promptly went blank at the sight of so many staring faces. For several seconds he merely blinked, mute and startled, until at last the words came back to his tongue. He took a deep breath. 'We're shutting down the tower.'

Professor Craft pushed her way to the front of the lobby. 'Mr Swift, what in God's name are you doing?'

'Hold on,' said Professor Harding. 'You're not supposed to be here, Jerome said—'

'There's a war going on,' Robin blurted. He winced as the words left his mouth; they were so clumsy, unpersuasive. He'd had a speech prepared, but suddenly he could remember only the highlights, and those sounded ridiculous even as he spoke them aloud. Across the lobby and along the balconies of the floors above, he saw alternating expressions of scepticism, amusement, and annoyance. Even Professor Playfair, now panting at the base of the stairs, looked more baffled than agitated. Robin felt dizzy. He wanted to vomit.

Griffin would have known how to compel them. Griffin was the storyteller, the true revolutionary; he could paint the necessary picture of imperial expansion, complicity, guilt, and responsibility with a handful of gutting phrases. But Griffin wasn't here, and the best Robin could do was to channel his dead brother's spirit.

'Parliament is debating military action on Canton.' He forced his voice to grow, to take up more space in the room than he ever had. 'There is no just pretext, apart from the greed of the trading companies. They're planning to force opium on the Chinese at gunpoint, and causing a diplomatic fiasco during my cohort's voyage was the excuse to do it.'

There, he'd said something that made sense. Around the tower, impatience changed to curiosity, confusion.

'What's Parliament got to do with us?' asked one of the fellows in Legal – Coalbrook or Conway, or something like that.

'The British Empire does nothing without our help,' said Robin. 'We write the bars that power their guns, their ships. We polish the knives of domination. We draw up their treaties. If we withdraw our help, then Parliament can't move on China—'

'I still don't see how it's our problem,' said Coalbrook or Conway.

'It's our problem because it's our professors who are behind it,' Victoire cut in. Her voice was shaky, but still louder, more sure than Robin's. 'They're running out of silver, this whole country's running a deficit, and some of our faculty think the way to fix it is by injecting opium into a foreign market. They'll do anything to push this through; they're murdering people who've been trying to leak it. They killed Anthony Ribben—'

'Anthony Ribben died at sea,' said Professor Craft.

'No, he didn't,' said Victoire. 'He's been in hiding, working to stop the Empire from doing exactly this. They shot him last week. And Vimal Srinivasan, Ilse Dejima, and Cathy O'Nell – go up to Jericho, go to the old building behind the forest past the bridge and you'll see the rubble, the bodies . . .'

This elicited murmurs. Vimal, Ilse, and Cathy were all well-liked in the faculty. The whispers grew; it was apparent now that they were not present, and no one could account for where they were.

'They're insane,' snapped Professor Playfair. He'd regained his composure, like an actor who'd remembered his lines. He pointed a dramatic, accusing finger at the two of them. 'They're insane, they're working with a band of rioting thieves, they ought to be in prison—'

But this seemed even more difficult for the room to swallow than Robin's story. Professor Playfair's booming voice, usually so engaging, had the contrary effect of making this seem like mere theatrics. No one else had a clue what the three of them were talking about; from the outside, it seemed as though they were all putting on a show.

'Why don't you tell us what happened to Richard Lovell?' Professor Playfair demanded. 'Where is he? What have you done with him?'

'Richard Lovell is one of the architects of this war,' Robin shouted. 'He went to Canton to obtain military intelligence from British spies, he's in direct contact with Palmerston—'

'But that's ridiculous,' said Professor Craft. 'That can't be true, that's—'

'We have papers,' Robin said. It crossed his mind, then, that those papers were now certainly destroyed or confiscated, but still, as rhetoric, it worked. 'We have quotes, proof – it's all there. He's been planning this for years. Playfair's in on it, ask him—'

'He's lying,' said Professor Playfair. 'He's rambling, Margaret, the boy's gone mad—'

'But madness is incoherent.' Professor Craft frowned, glancing back and forth between the two of them. 'And lies are self-serving. This story – it benefits no one, certainly not these two,' she said, pointing at Robin and Victoire, 'and it is coherent.'

'I assure you, Margaret—'

'Professor.' Robin appealed directly to Professor Craft. 'Professor, please – he wants a war, he's been planning it for years. Go and look in his office. In Professor Lovell's office. Go through their papers. It's all there.'

'No,' Professor Craft murmured. Her brows furrowed. Her eyes flickered across Robin and Victoire, and she seemed to register something – their hollow exhaustion, perhaps, the sag of their shoulders, or the grief seeping through their bones. 'No, I believe you . . .' She turned. 'Jerome? Did you know?'

Professor Playfair paused a moment, as if deliberating whether it was worth trying to keep up the pretence. Then he huffed. 'Don't act so shocked. You know what runs this tower. You knew the balance of power had to shift, you knew we had to do something about the deficit—'

'But to declare war on innocent people—'

'Don't pretend this is where you'll draw the line,' he said. 'You were just fine with everything else – it's not as if China has much to offer the world apart from its consumers. Why wouldn't we—' He stopped. He seemed to have realized his mistake, that he'd just validated their story.

It was too late. The atmosphere in the tower changed. The scepticism evaporated. Irritation turned to a dawning realization that this was not a farce, not a bout of hysteria, but something real.

The real world so seldom interfered with the tower. They didn't know what to do with it.

'We use the languages of other countries to enrich this one.' Robin gazed around the tower as he spoke. He was not trying to convince Professor Playfair, he reminded himself; he had to appeal to the room.

'We take so much knowledge that isn't ours. The least we can do is stop this from happening. It's the only ethical thing.'

'Then what are you planning?' asked Matthew Houndslow. He didn't sound hostile; only tentative, confused. 'It's in Parliament's hands now, as you said, so how—'

'We go on strike.'

Yes, he was on solid footing now; here was a question to which he knew the answer. He lifted his chin, tried to inject his voice with all the authority of Griffin and Anthony. 'We shut down the tower. From this day forward, no clients enter the lobby. No one creates, sells, or maintains silver bars. We deny Britain all translation services until they capitulate – and they will capitulate, because they *need* us. They need us more than anything. That's how we win.' He paused. The room was silent. He couldn't tell if he'd convinced them, couldn't tell if he was looking at expressions of grudging realization or incredulity. 'Look, if we all just—'

'But you'd need to secure the tower.' Professor Playfair gave a short, mean laugh. 'I mean, you'd have to subdue all of us.'

'I suppose we do,' said Victoire. 'I suppose we're doing that right now.'

Next came a very funny pause as it slowly dawned upon a building of Oxford scholars that whatever came next was a matter of force.

'You.' Professor Playfair pointed to the student nearest the door. 'Go and get the constables, let them in—'

The student didn't move. He was a second year – Ibrahim, Robin recalled, an Arabic scholar from Egypt. He seemed incredibly young, a baby-faced boy; were second years always that young? Ibrahim glanced to Robin and Victoire, then back at Professor Playfair, frowning. 'But, sir . . .'

'Don't,' Professor Craft told him, just as a pair of third years broke suddenly for the exit. One shoved Ibrahim against a shelf. Robin hurled a silver bar at the door. '*Explōdere*, explode.' A great, horrible noise filled the lobby; this time a screeching howl. The third years scrambled away from the door like frightened rabbits.

Robin pulled another silver bar from his front pocket and waved it above his head.

'I killed Richard Lovell with this.' He couldn't believe these words were coming out of his mouth. This was not him speaking; this was the ghost of Griffin, the braver, madder brother, reaching through the underworld to pull his strings. 'If anyone takes a step towards me, and if anyone tries to call for help, I'll destroy them.'

They all looked so terrified. They believed him.

That worried him. This had all been too easy. He'd been sure he would face more resistance, but the room seemed utterly subdued. Even the professors did not move; indeed, Professors Leblanc and De Vreese huddled together under a table, as if bracing for cannon fire. He could tell them to dance a jig, to rip the pages out of their books one by one, and they would obey.

They would obey because he threatened violence.

He couldn't remember why the thought of acting had scared him so before. Griffin was right – the obstacle was not the struggle, but the failure to imagine it was possible at all, the compulsion to cling to the safe, the survivable status quo. But the whole world was off its hinges now. Every door was wide open. They'd moved past the realm of ideas now, into the realm of action, and this was something Oxford students were wholly unprepared for.

'For God's sake,' snapped Professor Playfair. 'Someone apprehend them.'

A handful of graduate fellows stepped forward, looking uncertain. All Europeanists, all white. Robin cocked his head. 'Well, come on.'

What happened next was not dignified, would never be shelved next to great epics of valour and bravery. For Oxford's scholars were sheltered and coddled, armchair theorists who wrote of blood-stained battlefields with smooth and delicate hands. The seizure of Babel was a clumsy, silly clash of the abstract and the material. The fellows approached the table, reaching with hesitant arms. Robin kicked them away. And it felt like kicking at children, for they were too fearful to be vicious, and they weren't nearly desperate or angry enough to really hurt him. They seemed unsure of what they even wanted to do – pull him down, grab his legs, or simply graze his ankles – and so his retaliatory blows were, similarly, perfunctory. They were playing at a fight, all of them, amateur actors given a stage direction: *struggle*.

'Victoire!' he shouted.

One of the scholars had climbed up onto the table behind her. She spun around. The scholar hesitated a moment, looked her up and down, then threw a punch. But he hit like he only knew about the action in theory, like he only knew of its component parts – *plant feet, draw arm back, extend fist.* He'd misjudged his distance – the effect was nothing more than a light pat on Victoire's shoulder. She struck out with her left foot. He doubled over his shins, whining.

'Stop!'

The fracas ceased. Somehow, Professor Playfair had acquired a gun.

'Stop this silliness.' He pointed it at Robin. 'Stop this right now.'

'Go ahead,' Robin breathed. He had no idea where this ridiculous fount of courage came from, but he felt not a shred of fear. The gun, somehow, seemed more abstract than real, the bullet wholly incapable of touching him. 'Go ahead, I dare you.'

He was gambling on Professor Playfair's cowardice, on the fact that he might wield a gun, but he wouldn't pull the trigger. Professor Playfair, like every other Babel scholar, hated getting his hands dirty. He designed lethal traps – he never wielded the blades himself. And he didn't know how much will, or panic, it took to really kill a man.

Robin did not turn around, did not look to see what Victoire was doing. He knew. He spread his arms, keeping his eyes locked with Professor Playfair's. 'What'll it be?'

Professor Playfair's face tightened. His fingers moved, and Robin tensed, just as a shot rang out.

Professor Playfair reeled backwards, scarlet exploding across his middle. Screams erupted around the tower. Robin glanced back over his shoulder. And Victoire lowered one of Griffin's revolvers, smoke tendrils curling up around her face, her eyes enormous.

'There,' she breathed, chest heaving. 'Now we all know how it feels.'

Professor De Vreese dashed suddenly across the hall. He was going for Professor Playfair's gun. Robin jumped down off the table, but he was too far away – but then Professor Chakravarti threw himself at Professor De Vreese's side. They hit the floor with a *whumph* and began to wrestle – a clumsy, inelegant sight, two paunchy, middle-aged professors rolling around on the ground, their gowns flapping over their waists. Robin watched, astonished, as Professor Chakravarti wrenched the gun out of Professor De Vreese's grasp and pinned him down in a messy hold.

'Sir?'

'Received your message,' panted Professor Chakravarti. 'Very well done.'

Professor De Vreese jammed his elbow at Professor Chakravarti's nose. Professor Chakravarti lurched back. Professor De Vreese wriggled out of his hold, and the wrestling resumed.

Robin scooped the gun off the floor and pointed it down at Professor De Vreese.

'Stand up,' he ordered. 'Put your hands above your head.'

'You don't know how to use that,' Professor De Vreese sneered.

Robin pointed the gun at the chandelier and pulled the trigger. The chandelier exploded; glass shards sprinkled across the lobby. It was as if he'd shot into the crowd; everyone shrieked and cringed. Professor De Vreese turned and ran, but his ankle caught on a desk leg and he toppled backwards onto his bum. Robin reset the chamber, just as Griffin had shown him, and then pointed the gun at Professor De Vreese once again.

'This isn't a debate,' he announced. His whole body trembled, flush with the same vicious energy he'd felt when he'd first learned to shoot. 'This is a takeover. Would anyone else like to have a go?'

No one moved. No one spoke. They all shrank back, terrified. Some were crying; some had their hands clamped over their mouths, as if that were the only way to contain their screams. And all were watching him, waiting for him to dictate what came next.

For a moment the only sound in the tower was of Professor Playfair's moaning.

He glanced over his shoulder at Victoire. She looked as bewildered as she felt; her gun hung limp at her side. Deep down, neither of them had expected to actually get this far. Their visions of today had involved chaos: a violent and devastating last stand; a fracas that, in all likelihood, ended in death. They'd been prepared for sacrifice; they had not been prepared to win.

But the tower had been taken so very easily, just as Griffin had always predicted. And now they had to act like the victors.

'Nothing leaves Babel,' Robin declared. 'We put a lockdown on the silver-working tools. We stop routine maintenance on the city. We wait for the machine to grind to a halt, and hope they capitulate before we do.' He didn't know where these words were coming from, but they sounded good. 'This country can't last a month without us. We strike until they bend.'

'They'll set the troops on you,' said Professor Craft.

'But they can't,' said Victoire. 'They can't touch us. No one can touch us. They need us too badly.'

And that, the key to Griffin's theory of violence, was why they might win. They'd finally worked it out. It was why Griffin and Anthony had been so confident in their struggle, why they were convinced the colonies could take on the Empire. Empire needed extraction. Violence shocked the system, because the system could not cannibalize itself and survive. The hands of the Empire were tied, because it could not raze that from which it profited. And like those sugar fields, like those markets, like those bodies of unwilling labour, Babel was an asset. Britain needed Chinese, needed Arabic and Sanskrit and all the languages of colonized territories to function. Britain could not hurt Babel without hurting itself. And so Babel alone, an asset denied, could grind the Empire to a halt.

'Then what are you going to do?' demanded Professor De Vreese. 'Keep us hostage the entire time?'

'I hope you'll join us,' said Robin. 'But if you don't, you can leave the tower. Order the police away first, and then you can file out one by one. No one retrieves anything from the tower – you walk out with what's on your person."* He paused. 'And I'm sure you understand we'll have to destroy your blood vials if you go.'

As soon as he finished, a shuffle of bodies moved towards the door. Robin's heart sank as he counted the numbers. Dozens were leaving – all of the Classicists, all of the Europeanists, and nearly all of the faculty. Professor Playfair was carried out still moaning, slung ignominiously between Professor De Vreese and Professor Harding.

Only six scholars remained: Professor Chakravarti, Professor Craft, two undergraduates – Ibrahim and a tiny girl named Juliana – and two graduate fellows named Yusuf and Meghana, who worked in Legal and Literature respectively. Faces of colour, faces from the colonies, except for Professor Craft.

But this could work. They could sacrifice their hold on the talent if they retained control of the tower. Babel contained the greatest concentration of silver-working resources in the country: Grammaticas,

---

* This decision had been a matter of fierce debate between Robin and Victoire. Robin had wanted to hold all the scholars hostage; Victoire, instead, made the compelling argument that several dozen scholars were much more likely to comply with being forced out of a building at gunpoint than being trapped in a basement for weeks on end, with nowhere to bathe, do their laundry, or shit.

engraving pens, match-pair ledgers, and reference materials. And more than that, the *silver*. Professor Playfair and the others might establish a secondary translation centre elsewhere, but even if they could reconstruct everything they needed to maintain the country's silver-work from memory, it would take them weeks, perhaps months, to acquire materials on the scale necessary to replicate the functions of the tower. By then the vote would have already happened. By then, if all went to plan, the country would have already been brought to its knees.

'What now?' murmured Victoire.

Blood rushed to Robin's head as he stepped off the desk. 'Now we tell the world what's coming.'

At noon Robin and Victoire climbed up to the north balcony on the eighth floor. The balcony was largely decorative, designed for scholars who'd never internalized the concept of needing fresh air. No one ever stepped out there, and the door was nearly rusted shut. Robin pushed, leaning hard against the frame. When it swung suddenly open, he lurched out and found himself leaning over the ledge for one brief, terrifying moment before he regained his balance.

Oxford looked so tiny beneath him. A doll's house, a twee approximation of the real world for boys who would never have to truly engage with it. He wondered if this was how men like Jardine and Matheson saw the world – minuscule, manipulable. If people and places moved around the lines they drew. If cities shattered when they stomped.

Below, the stone steps at the front of the tower were alight with flames. The blood vials of all but the eight scholars who'd remained within the tower had been smashed against the bricks, doused with oil poured from unused lamps, and set aflame. This was not strictly necessary; all that mattered was that the vials were removed from the tower – but Robin and Victoire had insisted on ceremony. They had learned from Professor Playfair the importance of performance, and this macabre display was a statement, a warning. The castle was stormed, the magician thrown out.

'Ready?' Victoire placed a stack of papers on the ledge. Babel did not possess its own printing press, so they'd spent the morning laboriously copying out each of those hundred pamphlets. The declaration borrowed both from Anthony's coalition-building rhetoric and Griffin's philosophy of violence. Robin and Victoire had joined their voices – one an eloquent urge to link arms in a fight for justice, the other an uncompromising threat to those who opposed them – into a clear, succinct announcement of their intentions.

> *We, the students of the Royal Institute of Translation, demand Britain cease consideration of an unlawful war against China. Given this government's determination to initiate hostilities and its brutal suppression of those working to expose its motives, we have no other option to make our voices heard than to cease all translation and silver-working services by the Institute, until such time as our demands are met. We henceforth declare our strike.*

Such an interesting word, Robin thought, *strike.*[*] It brought to mind hammers against spikes, bodies throwing themselves against an immovable force. It contained in itself the paradox of the concept; that through nonaction, and nonviolence, one might prove the devastating consequences of refusing to accommodate those one relied upon.

Below them, Oxfordians were going about their merry way. No one glanced up; no one saw the two students leaning over the tallest point in the city. The exiled translators were nowhere in sight; if Playfair had sought the police, they had not yet chosen to act. The city remained serene, clueless as to what was coming.

> *Oxford, we ask you to stand with us. The strike will cause great hardships for the city in days to come. We ask you to direct your ire to the government that has made such a strike our only recourse. We ask you to stand on the side of justice and fairness.*

From there the pamphlets articulated the clear dangers of an influx of silver to the British economy, not only for China and the colonies, but for the working class of England. Robin did not expect anyone to read that far. He did not expect the city to support their strike; to the contrary, once the silver-work began breaking down, he expected they would hate them.

---

[*] The word *strike*, in relation to labour, originally had the connotation of submission. Ships would drop, or strike, their sails when surrendering to enemy forces or saluting their superiors. But when sailors in 1768 struck their sails in protest to demand better wages, they turned *strike* from an act of submission to a strategic act of violence; by withholding their labour, they proved they were in fact indispensable.

But the tower was impenetrable, and their hate did not matter. All that mattered was that they understood the cause of their inconvenience.

'How long do you think until they reach London?' asked Victoire.

'Hours,' said Robin. 'I think this reaches the first train headed from here to Paddington.'

They had chosen the unlikeliest of places for a revolution. Oxford was not the centre of activity, it was a refuge, decades behind the rest of England in every realm but the academic. The university was designed to be a bastion of antiquity, where scholars could fancy themselves in any of the past five centuries, where scandals and turmoil were so scarce that it made the University College newsletter if a red-breast began singing near the end of an exhaustingly long sermon at Christ Church.

But though Oxford was not the seat of power, it produced the occupants thereof. Its alumni ran the Empire. Someone, perhaps this moment, was rushing to Oxford Station with news of the occupation. Someone would recognize its significance, would see it was not a petty students' game but a crisis of national importance. Someone would get this in front of the Cabinet and the House of Lords. Then Parliament would choose what happened next.

'Go on.' Robin nodded to Victoire. Her Classical pronunciation was better than his. 'Let's see them fly.'

'*Polemikós*,' she murmured, holding a bar over the stack. 'Polemic. *Discutere*. Discuss.'

She pushed the stack off the ledge. The pamphlets took flight. The wind carried them soaring across the city; over spires and turrets down onto streets, yards, and gardens; flying down chimneys, darting through grates, slipping into open windows. They accosted everyone they came across, clinging to coats, flapping in faces, sticking persistently to satchels and briefcases. Most would bat them aside, irritated. But a few would pick them up, would read the strikers' manifesto, would slowly register what this meant for Oxford, for London, and for the Empire. And then no one would be able to ignore them. Then the entire world would be forced to look.

'Are you all right?' Robin asked.

Victoire had gone as still as a statue, eyes fixed on the pamphlets as if she could will herself to become a bird, to fly among them. 'Why wouldn't I be?'

'I – you know.'

'It's funny.' She did not turn to meet his eye. 'I'm waiting for it to hit, but it simply – it never does. Not like with you.'

'It wasn't the same.' He tried to find words that would comfort, that would make it out to be anything other than it was. 'It was self-defence. And he might still survive, it might – I mean, it won't be—'

'It was for Anthony,' she said in a very hard voice. 'And that's the last I ever want to speak of it.'

CHAPTER TWENTY-SEVEN

The seed ye sow, another reaps;
The wealth ye find, another keeps;
The robes ye weave, another wears;
The arms ye forge, another bears.

PERCY BYSSHE SHELLEY,
'Song to the Men of England'

The mood that afternoon was one of nervous apprehension. Like children who had kicked over an ants' nest, they now watched fearfully to see how awful the ramifications would be. Hours had passed. Surely the escaped professors had liaised with city policy-makers by now. Surely London had read those pamphlets by now. What form would the backlash take? They had all spent years trusting in the impenetrability of the tower; its wards, until now, had shielded them from everything. Still, it felt as if they were counting down the minutes to a vicious retaliation.

'They have to send in the constables,' said Professor Craft. 'Even if they can't get in. There will be some attempted arrest, surely. If not for the strike, then for—' She glanced at Victoire, blinked, and trailed off.

There was a brief silence.

'The strike is illegal too,' said Professor Chakravarti. 'The Combination of Workmen Act of 1825 suppresses the right to strike by trade unions and guilds.'

'We're not a guild, though,' said Robin.

'Actually, we are,' said Yusuf, who worked in Legal. 'It's in the founding documents. Babel alums and students comprise the Translators' Guild by virtue of their institutional affiliation, so by holding a strike we are in violation of the law, if you want to get technical about it.'

They looked round at each other, and then all at once burst out laughing.

But their good humour faded quickly. The association between their strike and the trade unions left a bad taste in all of their mouths, for the workers' agitations of the 1830s – brought about directly as the result of the silver industrial revolution – had met with resounding failure. The Luddites had ended up either dead or exiled to Australia. The Lancashire spinners were forced back to work to avoid starvation within a year. The Swing Rioters, by smashing threshing machines and setting barns on fire, had secured a temporary improvement in wages and working conditions, but these were promptly reneged upon; more than a dozen rioters were hanged, and hundreds were sent to penal colonies in Australia.

Strikers in this country never won broad public support, for the public merely wanted all the conveniences of modern life without the guilt of knowing how those conveniences were procured. And why should the translators succeed where other strikers – white strikers, no less – had failed?

There was at least one reason to hope. They were running on momentum. The social forces that had prompted the Luddites to smash machines had not disappeared. They had only grown worse. Silver-powered looms and spinning machines were getting cheaper and more ubiquitous, enriching none but factory owners and financiers. Each year they put more men out of work, left more families destitute, and maimed and killed more children in machines that operated more quickly than the human eye could track. The use of silver created inequality, and both had increased exponentially in England during the past decade. The country was pulling apart at the seams. This could not go on forever.

And their strike, Robin was convinced, was different. Their impact was larger, harder to patch over. There were no alternatives to Babel, no scabs. No one else could do what they did. Britain could not function without them. If Parliament did not believe it, then they would soon learn.

Still no policemen had appeared by evening. This lack of response baffled them. But soon logistical problems – namely, supplies and accommodation – became the more pressing matters at hand. It was clear now that they were going to be in the tower for quite some time, with no clear end date to their strike. At some point they were going to run out of food.

There was a tiny, rarely used kitchen in the basement, where servants had once lived before the Institute stopped housing its janitorial staff for free. Occasionally scholars ducked downstairs for a snack when working late. A foray into the cabinets produced a decent amount of nonperishables – nuts, preserves, indestructible tea biscuits, and dry oats for porridge. It wasn't much, but they wouldn't starve overnight. And they found many, many bottles of wine, left over from years of faculty functions and garden parties.

'Absolutely not,' said Professor Craft when Juliana and Meghana proposed bringing the bottles upstairs. 'Put those back. We need to keep our wits about us.'

'We need something to pass the time,' said Meghana. 'And if we're going to starve to death, we may as well go out drunk.'

'They're not going to starve us to death,' Robin said. 'They can't allow us to die. They can't hurt us. That's the point.'

'Even so,' said Yusuf. 'We've just declared our intention to break the city. I don't think we can just wander out for a hot breakfast, do you?'

Nor could they simply poke their heads outside and put in an order to the grocer's. They had no friends in town, no one who could act as their liaison with the outer world. Professor Craft had a brother in Reading, but there was no way of getting a letter to him, and nor was there a safe way for him to deliver foodstuffs up to the tower. And Professor Chakravarti, it turned out, had a very limited relationship with Hermes – he'd been recruited only after his promotion to junior faculty, after his ties to upper faculty rendered him too risky for deeper involvement – and he knew Hermes only through anonymous letters and drop points. No one else had responded to their beacon. As far as they knew, they were the only ones left.

'You two didn't think of this before you broke into the tower and started waving guns around?' asked Professor Chakravarti.

'We were a bit distracted,' said Robin, embarrassed.

'We – really, we were making it up as we went along,' said Victoire. 'And we didn't have much time.'

'Planning a revolution is not one of your strong suits.' Professor Craft sniffed. 'I shall see what I can do with the oats.'

Very soon a number of other problems arose. Babel was blessed with running water and indoor lavatories, but there was no place to shower. No one had an extra change of clothes, and there were of course no laundering facilities – all of them had their washing done by invisible scouts. Apart from a single cot on the eighth floor, which was used as an unofficial nap space by the graduate fellows, there were no beds, pillows, linens, or anything that might make for comfortable bedding at night except for their own coats.

'Think of it like this,' Professor Chakravarti said in a valiant attempt to lift their mood. 'Who doesn't dream of living in a library? Is there not a certain romance to our situation? Who among us would balk at a completely unhindered life of the mind?'

No one, it seemed, shared this fantasy.

'Can't we just duck out in the evenings?' asked Juliana. 'We can sneak out past midnight and be back by morning, no one will notice—'

'That's absurd,' said Robin. 'This isn't some kind of – of optional daytime activity—'

'We're going to smell,' said Yusuf. 'It'll be disgusting.'

'Still, we can't just keep going in and out—'

'Just once then,' said Ibrahim. 'Just for supplies—'

'Stop it,' snapped Victoire. 'Just stop it, all of you, will you? We all chose treason against the Crown. We'll be uncomfortable for some time yet.'

At half past ten, Meghana ran up from the lobby and breathlessly announced that London was sending a telegram. They crowded around the machine, watching nervously as Professor Chakravarti took down the message and transcribed it. He blinked at it for a moment, then said, 'They've more or less told us to shove it.'

'What?' Robin reached for the telegram. 'There's nothing else?'

'**PLEASE REOPEN TOWER TO REGULAR BUSINESS STOP**,' read Professor Chakravarti. 'That's all it says.'

'It's not even signed?'

'I can only assume it's coming direct from the Foreign Office,' said Professor Chakravarti. 'They don't take private messages this late.'

'There's no word about Playfair?' Victoire asked.

'Just the one line,' said Professor Chakravarti. 'That's it.'

So Parliament had declined to meet their demands – or indeed to take them seriously at all. Perhaps it was silly to hope the strike would produce a response so soon, before the lack of silver had taken effect, but they had hoped at least that Parliament would acknowledge the threat. Did the MPs think this whole thing would blow over on its own? Were they trying to prevent a general panic? Was this why not a single policeman had knocked on the door, why the green outside was as serene and empty as it had ever been?

'What now?' Juliana asked.

No one had an answer. They couldn't help feeling somewhat petulant, like toddlers who'd thrown tantrums but had not been rewarded for their efforts. All that trouble for such a curt response – it all seemed so pathetic.

They lingered around the telegraph machine for a few more moments, hoping it might spring to life with better news – that Parliament was greatly concerned, that they'd called a midnight debate, that crowds of protestors had flooded Trafalgar Square to demand the war be called off. But the needle remained still. One by one they slunk back upstairs, hungry and dispirited.

For the rest of the evening, Robin would occasionally step out onto the rooftop to peer over the city, scanning for any indication of change or unrest. But Oxford remained tranquil, undisturbed. Their pamphlets lay trodden in the street, stuck in grates, flapping pointlessly in the gentle night breeze. No one had even bothered to clean them up.

They had little to say to one another that night as they made their beds among the stacks, huddling under coats and spare gowns. The convivial atmosphere of that afternoon had vanished. They were all suffering the same unspoken, private fear, a creeping dread that this strike might do nothing but damn themselves, and that their cries would go unheard into the unforgiving dark.

Magdalen Tower fell the next morning.

None of them had anticipated this. They only worked out afterwards what had happened, after they'd checked the work order ledgers and realized what they could have done to prevent it. Magdalen Tower, the second-tallest building in Oxford, had relied since the eighteenth century on silver-facilitated engineering tricks to support its weight after centuries of soil erosion had eaten at its foundations. Babel scholars did routine maintenance on its supports every six months, once in January and once again in June.

In the hours that followed the disaster, they would learn that it was Professor Playfair who had overseen these biannual reinforcements for the past fifteen years, and whose notes on such procedures were locked in his office, inaccessible to the exiled Babel faculty, who had not even remembered Magdalen Tower's upcoming appointment. They would find in their letterbox a flurry of messages from the panicked members of the city council who had expected Professor Playfair the previous evening, and who discovered only the next day that he was laid up in hospital, pumped full of laudanum and unconscious. They would learn that one council member had passed the early hours of the morning banging frantically at Babel's door; only none of them heard or saw him, for the wards kept out all riffraff who might disrupt the scholars inside.

Meanwhile, the clock had run out on Magdalen Tower. At nine on the dot, a rumbling began at its base and spread through the entire city. At Babel, their teacups began clattering at breakfast. They thought they were experiencing an earthquake, until they rushed to the windows and saw that nothing was noticeably shaking except a single building in the distance.

Then they rushed to the rooftop and crowded around Professor Craft, who narrated what she saw from the telescope. 'It's – it's breaking apart.'

By now the changes were so great they could be seen with the naked eye. Tiles dripped off the roof like raindrops. Huge chunks of turrets peeled away and crashed to the ground.

Victoire asked what no one else dared. 'Do you think anyone's inside?'

If they were, at least they had ample time to get out. The building had been shaking for a good fifteen minutes now. This was their ethical defence; they did not let themselves consider the alternatives.

At twenty past nine, all ten of the tower's bells began to ring at once, without rhythm or harmony. They seemed to grow louder, building up to a terrible level; they reached a crescendo with an urgency that made Robin himself want to scream.

Then the tower collapsed, as simply and cleanly as a sandcastle kicked at the base. It took less than ten seconds for the building to fall, but nearly a minute for the rumbling to settle. Then, where Magdalen Tower had once stood was a great mound of brick, dust, and stone. And it was somehow lovely, unnervingly lovely because it was so awful, because it violated the rules of how things were supposed to move. That the city's horizon could, in an instant, be changed this dramatically was both breathtaking and awesome.

Robin and Victoire watched, hands clasped tight.

'We did that,' Robin murmured.

'That's not even the worst of it,' said Victoire, and he could not tell if she was delighted or scared. 'That's only the beginning.'

So Griffin was right. This was what it took: a show of force. If the people could not be won over by words, they would be persuaded by destruction.

Parliament's capitulation, they reasoned, was only hours away now. For wasn't this proof that the strike was intolerable? That the city could not ride out the tower's refusal of service?

The professors were not so optimistic.

'It won't speed things along,' said Professor Chakravarti. 'If anything, it'll slow the destruction down – they know they have to be vigilant now.'

'But it's a harbinger of things to come,' said Ibrahim. 'Right? What falls next? The Radcliffe Library? The Sheldonian?'

'Magdalen Tower was an accident,' said Professor Craft. 'But Professor Chakravarti is right. It'll put the rest of them on guard, covering for the effects that we've halted. It's a race against time now – they'll have regrouped somewhere else, surely, and they'll be trying to construct a new translation centre as we speak—'

'Can they do that?' asked Victoire. 'We've taken the tower. We have all the maintenance records, the tools—'

'And the silver,' said Robin. 'We have all the silver.'

'That will hurt, in time, but in the short term they will manage to plug the worst of the gaps,' said Professor Craft. 'They'll wait us out – we have porridge for a week at most, Swift, and what then? We starve?'

'Then we speed things up,' said Robin.

'How do you propose to do that?' asked Victoire.

'Resonance.'

Professor Chakravarti and Professor Craft exchanged a glance.

'How does he know about that?' asked Professor Craft.

Professor Chakravarti gave a guilty shrug. 'Might have shown him.'

'Anand!'

'Oh, what was the harm?'

'Well, *this*, clearly—'

'What is resonance?' Victoire demanded.

'Up on the eighth floor,' said Robin. 'Let's go, I'll show you. It's how the distant bars are maintained, the ones that aren't made for endurance. The centre to the periphery. If we remove the centre, then surely they'll begin to fail, won't they?'

'Well, there's a moral line,' said Professor Craft. 'Withholding services, resources – that's one thing. But deliberate sabotage—'

Robin scoffed. 'We're splitting ethical hairs over this? *This?*'

'The city would stop running,' said Professor Chakravarti. 'The country. It would be Armageddon.'

'But that's what we *want*—'

'You want enough damage to make the threat credible,' said Professor Chakravarti. 'And no more.'

'Then we'll remove just a few at once.' Robin stood up. His mind was made up. He did not want to debate this further, and he could see none of them did either; they were too anxious, and too afraid. They only wanted someone to tell them what to do. 'One by one, until they get the general idea. Would you like to pick which ones?'

The professors declined. Robin suspected it was too much for them to deconstruct the resonance rods by themselves, for they knew too well the consequences of what they did. They needed to preserve the illusion of innocence, or at least of ignorance. But they expressed no further opposition, and so that evening Robin and Victoire went together up to the eighth floor.

'A dozen or so, do you think?' Victoire suggested. 'A dozen every day, and we'll see if we need to scale up?'

'Perhaps two dozen to start,' said Robin. There must have been hundreds of rods in the room. He had the impulse to kick them all down, to just grab one and use it to bat down the others. 'Don't we want to be dramatic?'

Victoire shot him a droll look. 'There's dramatic, and then there's reckless.'

'This whole endeavour is reckless.'

'But we don't even know what *one* would do—'

'I only mean, we need to get their attention.' Robin pressed a fist into a palm. 'I want a spectacle. I *want* Armageddon. I want them to think that a dozen Magdalen Towers will fall every day until they listen to us.'

Victoire folded her arms. Robin didn't like the way her eyes were searching him, as though she'd seized on some truth that he didn't want to admit out loud.

'It's not revenge, what we're doing here.' She raised her eyebrows. 'Just so we're clear.'

He chose not to mention Professor Playfair then. 'I know that, Victoire.'

'Fine, then.' She nodded curtly. 'Two dozen.'

'Two dozen to *start*.' Robin reached down and pulled the nearest resonance rod from its fixture. It slid out with surprising ease. He'd expected some resistance, some noise or transformation symbolizing the break. 'Is it that simple?'

How slender, how fragile, the foundations of an empire. Take away the centre, and what's left? A gasping periphery, baseless, powerless, cut down at the roots.

Victoire reached out at random and pulled out a second rod, and then a third. 'I suppose we'll see.'

And then, like a house of cards, Oxford began to crumble.

The rapidity of its deterioration was stunning. The next day, all the bell-tower clocks stopped running, all frozen at precisely 6.37 in the morning. Later that afternoon, a great stink wafted over the city. It turned out silver had been used to facilitate the flow of sewage, which was now stuck in place, an unmoving mass of sludge. That evening, Oxford went dark. First one lamp-post started flickering, then another, and then another, until all of the lights on High Street went out. For the first time in the two decades since gas lamps were installed on its streets, Oxford passed the night shrouded in black.

'What did you two *do* up there?' Ibrahim marvelled.

'We only took out two dozen,' said Victoire. 'Two dozen only, so how—'

'This is how Babel was designed to work,' said Professor Chakravarti. 'We made the city as reliant on the Institute as possible. We designed bars to last for only several weeks instead of months, because maintenance appointments bring in money. This is the cost of inflating prices and artificially creating demand. It all works beautifully, until it doesn't.'

By the morning of the third day, transportation began breaking down. Most of the carts in England used a variety of match-pairs that played with the concept of speed. The word *speed* in modern English was specific to a sense of rapidity, but as a number of common phrases – *Godspeed, good speed to you* – proved, the root meaning, deriving with the Latin *spēs*, meaning 'to hope', was associated with good fortune and success, with the broader sense of seeking one's destination, of crossing great distances to reach one's goal. Speed-based match-pairs using Latin, or in rare cases Old Slavic, allowed carriages to travel more quickly without risk of accident.

But drivers had become too accustomed to the bars, and thus did not correct for when they failed. Accidents multiplied. Oxford's roads became blocked with overturned wagons and cabs that had taken corners too tightly. Up in the Cotswolds a small family of eight tumbled straight into a ravine because the driver had got used to sitting back and letting the horses take over during tricky turns.

The postal system, too, ground to a halt. For years, Royal Mail couriers with particularly heavy loads had been using bars engraved with the French-English match-pair *parcelle-parcel*. Both French and English had once used *parcel* to refer to pieces of land that made up an estate, but when it evolved to imply an item of business in both, it retained its connotation of small fragmentariness in French, whereas in English it simply meant a package. Fixing this bar to the postal carriage made the parcels seem a fraction of their true weight. But now these carriages, with horses straining under three times the load they were used to, were collapsing mid-route.

'Do you think they've caught on yet that this is a problem?' Robin demanded on the fourth day. 'I mean, how long is it going to take for people to realize this won't just go away on its own?'

But it was impossible to tell from within the tower. They had no way to gauge public opinion in either Oxford or London, except through the papers which, hilariously, were still delivered to the front door every morning. This was how they learned about the Cotswold family tragedy, the traffic accidents, and the countrywide courier slowdown. But the London papers made hardly any mention of the war on China or the strike, save for a brief announcement about some 'internal disturbances' at the 'prestigious Royal Institute of Translation'.

'We're being silenced,' Victoire said grimly. 'They're doing this on purpose.'

But how long did Parliament think it could keep things quiet? On the fifth morning, they were woken by a horribly discordant noise. It took some rooting through the ledgers to find out what was going on. Great Tom of Christ Church, the loudest bell in Oxford, had always sung a slightly imperfect B-flat note. But whatever silver-work regulated its sound had stopped working, and Great Tom now blared a devastating, eerie groan. By that afternoon, it was joined by the bells at St Martin's, St Mary's, and Osney Abbey, an ongoing, miserable, groaning chorus.

Babel's wards blocked out the sound somewhat, though by that evening they'd all learned to live with a constant, dreadful murmur seeping through the walls. They wore cotton in their ears to sleep.

The bells were a funeral dirge to an illusion. The city of dreaming spires was no longer. Oxford's degradation was visible – one could see it crumbling by the hour like a rotting gingerbread house. What became clear was how deeply Oxford relied on silver, how without the constant labour of its translation corps, of the talent it attracted from abroad, it immediately fell apart. It revealed more than the power of translation. It revealed the sheer dependence of the British, who, astonishingly, could not manage to do basic things like bake bread or get safely from one place to another without words stolen from other countries.

And still this was only the beginning. The maintenance ledgers were endless, and there were hundreds of resonance rods yet to be uprooted.

'How far are they going to let this go?' was the question they kept asking inside the tower. For they were all amazed, and somewhat horrified, that the city had still not acknowledged the real reason behind this strike; that Parliament had still not taken action.

Privately, Robin did not want this to end. He would never confess it to the others, but deep down, where the ghosts of Griffin and Ramy resided, he did not want a speedy resolution, a nominal settlement that only papered over decades of exploitation.

He wanted to see how far he could take this. He wanted to see Oxford broken down to its foundations, wanted its fat, golden opulence to slough away; for its pale, elegant bricks to crumble to pieces; for its turrets to smash against cobblestones; for its bookshelves to collapse like dominoes. He wanted the whole place dismantled so thoroughly that it would be as if it had never been built. All those buildings assembled by slaves, paid for by slaves, and stuffed with artefacts stolen from conquered lands, those buildings which had no right to exist, whose

ongoing existence demanded continuous extraction and violence –
destroyed, undone.

On the sixth day, they got the city's attention at last. A crowd assembled
at the base of the tower around midmorning, shouting for the scholars
to come out.

'Oh, look,' Victoire said sarcastically. 'It's a militia.'

They gathered round a fourth-floor window and peered down below.
Many of the crowd were Oxford students – black-robed young men
marching in defence of their town; scowling, chests puffed out. Robin
recognized Vincy Woolcombe by his shock of red hair, and then Elton
Pendennis, waving a torch above his head, shouting at the men behind
him as if leading troops onto a battlefield. But there were women too,
and children, and barkeeps and shopkeepers and farmers: a rare alliance
of town and gown.

'Probably we should go and talk to them,' said Robin. 'Else they'll be
out there all day.'

'Aren't you scared?' asked Meghana.

Robin scoffed. 'Are you?'

'There's quite a lot of them. You don't know what they'll do.'

'They're students,' said Robin. 'They don't know what they want
to do.'

Indeed, it seemed that the agitators had not thought through how
they would actually storm the tower. They were not even shouting in
unison. Most just milled around the green, confused, glancing around as
if waiting for someone else to give orders. This was not the angry mob of
unemployed workers that had threatened Babel's scholars over the past
year; these were schoolboys and townspeople for whom violence was a
wholly unfamiliar means of getting what they wanted.

'You're just going to walk out there?' Ibrahim asked.

'Why not?' Robin asked. 'May as well shout back.'

'Good Lord,' Professor Chakravarti said suddenly, voice tight. 'They're
trying to set this place ablaze.'

They turned back to the window. Now that the mob was drawing
closer, Robin could see they had brought wagons piled high with
kindling. They had torches. They had oil.

Were they going to burn them alive? Stupid, that would be so stupid
– surely they understood the whole point was that Babel could not be

lost, for Babel and the knowledge contained within it was precisely what they were fighting to reacquire. But perhaps rationality had fled. Perhaps there was only the mob, fuelled by the sheer fury that something they thought was theirs had been taken from them.

Some students started to pile kindling at the foot of the tower. Robin felt his first stab of worry. This was no idle threat; they really meant to set the place alight.

He shoved the window open and stuck his head outside. 'What are you doing?' he shouted. 'You burn us, and you'll never get your city in working order.'

Someone hurled a glass bottle at his face. He was too high up, and the bottle spiralled down before it came close, but still Professor Chakravarti yanked Robin backwards and slammed the window shut.

'All right,' he said. 'No sense reasoning with madmen, I think.'

'Then what are we going to do?' Ibrahim demanded. 'They're going to burn us alive!'

'The tower's made of stone,' Yusuf said dismissively. 'We'll be fine.'

'But the *smoke*—'

'We've got something,' Professor Chakravarti said abruptly as if only just remembering. 'Upstairs, under the Burma files—'

'Anand!' Professor Craft exclaimed. 'They're civilians.'

'It's self-defence,' said Professor Chakravarti. 'Justified, I think.'

Professor Craft peered back out at the crowd. Her mouth pressed in a thin line. 'Oh, very well.'

Without further explanation, the two of them made for the staircase. The rest glanced around at each other for a moment, at a loss for what to do.

Robin reached to open the window with one hand, fumbling around his inner front pocket with the other. Victoire grasped his wrist. 'What are you doing?'

'Griffin's bar,' he murmured. 'You know, the one—'

'Are you mad?'

'They're trying to burn us alive, let's not debate the morals—'

'That could set all the oil alight.' Her grip tightened, so much that it hurt. 'That'll kill half a dozen people. Calm down, will you?'

Robin put the bar back into his pocket, took a deep breath, and wondered at the hammering in his veins. He wanted a fight. He wanted to jump down there and bloody their faces with his fists. Wanted them to know exactly what he was, which was their worst nightmare – uncivilized, brutal, violent.

But it was over before it started. Like Professor Playfair, Pendennis and his sort were not soldiers. They liked to threaten and bluster. They liked to pretend the world obeyed their every whim. But at the end of the day, they were not meant for material struggle. They hadn't the faintest clue how much effort it might take to bring down a tower, and Babel was the most fortified tower on earth.

Pendennis lowered his torch and set light to the kindling. The crowd cheered as the flames licked up the walls. But the fire failed to take. The flames jumped hungrily, reaching with orange tendrils as if seeking a foothold, but pointlessly fell back again. Several students ran up to the tower walls in some badly thought-out attempt to scale them, but they scarcely touched the bricks before some unseen force hurled them back against the green.

Professor Chakravarti came panting down the stairs, bearing a silver bar that read विभाजित.* 'Sanskrit,' he explained. 'It'll split them.'

He leaned out of the window, observed the fracas for a moment, and then hurled the bar at the centre of the mob. In seconds, the crowd began to dispel. Robin couldn't quite tell what was going on, but there seemed to be an argument on the ground, and the agitators wore looks of alternating irritation and confusion as they milled around like ducks circling each other on a pond. Then, one by one, they drifted away from the tower; to home, to dinner, to waiting wives and husbands and children.

A small number of students lingered on for a little while. Elton Pendennis was still pontificating on the green, waving his torch above his head, yelling curses that they could not hear through the wards. But the tower, clearly, was never going to catch fire. The kindling burned pointlessly against the stone, and then spluttered out. The protestors' voices grew hoarse with shouting; their cries faltered, and then finally died out completely. By sunset, the last of the rabble had straggled home.

The translators did not have supper until nearly midnight; unseasoned gruel, peach preserves, and two tea biscuits each. After much begging, Professor Craft relented and permitted them to bring up several bottles

---

* The word विभाजित (*vibhājita*) makes use of the Sanskrit root विभिद् (*vibhid*), which has a variety of meanings including to disperse, to estrange, to unbind, and to alienate.

of red wine from the cellar. 'Well,' she said, pouring out generous glasses with a shaky hand. 'Wasn't that exciting.'

The next morning, the translators commenced the fortification of Babel.

They'd never been in any real danger the day before; even Juliana, who'd quietly cried herself to sleep, now laughed at the memory. But that prenatal riot was only the beginning. Oxford would continue to crumble, and the city would only hate them more. They had to prepare for next time.

They threw themselves into the work. Suddenly the tower felt just as it did during exam season. They sat in rows on the eighth floor, heads hunched over their texts, and the only sounds in the room were pages flipping and the occasional exclamation when someone stumbled upon a promising nugget of etymology. This felt good. Here at last was something to do, something that kept them from dawdling nervously as they awaited news from the outside.

Robin rooted through stacks of notes he'd found in Professor Lovell's office, which contained many potential match-pairs prepared for the China campaign. One excited him very much: the Chinese character 利 (lì) could mean to sharpen one's weapon, though it also carried connotations of profit and advantage, and its logogram represented grain being cut with a knife. Knives sharpened with the 利-*sharp* match-pair had frightfully thin blades, and unerringly found their targets.

'How is that useful?' asked Victoire when he showed her.

'It helps in a fight,' said Robin. 'Isn't that the point?'

'Do you think you're going to get in a knife fight with someone?'

He shrugged, annoyed and now a little embarrassed. 'It could come down to that.'

She narrowed her eyes. 'You want it to, don't you?'

'Of course not, I don't even – of course not. But if they get in, if it becomes strictly necessary—'

'We're trying to defend the tower,' she told him gently. 'We're just trying to keep ourselves safe. Not leave a field of blood in our wake.'

They began living like defenders under siege. They consulted classical texts – military histories, field manuals, strategic treatises – for ideas on how to run the tower. They instituted strict mealtimes and rations; no nibbling of the biscuits at midnight, as Ibrahim and Juliana had been caught doing. They hauled the rest of the old astronomy telescopes out onto the rooftop so they could keep watch over the deteriorating city. They set up a series of rotating two-hour surveillance shifts from the seventh- and eighth-floor windows so that when the next riots began, they'd see them coming from far away.

A day passed like this, and then another. It finally sank in that they'd passed the point of no return, that this was no temporary divergence; there would be no resumption of normal life. They emerged from here the victors, the harbingers of an unrecognizable Britain, or they left this tower dead.

'They're striking in London.' Victoire shook his shoulders. 'Robin, wake up.'

He bolted upright. The clock read ten past midnight; he'd just fallen asleep, preparing for a graveyard watch. 'What? Who?'

'Everyone.' Victoire sounded dazed, as if she couldn't believe it herself. 'Anthony's pamphlets must have worked – I mean, the ones addressing the Radicals, the ones about labour, because look—' She waved a telegram at him. 'Even the telegraph office. They say there've been crowds around Parliament all day, demanding that they withdraw the war proposal—'

'Who's *everyone*?'

'All the strikers from a few years ago – the tailors, the shoemakers, the weavers. They're all striking again. And there's more – there are dock workers, factory employees, gasworks stokers – I mean, really, *everyone*. Look.' She shook the telegram. 'Look. It'll be in all the papers tomorrow.'

Robin squinted at the missive in the dim light, trying to comprehend what this meant.

A hundred miles away, white British factory workers were crowding Westminster Hall to protest a war in a country they'd never stepped foot in.

Was Anthony right? Had they forged the most unlikely of alliances? Theirs was not the first of the antisilver revolts of that decade, only the most dramatic. The Rebecca Riots in Wales, the Bull Ring Riots in Birmingham, and the Chartist uprisings in Sheffield and Bradford just earlier that year had all tried and failed to halt the silver industrial revolution. The papers had made them out to be isolated outbursts of discontent. But it was clear now that they were all connected, all caught in the same web of coercion and exploitation. What was happening to the Lancashire spinners had happened to Indian weavers first. Sweating, exhausted textile workers in silver-gilded British factories spun cotton picked by slaves in America. Everywhere the silver industrial revolution had wrought poverty, inequality, and suffering, while the only ones who benefited were those in power at the heart of the Empire. And the grand accomplishment of the imperial project was to take only a little from so many places; to fragment and distribute the suffering so that at no point did it ever become too much for the entire community to bear. Until it did.

And if the oppressed came together, if they rallied around a common cause – here, now, was one of the impossible pivot points Griffin had spoken of so often. Here was their chance to push history off its course.

The first ceasefire offer came in from London an hour later: **RESUME BABEL SERVICES. FULL AMNESTY EVEN FOR SWIFT AND DESGRAVES STOP. OTHERWISE PRISON STOP.**

'Those are very bad terms,' said Yusuf.

'They're absurd terms,' said Professor Chakravarti. 'How ought we to respond?'

'I think we don't,' said Victoire. 'I think we let them sweat, that we just keep pushing them to the edge.'

'But that's dangerous,' said Professor Craft. 'They've opened up space for a dialogue, haven't they? We can't know how long it'll stay open. Suppose we ignore them and it closes—'

'There's something else,' Robin said sharply.

They watched the telegraph machine tap away in fearful, silent apprehension as Victoire took it down. '**ARMY ON ITS WAY STOP,**' she read. '**STAND DOWN STOP.**'

'Jesus Christ,' said Juliana.

'But what good does that do them?' Robin asked. 'They can't get through the wards—'

'We have to assume they can,' Professor Chakravarti said grimly. 'At least, that they will. We have to assume Jerome's helping them.'

This set off a round of frightened babbling.

'We've got to talk to them,' said Professor Craft. 'We'll lose the window of negotiation—'

Said Ibrahim, 'Suppose they put us all in prison, though—'

'Not if we surrender—' Juliana began.

And Victoire, firm, vehement: 'We can't surrender. We'll have gained nothing—'

'Hold on.' Robin raised his voice over the din. 'No – this threat, the Army – it all means it's working, don't you see? It means they're scared. On the first day they still thought they could order us around. But they've felt the consequences now. They're *terrified*. Which means if we can just hold on for a bit, if we can just keep this up, we'll win.'

CHAPTER TWENTY-EIGHT

What say you, then,
To times, when half the city shall break out
Full of one passion, vengeance, rage, or fear?

WILLIAM WORDSWORTH, *The Prelude*

The next morning they awoke to find that a set of barricades had mysteriously sprung up around the tower overnight. Great, tottering obstructions blocked up every major street leading towards Babel – High Street, Broad Street, Cornmarket. Was this the Army's work? They wondered. But it all seemed too slapdash, too haphazard to be an Army operation. The barricades were made of everyday materials – upturned carts, sand-filled barrels, fallen streetlamps, iron grillwork ripped away from the fences round Oxford's parks, and the stone rubble that had been gathering at every street corner as evidence of the city's slow deterioration. And what benefit did the Army obtain by fencing in their own streets?

They asked Ibrahim, who'd been on watch shift, what he'd seen. But Ibrahim had fallen asleep. 'I woke up a little before dawn,' he said defensively. 'By then they were already in place.'

Professor Chakravarti came rushing up from the lobby. 'There's a man outside who wants to talk to you two.' He nodded to Robin and Victoire.

'What man?' asked Victoire. 'Why us?'

'Unclear,' said Professor Chakravarti. 'But he was quite adamant he speaks to whoever's in charge. And this whole thing is your circus, isn't it?'

They descended to the lobby together. From the window they saw a tall, broad-shouldered, bearded man waiting on the steps. He didn't appear to be armed, nor particularly hostile, but his presence was baffling nonetheless.

He'd seen this man before, Robin realized. He wasn't carrying his sign, but he stood the same way he always had during the mill workers' protests: fists clenched, chin up, glaring determinedly at the tower as if he could topple it with his mind.

'For heaven's sake.' Professor Craft peeked out of the window. 'It's one of those madmen. Don't go out there, he'll attack you.'

But Robin was already pulling on his coat. 'No, he won't.' He had a suspicion of what was happening, and though he was afraid to hope just yet, his heart raced with excitement. 'I think he's here to help.'

When they opened the door,* the man courteously backed away, arms held high to show he had no weapon.

'What's your name?' asked Robin. 'I've seen you out here before.'

'Abel.' The man's voice was very deep; solid, like building stone. 'Abel Goodfellow.'

'You threw an egg at me,' accused Victoire. 'That was you, last February—'

'Yes, but it was only an egg,' said Abel. 'Nothing personal.'

Robin gestured to the barricades. The nearest one obstructed nearly the whole width of High Street, cutting off the main entrance to the tower. 'This is your work?'

Abel smiled. It was an odd sight, through that beard; it made him look briefly like a gleeful little boy. 'Do you like them?'

'I'm not sure what the point is,' said Victoire.

'The Army's on their way, haven't you heard?'

'And I don't see how this stops them,' said Victoire. 'Unless you're telling me you've also brought an army to man those walls.'

'It'll do a better job warding off troops than you think,' said Abel. 'It's not just about the walls – though they'll hold, you'll see. It's psychological. The barricades create the impression that there's a real resistance going on, while the Army currently thinks they'll be marching on the tower unopposed. And it emboldens our protestors – it creates a safe haven, a place to retreat.'

'And what are you out here protesting?' Victoire asked cautiously.

'The silver industrial revolution, of course.' Abel held up a crinkled, waterlogged pamphlet. One of theirs. 'Turns out we're on the same side.'

---

* Professor Craft had drawn Robin's and Victoire's blood and replaced their vials in the wall; they were now as free to enter and exit the tower as ever before.

Victoire cocked her head. 'Are we?'

'Certainly where industry is concerned. We've been trying to convince you of the same.'

Robin and Victoire exchanged a glance. They both felt rather ashamed now of their disdain for the strikers over the past year. They'd bought into Professor Lovell's claims, that the strikers were simply lazy, pathetic, and undeserving of basic economic dignities. But how different, really, were their causes?

'It was never about the silver,' said Abel. 'You realize that now, don't you? It was about the wage-cutting. The shoddy work. The women and children kept all day in hot airless rooms, the danger of untested machines the eye can't track. We were suffering. And we only wanted to make you see it.'

'I know,' Robin said. 'We know that now.'

'And we weren't there to harm any of you. Well, not seriously.'

Victoire hesitated, then nodded. 'I can try to believe that.'

'Anyhow.' Abel gestured at the barricades behind him. The movement was preciously awkward, like a suitor showing off his roses. 'We learned what you were up to, and thought we might come up and help. At least we can stop those buffoons from burning the tower down.'

'Well, thank you.' Robin was unsure what to make of this; he still couldn't quite believe this was happening. 'Do – do you want to come inside? Talk things over?'

'Well, yes,' said Abel. 'That's why I'm here.'

They stepped back through the door, and invited him in.

And so the battle lines were drawn. That afternoon commenced the strangest collaboration Robin had ever witnessed. Men who weeks ago had been screaming obscenities at Babel students now sat in the lobby among them, talking over tactics of street warfare and barrier integrity. Professor Craft and a striker named Maurice Long stood with their heads bent over a map of Oxford, discussing ideal locations for more barriers to block off Army entry points. 'Barricades are the only good thing we ever imported from the French,' Maurice was saying.* 'Over the

---

* The tactics of revolt spread fast. The British textile workers picked up these techniques of barricade from the 1831 and 1834 Canut revolts by silk workers in Lyon. Those revolts had been brutally repressed – but, crucially, they did not hold the backbone of the entire nation hostage.

wide roads, we want low-level obstructions – paving stones, overturned trees, that sort of thing. It takes time to clear, and it keeps them from bringing in horses or heavy artillery. And here, if we cut off the narrower access points around the quadrangle, we can keep them restricted to High Street . . ."*

Victoire and Ibrahim sat at a table with several other strikers, dutifully taking down notes on what sort of silver bars might best aid their defences. The word *barrels* came up quite a lot; Robin, eavesdropping, gathered they were planning to raid some wine cellars for structural reinforcements.†

'How many nights are you going to stay here?' Abel gestured around the lobby.

'As long as it takes,' said Robin. 'That's the key; they can try everything they've got, but they're hamstrung as long as we have the tower.'

'Do you have beds in here?'

'Not really. There's a cot we take turns using, but mostly we just curl up in the stacks.'

'Can't be comfortable.'

'Not at all.' Robin gave him a wry smile. 'Keep getting stepped on when someone heads down to use the toilet.'

Abel hummed. His eyes roved around the expansive lobby, the polished mahogany shelves, and the pristine marble flooring. 'Quite the sacrifice.'

*   *   *

---

* If this organizational competence strikes one as surprising, remember that both Babel and the British government made a great mistake in assuming all antisilver movements of the century were spontaneous riots carried out by uneducated, discontented lowlifes. For instance, the Luddites, so maligned as technology-fearing machine breakers, were a highly sophisticated insurrectionary movement, composed of small, well-disciplined groups who used disguises and watchwords, raised funds and gathered arms, terrorized their opponents, and carried out well-planned, targeted attacks. (And, while it is true the Luddite movement ultimately failed, it was only after Parliament had mobilized twelve thousand troops to put it down – more troops than had fought in the Peninsular War.) It was this level of training and professionalism that Abel's men brought to the Babel strike.

† *Barricade* comes from the Spanish *barrica*, meaning 'barrel', the basic building block of the first barricades. Besides their historical significance, barrels made for good barricade material for several reasons: they were easy to transport, easy to fill with sand or rocks, and easy to stack in ways that left portholes for snipers stationed behind them.

The British Army marched into Oxford that evening.

The scholars watched from the rooftop as red-coated troops rolled in a single column along High Street. The arrival of an armed platoon ought to have been a grand occasion, but it was hard to feel any real fear. The troops looked rather out of place among the townhouses and shops of the city centre, and the townspeople who turned out to cheer their arrival made them look more like a parade than a punitive military force. They marched slowly, making way for civilians crossing the street. It was all rather quaint and polite.

They halted when they reached the barricades. The commander, a richly mustachioed fellow decked out in medals, dismounted from his horse and strode to the first upturned wagon. He seemed deeply confused by this. He glanced around at the watching townspeople, as if awaiting some explanation.

'Do you think that's Lord Hill?' Juliana wondered.

'He's the Commander in Chief,' said Professor Chakravarti. 'They're not going to send in the Commander in Chief to deal with us.'

'They ought to,' said Robin. 'We're a threat to national security.'

'Don't be so dramatic.' Victoire hushed them. 'Look, they're talking.'

Abel Goodfellow strode out alone from behind the barricade.

The commander met Abel in the middle of the street. They exchanged words. Robin could not hear what they were saying, but the conversation seemed heated. It began in a civil manner, but then both men started gesticulating wildly; at several points he was afraid the commander was about to put Abel in handcuffs. At last they came to some agreement. Abel retreated behind the barricade, walking backwards as if making sure no one shot him in the back. The mustachioed commander returned to his battalion. Then, to Robin's amazement, the Army began to retreat.

'He's given us forty-eight hours to clear out,' Abel reported upon his return to the tower lobby. 'After that, he says they're going to forcibly clear the barricades.'

'So we've only got two days,' said Robin. 'That's not enough time.'

'More than that,' said Abel. 'This is all going to play out in fits and starts. They'll give another warning. Then another. Then a third, strongly worded this time. They'll drag their feet for as long as they can. If they were planning to storm us, they would have done so right then and there.'

'They were perfectly happy shooting on the Swing Rioters,' said Victoire. 'And the Blanketeers.'

'Those weren't riots over territory,' said Abel. 'Those were riots over policies. The rioters didn't need to hold their ground; when they were fired upon, they scattered. But we're embedded in the heart of a city. We've staked our claim on the tower, and on Oxford itself. If any of those soldiers accidentally strikes a bystander, this spirals out of their control. They can't break the barricades without breaking the city. And that, I think, Parliament cannot afford.' He rose to leave. 'We'll keep them out. You keep writing your pamphlets.'

So this, an impasse between the strikers and the Army at the barricades on High Street, became their new status quo.

When it came down to it, the tower itself would provide much better protection than Abel Goodfellow's hotchpotch obstructions could. But the barricades had more than mere symbolic value. They covered an area large enough to allow crucial supply lines in and out of the tower. This meant the scholars now got fresh food and fresh water (dinner that night was a bounty of fluffy white rolls and roast chicken), and it meant they had a reliable source for information on what was going on beyond the tower walls.

Despite all expectations, Abel's supporters grew in number over the following days. The workmen strikers were better at getting the message out than any of Robin's pamphlets. They spoke the same language, after all. The British could identify with Abel in a way they could not with foreign-born translators. Striking labourers from all over England came to join their cause. Young Oxford boys, bored with being cooped up at home and looking for something to do, turned up to the barricades simply because it seemed exciting. Women joined the ranks as well, out-of-work seamstresses and factory girls.

What a sight, this influx of defenders to the tower. The barricades had the peculiar effect of building community. They were all comrades in arms behind those walls, no matter their origins, and the regular deliveries of foodstuffs to the tower came with handwritten messages of encouragement. Robin had expected only violence, not solidarity, and he wasn't sure what to do with this show of support. It defied what he had come to expect of the world. He was scared to let it make him hope.

One morning he discovered Abel had left them a gift – a wagon deposited before the tower doors, piled high with mattresses, pillows, and homespun blankets. A scrawled note was pinned to the top. *This is on loan*, it said. *We'll want these back when you're done.*

Meanwhile, inside the tower, they devoted themselves to making London fear the costs of prolonged striking.

Silver afforded London all of its modern conveniences. Silver powered the ice-making machines in the kitchens of London's rich. Silver powered the engines of the breweries which supplied London's pubs, and the mills which produced London's flour. Without silver, the locomotives would cease to run. No new railways could be built. The water would run foul; the air would thicken with grime. When all the machines that mechanized the processes of spinning, weaving, carding, and roving ground to a halt, Britain's textile industry would wholly collapse. The entire country faced possible starvation, for there was silver in the plough-frames, seed drills, threshing machines, and drainage pipes throughout Britain's countryside.*

These effects would not be fully felt for months. There were still regional silver-working centres in London, Liverpool, Edinburgh, and Birmingham, where Babel scholars who hadn't dazzled enough during their undergraduate years to win fellowships eked out a mundane living fiddling with the bars invented by their more talented peers. These centres would function as a stopgap in the interim. But they could not

---

* Crucially, everything that ran on steam power was in trouble. Professor Lovell, it turned out, had made the majority of his fortune by turning steam power from a fussy and complicated technology to a reliable source of energy that powered nearly the whole of the British fleet. His great innovation had actually been quite simple: in Chinese, the character for *vapour* was 气 (*qì*), which also bore connotations of spirit and energy. When installed on the engines devised by Richard Trevithick some decades earlier, it produced a shocking amount of energy at a fraction of the cost in coal. (Researchers in the 1830s had explored applications of this match-pair in aerial transportation, but they hadn't got very far as the balloons kept either exploding or shooting into the stratosphere.)

This single invention, some argued, explained Britain's victory at Trafalgar. Now all of England ran on steam. Steam locomotives had displaced many horse-drawn vehicles; steam-engine ships had mostly displaced sails. But Britain had very few Chinese translators indeed, and, with the exception of Robin and Professor Chakravarti, all the other translators were, unhelpfully, dead or abroad. Without scheduled maintenance, steam power would not fail to work entirely, but it would lose its unique power; it's incredible efficiency that put British ships in a league beyond anything the American or Spanish fleets could achieve.

fully make up the deficit – especially since, crucially, they did not have access to the same maintenance ledgers.

'Don't you think they'll remember?' asked Robin. 'At least, the scholars who walked out with Professor Playfair?'

'They're academics,' said Professor Craft. 'All we know is the life of the mind. We don't remember anything unless it's written in our diaries and circled several times over. Jerome will do his very best, supposing he's not still drugged up from surgery, but too much will slip through the cracks. This country's going to pieces in months.'

'And the economy is going to fail even more quickly than that,' said Yusuf, who, alone among them, actually knew something about markets and banking. 'It's all the speculation, see – people have been going mad buying shares in railways and other silver-powered industries in the past decade because they all think they're on the verge of getting rich. What happens when they realize all those shares will come to naught? The rail industry might take months to falter. The markets themselves will fail in weeks.'

Market failure. The thought was absurd, yet tantalizing. Could they win this with the threat of a stock market collapse and the inevitable bank run?

For that was the key, wasn't it? For this to work, they had to frighten the rich and powerful. They knew the strike would have a disproportionate impact on the working poor; those living in the dirtiest, most crowded parts of London, who could not simply pack up and escape to the country when their air blackened and their water grew foul. But in another important sense, silver scarcity would most acutely hit those who had the most to gain from its development. The newest buildings – the private clubs, the dance halls, the freshly renovated theatres – would collapse first. London's shabby tenements were built from ordinary lumber, not foundations enhanced by silver to support weight much heavier than natural materials could. The architect Augustus Pugin was a frequent collaborator of Babel's faculty, and had made great use of silver bars in his recent projects – Scarisbrick Hall in Lancashire, the Alton Towers renovation, and most notably, the rebuilding of the Palace of Westminster after the 1834 fire. According to the work-order ledgers, all these buildings would fail by the end of the year. Sooner, if the right rods were pulled away.

How would London's wealthy respond when the ground gave way beneath their feet?

The strikers gave fair warning. They loudly advertised this information. They wrote endless pamphlets, which Abel communicated to associates in London. *Your roads will fail*, they wrote. *Your water will run dry. Your lights will go dark, your food will rot, and your ships sink. All this will come to pass, unless you choose peace.*

'It's like the Ten Plagues,' Victoire observed.

Robin had not cracked open a Bible in years. 'The Ten Plagues?'

'Moses asked Pharaoh to let his people go,' said Victoire. 'But Pharaoh's heart was unyielding, and he refused. So the Lord cast ten plagues on the Pharaoh's land. He turned the Nile to blood. He sent locusts, frogs, and pestilence. He cast all of Egypt into darkness, and through these feats he made Pharaoh know his power.'

'And did Pharaoh let them go?' Robin asked.

'He did,' said Victoire. 'But only after the tenth plague. Only after he had suffered the death of his firstborn son.'

Occasionally the effects of the strike reversed themselves. Sometimes the lights would flicker back on for a night, or a patchwork of roads would clear up, or news would spread that clean water silver-work was now available and selling at exorbitant prices in certain neighbourhoods of London. Occasionally the disaster the ledgers predicted did not come to pass.

This was not a surprise. The exiled scholars – Professor De Vreese, Professor Harding, and all the faculty and fellows who had not remained in the tower – had regrouped in London and established a defence society to counteract the strikers. The country now lay in the throes of an invisible battle of words and meaning; its fate teetered between the university centre and the desperate, striving periphery.

The strikers were not concerned. The exiles could not win; they simply lacked the tower's resources. They could stick their fingers in the mud. They could not stop the river from flowing, nor the dam from bursting.

'It's very embarrassing,' Victoire observed one afternoon over tea, 'how much it all depends on Oxford, in the end. You'd think they would have known better than to put all their eggs in one basket.'

'Well, it's just so funny,' said Professor Chakravarti. 'Technically, those supplementary stations do exist, precisely to alleviate such a crisis of dependence. Cambridge, for example, has been trying to establish a rival programme for years. But Oxford wouldn't share any resources.'

'Because of scarcity?' Robin asked.

'Because of jealousy and avarice,' said Professor Craft. 'Scarcity's never been an issue.' We simply don't like the Cambridge scholars. Nasty little upstarts, thinking they can make it on their own.'

'No one goes to Cambridge unless they can't find a job here,' Professor Chakravarti said. 'Sad.'

Robin cast them an amazed look. 'Are you telling me this country's going to fall because of academic territoriality?'

'Well, yes.' Professor Craft lifted her teacup to her lips. 'It's Oxford, what did you expect?'

Still Parliament refused to cooperate. Every night the Foreign Office sent them the same telegram, always worded in precisely the same way, as if shouting a message over and over again could induce obedience: CEASE STRIKE NOW STOP. In a week, these offers stopped including an offer of amnesty. Shortly after that, they came with a rather redundant threat attached: CEASE STRIKE NOW STOP OR ARMY WILL TAKE BACK THE TOWER STOP.

Very soon the effects of their strike became deadly.[†] One of the major breaking points, it turned out, was the roads. In Oxford, but even more so in London, traffic was the dominant problem facing city officials – how to manage the flow of carts, horses, pedestrians, stagecoaches, hackney carriages, and wagons without gridlock or accidents. Silver-work had kept pile-ups at bay by reinforcing wooden roads, regulating turnpikes, reinforcing toll gates and bridges, ensuring smooth turns by carts, replenishing the water pumps meant for suppressing dust, and keeping

---

[*] The Baresch alphabet used on the resonance rods, for instance, is not strictly necessary to their function; it was created by Babel scholars solely so that its proprietary resonance technology would remain inscrutable to outsiders. It is astounding, in truth, how much of academia's perceived resource scarcity is artificially constructed.

[†] Abel brought them a running stream of gruesome updates. On the Cherwell, a houseboat collided with a transport barge when the navigation systems of both failed, causing a steaming pile-up in the middle of the river. Three people died, trapped in submerged cabins. Up in Jericho, a four-year-old child was crushed under the wheels of a carriage which ran amok. Out in Kensington, a seventeen-year-old girl and her lover were buried alive when the ruins of a church tower collapsed above them during a midnight tryst.

horses docile. Without Babel maintenance, all of these minute adjustments began to fail one by one, and dozens died as a result.

Transportation tipped the domino that led to a slew of other miseries. Grocers could not stock their shelves. Bakers could not obtain flour.
Doctors could not see their patients. Solicitors could not make it to court.
A dozen carriages in London's richer neighbourhoods had made use of
a match-pair by Professor Lovell that played on the Chinese character
辅 (*fǔ*), which meant 'to help' or 'to assist'. The character had originally
referred to the protective sidebars on a carriage. Professor Lovell had
been due in London to touch them up mid-January. The bars failed. The
carriages were now too dangerous to drive.*

Everything they knew would transpire in London was already happening in Oxford, for Oxford, by proximity to Babel, was the most
silver-reliant city in the world. And Oxford was rotting. Its people were
going broke, they were hungry, their trades had been interrupted, their
rivers were blocked up, their markets had shut down. They sent out to
London for food and supplies, but the roads had become perilous, and
the Oxford-to-Paddington line was no longer running.

The attacks on the tower redoubled. Townspeople and soldiers
together crowded the streets, shouting obscenities at the windows, skirmishing with men at the barricades. But it made no difference. They
could not hurt the translators, who were the only people who could end
their misery. They could not get past the tower's wards, could not burn
it down or set explosives at its base. They could only beg the scholars
to stop.

We only have two demands, Robin wrote in a series of pamphlets, which
had become his way of responding to the town's outcries. *Parliament
knows this. Refusal to go to war, and amnesty. Your fate lies in their hands.*

He requested that London capitulate before all these things came to
pass. He hoped, and knew, they would not. He had fully converted now
to Griffin's theory of violence, that the oppressor would never sit down
at the negotiating table when they still thought they had nothing to

---

* On a Wednesday, two carts collided, one of which was loaded with barrels of fine
brandy. When the sweet fumes leaked out onto the street, a small crowd of bystanders rushed in to scoop up the brandy with their hands, and it was all good fun until
a man with a lit pipe walked into the fray, turning the street into a conflagration of
people, horses, and exploding barrels.

lose. No; things had to get bloody. Until now, all threats had been hypo-thetical. London had to suffer to learn.

Victoire did not like this. Every time they ascended to the eighth floor, they quarrelled over which resonance bars to pull out, and how many. He wanted to deactivate two dozen; she wanted only two. Usually, they settled on five or six.

'You're pushing things too fast,' she said. 'You haven't even given them a chance to respond.'

'They can respond whenever they like,' said Robin. 'What's stopping them? Meanwhile, the Army's already here—'

'The Army's here because you pushed them to it.'

He made an impatient noise. 'I'm sorry I won't be squeamish—'

'I'm not being *squeamish*; I'm being prudent.' Victoire folded her arms. 'It's too fast, Robin. It's too much all at once. You need to let the debates settle. You need to let public opinion turn against the war—'

'It's not enough,' he insisted. 'They won't reason themselves into justice now when they never have before. Fear's the only thing that works. This is just *tactics*—'

'This is not coming from tactics.' Her voice sharpened. 'It's coming from grief.'

He couldn't turn around. He didn't want her to see his expression. 'You said yourself you wanted this place to burn.'

'But even more,' said Victoire, placing a hand on his shoulder, 'I want us to survive.'

It was impossible to say, in the end, how much of a difference the pace of their destruction really made. The choice remained with Parliament. The debates continued in London.

No one knew what was going on inside the House of Lords, except that neither the Whigs nor the Radicals felt good enough about their numbers yet to call a vote. The papers revealed more about public senti-ment. The mainstream rags expressed the opinion Robin had expected, which was that the war on China was a matter of defending national pride, that invasion was nothing more than a just punishment for the indignities imposed by the Chinese on the British flag, that the occu-pation of Babel by foreign-born students was an act of treason, that the barricades in Oxford and the strikes in London were the work of brutish malcontents, and that the government ought to hold firm against their demands. Prowar editorials stressed the ease with which China would be defeated. It would only be a little war, and not even a proper war at that; all it took was the ignition of several cannons and the Chinese would admit defeat within a day.

The papers could not seem to make up their minds about the translators. The prowar publications offered a dozen theories. They were in cahoots with the corrupt Chinese government. They were co-conspirators of mutineers in India. They were malicious ingrates with no agenda at all except a desire to hurt England, to bite the hand that had fed them – and this required no further explanation, for it was a motive that the British public were all too ready to believe. *We will not negotiate with Babel*, promised members of Parliament on both sides. *Britain does not bow to foreigners.**

Yet not all the papers were against Babel or for the war. Indeed, for every headline that urged swift action in Canton, there was another by a publication (albeit smaller, more niche, more radical) that called the war a moral and religious outrage. The *Spectator* accused the prowar party of greed and profiteering; the *Examiner* called the war criminal and indefensible. JARDINE'S OPIUM WAR A DISGRACE, read one headline by the *Champion*. Others were not so tactful: DRUGGY MCDRUGGY WANTS HIS THUMBS IN CHINA read the *Political Register*.

---

* The papers always referred to the strikers as foreign; as Chinamen, Indians, Arabs, and Africans. (Never mind Professor Craft.) They were never Oxfordians, they were never Englishmen, they were travellers from abroad who had taken advantage of Oxford's good graces, and who now held the nation hostage. *Babel* had become synonymous with *foreign*, and this was very strange, because before this, the Royal Institute of Translation had always been regarded as a national treasure, a quintessentially English institution.

But then England, and the English language, had always been more indebted to the poor, the lowly, and the foreign than it cared to admit. The word *vernacular* came from the Latin *verna*, meaning 'house slave'; this emphasized the nativeness, the domesticity of the vernacular language. But the root *verna* also indicated the lowly origins of the language spoken by the powerful; the terms and phrases invented by slaves, labourers, beggars, and criminals – the vulgar cants, as it were – had infiltrated English until they became proper. And the English vernacular could not properly be called domestic either, because English etymology had roots all over the world. *Almanacs* and *algebra* came from Arabic; *pyjamas* from Sanskrit, *ketchup* from Chinese, and *paddies* from Malay. It was only when elite England's way of life was threatened that the true English, whoever they were, attempted to excise all that had made them.

Every social faction in England had an opinion. The abolitionists put
out statements of support for the strikers. So too did the suffragists,
though not quite so loudly. Christian organizations printed pamphlets
criticizing the spread of an illegal vice to an innocent people, though the
prowar evangelists responded with the supposedly Christian argument
that it would in fact be God's work to expose the Chinese people to
free trade.

Meanwhile, Radical publications made the argument that the opening
up of China was antithetical to the interests of workers in northern
England. The Chartists, a movement of disillusioned industrial and artisanal workers, came out most strongly in support of the strikers; the
Chartist circular *The Red Republican*, in fact, put out a headline calling
the translators heroes of the working class.

This gave Robin hope. The Radicals were, after all, the party that the
Whigs needed to appease, and if such headlines could convince the
Radicals that war was not in their long-term interests, then perhaps all
this could be resolved.

And indeed, the conversation about the dangers of silver-work had
fared better in the court of public opinion than did the conversation
about China. Here was an issue that was close to home, that affected
the average Briton in ways he could understand. The silver industrial
revolution had decimated both the textile and agricultural industries.
The papers ran piece after piece exposing the horrific working conditions inside silver-powered factories (although these had their rebut-
tals, including one refutation by Andrew Ure, who argued that factory
workers would feel a good deal better if they only consumed less gin and
tobacco). In 1833, the surgeon Peter Gaskell had published a thoroughly
researched manuscript entitled *The Manufacturing Population of England*,
focusing chiefly on the moral, social, and physical toll of silver-working
machinery on British labourers. It had gone largely unheeded at the
time, except by the Radicals, who were known to exaggerate everything.
Now, the antiwar papers ran excerpts from it every day, reporting in
grisly detail the coal dust inhaled by small children forced to wriggle into
tunnels that adults could not, the fingers and toes lost to silver-powered
machines working at inhuman speeds, the girls who'd been strangled by
their own hair caught in whirring spindles and looms.

The *Spectator* printed a cartoon illustration of emaciated children
being crushed to death under the wheels of some nebulous contraption,

which they captioned **WHITE SLAVES OF THE SILVER REVOLU-TION**. In the tower, they laughed themselves silly over this comparison, but the general public seemed genuinely horrified. Someone asked a member of the House of Lords why he supported exploiting children in factories; he replied quite flippantly that employing children under the age of nine had been outlawed in 1833, which led to more general outcry over the suffering of ten- and eleven-year-olds in the country.

'Is it really as bad as all that?' Robin asked Abel. 'The factories, I mean.'

'Worse,' said Abel. 'Those are just the freak accidents they're reporting on. But they don't say what it's like to work day after day on those cramped floors. Rising before dawn and working until nine with few breaks in between. And those are the conditions we *covet*. The jobs we wish we could get back. I imagine they don't make you work half as hard at university, do they?'

'No,' said Robin, feeling embarrassed. 'They don't.'

The *Spectator* story seemed to greatly affect Professor Craft in particular. Robin found her sitting with it at the tea table, red in the eyes, long after the others had finished their breakfast. She hastily wiped her eyes with a handkerchief when she saw him approach.

He sat down beside her. 'Are you all right, Professor?'

'Oh, yes.' She cleared her throat, paused, then nudged the paper. 'It's just . . . it's a side of the story we don't often think about, isn't it?'

'I think we all got good at choosing not to think about certain things.'

She seemed not to hear him. She stared out of the window at the green below, where the strikers' protest grounds had been turned into what looked like a military camp. 'My first patented match-pair improved the efficiency of equipment at a mine in Tyneshire,' she said. 'It kept coal-laden trolleys firmly on their tracks. The mine owners were so impressed they invited me up for a visit, and of course I went; I was so excited about contributing something to the country. I remember being shocked at all the little children in the pits. When I asked, the miners said that they were completely safe, and that helping out in the mines kept them from trouble when their parents were at work.'

She took a shaky breath. 'Later they told me that the silver-work made the trolleys impossible to move off the tracks, even when there were people in the way. There was an accident. One little boy lost both his legs. They stopped using the match-pair when they couldn't figure out a workaround, but I didn't give it a second thought. By then I'd received my fellowship. I had a professorship in sight, and I'd moved on to other, bigger projects. I didn't think about it. I simply didn't think about it, for years, and years and years.'

She turned back towards him. Her eyes were wet. 'Only it builds up, doesn't it? It doesn't just disappear. And one day you start prodding at what you've suppressed. And it's a mass of black rot, and it's endless, horrifying, and you can't look away.'

'Jesus Christ,' said Robin.

Victoire glanced up. 'What is it?'

They were holed up in an office on the sixth floor, poring through the ledgers to find portents of future disasters. They'd already been through the Oxford town appointments up to the next year. London's maintenance schedules were harder to find – Babel's bookkeeping was astonishingly bad, and the categorization system used by its clerks seemed not to be organized by date, which would have been logical, or by language, which would have made less but at least some sense, but by the postal code of the London neighbourhood in question.

Robin tapped his ledger. 'I think we might be close to a breaking point.'

'Why?'

'They're due for maintenance on Westminster Bridge in a week. They contracted for silver-work at the same time that the New London Bridge was built in 1825, and the bars were meant to expire after fifteen years. That's now.'

'So what happens?' asked Victoire. 'The turnstiles lock in?'

'I don't think so, it was quite a major . . . *F* is code for *foundation*, isn't it?' Robin trailed off, then fell silent. His eyes darted up and down the ledger, trying to confirm what was in front of him. It was quite a large entry, a list of silver bars and match-pairs in various languages that stretched nearly half a page. A good number of them had corresponding numbers in a subsequent column – an indication they employed resonance links. He turned the page, then blinked. The column continued over the next two pages. 'I think it just falls right into the river.'

Victoire leaned back and exhaled very slowly, deflating.

The implications were enormous. Westminster Bridge was not the only bridge to cross the Thames, but it saw the heaviest traffic. And if Westminster Bridge fell into the river, then no steamers, no house-boats, no sculls or canoes would be able to get around the wreckage. If Westminster Bridge went down, the whole city stopped moving.

And in the weeks to come, when the bars that kept the Thames clean of sewage and pollution from gas factories and chemical works at last expired, the waters would revert to a state of diseased and putrid fermentation. Fish would float belly-up to the surface, dead and stinking. Urine and feces, already moving sluggishly through sewer drains, would solidify.

Egypt would suffer her ten plagues.

But as Robin explained this, Victoire's face mirrored none of his glee. Rather, she was looking at him with a very odd expression, brows furrowed and lips pursed, and it turned his insides with discomfort.

'It's Armageddon,' he insisted, spreading his hands in the air. How could he make her see? 'It's the worst possible thing that could happen.'

'I know,' she said. 'Except once you've played it, we've nothing left.'

'We won't need anything else,' he said. 'We only need to turn the screws once, to push them to the limit—'

'A limit you know they'll ignore? Please, Robin—'

'Then what's the alternative? Defanging ourselves?'

'It's giving them *time*, it's letting them see the consequences—'

'What more is there to see?' He had not meant to yell. He took a deep breath. 'Victoire, please, I just think we need to escalate, otherwise—'

'I think you want it to fall,' she accused. 'I think this is just retribution for you, because you want to see it fall.'

'And why *not*?'

They'd had this argument before. The ghosts of Anthony and Griffin loomed between them: one guided by the conviction that the enemy would at least act in rational self-interest, if not altruism, and the other guided less by conviction, less by telos, and more by sheer, untrammelled rage.

'I know it hurts.' Victoire's throat pulsed. 'I know – I know it feels impossible to move on. But your motivating goal cannot be to join Ramy.'

A silence. Robin considered denying this. But there was no point lying to Victoire, or to himself.

'Doesn't it kill you?' His voice broke. 'Knowing what they've done? Seeing their faces? I can't imagine a world where we coexist with them. Doesn't it split you apart?'

'Of course it does,' she cried. 'But that's no excuse not to keep living.'

'I'm not trying to die.'

'What do you think making this bridge collapse does, then? What do you think they'll do to us?'

'What would you do?' he asked. 'End this strike? Open up the tower?'

'If I tried,' she said, 'could you stop me?'

They both stared at the ledger. Neither of them spoke for a very long time. They did not want to follow this conversation where it might lead. Neither of them could bear any more heartbreak.

'A vote,' Robin proposed at last, unable to take this any longer. 'We can't – we can't just break the strike like this. It's not up to us. Let's not decide, Victoire.'

Victoire's shoulders sagged. He saw such sorrow on her face. She lifted her chin, and for a moment he thought she might argue further, but all she did then was nod.

The vote came out narrowly in Robin's favour. Victoire and the professors were against; all the students were for. The students agreed with Robin that they had to push Parliament to the breaking point, but they were not thrilled about it. Ibrahim and Juliana both hugged their arms against their chest as they voted, as if shrinking from the idea. Even Yusuf, who usually took great pleasure in helping Robin compose threatening pamphlets to London, stared down at his feet.

'So that's that,' said Robin. He'd won, but it did not feel like such a victory. He could not meet Victoire's eye.

'When does this happen?' Professor Chakravarti asked.

'This Saturday,' Robin said. 'The timing's marvellous.'

'But Parliament isn't going to capitulate by Saturday.'

'Then I suppose we'll hear about the bridge when it's collapsed.'

'And you are comfortable with this?' Professor Chakravarti glanced about, as if trying to gauge the moral temperature of the room. 'Dozens of people will die. There are whole crowds there trying to get on boats at all times of day; what happens when—'

'That's not our choice,' said Robin. 'It's theirs. It's inaction. It's killing by letting die. We're not even touching the resonance rods, it's going to fall on its own—'

'You know very well that doesn't matter,' said Professor Chakravarti. 'Don't mince the ethics. Westminster Bridge falling down is your choice. But innocent people can't determine the whims of Parliament.'

'But it's their government's duty to look out for them,' said Robin. 'That's the entire point of Parliament, isn't it? Meanwhile, we don't have the option of civility. Or grace. It's an indiscriminate torch, I'll admit that, but that's what the stakes demand. You can't put the moral blame on me.' He swallowed. 'You can't.'

'You are the proximate cause,' insisted Professor Chakravarti. 'You can make it stop.'

'But that's precisely the devil's trick,' Robin insisted. 'This is how colonialism works. It convinces us that the fallout from resistance is entirely our fault, that the immoral choice is resistance itself rather than the circumstances that demanded it.'

'Even so, there are lines you can't cross.'

'Lines? If we play by the rules, then they've already won—'

'You're trying to win by punishing the city,' said Professor Chakravarti. 'That means the whole city, everyone in it – men, women, children. There are sick children who can't get their medicine. There are whole families with no income and no source of food. This is more than an inconvenience to them, it's a death threat.'

'I know,' said Robin, frustrated. 'That's the point.'

They glared at each other, and Robin thought he understood now the way that Griffin had once looked at him. This was a failure of nerve. A refusal to push things to the limit. Violence was the only thing that brought the colonizer to the table; violence was the only option. The gun was right there, lying on the table, waiting for them to pick it up. Why were they so afraid to even look at it?

Professor Chakravarti stood. 'I can't follow you down this path.'

'Then you ought to leave the tower,' Robin said promptly. 'It'll help keep your conscience clear.'

'Mr Swift, please, listen to reason—'

'Turn out your pockets.' Robin raised his voice, speaking over the ringing in his ears. 'Take nothing with you – not silver, not ledgers, not notes you've written to yourself.' He kept waiting for someone to interrupt him; for Victoire to intervene, to tell him he was wrong, but no one spoke. He took this silence as tacit approval. 'And if you leave, I'm sure you know, you can't come back.'

'There is no path to victory here,' warned Professor Chakravarti. 'This will only make them hate you.'

Robin scoffed. 'They can't hate us any more than they do.'

But no, that was not true; they both knew it. The British did not hate them, because hate was bound up with fear and resentment, and both required seeing your opponent as a morally autonomous being, worthy of respect and rivalry. The attitude the British held towards the Chinese was patronizing, was dismissive; but it was not hatred. Not yet.

That might change after the bridge fell.

But then, Robin thought, invoking hatred might be good. Hatred might force respect. Hatred might force the British to look them in the eyes and see not an object, but a person. *Violence shocks the system*, Griffin had told him. *And the system cannot survive the shock.*

'*Oderint dum metuant*,' he said.* 'That's our path to victory.'

'That's Caligula,' said Professor Chakravarti. 'You're invoking *Caligula*?'

'Caligula got his way.'

'Caligula was assassinated.'

Robin shrugged, wholly unbothered.

'You know,' said Professor Chakravarti, 'you know, one of the most commonly misunderstood Sanskrit concepts is *ahimsa*. Nonviolence.'

'I don't need a lecture, sir,' said Robin, but Professor Chakravarti spoke over him.

'Many think *ahimsa* means absolute pacifism, and that the Indian people are therefore a sheepish, submissive people who will bend the knee to anything. But in the *Bhagavad Gita*, exceptions are made for a *dharma yuddha*. A righteous war. A war in which violence is applied as the last resort, a war fought not for selfish gain or personal motives but from a commitment to a greater cause.' He shook his head. 'This is how I have justified this strike, Mr Swift. But what you're doing here is not self-defence; it has trespassed into malice. Your violence is personal, it is vindictive, and this I cannot support.'

Robin's throat pulsed. 'Then take your blood vial before you go, sir.'

Professor Chakravarti examined him for a moment, nodded, and then began turning out the contents of his pockets onto the middle table. A pencil. A notebook. Two blank silver bars.

Everyone watched, silent.

---

* 'Let them hate, so long as they fear.'

Robin felt a flash of irritation. 'Would anyone else like to voice a complaint?' he snapped.

No one else said a word. Professor Craft stood and walked away up the stairs. A moment later, Ibrahim joined her, then Juliana; and then the rest until only Robin and Victoire stood in the lobby, watching Professor Chakravarti stride down the front steps towards the barricades.

CHAPTER TWENTY-NINE

How the Chimney-sweepers cry
Every blackning Church appalls,
And the hapless Soldiers sigh
Runs in blood down Palace walls

WILLIAM BLAKE, 'London'

The mood in the tower turned sombre after Professor Chakravarti left.

In the early days of the strike, they'd been too occupied with the exigencies of their situation – with pamphleteering, ledgers research, and barricade fortifications – to pay attention to the sheer danger they were in. It had all been so monumental, so unifying. They'd delighted in each other's company. They'd talked long into the nights, learning about one another, marvelling at how astonishingly similar their histories were. They'd been plucked from their motherlands at a very young age, thrown into England, and instructed to thrive or be deported. So many of them were orphans, all ties to their countries severed except that of language.*

But the frantic preparations of those early days had now given way to gloomy, suffocating hours. All the pieces had been laid on the board; all hands were shown. They had no threats left to make other than ones they'd already shouted from the rooftops. What stretched before them now was only time, a ticking down to the inevitable collapse.

---

* But that was part of the genius of Babel. By keeping them isolated, by distracting them with coursework so that they never had the chance to form bonds outside their cohort, it had cut off all avenues towards meaningful solidarity, had made them believe for so long that they were the only ones caught in their particular web.

They'd issued their ultimatum, sent out their pamphlets. Westminster Bridge fell in seven days, unless. Unless.

This decision had left a bad taste in their mouths. They'd said all there was to say, and no one wanted pick apart the implications. Introspection was dangerous; they only wanted to get through the day. Now, more often than not, they drifted to separate corners of the tower, reading or researching or doing whatever it was they did to make the time pass. Ibrahim and Juliana spent all their waking hours together. Sometimes the rest of them speculated whether the two might be falling in love, but they found they could never sustain that conversation; it made them think of the future, of how this might all end up, and that made them too sad. Yusuf kept to himself. Meghana occasionally took tea with Robin and Victoire, and they would exchange stories about their over-lapping acquaintances – she'd graduated recently, and had been close to both Vimal and Anthony – but as the days drew on she also started withdrawing into herself. And Robin wondered, sometimes, whether she and Yusuf were now regretting their decision to stay.

Life in the tower, life on strike – at first so novel and strangely excit-ing – took on a routine, monotonous air. Things were hard going at first. It was both funny and embarrassing, how little they'd learned about how to keep their living quarters in order. No one knew where the brooms were kept, so the floors remained dusty and littered with crumbs. No one knew how to do laundry – they tried producing a match-pair using the word *bleach* and words derived from the Proto-Indo-European root *bhel* ('shining white, to flash, to burn'), but all this did was temporarily turn their clothes white and scorching-hot to the touch.

They still congregated for meals three times a day on the hour, if only because that made rationing simpler. Their luxury items had quickly dis-appeared. There was no coffee after the first week; they were close to running out of tea by the second. Their solution to this was to dilute the tea more and more until they were drinking little more than slightly dis-coloured water. There was no milk or sugar to speak of. Meghana argued they ought to just enjoy the last few teaspoons in a properly, full-brewed cup, but Professor Craft vehemently disagreed.

'I can give up milk,' she said. 'But I cannot give up tea.'

Victoire was Robin's anchor during that week.

She was furious with him, he knew. The first two days they spent together in begrudging silence – but together, still, because they needed each other for solace. They spent hours by the sixth-floor window, sitting shoulder to shoulder on the floor. He did not press his point. She made no recriminations. There was nothing more to say. The course was set.

By the third day the silence became unbearable, so they began to talk; small nothings at first, and then everything that came to mind. Sometimes they reminisced about Babel, about the golden years before everything turned upside down. Sometimes they suspended reality, managed to forget everything that had happened, and gossiped about their college days as if the most important matter at hand was whether Colin Thornhill and the Sharp twins would get into fisticuffs over Bill Jameson's pretty, visiting sister.

It was four days before they could bring themselves to broach the subject of Letty.

Robin did it first. Letty had lingered in the back of both their memories like a festering sore they didn't dare touch, and he couldn't keep circling around it anymore. He wanted to take a burning knife and dig into the rot.

'Do you think she was always going to turn on us?' he asked. 'Do you think it was difficult for her, what she did?'

Victoire didn't need to ask who he meant. 'It was like an exercise in hope,' she said after a pause. 'Loving her, I mean. Sometimes I'd think she'd come around. Sometimes I'd look her in the eyes and think that I was looking at a true friend. Then she'd say something, make some off-the-cuff comment, and the whole cycle would begin all over again. It was like pouring sand into a sieve. Nothing stuck.'

'Do you think there's anything you could have said that might have changed her mind?'

'I don't know,' said Victoire. 'Do you?'

His mind did what it always did, which was to summon a Chinese character in lieu of the thought he was afraid of. 'When I think of Letty, I think about the character *xì*.' He drew it in the air for her: 隙. 'It's most commonly used to mean "a crack or a fissure". But in Classical Chinese texts, it also means "a grudge, or a feud". According to rumours, the Qing Emperor uses a bar engraved with the *xì-feud* match-pair installed under a stone mural of the imperial lineage. And when cracks appear, it shows that someone is plotting against him.' He swallowed. 'I think those cracks were always there. I don't think there's anything we could have done about them. And all it took was pressure for the whole thing to collapse.'

'You think she resented us that much?'

He paused, deliberating the weight and impact of his words. 'I think she killed him on purpose.'

Victoire observed him for a long moment before she responded, simply, 'Why?'

'I think she wanted him dead,' he continued hoarsely. 'You could see it on her face – she wasn't scared, she knew what she was doing, she could have aimed at any one of us, and she knew it was Ramy she wanted.'

'Robin ...'

'She loved him, you know,' he said. The words came out of him like a torrent now; the floodgates were broken, and the waters could not be stopped. No matter how devastating, how tragic, he had to say it out loud, had to burden someone else with this awful, awful suspicion. 'She told me, the night of the commemoration ball – she spent nearly an hour weeping into my shoulder because she wanted to dance with him, and he wouldn't even look at her. He never looked at her, he didn't ...' He had to stop; his tears threatened to choke him.

Victoire gripped his wrist. 'Oh, Robin.'

'Imagine that,' he said. 'A brown man refuses an English rose. Letty couldn't bear that. The humiliation.' He wiped his sleeve against his eyes. 'So she killed him.'

Victoire said nothing for a long time. She gazed out over the crumbling city, thinking. At last, she pulled a rumpled piece of paper from her pocket and pressed it into his hand. 'You should have this.'

Robin unfolded it. It was the daguerreotype portrait of the four of them, folded and refolded so many times that thin white lines crisscrossed the image. But their faces were printed so clearly. Letty, glaring proudly, her face a bit strained after such a long time. Ramy's hands affectionately on both her and Victoire's shoulders. Victoire's half-smile; chin tilted down, eyes raised and luminous. His own awkward shyness. Ramy's grin.

He took a sharp breath. His chest tightened, as if his ribs were constricting, squeezing his heart like a vice. He hadn't realized he could still hurt so much.

He wanted to rip it to shreds. But it was the only remaining likeness he had of Ramy.

'I hadn't realized you'd kept it.'

'Letty kept it,' said Victoire. 'She kept it framed in our room. I took it out the night before the garden party. I don't think she noticed.'

'We look so young.' He marvelled at their expressions. It seemed like a lifetime had passed since they'd posed for that daguerreotype. 'We look like children.'

'We were happy then.' Victoire glanced down, fingers tracing their fading faces. 'I thought about burning it, you know. I wanted the satisfaction. At Oxford Castle I kept taking it out, studying her face, trying to see . . . to see the person that would do this to us. But the more I look, the more I . . . I just feel sorry for her. It's twisted, but from her perspective, she must think she's the one who lost everything. She was so alone, you know. All she wanted was a group of friends, people who could understand what she'd been through. And she thought she'd finally found that in us.' She took a shaky breath. 'And I suppose, when it all fell apart – I suppose she felt just as betrayed as we did.'

Ibrahim, they noticed, spent a great deal of time writing in a leather-bound notebook.

'It's a chronicle,' he told them when asked. 'Of what happened inside the tower. Everything that was said. All the decisions that were made. Everything we stood for. Would you like to contribute?'

'As a co-author?' asked Robin.

'As an interview subject. Tell me your thoughts. I'll write them down.'

'Perhaps tomorrow.' Robin felt very tired, and for some reason the sight of those pages of scribbles filled him with dread.

'I only want to be thorough,' said Ibrahim. 'I've got Professor Craft's and the graduate fellows' statements already. I just thought – well, if this all turns upside down . . .'

'You think we're going to lose,' said Victoire.

'I think no one knows how this is going to end,' said Ibrahim. 'But I know what they'll say about us if it ends badly. When those students in Paris died at the barricades, everyone called them heroes. But if we die here, no one's going to think we're martyrs. And I just want to make sure some record of us exists, a record that doesn't make us out to be the villains.' Ibrahim glanced at Robin. 'But you don't like this project, do you?'

Had he been glaring? Robin hastily rearranged his face. 'I didn't say that.'

'You look repelled.'

'No, I'm sorry, I just . . .' Robin didn't know why he found it so hard to put the words together. 'I suppose I just don't like thinking of us as history when we haven't even yet made a mark on the present.'

'We've made our mark,' said Ibrahim. 'We're already in the history books, for better or for worse. Here's a chance to intervene against the archives, no?'

'What sort of things are going in it?' Victoire asked. 'Broad strokes only? Or personal observations?'

'Anything you like,' said Ibrahim. 'What you had for breakfast, if you want. How you while away the hours. But I'm most interested, of course, in how we all got here.'

'I suppose you want to know about Hermes,' said Robin.

'I want to know everything you'd care to tell me.'

Robin felt a very heavy weight on his chest then. He wanted to start talking, to spill out everything he knew and have it preserved in ink, but the words died on his tongue. He didn't know how to articulate that the problem was not the existence of the record itself, but the fact that it wasn't enough, that it was such an insufficient intervention against the archives that it felt pointless.

There was so much to say. He didn't know where to begin. He had never thought before about the lacuna of written history they existed in and the oppressive swath of denigrating narrative they fought against, and now that he did, it seemed insurmountable. The record was so blank. No chronicle of the Hermes Society existed at all except this one. Hermes had operated like the best of clandestine societies, erasing its own history even as it changed Britain's. No one would celebrate their achievements. No one would even know what they were.

He thought of the Old Library, destroyed and dismantled, all those mountains of research locked away and hidden forever from view. He thought of that envelope, lost to ash; of the dozens of Hermes associates who'd never been contacted, who might never know what had happened. He thought of all those years Griffin spent abroad – fighting, struggling, railing against a system that was infinitely more powerful than he was. Robin would never know the full extent of what his brother had done, what he'd suffered. So much history, erased.

'It just scares me,' he said. 'I don't want this to be all we ever were.'

Ibrahim nodded to his notebook. 'Worth getting some of it down, then.'

'It's a good idea.' Victoire took a seat. 'I'll play. Ask me anything. Let's see if we can change some future historian's mind.'

'Perhaps we'll be remembered like the Oxford Martyrs,' said Ibrahim. 'Perhaps we'll get a monument.'

'The Oxford Martyrs were tried for heresy and burned at the stake,' said Robin.

'Ah,' said Ibrahim, eyes twinkling. 'But Oxford's an Anglican university now, isn't it?'

Robin wondered in the days that followed if what they'd felt that night was a shared sense of mortality, akin to how soldiers felt sitting in trenches at war. For it was war, what was breaking out on those streets. Westminster Bridge had not fallen, not yet, but the accidents continued and the shortages grew worse. London's patience was strained. The public demanded retribution, demanded action, in some form or another. And since Parliament would not vote no on the China invasion, they simply increased their pressure on the Army.

It appeared the guardsmen had orders to leave the tower itself alone, but were permitted to aim at individual scholars when they got the chance. Robin stopped venturing outside when a rendezvous with Abel Goodfellow was interrupted by a spate of rifle fire. Once, a window shattered next to Victoire's head when she was searching the stacks for a book. They all dropped to the floor and crawled on hands and knees to the basement, where they were protected by walls on all sides. Later they found a bullet lodged in the shelf just behind where she'd been standing.

'How is this possible?' demanded Professor Craft. 'Nothing penetrates these windows. Nothing gets through these walls.'

Curious, Robin examined the bullet: thick, warped, and unnaturally cold to the touch. He held it up to the light and saw a thin band of silver lining the base of the casing. 'I suppose Professor Playfair thought of something.'

That raised the stakes. Babel was not impenetrable. This was not a strike any longer, but a siege. If the soldiers broke through the barricades, if soldiers wielding Professor Playfair's inventions reached the front door, their strike was effectively over. Professor Craft and Professor Chakravarti had replaced Professor Playfair's wards on their first night in the tower, but even they admitted they were not as good at this as Professor Playfair had been; they were not sure how well their own defences would hold up.

'Let's stay away from windows from now on,' Victoire suggested.

For now the barricades held, though outside, the skirmishing had turned vicious. Initially Abel Goodfellow's strikers had fought a purely defensive war from behind the barricades. They reinforced their structures, they ran supply lines, but they did not provoke the guardsmen. Now the streets had turned bloody. Soldiers fired regularly now on the barricaders, and the barricaders struck back in turn. They made incendiary devices with cloth, oil, and bottles and hurled them at the Army camps. They climbed the rooftops of the Radcliffe Library and the Bodleian, from which they threw paving stones and poured boiling water onto the troops below.

It shouldn't have been so evenly matched, civilians against guardsmen. In theory, they shouldn't have lasted a week. But many of Abel's men were veterans, men discharged from an army falling into disrepair after the defeat of Napoleon. They knew where to find firearms. They knew what to do with them.

The translators helped. Victoire, who'd been reading furiously through French dissident literature, composed the match-pair élan-*energy*, the latter of which bore connotations of a particular French revolutionary zeal, and which could be traced back to the Latin *lancea*, meaning 'lance'. Carried through was an association with throwing and momentum, and it was this latent distortion into the English *energy* that helped the barricaders' projectiles fly further, hit truer, and make more of an impact than bricks and cobblestones ought to have been able to do.

They'd come up with a few wilder ideas which bore no fruit. The word *seduce* came from the Latin *seducere*, meaning 'to lead astray', from which the late-fifteenth-century definition 'to persuade one to abandon their allegiance' came about. This seemed promising, but they could not think of a way to manifest it without sending the girls into the front lines, which no one was willing to suggest, or dressing up Abel's men in women's clothes, which seemed unlikely to work. There was also the German word *Nachtmahr*, a now rarely used word for 'nightmare', which also referred to a malicious entity that sat upon the sleeper's chest. Some experimentation proved this match-pair made bad dreams worse when one had them, but seemed unable to induce them in the first place.

One morning, Abel showed up in the lobby with several long, slender cloth-wrapped parcels. 'Can any of you shoot?' he asked.

Robin imagined aiming one of those rifles at a living body and pulling the trigger. He wasn't sure that he could do it. 'Not well.'

'Not with those,' said Victoire.

'Then let some of my men in there,' said Abel. 'You've got the best vantage point in the city. Pity if you don't use it.'

Day after day, the barricades held. Robin found it amazing that they didn't shatter under the weight of the near constant cannon fire, but Abel was confident they could hold out indefinitely as long as they kept scrounging up new materials to bolster the damaged sections.

'It's because we've built them in V-shaped structures,' he explained. 'The cannonballs hit the protrusion, which only packs the materials in more tightly.'

Robin was sceptical. 'They can't hold forever, though.'

'No, perhaps not.'

'And what happens when they come pouring through?' Robin asked. 'Will you flee? Or will you stay and fight?'

Abel was quiet for a moment. Then he said, 'At the French barricades, revolutionaries would march up to the soldiers with their shirts open and shout at them to shoot, if they dared.'

'Did they?'

'Sometimes. Sometimes they shot them dead on sight. But other times – well, think about it. You're looking someone in the eyes. They're around your age, or younger. From the same city. Possibly the same neighbourhood. Possibly you know them, or you see in their face someone you could know. Would you pull the trigger?'

'I suppose not,' Robin admitted, though a small voice in his mind whispered, *Letty did*.

'Every soldier's conscience has a limit,' said Abel. 'I suppose they'll try to arrest us. But firing on townspeople? Carrying out a massacre? I'm not so sure. But we'll force that split. We'll see what happens.'

It will all be over soon. They tried to reassure themselves at night when they looked out over the city, saw the torchlight and cannon fire burning bright. They needed only to hold out until Saturday. Parliament could not sustain this any longer than they could. They could not let Westminster Bridge fall.

Then, always, the strange, tentative imagining of what a ceasefire might look like. Should they write up a contract with terms of amnesty? Yusuf took charge of this, drafting a treaty that saved them from the gallows. When the tower resumed normal functioning, would they be a part of it? What did scholarship look like in the age after empire, when they knew Britain's silver stores would dwindle into nothing? They had never considered these questions before, but now, when the outcome of this strike stood on a razor's edge, their only comfort was in prognosticating the future in such detail that it seemed possible.

But Robin couldn't bring himself to try. He couldn't bear those conversations; he excused himself whenever they occurred.

There was no future without Ramy, without Griffin, without Anthony and Cathy and Ilse and Vimal. As far as he was concerned, time had stopped when Letty's bullet had left the chamber. All there was now was the fallout. What happened after was for someone else to struggle through. Robin only wanted it all to end.

Victoire found him on the rooftop, hugging his knees to his chest, rocking back and forth to the sound of gunfire. She sat down beside him. 'Bored with legal terminology?'

'It feels like a game,' he said. 'It feels ludicrous – and I know this, all of this, was ludicrous to begin with, but that – talking about after – just feels like an exercise in fantasy.'

'You have to believe there's an after,' she murmured. 'They did.'

'They were better than us.'

'They were.' She curled around his arm. 'But it all still wound up in our hands, didn't it?'

CHAPTER THIRTY

Westminster Bridge fell.[*]

---

[*]

London was sleeping when the bridge fell. London was still and unaware; was as Wordsworth wrote, 'all bright and glittering in the smokeless air'; was wearing like a garment 'the beauty of the morning; silent, bare'.

Later, Oxford residents would claim that they, too, knew the moment that Westminster Bridge had fallen – this despite the cities being over a hundred miles apart, and there being no building tall enough to see London from that distance. Regardless, dozens of witnesses claimed – perhaps due to group hallucination, or perhaps an invisible effect of the resonance rods – that they heard it breaking before it collapsed.

'It was this terrible feeling that gnawed at your gut,' said Professor Harrison Lewis, Merton College, Natural Philosophy. 'The most intense dread. You knew something was about to happen, and you only later learned what.'

Eyewitness accounts from London herself described it as a great rumbling.

'Like the stones were screaming,' said Mrs Sarah Harris, washerwoman. 'They seemed to be telling you to get away, and Heaven knows I listened.'

This was a city used to bridges falling into disrepair, mind. London Bridge had become unusable at least thrice in her history – once by ice, and many times by fire. But London Bridge, despite the songs, had only ever partially collapsed. It had never fallen plumb into the water.

Westminster Bridge did.

'It was so very clean,' said Mr Monks Creedy, chimney sweep. 'One moment it was in the air. And then it wasn't.'

It did not fall without warning. Eyewitnesses reported that the stones grumbled for twenty minutes before, and this gave most pedestrians time to flee to either end. Two steamships were crossing beneath when the rumbling began, and both tried to clear the bridge – one by reversing, and the other by accelerating ahead. The result was a traffic pile-up that trapped both ships, and many other boats, right beneath the bridge.

'It was like Jericho when the walls came down,' said Mr Martin Green Esq., solicitor. 'It was so neat. Like it all fell at the call of some invisible trumpet.'

The human toll remains under debate, for there is the uncertain number of pedestrians on the bridge at the moment of collapse (at least sixty-three, including one MP who had in fact been against the war), the victims on the ships below, and those who died in the river accidents that followed.

'I saw a lady yelling by the bank,' said Mrs Sue Sweet, housekeeper. 'She was screaming for this houseboat to come and fetch her. Only the houseboat was too far away, and by the time she thought to run, the stones were upon her.'

When asked if she thought the fall of Westminster Bridge might advance the translators' cause, Mrs Sweet said, 'No. I don't think they did this. No man could do this. Something like this could only be an act of God.

CHAPTER THIRTY-ONE

W estminster Bridge fell, and Oxford broke out in open warfare.
They were crowded around the telegraph machine, waiting
anxiously for an update, when one of the gunmen rushed in from
upstairs and caught his breath before announcing, 'They've killed a girl.'

They followed him to the rooftop. With his naked eye Robin could
see a commotion up north in Jericho, a frenzied movement of the crowd,
but it took a moment of fumbling with a telescope before he honed in
on what the gunmen were pointing at.

Soldiers and labourers at the Jericho barricade had just exchanged
fire, the gunman told them. Usually this led to nothing – warning shots
echoed throughout the city at all times, and the sides usually took turns
firing before retreating back down behind the barricades. Symbolic; it
was all supposed to be symbolic. But this time a body had toppled.

The telescope lens revealed a startling amount of detail. The victim
was young, she was white, she was fair-haired and pretty, and the blood
blossoming from her stomach stained the ground a vivid, unmistakable
scarlet. Against the slate-grey cobblestones, it looked like a flag.

She wasn't wearing trousers. The women who'd joined the barricades
usually wore trousers. She had on a shawl and a flowing skirt, and an
upturned basket still hung from her left arm. She could have been on
her way to buy groceries. She could have been on her way home to a
husband, to parents, to children.

Robin straightened up. 'Was it—'

'It wasn't us,' said the other gunman. 'Look at the angle. She's turned
away from the barricades. It wasn't one of ours, I tell you.'

Shouts from below. Shots whistled above their heads. Startled, they
hurried back down the stairs into the safety of the tower.

They congregated in the basement, huddled nervously, eyes darting around like frightened children who had just done something very naughty. This was the first civilian casualty of the barricades, and it was momentous. The line had been breached.

'It's over,' said Professor Craft. 'This is open warfare on English soil. This all needs to end.'

A debate broke open then.

'But it wasn't our fault,' said Ibrahim.

'They don't care if it's our fault,' said Yusuf. 'We started it—'

'Then do we surrender?' demanded Meghana. 'After all this? We just stop?'

'We don't stop,' said Robin. The strength of his voice stunned him. It came from someplace beyond him. It sounded older; it sounded like Griffin's. And it must have resonated, for the voices quieted, and all faces turned towards him, scared, expectant, hopeful. 'This is when the tides turn. This was the most foolish thing they could have done.' Blood thundered in his ears. 'Before, the whole city was against us, don't you see? But now the Army's messed up. They've shot one of the towns-folk. There's no coming back from that. Do you think Oxford's going to support the Army now?'

'If you're right,' Professor Craft said slowly, 'then things are about to get much worse.'

'Good,' said Robin. 'As long as the barricades hold.'

Victoire was watching him with narrowed eyes, and he knew what she suspected – that this did not weigh on his conscience at all, that he wasn't nearly as distressed as the others.

Well, why not admit it? He was not ashamed. He was right. This girl, whoever she was, was a symbol; she proved that empire had no restraints, that empire would do anything to protect itself. *Go on*, he thought; *do it again; kill more of them; turn the streets red with the blood of your own. Show them who you are. Show them their whiteness won't save them*. Here, at last, was an unforgivable offence with a clear perpetrator. The Army had killed this girl. And if Oxford wanted vengeance, there was only one way to get it.

That night Oxford's streets exploded into proper violence. The fighting started at the far end of the city, at Jericho where the first blood was shed, and gradually spread as more and more points of conflict developed. The cannon fire was constant. The whole city was awake with shouts and rioting, and Robin saw on those streets more people than he had ever imagined lived in Oxford.

The scholars clustered by the windows, peeking out in between spates of sniper fire.

'This is insane,' Professor Craft kept whispering. 'Absolutely insane.'

Insane was not enough to cover it, Robin thought. English was insufficient to describe all this. His mind wandered to old Chinese texts, the idioms they employed about dynastic collapse and change. 天翻地覆; *tiānfāndìfù*. The heavens fell, and the earth collapsed in on itself. The world turned upside down. Britain was spilling its own blood, Britain was gouging out its own flesh, and nothing after this could go back to the way it had been before.

At midnight Abel summoned Robin to the lobby.

'It's over,' he said. 'We're nearing the end of the road.'

'What do you mean?' Robin asked. 'This is good for us – they've provoked the entire city, haven't they?'

'It won't last,' said Abel. 'They're angry now, but they're not soldiers. They've got no endurance. I've seen this before. By the early hours of the night, they'll start straggling home. And I've just had word from the Army that at dawn, they'll start firing on whoever's still out there.'

'But what about the barricades?' Robin asked, desperate. 'They're still up—'

'We're down to the last circle of barriers. High Street is all we've got. There's no pretence of civility any longer. They'll break through; it's not a question of if, but when. And the fact is, we're a civilian uprising and they're a trained, armed battalion with reinforcements to spare. If history is anything to go by, if this really does become a battle, then we're going to get crushed. We aren't keen on a repeat of Peterloo.'* Abel sighed. 'The illusion of restraint could only ever last so long. I hope we've bought you time.'

'I suppose they were happy to fire on you after all,' said Robin.

Abel cast him a rueful look. 'I suppose it doesn't feel good to be right.'

'Well then.' Robin felt a roil of frustration but forced it down; it wasn't

---

* The Peterloo Massacre of 1819, the largest immediate effect of which was to provoke a government crackdown on radical organizing. The cavalry rushed a crowd agitating for parliamentary representation, crushing men, women, and children alike under their hooves. Eleven died.

fair to blame Abel for these developments, nor was it fair to ask him to stay any longer, when all he would face was near certain death or arrest. 'Thank you, I suppose. Thank you for everything.'

'Hold on,' said Abel. 'I didn't come just to announce we were abandoning you.'

Robin shrugged. He tried not to sound resentful. 'It'll be over very quickly without those barricades.'

'I'm telling you this is your chance to get out. We'll start ferrying people away before the shooting gets properly vicious. A few of us will stay to defend the barricades, and that'll distract them long enough to get the rest out to the Cotswolds, at least.'

'No,' Robin said. 'No, thank you, but we can't. We're staying in the tower.'

Abel arched an eyebrow. 'All of you?'

What he meant: *Can you make that decision? Can you tell me everyone in there wants to die?* And he was right to ask, because no, Robin could not speak for all seven remaining scholars; in fact, he realized, he had no idea what they would choose to do next.

'I'll ask,' he said, chastened. 'How long—'

'Within the hour,' said Abel. 'Sooner, if you can. Would rather not tarry.'

Robin steeled himself a moment before going back upstairs. He didn't know how to tell them this was the end. His face kept threatening to crumple, to reveal the scared boy hiding behind the ghost of his older brother. He had roped all these people into this last stand; he could not bear the sight of their faces when he told them it was over.

Everyone was on the fourth floor, clustered at the east window. He joined them. Outside, soldiers were marching forth on the lawn, advancing at an oddly hesitant pace.

'What are they doing?' wondered Professor Craft. 'Is this a charge?'

'You'd think they'd charge with more of them,' said Victoire.

She had a point. More than a dozen troops had halted on High Street, but only five soldiers proceeded the rest of the way towards the tower. As they watched, the soldiers parted, and a solitary figure stepped through their ranks up to the final remaining barricade.

Victoire drew in a sharp breath.

It was Letty. She waved a white flag.

CHAPTER THIRTY-TWO

She sate upon her Dobie,
To watch the Evening Star,
And all the Punkahs as they passed
Cried, 'My! How fair you are!'

EDWARD LEAR,
'The Cummerbund'

They sent everyone else upstairs before they opened the door. Letty was not here to negotiate with the crowd; they would not have sent an undergraduate to do so. This was personal; Letty was here for a reckoning.

'Let her through,' Robin told Abel.

'Pardon?'

'She's here to talk. Tell them to let her through.'

Abel spoke a word to his man, who ran across the green to inform the barricaders. Two men climbed on top of the barricade and bent down. A moment later Letty was lifted over the top, then lowered none-too-gently down onto the other side.

She made her way across the green, shoulders hunched, flag trailing behind her on the pavement. She did not raise her eyes until she met them at the threshold.

'Hello, Letty,' said Victoire.

'Hello,' Letty murmured. 'Thank you for seeing me.'

She looked miserable. She had clearly not been sleeping; her clothes were dirty and rumpled, her cheeks hollow, and her eyes red and puffy from crying. The way she hunched her shoulders around her, as if flinching from a blow, made her look very small. And despite himself, despite everything, all Robin wanted then was to give her a hug.

This instinct startled him. As she'd approached the tower he'd entertained, briefly, the thought of killing her – if only her death did not
doom them all, if only he could just throw his own life into the bargain.
But it was so hard to look at her now and not see a friend. How could
you love someone who had hurt you so badly? Up close, staring her in
the eyes, he had trouble believing that this Letty, their Letty, had done
the things she had. She looked grief-stricken, vulnerable, the wretched
heroine of a terrible fairy tale.

But that, he reminded himself, was the advantage of the image Letty
occupied. In this country, she had the face and colouring that inspired
sympathy. Among them, no matter what happened, Letty alone could
walk out of here innocent.

He nodded at her flag. 'Here to surrender?'

'Here to negotiate,' she said. 'That's all.'

'Then come in,' said Victoire.

Letty, invited, stepped through the door. It slammed shut behind her.

For a moment the three of them only looked at each other. They stood
uncertain in the middle of the lobby, an unbalanced triangle. It felt so
fundamentally wrong. There had always been four of them; they had
always come in pairs, an even set, and all Robin could think of was the
acute absence of Ramy among them. They were not themselves without
him; without his laughter, his quick, easy wit, his sudden turns of conversation that made them feel like they were spinning plates. They were
no longer a cohort. Now they were only a wake.

Victoire asked, in a flat and toneless voice, 'Why?'

Letty flinched, but only just barely. 'I had to,' she said, chin high,
unwavering. 'You know it's all I could have done.'

'No,' said Victoire. 'I don't.'

'I couldn't betray my country.'

'You didn't have to betray us.'

'You were in the thrall of a violent criminal organization,' said Letty.
The words came out so smoothly Robin could only assume they had
been rehearsed. 'And unless I pretended I agreed with you, unless I
played along, I didn't see how I was going to get out of there alive.'

Did she truly believe that? Robin wondered. Was that how she'd
always seen them? He couldn't believe these words were coming out
of her mouth, that this was the same girl who'd once stayed up late
with them, laughing so hard their ribs had ached. Only Chinese had a

character that encapsulated how much simple words could hurt: 刺, *cì*, the character for thorns, for stabs, for criticism. Such a flexible character. In a phrase, 刺言, 刺語, it meant 'barbed, stinging words'. 刺 could mean 'to goad'. 刺 could also mean 'to murder'.

'So what's this, then?' Robin asked. 'Parliament's had enough?'

'Oh, Robin.' Letty gave him a plaintive look. 'You need to surrender.'

'I'm afraid that's not how negotiation works, Letty.'

'I mean it. I'm trying to warn you. They don't even want me to be here, but I begged them, I wrote to my father, I pulled every string I had.'

'Warn us about what?' Victoire asked.

'They're going to storm the tower at dawn. And they're going to destroy your resistance with guns. No more waiting. It's over.'

Robin crossed his arms. 'Good luck with getting their city back, then.'

'But that's just it,' said Letty. 'They've held back because they thought they could starve you out. They don't want you dead. Believe it or not, they don't like shooting at scholars. You're all very useful, you're right about that. But the country can't stand it anymore. You've pushed them to the edge.'

'Seems like the logical thing then would be to agree to our demands,' said Victoire.

'You know they can't do that.'

'They're going to destroy their own city?'

'Do you think Parliament cares what you destroy?' Letty demanded, impatient. 'Those men aren't bothered about what you're doing to Oxford, or to London. They laughed when the lights went dark, and they laughed when the bridge fell down. Those men *want* the city destroyed. They think it's grown too big and unwieldy already, that its dark, squalid slums are overriding all its civilized boroughs. And you know it's the poor who will suffer the most. The rich can ride out to the country and stay on their summer estates where they'll have clean air and clean water until spring. The poor will die in droves. Listen, you two. The people who run this country care more about the pride of the British Empire than they do mild inconveniences, and they'll let the city collapse before they bow to the demands of what they see as a handful of – of Babblers.'

'Say what you mean,' said Victoire.

'Of foreigners.'

'That's quite a sense of pride,' said Robin.

'I know,' said Letty. 'It's what I grew up with. I know how deep it runs. Believe me on this. You have no idea how much they're willing to bleed for the sake of their pride. These men let Westminster Bridge fall. What else can you threaten them with?'

Silence, then. Westminster Bridge was the trump card. What rebuttal could they offer?

'So you mean to talk us into our deaths,' Victoire said finally.

'I don't,' said Letty. 'I mean to save you.'

She blinked, and suddenly tears traced two thin, clear lines down her face. This was not an act; they knew Letty could not act. She was heartbroken, truly heartbroken. She loved them; Robin did not doubt it; at least she really believed that she loved them. She wanted them safe and sound, only her version of a successful resolution was to put them behind bars.

'I didn't want any of this,' she said. 'I just want things to go back to the way they were. We had a future together, all of us.'

Robin bit back a laugh. 'What did you imagine?' he asked quietly. 'That we would keep eating lemon biscuits together while this country declared war on our motherlands?'

'They're not your motherlands,' said Letty. 'They don't have to be.'

'They *do* have to be,' said Victoire. 'Because we'll never be British. How can you still not understand? That identity is foreclosed to us. We are foreign because this nation has marked us so, and as long as we're punished daily for our ties to our homelands, we might as well defend them. No, Letty, we can't maintain this fantasy. The only one who can do that is you.'

Letty's face tightened.

The truce was over; the walls were up; they had reminded her why she'd abandoned them, which was that she could never really, properly, be one of them. And Letty, if she could not belong to a place, would rather tear the whole thing down.

'You realize that if I walk out of here with a no, they'll come in prepared to kill all of you.'

'But they can't do that.' Victoire glanced at Robin as if for confirmation. 'The whole point of this strike was that they need us; they can't risk us.'

'Please understand.' Letty's voice hardened. 'You gave them a headache. Well done you. But you are, in the end, expendable. All of you. Losing you would be a minor setback, but the imperial project involves more than a few scholars. And it will span more than a few decades. This nation is trying to achieve what no other civilization has done through-out history, and if mowing you down means a temporary delay, then they'll do it. They'll train new translators.'

'They won't,' said Robin. 'No one will work for them after this.'

Letty scoffed. 'Of course they will. We knew very well what they were up to, didn't we? They told us on the very first day. And we still loved it here. They'll *always* be able to find new translators. They'll relearn what they lost. And they'll just keep going, because no one else will be there to stop them.' She seized Robin's hand. The gesture was so sudden, so shocking that he didn't have time to pull away. Her skin was icy cold, her grip so strong he was afraid she might snap his fingers off. 'You can't change things if you're dead, Birdie.'

Violently, he shook her off. 'Don't call me Birdie.'

She pretended not to hear this. 'Don't lose sight of your end goal. If you want to fix the Empire, your best course is to work within it.'

'Like you do?' asked Robin. 'Like Sterling Jones did?'

'At least we're not wanted by the police. At least we have the freedom to act.'

'Do you think the state's ever going to change, Letty? I mean, have you ever thought about what happens if you win?'

She shrugged. 'We will win a quick, bodiless war. And after that, all the silver in the world.'

'And then what? Your machines get faster. Wages fall. Inequality increases. Poverty increases. Everything Anthony predicted will happen. The revels will be unsustainable. What then?'

'I suppose we'll cross that bridge when we get to it.' Letty's lip curled. 'As it were.'

'You won't,' said Robin. 'There's no solution. You're on a train that you can't jump off, don't you see? This can't end well for anyone. Liberation for us means liberation for you as well.'

'Or,' said Letty, 'it'll just keep going faster and faster, and we'll let it, because if the train's speeding past everyone else, we may as well be riding it.'

There was no arguing with that. But, if they were being honest with themselves, there had never been any arguing with Letty.

'This isn't worth it,' Letty continued. 'All those bodies in the streets –
and for what? To *make a point*? Ideological righteousness is well and fine,
but by God, Robin, you're letting people die for a cause you must know
is bound to fail. And you *will* fail,' she continued, relentlessly. 'You don't
have the numbers. You don't have the public support, you don't have the
votes, and you don't have the momentum. You don't understand how
determined the Empire is to reclaim its silver. You think you're prepared
to make sacrifices? They will do *anything* it takes to smoke you out. You
should know that they don't plan on losing all of you. They just need to
kill some of you. They'll take the rest prisoner, and then they'll break
your strike.

'Tell me – if you'd just seen your friends die, if you had a gun pointed
at your head, wouldn't you go back to work? They've already arrested
Chakravarti, you know. They'll torture him until he cooperates. Go on,
tell me – when push comes to shove, how many people in this tower are
going to stick to their principles?'

'We're not all as spineless as you,' said Victoire. 'They're here, aren't
they? They're with us.'

'I ask again. How long do you think that'll last? They haven't yet lost
one of their own. How do you think they'll feel when the first body of
your revolution hits the floor? When there's a gun to *their* temple?'

Victoire pointed to the door. 'Get out.'

'I'm trying to save you,' Letty insisted. 'I'm your last shot at salvation.
Surrender now, come out peacefully, and cooperate with restoration.
You won't be in prison for long. They need you, you said it yourself –
you'll be back at Babel in no time, doing the work you always dreamed
of. It's the best offer you'll get. That's all I came here to say. Take it, or
you'll die.'

Then we'll die, Robin almost said, but stopped himself. He couldn't
sentence everyone upstairs to death. She knew that.

She had them beat. There was no arguing their way out of this. She
had them utterly cornered; there was nothing she hadn't foreseen, no
more tricks to pull out of their sleeves.

Westminster Bridge had fallen. What more could they threaten?

He hated what came out of his lips next. It felt like surrender, like
bowing. 'We can't decide for them all.'

'Then call a meeting.' Letty's lip curled. 'Poll the room, get a consen-
sus with whatever little form of democracy you've got running here.'

She placed the white flag down on a table. 'But have an answer for us by dawn.'

She turned to go.

Robin rushed forward. 'Letty, wait.'

She paused, one hand on the door.

'Why Ramy?' he asked.

She froze. She looked like a statue; under the moonlight, her cheeks shone a pale, marble white. This was how he should always have seen her, he thought. Cold. Bloodless. Devoid of anything that made her a living, breathing, loving, hurting human being.

'You aimed,' he said. 'You pulled the trigger. And you're a terribly good shot, Letty. Why him? What did Ramy ever do to you?'

He knew what. They both knew; there was no question. But Robin wanted to give it a name, wanted to make sure Letty knew what he knew, wanted to pull the memory fresh between them, sharp and vicious, because he could see the pain it brought to Letty's eyes and because she deserved it.

Letty stared at him for a long time. She did not move, save for the rapid rise and fall of her chest. When she spoke, her voice was high and cold.

'I didn't,' she said; and Robin could tell from the way she narrowed her eyes and drawled her words, punctuating them just so, like daggers, what was going to come next. His own words, thrown back in his face. 'I didn't think at all. I panicked. And then I killed him.'

'Murder's not that simple,' he said.

'It turns out it is, Birdie.' She cast him a scornful look. 'Isn't that how we got here?'

'We loved you,' Victoire whispered. 'Letty, we would have died for you.'

Letty did not answer. She turned on her heel, threw the door open, and fled into the night.

The door slammed shut, and then there was silence. They weren't ready to take the news upstairs. They didn't know what they could say.

'You think she means it?' Robin asked finally.

'She absolutely does,' said Victoire. 'Letty doesn't flinch.'

'Then do we let her win?'

'How,' Victoire asked slowly, 'do you think we make her lose?'

An awful weight hung between them. Robin knew his answer, only not how to utter it. Victoire knew everything in his heart except this. It was the one thing he'd concealed from her – in part because he did not want to make her share this burden, and in part because he was afraid of how she might respond.

Her eyes narrowed. 'Robin.'

'We destroy the tower,' he said. 'And we destroy ourselves.'

She didn't flinch; she only seemed to deflate, as if she'd been waiting for confirmation. He hadn't pretended as well as he'd thought; she'd expected this from him. 'You can't.'

'There's a way.' Robin misinterpreted her words on purpose, hoping, rather, that her objection was one of logistics. 'You know there is. They showed us at the very beginning.'

Victoire went very still then. Robin knew what she was imagining. The shrill, vibrating bar in Professor Playfair's hands, screaming as if in pain, shattering into a thousand sharp, glinting pieces. Multiply that over and over. Instead of a bar, imagine a tower. Imagine a country.

'It's a chain reaction,' he whispered. 'It'll finish the job on its own. Remember? Playfair showed us how it's done. If it so much as touches another bar, the effect transmits across the metal. It doesn't stop, it just keeps going, until it renders all the silver unusable.'

How much silver lined the walls of Babel? When this was over, all those bars would be worthless. Then the cooperation of the translators wouldn't matter. Their facilities would be gone. Their library, gone. The Grammaticas, gone. Their resonance rods, their silver, useless, gone.

'How long have you been planning this?' Victoire demanded.

'Since the beginning,' he said.

'I hate you.'

'It's the only way we have left to win.'

'It's your suicide plan,' she said angrily. 'And don't tell me that it's anything but. You want this; you've always wanted this.'

But that was just it, Robin thought. How did he explain the weight crushing his chest, the constant inability to breathe? 'I think – ever since Ramy and Griffin – no, ever since Canton, I . . .' He swallowed. 'I've felt I didn't have the right.'

'Don't say that.'

'It's true. They were better men, and they died—'

'Robin, that's not how it works—'

'And what did I do? I lived a life I shouldn't have, I had what millions of people didn't – all that suffering, Victoire, and the whole time I was drinking champagne—'

'Don't you dare.' She raised a hand as if to slap him. 'Don't tell me you're just some fragile academic who can't handle the weight of the world now that you've seen it – that's absolute *tripe*, Robin. You're not some foppish dandy who faints at the first mention of suffering. You know what those men are? They're cowards, romantics, idiots who never did a thing to change the world they found so upsetting, hiding away because they felt so guilty—'

'Guilty,' he repeated. 'Guilty, that's exactly what I am. Ramy told me once that I didn't care about doing the right thing, that I just wanted to take the easy way out.'

'He was right,' she said fiercely. 'It's the coward's way, you know it—'

'No, listen.' He gripped her hands. They were trembling. She tried to pull away, but he squeezed her fingers between his. He needed her with him. Needed to make her understand, before she hated him forever for abandoning her to the dark. 'He's right. You're right. I know it, I'm trying to say it – he was right. I'm so sorry. But I don't know how to go on.'

'Day by day, Birdie.' Her eyes filled with tears. 'You go on, day by day. Just as we've been doing. It's not hard.'

'No, it's – Victoire, I can't.' He didn't want to cry; if he started crying, then all his words would disappear and he would never manage to say what he needed to. He ploughed through before his tears could catch up. 'I want to believe in the future we're fighting for, but it's not there, it's just *not there*, and I can't take things day by day when I'm too horrified by the thought of tomorrow. I'm underwater. And I've been underwater for so long, and I wanted a way out, but couldn't find one that didn't feel like some – some great abdication of responsibility. But this – this is my way out.'

She shook her head. She was weeping freely now; both of them were. 'Don't say this to me.'

'Someone's got to speak the words. Someone has to stay.'

'Then aren't you going to ask me to stay with you?'

'Oh, Victoire.'

What else was there to say? He could not ask this of her, and she knew he would never dare. Yet the question hung between them, unanswered.

Victoire's gaze was fixed steadily on the window, at the black lawn outside, at the torchlit barricades. She cried, steadily and silently; the tears kept streaming down her cheeks and she kept wiping them away, pointlessly. He couldn't tell what she was thinking. This was the first time, since all this had started, that he couldn't read her heart.

At last she took a deep breath and lifted her head. Without turning around, she asked, 'Did you ever read that poem the abolitionists love? That one by Bicknell and Day. It's called *The Dying Negro*.'

Robin had read it, in fact, in an abolitionist pamphlet he'd picked up in London. He'd found it striking; he still remembered it in detail. It described the story of an African man who, facing the prospects of capture and return to slavery, killed himself instead.[*] Robin had found it romantic and moving at the time, but now, seeing Victoire's expression, he realized it was anything but.

'I did,' he said. 'It was – tragic.'

'We have to die to get their pity,' said Victoire. 'We have to die for them to find us noble. Our deaths are thus great acts of rebellion, a wretched lament that highlights their inhumanity. Our deaths become their battle cry. But I don't want to die, Robin.' Her throat hitched. 'I don't want to die. I don't want to be their Imoinda, their Oroonoko.[†] I don't want to be their tragic, lovely lacquer figure. I want to live.'

She fell against his shoulder. He wrapped his arms around her and held her tight, rocking back and forth.

'I want to live,' she repeated, 'and live, and thrive, and survive them. I want a future. I don't think death is a reprieve. I think it's – it's just the end. It forecloses everything – a future where I might be happy, and free. And it's not about being brave. It's about wanting another chance. Even if all I did was run away, even if I never lifted a finger to help anyone else as long as I lived – at least I would get to be happy. At least the world might be all right, just for a day, just for me. Is that selfish?'

Her shoulders crumpled. Robin held her tight against him. What

---

[*] 'Arm'd with thy sad last gift – the pow'r to die! / Thy shafts, stern fortune, now I can defy.' (Thomas Day and John Bicknell, 1775)

[†] In (the white Englishwoman) Aphra Behn's 1688 romantic novel *Oroonoko*, the African prince Oroonoko kills his lover Imoinda to save her from being violated by the English military forces against whom they are revolting. Oroonoko is later captured, bound to a post, quartered, and dismembered. *Oroonoko*, and its theatrical adaptation by Thomas Southerne, were received at the time as a great romance.

an anchor she was, he thought, an anchor he did not deserve. She was his rock, his light, the sole presence that had kept him going. And he wished, he wished, that was enough for him to hold on to.

'Be selfish,' he whispered. 'Be brave.'

CHAPTER THIRTY-THREE

The hour of departure has arrived, and we go our ways – I to die, and you to live. Which is better God only knows.

PLATO, *Apology*, trans. Benjamin Jowett

'The whole tower?' asked Professor Craft.

She was the first to speak. The rest of them stared at Robin and Victoire in varying states of disbelief, and even Professor Craft seemed like she was still wrapping her mind around the idea as she spoke its implications out loud. 'That's decades – *centuries* – of research, that's everything, buried – lost – oh, but who knows how many . . .' She trailed off.

'And the ramifications for England will be much worse,' said Robin. 'This country runs on silver. Silver pumps through its blood; England can't live without it.'

'They'd build it all back—'

'Eventually, yes,' said Robin. 'But not before the rest of the world has time to muster a defence.'

'And China?'

'They won't go to war. They won't be able to. Silver powers the gunships, you see. Silver feeds the Navy. For months after this, perhaps years, they'll no longer be the strongest nation in the world. And what happens next is anyone's guess.'

The future would be fluid. It was just as Griffin had predicted. One individual choice, made at just the right time. This was how they defied momentum. This was how they altered the tracks of history.

And in the end, the answer had been so obvious – to simply refuse to participate. To remove their labour – and the fruits of their labour – permanently from the offering.

'That can't be it,' said Juliana. Her voice trailed up at the end; it was a question, not a declaration. 'There's got to be – there must be some other way—'

'They're storming us at dawn,' said Robin. 'They'll shoot a few of us to make an example, and then hold the rest of us at gunpoint until we start repairing the damage. They'll put us in chains, and they'll put us to work.'

'But the barricades—'

'The barricades will fall,' whispered Victoire. 'They're just walls, Juliana. Walls can be destroyed.'

Silence first; then resignation, then acceptance. They already lived in the impossible; what more was the fall of the most eternal thing they'd ever known?

'Then I suppose we'll have to get out fast,' said Ibrahim. 'Right after the chain reaction starts.'

But you can't get out fast, Robin almost said before he stopped himself. The rejoinder was obvious. They couldn't get out fast, because they couldn't get out at all. A single incantation would not do. If they were not thorough, the tower might collapse partway, but its remains would be salvageable, easily repurposed. The only things they would have inflicted would be expense and frustration. They would have suffered for nothing.

No; for this plan to work – to strike a blow against empire from which it could not recover – they had to stay, and say the words again and again, and activate as many nodes of destruction as they could.

But how did he tell a room full of people that they needed to die?

'I . . .' he started, but the words stuck in his throat.

He didn't have to explain. They'd all figured it out; they were all reaching the same conclusion, one after the other, and the change in their eyes was heartbreaking.

'I'm going through with it,' he said. 'I'm not asking all of you to come with me – Abel can get you out if you won't – but all I mean is . . . I just – I can't do it by myself.'

Victoire looked away, arms crossed.

'We won't need everyone,' he continued, desperate to fill the silence with words because, perhaps the more he spoke it, the less awful it sounded. 'I suppose a diversity of languages would be good, to amplify the effect – and of course, we'll want people standing in all corners of the tower, because . . .' His throat pulsed. 'But we don't need everyone.'

'I'll stay,' said Professor Craft.

'I . . . thank you, Professor.'

She gave him a wobbly smile. 'I suppose I wasn't going to get tenure on the other side of this anyhow.'

He saw them all making the same calculation then: the finality of death against the persecution, prison, and possible execution they would face on the outside. Surviving Babel did not necessarily mean survival. And he could see them asking themselves if they could come to terms, now, with their own deaths; if that would, in the end, be easier.

'You're not afraid,' Meghana told him, asked him.

'No,' said Robin. But that was all he could say. He didn't understand his heart himself. He felt resolved, but perhaps that was only the adrenaline; perhaps his fear and hesitation were only pushed temporarily behind a flimsy wall, which would shatter upon closer examination. 'No, I'm not, I . . . just – I'm ready. But we won't need everyone.'

'Possibly the younger students . . .' Professor Craft cleared her throat. 'The ones who don't know any silver-working, I mean. There's no reason—'

'I want to stay.' Ibrahim cast Juliana an anxious glance. 'I don't . . . I don't want to run.'

Juliana, pale as paper, said nothing.

'There is a way out?' Yusuf asked Robin.

'There is. Abel's men can ferry you out of the city, they've promised; they're waiting for us. But you'll have to go as soon as you can. And then you'll have to run. I don't think you'll ever be able to stop running.'

'There are no terms of amnesty?' Meghana asked.

'There are if you work for them,' said Robin. 'If you help them restore things back to how they were. Letty made that offer, she wanted you to know. But you'll always be under their thumb. They'll never let you go. She intimated as much – they'll own you, and they'll make you feel grateful for it.'

At this, Juliana reached out and took Ibrahim's hand. He squeezed her fingers. Both their knuckles turned white, and the sight of this was so intimate that Robin blinked and glanced away.

'But we can still run,' said Yusuf.

'You can still run,' said Robin. 'You wouldn't be safe anywhere in this country—'

'But we could go home.'

Victoire's voice was so soft that they could barely hear her. 'We can go home.'

Yusuf nodded, considered this a moment, and then moved to stand beside her.

And it was that simple, the determination of who fled and who died. Robin, Professor Craft, Meghana, Ibrahim, and Juliana on one side. Yusuf and Victoire on the other. No one pleaded or begged, and no one changed their minds.

'So.' Ibrahim looked very small. 'When—'

'Dawn,' said Robin. 'They're coming at dawn.'

'Then we'd better stack the bars,' said Professor Craft. 'And we'd better place them properly, if we only get one go.'

'What's the word?' Abel Goodfellow demanded. 'They're inching right up to us.'

'Send your men home,' Robin said.

'What?'

'As quick as you can. Get out of the barricades and go on the run. There's not much time. The Guards – they don't care about casualties anymore.'

Abel registered this, then nodded. 'Who's coming with us?'

'Just two. Yusuf. Victoire. They're saying their goodbyes, they'll be ready soon.' Robin pulled a wrapped parcel from inside his jacket. 'There's also this.'

Abel must have read something in his face, heard something in his voice, because his eyes narrowed. 'And what are the rest of you up to in there?'

'I shouldn't tell you.'

Abel raised the parcel. 'Is this a suicide note?'

'It's a written record,' said Robin. 'Of everything that's happened in this tower. What we stood for. There's a second copy, but in case it gets lost – I know you'll find some way to get this out there. Print it all over England. Tell them what we did. Make them remember us.' Abel looked like he wanted to argue, but Robin shook his head. 'Please, my mind's made up, and there's not much time. I can't explain this, and I think it's best if you don't ask.'

Abel watched him for a moment, then seemed to think better of what it was he was about to say. 'You'll end this?'

'We're going to try.' Robin's chest felt very tight. He was so exhausted; he wanted to curl up on the ground and go to sleep. He wanted this to be over. 'But I can't tell you more tonight. I just need you to go.'

Abel thrust out his arm. 'Then this, I suppose, is goodbye.'

'Goodbye.' Robin grasped his palm and shook it. 'Oh – and the blankets, I forgot—'

'Think nothing of it.' Abel wrapped his other hand over Robin's. His grip was so warm, solid. Robin felt a catch in his throat; he was grateful that Abel was making this easy, that he hadn't forced him to justify himself. He had to go swiftly, resolute to the very end.

'Good luck, Robin Swift.' Abel squeezed his hand. 'God be with you.'

They spent the hours before dawn arranging hundreds of silver bars into pyramids at vulnerable points around the tower – around the base supports, beneath the windows, along the walls and bookshelves, and in veritable pyramids around the Grammaticas. They could not predict the scope, the scale, of the destruction, but they would prepare for it as well as they could, would make it near impossible to salvage any material from the remains.

Victoire and Yusuf left an hour after midnight. Their farewells were brief, constrained. It was an impossible parting; there was too much and yet nothing to say, and there was a sense that everyone was holding back for fear of opening the floodgates. If they said too little, they would regret it forever. If they said too much, they'd never bring themselves to part.

'Safe travels,' Robin whispered, embracing Victoire.

She choked out a laugh. 'Yes. Thank you.'

They clung to each other for a long time, long enough that at last, once everyone had left to give them privacy, they were the only two standing in the lobby. Finally she stepped back, glanced round, eyes darting back and forth as if she was unsure whether to speak.

'You don't think this will work,' said Robin.

'I didn't say that.'

'You're thinking it.'

'I'm just terrified that we'll make this grand statement.' She lifted her hands, let them fall. 'And they'll see it only as a temporary setback, something to recover from. That they'll never understand what we meant.'

'For what it's worth, I don't think they were ever going to listen.'

'No, I don't think they were.' She was crying again. 'Oh, Robin, I don't know what to—'

'Just go,' he said. 'And write to Ramy's parents, will you? I just – they ought to know.'

She nodded, gave him one last, tight squeeze, and then darted out the door to the green where Yusuf and Abel's men were waiting. One last wave – Victoire's stricken expression under the moonlight – and then they were gone.

Then there was nothing to do but wait for the end.

How did one make peace with one's own death? According to the accounts of the *Crito*, the *Phaedo*, and the *Apology*, Socrates went to his death without distress, with such preternatural calm that he refused multiple entreaties to escape. In fact, he'd been so cheerfully blasé, so convinced that dying was the just thing to do, that he beat his friends over their heads with his reasoning, in that insufferably righteous way of his, even as they burst into tears. Robin had been so struck, upon his first foray into the Greek texts, by Socrates's utter indifference to his end.

And surely it was better, easier to die with such good cheer; no doubts, no fears, one's heart at rest. He could, in theory, believe it. Often, he had thought of death as a reprieve. He had not stopped dreaming of it since the day Letty shot Ramy. He entertained himself with ideas of heaven as paradise, of green hills and brilliant skies where he and Ramy could sit and talk and watch an eternal sunset. But such fantasies did not comfort him so much as the idea that all death meant was nothingness, that everything would just stop: the pain, the anguish, the awful, suffocating grief. If nothing else, surely, death meant peace.

Still, facing the moment, he was terrified.

They wound up sitting on the floor in the lobby, taking comfort in the silence of the group, listening to each other breathe. Professor Craft tried, haltingly, to comfort them, surveying her memory for ancient words on this most human of dilemmas. She spoke to them of Seneca's *Troades*, of Lucan's Vulteius, of the martyrdom of Cato and Socrates. She quoted to them Cicero, Horace, and Pliny the Elder. *Death is nature's greatest good. Death is a better state. Death frees the immortal soul. Death is transcendence. Death is an act of bravery, a glorious act of defiance.*

Seneca the Younger, describing Cato: *una manu latam libertati viam faciet.*[*]

Virgil, describing Dido: *Sic, sic iuvat ire sub umbras.*[†]

None of it really sank in; none of it moved them, for theorizing about death never could. Words and thoughts always ran up against the immovable limit of the imminent, permanent ending. Still, her voice, steady and unflinching, was a comfort; they let it wash over their ears, lulling them in these final hours.

Juliana glanced out of the window. 'They're moving across the green.'

'It's not dawn,' said Robin.

'They're moving,' she said simply.

'Well then,' said Professor Craft, 'We'd better get on with it.'

They stood.

They would not face their ends together. Each man and woman to their station – to the pyramids of silver distributed on different floors and different wings across the building, positioned thus to reduce the chances that any part of the tower might remain intact. When the walls tumbled down upon them, they would be alone, and this was why, as the moment drew near, it felt so impossible to part.

Tears streamed down Ibrahim's face.

'I don't want to die,' he whispered. 'There must be some other – I don't want to die.'

They all felt the same, a desperate hope for some chance of escape. In these last moments, the seconds weren't enough. In theory this decision they'd made was something beautiful. In theory they would be martyrs, heroes, the ones who'd pushed history off its path. But none of that was a comfort. In the moment, all that mattered was that death was painful and frightening and permanent, and none of them wanted to die.

But even as they trembled, not one of them broke. It was only a wish, after all. And the Army was on its way.

'Let's not tarry,' said Professor Craft, and they ascended the stairs to their respective floors.

Robin remained in the centre of the lobby beneath the broken chandelier, surrounded by eight pyramids of silver bars as tall as he stood.

---

[*] 'With one hand he will make an open path for freedom.'

[†] 'Thus, thus it helps to go beneath the shadows.'

He took a deep breath, watching the second hand tick across the clock above the door.

Oxford's bell towers had long gone mute. As the minute drew near, the only indication of the time was the synchronized ticking of the grandfather clocks, all positioned in the same place on every floor. They'd chosen six o'clock on the dot; an arbitrary time, but they needed a final moment, an immovable fact on which to fix their will.

One minute to six.

He loosed a shaky breath. His thoughts flew about, casting desperately for anything to think about that was not this. He landed not on coherent memories but on hyperspecific details – the salty weight of the air at sea, the length of Victoire's eyelashes, the hitch in Ramy's voice just before he burst out into full-bellied laughter. He clung to them, lingered there as long as he could, refused to let his mind go anywhere else.

Twenty seconds.

The warm grittiness of a scone at Vaults. Mrs Piper's sweet, floury hugs. Buttery lemon biscuits melting into nectar on his tongue.

Ten.

The bitter taste of ale, and the biting sting of Griffin's laughter. The sour stink of opium. Dinner at the Old Library; fragrant curry and the burnt bottoms of oversalted potatoes. Laughter, loud and desperate and hysterical.

Five.

Ramy, smiling. Ramy, reaching.

Robin placed his hand on the nearest pyramid, closed his eyes, and breathed, '*Fānyì*. Translate.'

The sharp ring echoed through the room, a siren's screech, reverberating through his bones. A death rattle, resounding all the way up and down the tower, for everyone had carried out their duty; no one had balked.

Robin exhaled, trembling. No space for hesitation. No time for fear. He moved his hand to the bars in the next pile and whispered again. '*Fānyì*. Translate.' Again. '*Fānyì*. Translate.' And again. '*Fānyì*. Translate.'

He felt a shifting beneath his feet. He saw the walls trembling. Books tumbled off the shelves. Above him, something groaned.

He thought he'd be scared.

He thought he'd be fixated on the pain; on how it might feel when eight thousand tons of rubble collapsed on him at once; on whether death might be instant, or whether it might come in horribly small increments when his hands and limbs were crushed, when his lungs struggled to expand in an ever-tinier space.

But what struck him most just then was the beauty. The bars were singing, shaking; trying, he thought, to express some unutterable truth about themselves, which was that translation was impossible, that the realm of pure meaning they captured and manifested would and could not ever be known, that the enterprise of this tower had been impossible from inception.

For how could there ever be an Adamic language? The thought now made him laugh. There was no innate, perfectly comprehensible language; there was no candidate, not English, not French, that could bully and absorb enough to become one. Language was just difference. A thousand different ways of seeing, of moving through the world. No; a thousand worlds within one. And translation – a necessary endeavour, however futile, to move between them.

He went back to his first morning in Oxford: climbing a sunny hill with Ramy, picnic basket in hand. Elderflower cordial. Warm brioche, sharp cheese, a chocolate tart for dessert. The air that day smelled like a promise, all of Oxford shone like an illumination, and he was falling in love.

'It's so odd,' Robin said. Back then they'd already passed the point of honesty; they spoke to one another unfiltered, unafraid of the consequences. 'It's like I've known you forever.'

'Me too,' Ramy said.

'And that makes no sense,' said Robin, drunk already, though there was no alcohol in the cordial. 'Because I've known you for less than a day, and yet . . .'

'I think,' said Ramy, 'it's because when I speak, you listen.'

'Because you're fascinating.'

'Because you're a good translator.' Ramy leaned back on his elbows. 'That's just what translation is, I think. That's all speaking is. Listening to the other and trying to see past your own biases to glimpse what they're trying to say. Showing yourself to the world, and hoping someone else understands.'

The ceiling was starting to crumble; first streams of pebbles, then whole chunks of marble, exposing planks, breaking beams. The shelves collapsed. Sunlight streaked the room where before there had been no windows. Robin looked up and saw Babel, falling in and upon him, and beyond that, the sky before dawn.

He shut his eyes.

But he'd waited for death to come before. He remembered this now - he knew death. Not so abruptly, no, not so violently. But the memory of waiting to fade was still locked in his bones; memories of a stale, hot room, of paralysis, of dreaming about the end. He remembered the stillness. The peace. As the windows smashed in, Robin shut his eyes and imagined his mother's face.

She smiles. She says his name.

EPILOGUE

Victoire

Victoire Desgraves has always been good at surviving.

The key, she has learned, is refusing to look back. Even as she races north on horseback through the Cotswolds, head bent against the whipping branches, some part of her wants to be in the tower, with her friends, feeling the walls come down around them. If they must die, she wants them to be buried together.

But survival demands severing the cord. Survival demands she look only to the future. Who knows what will happen now? What happened in Oxford today is unthinkable, its ramifications unimaginable. There is no historical precedent for this. The juncture is shot. History, for once, is fluid.

But Victoire is familiar with the unthinkable. The liberation of her motherland was unthinkable even as it happened, for no one in France or England, not even the most radical proponents of universal freedom, believed that slaves – creatures they never thought fell under their categories of rational, rights-holding, enlightened men – would demand their own liberation. Two months after news broke of the August 1791 uprising, Jean Pierre Brissot, himself a founding member of the Amis des Noirs, announced to the French Assembly that this news must be false, for as anyone knew, slaves were simply incapable of such rapid, coordinated, defiant action. A year into the revolution, many still believed that soon the unrest would be quelled, that things would go back to normal, for *normal* meant white dominance over Blacks.

They were, of course, wrong.

But who, in living history, ever understands their part in the tapestry? For the better part of her life, Victoire was not even aware she hailed from the world's first Black republic.

Here is all she knew, before Hermes:

She was born in Haiti, Ayiti, in 1820, the same year that King Henry Christophe, fearing a coup, took his own life. His wife and daughters fled to the home of an English benefactor in Suffolk. Victoire's mother, a maid of the exiled queen, went with them. She referred to this always as their great flight and, once she set foot in Paris, refused ever to think again of Haiti as home.

Victoire's understanding of Haitian history is of curses in the night; of a magnificent palace named Sans Souci, home to the first Black king in the New World; of men with guns; of vague political disagreements she does not understand that, somehow, uprooted her life and sent her across the Atlantic. As a child she knew her motherland as a place of violence and barbaric power struggles, for that is how they spoke of it in France, and that was what her exiled mother chose to believe.

'We are lucky,' whispered her mother, 'that we survived it.'

But her mother did not survive France. Victoire never learned how her mother, a free-born woman, was sent from Suffolk to work in the household of a retired Parisian academic, Professor Emile Desjardins. She does not know what promises her mother's friends made her, whether or not money changed hands. She knows only that in Paris, at the Desjardins estate, they were not allowed to leave – for here, forms of slavery still existed, as they did all over the world; a twilight condition, the rules unwritten but implied. And when her mother fell ill, the Desjardinses did not send for a doctor. They merely closed the door to her sickroom and waited outside until a maid went in, felt for her breath and pulse, and announced she had expired.

Then they locked Victoire in a cupboard and did not let her out, for fear the illness would catch. But the contagion took the rest of the household regardless, and once again the doctors were powerless to do anything but watch it run its course.

Victoire survived. Professor Desjardins's wife survived. His daughters survived. The professor himself died, and with him, Victoire's only connection to the people who purported to love her mother, and had yet somehow sold her away.

The house fell into disrepair. Madame Desjardins, a tight-faced blonde woman, kept bad accounts and spent prodigiously. Money was tight. They fired the maid – why keep one, they argued, when they had Victoire? Overnight Victoire became responsible for dozens of tasks:

keeping the fire, polishing the silver, dusting the rooms, serving the tea. But these were not tasks she'd been trained to fulfil. She'd been raised to read and compose and interpret, not manage a household, and for this they scolded and beat her.

She found no comfort from Madame Desjardins's two little daughters, who took great delight in announcing to houseguests that Victoire was an orphan they'd rescued from Africa. 'From Zanzibar,' they would sing in unison. '*Zaaanzibar!*'

But it was not so bad.

It was not so bad, they told her, compared with her native Haiti, which was overrun with crime, which was being driven to poverty and anarchy by an incompetent and illegitimate regime. You are lucky, they said, to be here with us, where things are safe, and civilized.

This she believed. She had no way of knowing anything else.

She might have run away, but Professor and Madame Desjardins had kept her so sheltered, so isolated from the world outside that she had no idea she had the legal right to be free. Victoire had grown up in the great contradiction of France, whose citizens in 1789 had issued a declaration of the rights of man but had not abolished slavery, and had preserved the right to property including chattel.

Liberation was a string of coincidences, of ingenuity, resourcefulness, and luck. Victoire went through Professor Desjardins's letters, looking for a deed, some proof that he did own her and her mother. She never found it. But she did learn about a place named the Royal Institute of Translation, a place he'd trained at in his youth, a place he'd written to about her, in fact. He'd told them about the brilliant little girl in his household, about her prodigious memory and talent for Greek and Latin. He'd intended to show her around Europe on tour. Perhaps they might be interested in an interview?

And so she created the conditions of her own freedom. When Professor Desjardins's friends at Oxford finally wrote back, expressing that they would be very happy to have the talented Miss Desgraves at the Institute, and that they would pay the way, it felt like such an escape.

But the true liberation of Victoire Desgraves did not happen until she met Anthony Ribben. It was not until her induction to the Hermes Society that she learned to call herself Haitian at all. She learned to take pride in her Kreyòl, patchy, half-remembered, barely distinguishable from her French. (Madame Desjardins used to slap her whenever she spoke in Kreyòl. 'Shut up,' she would say, 'I told you, you must speak French, the Frenchman's French.') She also learned that to much of the rest of the world, the Haitian Revolution was not a failed experiment but a beacon of hope.

She learned revolution is, in fact, always unimaginable. It shatters the world you know. The future is unwritten, brimming with potential. The colonizers have no idea what is coming, and that makes them panic. It terrifies them.

Good. It should.

She's not sure where she's headed now. She has some envelopes in her coat pocket: parting words of advice from Anthony and the code names of several contacts. Friends in Mauritius, in the Seychelles, and in Paris. Perhaps one day she'll head back to France, but she's not quite ready yet. She knows there's a base in Ireland, though at the moment she'd quite like just to be off the continent. Perhaps one day she'll go home and see, with her own eyes, the historical impossibility of free Haiti. Right now she's boarding a ship to America, where people like her are still not free, because it was the first vessel that she could book passage on, and because she needed to get out of England as quickly as she could.

She has the letter from Griffin that Robin never opened. Meanwhile she's read it so many times she's memorized it. She knows three names – Martlet, Oriel, and Rook. She can see in her mind's eye the final sentence, scrawled before the signatures like an afterthought: *We're not the only ones.*

She doesn't know who these three are. She doesn't know what this sentence means. She'll find out, one day, and the truth will dazzle and horrify her. But for now they are only lovely syllables that signify all sorts of possibilities, and possibilities – *hope* – are the only things she can cling to now.

She has silver lining her pockets, silver in the inseams of her dress, so much silver on her person that she feels stiff and heavy when she moves. Her eyes are swollen from tears, her throat sore with stifled sobs. She has the faces of her dead friends engraved in her memory. She keeps imagining their last moments: their terror, their pain as the walls came crumbling down around them.

She does not, *will* not let herself think of her friends as they were, alive and happy. Not Ramy, torn down in his prime; not Robin, who brought down a tower upon himself because he couldn't think of a way to keep on living. Not even Letty, who remains alive; who, if she knows Victoire lives too, will hunt her to the ends of the earth.

Letty, she knows, cannot allow her to roam free. Even the idea of Victoire is a threat. It threatens the core of her very being. It is proof that she is, and always was, wrong.

She won't let herself grieve that friendship, as true and terrible and abusive as it was. There will come a time for grief. There will come many nights on the voyage when the sadness is so great it threatens to tear her apart; when she regrets her decision to live; when she curses Robin for placing this burden on her, because he was right: he was not being brave, he was not choosing sacrifice. Death is seductive. Victoire resists.

She cannot weep now. She must keep moving. She must run, as fast as she can, without knowing what is on the other side.

She has no illusions about what she will encounter. She knows she will face immeasurable cruelty. She knows her greatest obstacle will be cold indifference, born of a bone-deep investment in an economic system that privileges some and crushes others.

But she might find allies. She might find a way forward.

Anthony called victory an inevitability. Anthony believed the material contradictions of England would tear it apart, that their movement would succeed because the revels of the Empire were simply unsustainable. This, he argued, was why they had a chance.

Victoire knows better.

Victory is not assured. Victory may be in the portents, but it must be urged there by violence, by suffering, by martyrs, by blood. Victory is wrought by ingenuity, persistence, and sacrifice. Victory is a game of inches, of historical contingencies where everything goes right because they have made it go right.

She cannot know what shape that struggle will take. There are so many battles to be fought, so many fights on so many fronts – in India, in China, in the Americas – all linked together by the same drive to exploit that which is not white and English. She knows only that she will be in it at every unpredictable turn, will fight until her dying breath.

'*Mande mwen yon ti kou ankò ma di ou,*' she'd told Anthony once, when he'd first asked her what she thought of Hermes, if she thought they might succeed.

He'd tried his best to parse Kreyòl with what he knew of French, then he'd given up. 'What's that mean?'

'I don't know,' said Victoire. 'At least, we say it when we don't know the answer, or don't care to share the answer.'

'And what's it literally mean?'

She'd winked at him. 'Ask me a little later, and I'll tell you.'

*   *   *

ACKNOWLEDGEMENTS

Babel is about infinite worlds of languages, cultures, and histories – many of which I do not know – and its writing would not have been possible without the friends who shared their knowledge with me. Many, many thanks are in order:

First, to Peng Shepherd, Ehigbor Shultz, Farah Naz Rishi, Sarah Mughal, and Nathalie Gedeon for helping me ensure that Robin, Ramy, and Victoire were written with detail and compassion. To Caroline Mann and Allison Resnick for their Classics expertise; to Sarah Forssman, Saoudia Ganiou, and De'Andre Ferreira for their help with translations; and to my dear professors at Yale – in particular Jing Tsu, Lisa Lowe, and Denise Ho – for shaping my thinking about coloniality, post-coloniality, and the bearing of language on power.

I am supported by the most wonderful teams at Harper Voyager on both sides of the pond. Thank you to my editors, David Pomerico and Natasha Bardon; as well as to Fleur Clarke, Susanna Peden, Robyn Watts, Vicky Leech, Jack Renninson, Mireya Chiriboga, Holly Rice-Baturin, and DJ DeSmyter.

Thank you to the artists who made *Babel* look the way it does: Nico Delort, Kimberly Jade McDonald, and Holly Macdonald.

Thank you also to Hannah Bowman, without whom none of this would be possible, and the entire team at Liza Dawson Associates – especially Havis Dawson, Joanne Fallert, Lauren Banka, and Liza Dawson.

Thank you to Julius Bright-Ross, Taylor Vandick, Katie O'Nell, and the Vaults & Garden cafe, who made those strange, sad months in Oxford bearable. And thank you to the New Haven homies – Tochi Onyebuchi, Akanksha Shah, and James Jensen – for the pizzas and the laughs. All hail the Great Egg.

Thank you to Tiff and Chris for helping run Coco's Cocoa, a most wonderful interdimensional, magical dog-owned café at which most of this manuscript was written.

Thank you to Bennett, who was the best company I could have asked for during that long, lonely, terrible year in which *Babel* came together, and whose counsel shaped so many details of this story. He would like everyone to know that he named the book, as well as the Hermes Society, for while I have a sense for the literary, he has a sense for the awesome.

Finally, thank you to Mom and Dad, to whom I owe everything.